DRAGON HUNTERS

BOOKS BY MARC TURNER

When the Heavens Fall

DRAGON HUNTERS

MARC TURNER

A Tom Doherty Associates Book
New York

DRAGON HUNTERS

Copyright © 2016 by Marc Turner

All rights reserved.

Map by Rhys Davies

A Tor Book
Published by Tom Doherty Associates, LLC
175 Fifth Avenue
New York, NY 10010

www.tor-forge.com

Tor® is a registered trademark of Tom Doherty Associates, LLC.

Library of Congress Cataloging-in-Publication Data

Turner, Marc.
    Dragon hunters / Marc Turner.—First Edition.
        p. cm.
    ISBN 978-0-7653-3713-9 (hardcover)
    ISBN 978-1-4668-3121-6 (e-book)
    I. Title.
    PR6120.U775D73 2016
    823'.92—dc23

                                          2015031511

Our books may be purchased in bulk for promotional, educational, or business use. Please contact your local bookseller or the Macmillan Corporate and Premium Sales Department at 1-800-221-7945, extension 5442, or by e-mail at MacmillanSpecialMarkets@macmillan.com.

First Edition: February 2016

Printed in the United States of America

0 9 8 7 6 5 4 3 2 1

FOR DAD,

who must be reading the Karmel storyline
and scratching his head at where that came from

CONTENTS

DRAMATIS PERSONAE

The Olairian Court

Imerle Polivar, emira of the Storm Council

Pernay Ord, chief minister

Jambar Simanis, a Remnerol shaman

Mili and Tali, the emira's twin bodyguards

The executioner

Mazana Creed, a Storm Lady

Dutia Beauce Carlyn, commander of Mazana Creed's forces

Greave, Mazana Creed's bodyguard

Kiapa, Mazana Creed's bodyguard

Uriel, Mazana's half brother

Gensu Sensama, a Storm Lord

Polin Sensama, Gensu's son

Cauroy Blent, a Storm Lord

Thane Tanner, a Storm Lord

Mokinda Char, a Storm Lord

Dutia Elemy Meddes, commander of the Storm Guards

Septia Cilin Rai, a soldier

Orsan, a water-mage

Erin Elalese

Senar Sol, a Guardian

Li Benir, a dead Guardian, Senar's former mentor

Jessca, a dead Guardian

Avallon Delamar, emperor of Erin Elal

Chameleons

Caval Flood, the Chameleon high priest of the Storm Isles

Karmel Flood, a Chameleon priestess, sister to Caval

Pennick Flood, a Chameleon priest, Caval and Karmel's father

Veran Beck, a former Chameleon priest

Foss, the Chameleon weaponsmaster

Wick, a Chameleon priest, Keeper of the Keys

Aminex, the Chameleon high priest of Seygreen

Watchmen

Quina Hilaire Desa, commander of the Watch

Septia Kempis Parr

Corrick, Kempis's former partner, now dead

Sniffer

Loop

Duffle

Pompit

Gilgamarians

Kalisch Rethell Webb, first speaker of the Gilgamarian Ruling Council

Kalischa Agenta Webb, Rethell's daughter

Zelin Webb, Rethell's dead son

Lydanto Hood, Gilgamarian ambassador to the Storm Isles

Trita Warner Sturge, commander of Rethell's forces

Balen, a water-mage

Iqral, a soldier

Jayle, a soldier

Others

The Spider, a goddess

The Chameleon, a god

Piput Da Marka, governor of Dian

Colm Spicer, a nobleman

Inneez, a merchant

Enli Alapha, a merchant

Enix, a boatman

Sticks, a pirate

Irlon, a spirit

Darbonna, a librarian of the Founder's Citadel

The Lord of Hidden Faces, a god of mysterious origins

Artagina, high priest of the Lord of Hidden Faces

Samel Fletch, a merchant

Farrell Fletch, Samel's son

Selis, an air-mage

Fume, an elder god

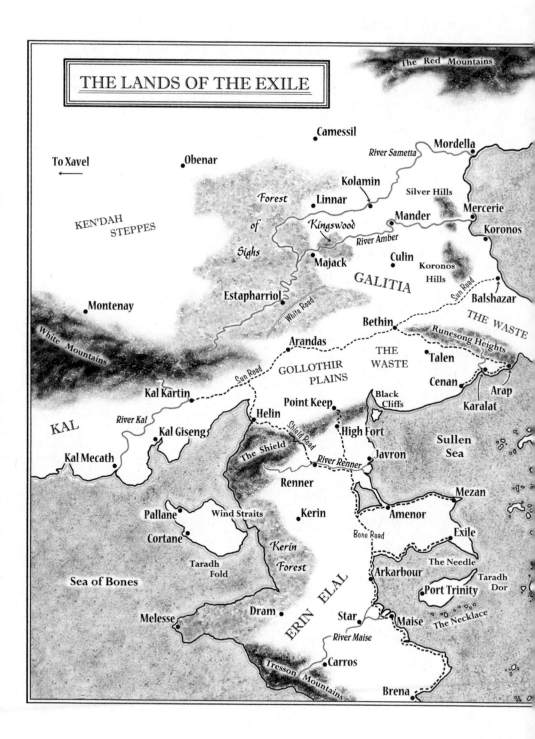

THE LANDS OF THE EXILE

The Red Mountains

Camessil

Mordella

River Sametta

To Xavel

Obenar

Kolamin

Silver Hills

Forest

Linnar

Mander

Mercerie

KEN'DAH
STEPPES

of

Kingswood

River Amber

Koronos

Sighs

Majack

Culin

Koronos
Hills

GALITIA

Estapharriol

Montenay

White Road

Bethin

Balshazar

THE WASTE

White Mountains

Arandas

GOLLOTHIR
PLAINS

THE
WASTE

Runesong Heights

Talen

Sun Road

Point Keep

Cenan

Arap

Kal Kartin

Helin

Black
Cliffs

Karalat

KAL

River Kal

Kal Giseng

Shield Road

High Fort

Sullen
Sea

Kal Mecath

The Shield

River Renner

Javron

Renner

Mezan

Pallane

Wind Straits

Kerin

Amenor

Exile

Cortane

Bone Road

Kerin
Forest

ERIN ELAL

The Needle

Taradh
Fold

Arkarbour

Taradh
Dor

Sea of Bones

Dram

Star

Port Trinity

Melesse

Maise

The Necklace

River Maise

Carros

Tresson Mountains

Brena

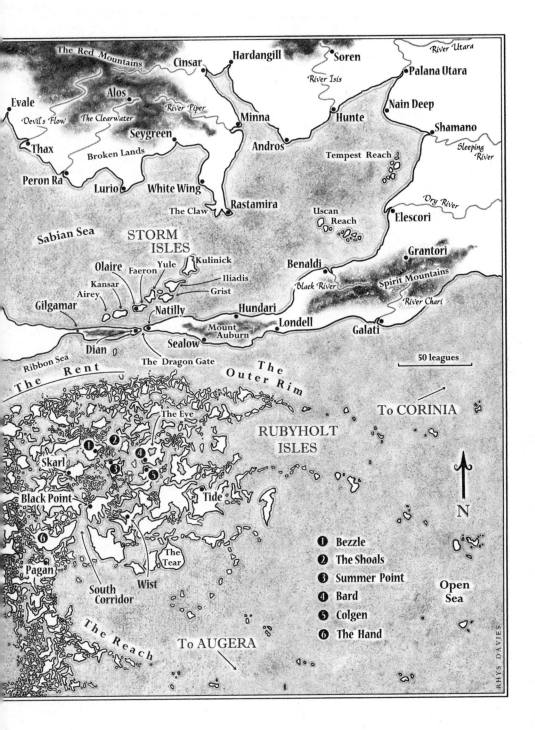

The Red Mountains
Cinsar
Hardangill
Soren
River Utara
Palana Utara
River Isis
Evale
Alos
River Piper
Nain Deep
Devil's Flow
The Clearwater
Minna
Hunte
Shamano
Seygreen
Andros
Sleeping River
Thax
Broken Lands
Tempest Reach
Peron Ra
Lurio
White Wing
Dry River
The Claw
Rastamira
Uscan Reach
Elescori
Sabian Sea
STORM ISLES
Kulinick
Grantori
Olaire
Yule
Benaldi
Faeron
Iliadis
Spirit Mountains
Kansar
Grist
Black River
River Chari
Airey
Gilgamar
Natilly
Hundari
Londell
Galati
Mount Auburn
Dian
Sealow
50 leagues
Ribbon Sea
The Dragon Gate
The Outer Rim
The Rent
The Eye
To CORINIA
RUBYHOLT ISLES
Skarl
Black Point
Tide
Pagan
The Tear
N
South Corridor
Wist
The Reach
To AUGERA

❶ Bezzle
❷ The Shoals
❸ Summer Point
❹ Bard
❺ Colgen
❻ The Hand

Open Sea

RHYS DAVIES

PROLOGUE

THROUGH THE eye slits of her mask, the woman studied the Chameleon priest. Standing motionless in the darkness beyond the doorway, he blended in seamlessly with the other shadows. With his power employed he would have been invisible to eyes other than the woman's. His gaze lingered on her before moving off to scan the room in which she waited. He took in its walls with their carvings of masked and animal-headed figures, its headless statue of a winged creature in the southwest corner, its large arched window in the wall behind the woman.

Then he surrendered his power and entered the chamber. Potsherds and shattered floor tiles crunched beneath his sandals. He advanced to within a dozen paces of the woman.

"That's close enough," she said, her hand straying to the hilt of her sword.

He halted.

The moonlight spilling through the window to his right gave one side of his face a ghostly sheen. So deeply was the darkness gathered in his sunken eyes that it seemed as if he'd brought some of the shadows in with him from the passage. The gray streaks in his hair gave him the look of a man old before his time. He carried no weapons—as she had insisted in her message. Round his lower arms were armguards of blackened metal.

The silence dragged out. The woman could hear the hiss of waves breaking against the Natillian cliffs, then over that the *clang, clang,*

clang—regular as a shipwright's hammer—of a sea dragon ramming its head into the Dragon Gate. The floor trembled.

When the priest spoke, his voice was scratchy from lack of use. "This used to be a temple of the Lord of Hidden Faces."

The woman smiled behind her mask. The priest would be feeling uncomfortable in another god's abode, she knew, no matter that the shrine had long since been abandoned. There was an emptiness to the place that was more than just the stillness of the night. The air in the chamber felt thin, as if it had passed through the lungs of too many people.

"Strange place for a meeting," the priest added.

"I like it here. It's quiet."

"Also gives you access to the rooftops in case you need to make a sharp exit."

"I hadn't noticed. Now, where is my payment?"

From a pocket in his robe the priest produced a perfume bottle made of pearlshell. The woman could sense the protective sorcery invested in the container to protect it from its contents.

"Put it on the floor and step back."

He did as he was bid.

The woman edged forward, her gaze not leaving the priest, then picked up the bottle before retreating. She withdrew the stopper and sniffed its contents. The metallic sharpness of dragon blood made her eyes water. Replacing the stopper, she gave the bottle a shake.

"A little less in here than we agreed, I think, but still enough to set me up far beyond the reach of your mistress."

The priest's eyes narrowed. "My mistress?"

"Oh, come now, how many people in the Sabian League can lay their hands on dragon blood at short notice? How many of those people have an interest in the information on this scroll?" She tossed the parchment in her left hand onto the floor. "It's all there—everything you need to know about the Dianese citadel."

He made no move to collect it. "Tell me."

The woman considered, then began speaking. She told the priest about the guard postings and squad rotations, about the bastions along the fortress's outer walls, about the invisible pockets of sorcerously condensed air scattered about the guardhouse to ensnare intruders.

"What about the chamber with the mechanism that raises the Dragon Gate?" the priest said when she had finished.

The woman laughed. "You haven't been listening, have you? You won't make it as far as the fortress's grounds, never mind the control room. In the week leading up to Dragon Day, the number of soldiers patrolling the outer wall is trebled. All of the gates are sealed, except for the main gate, which is guarded by fifty of the governor's elite." The corners of her mouth turned up. "Not even the Chameleon god himself could slip through undetected."

"Humor me."

Humor him? Judging by the priest's dour demeanour, she stood as much chance of doing that as *he* did of piercing the citadel's defenses. "The door to the control room is locked from the inside," she said, "and the corridor leading to it is guarded by twenty soldiers. Two more soldiers are stationed inside the chamber itself. Then there are the men whose job it will be to raise the gate." She lifted the bottle of dragon blood as if toasting him before slipping it into a pocket. "I almost feel bad taking this from your mistress. The information she has paid for is useless to her."

"The more closely a place is guarded, the less wary are the soldiers who're watching it."

"If you say so."

A scratching sound came from the doorway through which the priest had entered. He looked across. The woman followed his gaze, but it was only a rat nosing along the passage outside.

She said, "One more thing you should know—"

The priest sprang to the attack.

For a heartbeat the woman stood frozen in surprise. Then she pushed herself into motion. She'd been careful to keep her distance from the man, yet he closed the gap between them so quickly she barely had time to draw her sword. Her backhand slash was deflected by one of the priest's armguards. Before she could recover her blade, his hand closed around her wrist. The fingers of his other hand formed a spear that jabbed toward her throat. She swayed aside.

Too late.

Pain exploded in her neck. She tried to draw a breath, but her throat felt as if a rock had lodged in it. She tried to scream, but all that came out was a wheeze. The priest's hand about her wrist twisted and squeezed, and her sword slipped from her fingers. She tried to pull loose from his grip, but he was too strong. She flailed with her free arm, hoping to catch him a chance blow, but he ducked and moved behind her.

A kick to the back of her legs, and she fell to her knees. Her sword lay on the floor, but when she reached for it, the priest curled an arm round her neck and hauled her back. The pressure on her wounded throat caused another stab of agony. Black spots flashed before her eyes. She bucked and heaved, but there was no give in her attacker's arm. She opened her mouth to try to reason with him, but the words would not come.

The pressure on her throat intensified.

Darkness gathered at the edges of her vision.

Fingers fluttering, the goddess known as the Spider looked down at the woman's corpse.

Since throttling his victim, the Chameleon priest had made himself busy. After retrieving the bottle of dragon blood, he'd removed the woman's rings and the fishbone charm round her neck. Next he had stripped her naked and checked her body for distinguishing scars or birthmarks. Finally he'd used the pommel of her sword to smash her mask and the face beneath it into bloody ruin. And all so she wouldn't be identified by her masters at the Dianese citadel, for surely the disappearance of someone so familiar with the workings of the fortress would not go unnoticed.

A reasonable assumption, but wrong, as it turned out.

The goddess waved her fingers, and the illusion of the woman's corpse, along with the pool of blood beneath it, faded to nothing.

"Perrrfect."

Looking out of the window, the Spider saw the priest leave the temple and move along Gable Street, hugging the walls of the Elissian Sanctum. He'd been clever, she conceded, to keep the woman talking until the rat distracted her. Even though the goddess had suspected he would attack, his speed had still caught her off guard. Doubtless he was wondering what his victim had intended to reveal with her final words—*One more thing you should know*—but he'd already made his move by then, and he could hardly have broken off his assault to let the woman finish her sentence. The Spider smiled. If he made it as far as the Dianese control room, he'd be in for a surprise—a surprise that could jeopardize the success of both his and the goddess's own schemes. But that only added more spice to the pot.

The rhythmic clang of the dragon bashing its head into the Dragon Gate started up again. Strange that one of the creatures should stray so far north at this time of year. Usually they prowled the Southern Wastes until they were lured here at the end of the summer in readiness for the Dragon Hunt. The goddess's fingers fluttered. Dragon Day and all it presaged was still months away, but she would have to be patient. Today she had set a spark to the kindling. Soon it would grow into a fire that swept the length and breadth of the Sabian League.

And where chaos ruled, there was only one place for the Spider to be.

Right at its heart.

Part I

The Drowning City

CHAPTER 1

THE TIME had come for Senar Sol to learn his fate.

The Guardian had known it as soon as the bolts of his cell door were thrown back, for this was the first time it had happened in all the months he had been imprisoned. He pushed himself to his feet, found his legs were trembling. How long had he been a captive? How long since he'd stepped through the Merigan portal and swapped Emperor Avallon Delamar's knife at his back for a sword at his throat? The best part of a year, he realized, for through the bars across his room's window he had seen autumn, winter, spring, and much of summer pass by. As the weeks of his imprisonment had turned into months, he'd begun to wonder if his jailers would just leave him there to rot. But then why had they kept passing food and water through the grille of his cell door? Why bother keeping him alive at all?

Something told him he was about to find out.

The door opened and torchlight flooded through the doorway, banishing the gloom about the cell. Senar squinted into the light. A balding man entered—the same man to whom the Guardian had surrendered his sword on stepping through the Merigan portal all those months ago to find himself surrounded by enemy soldiers. The guard wore leather armor covered with metal plates that overlapped like fish scales. In one hand he held a sword with a blade made from the snout of a sawfish. Three stripes on his left shoulder marked him as an officer. Senar searched his gaze for any hint as to what his coming here signified, but the man's expression was masked. He gestured to the open doorway.

Senar scratched at the stubs that were all that remained of the two smallest fingers of his left hand. Beyond the officer waited an escort of no fewer than twelve soldiers. High honor, indeed. Another time, odds of thirteen to one would have meant nothing to the Guardian, but he rejected the idea of attacking for the same reason he'd yielded up his blade after he passed through the portal three seasons ago: even if he could defeat the guards facing him, what about the reinforcements that would inevitably come? And what was the point in trying to escape when he didn't know what lay beyond the four walls of his cell, didn't even know in which city of which empire he was imprisoned? Then there was the fact that his time in captivity would have left his skills as rusty as the hinges of his cell door. No, he would not throw his life away while his captors' intentions remained unclear.

Not when he still had unfinished business with the emperor who had sent him here to die.

Why, then, when the officer beckoned him through the door again did Senar hold back? A smile touched his lips. He had been a prisoner all this time, yet now when he was offered a glimpse of freedom, he hesitated? Better the gallows than this lingering death of the spirit he'd endured these past few months. Though he might see things differently, of course, when he was swinging from the noose.

He hadn't been heedless of the risks of traveling through the Merigan portals when he stepped through all those months ago. Only two such gateways had been found in Erin Elal—at Bastion and at Amenor—but there were innumerable others beyond the borders of the empire. And while the symbols etched into each portal's architrave denoted the destinations to which one could travel, the emperor's scholars had yet to decipher the code behind those symbols. Senar's destination had been chosen at random, and if that destination had proved to be a gateway that no longer existed, his journey to it would have killed him instantly. Even if the passage had not proved immediately fatal, Senar could have been transported to any one of a hundred different kingdoms, thousands of leagues from home. Few of those kingdoms would look kindly on visitors dropping by unannounced.

So where *had* the portal brought him? He hadn't had any visitors in his time here, so no help there. Nor had his captors left any clues in his cell, for the books of poetry and philosophy he'd been given were written in the common tongue by authors from numerous different cultures. Badly written, as it happened. He'd tried looking out of his cell's window for clues, but there was only so much information he could deduce from the blank wall opposite. From time to time he'd heard people talking outside, but never clearly enough to make out their words. And why? Because they were drowned by the sound of the sea.

The sea.

Senar had come to know its many voices in the months he'd been a prisoner. At times its gentle gurgle put him in mind of sleepy days spent fishing with his father in the sheltered bays east of Amenor—before his father had died. At other times it would rage in the grip of a storm so savage it seemed the Furies themselves were battering at the shutters. Those storms had been one of the things to awaken in Senar a suspicion as to his location. Then there was the style of the armor and sword worn by the officer before him, together with the emblem on the man's breast of a shaft of silver lightning over a storm cloud.

The Storm Isles—that was where the clues were leading him.

Throughout his imprisonment, he had tried to remember everything he'd heard of that empire. Located in the Sabian Sea to the north and east of Erin Elal, the Storm Isles were a chain of islands ruled by a fellowship of water-mages—the Storm Lords—that held in its thrall a confederation of cities known as the Sabian League. In return for the Storm Lords protecting the League's shipping from pirates, as well as from the supernatural storms that swept down from the Broken Lands, the League's members paid tribute to the Storm Lords. The Storm Lords' seat of government was the city of Olaire on the island of Faeron, a handful of leagues from the fabled Dragon Gate that spanned the Cappel Strait between Dian and Natilly.

The Dragon Gate. Just to speak the name in his mind made Senar's pulse quicken. Once each year the gate was raised to allow a sea dragon to pass into the Sabian Sea. Awaiting it would be ships from the Storm Isles and the cities of the Sabian League, and they would hunt the creature for the honor and riches that came to the vessel that slew it. *Dragon Day.* Two words that inspired awe even in Erin Elal.

The balding officer gestured again to the open door, and Senar glanced down at his clothes. They were the same clothes he'd arrived in last year. He looked like a beggar, and he smelled like one too, but if they'd been going to kill him, surely they'd have let him wash and change first. Die with a little dignity, and all that. He stepped through the doorway.

To his right stretched a passage that was featureless but for several closed doors to either side. At the end of the passage was another door, and beyond it was a corridor that seemed cavernous to Senar after the confines of his cell. Its floor was covered by a blue and white mosaic so artfully crafted that, for an improbable moment, the Guardian thought he was standing on a frothing tide.

The officer led the way through a maze of passages. Senar's legs ached as he struggled to keep pace, but then the months of captivity would have left a few creases it would take time to iron out. The sound of the sea grew louder until eventually he came to a corridor where the boom of waves made it feel as if he were inside a drum. The wall to his right had no windows and was imbued with such powerful water-magic he suspected the sea lay just the other side.

And where there was powerful water-magic, there were powerful water-mages.

The Storm Isles. It has to be.

If Senar's theory concerning his location was correct, the news was both good and bad. Good in that if he ever got the chance to return home, Erin Elal was only a few weeks' travel away.

But bad for the same reason. For even though Emperor Avallon Delamar had yet to lock horns with the Storm Lords, it could only be a matter of time. Over the past decade Erin Elal had fought its northwestern neighbor, Kal, to a standstill, and while Avallon would never abandon his ambition to conquer the Kalanese empire, the loosely allied nations to the northeast of Erin Elal surely represented easier pickings. If the emperor were to learn of the Merigan portal in the Storm Isles, the strategic advantages he would gain from a back door to the Storm Lords' empire could not be overstated.

So why am I still alive?

The question had plagued him throughout his imprisonment. Even if his captors were ignorant as to his identity—and doubtless they were, since no one had bothered to question him—why take the risk of keeping him alive? Why not kill him and be done with it?

Of course, that could be what was about to happen.

The balding officer—a Storm Guard, Senar supposed, if these were indeed the Storm Isles—came to a staircase, and the Guardian followed him up into blistering sunshine. Shielding his eyes against the glare, he stepped onto the roof of the corridor he had been walking along moments ago. He was on a terrace overlooking the sea. The terrace stretched for hundreds of paces in either direction, ending to the east in black cliffs and to the west in a rocky shoreline. Its tiles were slick with spray. Immediately to the south Senar saw the roofs and courtyards of a sprawling building complex. Beyond lay a hill, its lower slopes crowded with white-plastered houses that gave way to trees near the hill's summit.

To the Guardian's left stood five figures, all staring down into a courtyard. They turned as he approached. At the center of the group was a woman with skin so pale she might never have set foot outdoors before. Her hair was gray—a curious detail, since she looked only a few years older than Senar. Her blue eyes were as cold as glacial pools, and perhaps ice ran through her veins as well, for her face showed not a bead of sweat in spite of the crushing heat.

To her right stood two young women, identical twins. And a handspan taller than Senar. He disliked them instinctively. Each wore a sword strapped to her waist, and one of them was holding Senar's scabbarded blade. To the other side of the gray-haired woman was a bearded man wearing a brown shirt and trousers. The whites of his eyes were gray, marking him as an oscura addict. Beside him stood a one-eyed old man with the olive skin of a Remnerol. Like all Remnerol, he was missing the little fingers of both hands. In his left hand he held a black bag. When a gust of wind tugged at the bag, its contents made a clacking noise. *Bones.* A shaman, then, for the elders of the Remnerol tribes were said to be able to read the future in the cast finger bones of their kinsmen.

The Storm Guard officer bowed to the gray-haired woman. "The prisoner as you ordered, Emira," he said, raising his voice to make himself heard above the sound of a wave striking the seawall. The spray thrown up cooled Senar's skin.

The emira inclined her head, and the soldier retreated.

So this was Imerle Polivar, leader of the Storm Lords and reputedly the most powerful water-mage ever to have sat Olaire's throne; the woman who had brought to an end an ancient dispute between the Storm Isles and the city of Hunte by draining Hunte's harbor and diverting the river that ran through it; who had destroyed the stronghold of the notorious pirate lord Kapke Kar in the Uscan Reach by pummelling the fortress with waves of water-magic until it slipped into the sea. Of the woman *behind* the legend, Senar had heard nothing, but all the clues as to her temper were there in her thin mouth and wintry gaze.

The emira studied the Guardian with the same scrutiny with which he regarded her. Then she turned to look down into the courtyard. Senar followed her gaze. At the center of the yard was a wooden post. Tied to it was a stocky man with gray-green skin, naked but for a loincloth. His hands and feet were webbed, and there were gills on his cheeks. *An Untarian.* Beyond the prisoner, another figure entered the courtyard. Senar did a double take. The man was a giant, half again as tall as the soldiers standing guard along the walls. At first Senar thought he was wearing armor, but when he looked closer . . .

Matron's mercy. Years ago, in the Tresson Mountains, Senar had encountered an Uddin tribe who mixed molten iliafa ore with rose blood to create a metal that could be spun into threads as supple as string yet as strong as steel. For every enemy defeated in single combat, the tribe's warriors would stitch one of these strands through the skin of their upper arms. The giant below Senar, however, had woven the threads across his entire body from the bottom of his ankles to the top of his neck to form a metallic skin that shimmered as he walked. Over his arms, legs, and chest, black hairs sprouted from between the strands. The hilt of a sword was visible over his left shoulder.

He halted beside the Untarian and looked up at the emira.

She nodded.

Senar glanced from Imerle to the prisoner. *It seems a show has been put on for me.*

The Untarian must have known what was coming, for he started pulling against his bonds. The giant placed a paw on his right shoulder before bending until his face was level with the other man's. The prisoner gabbled in a language Senar did not recognize. His words had a pattern to them, as if he was chanting some mantra.

On the giant's left hand was a metal gauntlet with long curved talons. He lifted the gauntlet to the Untarian's chest and drew its claws across his skin. They left threads of blood in their wake.

The prisoner's voice grew louder, his eyes bright with defiance.

The giant bared his lips in a snarl.

Then he pulled back his gauntleted hand and plunged its talons into the Untarian's chest over his heart.

Senar's expression tightened. The prisoner's gasp was barely audible above the sound of cracking bones. Blood bubbled at the corners of his mouth, and he slumped against his bindings. He managed another few words of his mantra before his voice abruptly faded as if he'd run out of breath. Five metal claws in your chest would do that, though, the Guardian supposed. *Poor sod,* Senar thought. What crime had the man committed to warrant such a punishment? Perhaps no more than to be brought before Imerle on the day Senar was released, for the spectacle had clearly been intended as a warning to the Guardian of what would happen if his answers to the emira's questions failed to please.

When the emira spoke, her voice was as sibilant as the sea. "We are Imerle Polivar, emira of Olaire and first of the Storm Lords."

We? The woman referred to herself in the plural? But then doubtless she had an ego big enough for two.

The emira nodded toward the oscura addict and continued, "This is our chief minister, Pernay Ord, and beside him"—she indicated the Remnerol—"is our seer, Jambar Simanis." She paused as if expecting Senar to introduce himself, but when he kept silent she glanced at his halfhand and added, "And you are Senar Sol, member of the Guardian Council of Erin Elal and former apprentice of Li Benir. A diplomat, a spy, an assassin. Which of those three are you here, we wonder?"

Senar rubbed the stubs of his missing fingers. So it was his halfhand that had given him away? His mouth twitched. With the aim of hiding his identity, he had spent countless bells during his captivity inventing an alter ego with a history as rich and detailed as his own. Now, within the space of a few heartbeats, Imerle had rendered his efforts redundant. He had to smile, though. People who couldn't laugh at themselves were missing out on a rich vein of humor. In response to her question, he gave his best bow and said, "Here, Emira, I am naught but your prisoner."

"Why were you sent through the Merigan portal?"

So that was the end of the small talk, apparently. Senar was silent, considering. He didn't want to volunteer information unnecessarily, but neither did he want to be caught being economical with the truth.

"If you know about me, you will know of the history between the Guardians and Emperor Avallon Delamar—"

"We did not ask you to tell us what we already know," Imerle cut in. "We are aware of what happened on the night of the Betrayal. We are aware of your opposition to the emperor, and the reasons why Avallon chose *you* to travel through the gateway. Our question is, why were you sent *here*?"

"I was not sent *here*. I was sent to wherever the portal took me."

"Meaning?"

"Meaning the emperor has been trying to rid himself of the Guardians for years. The opportunity to pluck a few thorns from his flesh by sending us through the gateway was too tempting to pass up."

"You are saying Avallon has no interest in navigating the portals?"

"I am saying his professed intention of using the Guardians to decipher the portal's code is incidental—"

"A moment." It was the chief minister's turn to interrupt. "The code? You mean the symbols on the gateway's architrave?"

The Guardian nodded.

"What is the symbol for Olaire?"

"I do not know. As I stepped through the portal, the symbol was hidden from me by Avallon's pet mages."

"And the symbol for Amenor—the city from which you traveled?"

"If I knew that, would I not have used the gateway here to return to Erin Elal when I was confronted by your soldiers?"

Pernay threw up his hands. Yes, how dare Senar bring his logic and good sense here? "This is absurd!" the chief minister said. He looked at the emira, then pointed a finger at the one-eyed Remnerol. "He plays you for a fool!"

The Remnerol smiled inanely. "Your barbs strike at my heart, yet my bosom is armored in the steel of righteousness."

Pernay shook his head in disgust. To Imerle he said, "You would place your faith in this . . . this—"

The emira silenced him with a look.

There was plenty going on here that Senar did not understand, but before he could think on it, he noticed a flicker of movement in the courtyard. The dead Untarian had begun thrashing against his bonds once more. And since there was no question of the man still being alive, that could only mean . . . *dragon blood*. The claws of the giant's gauntlet must have been dipped in the poison. Dragon blood was said to scar not just the flesh but also the soul, ensuring the victim's suffering extended beyond his passage through Shroud's Gate.

A reminder, as if one were needed, that Senar would have to be on his best behavior.

Imerle said, "You say it was Avallon who ordered you through the portal."

"Correct."

"We were of the understanding the Guardians served the empire of Erin Elal, not its emperor."

"To Avallon the distinction has ceased to have any meaning."

"And you value his opinion above your own?"

Senar frowned. "Your point is well made. A few years ago his view would have carried little weight with our Council, but the Guardian order has fallen far in that time. The emperor has made sure of it."

"You hold him accountable for your losses?"

Damned right he did. "He has never acted openly against us, but neither has he passed up any opportunity to whittle down our numbers."

"Even if by doing so he weakened Erin Elal?"

"The emperor cares not if his horse dies under him, so long as he remains in the saddle."

"So we understand. In the last two years over a hundred Guardians have been lost, yes? Including your master, Li Benir."

Senar felt the familiar anger bubble up inside him. He took a breath and let it out slowly. The emira was trying to provoke a reaction in him, but he could not afford to let her succeed. Best behavior, he reminded himself. And at least his spell in captivity had given him time to grieve properly over Li Benir, and Jessca, and other friends lost.

Imerle said, "And yet in spite of Li Benir's death, when the emperor orders you through the portal, you obey. Why?"

"The word 'no' is not one Avallon recognizes." In hindsight, Senar should have been suspicious of the emperor's intent when he was summoned to Amenor, but then Senar had long thought himself too important for Avallon to try strong-arming him through the portal. Maybe he still did. Conceited, perhaps? To that charge he had to hold up his hands. Or a hand and a half at least. Thirty of the emperor's Breakers had quickly disabused him of his pretensions.

The emira said, "Six Guardians were sent through the Merigan

portal before you, is that not so? Considering your enmity toward
Avallon, you must have known he might make you the seventh."

"You think I should have run? To where? To do what?"

"The Guardians are all you know."

"The Guardians are all I *have* known, yes." After the death of his
father thirty years ago, the Guardians had become the only family
Senar had.

"Then you must be anxious to return to Erin Elal."

Senar was under no illusions on that score. Trapped as he was on
an island of water-mages, the chances of him escaping to the main-
land were slim at best. More to the point, whatever Imerle's reasons
for keeping him alive thus far, they would count for nothing unless he
could convince her his old allegiances were dead. "Return, Emira? So
the emperor can send me somewhere else through the portal?"

"So you can avenge Li Benir's death. So you can help the Guardians regain their preeminence."

"The Guardians are finished." It was hard for Senar to say the
words, but he couldn't let any sentiment show in his voice. Even though
he feared it might be true. What had happened back home in the
months he'd been away? Somehow he doubted the emperor's campaign
against the Guardians had stopped just because Senar was out of the
picture. "Even if Avallon does not disband the order, he will make
sure its numbers never return to what they were."

"And you are just going to stand aside and let that happen?"

"There is nothing I can do to prevent it." He paused. "That does
not mean, though, that I will forget the part the emperor played in
the Guardians' demise."

Imerle turned back to the courtyard. The Untarian's body had been
untied from the post and was now being dragged away by two soldiers. The executioner stood to one side, staring at nothing.

"If revenge is what you seek," the emira said, "you have come to
the wrong place. We have no quarrel with Erin Elal."

"Not yet, perhaps."

Pernay sneered. "Would you have us believe Avallon has set his
sights on the Storm Isles? Is he in the habit of confiding his plans in
you, then?"

Senar caught the man's gaze and held it. "If you've done your
homework on me, you'll know I was sent to Balshazar three years ago

to sound out the city's Ruling Council on the possibility of joining the emperor's Confederacy against the Kalanese."

"Balshazar is not a Storm Lord city."

"But it *is* part of the Sabian League. It pays you tribute. If Avallon were to gain a hold on the city, do you think he would continue paying? And if Balshazar refused to pay, would that not set a dangerous precedent?" Senar turned to gauge Imerle's reaction to his words, found her expression as blank as a slab of ice. "But whatever plans the emperor has concerning the Storm Isles, there is one thing of which you can be certain. He is not a man to settle for what he already has."

Into the silence that followed came footfalls, and Senar looked across to see the balding Storm Guard officer approaching. He halted a few paces away.

"Forgive my interruption, Emira. Mazana Creed's ship has just docked at the harbor."

Mazana Creed? A name Senar had heard before, but where?

Imerle had gone still. "Mazana Creed. You are sure, Septia?"

"That is the message I was given."

When the emira exchanged a glance with Pernay, Senar noticed with a start that a smoldering flame had kindled in her eyes. And not the sort of flame that left him feeling any warmth, either. He'd thought it a reflection of a fire behind him, but no, the flame was actually within the orbs themselves. When she looked back at him, he knew the time of his judgment was upon him. He scratched at the stubs of his missing fingers. What could he say to sway her decision? In an effort to persuade her of his usefulness he had exaggerated the threat posed by Avallon, but the longer Imerle's gaze bored into him, the more he suspected she was no more taken in by his deception than she was by his feigned indifference to the Guardians' plight.

He looked at his sword in the hands of one of the twin sisters and saw she was holding it by the scabbard, not the hilt. Did she know he could use his Will to summon the blade to him? Li Benir, the consummate diplomat, used to say that if you had to draw your sword you'd already lost. And the reality was, there was no chance of Senar fighting his way clear of this terrace—when you were standing a handful of paces from the sea, you didn't take on a water-mage of Imerle's repute and expect to walk away from it. But there were different types of losing, Senar reckoned, and any death at the hands of the emira or the twin swordswomen beat losing a lump of his chest to that metal giant in the courtyard.

You had to take your consolations where you found them.

His look at the weapon had not gone unnoticed by Imerle. She smiled faintly. "Perhaps we should adjourn to the throne room to greet Mazana," she said. "Join us, Guardian."

It took a heartbeat for her words to sink in. Was he to be spared, then?

"Emira—" the chief minister began.

Imerle waved him to silence. "Do you know," she said to Senar, "why we kept you imprisoned for so long?"

He shook his head.

"How many months has it been since you came through the portal? Nine? Ten?"

It was Pernay who answered. "Ten."

"A man could travel far in that time; is that not so, Guardian?"

"He could," Senar said cautiously.

"Aside from the Storm Guards who saw you arrive, the only people who know how you came to be in Olaire are those here now, and they can be relied on to keep the information to themselves. We trust the same can be said of you."

Senar paused, thinking. There was a certain logic to Imerle's reasoning. When Avallon discovered Senar was in Olaire, all he would know for certain was that the portal to which the Guardian had journeyed was within ten months' travel of the Storm Isles. Yet if Senar were to reveal the truth of what had happened here . . . *I'm missing something.* It was clear the emira didn't trust him, so why was she taking a chance on his silence? True, she could prevent him from leaving the island, but how could she stop him sending a message to Erin Elal if he chose to do so?

Senar's gaze shifted to the Remnerol shaman. What had Pernay said to Imerle earlier? *He plays you for a fool.* Somehow Jambar had convinced the emira to spare Senar's life, but why?

Rousing himself, the Guardian looked back at Imerle. There was an expectation in her eyes, and Senar knew what she wanted to hear. He had no hesitation in speaking the words, though if his hands hadn't been on show he would have been crossing his fingers. Or the fingers he had left, that is.

"My sword is yours, Emira," he said.

———————

The Chameleon priestess, Karmel, crept a step closer to her target. Elarr stood ten paces away, the back of his shirt emblazoned with a dark butterfly of sweat. Unlike Karmel he was pale-skinned, and as he turned toward her she saw his face was flushed. His eyes seemed to fix on her, but with her power employed Karmel knew she would be invisible to him while she remained still. Sure enough, the initiate's gaze was already sliding away to the east.

The priestess scanned the temple courtyard with its carpet of broken glass. Near the eastern edge was a huge sand-glass, its top globe now all but empty of sand. Beyond, in the shade of a colonnade, a small crowd of Karmel's fellow priests and priestesses had gathered to watch the contest, for unlike a mere initiate such as Elarr they would be able to track her movements as she closed in on her adversary. Imrie was there with her mismatched sandals. Beside her stood Colley, the belt of his robe drawn so tightly round his waist it was a wonder he could breathe. Both were watching the scene intently. The object of the game she was playing was to reach the center of the courtyard and touch her opponent without being spotted, yet most Chameleons never made it that far. The best they could hope for was to go a turn of the glass undetected.

Before commencing the game Karmel had removed her sandals, and the courtyard's flagstones burned beneath her feet. The ground would be cooler ahead and to her right in the shadow of Vaulk's Tower. The priestess had rejected an approach from that direction, though, because if she'd been in Elarr's shoes she would have expected her hunter to come from there. Time had proved the wisdom of her choice. Since the start of the game Elarr had concentrated his attention on that side of the square, and as he looked that way again Karmel stepped forward, easing her weight onto the ball of her left foot before settling back on the heel. All the while her gaze was on her opponent, not on the ground in front of her. Earlier she'd mapped out a mental path through the glass, but she was still taking a risk in moving without checking for shards. It was a risk she had to take, though, for by keeping Elarr in her sights she gave herself a chance of stopping if he spun round unexpectedly.

As he had a habit of doing.

Karmel glanced again at the sand-glass. Judging by the level of the grains she had already exceeded her best time, but that was hardly surprising considering who her opponent was. The gangly youth, Elarr, was flintcat-quick, and he was taking care to ensure his movements never settled into a pattern, that his gaze never rested for long in one place. She'd known what to expect from him, obviously, for she had danced this dance with him once before—a contest six months ago from which she'd emerged victorious, but only after two turns of the glass. Why, then, had she chosen Elarr of all the initiates as an adversary today?

For the same reason she'd opted to have broken glass scattered on the ground: she needed a challenge. Because if she could defeat an opponent such as Elarr when he knew he was being hunted, how much simpler would it be to bring down an unsuspecting target when she was finally trusted with a mission beyond the temple walls?

Patches of shadow glided across the courtyard as a flock of lime-wings passed overhead. To the west the flags of the Ingar counting-house fluttered in the breeze. Thinking to take advantage of the cover offered by the sound, Karmel raised her right foot to step forward—

Elarr turned, his sandals scuffing on the flagstones.

The priestess froze.

Something had drawn the initiate's gaze. That something could not have been Karmel, though, for Elarr was looking toward the scriptorium's archway on her left. For an instant she considered lowering her leg, then rejected the idea in case her opponent spied her in his peripheral vision.

She waited.

Footsteps approached from the archway. Elarr's mouth opened as he recognized the newcomer, and he touched the fingers of both hands to his forehead in a gesture of deference.

Curious, Karmel followed his gaze—moving her eyes, not her head.

Then frowned.

Beneath the western colonnade stood her brother, Caval. The high priest always claimed it was coincidence that brought him to this part of the temple when Karmel was playing the game, but the priestess knew otherwise. He'd been here the last two times she'd tasted defeat, and Karmel suspected he'd had a hand in both failures. It would be easy for him to sabotage her efforts, after all; all he had to do was allow his gaze to linger on her and thus give Elarr a clue as to her whereabouts. If Karmel was going to reach the youth now, before

Caval interfered, she would have to take more risks than she'd intended.

Perhaps that was no bad thing, though. Since her brother had gone out of his way to seek her out, it seemed only fair she entertain him properly.

A breeze stirred the leaves of a tree in the southwest corner of the courtyard, and their rustle blended with the susurration of the distant sea. Still balanced on one leg, Karmel looked at Elarr. The initiate had dragged his gaze from Caval and was now staring at something behind Karmel. A needlefly buzzed past his face, and he swiped at it with a stick in his right hand—the stick with which he must strike Karmel to bring the game to an end. The priestess worked saliva into her mouth. The muscles of her thighs were beginning to tremble from keeping her leg up, but she wasn't yet concerned—such twitches would be imperceptible to Elarr so long as they remained minor.

From beside her right ear another needlefly's whine sounded. The insect settled like the touch of a feather on her arm. She silently swore as she felt its stinger pierce her skin. The needlefly's body darkened and puffed out as it drew in her blood. Her flesh round the bite began to blister. The urge to scratch the swelling was strong, but Karmel ignored it. A breath of air tugged at her, and it took all her concentration to keep her balance. Her leg muscles were cramping. She reckoned she had only heartbeats before her strength gave out. Elarr would have to turn away soon, though. The longer he went without seeing her, the more he would worry she was creeping up on him from behind.

Gritting her teeth, she waited for some sight or sound to snare the youth's attention. Who knew, maybe Imrie or Colley would do something to distract him. It was against the rules for spectators to interfere, of course—but it wasn't breaking the rules if you didn't get caught.

Her friends, though, seemed to be enjoying her discomfort. Colley in particular was grinning. But then maybe he had every right to, since when he'd played this game last week, Karmel had sprinkled pepper on the ground to make him sneeze. Pranks were common among the younger priests and priestesses at the temple. Indeed, they were expected.

Not today, though. Not when there was glass on the floor that Karmel could step on.

Just then the sands of the timer ran out, and two female initiates scampered over to it from the eastern colonnade. As they wrestled the glass end over end, Elarr looked toward them. It was the opportunity Karmel had been waiting for. Lowering her leg, she took two paces forward, praying she hadn't left sweaty footprints on the flagstones behind.

The needlefly on her arm took flight. It flitted across Elarr's field of vision, and he waved his stick at it.

Karmel was now only half a dozen paces from her opponent but these last few steps would be the most difficult, for the closer she came to Elarr, the greater was the chance of him seeing her when she moved. Some sixth sense must have warned him she was near, because he began thrusting out with his stick in all directions as if he were play-fighting an imaginary foe. Safely beyond range, Karmel considered her next move. Immediately ahead the ground was blanketed in a covering of glass so thick she could see no way through. If she stepped over it to clearer ground, the initiate would surely hear her foot coming down. If she went round, though, she would have to plot a new path to her opponent. And if she was looking down at the flagstones, she couldn't also be watching Elarr.

Fortunately she had a plan. It would mean trusting more to luck than she would have liked, but with Caval standing by to spoil her game, what choice did she have?

Elarr turned to survey the courtyard again. When his back was to Karmel, she bent down and snatched up a shard of glass from the ground. Her pulse was racing, but her thoughts remained calm. Truth be told, she was starting to enjoy herself. The thrill of the hunt was back: the buzz that came from feeling the gazes of the watchers— Caval included—upon her, from seeing her opponent's frustration as she crept closer.

Karmel rose and advanced, her right foot touching down in the space the shard of glass had occupied.

So far, so good.

Now, though, she would need a touch of the Lady's fortune, for there was no way of knowing how Elarr would react to what she planned to do. On the previous occasion she'd hunted the youth, she'd duped him into turning away at the critical moment by throwing a fragment of glass onto the flagstones behind him. When he'd spun toward the sound—thinking, no doubt, that Karmel had inadvertently disturbed the carpet of glass—the priestess had sprung forward to touch him on the back.

If it worked last time . . .

Karmel tossed the shard of glass onto the ground. It made a tinkling noise.

Elarr smiled. He must have remembered the ruse she'd played in their last encounter, for he turned not toward the sound but away from it, plainly expecting a repeat of the priestess's deception.

As Karmel had hoped he would.

For she had thrown the shard not *beyond* the initiate, but merely a pace ahead and to one side of her. Elarr, by turning away from the noise, had put his back to the priestess, and two quick steps now brought her behind him. She rested a hand on his left shoulder.

"Better luck next time," she said.

Elarr groaned, his head dropping.

The sound of crunching glass marked Caval's approach, and Elarr bowed to the high priest before scurrying away. Karmel searched her brother's gaze for some hint of approval at what he'd seen, but there was nothing. There had been a time when they were able to share in each other's successes; now Caval seemed to treat her victories as if they'd come at his expense. His beard was freshly oiled, and his shoulder-length hair was held back from his eyes by a silver band. He halted before Karmel.

"Impressive," he said, though his tone gave the lie to his words. He stroked his crooked nose. "I think there must be something wrong with your sand-glass, though. I noticed the initiates turning it earlier. Surely it hasn't taken you half a bell to finish the game."

"The only problem with the sand-glass is that *I* haven't fixed it so the grains run more slowly."

"Still obsessed with beating my time?"

"You mean once wasn't enough?"

"Ah, you are referring to your efforts last month against that girl— Silina, wasn't it? I had understood the point of the game was to touch your opponent *before* she touches you, not at the same time."

"Silina got lucky. Luck-y."

"Either that or she heard you approach."

"She couldn't have done, because I made no sound. She must have heard something else and thought it was me."

"I can see why you would want to believe that," Caval said, smiling his gap-toothed smile.

Karmel scratched at her needlefly bite. There was something

unconvincing about that smile, just as there had been something unconvincing about the whole exchange. It was as if the high priest's
jousting had been done for her benefit—as if he'd merely been going
through the motions. The old banter between them didn't feel the same
anymore. Too often there was an edge to their words that could cut.

At the edge of the eastern colonnade hovered two initiates with
brooms ready to sweep the glass from the courtyard. A further two
acolytes were carrying the sand-glass toward the scriptorium with
stilted steps.

"Walk with me," Caval said to Karmel, setting off for an archway
on the far side of the square.

The priestess bridled at the note of command in his voice but
followed him all the same. She had left her sandals next to a pool of
water by the arch Caval was heading for, and she paused to wash her
feet before slipping on her shoes. Imrie and Colley waited to her right.
Karmel nodded to them, but there was no time to talk. Her brother
had gone on ahead, and she hurried through the arch to catch up
to him.

A chill hung about the temple's passages. Karmel's sweat cooled
against her skin. In front Caval passed the doorway to the Quillery,
acknowledging with a raised hand a greeting from within. His footsteps echoed along the corridor, one moment as loud as if he were
walking beside Karmel, the next so soft he might have been at the
other end of the temple. The sorcery invested in the shrine's walls was
responsible, the priestess knew—it could play such tricks on the senses.
Even now the walls rippled as Caval strode by, briefly taking on the
hue of his black robe before fading once more to white.

Karmel drew alongside her brother. "Did you know Mother is in
Olaire?" she said.

Their mother had always been a distant figure in their childhood—
emotionally as well as geographically. Too often she'd abandoned them
to their father's care while she disappeared on some mission or other.
Recently she'd tried to ingratiate herself into their lives, but neither
Karmel nor Caval had let her. It was easy to play mother now that her
children had earned independence from their father. Parenthood
wasn't supposed to be easy, though. And Karmel wouldn't forgive
her mother for being absent through the difficult times.

"I know now," Caval replied.

"I would have thought as high priest—"

"Ah, Anla reports to the emira now, not me. Imerle has been keeping her busy in the east, spying on the new pasha of Hunte."

At the end of the corridor they entered a courtyard and followed its colonnade round to the left. At the center of the square a *mithreni* initiation ceremony was under way, and a statue of the Chameleon throbbed in and out of focus as six priests circled it with outstretched hands. The slap of Karmel's sandals drew a scowl from the bearded *mithren* leading the ritual. Karmel gave him a wave.

"She asked if she could see you," she said to Caval as they reached the next passage.

"The emira?"

"No. Mother."

"Maybe she wants to remind herself what I look like."

Karmel smiled sweetly. "Or maybe she has a message for you from Father."

They had arrived at Caval's quarters. He pushed open the door.

"Well?" Karmel said. "What shall I tell her?"

"Tell her I have not forgotten."

She pretended ignorance. "Forgotten what?"

A coldness entered her brother's eyes, and Karmel wondered if she'd pushed him too far. That was always her problem: not knowing when to stop. But then when Caval's moods slipped as quickly as they did, it could be hard sometimes to tread the line between teasing and taunting. Sometimes that line could shift midsentence. Karmel tried to think of some quip that would take the sting out of her words, but Caval had already walked into his quarters.

Karmel trailed him inside.

She felt a familiar knot in her stomach as she stepped over the threshold. These chambers had belonged to their father, Pennick, until Caval deposed him as high priest in a bloodless coup last year. Since then Caval had tried to erase all marks of his predecessor. Gone were the grim-faced images of the Chameleon glaring down from the walls; the gnarled fellwood furniture; the stale odor of sweat and old blood. In their place were white-plastered walls adorned with Elescorian tapestries; bookcases filled with books on philosophy, history, and mercantile law; and covering the floor was a mosaic showing the Dragon Gate rising over the Sabian Sea. Yet even though Caval had been high priest for more than a year, the room seemed to Karmel to have an . . . impermanence to it. As if behind the plaster on the walls, the cold gray stone of Pennick's time was just waiting to be exposed once more.

For all her brother's changes, the room's most striking feature remained its transparent, west-facing wall, pulsing with sorcery. That sorcery meant that while Caval's chambers appeared from this side to be open to the elements, anyone outside staring back at the building would see only a blank wall. Karmel looked down on Olaire's black-tiled roofs. Years ago the Chameleon Temple had stood alone on the flank of Kalin's Hill, but with the sea having risen to flood the low-lying districts of the city, a tide of humanity had swept up the slope to surround the shrine. Dominating the skyline to the northwest was the Founder's Citadel, while farther south and east were the guildhouses, the mercantile courts, and the embassies of the Commercial District. One of the embassies was hosting a reception, and a dozen figures were gathered on a second-floor balcony. Some of those people seemed to be looking back at Karmel, but there was no way they would be able to see her.

The high priest had seated himself behind his desk, and Karmel sat down opposite him. He gazed down on Olaire as if he'd forgotten she was there, but then doubtless he liked having her wait on him. He rubbed his left shoulder—the shoulder that had never healed properly even after all these years—and Karmel's face twisted as she saw again the blow that had broken his collarbone, heard her father's voice gasping the Chameleon's name over and over in time to the rising and falling of his cane . . .

Caval's gaze focused on her. "I have a task for you," he said. "One uniquely suited to your talents."

Karmel blinked. "Flattery, Caval? You must need my help very badly indeed."

"You are familiar with Piput Da Marka, the governor of Dian?"

"I know the name."

"Ah, then you must be aware of the trouble he's been stirring up for the emira recently."

"Remind me." In truth, the politics of the Sabian League always made Karmel's eyes glaze over.

Caval's smile was knowing. "Since coming to power, Imerle has been steadily increasing the Sabian cities' tribute—this year alone she raised it by two hundred and fifty imperial talents—and Piput has finally had the temerity to object. With the Dragon Gate barring the dragons from the Sabian Sea, and the storms from the Broken Lands having abated of late, the Storm Council's only function, as Piput sees it, is to protect Sabian shipping from piracy." He spread his hands. "And since piracy is on the increase, Piput has been left wondering whether Imerle is really earning her keep."

The sun was bright in Karmel's eyes through the transparent wall, yet she could not feel its heat, nor detect the touch of the wind that rustled the branches of the ketar trees a short distance away. "So?"

"So he has been finding support among the leaders of the other Sabian cities. Muted support, it must be said, for while those leaders are keen to reduce their tribute, they are more anxious still not to draw the emira's eye."

Karmel could see where this was heading. "Imerle wants Piput taken down a peg or two."

Caval nodded. "She believes—rightly, I suspect—that if Dian's governor were to lose face with his allies, his cause would flounder."

The priestess was silent, considering. Then it came to her. "Dragon Day," she said.

"Very good. On Dragon Day the heads of every city in the Sabian League will converge on Dian and Natilly for the Dragon Hunt. If the Dragon Gate should fail to rise, thus depriving those leaders of their day of sport . . ."

Karmel's voice betrayed her doubt. "Fail to rise? You are the historian, I know, but as I recall, the gate hasn't failed to rise in more than three hundred years."

"Three hundred and eighty-six, to be precise. Oh, there have been plenty who wanted to stop it in that time. The Rubyholters tried to smuggle some men into the citadel a few years back. But tricking your way past the guards is going to be harder than just putting on a hat and claiming your name has been missed off the guest list."

"And that's where I come in?"

"Correct." Caval looked down at the floor mosaic of the Dragon Gate. "For the gate to rise, the hoisting mechanisms in both Dian and Natilly must be operated simultaneously. Which means it just takes one of those mechanisms to malfunction and Dragon Day will be over before it has started."

"As easy as that?"

"Ah, I never said it would be easy. In two days' time the citadel will be crawling with soldiers, and even if you make it past the outer wall you still have to get to the fortress's control room where the hoisting mechanism is located. Then there is the small matter of escaping afterward through a citadel up in arms. Of course, if you think I should find someone else . . ."

Karmel ran a hand through her short-cropped hair. Her brother was trying to play on her pride, but he needn't have bothered. For months she'd been waiting for a chance such as this to prove herself, and she would have accepted the mission whatever the dangers. What was the point of all her training, after all, if she did nothing with it? It felt sometimes as if Caval was trying to protect her, but at other times it felt like he was holding her back. A voice inside her urged caution, though. Caval had never before trusted her with an assignment of note, yet now he would trust her with *this*? Breaking into the Dianese citadel? On Dragon Day? She shifted in her seat. Even for a Chameleon it sounded . . . ambitious. "What happens if I get caught?"

"I wouldn't advise that."

"I mean, aren't you taking a risk in sending your sister? If I should be seen, the finger of suspicion will point at you."

"Whether it's you or another Chameleon, the suspicion will be the same."

"Then why did you choose me?" Karmel said, knowing the answer but wanting to hear it from him.

The high priest did not respond.

Karmel gave him an impish look. "It's all right, Caval—you can say it. I'm good. I may even be better than you. Of course we'll never know for sure if you keep refusing to spar with me."

Her brother's voice was bitter. "And that's the height of your ambition? To outdo me?"

Not that it mattered, obviously. However many times she challenged Caval, he would always find an excuse not to face her. It wouldn't do, after all, for a high priest to be beaten by one of his juniors. More to the point, it wouldn't do for a brother to be beaten by his little sister. "What about the emira? What's in it for her?"

"I've already told you. Piput gets the wind taken out of his sails—"

"Oh, come on, you can do better than that. Imerle's time as emira is up at the end of this year, meaning Piput will soon become her successor's problem. Why should she care about what tribute Dian pays when she won't be there to receive it?"

"Won't she?"

At first Karmel thought Caval was mocking her, but when his gaze held steady on hers, she realized she'd read him wrong. She leaned back in her chair. So Imerle was planning a coup, was she? For weeks the city had been alive with rumors of a plot. But then there were always rumors when an emir or emira's tenure came to an end, and none of those rumors had ever come to anything before. With good reason, too: however powerful the head of the Storm Council might be, there were five other Storm Lords to oppose them. The fact Imerle intended to risk those odds was surprising enough . . . but more surprising still was the fact she had apparently confided her plans in Caval. It was less than a year, after all, since her brother had first approached the woman to offer his services.

Caval made to rise, but Karmel remained seated. "Dragon Day is, what, three days away? If I'm supposed to infiltrate the Dianese citadel in that time, we're cutting things a little fine."

"Ah, that's why you're leaving tonight."

"Who else is coming?"

The high priest stared at her.

Karmel grinned. "I may be good, Caval, but even *I* need someone to carry my bags."

"His name is Veran."

"A Chameleon?"

"Of sorts."

"Meaning?"

"Why don't you ask him yourself. You'll be meeting him soon enough." The high priest's gap-toothed smile was back, but there was no more humor in it this time than there had been the last. "I'm sure he'll be only too happy to answer your questions."

CHAPTER 2

SEPTIA KEMPIS Parr knew he was in trouble the moment he saw the quina's clerk, Pompit, smile at him.

Only one person in the world smiled like that. Pompit's top lip curled back as if he were offering his upper teeth for inspection, giving his face an expression of such smugness the septia wanted to slap it with a closed first. Right now, though, he had more important things on his mind, like what in the Nine Hells he was doing here. Quina Hilaire Desa's messenger had said she wanted to see him, but not why.

Kempis was damned if he was going to ask Pompit. Instead he crossed to a chair beside the left-hand wall and sat down. To Pompit's right was the door to Hilaire's office, and from behind it Kempis heard voices—a woman's and a man's. The quina's was simple enough to identify, but the man's was not one the septia recognized. Then Hilaire's laughter rang out, and Kempis's face fell. The only jokes the quina laughed at were those of her superiors. A coincidence that Kempis had been summoned when Hilaire's mysterious visitor was here? Not if Pompit's smile was anything to go by.

The septia thought back over the things he'd done recently that might have caught the eye of someone in high places. There was that business this morning with the merchant who'd tried to clear a path through the crowds in Hare Lane with his riding whip, but even if the man had identified Kempis as the one who'd unfastened his saddle's girth-strap, there was no way he could have tracked him down so swiftly. Then there was the matter of the debts Kempis had racked up while investigating the bloodbath at Lappin's gambling den. The septia was already down a month's wages, but surely he had too much dirt on Lappin for the den's owner to risk tattling on him.

There was another possibility, of course. Maybe someone had finally tracked down Corrick's killer and was here to share the good news. It was more than six months since Kempis's partner had taken a crossbow bolt through the neck and spent his last heartbeats coughing blood onto the septia's boots. New boots they'd been, as well. The two Watchmen had been patrolling Olaire's Wharf District when they'd seen three hooded men creeping along Ravens Alley. One of the strangers was plainly a blueblood, because he wore so much gold on his fingers Kempis was surprised his knuckles didn't drag on the ground. The other figures must have been the man's bodyguards—Storm Guards, no less, judging by the fish-scale armor they'd been wearing. Corrick had insisted on following them, and Kempis had reluctantly tagged along. They'd trailed the strangers to the flooded streets of the Shallows where the blueblood and his minders had boarded a boat.

Kempis hadn't seen the crossbowmen who'd fired at Corrick and at him. He should have known the bastards were there, though, for how many bluebloods went strolling through the Wharf District with just two bodyguards for company? Kempis had been hit in the shoulder. He'd escaped by taking refuge in one of the partly submerged houses on Flask Street. When he didn't reappear with the rising tide, the crossbowmen must have thought he'd drowned inside. The septia had certainly felt on the threshold of Shroud's Gate next morning when he crawled bloody and shivering from the water.

It was several weeks before Kempis had recovered from his ordeal. The wound to his side had healed quickly enough, but the same could not be said of the mental scars left by his first dip in the sea since a kris shark had nibbled on his thigh twenty years ago. Because the blueblood's minder had been a Storm Guard, the emira had insisted on her personal soldiers investigating the incident. Needless to say they'd never caught Corrick's killer, and by the time Kempis was on his feet again the trail had gone cold. Not that the septia was in any hurry to avenge his partner. The fool had got what was coming to him for sticking his nose where it wasn't wanted. Nothing good ever came of mixing with the bluebloods.

Which made the presence next door of one of their kind all the more troubling.

Another peal of Hilaire's laughter sounded. It crossed Kempis's mind to listen at the door in case he could hear what was being said, but one glance at Pompit put an end to the idea. The clerk was still grinning. Evidently he'd been warned a blueblood would be visiting, because his uniform looked as pristine as if it had been sewn this morning. He sat behind a desk made from a wood as dark as Kempis's skin. He must have been sitting on a cushion, for his feet dangled half a handspan above the floor.

Kempis pushed himself to his feet.

Pompit said, "A bit restless, are we, Septia?"

"Just stretching my legs."

On the clerk's desk were piles of papers arranged with geometric precision, all written in an orderly hand any scribe would be proud of. The piece of parchment on top of the nearest pile was a requisition order for swords, helmets, and breastplates. The paper next to it concerned the sighting of a ship flying no flag off the western shore of the island. When Kempis lifted the parchment for a closer look, Pompit snatched it from him, then began rubbing at a smudged thumbprint the septia had left in one corner. In a vase to the clerk's right stood a bunch of dewflowers, their scent doubtless intended to mask the stink of excrement coming from the open window to Kempis's left. The whole city reeked like a blocked latrine today. On the septia's walk through the Wharf District the stench had been strong enough to conceal even the smell of fish from the market in Crofters Lane.

Through the window Kempis heard a clash of wooden swords in the Watchstation's exercise yard. Then above that . . .

Footfalls from the quina's office.

Kempis spun round just as the door opened. A cloud of perfume engulfed him. Through watering eyes he saw Hilaire standing in the doorway. She had found a medal from somewhere and pinned it to her breast. Her long brown hair was held up by jeweled pins. On her face was a smile left over from her discussion with her guest—a smile that faded as she took in Kempis's unkempt hair and crumpled uniform. Her mouth opened and closed, and he thought that she would slam the door in his face. Instead she gestured him into her office with a look that warned him to be a good boy.

Kempis glanced past her.

And inwardly groaned.

Standing in front of Hilaire's desk was a middle-aged man with gray eyes, a gray mustache, and a few strands of gray hair carefully arranged across his skull in an effort to conceal his baldness. Dutia Elemy Meddes. The head of the Storm Lords' forces in Olaire stood rigidly at attention as if Kempis were his superior come to inspect him. Kempis's hackles rose. True, Gray-Face had a reputation for fairness, but after that business with Corrick in the Shallows the septia couldn't look at a Storm Guard without wondering if he owed him a crossbow bolt in the shoulder.

Hilaire closed the door behind Kempis and strode to her desk. The windows along the wall behind were closed against the city's stink, and the air in the room was as stuffy as the dutia.

"Sir," Hilaire said to Elemy, her voice unrecognizable from the harsh Olairian drawl Kempis was used to. "Allow me to introduce Septia Kempis Parr. Kempis, this is Dutia Elemy Meddes."

Kempis hesitated. Was he supposed to bow or salute or just shake the man's gray hand? In the end he gave him a nod. "Good of you to deliver the news yourself, sir."

Gray-Face cast a critical eye over the septia. "News?"

"About Corrick. It's been months since he died, right? Emira's personal guard can't have drawn a complete blank in that time."

Hilaire came to Elemy's rescue. "Corrick was Kempis's former partner, sir. The one I was telling you about."

Gray-Face said, "Ah, yes, an unfortunate business. Alas, it seems the emira's soldiers have made no progress. The case has been closed."

Was it possible to close something that had never been opened? Kempis was about to ask when Hilaire hurriedly said, "Kempis has a new partner now, isn't that so, Septia?"

Kempis nodded. "Sniffer, we call her," he said to Elemy.

"Why, may I ask?"

" 'Cause that's her name."

Hilaire leapt into the breach once more. "One of the Untarians, sir. Even for her kind she has a remarkable ability to follow a trail through water. If a fugitive so much as steps in a puddle, Sniffer can track his footsteps across the length and breadth of the city."

Kempis's eyes narrowed. The only reason Hilaire had to talk up his team was because there was work in the offing. He was starting to feel like he was being interviewed for a job he didn't want. "Of course, ain't no guarantee Sniffer will be around much longer," he said. "Just a few days now and her sentence ends."

Elemy raised an eyebrow. "Sentence?"

"Sniffer's one of our probationers. Didn't the quina tell you? It were either serve her time behind bars or in the Watch. If you ask me, she made the wrong choice."

Gray-Face looked at Hilaire. "What did she do?"

"She, ah . . . accosted the son of one of the magisters."

"*Grand* Magister Dewar, weren't it?" Kempis said. His gaze shifted to Elemy's poorly concealed bald pate. "Not wanting to split hairs, or anything."

Hilaire bailed manfully. "A little youthful exuberance—"

"Tell that to the cutter who stitched the poor sod up afterward. Handy with her knives, is Sniffer. Sliced the lad so bad that when the cutter were finished with him he looked like one of them Alosian patchwork dolls." An exaggeration, obviously. As Sniffer had explained it to Kempis, the boy's only injury had been self-inflicted when he attempted to draw his sword. The septia's gaze returned to Elemy's scalp. "Escaped with his life by a hairbreadth, you might say."

The dutia looked across at Hilaire, but for once she had no inspiration to offer. "Well," he began, then ran out of things to say. "Yes, well," he tried again. "At least this Sniffer should be well-acquainted with the workings of the criminal mind, eh, Quina?"

Hilaire's burst of laughter had a note of desperation in it.

Elemy sank into one of the chairs in front of the quina's desk, and Hilaire also sat. When Kempis made to do likewise, she shot him a look that froze him solid.

Gray-Face appeared not to notice. "What of yourself, Septia? I understand you have something of a talent too for hunting down lawbreakers."

It was Hilaire who answered. "Indeed so, sir. Kempis is able to sniff out a mage anywhere in the city."

"Not mages, *magic*," Kempis said. Then, to Elemy, "Sorcery leaves ripples I can sense if I get to the source of the power quick enough."

"Quickly? How quickly?"

"Depends on how strong the magic is."

A needlefly landed on the dutia's gleaming skull, and he waved a hand at it. "And if you detect a mage's signature, you will recognize it if you encounter it again?"

"I know shit when I smell it," Kempis said, then as an afterthought added, "Sir."

"You are not a magician yourself, though. Is that correct?"

"Hells, no. Ain't no one ever taught me this stuff. When I sense sorcery, it's instinctive. A feeling like"—Kempis pretended to consider, his eyes flickering once more to Elemy's bald pate—"like hairs standing up on the back of my neck."

Gray-Face's furrowed brow suggested the penny had finally dropped.

Hilaire cleared her throat. "You are familiar with Bedel, sir? The madman who terrorized the city last year?"

"I know the name," Elemy said, tearing his gaze from Kempis.

"Bedel was a lowborn trader in sun pearls who had an ax to grind with guild master Thetharo. Thetharo refused to pay Bedel for a shipment of pearls he claimed never to have received. Bedel's efforts to extract money from Thetharo in the courts proved unsuccessful—"

"There's a shock," Kempis muttered.

"So Bedel decided to take matters into his own hands. Unbeknownst to Thetharo, Bedel was a blood-mage, and he began butchering members of the guild master's family, then bathing in the blood of each victim in order to acquire the power to subdue his next target."

"Hair-raising stuff," the septia said.

"Kempis was the man who succeeded in tracking Bedel down when all others had failed."

Elemy nodded absently. The sun pouring through the window to his left had breathed some color into his gray skin. The dutia must have been concerned for his complexion, though, because he rose and moved to stand in the shadows. "Is there anyone else on your staff," he said to Hilaire, "who has this ability to track magic?"

"I'm afraid not, sir."

The needlefly was now buzzing round Kempis's head, but he ignored it. It was clear Elemy was weighing up whether to entrust him with a mission, and Kempis searched for a way to swing the decision against him. He'd run out of hair gags, though. And something told him if his antics thus far hadn't sent Elemy running for the hills, then nothing would. Sure enough the dutia's shoulders slumped, and Kempis knew his fate was sealed. The only consolation was that Gray-Face seemed as happy about the whole business as Kempis himself was.

"You are familiar, Septia," Elemy said, "with the fellowship of water-mages known as the Drifters? Their job, amongst other things, is to ensure the sea in the Shallows continues to circulate, thus preventing the accumulation of nightsoil and other unpleasantries."

Kempis smirked. *Nightsoil*. He'd have to remember that one.

"As you may have deduced," Elemy went on, "the Drifters on duty last night failed to carry out their responsibilities." When Kempis returned his look blankly, Elemy wrinkled his nose and said, "You must have noticed the smell."

"I thought that was Pompit, sir."

Hilaire's voice was cold. "Three Drifters were murdered in the early hours this morning, Septia—one in Waterside Road, one in Char Lane, and one in Stocks Alley. The killer got sloppy with his last victim because he left a couple of witnesses behind."

"We got a description?"

"No. One of the witnesses, though, mentioned seeing the assassin . . . disappear after the killing."

"Disappear as in do a runner?"

"Disappear as in disappear."

"Right. Puff of smoke, was it?"

Hilaire did not reply.

Kempis looked from the quina to Elemy then back again, expecting one of them to continue the brief. When it became clear they were waiting for *him* to speak he said, "That's it? That's all you've got?"

Gray-Face paused, then nodded to Hilaire.

"We lost another Drifter the night before last," she said, "along with some water-mage in from Cinsar. The night before that it was a stormcaller from the Uscan Reach. We thought nothing of their deaths at the time, but now . . ."

"You reckon someone has a bone to pick with water-mages?"

Elemy said, "That is for you to determine. In case it has slipped your mind, the Storm Lords are also water-mages, and it just so happens Mazana Creed's ship docked in the harbor quarter of a bell ago. With Dragon Day approaching, the other Storm Lords are likely not far behind."

"It's one hell of a step up from a Drifter to a Storm Lord."

"And I intend to ensure the assassin never makes it. Last night's sighting of the killer is the only lead we have, so I suggest you begin your inquiries at the scene of the third Drifter's murder. If the assassin did just . . . disappear, it is safe to assume sorcery is involved. But we will know for certain if you detect any of those ripples you mentioned earlier."

"And if I find nothing?"

Elemy's expression made it plain he thought that unlikely. "When you track the assassin down, I want him brought in alive. I have questions."

"I'll try to keep Sniffer on her leash."

The crash of wooden swords in the Watchstation's exercise yard sounded suddenly loud. There was a strangled shriek and a stream of curses so colorful they brought a glow to Hilaire's cheeks.

Gray-Face's gaze remained fixed on Kempis. "I trust I don't need to tell you the Storm Lords will be most grateful if you succeed in catching the perpetrator."

Kempis made a sour face. He'd had a taste of blueblood gratitude before, and it hadn't agreed with him one bit. Last month he'd intercepted a thief climbing through one of the windows of Magister Nayak's home, and the judge had shown his appreciation by presenting Kempis with a bill for a statue destroyed in the ensuing struggle. On this occasion, though, it was clear from Hilaire's look who'd be taking any credit that was going.

"Well, then, that's settled," Gray-Face said, marching toward the door. "Keep me informed of developments, Quina."

"Of course, sir," Hilaire replied, moving round her desk. In her rush to open the door for Elemy she almost bundled Kempis from his feet. She trailed the dutia outside.

"I should be making a move too," Kempis said. "Them ripples won't be getting any stronger . . ."

Hilaire shut the door on him.

He scowled, knowing what was coming next.

Another peal of Hilaire's laughter sounded from Pompit's room, followed by a moment of silence. Then the quina reentered the office and slammed the door behind her. Her hands were clenched into fists. She looked Kempis up and down once more, her expression darkening all the while.

"Gods below, Septia," she said, "did you spend the night in a gutter? And where in the Sender's name are your stripes?"

"Must have come loose," Kempis replied, hoping she wouldn't ask him to turn out his pockets.

Hilaire jabbed a finger at his chest. "Unless you want them to come loose permanently, you're going to give this case your undivided attention. You don't rest until the killer is caught, you understand? You don't eat, you don't sleep, hells, you don't take a shit until this is over . . ."

Inspiring stuff, but Kempis was only half listening. It wasn't as if he needed any encouragement to catch the assassin. The sooner he was out of the blueblood spotlight, the better.

". . . and until the killer is in one of our cells, I'm going to be over you like a rash . . ."

An unpleasant image stirred in Kempis's mind—one he suspected he wouldn't be able to shift for days.

". . . you stay away from the dutia, do you hear me?" Each of the quina's words was accompanied by another poke of her finger. "If you sense one of those sorcerous ripples, you report it to me. You hear a whisper from one of your sources, I want to know. And when you track down the killer, you don't move against him unless I'm there . . ."

Normally Kempis would have been happy to have another pair of eyes watching his back. In Hilaire's case, though, he suspected it was just so she could decide where to bury her knife.

The pep talk ended, and the quina tugged loose the medal pinned to her breast and slung it onto the desk. "Anything you need, you come to me. In the meantime I'm giving you Loop and Duffle."

"I don't want—"

"I don't care what you want, you'll take them anyway."

Kempis frowned. It was bad enough nursemaiding Sniffer, now he had two more fools to dog his heels? "That business at Lappin's gambling den—"

"Has been reassigned. Nothing gets in the way of this job, do I make myself clear?" Hilaire looked him up and down a final time, then shuddered. "I've sent Loop and Duffle ahead to secure the crime scene. Sniffer should be on her way there as we speak. Now, get out of here, Septia. You've got work to do."

Senar Sol trailed the emira's party down the steps from the roof terrace and along the palace corridor. He kept expecting a squad of Storm Guards to pounce on him, but for the time being it seemed his stay of execution was a genuine one. The emira came to a set of double doors in the wall holding back the sea. Two Storm Guards tugged the doors open to reveal a shimmering barrier of water. Imerle gathered her power, and Senar watched openmouthed as that barrier receded to form a passage bounded above and to either side by the sea, and below by a mosaic path that sloped down into the deep. The emira, Pernay, and Jambar set off along it, and the Guardian followed.

All about, the sea was bright with trapped sunlight. Senar reached out a hand to one of the walls and felt a tingle of sorcery as his fingers entered the water. A warm wind was at his back, and when he looked behind he saw the seawall covered in swaying fireweed. After thirty paces the passage opened out into a chamber that was still expanding like an air sac. Here too the walls and ceiling comprised barriers of water, while covering the floor was a mosaic depicting a hugely muscled blue-skinned figure clutching a fish-spine sword— the Sender, Senar presumed. The god was battling a shadowy, many-tentacled beast with a scaled hide. Threads of watery light shifted across the image, making it appear as if the combatants were in motion. Beyond the edges of the mosaic, the seabed fell away on all sides.

Set into the floor near the far wall were six thrones made from the vast yellowed bones of some creature—a dragon, probably. The beast's teeth, each a handspan long, crowned the back pieces of the chairs. Imerle settled into the throne left of center, and the chief minister sat to her right. The Remnerol shaman moved behind them. Unsure where to stand, Senar took up a position apart from the others beside the left-hand wall. Strange how he could be among people once more, yet feel no less alone than he'd felt during his captivity.

The throne room was a different kind of cold and gray from the Guardians' Sacrosanct, but a flood of memories still came pressing in upon him, sharper than he'd endured them for months: he saw again the time he'd first got past Li Benir's guard in a duel, and the smile in his master's eyes afterward; the day he'd met Jessca; the time he'd stood in the Great Hall and been sworn in as a member of the Council, his sense of pride tainted by the knowledge that his seat was available only because of the Guardians' losses in the Betrayal. He forced the recollections down. Sometimes memories warm you, but more often they serve only to remind you of things lost. To live with the past, you need to have a future too.

Pernay was whispering to the emira, and a certain steel in her eyes suggested sparks would fly in the imminent meeting with Mazana Creed. A part of Senar wondered why, but another part warned him to keep a tight rein on his curiosity. His only interest in the Storm Isles' business was in steering a safe course through it until an opportunity to slip away presented itself. For he *would* find a way to get back home. He must. The "how" could wait for another day.

And yet, what was there in Erin Elal for him to return to? Li Benir, Jessca, Ul Rettel, all dead. Erilon retired. Jeng Elesar and Amad Adala gone through the Merigan portal ahead of Senar. Most likely the rest of the order would soon go Shroud's way too, if indeed it hadn't done so already. Perhaps it was a blessing he wouldn't be around to witness the death stroke when it fell. Perhaps he should be grateful for this chance to start over.

The twin swordswomen approached. Blond-haired and thin as willow reeds, they walked with the grace of dancers, yet their arms showed knotted muscles beneath tanned skin. Up close, they seemed even taller than they had on the roof terrace. One of the women was holding Senar's sword.

"Your blade, Guardian," she said, offering him the weapon.

Senar accepted it with a bow. Gods, that felt better. "My thanks." He looked between the sisters. "You are the emira's bodyguards?"

"We are," the one who'd given him his sword said.

"Amongst other things," the other added.

"I am called Tali."

"And I am Mili."

Senar studied their faces but could see no difference in their fine-boned features. Evidently conscious of his scrutiny Tali said, "We are identical . . ."

". . . except for our scars."

"Perhaps we will . . ."

". . . show you some time."

If Senar had been minded to look he suspected he could have seen for himself, because the wispy material of the women's susha robes left little to the imagination.

Tali reached up a hand to stroke his cheek. "So pretty."

Senar flinched, then hastily said, "Who is this Mazana Creed the Storm Guard mentioned?"

Mili shrugged, uninterested. "A Storm Lady."

"And not a favorite of the emira, I take it."

"The emira has no favorites . . ."

". . . unless it is us, of course."

"Of course." Senar looked between the twins again. "I am curious, how do the two of you converse when the other is not around to finish your sentences?"

"We will never know, Guardian . . ."

". . . we do everything together."

Tali leaned in close, smiling. "Everything."

Senar was saved from having to respond by the arrival of the executioner. The threads of metal across the giant's shoulders and at the top of his back glowed softly, and as he passed Senar the Guardian felt a wash of heat. Moments later four other figures entered the chamber. In front was a woman with copper-colored hair. She wore a red dress cut just the right side of indecent, and she walked with a muscular stride that had her companions hastening to keep up. Around her neck was a chain from which hung a jewel that must have been invested with air-magic, for it shone like a star in the meager light.

Behind her came three men. The first was barrel-chested and wore a puffed blue shirt and leggings. His black hair was braided close to his scalp, and his small, close-spaced eyes kept flickering to his female companion as if he feared she might steal away when his head was turned. Next to him was a tall, blond-haired man with an ageless face and skin as bronze as the cuirass he wore. His left arm from the hand to the elbow was a lighter tan than the rest of his body. The third man walked with a pronounced stoop. His teeth were stained with blackweed, and his shirt was open to his navel. A curious fashion, that. What was the point in having clothes if you didn't actually *wear* them?

The woman halted her party just inside the chamber, then stepped into the center like an actor taking to the stage. Her gaze lingered on Senar before shifting to the emira. "Imerle," she said. "So good to see you again. Allow me to present my companions. You know my dutia, Beauce"—she indicated the black-toothed man. "To his left is Greave"—the fat man—"and to his right, Kiapa"—the man in the cuirass.

Imerle did not spare them a glance. "Why are you here, Mazana?"

Ignoring the question, the Storm Lady looked from the emira to Senar, then back again. "Aren't you going to introduce us?"

Imerle hesitated. "This is Senar Sol, a Guardian from Erin Elal."

"A Guardian," Mazana repeated, crossing to stand before him. She offered him her left hand. There was something in her gaze that left him acutely aware of the shabbiness of his clothes. "And what business does the acquisitive Emperor Avallon Delamar have in the Storm Isles?"

Senar lifted her hand to his lips. "The *business* here is not the emperor's but mine," he said. "As is the pleasure."

The Storm Lady's lips quirked.

Imerle said, "You have not answered our question. Why are you here?"

Mazana withdrew her hand. "Why? I come as summoned, obedient as ever to your orders."

"Summoned?"

"Your summons, my dear. Surely you remember sending it."

Silence.

Senar was watching Mazana. She glanced at Pernay before looking back at the emira and rolling her eyes. "You didn't know? Really, Imerle, you must keep our esteemed chief minister on a tighter rein. I appreciate the two of you are close but—"

"What are you talking about?" Pernay cut in. "No summons was sent."

"I received it two days ago. The parchment bore the emira's mark."

"You have it here?"

Mazana looked at her three companions. "Did we bring it?"

The black-toothed dutia made to spit on the floor, then stopped himself. "We left it behind."

Mazana turned back to Pernay. "We left it behind."

"Of course you did."

"You flatter yourself if you think I would choose to come here of my own volition."

"Enough of this! We are tired of your games!"

The Storm Lady's eyes glittered. "If you are so sure I'm playing you false, Chief Minister, perhaps you can explain why the flagship of our perfumed friend, Cauroy, came in to dock just as I was disembarking."

Pernay regarded her skeptically before looking to the emira for guidance. Imerle's eyes, though, were closed, and after a moment the chief minister pushed himself to his feet. "What did this summons say?" he asked Mazana.

"The clue is in the word 'summons.' "

Senar cleared his throat to cover a chuckle.

"I meant precisely!"

"*Precisely* it said that I was required to present myself here today. Really, Chief Minister, the dots aren't so hard to join up if you try."

Pernay's hands were shaking, and he clasped them behind his back. "The parchment bore the emira's mark but not her signature, I take it."

"Indeed."

"And you did not think that strange?"

Mazana waved a languid hand. "I have been thinking of little else these last two days." An idea seemed to come to her. "Perhaps it was our quarrelsome colleague Gensu who called this gathering. Perhaps he wants to reopen the question of your employment." The Storm Lady looked at Imerle, her expression hardening. "Or perhaps *I* am not the one playing games here."

Senar frowned. *Gensu?* Another Storm Lord? The names slipped his mind even as he heard them, and no one was bothering to provide him with a commentary. But he didn't need to know who the players were in order to learn from Mazana and Pernay's exchange. The suspicion on both sides was palpable, as was the dislike. Mazana had appeared genuinely surprised to discover the emira knew nothing of the summons, but she had quickly recovered her poise and now seemed to be taking great pleasure in goading the chief minister. As for Pernay, his hostility suggested he and Mazana were resuming a long-standing feud—though Senar suspected the feud was in truth between Mazana and Imerle, and that Pernay was simply shielding his mistress from the brunt of the other woman's verbal barbs.

The emira finally opened her eyes. Flames smoldered in their depths. "Whatever the explanation, Mazana, it appears you have had a wasted journey. Don't let us keep you."

"Thoughtful of you as ever, but I think I will stay awhile. Perhaps one of the other Storm Lords will have an answer to this mystery when they get here."

"Oh? You know for certain that they all received a summons?"

A slip, that, by Mazana? If so, she wasn't about to acknowledge it. "It would seem a fair assumption. Now, if you don't mind, I think I will retire to my house to freshen up. Perhaps by the time I return you will have remembered why you sent the summons."

The skirt of her dress swirled about her legs as she spun round. Her companions parted for her. As she disappeared along the underwater passage, Beauce and Kiapa set off in pursuit. Greave hesitated an instant before following, as if he had been expecting an invitation to speak. Senar found himself missing the Storm Lady already, if only because the emira and her crowd mistrusted the woman even more than they mistrusted him.

The double doors leading to the palace closed with a boom.

Pernay threw himself into his chair. "The bitch is hiding something, I swear it!"

Senar was not so sure. Thinking back to the cut of Mazana's dress, he felt, to the contrary, that the Storm Lady was revealing too much.

The shaman said, "If Mazana is right, and the other Storm Lords are heading here, what does she gain by calling them together?"

"If we knew that," Pernay snapped, "we wouldn't be having this conversation!"

"I meant, there is sense in what she says. Gensu has more reason—"

"Then why was the emira's mark on the summons? Gensu has never shied from putting his name to his grievances before. No, this melodrama stinks of Mazana's work."

A kris shark was now prowling the seas behind the executioner. The giant appeared unaware of its presence, and Senar found himself wondering whether the fish's teeth could penetrate the man's armor. Or if anything could, for that matter.

Pernay was saying to Jambar, ". . . you're supposed to be a shaman, aren't you? How is it your arts failed to forewarn you of Mazana's coming?"

Jambar sighed. "I have been agonizing over that same question. Alas, the days leading up to Dragon Day are ever a blur to me."

Senar's heart skipped a beat. *Dragon Day.* It was close, then? He'd always thought he'd liked to see the Hunt one day. Now he was reconsidering.

Jambar went on, "The convergence of so many formidable powers on our fair city has muddied the waters of my prescience."

Pernay turned to Imerle. "Whoever is behind this, the timing of the summons can be no coincidence. Our plans—"

The emira raised a hand to cut him off. And just as things were getting interesting, too. "Guardian," she said, "we would hear your thoughts."

Suddenly the spotlight was back on Senar. The Guardian shifted under Imerle's regard. Had she expected him to follow all this enough to express an opinion? "If Mazana Creed's performance here was just a performance in truth, then it was masterful. But I do not know enough about the other players to judge the pattern of the game."

Pernay spoke. "Could the woman's companions be relevant? What do we know of them?"

"The bronze-skinned man is an Everlord," Senar said. "His left arm below the elbow was less tanned than the rest of his body, suggesting the limb has been severed recently and grown back. The new skin has not yet darkened to match the old."

"And the other man? The fat one?"

Senar raised an eyebrow at his tone. "You will have to forgive me, Chief Minister. The view from my cell was somewhat limited."

Pernay scowled.

The emira said, "Guardian, go to her."

Senar blinked. "To Mazana?"

"See what you can find out about her schemes, then report back to us."

He hadn't seen *that* coming. He'd assumed Imerle would want him close at hand so she could keep a fiery eye on him. More to the point, there was no reason to think Mazana would be more forthcoming with Senar that she'd been with the emira. But then he was beginning to suspect Imerle's order had as much to do with getting him out of the throne room as it did with obtaining information.

"As you command," he said. "Mazana will surely guess, though, why you have sent me to her. What if she turns me away?"

Imerle smiled with her usual warmth. "Somehow we think that is the least of your concerns."

Judging by the rate at which the sea had crept inland over recent years, Kempis reckoned the brothel had only a few months left before the water claimed its ground floor. The waves lapping at the road already reached to within half a dozen paces of the building's doorway. Three stories high, the brothel tilted precariously over the alley onto which it fronted. From its upper windows leaned painted ladies who shouted abuse at Kempis as he strode beneath.

In front of the building, Loop and Duffle flanked a pale-skinned nobleman in gaudy green silks with a face so bruised it looked like he'd run into a wall. Loop was the closest thing the Watch had to a mage. He'd been in the job as long as Kempis had, though strangely this would be the first time they'd worked together on a case. Duffle, like Sniffer, was a thief seeing out his sentence in the Watch, and Kempis suspected the youth was using the time as work experience to find out how the other side operated. Even barefooted, Duffle towered over Loop and the noble. The youth's uniform—the largest the Watch's quartermaster had been able to find—was a finger's width too short for him at the wrists and ankles.

A breeze blew off the sea, carrying on it the stench of excrement. The water had a sheen to it. Bobbing on the surface were clinking bottles, scraps of wood, torn fishing nets, even a boot missing its sole. A pace from the water's edge was a bloody sheet covering what had to be a corpse. Taking a look at the package meant getting closer to the sea than Kempis would have liked, but he gritted his teeth and crouched beside the body. He lifted a corner of the sheet. Sharks must have been at the corpse, because its left arm was missing. Its facial features were unrecognizable, but the contours of the body were unmistakably those of a woman.

Loop approached. "That one ain't ours, Septia. The lass here washed up half a bell ago while we was waiting for you to show."

Now he tells me. Kempis let the sheet fall and rose. "So where's the Drifter?"

"Taken away to be put on ice. Body was getting a bit ripe in the heat."

"You saw it?"

Loop spat into his hands and ran them through his hair. "Yeah, pro job. One stab through the heart, nice and clean." He almost sounded disappointed.

Kempis looked at the pale-skinned man standing next to Duffle. "Who's the blueblood?"

"Witness, sir."

Kempis took in the dandy's bruised face. "Didn't like his answers to your questions, eh?"

"Weren't my work. Couple of lads in the Duskwatch caught him running from the scene. Mistook him for the killer and, er, got a bit carried away. Knocked him out cold for a couple of bells."

"What about the other witness Hilaire mentioned?"

"One of the whores. Not spoken to her yet—too shook up."

"Where is she now?"

"Inside. Went to lie down."

"I bet she did."

"You want me to find her?"

Kempis nodded, and the mage scuttled away. Farther along the alley a fat man wearing furs waddled into view from a side street. Seeing the septia, he smoothly reversed course and disappeared. A heartbeat later Sniffer emerged from the street he'd taken. In her webbed hands was a raw, half-eaten runefish, its flesh a gray-green to match the Untarian's skin. As she drew up before Kempis she picked a fish bone from her teeth and flicked it away. She was whistling through her gills, and the septia shot her a look to silence her.

"What we got?" she said.

Before Kempis could respond, a new voice spoke. "You, man! You are Septia Kempis Parr?" The pale-skinned noble shook off Duffle and strode forward. His right eye was swollen shut, and his hair was crusted with blood. To his shattered nose he held a handkerchief spotted with more blood. "Well? Answer me, man!"

Kempis bristled at the dandy's tone. He'd have to play this carefully, though, since Duffle had evidently given the blueblood his name. "And you are?"

"Colm Spicer," the noble replied with the arrogance of all those born into privilege. He looked for a flicker of recognition in Kempis's eyes, then added, "Of House Spicer. The largest actuary in Olaire!"

"Of course. Can't think how I missed you. Must have been the bruising to your face that threw me, sir."

Colm did not react to his irony. But then it was amazing the shit you could get away with just by adding "sir" at the end of a sentence.

"I demand justice!" the man said. "Your men attacked me without provocation. I want them whipped! Whipped, do you hear me!"

Spittle flew from his mouth, and Kempis wiped a hand across his face.

"I can describe the perpetrators to you," Colm continued. "One had a scar along his jaw. Potter, I think his friend called him—"

"Please, sir," Kempis interrupted, holding up a hand. "I'll need to take a full statement, but this ain't the time or the place. If you like, I could call round your house later."

The noble cast a glance at the brothel before licking his lips. "Is that really necessary?"

"Absolutely. Like to do things by the book, me. Ain't that right, Sniffer?"

The Untarian nodded as she tore off another mouthful of fish.

Kempis looked at the blueblood's left hand and saw a wedding band on his ring finger. "If you ain't in, I'll speak to your missus, shall I?"

Colm stared down at the ring.

"Or if you'd prefer, we could continue this in my office. I'm a reasonable man, sir. You can rely on me and the lads for discretion, but I'd worry someone might see you going into the Watchstation and ask questions."

Colm studied Kempis, then ground his teeth together. "Never mind."

The septia slapped him on the back. "Good of you, sir. I'm sure the lads meant no harm. I'll have a word with them if you like, make certain it don't happen again." The only thing he'd be telling Potter when he caught up with him was to watch his back. Bluebloods weren't the types to let grudges slip. "What brings you to this part of the city, if you don't mind me asking?"

Colm watched with sick fascination as Sniffer bit into the runefish's egg sac and used her tongue to tease out the roe. She showed her black teeth to him, and he came to suddenly before swinging his gaze to Kempis. "Excuse me?"

"What were you doing in the Shallows?"

"I'd left the Round and was making my way to the Temple District when I must have, uh, lost my bearings."

"Temple District is *up* the hill from the Round. Strange you should find yourself all the way down here."

"Ah, yes." The noble paused. "There's a shortcut I sometimes use. Well, not a shortcut as such—"

"Keep digging, sir," Sniffer cut in. "I'm sure you'll be out of that hole in no time."

Colm glared at her.

"This Drifter," Kempis said. "You get a good look at who did for him?"

"I already told your colleague—"

"And now you're going to tell me. So, did you get a look at the killer?"

"Of course not! It happened just after the fourth bell. Pitch bloody dark, it was!"

"Explains how you got lost."

The noble searched Kempis's expression for mockery.

"The assassin," Kempis prompted.

"She was standing—"

"*She,* sir?"

"I know a woman when I see one. Her build, her poise, her bearing."

"Where exactly did you see her?"

"There," the noble said, pointing down the alley, "at the corner of the next building."

"In the sea, then."

"I heard a splash when the Drifter's body hit the water. That's what caught my attention in the first place. The killer was crouching beside the man, checking for a pulse."

"How far away were you?"

"A dozen paces, maybe."

"A dozen paces," Sniffer mused aloud. "That would put you in the doorway to the brothel."

Colm groped for a retort.

Kempis gauged distances. "A dozen paces, and you saw nothing of her face?"

"She was wearing a hood. All I remember were her eyes. Bright blue, they were. So bright they glowed in the dark."

"She saw you too?"

"Our gazes locked. Then she disappeared."

"Disappeared." Kempis let the word linger on his tongue. "It was dark, sir. You said so yourself."

"She disappeared, I tell you! One moment she was there; the next, she was gone."

Sniffer leaned forward and sniffed his breath. "Been drinking, have we?"

"No."

"A little blackweed, perhaps?" Kempis said.

"No, damn you! I know what I saw."

"Then why did you run?"

"What?"

"The Duskwatch lads you bumped into said you were running. Why run if the killer had already gone?"

"Because I heard a woman in the . . . brothel scream. With the assassin flown, I didn't want to be mistaken for the Drifter's killer. And from the reception I was given by your thugs, I'd say my fears were well-founded." Colm's nose started to bleed again. A drop fell onto his shirt, and he tutted as he brushed at the silk. "Now, if we're done here, I'd like to get my wounds seen to."

Kempis nodded. "I know where to find you if I think of anything else."

The noble grunted.

"Just one more question," the septia said as Colm turned away. "You say you didn't get a good look at the assassin before she vanished. Any chance *she'd* recognize *you* if she saw you again?"

Kempis chuckled as the other man retreated, white-faced, peering into every shadowy doorway he passed.

Sniffer moved to the waterline and stared toward the Deeps. Kempis joined her, his stomach aflutter. A group of people had collected on the roof of one of the buildings—a yellow-plastered house covered with graffiti. In the distance was a small boat. An old man paddled it with a plank of wood, scavenging amid the floating detritus.

Sniffer took a final bite from her runefish before tossing it into the water. She crouched beyond the reach of the waves, her gills flaring as she tested the air.

"Sense anything?" Kempis asked, turning his back on the sea.

"Just Loop," Sniffer said. She nodded at the corpse under the sheet. "He left footprints when he dragged out the fish food."

"And the killer?"

"Went in but didn't come back out. Not here, at least." The Untarian straightened. "What about you?"

What indeed? Kempis closed his eyes and tried to relax his mind. It wasn't easy with the buzz of salt-stingers in his ears, but after a while he detected ripples of sorcery on the air. He'd been just eight when he discovered he had the ability to sense magic. Growing up next door to a featherwitch in the Wharf District, he'd had to endure all manner of energies drifting through the wall of his mother's hut. At first the sorcerous ripples had sat so ill on his stomach that he'd thrown up every day for a month. He still had no idea where the talent came from—from his father, most likely, since his mother had never shown any trace of it. Maybe one day he'd learn the truth. But only if his mother ever remembered who his father was.

Kempis focused on the ripples in the alley. The dead Drifter's water-magic was simple enough to distinguish, but there was something else too. Something alien. All sorcerers drew in energy to fuel their power. Until now Kempis had always been able to get a sense of the source of that energy—the prickling heat of fire-magic or the spine-tingling chill of necromancy. Here, though, all he got was a vague feeling of incongruity, as if when he opened his eyes he would find himself somewhere else.

"Well?" Sniffer said.

The septia shrugged.

"Chameleon, perhaps?"

"No."

"Illusion, then. The assassin could have hidden herself when she was spotted."

"I know what an illusion smells like," Kempis said, opening his eyes. "This is new."

Footfalls marked the approach of Loop and Duffle. Loop was frowning at the sky.

"Don't like the look of them clouds, Septia. There's rain on the way, mark my words."

Kempis followed his gaze. And blinked. The sky was a dazzling vista of blue broken only by a few wisps of white. "Mage," he said, "what sorcerers can transport themselves from one place to another?"

"Can't be done."

"I'm smelling it now, man!"

Loop considered. "It's said where enough magic is unleashed, it can burn a way through to wherever the sorcerer gets his power from. But that kind of magic—"

"Ain't wielded by someone who goes round sticking holes in Drifters," Kempis finished. In any event, if such a portal *had* been opened, wouldn't it still be here?

Kempis scratched his grizzled chin. The fact the assassin's magic was something he hadn't encountered before meant a new player had come to Olaire. Kempis shouldn't have any trouble recognizing her signature if he came across it again. The problem was, he had no way of knowing where the assassin had vanished herself *to*. And when he next caught a whiff of her sorcery, that wouldn't help him track her down if all it signified was that she'd done another disappearing act. He turned to Loop. "Find anything out from the whore?"

"Says she saw the Drifter get stabbed, but not the face of the person who done it."

Kempis looked at Sniffer. "What about the other Drifters that were killed? Anyone see what happened?"

The Untarian shook her head. "I stopped by the two scenes before I came here. No one saw a thing."

Not that they're admitting to. Above Kempis one of the brothel's windows was thrown open. A woman stuck her head out. Her face was plastered in white makeup except for her blood-red lips. She began screaming at the septia—something about scaring away her girls' custom. Kempis paid her no mind. "How do we know it's just one assassin we're looking for? Sniffer, how were the other Drifters done in?"

"Single blade thrust through the heart, just like the one here."

"Times?"

"There was a bell between the first and second stabbings, half a bell between the second and third. It's the same killer, sir."

A wave broke round Kempis's boots. He took a hurried step away from the sea, earning himself a snort from Sniffer. "Right, here's what we're going to do." He jabbed a finger at the Untarian. "You, go and find me some witnesses to the first two killings. Ain't no way two Drifters get pricked in the Shallows without anyone seeing or hearing nothing. Start with whichever bastards picked the bodies clean." He swung to Loop. "You, find out which mages can make themselves disappear into thin air. Ask round at the Watchstation. Hells, go to the library at the Founder's Citadel if you have to."

"But I can't read."

"So it'll be a challenge."

Duffle came to attention. "What about me, sir, Septia, sir?"

"Get back to the Watchstation and sort out a few lads to keep an eye on the Drifters tonight. Nothing too conspicuous, mind. I don't want them scaring the assassin off before she shows."

"Where will you be, sir, Septia, sir?"

"Think I'll drop in on an old friend of mine. This is a pro job, right? Means someone will have paid for it, and paid big since the assassin dabbles in sorcery. Can't be many people in Olaire who can organize this shit. Maybe Inneez can point me in the direction of one of them."

The others turned away.

"Oh, and, Duffle," Kempis said, bringing the youth up short, "if you ever give my name to a blueblood again I'll cut your arms and legs down till they fit that Shroud-cursed uniform of yours, got it?"

Chapter 3

STANDING AT the prow of her father's galleon, the *Crest*, Kalischa Agenta Webb studied the waterway leading to Olaire's harbor. To either side of the ship black-tiled roofs rose from the sea, draped in fireweed and beaded with spray. Farther ahead the upper floors of flooded buildings could be seen protruding from the waves, their white plaster fascias peeling to reveal black stone underneath. From the windows of those buildings, faces looked back at Agenta, and more people watched from atop the roofs: a shaven-headed man who wolf whistled at the kalischa—so flattering; an Untarian woman hanging washing from a line between two chimney stacks; four children gathered about a honeyfish sizzling on the sun-drenched roof tiles.

On the deck behind, Agenta heard the *Crest*'s crew scuttling about in response to the captain's bellowed orders. From below came a rhythmic splashing as the galleon's oars dipped and lifted in time to the beat of a drum. Then a creak of boards sounded as Agenta's father came to stand beside her. Rethell's face glistened with sweat, and his hair was plastered to his scalp. For a while he and the kalischa stood in silence. Not a comfortable silence, but a customary one.

"Last time I was in Olaire," he said finally, "the old harbor was still in use—to the south of here. When the sea rose to claim it, a new one was built inland. It's said the Storm Lords had to dig through a hundred armspans of rock to make the harbor deep enough for ships."

Agenta looked at the partly submerged houses all about. "What caused this?" she asked. Her father had spent so much time telling her about the city before, she supposed she should *try* to appear interested. "If water levels had risen here, they would have risen in Gilgamar too."

"Olaire is slipping into the sea, has been for decades. The Untarians say a fire demon is imprisoned in a mountain to the east, and that in its struggles to free itself it is shaking the island apart."

"And the real reason?"

Rethell shrugged.

The thrum of the distant harbor was growing. As the *Crest* turned a bend in the waterway—the Causeway, Rethell had called it—Agenta saw a forest of masts above a line of warehouses. She scanned the city beyond. Dominating the district to the northwest was a brooding fortress, while farther south a circular edifice towered over the buildings round it. It was capped by a dome of glass that sparkled in the sunlight. Agenta nodded at it. "Is that the palace?"

Rethell shook his head. "The palace is on the coast to the north. That domed building is the Round—the Storm Lords' principal countinghouse. When the wind picks up you can make out the flags of the embassies round it, and to the west is the Mercantile Court—see that building with the steepled roof?"

"I suspect we'll be seeing a lot more of it in the days to come."

Her father's expression tightened. "Have faith, Agenta. Imerle will deal."

The kalischa held back a smile. *Faith?* What was faith but the last bastion of those who had abandoned all grip on reason?

"The year before last," Rethell went on, "Locio Low lost a ship to a storm off Peron Ra. The Storm Council paid up within a week."

"What cargo was the ship carrying?"

"Fellwood."

"Worth, what? A few thousand imperial sovereigns the lot? Our duskstones are worth a thousand times that. Somehow I doubt the emira will be so helpful when she is presented with our bill."

"Then I will just have to convince her. I knew her father from the time he ran the sea lane to Palana Utara. He made a name for himself driving pirates onto the rocks off the Claw and was raised to the Storm Council when Lord Forte caught a stray arrow on Dragon Day. A formidable man."

"There was a time people would have said the same of you."

Rethell continued as if he hadn't heard. "There's history between the Storm Lords and Gilgamar, yes, and this dispute over the Levy couldn't have come at a worse time. But Imerle is too smart to risk alienating the Ruling Council while Piput is stirring up trouble in Dian. If she'll see us today—"

"If?" Agenta cut in. "Since when has that word been in your vocabulary?" She waited for him to respond, then added, "If you have no stomach for this fight, perhaps you should let me do the talking when we get to the palace."

For a heartbeat she thought she saw anger spark in Rethell's eyes, but it was only the sun reflecting in them. He turned and walked back to the quarterdeck.

Agenta watched him go. She'd hoped her words would provoke some reaction in him, but it seemed even her taunting could not rekindle his old fire—a fire he would need today in his confrontation with Imerle. It was not hard to deduce the reason for his reserve. It was almost a year since her brother, Zelin, had died. Even Agenta had found her thoughts straying back at unguarded moments to the memory of his final days: of his eyes weeping blood as he screamed out his last breaths; of Rethell sitting at his bedside, clinging to his hand as if that contact alone could keep Zelin's soul from fleeing his body. For Agenta the memories held no more sting than the bite of a needlefly, because the numbing effect of the tollen drug she'd taken had long since robbed them of meaning. Rethell's mood, by contrast, had spiraled steadily down as the anniversary of Zelin's death approached. But then her father had lost far more than Agenta had that day. For with Agenta's mother having passed through Shroud's Gate a few months previously, within the space of a year Rethell had lost the two people in the world who mattered to him most.

A shouted curse brought the kalischa back to the present. She looked down to see a fisherman frantically rowing his boat out of the *Crest*'s path. Ahead the Causeway widened as it entered the harbor. Judging by the flags fluttering in the breeze, every city in the Sabian League was represented here in readiness for Dragon Day. It took the *Crest*'s captain quarter of a bell to secure a berth. Rethell sent a runner to the palace to request an audience with the emira, then hailed a sedan. Agenta took the seat opposite him amid a fog of perfume that did nothing to mask the smell of sweat from the sedan's previous occupant. Sensing her father did not want to talk, she settled back on the gilded cushions and let the sounds of the harbor wash over her:

the hammering of shipwrights from the dry docks to the north, the lowing of temlocks unloading cargos, the cries of hawkers selling manabread or honeyfish or blue oysters.

As the sedan moved clear of the harbor, Agenta tugged back one of the curtains and looked out on the city. Olaire might have been the jewel in the Storm Lord crown, but it was a jewel no less tarnished than any other capital. A stream of slurry ran down the center of the main street, and the alleys to either side were choked with rubbish. And while the buildings fronting the road possessed an unmistakable grandeur with their wrought iron gates and wide staircases leading up to doors framed by columned porticos, it was a grandeur that had decayed to leave crumbling, salt-rimed fascias and weed-infested grounds. Still, at least the street corners here weren't cluttered with tollen addicts as they were in Gilgamar—addicts who had served as an unwelcome reminder of the cravings gnawing at Agenta's guts.

Over the drone of the crowds she heard Trita Warner Sturge and his men shouting to clear a path. Still the sedan seemed to spend as much time stationary as it did on the move, and the chair pitched and swayed as it was jostled by the throng. After half a bell the sedan began to climb above the stench of salt and humanity. When it reached the foot of Kalin's Hill the crowds thinned, and the sedan's pace increased. Here the streets were wider and tree-lined. Agenta looked for the Round and caught a glimpse of its glass roof between the Erin Elalese and Androsian embassies.

Another quarter-bell and the roads became so steep the kalischa, sitting with her back to the direction of travel, had to hold on to her seat to stop herself falling into her father's lap. A breeze set the curtains ruffling, carrying on it a haze of dust. When Agenta looked back the way they'd come she saw a shimmering expanse of roofs stepping down to the harbor like a giant's stairwell. A Thaxian ship was being towed along the Causeway by two rowboats. Beyond, the sea sparkled like a jewel of a million facets. Easy up here to forget the stink and the bustle and the privation of the lower city, but that was the point, wasn't it?

Agenta looked at her father and saw his eyes were closed, his features quiet—too quiet considering the importance of what they would be discussing with the emira. The loss of their cargo of duskstones had left a gaping hole in the family's finances. More troubling, though, was the damage it would cause to Rethell's standing if he was unable to recover the cargo's worth. Agenta's smile was wry. Two decades it had taken her father to claw his way to the top of the human slagheap that called itself Gilgamar's Ruling Council, yet now all he'd worked for stood to be snatched away in an instant. But then nothing was meant to last. The kalischa had learned that lesson from her brother's death and her mother's before that. She'd said as much to Rethell when they set out for Olaire. She'd even argued against coming, yet now that she was here she couldn't deny a prickle of anticipation. And not just at the prospect of meeting the vaunted Imerle Polivar either. For too long her father had kept her cooped up in their home at Gilgamar on the strength of mere rumors of a Seeker conspiracy against her. Surely he couldn't object if she did a little exploring while she was here?

The sedan passed through the gates of the palace. Set in immaculately groomed gardens, the palace was a single-story building so nondescript that Agenta thought she and Rethell had been brought to the servants' entrance. Standing beside a fountain with a statue of a sea dragon at its center was an elderly, pinch-faced courtier waiting to take them to the throne room. Agenta had expected to have to wait for an audience, but it seemed the emira had agreed to meet them straightaway. Had Imerle foreseen their coming? *Foreseen and prepared for, most likely.*

The courtier told Warner and his men to wait outside before setting off through the palace's corridors with Agenta and Rethell in tow. His pace was so measured it was all the kalischa could do not to take him by the arm and hurry him along. When he finally brought them to the underwater passage leading to the throne room, Agenta had to stop herself gawping like some moonstruck youngling. The throne room itself was even more breathtaking, with its glassy ceiling and rippling walls. To the east the kalischa saw the rotting bones of a sunken galley, while from above and behind came the muted crash of waves.

At the opposite end of the room were three figures. Agenta's gaze passed over the metal-clad giant and the man with the gray eyes of an oscura addict—Chief Minister Pernay Ord, her father whispered—before coming to rest on the emira. Imerle's eyebrows were arched in a way that gave her a perpetual look of mild surprise, and there was a calculation in her expression that put Agenta in mind of a hafters player, forever weighing each move and countermove. A thinker, then.

Someone not given to hasty judgment. And doubtless a more daunting adversary for that.

The pinch-faced courtier departed without announcing Agenta and her father, so Rethell bowed and said, "Emira, I am Kalisch Rethell Webb of Gilgamar. This is my daughter, Agenta."

Imerle's gaze swung to the kalischa. "So you are the one. The newest member of the Seekers."

"Those allegations were never proved," Rethell said stiffly.

Never proved? A stirring defense, that. "The Seekers are no friends of mine," Agenta told the emira.

"And the other . . . rumor we heard? That they put a price on your head?"

"Why, are you looking to collect?"

"Not at all. We were just wondering what you could have done to upset them so. Since you were never one of their number, of course."

Agenta smiled. She'd score that first round even.

Rethell appeared keen to change the subject. "I am grateful to you, Emira, for seeing us at such short notice."

"Why would we not? The Storm Council is anxious to know why Gilgamar has withheld its tribute."

"Gilgamar has paid the Levy, just at last year's rate."

"You think the uplift is unwarranted?"

"My *Council's* position," Rethell said, "is that it wishes clarification on certain issues before settling the amount in full. The Levy has nearly doubled in three years, yet the storms from the Broken Lands have abated and the dragons remain barred behind the Dragon Gate."

Imerle's face was impassive. "Your *Council's* position, Kalisch? You are the head of that Council, are you not? And yet here you are, distancing yourself from its decisions."

"I am the Council's spokesman, not its leader."

"Such a humble man."

"In any event," Rethell went on, "I did not come to discuss the Levy—the Ruling Council will make formal representations to you in due course. I am here on a personal matter."

"Oh?" Pernay said, the glint in his eyes suggesting to Agenta he knew what was coming.

"I am referring to the disappearance of my ship, the *Gadfly*. It was lost off Rastamira three weeks ago with its cargo of duskstones."

"You have come to claim compensation?"

"Yes."

"Then you must have taken a wrong turn on your way to the Mercantile Court. I can direct you there, if you wish."

"I was hoping that would not be necessary."

Pernay chuckled. "Of course. Why bother with courts at all? Why not open the treasury to every beggar who comes before us with hands outstretched?"

Agenta winced, awaiting her father's inevitable outburst. In Gilgamar's council chamber it was said the echoes of his voice could be heard several bells after he'd finished speaking, and that the fierceness of his temper was matched only by the strength of his look. Last year Agenta had seen him carry a debate by glaring at an opponent until the man's conviction fled and his words dried up. That was before Zelin's death, though. The loss of his son had cut Rethell deeply, and judging by the whiff of disdain in the throne room, both the emira and Pernay could smell blood.

"How was your ship lost?" Imerle said.

"I cannot be certain," Rethell replied. "There were no survivors."

The chief minister snorted. "No witnesses, you mean. The Storm Council does not compensate traders for piracy by their own crew."

Rethell's gaze remained on the emira. "I have a copy of Cinsar's harbor log stamped with the harbormaster's mark."

"Proving only that the *Gadfly* set sail from that port," Pernay said. "Can you also prove it never arrived at its destination?"

Agenta laughed. "And how are we supposed to show that? With an empty page in Gilgamar's harbor log?"

Rethell struck a more reasonable tone. "As I understand the law, Chief Minister, since I can prove the ship set sail from Cinsar, it is for you to show the shipment *did* arrive in Gilgamar, rather than for me to show it did not."

Pernay made to respond, but the emira held up a hand. "The kalisch is correct, of course. And even if he were not, one need only take a stroll through Olaire's Jewelry Quarter to see the *Gadfly*'s cargo did not reach its intended destination. In case you were unaware, Kalisch, Olaire's markets have been flooded with duskstones this past fortnight. It is too much of a coincidence, surely, for them to be anything other than your missing shipment."

Agenta cocked her head. "You accept our claim, then?" she said, waiting for the catch.

"Some elements of it, yes."

"*Some* elements?"

"The law is clear," Rethell said. "In return for payment of the Levy, the Storm Lords guarantee the safety of all Gilgamarian shipping in the Sabian Sea."

"In return for payment of the Levy, yes. And since you have not paid the Levy in full . . ."

There was a note to Imerle's voice Agenta couldn't place, and the kalischa found herself wondering if the woman knew more about this affair than she was letting on. The Storm Lords were rumored to be responsible for most of the piracy in the Sabian Sea. Agenta wouldn't have put it past the emira to specifically target Gilgamarian ships now that the Ruling Council had withheld part of its tribute.

Pernay said, "Even if the Storm Lords were to honor your claim, there remains the question of what compensation is payable. You will appreciate the price of duskstones has fallen significantly with the glut in supply. I fear the value of your cargo would be worth far less now than it was when the *Gadfly* set sail."

Rethell said, "Compensation is payable at the value of the goods *before* they were lost, Chief Minister, not after."

"If you say so."

Silence.

Rethell looked from Pernay to the emira then back again, his face hardening all the while. Maybe now Agenta would get to witness the outburst she'd been anticipating. Instead her father said, "I see we are wasting our time here."

Finally the message had got through. And neither Imerle nor Pernay was disputing his charge.

Agenta watched her father spin on his heel and make his way toward the underwater passage. An ignominious withdrawal, but what had he expected, throwing himself on the emira's charity like that? There was nothing worse than a man come seeking a handout.

As the sound of her father's footsteps receded, Agenta looked at Imerle.

The emira raised an eyebrow, and the kalischa shrugged before turning to follow him.

Kempis had been waiting in an alley opposite Inneez's house for more than two bells. The shadows he'd sheltered in when he arrived had now melted away to leave him exposed to the midday sun. He was tempted to abandon his vigil, but of all his sources, Inneez was most likely to be able to point him at whoever had arranged the contracts on the Drifters. Nothing went on in Olaire—nothing shady at least—without the merchant hearing of it.

The street in front of Inneez's house was lined with ketar trees, and between the trunks were stalls selling sandals, susha robes, spices, and jewelry crafted from fish bones or podfish carapaces. The space usually filled by Inneez's stand was taken up by that of a merchant trading in Elescorian carpets who was haggling with a blueblood over a rug. To the right was a stall of cages containing Shamanon toy dogs of a hundred different sizes and colors. Their yapping rose in pitch as a Hundari tribesman strode past holding skewers of steaming meat. *Probably recognize their own when they smell them.*

Kempis swung his gaze to Inneez's house. Its ground-floor windows were boarded, and countless tiles were missing from its roof. Twenty years ago this district had been one of the most sought-after in Olaire, but the rising of the Sabian Sea, and with it the creation of the Deeps and the Shallows, had seen the great and the good move away from the coast and up the slopes of Kalin's Hill. Now the flooded districts were a hotbed of lawlessness. There were many theories as to why the sea was creeping higher, but to Kempis's mind the reason was clear: the Storm Lords. It was a clever scam, he conceded—raise the sea to drive down property prices, buy up houses on the cheap, then lower the water levels again and sell at a profit. The only real mystery here was why more people hadn't seen through the swindle.

The blueblood arguing over the rug brought negotiations to an end by backhanding the merchant across the face and walking away with his prize. No one stopped him. Even the merchant was too busy trying to stem the flood of blood from his busted nose to complain.

It was a similar incident fifteen years ago that had seen Kempis join the Watch. On that occasion it had been the septia's uncle who was struck. In Yollip's case, the blow had knocked him to the ground where he'd smashed out his brains on a kerb. Kempis had seen it happen. So had a hundred other people, but the blueblood responsible had never faced charges. A naive Kempis had thought that by joining the Watch he might change that. Nine months of banging his head against a wall of blueblood partisanship had followed. So in the end he'd tracked down the culprit and executed his own secret form of justice.

He could have left the Watch then. Except that afterward there had been an investigation into the blueblood's demise—and this one had been most thorough. Kempis had had to stick around to muddy the waters. He was still trying to get himself unstuck even now.

As the noble with the stolen rug sauntered off, Kempis committed his face to memory.

A splash of color in the crowd to his right caught the septia's eye. He recognized Inneez from his rolling gait and the stained yellow silks that swathed his huge frame. One pudgy hand was stuffing sweetmeats into his mouth. Some instinct must have made him glance in Kempis's direction, and the septia shrank back into the alley. To conceal his uniform he had borrowed a hooded susha robe from one of the stalls in the Salter Bazaar a few streets back. There was no way Inneez could have pierced the shadows of his cowl, and even if he had, what was the fat man going to do, run?

When Kempis risked another look out, he saw Inneez had made it to the steps of his house. The merchant drew a key from a pocket and began to climb the stairs.

Kempis slipped from his hiding place and jostled his way through the crowd in the main street. An Untarian woman flared her gills at him as he pushed past. He darted in front of a cart drawn by two tem-locks, causing the animals to snort and toss their heads. The driver swore.

Inneez had reached his door and now looked over his shoulder to discover the cause of the commotion. Suddenly he was fumbling his key in his haste to put it into the lock. Kempis picked up his pace. Reaching the stairs, he bounded up them just as Inneez opened the door and stepped through. The septia got his boot in the door as it was closing and grunted as the wood slammed into his foot. He threw his weight against the door and sent Inneez stumbling back before following him inside and closing the door behind.

He found himself in a dusty room. The walls to either side were lined with glass cabinets, while ahead and to his left was a table. The remainder of the room was veiled in shadow. Inneez turned to confront him, his face illuminated by threads of light filtering between the boards over the windows. He had grown a third chin since Kempis last saw him, and there was a scar below his left eye. A knife materialized in his right hand.

"Put that away," Kempis said, pulling down his hood.

The merchant's eyes softened. "Ah, it is you, Septia. I didn't recognize you, my friend."

Kempis's face twisted. All of the Inneezes in Olaire wanted to be his friend, but he had no more use for *their* friendship than he had for anyone else's. "You've got some explaining to do. Your tip-off about Javon and the stolen blackweed . . ."

"You did not find the blackweed, *mesa*?"

"Oh, I found the blackweed, all right—ten crates of the stuff, just as you said. When I followed the shipment to that warehouse in Grange Street, though, imagine my surprise when I find not Javon waiting for it, but Hegan Harl. You two have history, right?"

The merchant spread his hands. "The fickleness of fate."

"I don't like being used to settle your scores, Inneez. You owe me."

The fat man's expression was pained. "Friends should never speak of debts, *mesa*." He looked at the table to his right. "What's mine is yours."

Kempis followed his gaze. On the table was a collection of objects including what appeared to be a shield fashioned from the shell of a giant turtle. At the back, a strap had been fixed to the center, and there was a handle by its rim. The septia slipped his left arm through the strap and gripped the handle. There was a stain on the front of the shield. "You might at least have wiped the blood off!"

Inneez began lighting the candles about the room. "That shield is made from a scale of a khalid esgaril. Impervious to steel, fire, even sorcery."

"Then how did you make the holes for the strap and the handle?"

The merchant's smile wavered. "Inneez is a resourceful man."

Kempis replaced the shield on the table. Beside it was a silver necklace with a purple jewel. He brushed the jewel with a finger.

"A rare piece," Inneez said in a reverential tone. "Blessed by the White Lady herself. So long as the pendant hangs about your neck, you will never take a mortal wound."

"Right. So if I recover from the wound, the White Lady gets the credit, but if I don't, there ain't no one around to come looking for a refund."

"You like it? Take it as my gift to you."

Truly worthless, then. "I didn't come here for your useless trinkets. I came for information."

"Ah! My most valuable commodity!"

"You heard about the Drifters, I take it."

Inneez lit a final candle before moving to stand by the table. The room filled with the scent of moonblossom. "A most regrettable business."

"Friends of yours, were they?"

"All men are my friends."

"You'll be keen to help me find out who killed them, then."

Inneez smiled faintly. Taking out a jar from one of the folds in his robe, he withdrew a sweetmeat and placed it in his mouth. As he chewed, he gazed at Kempis with an expression showing both wariness and curiosity.

The septia hesitated. Whatever he told the merchant would be round the whole city by nightfall, but then knowing Inneez he'd probably heard the story already from someone at the Watchstation.

"It was a pro job," Kempis said at last. "Killer used sorcery."

"What manner of sorcery?"

"Who's asking the questions here? How do I go about hiring me an assassin who uses magic?"

"*Mesa* has forgotten our conversation from last year? The disciples of the Antlered God—"

"I know the Lord of the Hunt's work. This weren't it."

Inneez licked his fingers. "Alas, I am but a humble merchant."

"Then point me in the direction of someone who isn't."

The fat man's look said he hoped he'd misheard.

Outside, the dogs in the cages started yapping. Inneez placed his jar of sweetmeats on the table and crossed to the window before peering through a gap in the boards.

"Relax," Kempis said, gesturing to his hood. "I came wearing this, remember." He paused. "Of course, I ain't decided whether I'll be wearing it when I leave."

Inneez swung round. "Our usual arrangements—"

"There weren't time."

"If someone saw you come here . . ." The merchant clasped his hands together and turned back to the window. When he spoke again, his voice had lost its affable note. "These are serious people, *mesa*."

The septia helped himself to a sweetmeat. "So am I."

"Serious people who value their privacy."

"I want a word, is all. For all you know, I might have work for them meself."

"On a septia's salary?"

He's got me there. "Give me a name."

"You'll put a target on *both* our backs."

"A name, Inneez. Otherwise I'll get it from someone else, and when I talk with whoever you're protecting I'll make sure *your* name comes up."

The merchant did not respond.

The dogs' yapping had risen to a cacophony. Inneez peered out into the street again. Had he seen something to trouble him, or was he simply playing for time? Kempis resisted an urge to join him at the window. Instead he helped himself to another sweetmeat. He couldn't see Inneez's hands, and he remembered the knife from earlier. Was the merchant desperate enough to try something stupid? When you backed a flintcat into a corner, like as not it showed its claws.

Inneez turned to face him. His dark eyes glittered in the candle-light. He looked about the room as if taking in its details for the last time. "I can trust your discretion, Septia?"

"I'm a reasonable man."

The merchant stared at him as if he could read the septia's intent in his eyes. Kempis returned his gaze without blinking. Finally Inneez sighed. "The man you want is called Enli."

"Last name?"

"I don't know."

"Perfect. I'll just grab me a copy of the census and start at 'A.'"

"He has an address in Dalamine Street. Near the Round."

"*The* Dalamine Street?"

"Like I said, these are serious people."

"What's his front?"

"Spices. Ganda from Soren, blayfire from Kal Kartin. He is the principal broker for Fitch and Rambler, as well as the Excel cartel in Palana Utara."

The names meant nothing to Kempis, but then he'd always made it his business to keep out of blueblood affairs. Now it seemed he would have to tread on a few pedicured toes. *Assuming, of course, Inneez isn't spinning me a line.*

"If you're making this up, Inneez, I'll be back for you. You can go deep under, but you'll have to come up for air eventually. And when you do, I'll be waiting for you."

The merchant's expression was hurt. "We're even now, *mesa*? No more debts between us, yes?"

Kempis put another sweetmeat into his mouth. "Friends should never talk of debts."

The doorway to Ambassador Lydanto Hood's office was covered by a curtain of crystals that tinkled as Agenta led her father through. To her left the ambassador sat behind a desk with his nose in a book. He looked up as she entered, then glanced about as if unsure where he was. A moment later he roused himself, setting his book down before rising and making his way round the desk with such haste he banged his hip on a corner.

He bowed to Rethell before taking Agenta's hand and lifting it to his lips. "Kalischa," he said in his harsh Grantorian accent. "I am enchanted to be seeing you again."

"Ambassador."

His look turned grave, and Agenta braced herself for the inevitable.

"I am most sorry to be hearing about the death of your brother," he said. "His exuberance was an example to us all."

A hundred quips came to the kalischa's mind, but she had learned the safest thing to do in these situations was to match the ambassador's weighty expression and mumble a thank-you. Why was it that no matter how many people plagued her with their good wishes, there were always more waiting round the corner? As if the best way to help someone get over a bereavement was to bring it up as often as possible.

The black bags under Lydanto's eyes suggested he'd endured a sleepless night, yet his posting to Olaire was evidently agreeing with him, for his stomach had expanded to overhang his belt and his nose was even rosier than Agenta remembered it. His extravagantly curled mustache was wilting in the heat. Years ago he had been a rising star on Gilgamar's Ruling Council until he'd lost his seat following some misadventure, the details of which Agenta had never learned. Bankrupt and in disgrace, Lydanto had faced a spell in the Carsian Mines to settle his debts. Then Rethell had paid off his creditors and taken him in as tutor to Agenta and Zelin. Two years later the Grantorian's return to favor was completed when he was appointed ambassador to Olaire.

Agenta had been sad to see him go. He'd taught her history and accounts, and about the machinations of the Ruling Council. But he'd also taught her how to brew juripa spirits so strong they could fell a temlock. And how to mix rum and ganja fire to form a tonic that exploded when lit. He'd even tried drinking the stuff once and lost his voice for four days afterward. Meeting him again was worth the journey to Olaire alone.

Lydanto ushered Agenta and her father to two chairs in front of his desk, then lurched to a table on the opposite wall. On the table was a collection of decanters and glasses. Most of the glasses had been used, as if the Grantorian had just finished hosting a gathering. A gathering of one, if Agenta remembered his drinking habits correctly.

"Can I be offering you a drink?" Lydanto asked her.

"I'd say 'whatever you're having,' but I want to be able to walk out of here when we're finished."

The ambassador chuckled, then lifted a decanter filled with a thick black liquid. The way it clung to the sides of the decanter reminded Agenta uncomfortably of tollen. "The Olairians are having a delicacy," Lydanto said. "Apilone, it is called, made from the ink of the apil fish—"

"Water will be fine," Agenta cut in.

"Of course. And for you, Kalisch?"

Rethell shook his head. Slumped in his chair, he looked like he'd lost another member of his family. Though since Agenta was now all the family he had, perhaps not.

"Do you mind if I . . . ?" Lydanto said, already pouring himself a glass of apilone. He offered the water glass to Agenta before picking up the other and seating himself at the desk. On it was a tray with an untouched bowl of honeyfish soup. Lydanto lifted the tray and placed it on the floor behind his desk. Behind and to the Grantorian's left was another doorway, covered, as the door to the office was, by a crystal curtain.

Agenta nodded at it. "These crystal curtains . . . are they a local custom?"

"Soon I am thinking they will be. Olaire is suffering from an infestation of Chameleon priests."

"Oh?"

"A year ago the priesthood was arriving at an understanding with the emira. Since that time they are more and more being found in places where they should not be. With these curtains, what I am not seeing I can at least be hearing."

"What you are not seeing? I thought Chameleons were only invisible for so long as they are standing still."

"So they are. Yet if one were to be coming into the room when my back was turned . . ."

Agenta sipped her water. "You think the emira is employing them as spies?"

"Assassins too, I am hearing."

"I thought the Storm Lords' charter prohibited associations with deities."

"*Formal* associations, yes. But while the Chameleon high priest is never straying far from the side of Imerle, who is to say their association is anything more than friendship? Or that the emira is not a devotee of the god?" Lydanto stroked his mustache. "Imerle has been proving herself adept at exploiting the areas of grayness in the charter."

"As we have just witnessed for ourselves," Agenta said. Since her father was intent on wallowing in self-pity, it seemed the storytelling duties would fall on the kalischa, so she told Lydanto about the meeting in the throne room.

"Misfortune most unhappy," the ambassador said, turning to Rethell. "Though you are not the only one to be finding yourself in such a predicament, if that is being of any consolation."

"It isn't," Rethell muttered.

"The Mercantile Court is—how do you say?—bursting from the seams with people seeking compensation for lost ships. Yet none of them has seen so much as a copper clipping. The Master of Courts is drowning each case in technicalities, bamboozling the claimants with trivialities of form and procedure." He rubbed his hands together. "I will be representing your interests, of course. Strictly speaking, I am Gilgamar's representative in Olaire, not yours, but I am seeing no conflict of interest in this."

Just as Agenta was seeing no hope of success. What were the courts, after all, but a way to give a ruler's wants a veneer of false legitimacy?

Rethell shook himself. "Was I right in what I said to the chief minister? About compensation for the duskstones being calculated according to their value before they were stolen?"

"An excellent question!" Leaning back, Lydanto reached for one of the books on a bookcase behind him. He leafed through it, then slapped a page with the back of his hand. "Ah, yes! Here it is. The *Axmarl* and its cargo of Elescorian brandy, lost three years ago to a storm off Andros. The owner of the ship sought to argue the value of the cargo had *increased* since the ship went down, and it was the Master of Courts—this is excellent!—who was successfully arguing—"

Rethell brought one hand down in a chopping motion. "If I am forced to play this out, how long before the court reaches a judgment?"

"Perhaps a year," the ambassador said, his voice bright with excitement. "The issues are fascinating, no?"

"Not all bad news, then," Agenta said.

Lydanto's smile this time was strained. He closed his book. "As for Gilgamar's Ruling Council withholding part of its tribute . . . perhaps it would be better if the Levy were settled in full before your case is coming to court."

Rethell stood up and began pacing the room. "You think it is that easy? My opponents on the Council will have heard by now about the *Gadfly*'s disappearance. Their opposition to paying the Levy will become stronger once they realize what I stand to lose."

That was the way things went in Gilgamar: one man's misfortune was always another man's opportunity for gain. The nobles on the Council would stop at nothing to trick and claw their way to the top. So, when the rumor had surfaced about Agenta becoming a Seeker, the other Council members had been quick to jump on it. For all the kalischa knew, it had been one of them who had spread the story in the first place.

It was all nonsense, of course. The Seekers were fanatics. The drugs they peddled dulled the senses of the masses, but only by robbing them of their emotions, their memories. The Seekers reveled in that fact. It was their way of fighting back, they said, against the hardships inflicted by the ruling elite. They had asked Agenta to join them, no doubt hoping to use her family's name to further their crusade. The kalischa, though, had no interest in joining any cause, even one as destructive as the Seekers'.

She swirled the water in her glass. "What I don't understand is why Imerle is contesting this at all. She is coming to the end of her time as emira, right? So why does she care about our case? Soon the money won't be hers to lose."

Lydanto said, "Strictly speaking, the money is belonging to the Storm Lords, not Imerle, but your point is still valid." He drained his glass and cast a longing look at the decanters. "There are whisperings the emira is plotting to hold on to power, but I am believing that is all they are: whisperings. Nevertheless, it is clear *something* is afoot."

It was a moment before Agenta saw his meaning. "The backlog in the courts."

"Precisely. Your real problem, Kalischa, is not so much the delaying tactics of Imerle but rather how many petitions have been filed at the court—more than twenty in the past month alone. Clearly whichever pirate is responsible for the hijackings is an individual most capable. And yet, a pirate commanding a fleet large enough to seize so many ships, and who is able to evade capture by the Storm Lords? I am—how do you say?—smelling the rat."

"Does it have to be the emira behind this? Could it be another of the Storm Lords?"

"Most certainly. But there are other reasons for thinking Imerle is being up to no good. A rumor has reached me that she is taking out loans with certain merchants in Olaire."

Rethell stopped pacing. "She is borrowing to settle the claims brought against her?"

"No—liability rests with the Storm Lords, not the emira. These loans are to Imerle personally."

Agenta considered this. If the stories of the emira plotting to remain in power were correct, it was not difficult to imagine what she wanted money for . . . An idea came to her. "Perhaps there is a way we can use these loans to our advantage."

Lydanto raised an inquiring eyebrow.

"Whatever their purpose, it is fair to assume Imerle wants to keep their existence a secret. If we can find a way to link the loans to our duskstones, maybe the emira will settle rather than have her financial dealings investigated in court."

Rethell looked at Lydanto. "Can it be done?"

"Perhaps, Kalisch, if one of the merchants lending to Imerle has also been purchasing the stolen duskstones." The ambassador finally succumbed to temptation and crossed to the table with the decanters. "I will need to be making inquiries at the Round."

"Later," Rethell said. "First, I have another task for you."

Lydanto paused. "Task?"

"The emira said Olaire's markets have been flooded with dusk-stones this past week. So where are they coming from?"

"You mean where are the attackers of your ship hiding them?" The ambassador refilled his glass with apilone. "The Deeps, I am thinking. Ever since the district was being flooded by the sea, it has become home to all manner of undesirables. But if your concern is to discover whether the duskstones in Olaire are from the *Gadfly,* you can easily be buying one in the Jewelry Quarter."

"I'm more interested in who is selling them. The pirates can't have flogged the whole shipment already, so let's make it known we're in the market for whatever they've got left. If we dangle a big enough hook, maybe someone will bite."

Agenta set down her glass. After all this talk of courts and loans, things were suddenly looking a good deal more interesting. "Can you arrange a meeting with whoever is selling the stones?" she asked Lydanto. "Discreetly, of course."

"I am sure I can be sorting something out."

The kalischa turned to her father. "I'll go." She'd wanted to see the sights of Olaire, hadn't she? The Deeps certainly counted in that respect. And if it came with a little danger attached, then all the better.

Rethell nodded.

Agenta covered her surprise. Just like that he said yes? She'd expected him to squirm and to deliberate and to find some excuse to send someone in her place—to try to protect her as he'd been unable to protect Zelin. Then again, why should he? She wasn't her brother, after all.

"Take Warner and Balen with you," was all he said.

CHAPTER 4

SENAR HAD been waiting for what seemed like an eternity for an audience with Mazana Creed. The first time he'd presented himself at her house he'd been told that she had come and gone, and would not be returning until dusk. Then, when he went back at the eighth bell, he was left waiting in a corridor with dark wooden wall panels so highly polished he could see his reflection in them. The last of the day's light trickled through windows along the passage to his left. As the shadows deepened, his eyelids grew heavy. During his imprisonment he'd worked hard to maintain his fitness—at least so far as the confines of his cell would allow—but already the strains of the day were beginning to weigh on him.

From behind a door to his right came raised voices, muffled laughter, breaking glass. With each sound, a serving-girl sweeping the floor to his left cast a fearful glance at the door. She could not have seen Senar standing motionless in the gloom, for when he rubbed his eyes she gave a squeal and bolted along a side passage. The Guardian listened to the flap of her sandals die away, wishing he too could make tracks. On his way to Mazana's house he'd seen the masts of the ships docked in the harbor to the west, but he had no coin to buy passage out, and what were his chances of stowing away on a vessel and staying hidden for the duration of the crossing? And while he hadn't noticed any of Imerle's lackeys following him, the watchers would surely be close. No, better to bide his time until the emira's guard slipped. *Best behavior, remember.*

A cheer sounded in the next room, and a memory stirred in Senar of the time during the fifth Kalanese campaign when he had traveled with his master, Li Benir, to an enemy encampment near Kal Kartin to deliver Avallon's offer of a ceasefire. The two Guardians had waited in an anteroom of the enemy commander's tent, choking on dust and listening to the tent flaps crack in the wind. All the while, Li Benir had stood quietly with his hands clasped behind his back, a flicker of a smile on his face as he watched Senar pace back and forth. The Kalanese's hatred of Erin Elal was such that any Guardian captured would be skinned alive and buried to the neck for the bone ants to feast on. By the end of the night, though, Li Benir had had the Kalanese toasting him with ganga fire as they sat cross-legged on heaped sandclaw pelts. In response to one of Li Benir's jests, even the wizened soulcaster squatting across from Senar had cracked a toothless grin. But then Senar's master had always been adept at using his Will to influence the thoughts of others. For all Senar's strength, it was a skill he had never grasped.

What he wouldn't have given to have Li Benir with him now. Or just to know his master was alive—

He started as the door beside him opened to let out a babble of noise. Mazana's black-toothed dutia, Beauce, appeared. "You ready for this, lad?" he said.

Senar pushed himself away from the wall. Was he supposed to feel intimidated, then? It was good to know what was expected of him, if only so he could make a point of doing the opposite. "Lead on."

Instead, the dutia stepped to one side and gestured for Senar to enter. As the Guardian moved past, Beauce slapped him on the back.

Senar found himself in a chamber of a similar size to the emira's throne room. It smelled of musty furniture and smoke from the wall torches. The walls were crammed with portraits of brooding figures looking down with sullen eyes. The floor was dominated by a mosaic showing a sea dragon alongside a three-masted galley. The creature's tail had flicked the ship several armspans into the air, and figures were tumbling from the deck into the waters below. To the left edge of the mosaic was a smashed bottle. A woman lay facedown amid pieces of glass, her blood mixing with whatever liquid the bottle had contained to run pink between the mosaic's stones.

Mazana Creed reclined on a divan at the far end of the room. The light from the wall torches accentuated the strong lines of her face.

There were spots of color on her cheeks, and in one hand she clutched a near-empty wineglass. She looked like she wanted to be here about as much as the Guardian did. A slit in her dress revealed her bare legs.

Beauce moved past Senar and settled on a divan to her left. Around him stood a cluster of soldiers in blue uniforms bearing on their breasts the insignia of a red lightning bolt over a storm cloud. On a divan to the Storm Lady's right lounged the fat man, Greave, who had accompanied her to the throne room, while behind her stood the Everlord, Kiapa. One of Kiapa's hands rested on the right shoulder of a girl who wore about her neck a collar with bells on it. The bells tinkled as the girl swayed from side to side, her dead eyes staring through Senar as he halted at the center of the mosaic.

He bowed to Mazana. "My Lady."

Mazana took a sip of wine. "Guardian, what a pleasant surprise. What brings you to my humble abode?"

"The emira sent me."

"To spy on me?"

There seemed little point in denying it. "Correct."

Mazana's eyes glinted with amusement. "You're not very good at this, are you?"

Senar shrugged. "I can only play the cards I am dealt."

"And if I should send you back to Imerle?"

"My Lady is too kind."

He was rewarded with a half smile.

Greave was on his feet. "Hear that, lads?" he said to the room. "The fool here reckons our little hellcat is a Shroud-cursed *lady*." He seated himself on Mazana's divan, leering. Then he plunged his hand down the front of her dress.

Beauce growled and sat forward. Senar's right hand shifted to the hilt of his sword.

"Remove your hand, Greave," Mazana said softly, "or I will remove it for you."

The fat man stared at her for a moment before pulling back his arm. He had withdrawn his hand into the sleeve of his shirt. "Remove me hand, she said!" he rumbled, showing his sleeve to a dozen rough-cut men and women on his side of the room. "I hear and obey!"

Raucous laughter greeted his words. Senar managed to contain his own mirth. The soldiers gathered about Beauce weren't laughing

either, he noticed. He relaxed his grip on his sword hilt, but the movement must have caught Greave's eye, for the man bared his teeth and
approached. Closer now, Senar could see he'd been wrong to dismiss
him as fat, because there were cords of muscle in his neck, and he
moved with the agility of a swordsman. He was a handspan taller
than Senar and the same again as wide.

"Guardian, ain't it?" Greave sneered, sizing him up. At Senar's
height, it didn't take long. "I've heard about yer kind."

"Not enough, it seems."

"Yer reckon the emira can protect yer here, pretty boy?" He jabbed
a finger into Senar's chest. "If Imerle gave a shit for yer worthless
hide, she wouldnta thrown yer to the lions."

Senar could feel Mazana's gaze upon him. His voice was flat. "I
see no lions."

The Storm Lady spoke. "You are talking to the once champion of
Bethin's blood pits. No one before or since has matched his thirty-
one fights undefeated."

"Indeed. The pits, you say." Maybe Senar should have been trying
harder not to wind the man up, but somehow he just couldn't do it.

Mazana chuckled, then said to Greave, "It appears the Guardian
isn't impressed."

"Makes two of us."

Beauce pushed himself to his feet. "Fighting talk, gentlemen.
Seems to me there's only one way to sort this out: a duel to first blood,
here and now."

Senar's eyes narrowed. A duel? Mazana was regarding him
shrewdly, and it dawned on him that he might have blundered into a
trap. For while the Storm Lady could easily have just sent him back
to Imerle, sending back a corpse conveyed a stronger message. If it
was a trap, though, Greave had apparently not been in on the plan, for
he was frowning at Mazana. Judging by the smell of juripa spirits on
his breath he'd been drinking heavily, and while some warriors preferred to fight drunk, none of those lived to contest thirty-one duels.
He couldn't, however, back down without losing face, for the men and
women on his side of the room were shouting encouragement. *As
Mazana was no doubt counting on.* Had the duel been orchestrated
to put Greave in his place, then, not Senar?

The Guardian grimaced. He'd pledged his blade to the emira, yet
already he was fighting Mazana's battles for her. But then what other

option was there? If he declined the duel, the Storm Lady would surely dismiss him, and in spite of what he'd said earlier he had no wish to return to Imerle empty-handed. Another time he might have welcomed the chance to teach Greave some civility, but the fact he'd let himself be so easily manipulated left a sour taste in his mouth. Still, if he had to go through with his, he would at least pretend it was by his choice, not Mazana's, and so he forced a smile and said, "Why not?"

Greave emptied the contents of his nostrils onto the floor. Clearly he'd learned not just his combat skills in the pits, but also his manners. He crossed to the divan he'd been lying on. On the ground beneath it was a fish-spine sword made of blue steel with toothlike barbs along the blade. The champion picked up the weapon, then smirked when he caught Senar looking at it. "Arena rules?"

"Are there such things?" the Guardian said, drawing his sword and raising it in a salute.

His opponent attacked.

Grunting as each strike landed, Greave forced Senar to retreat with a series of cuts and thrusts. There was weight behind his blows, but the juripa spirits must have slowed his reactions, for when Senar counterattacked with a stab to the abdomen, Greave only just parried in time. As their swords met, the champion turned his wrist, and Senar's weapon snagged on the barbs of the other man's blade. When the Guardian stepped back to disengage, Greave followed him, his left fist swinging for Senar's face.

The Guardian swayed aside.

So far, so comfortable.

Senar circled to the right, the shouts of the champion's followers loud in his ears. He would have to finish this quickly. Ordinarily he preferred to take time to assess his opponent's technique, but the months of captivity had sapped his strength, and his sword arm was already aching. If Greave had known of his weakness he would probably have played a waiting game. Instead he pressed forward, aiming a slash to Senar's chest which the Guardian blocked. The force of the impact knocked him back a step.

Glass crunched beneath his heel.

In Senar's mind's eye he saw again the woman lying facedown amid the pieces of broken bottle, and he knew without looking that her body would be close behind. Greave had no doubt driven him toward her, hoping the Guardian would trip over her. Senar needed to make some room, so when his opponent attacked again, he ducked under a head-high cut, then lashed out with a Will-strike to Greave's chin. The champion's head rocked back—more in surprise, Senar suspected, than from the power of the blow. Greave had claimed to know about Guardians, but he was clearly ignorant on the workings of the Will, for he retreated hurriedly, looking about for the source of the unseen attack.

Senar stepped into the center of the mosaic.

Greave strode forward once more, roared on by his followers. His sword came whistling round. A duel to first blood Beauce had said, but it was plain from Greave's strokes that the champion didn't care if Senar's first blood was his last. Then, midstroke, Greave changed the angle of his sword's swing and released his blade before snatching for the hilt with his left hand. His right hand, meanwhile, reached for Senar's sword. Doubtless Greave had intended to grab the Guardian's weapon and thus prevent him from parrying an attack from the fish-spine blade now in his left hand. A nice trick, but the juripa spirits must have spoiled it, for Greave's right hand missed Senar's sword and his left fumbled at the hilt of his own blade, only grasping it at the second attempt.

Senar had plenty of time to block the cut that followed.

With Greave's sword now in his wrong hand, the Guardian saw his chance to seize the initiative. He feinted low, then attacked high with a thrust meant to graze his opponent's right arm. The champion brought his blade up to parry, but Senar used a nudge of his Will to slow the weapon. *Got you.*

His sword glanced off Greave's arm with a scrape of metal.

Senar stepped back, uncertain.

The champion lowered his blade, his gaze shifting from the Guardian to his arm. Senar's sword had made a gash in his shirt, but no blood welled up to soak the cloth. Instead Senar saw a glint of silver through the tear. Scales? Evidently his opponent was wearing armor beneath his puffed shirt.

Greave grinned. "First blood, remember."

He launched himself forward.

The shouting of his followers had died away to leave a charged silence broken only by the clang of swords. The wall torches cast wild shadows across the mosaic. Senar was panting now, but at least the longer the duel went on, the more his mastery of the Will would return. In his early days as an initiate at the Sacrosanct, Senar's weaponsmasters had considered him the runt of the litter because of his size, yet even then his control of the Will had let him defeat stronger, more practiced, opponents. Using the Will was like wielding a second weapon, and a flick of his mind now drove Greave back. Senar worked an opening to his adversary's left leg. He feinted to it to bring the champion's blade flashing down. Another touch of the Guardian's power added momentum to the other man's swing, overbalancing him.

Senar stepped to his right and lunged with his sword for Greave's face. No armor there. Greave did not have time to recover his blade, so he threw his head back in an effort to evade the attack.

Too late.

Senar's sword sliced open his left cheek and nicked the lobe of his ear.

Behind, Mazana flinched as a thread of the champion's blood spattered her face.

And that concludes today's lesson. Normally Senar didn't like to gloat, but for the champion he'd make an exception.

Greave's eyes were wide with surprise, and his sword, poised now for a thrust at Senar's midsection, wavered in the air. The Guardian moved back, but didn't lower his weapon. No way he trusted Greave to take defeat graciously. Someone to his right began a slow, mocking handclap. Greave lifted a hand to his wounded cheek. He stared, disbelieving, at his bloody fingers. When he finally looked at Senar again, his lips were drawn back in a snarl.

"A shallow victory, Guardian," he said. "In giving that cut, yer left yerself open to a killing stroke. Me next thrust would have gutted yer like a bayfish."

Not true, as it happened, for Senar would have blocked the move with his Will. But that was hardly the point, as Greave well knew. "How did you put it? 'First blood, remember.'"

"Out!" Mazana said. "Everybody out! I wish to speak to the Guardian alone. You too, Greave," she added when the man lingered.

Beauce was the first to move, chuckling as he headed for the door through which Senar had entered. His soldiers fell in behind. The Everlord went next, guiding the manacled girl before him. Greave and his followers went more slowly. Two of them seized an ankle each of the woman lying on the floor. As they dragged her across the mosaic, a red smear was left in her wake.

The door closed to leave Senar alone with Mazana.

Interesting development.

The Storm Lady was watching him, and he returned her look evenly, waiting for her to speak. Instead she rose, then wiped Greave's blood from her face with a sleeve and crossed to stand in front of a painting of a man mounted on a palimar. Two daggers protruded from the canvas, one from the rider's forehead, the other from his left cheek. There were more slashes round his chin and neck. Mazana reached up and seized the hilt of the knife piercing his forehead. Twisting it from side to side, she tugged it free. For a while she weighed the blade in her hand as if she was considering stabbing it into the canvas once more.

When the Guardian studied the painting, he saw the rider had Mazana's copper-red hair and sardonic smile. "Your father?" he said, sheathing his sword. He couldn't put his finger on it, but something told him they shared a difficult relationship.

She nodded. "He's dead. He died six years ago."

"I'm sorry."

"Don't be. He taught me never to let my thoughts be governed by compassion or sentiment. To be unrelenting in my ambition, and ruthless in my dealings with friend and foe alike." She paused. "So one day I took him at his word and slipped red solent into his wine."

Senar's expression darkened. She'd killed her father? And apparently she saw no shame in the act either. Senar's own father had died on a mission when Senar was seven; his loss was stamped all over Senar's childhood. All he remembered of the man were snatched images, but they were no less valued for that.

"What did you want to speak to me about?" he asked Mazana coolly.

Ignoring the question, Mazana strode to a door along the wall to her left and stepped through. Senar followed. Beyond was a passage, and with slow steps the Guardian trailed Mazana along it and through a door at the far end. He entered a bedroom and halted just inside. More and more . . . interesting. Dominating the right-hand wall was a four-poster bed with curtains of white silk. In a smaller bed beside it was a red-haired boy, curled up in sleep. Mazana crossed to a wardrobe against the far wall, tossing her knife onto a chair. Then, with her back to Senar, she released a clasp at her left shoulder. Her dress fell away to pool at her feet.

Senar averted his gaze and found himself looking through an open window at a sky streaked crimson by the setting sun. Whatever game Mazana was playing, he wanted no part of it.

Moments later the Storm Lady crossed his line of sight. She now wore a cream nightgown that swept the floor tiles as she walked. She moved to a desk beneath the window. On the desk was a decanter filled with a clear liquid, and the Storm Lady filled two glasses before crossing to join Senar. The jewel invested with air-magic was still round her neck. It sparkled in the half-light, and Mazana's eyes were no less bright as they focused on the Guardian. She gave him one of the glasses. The smell of juripa spirits reached him.

"You think the summons was sent by me?" Mazana asked suddenly.

A smudge of Greave's blood remained below her hairline, and Senar resisted an impulse to wipe it clean. "I think it was not sent by the emira."

"And I think Imerle is more cunning than you give her credit for. You're aware her rule is coming to an end?"

Senar shook his head. He had known each Storm Lord held the title of emir or emira for five years before making way for a colleague, but he did not know when Imerle's term finished, nor for that matter where Mazana fitted into the succession.

The Storm Lady said, "Her tenure concludes at the end of this year. Then Gensu takes up the reins, and the great Imerle Polivar passes into obscurity to wait twenty-five years for her turn to come again. You backed the wrong horse, Guardian." She cocked her head. "Unless, of course, you know something I don't."

Senar was silent, unsure what she was hinting at. "You think the emira is plotting to hold on to power?"

"When you've stood on top of the mountain for so long, it must be difficult to climb down and watch another take your place. And twenty-five years is a not inconsiderable time to wait, don't you think?"

"How long is it before your own turn comes round?"

Mazana smiled but did not respond. A breeze was stealing in through the open window to Senar's left. As the Storm Lady went to close it she stepped in front of a torch, and its light seeped through her gown, making it appear as insubstantial as smoke.

"Poor Imerle," Mazana said. "Such a sad and broken woman. You know her history, of course?"

"I have a feeling you are going to tell me," Senar muttered. The emira had sent him here for information, but thus far all he'd found out was what Mazana wanted him to know.

"Imerle was a powerful sorceress even as a child, but she had the misfortune to grow up when her father was at war with another Storm Lord. She was made to help her father wreak destruction on his enemy's fleet. Hundreds died." Mazana drank from her glass. "Then she was captured. Her jailers made threats against her in the hope they could bring her father to the negotiating table, but he left her to rot in a cell. Two years it took for the conflict to run its course. The ordeal left Imerle afraid of the dark, so much so that she now sleeps in a brightly lit room, and always with others present—the twins, mostly." Her eyes twinkled. "You can imagine the rumors that has led to."

Senar cleared his throat. "The emira is the strongest of the Storm Lords?"

"Yes. She is an archmage—you must have noticed her flaming eyes. All water retains within it the memory of the fires it has quenched. The most powerful water-mages are able to draw that fire out and shape it."

"Is she stronger than all of the other Storm Lords combined?"

"Hardly."

"Then if she were plotting against you, why would she bring all her rivals together in one place? Why not attack each of them while they are alone?"

"Perhaps because she has a plan to dispose of us all at once."

From somewhere in the house cheers sounded, followed by a burst of laughter. The Guardian set his glass down untouched on a table to his left, ignoring Mazana's amused expression. The time had come to steer the conversation in a direction of his choosing, for while he had no wish to become embroiled in the intrigues of Imerle's court, he knew he should take this opportunity to find out more about the key players—even if it was just Mazana's skewed view of them. "You mentioned Gensu in the throne room earlier. Something about the chief minister's employment?"

Mazana considered before answering. "Throughout the history of the Storm Lords, the machinery of state—the army, the courts, the administration—has remained independent of the emir or emira. The thinking was that if the most powerful people in Olaire owed their loyalty to the Storm Lords, as opposed to the leader personally, it would be more difficult for that leader to hang on to power at the end of their tenure. Generally that neutrality has been respected." She drained her glass. "But not always."

"You don't think the chief minister is neutral?"

"Not unless you count fathering a child on Imerle neutral, no. Oh, I have no proof of that, but rumors abound, and this time they weren't even started by me." She rolled her empty glass between her hands. "Imerle lost her daughter three years ago to a fever, and it broke her mind. Such a tragedy."

Odd, Mazana didn't sound all that regretful. "And so Gensu tried to have Pernay removed from office?"

"He nearly succeeded, too. The vote was tied three all, so the emira's casting vote held sway."

"If the case against the chief minister was as clear as you say, how did he hold on to his position?"

"Imerle's predecessor, Mokinda, has always been in her pocket."

"And the third vote in Pernay's favor?"

"Mine, naturally."

Senar scratched at the stubs of his missing fingers. Mazana had voted to keep Pernay in office even though by doing so she strengthened Imerle's hand? Why? *Perhaps for no other reason than to keep the emira guessing,* he thought sourly. *As she has me doing.*

The boy in the small bed murmured in his sleep. When Mazana looked down on him, her eyes lost some of their hardness.

"Your son?" Senar asked in a low voice.

"My half brother, Uriel." Mazana reached down to brush a strand of hair from the boy's forehead. "My father always wanted a son to continue his dynasty, even set my mother aside when it became clear she could not give him one."

"And you feared he would do the same to you when Uriel was born?" Was it for power, then, that she had killed him? Senar didn't think so. Mazana was trying to hide it, but her eyes held a pain that hinted at something more. Senar was tempted to ask her about it, but he knew it wasn't his place.

"No," she replied. "He had already sent me to live in Olaire. I hadn't set eyes on him for years before I poisoned him."

Senar looked at Uriel. "So you brought the boy up yourself? What of his mother?"

Mazana's raised eyebrow was all the answer Senar needed.

Seeing his expression the Storm Lady said, "You disapprove, Guardian? Or perhaps you would have killed the boy as well?"

"I am wondering why *you* did not."

"Oh, please, don't put me on a pedestal." Uriel stirred once more, and Mazana's voice softened. "He's just a boy now, but one day he will learn that I killed his mother and father." She shrugged, then added in a whisper, as if to herself, "What choice do I have?"

Senar nodded. "Your father taught you well."

"My father taught me not to let my emotions govern my judgment. A lesson I'd have thought you would approve of."

"Meaning?"

"Meaning you're a long way from home. A man does not go walking in the cold when he has a fire in his hearth to keep him warm."

She could not know, of course, about Senar's passage through the Merigan portal, or of his reasons for being in Olaire. For a heartbeat he wanted to tell her. "The decision to come here was not mine."

"And yet you don't seem in any hurry to leave." Mazana approached to within a pace of Senar. Along with the smell of juripa spirits, the Guardian caught the scent of mirispice. "Is there anyone in Erin Elal wondering what you are doing now or when you will return?"

Senar kept his silence. That barb, at least, had found its mark, though not for the reason she had intended.

Mazana must have taken his silence for confirmation, for she turned away and said, "I thought not. Close the door on your way out, Guardian."

Karmel followed her brother along a ledge that clung to the cliff. A dozen armspans below, waves pummeled the rocks, shattering into clouds of spray that glistened in the moonlight. One of those waves set the ledge shuddering, and Karmel stumbled. She reached out a hand to the cliff to steady herself, only to scrape her knuckles on a jagged protrusion. On the path ahead was a mound of stones. Beyond it Caval had stopped to offer his hand, but the priestess ignored him and scrambled over unaided.

On leaving the temple earlier Caval hadn't bothered to mention they would be going rock-climbing, yet Karmel was becoming all too accustomed to her brother's . . . reticence. Their conversation this morning had left countless questions unanswered, but Caval had dismissed her before she could ask them, citing important temple business. For the rest of the day he had been impossible to track down, so on the walk to the shore Karmel had pressed him for more information. How, for example, was she supposed to sneak into Dian's citadel with barely a day to scout the place, and how was she going to disable the mechanism that raised the Dragon Gate? Caval, though, had refused to discuss the mission until they were clear of Olaire, and by the time they reached the coast the hiss of the sea, together with the unevenness of the path, had made conversation out of the question.

Karmel's brow furrowed. Something had been troubling her on the walk. It wasn't that she knew so little about the mission, for doubtless the Chameleon priest accompanying her—Veran—would be better informed. No, what concerned her was that there hadn't been time for Caval to give her fuller instructions. She wondered if she hadn't been her brother's first choice for this mission—if she was filling in for another Chameleon who had backed out at the eleventh hour. And why had her predecessor withdrawn? Perhaps because of something Caval hadn't yet had a chance to tell Karmel about?

How convenient.

All day Karmel had felt like she should be doing something to prepare for the mission. She'd had no idea what, though, so instead she had returned to the routine of her temple duties: weaponwork with Foss, theology with Scale. Colley knew her well enough to sense something was amiss, but Karmel had been warned not to breathe a word about the mission, so she'd refused to answer his questions. The secret had swelled inside her like a drawn breath until she'd been forced to go to the Gray Room and whisper it to the statue of the Changeling. Then, as she was leaving, she had been cornered by that old fossil, Zilva, and bored witless by his tales of braving the Shark Run in the Rubyholt Isles. All in all it had been one of the longest days of Karmel's life.

Yet when the time had finally come for Caval to collect her, it had still seemed too soon.

The ledge along the cliff became a track that curled down to a beach of gray stones strewn with fireweed. A pace above the waterline stood a black man—Veran, Karmel assumed—staring out to sea. Drawn up beside him was an undecked boat fifteen paces long. As the priestess reached the beach, she tugged Caval's sleeve and pointed at the craft. "I'm traveling in *that*?" She'd expected a mode of transport more in keeping with the prestige of the mission. The emira's flagship, perhaps.

Her brother ignored the question. "When you're finished in Dian, I want you to go to ground for a few days until the dust settles."

"What am I supposed to do in Dian for a few days?"

"Ah, whatever you like, so long as it doesn't involve the Chameleon Temple there. No one is to know you're in the city."

"You haven't told anyone I'm going?"

Caval looked away. "The fewer people who learn about the mission, the less chance there is of a loose tongue letting something slip."

Karmel covered a smile. A loose tongue, indeed. The truth was, her brother didn't want anyone knowing about her role in the operation so he could take credit for her success afterward. Not that she would let him, of course. She wasn't about to pass up this opportunity to catch the eye not just of the emira but also of those Chameleons at the temple who when they looked at her saw only the sister of the high priest. For too long she'd lingered in her brother's shadow.

"I'm aware," Caval said, "that you haven't been properly briefed about the mission. There hasn't been time. Veran will fill you in on the details." He glanced across. "You're to do as he tells you out there, understood?"

"So long as he doesn't—"

"No," Caval cut in. "You'll do as you're told, or we end this now."

End this now? If by that he meant he would stand Karmel down, he was surely bluffing, for where was he going to find a replacement at such short notice? So intense was his gaze, though, that the priestess's retort died on her lips. She inclined her head.

Caval studied her, then nodded in turn. "Wait here," he said, setting off down the beach toward Veran.

He approached the other man as if Veran were some cinderhound prone to bite—swinging round to come from one side before halting several paces away. The high priest had swapped his robes of office for a plain shirt, trousers, and cloak, yet still he cut a commanding figure beside the shorter Veran in his tattered kalabi robe. Veran did not acknowledge Caval's presence. Instead he remained looking out to sea, his arms crossed over his chest.

A gust of wind swept along the beach, setting Karmel's robes flapping. She could hear the two men's voices but not what they were saying. Caval appeared to be doing most of the talking, though. The priestess frowned. What did her brother have to say to Veran? Most likely he was giving him final instructions regarding the mission, but then why had he told Karmel to wait here?

She had just resolved to join the two men when Caval turned and beckoned her forward.

He came to meet her halfway down the beach. The hem of his cloak was wet from the surf. Karmel looked expectantly at Veran, but Caval did not reveal what he'd been discussing with the other man. He made to speak, then changed his mind. The silence dragged out. Karmel realized she was fiddling with the cuff of her sleeve, and she clasped her hands together to still them.

"Aren't you going to wish me luck?" she said.

"Ah, will you need it?"

"No," she said, trying to sound confident.

A smile touched the corners of Caval's mouth, but it quickly faded. "Stay close to Veran. He'll take care of you."

The time had come for them to part. Karmel found herself searching for something to say that would keep her brother here longer, but her mind was blank. The waves fretted at the beach. Caval watched her. For a heartbeat Karmel thought he was going to step forward and embrace her, but it was only the wind ruffling his cloak, not a movement of his body that she'd seen. His expression was hidden by the shadows of his hood. Karmel could see his eyes, though, glassy with reflected moonlight. There was something in them she did not recognize, but before she could focus on it Caval broke her gaze.

Stepping past her, he walked up the beach toward the track.

Her stomach churning, the priestess watched him until he reached the cliff ledge. He did not look round.

No turning back now.

Stones crunched beneath Karmel's sandals as she went to join Veran. He was still staring out to sea. He could only be a few years older than Caval, but his hair was streaked with gray. There was something of the banewolf in his angular features and in the yellowish cast to his eyes.

A wave broke cold over Karmel's feet as she waited. "Are you hoping Dian will come to us?" she said at last.

Veran swung to confront her. His face was thin, his cheeks hollow, but there was a strength to his gaze that made the priestess want to look away. Which made her all the more determined not to. He gestured to the boat. "Get in," he said.

"Since you ask so nicely."

Karmel climbed into the craft, wrinkling her nose at the stench of rotting fish. The boat had a mast with a single sail and a bench with a pair of banked oars. The priestess stored her pack beneath the bench before moving to the bow. Here she caught another smell—caulking. Fresh, too. No doubt it was only thing holding the boat together.

Veran set his shoulder to the stern of the craft and pushed. Stones skittered beneath his feet. The boat shifted forward a fraction . . .

And stuck.

The priest snorted and leaned into the transom once more. Veins stood out on his forehead. Still the boat remained wedged.

"Put your back into it," Karmel suggested helpfully.

There was a groan of wood. Then the craft lurched forward into the sea, flinging up a plume of spray.

Thrown off balance, Karmel fell backward and jarred her elbows on the bottom of the boat. When she put her hands down for support, she felt the sting of a splinter in her palm. Her tension came bubbling up. *Curse it all!* Her first mission, and already it seemed like one indignity piled atop another. Somewhere, she suspected, Caval would be laughing. For all she knew, this whole thing—this talk of the emira plotting to remain in power, him trusting her with the assignment—could be some elaborate joke at her expense. Maybe Veran would sail round the island a couple of times and arrive back here to find her brother waiting for her, grinning.

It was what Karmel would have done in his position.

Veran continued to push on the transom until the waves came up to his waist. Then he placed his hands on the gunwale and sprang inside. Settling himself on the oar-bench, he unlimbered the oars and heaved upon them. The muscles of his arms knotted with each stroke. To the sound of crashing water, the boat labored out into the bay.

Veran was facing away from Karmel, so she was spared having to endure his stare as she looked back at the shore. The sea reached white fingers onto the beach, erasing the gouge left by the boat's keel. Karmel scanned the cliff ledge for Caval. She thought she saw a shadowy form pass in front of one of the caves in the rock face, but it must have been a trick of the light, for the figure did not reappear along the track beyond the opening.

To Karmel's left Olaire was visible above a rocky promontory. The Round's dome was easy to spot, as were the beacons at the mouth of the Causeway. When the priestess searched Kalin's Hill for the Chameleon Temple, though—it seemed oddly important that she catch a final glimpse of it—she could not make it out. As daughter to the former high priest, the temple had been her home throughout her childhood—the only home she'd ever known. She continued to look for it until the boat neared the mouth of the bay, but the darkness clung stubbornly to the hillside, and Karmel fought to shake off a premonition she would not see the temple, or her brother, again.

Shivering, she wrapped her cloak about her shoulders.

The noise of waves breaking on the shore faded, to be replaced by the splash of oars and the slap of water on the boat's hull. From the direction of Olaire came the clang of a crescent-bell, indicating that somewhere in the Shallows' flooded streets a saberfin had been sighted. Lights showed in the windows of the buildings in the Deeps, and their glow reflected off the sea in smears of watery gold. As the boat's course took it closer to the headland, those lights disappeared behind the promontory. Soon all that remained to mark Olaire's presence was a paling of the night sky.

Karmel realized abruptly that her buttocks were wet, and she placed her palm on the planks beneath her. The wood was damp. Rising, she spied a trickle of water running along the boards toward the bench where Veran sat.

"We're taking on water—"

"Silence, girl!"

"My name is Karmel . . ." the priestess began, louder than she'd intended.

Her voice trailed off.

Veran's oars had gone still. He was looking to the west, to where the promontory fell away into the sea. From the other side materialized a small boat under sail, less than fifty armspans away. It was heading this way. Karmel silently swore. Someone was following them! Had the other Storm Lords found out about the mission and moved quickly to put an end to it? Even through her panic, she knew that made no sense. If it had been the Storm Lords pursuing them, would they have given chase in a craft even more wretched than Karmel's?

Then she noticed the crayfish baskets stacked in the boat's stern. *Just a fishing boat,* she assured herself. Any moment now its owner would see them and turn aside.

Even as the thought came to her a curse sounded across the waves, and the craft's occupant—an Untarian male with fishbone piercings in his nose and ears—reached for the tiller. The boat's bow swung round.

Veran looked from the fisherman to Karmel. "Shut him up," he said, glancing at the baldric of knives across her chest.

The priestess stared at him. Was he serious? "Do you hear him talking?" she asked.

Veran's face twisted in disgust.

Karmel's mind struggled to keep up with what happened next. Her companion reached under the oar-bench and straightened with a throwing knife of his own in his hand. His meaning had been clear when he told her to silence the fisherman, yet a part of Karmel still hadn't believed he would go through with it.

He spun and threw the blade in one motion. A glittering point of silver flashed over the waves.

Karmel didn't see the dagger strike its target, only heard the fisherman's choked gasp. He raised his hands to his neck, then staggered back and toppled over the gunwale, hitting the sea with a splash. The fishing boat slewed to the west, its sail falling limp.

For a while Karmel could only gape at the man's body in the water, aghast. *He's dead,* she thought stupidly. And for what? Because he'd seen their boat? At such a distance he couldn't have made out their faces, and even if he had, he wouldn't have remembered them. And yet, through her shock and disquiet she found herself admiring the skill of Veran's throw. He'd found his mark in near blackness and with the boat rocking beneath him . . .

Lucky bastard.

The priest reseated himself on the oar-bench and hauled on the oars again. "You owe me a throwing knife," he said between strokes. His voice showed not a flicker of emotion at the fisherman's murder.

"What?"

"Untarian's blood is on your hands. I wouldn't have had to silence him if you hadn't bleated your name."

She had said it, hadn't she? Karmel was caught between guilt and indignation, but the indignation won out. "And I wouldn't have spoken my name if you hadn't called me 'girl.' In any case, there's no way the man would have heard. No way."

"Ain't taking no chances. No witnesses, Caval said."

"And you don't think questions will be asked when his body washes up on shore?"

"Currents will take him east to Ebony Bay. We'll be halfway to Dian before he's found."

"If we haven't sunk first," Karmel said, eyeing the water that was pooling at the bottom of the boat.

"Then start bailing."

"With what? My hands?"

"With your Shroud-cursed mouth if I had my way," Veran muttered.

Karmel groped for a reply, but none came.

A tattered banner of cloud floated across the moon, and the silvery waves faded to black. The priestess peered toward where the fisherman's corpse would be, but she couldn't make it out in the gloom. She swung her gaze south, hoping for a glimpse of Dian or Natilly. All she could see, though, was an empty waste of pitching water. The Dragon Gate was, what, twenty leagues from Olaire? With a favorable wind they might reach it within a dozen bells . . . unless Veran decided to slow their passage so they arrived unseen at nightfall tomorrow.

Karmel took a breath and blew it out. There would be sense in that, she had to admit. A day then, probably, before she could leave behind this leaking heap of driftwood. A day before she'd be free of the stink of fish and tar.

She cast a look at Veran's back.

Something told her it would feel like much longer.

CHAPTER 5

THE DOOR to Jambar's quarters opened even as Senar raised a hand to knock. Inside, Jambar stood watching him with the same inane smile Senar remembered from their encounter on the roof terrace—a smile vaguely unsettling in its false sincerity.

"Come in, Guardian."

Senar raised an eyebrow. He hadn't told the old man he was coming, but then the Remnerol was a shaman, wasn't he? Evidently he'd foreseen Senar's arrival. It occurred to Senar that Jambar was probably the closest thing he had to a kinsman in this place, because the Remnerol homeland fell within the borders of the Erin Elalese empire. He felt no sense of fellowship to the old man, though, for the loyalty of the Remnerol clans had always been bought with the sword. Senar had done some of the buying himself. He'd lost some good friends in those campaigns.

He followed Jambar into his chambers and found himself in a room ten paces square. There was a barred door to his right and a window on the opposite wall. To the left was a cot with a straw mattress, while in the center of the floor was a lopsided table and a chair. The room was devoid of personal adornment, as though the shaman were merely a guest. *Or he thinks he might one day have to leave in a hurry.*

"Modest quarters you have here," the Guardian said.

"Of my own choosing. The more a man deprives himself of worldly goods, the more his own goodness grows."

Senar searched the Remnerol's face for mockery but saw nothing beyond the simple smile.

Jambar crossed to the table and sat down on the chair. On the table was a round wooden board with a silver rim. Painted on the board were white runes arranged in circles that extended outward from a large central character—an inverted cross over an ellipse. Beside the board were twenty knuckle bones. One pair of knuckles, Senar noticed, was black. One was twice the size of the others. His gaze lingered on the large pair. "I thought a Remnerol shaman used only the bones of his clansmen in his readings."

"Most do."

"Using other people's bones increases your powers?"

The old man nodded. "The more powerful the bones' former owners, the greater accuracy they give to my readings. There are millions of possible futures, Guardian. Every act of every person affects what is to come. As my powers increase, I am better able to pinpoint the actions that shape those futures."

"And where did you find a giant's bones?"

"Why, in a giant's grave, of course," Jambar said, picking up a handful of the knuckles and placing them in a bag.

There was a smell in the air, Senar noticed: sweat and wet hair and something else he couldn't place. It reminded him of his own stink yesterday after ten months in a cell. "I have often wondered at the source of a shaman's power," he said. The Remnerol wars had given him good cause. Part of the trouble with fighting the tribes was that they always knew you were coming. There was no such thing as catching the Remnerol off guard. "All sorcery requires energy to fuel it, correct? Yet bone is dead. What energies can there be in bone for a shaman to draw on?"

"A good question," Jambar said. "And I would be glad to tell you the answer—after *you* have told *me* how Guardians are able to summon power from mere thought."

Senar made a sour face. Soon it would be no mystery. The Guardians had protected the knowledge for centuries, but now Avallon wanted his Breakers to be trained in the Will. How long before someone yielded the secret to the Kalanese? Avallon's shortsightedness would bring the empire to its knees.

When he suggested as much to Jambar, though, the shaman said, "Denounce your own emperor, would you? Are you so blessed with friends here that you must look for enemies among your own kins-men?"

"Avallon betrayed us."

"Because he took the Guardians' power before you could take his? What you resent is the fact that he won."

Senar bit back a retort. What did the old man know about the Sacrosanct's business? The Guardian Council had never wanted the emperor's power for itself. Its concern had been only to keep Avallon in check and to maintain its independence in the face of the emperor's ever more insistent demands for allegiance. Avallon had disturbed a balance that had existed for millennia, and all in the name of his ambition. Senar kept his silence, though, knowing that his words would be wasted on the shaman.

And that there might just be a grain of truth in the old man's charge.

The strange smell was becoming stronger, and the Guardian crossed to the window for some fresh air. Beyond was a courtyard much the same as the one in which he'd seen the giant execute the Untarian. In the distance he heard the murmur of the sea along with the bump of something wooden against the seawall.

"What did you say to the emira about me? Yesterday on the terrace . . . Pernay said, 'He plays you for a fool.'"

Jambar sighed. "The chief minister dislikes me, it is true, but con-demnation does not make a man evil any more than praise makes him good. I deem it a beneficial thing that people think ill of me even when I mean well. Such opposition is an aid to humility, for it shelters me from pride."

Again Senar looked for mockery, and again he saw nothing. It had to be there, though, didn't it? No one could truly believe the nonsense the shaman was coming out with.

"I am not stupid," he said. Whatever the evidence to the contrary. "Nor is Imerle. If word gets back to Avallon that I am here, he may come to realize there is a back door to the Storm Isles. Why should the emira risk letting me live?"

"You think I convinced her to spare you? Do you consider your-self in my debt, then?"

"You saw something in the bones, didn't you? Something in my future."

The Remnerol spread his hands, his smile unwavering. "Dragon

Day is almost upon us. As I said in the throne room, the days ahead are little more than a blur to me."

"And yet you knew I was coming to see you just now."

"It takes no skill to interpret the meaning of approaching foot-steps."

Just as it took no skill to figure out the old man was keeping some-thing back. "If the next two days are a blur, what about *after* Dragon Day?"

The shaman shifted in his seat. "Time is a river, Guardian. No sooner does one thing come into sight than it is hurried past and another is borne along, only to be swept away in turn."

In other words, he knows nothing. A thought came to Senar. "What of your own fate?"

Jambar's smile flickered but held.

"You must have seen something of yourself after Dragon Day," the Guardian pressed. Then, when Jambar did not respond, Senar nodded and said, "It cannot be easy witnessing one's own death—"

"I see everyone's death," the shaman cut in, "a hundred times over." There was an edge to his voice his inane smile could not con-ceal. Good. The more Senar rattled the old man, the more chance there was of something being shaken loose. "Would you like to know the manner of your own passing? Who strikes the killing blow?"

"Nothing is certain. You said so yourself, all you see is possi-bilities."

"The difference between us is that *I* have prior warning of those possibilities and thus an opportunity to influence them."

There was no arguing that, and Senar realized belatedly he might have made a mistake in baiting the old man. Not because of their shared kinsmanship, but because the shaman's gift of prescience could have made him a useful ally. Too late for that now. Then again, alliances were founded on trust, and that was not a word he would ever associate with the old man. "Then I had best disturb you no longer," he said, making for the door. "Two days does not give you long to think of a way to cheat Shroud."

He left the Remnerol smiling.

Outside in the corridor, the Guardian's mind raced. Jambar had neither confirmed nor denied Senar's suspicions over the shaman sparing him from Imerle, but the Guardian was convinced the old man knew something he wasn't sharing. Was Imerle in danger? Was

Senar destined to save her? But save her from whom? And if he did so, wouldn't that mean he had outlived his usefulness?

One thing was certain, a storm was brewing in Olaire. The warning signs were not difficult to read: the approach of Dragon Day; the assassinations in the Shallows that Senar had heard about; the gathering of the Storm Lords in answer to the mysterious summonses. There was a connection there if only he could see it. While he remained in the dark, he would have to watch Jambar carefully. If anyone was going to end up on the winning side it was the shaman, and Senar intended to be there with him.

At the moment he didn't even know what the Shroud-cursed sides were.

Footfalls sounded along the corridor, and he looked up to see the chief minister. Pernay halted. "What are you doing here?"

Yes, that would take some explaining. Senar should long since have reported to the emira about his meeting with Mazana Creed, but he'd had much more important business to attend to—such as tracking down a decent tailor and making an enemy of the Remnerol.

"I seem to have lost my way," he said. "I was looking for the throne room."

Pernay's gaze flickered to the Remnerol's door. "Do not be fooled by the shaman's false humility and crass philosophy. He is an abomination. In the past month alone, three servants sent to convey messages to him have disappeared."

"And yet here you are."

The chief minister continued as if he had not heard. "The emira should have disposed of him long ago."

"Perhaps she knows better than to try. Doubtless Jambar would see the ax falling before it was even raised."

"If he weren't a complete charlatan, yes." Pernay's hands were shaking, and he hid them behind his back. "What did you learn from Mazana Creed?"

"Little," Senar conceded. "She continues to protest her innocence over the summonses, but if she did not send them, I suspect she knows who did." He paused as a serving-girl scuttled by. "I was, however, able to find out something about her companion, Greave. He is a former champion of the blood pits in Bethin. He is also, I believe, not so much Mazana's bodyguard as her associate, for he appears to command a sizable following within her entourage."

The chief minister's look seemed to say, *Is that all?* but then what had he expected, the Storm Lady's signed confession over the summonses? "Stay close to her, Guardian," he said at last. "Mazana is too shrewd to let slip whatever twisted scheme she has dreamed up, but your presence may force her to tread softly."

Senar frowned. He had hoped last night's encounter with Mazana would be his last—and hoped it wasn't, all at the same time. "What news of the other Storm Lords?" he asked.

"They are here now, barring Gensu."

"And they all deny sending the summonses?"

"Of course."

"That leaves Gensu, then."

"And yet if he *is* the one who called this gathering, does it not seem strange he should be the last to show his face?" Pernay shrugged aside his own question. "A conference has been called for this evening, by which time Gensu will no doubt have arrived. We will sort this out then. In the meantime, I will report your words about Mazana to the emira." He smiled without humor. "No need for you to continue your search for the throne room."

The chief minister turned to knock on Jambar's door.

It was already opening.

Karmel opened her eyes. The powder-blue sky told her it was morning, yet it felt like only heartbeats had passed since she'd nodded off. The spare cloak she had used to plug the leak in the hull must have done its job, because there was only a finger's width of water sloshing about in the boat. *Only.* That water, though, had seeped into her shirt and trousers to leave them drenched and stinking as strongly of fish as if she'd been hauled out of the water in one of the boat's nets. Still, at least she had a change of clothes in her pack.

Then she remembered she'd stored her gear under the oar-bench—where the water was deepest. Doubtless it too was now soaked through.

Scowling, she looked at Veran. The priest sat cross-legged on the bench, facing her. His eyes were closed, and he was breathing deeply, but Karmel could tell he wasn't asleep because with the fingers of his left hand he was turning round and round a Chameleon ring on the index finger of his right. She took the opportunity to study him more closely. There were bruises beneath his eyes and worry lines across his forehead. Whatever his prowess with his throwing knives, he was clearly less than capable with a sword because his forearms were crisscrossed with scars. There was another scar running from his right ear to the neckline of his kalabi robe. Karmel noticed he wasn't wearing a blade and that hers was the only sword in the boat. If trouble came calling, what was he planning to do, dazzle his enemies with his charm?

Veran had evidently been careful to avoid the main shipping lanes between Olaire and the Dragon Gate because Karmel could see just half a dozen boats on the sea around her, and none of those vessels were close enough for their passengers to make out the Chameleons' faces. Dian and Natilly were to the south, perched atop the cliffs that flanked the Dragon Gate. Still leagues away, the gate itself was visible only as a continuation of those cliffs, giving Karmel the impression that she was sailing toward an unbroken wall of rock. Above Dian and Natilly, flocks of limewings swirled on the breeze like carrion birds over a battlefield.

Karmel retrieved her pack from under the oar-bench and took out her throwing knives and a cloth. Drawing one of the blades, she began to polish it.

Veran did not stir.

"Perhaps now would be a good time," the priestess said, "to tell me more about our mission."

Her companion's eyes remained shut. "We'll talk in Dian."

"Are you worried the fish might overhear?"

No reply.

Karmel bit down on her irritation. There was no reason for him to keep the information from her, except that it made him feel like a big man to do so. It was clear he saw her not so much as a partner but as an underling. Worse, he expected her to feed off the scraps she was given and be thankful for them. It was time to set him straight on that. "Whose place did I take on this mission?" She'd pondered that question last night while she was waiting for sleep to come. The names weren't difficult to conjure up: Foss undoubtedly, Zaman, maybe even Wick.

Veran opened his eyes. He stared at her blankly.

"There's no way," she went on, "Caval would have given me such short notice unless I was stepping into someone else's shoes. No way."

"Why don't you ask your brother?"

She made a show of looking round the boat before her gaze finally came to rest on the sailcloth cover beside her pack. "Is he hiding under there?"

Again, no response.

Off the port quarter a single-masted galleon flying the gold-and-silver-striped flag of the Goldsmiths' Guild came into view. It must have had a water-mage on board, for it rode the crest of a wave several armspans high. In a matter of heartbeats it drew level with the Chameleons' boat, and both Karmel and Veran turned their faces away. The edge of the sorcerous wave broke against the craft, setting it rocking. Karmel watched the ship speed southward, then looked at Veran.

"I didn't get a chance in Olaire to ask Caval about you—"

"Good."

"So I did some asking round at the temple instead. Respected, I was told, but nothing more. Apparently you left the priesthood last year, and no one seems in any hurry to talk you into returning. No one. Naturally I was curious why someone who had turned his back on the Chameleon would agree to go on this mission . . ." She left the thought hanging.

"None of your business."

"I thought you'd say that, so I did a little digging." Glancing at Veran's left hand, she saw a gold wedding band on his ring finger. "Rumor has it your wife fell ill after you walked out on us. That's when you requested an audience with Caval, right?"

Veran closed his eyes as if to signal the conversation was at an end, but Karmel was just getting started.

"I'm guessing you thought it was no coincidence that your wife fell sick after you abandoned the priesthood. That the Chameleon was responsible for her illness."

Her companion was a long time in answering. "I thought he might heal her."

"And did he?"

"Her sickness lifted. For a while."

"So you believed in him enough to go begging for his aid, but not enough to credit him with your wife's improvement when it came?"

"I know he could heal her if he wanted to. Just ain't sure he gives enough of a damn to lift a hand."

"But you *want* to believe, don't you? Why else would you have gone to Caval for help? Why else would you still be wearing that ring you keep twiddling?"

No reply.

Karmel's anger was building. She was prodding him in the hope it would make him open up, but no matter what she said she was met by a wall of indifference. It was almost as if he couldn't be bothered to react to her goading. "There's more to the story, though, isn't there?" she said. "You go to see Caval, and afterward your wife's condition improves—briefly. Then a few weeks ago you come to see my brother a second time, and now here you are." She leaned forward. "You know what I think?"

Silence.

"I think after you visited Caval that first time, you agreed to do something for him in exchange for the Chameleon healing your wife. Then, when her sickness returned, you came back to the temple and were told if you wanted more help you'd have to take a trip to Dian, maybe pay a little visit to the citadel while you were there. How am I doing so far?"

Veran's fingers were white where they gripped his Chameleon ring. "You ever seen someone struck down by the gray fever, girl?"

Karmel shook her head.

"Then you're lucky. First your limbs swell up so bad you can't move. Then your tongue swells up, so you can't speak. Eventually your throat swells up, so you can't breathe. Ain't no one ever caught the gray fever that's recovered from it. Ain't no one taken less than a year to die from it either."

Karmel pitied his wife, but she couldn't find it in herself to do the same for the priest. Most likely his wife had just a few more months among the living. Though no doubt Veran was foolish enough to think it might be longer. "When you last did what the Chameleon wanted, your wife's symptoms eased for only a short while. What makes you think this time will be any different?"

Veran did not respond, but from the set of his mouth he knew it wouldn't.

"Poor Veran," Karmel said. "A few months ago you must have thought you were free of the Chameleon forever. Instead your wife's illness means you're as much his servant now as you ever were."

Veran half rose from the oar-bench, his eyes flashing. Nerve touched. For an uncomfortable moment Karmel was grateful she was holding one of her throwing knives. Then the fire in the priest's gaze died, and he sat down again. A heavy silence settled on the boat. Karmel found herself disinclined to break it. Part of her wanted to take back her words, but another part feared it would make her look weak. She finished polishing her first throwing knife and took out a second.

In the distance the guild ship passed close to a red-sailed catboat, throwing up a shower of spray that drenched the smaller craft's passengers. Curses rang out across the water.

"You ever spoken to your god before?" Veran said suddenly. "He ever answer any of your questions?"

The change of subject took Karmel aback momentarily. "I'll let you know when I think of something to ask him."

Her companion's look was a mixture of disgust and disbelief. "You never stopped to ask yourself why we're doing what we're doing? What interest does the Chameleon have in what tribute Piput's paying? Who do we serve now, the god or the emira?"

"You serve my brother."

"And who does *he* serve?"

The priestess laughed. "You think it might be Imerle? Caval could never remain high priest if he wasn't doing what the Chameleon wanted. Never."

"So your father wasn't doing what the Chameleon wanted when he was kicked out, is that it?"

Karmel stared at him, unsure what he was getting at. When Pennick was high priest, he'd been despised by his fellows for his cruelty and aloofness, but no one had ever questioned his devotion to the Chameleon.

Veran nodded as if she'd spoken the thought aloud. "Why would the Chameleon want Caval as high priest instead of your father? Caval, a man who'd been a mere initiate a few years previously. A man prepared to betray his own flesh and blood—"

"What do you know of betrayal?" Karmel cut in, surprised at the vehemence in her voice. "Were you there when my father gave Caval his gap-toothed smile? Were you there when he beat him so badly he coughed blood for a fortnight?" And all because he'd failed to recite the Benediction perfectly. All six hundred and thirty-four lines of it.

Veran shook his head.

"Then maybe you should keep your mouth shut instead of talking of things you know nothing about."

"Right," the priest muttered. "Forgot you had the monopoly on that."

Karmel mastered herself with an effort. Veran was trying to provoke her, just as she had provoked him. And he'd succeeded far too easily for the priestess's liking. "When my brother was young, he wanted nothing to do with the priesthood. My father had to beat it into him." She drew another throwing knife. "So you tell me, how exactly did Caval betray him? He did what our father always wanted—he followed in his footsteps and became high priest."

Veran was stony-faced. "The Chameleon doesn't give a shit about family spats. He wouldn't have raised Caval up just so your brother could settle a score with Pennick."

"So?"

"So the only reason the god would want a changing of the guard is because Caval offered him something your father couldn't."

"What if he did?" Karmel said, trying to appear uninterested. Truth be told, she had long suspected there was more to her brother's rise to preeminence than he'd admitted. Throughout his childhood he had resisted taking his final vows, yet within six years of doing so he'd become the most powerful man in Olaire's priesthood? There was a time when Karmel had felt hurt that he hadn't told her the full story. But she wasn't going to sit there and listen to a stranger like Veran—a man who had turned his back on the temple, no less—throw mud at her brother.

Veran said, "Maybe I'd like to know what deal Caval struck with the Chameleon. Maybe I'd like to know just what it is I'm supposed to be fighting for now."

"You'd question the will of your god?"

"If it means we become the emira's playthings, damned right I would."

Karmel wondered if his wife shared his high ideals.

An urge took her to shake out some of the kinks the night's sleep had left in her body, and so she returned her throwing knives to her pack and moved to the bow. Taking off her sandals, she ran a hand along the prow to check for splinters, then stepped up. The breeze was strong at her back. She remained still for a time, settling the sea's rhythm in her mind. With a final breath to compose herself, she took her right foot in her hand on that side and lifted her leg.

A creak sounded as Veran rose from the oar-bench, followed by a snap of canvas as he trimmed the sail. Karmel sought to put him from her mind, but his words from earlier came back to her. *Maybe I'd like to know just what it is I'm supposed to be fighting for now.* All this talk of uncertainty in Caval's leadership, of lost faith in the direction the priesthood was taking, was no more than a smoke screen, Karmel knew. His real motives for leaving the temple would be far less noble. Perhaps he'd enjoyed greater privileges under the old regime than the new, or perhaps he had seen himself as a more worthy successor to Pennick than Caval.

History had proved him wrong. Caval's association with Imerle had opened up countless opportunities for the advancement of the Chameleon order, yet there would always be those among the priesthood—the meek, the small-minded—who lacked the vision to see those chances for what they were. Who had grown comfortable in their laziness and now resisted change because they feared losing their influence to younger, more ambitious colleagues. Colleagues more deserving of basking in the god's favor.

Colleagues like Karmel, perhaps.

Or maybe Veran's problem was simpler. Maybe he'd been so long at the sharp end of the Chameleon's dealings with his enemies that he'd lost his nerve.

When she suggested as much to Veran, he grunted and said, "You ever killed a man before?"

Karmel held her pose for another heartbeat, then lowered her right leg and raised her left. Off the port bow a school of silverfins flitted through the foam-specked water. "Of course." The first time had been last year when a gang of deadbeats had insulted the temple by scrawling graffiti over its walls. Karmel had been among those sent to hunt them down.

"Not with those pretty throwing knives of yours. Up close, so you could see the whites of his eyes."

"I've defeated enough opponents in my training at the temple. I see no reason why the real thing should be any less easy."

"You better hope it never gets easy."

Karmel sensed a lecture coming. She got enough of those in the temple. "Was it easy when you silenced that fisherman yesterday?"

"No easier, I reckon, than when you killed that boy in the duel to become Honorary Blade."

Karmel started, almost losing her balance. "You were there?" The contest for the privilege of carrying the Chameleon's sword had taken place at the temple three months ago—*after* Veran had left the priesthood—so what had he been doing there?

Veran said, "Others might think it was a mistake when you crushed the lad's windpipe with that thrust, but you had your blade well enough under control before then. What was the matter, girl? Did he forget to stain his knees before you when you took up your positions?"

Karmel kept her expression even. The episode was one she'd tried hard to forget, but now she saw again the closing exchanges of the duel, pictured Vallans's face turning blue as he clawed at his throat. More clearly, though, she remembered the stink of his body when his bowels opened. She hadn't been able to get the smell out of her nose for days. No doubt in Vallans's final moments he'd regretted the taunts he'd whispered to her as they touched their wooden blades at the start of the fight, as well as his attempts to intimidate her in the days leading up to the contest. Afterward his family had accused her of killing him deliberately, but it was an accusation Karmel had always denied. And it *had* been a misjudgment, hadn't it? She would never have slain him on purpose. When she spoke to Veran she tried to sound offhand. "Even the best swordsmen make mistakes. Even the best."

The priest grunted.

"You question my abilities?" she said, angry again. It seemed Veran had a gift for bringing out the worst in her.

"Sparring ain't the same as fighting."

Karmel had heard those words a dozen times from a dozen of her fellow priests and priestesses, yet if Veran and those others thought they were better than Karmel, why had they not entered the contest? "I'm the youngest Chameleon ever to become Honorary Blade. Even my brother fears to face me."

"I've seen your brother fight. He would cut you into strips."

"Of course he would." Karmel lowered her leg. "*That's* why he turns me down every time I ask to spar with him." Tucking her shirt into her trousers, she bent down to place her hands on the prow and swung her legs up into a handstand. Blood rushed to her head.

"Get down from there," Veran snapped. "We're supposed to be fishermen, not Shroud-cursed acrobats."

Karmel ignored him. "In any case, I hardly think someone with as many scars as you is in any position to judge another swordsman's skill."

"Those scars were earned. Every one is a fight I've walked away from."

"A fight in which your defenses were breached, you mean. Do you see any scars on me?"

"One for each scrap you've been in," Veran muttered.

Karmel pretended she hadn't heard. Did the fool really think she was green just because she hadn't been knocked about like he had? Did he believe his scars were some badge of honor—

The boat lurched to the left, and the priestess found herself toppling forward. Tightening her grip on the prow, she arched her back in an effort to restore her balance, but to no avail. Her fall was going to land her in the path of the boat, so she pushed off with both hands and twisted to the right. She hit the sea on her back and took a half breath before the cool, sun-bright waves closed around her, filling her ears with watery silence.

She resurfaced, spluttering, off the starboard beam and draped her arms over the gunwale.

Veran watched from the oar-bench. His face was impassive, but Karmel could swear there was a twinkle in his eye as he said, "Sorry, girl, hand must have nudged the tiller by mistake. Even the best sailors, and all that."

The door to Enli Alapha's offices was made of glass, but then a man who represented assassins had little need to worry about thieves, Kempis supposed. Pushing the door open, he entered a reception area dominated by a desk so high it resembled a bar at an inn. Behind the desk sat a middle-aged woman with immaculately coiffured hair and the longest nose Kempis had ever seen. As he entered with Sniffer, the woman looked them up and down as if she'd just scraped them off the sole of her sandal.

"Good evening," she said.

Kempis strode to a door on his left.

"Excuse me, sir! Excuse me!"

The septia entered the room beyond and found himself in an office lit by torches set into wall niches. Behind a desk at the far end sat an old man—Enli Alapha, Kempis assumed—wearing a robe trimmed with flintcat fur. The merchant's eyes were a blue so pale the irises were almost indistinguishable from the whites. A beard jutted from his chin, and a mole sprouted from the left side of his nose. He was writing with a quill pen in a leather-bound book.

The office was blessedly cool after the sapping night heat. Judging by the trace of sorcery in the room, an air-mage had been employed to keep the air circulating. The office was filled with the smell of exotic spices, but it couldn't mask a certain whiff of self-righteousness that set Kempis's nostrils twitching.

The receptionist appeared behind him. Enli Alapha waved her away. He took in Kempis's uniform and gave a wintry smile. "Can I help you, Watchman?"

"Nice setup you have here," Kempis said, sitting in one of the chairs in front of the desk. He shot a glance at Sniffer, who had trailed him inside. "Didn't know there was so much money in spices."

The Untarian nodded. "The man must be making a *killing*," she said.

Kempis frowned. "I make the jokes round here."

"You do? I hadn't noticed."

Enli's smile had not wavered. "I don't believe I've had the pleasure."

Kempis ignored the unspoken question. No Duffle here to give his name away. There was a row of glass containers on the desk, each containing a different spice. The septia lifted the nearest and sniffed its contents through the holes in the top, then winced as he recognized the smell of blayfire. He put the container down. "I'm looking for a client of yours," he said to the merchant.

"Indeed? Alas, you appreciate my clients expect from me the highest levels of confidentiality. Since I am a member of the Merchant's Guild, though, certain details of my contracts are kept at the Round."

"Yes, they are, aren't they? As it happens I've spent a night and a day going through your records. Fascinating stuff." Kempis took a roll of parchment from his cloak and tossed it onto the desk. "You know what really bugs me?"

Enli steepled his hands. "I'm on tenterhooks."

"Anolamies."

"Anomalies?"

"Them too. Take, for example, a cargo of ganda spice from Palana Utara. Thirty thousand imperial sovereigns' worth, to be precise. Is this ringing any bells?" He gestured to the parchment. "Hamilla, your buyer was called. Placed the contract with you last year, on the eve of Dragon Day. You signed an endorsement to say you'd got his silver, but here's the strange thing: when I checked the harbor log to see when the spices arrived in Olaire, I found no record of the ship carrying them ever docking."

Enli went back to writing in his book. "Clearly a mistake on the part of the harbormaster. Since the buyer paid for the spices, it seems fair to assume the cargo arrived, wouldn't you agree?"

"So I told my colleague here," Kempis said, nodding at Sniffer. "Just to dot the *i*'s, though, I went to check with your buyer at the address in the contract. And guess what? Seems no one there ever heard of a Hamilla, or of you for that matter."

Enli gave his wintry smile again. "You've got me, Watchman. I confess it. I filed particulars of a contract that didn't exist in order to overstate my earnings and thus inflate my tax bill. I'm surprised more people aren't doing it."

Kempis scowled. That was the problem with being too clever: you started thinking everyone around you was stupid. Evidently Enli was receiving large sums of money for brokering deals on behalf of his assassin clients and disguising the payments as fees for nonexistent spice cargos. It seemed no one had had cause to question the legitimacy of those fees before now, and Kempis suspected the irregularities would never have come to light but for Inneez's tip-off. It had taken the septia the best part of a day to find even one suspicious dealing among dozens of regular transactions.

The blayfire Kempis had sniffed was making his nostrils feel like they were on fire. He sneezed into a sleeve. Enli withdrew a handkerchief from a pocket and passed it to him. The septia dabbed at his nose. In response to the merchant's earlier words he said, "Oh, I reckon the contracts existed. What I ain't clear on is exactly what you were paid *for*."

Sniffer had crossed to the wall on Kempis's right. It was filled from floor to ceiling with drawers. Pulling one open, she withdrew a card.

"Of course," Kempis went on, "could be a perfectly innocent explanation for all this. Does make me wonder, though, how many more inconsistencies I might find if I kept digging."

Enli's pen paused over his book. His gaze flickered to Sniffer but his expression said "cold, cold," as in a children's game, so either the Untarian was looking in the wrong place or the merchant had figured out she couldn't read.

Kempis raised his voice. "Perhaps you should work your way down from the top," he said to Sniffer. "You know, start with the ones hardest to reach."

Enli put his quill pen in its ink pot, then scratched the mole on his nose. "You never said how I could help you."

"I need to make a problem go away—"

"I share your sentiments."

"And I'm reliably informed you're the man who can help."

"Informed by whom?"

Kempis did not reply. The heat in his nostrils was becoming more intense. "Any of your . . . clients Drifters, by any chance?"

"Somehow I doubt a Drifter could afford my services."

Sniffer closed a drawer and opened another. "What about clients with interests in the Shallows?"

Enli shrugged. "Spices are a popular commodity. You can't expect me to know everyone in the trade."

"Ah," Kempis said, "but I'm talking about a very particular person." He thought back to Colm Spicer's account of how the assassin had vanished after killing the Drifter. "Someone who is also skilled at making problems . . . disappear."

"I'm sure if I had such a client I would know."

Kempis looked at Sniffer. "You see that?"

"Sure did."

Enli's eyes narrowed. "See what?"

"My point exactly," Kempis said. "The way I look at it, if there were someone new to the game out there—someone working your patch—you should be twisting my arm to find out more. And yet you don't even bat an eyelid."

The merchant's expression gave nothing away. "Let us imagine for the sake of argument that I do have a client with an interest in the Shallows. How do you think such an individual would react to your taking an interest in their interest?"

Kempis looked at Sniffer. "That sound like a threat to you?"

"Sure did."

The old man tugged at the hairs on his mole. "Of course, I would never presume to make threats to a Watchman, but again, for the sake of argument, if I were to do so, do you doubt I would be able to make good on them?"

The septia bared his teeth. "And do *you* doubt someone would come looking for payback if you did?"

"Just as there would be repercussions if I were to compromise the privacy of a client."

Kempis's nose was running, and he blew a thunderous blast into Enli's handkerchief. "I ain't interested in your damned client—I know who she is already," he lied. "I ain't even interested in you, hard though that must be on your ego. I want to know who's paying your bill."

"Ah, you want the next up in the food chain."

"If you like." The septia offered the merchant back his handkerchief.

Enli regarded it with a raised eyebrow. "But that's the problem, isn't it? The next *up* in the food chain is invariably a bigger fish."

"Then you'll just have to find another pond to swim in. Either way, your client's actions stop now, understood?"

"I have no way of contacting—"

"Understood?"

Enli pursed his lips.

Kempis had to admire the old man's composure. Usually with bluebloods, once you stripped away the bluster you found precious little underneath. The merchant was made of sterner stuff. He'd break eventually, though. They all did. "I'll leave you to think things over," Kempis said, rising from his seat.

Enli blinked. Obviously he'd been expecting to continue their conversation at the Watchstation, but Kempis reckoned the old man had said as much as he was going to say. Let him think he'd been given a reprieve. Let him think he had an opportunity to put his house in order before the septia came calling again. When he made his next move, Kempis would be waiting.

He gestured to Sniffer and made for the door.

Outside, he headed for the nearest alley that offered a view of the merchant's offices. Sniffer drew up beside him.

"What are you playing at, sir?" she said. "Ain't no way he's gonna sell out his employer. If we brought him in—"

"He'd clam up tight as Hilaire's asshole. Then what would we do? We can prove he's received dodgy payments, but we can't prove what they're for. This way, if we're lucky, he may do something stupid—like try to warn the assassin we're on to her." It wasn't as if Kempis had any other cards up his sleeve. Loop had drawn a blank in trying to find out what magic the killer was using, and Sniffer had failed to track down a single witness to the murders of the first two Drifters.

"And if you're wrong?" Sniffer nodded toward Enli's offices. "Lot of torches in that room, sir. Maybe he's in there now feeding the evidence to the steam-maker."

From his vantage point Kempis could make out the window to the old man's office. Perhaps it was his imagination, but the light inside *did* appear to brighten suddenly. "You think he's got a card in there with all his shady contacts written out on it? Addresses too, maybe?"

Sniffer pressed on. "You still carrying them stripes in your pocket? Maybe you should ask the merchant to add them—"

"You got something useful to say, let's hear it," Kempis cut in. "Until then, put a bung in it."

"Is it much farther?" Agenta asked, feeling six years old again.

The boatman, Enix, spat into the water. "Nearly there."

The kalischa eyed him speculatively. He'd said the same thing quarter of a bell ago, and she suspected he was taking a deliberately circuitous route through the flooded alleys to stop her retracing her steps later. Not that there was any chance of that: there were no landmarks in the Deeps that Agenta could fix on, and with the place shrouded in darkness, each building looked much the same as the next.

Barely a breath of wind ruffled the water. The noise and color of the Shallows had faded behind, and all was quiet but for the splash of Enix's oar, the creak of the boat, the buzzing of the needleflies and salt-stingers. Ahead the street was blocked by a collapsed building, so the boatman steered his craft into a side alley so narrow the gunwales scraped the walls. Just visible above the water was a net draped between two houses. Enix lifted his oar and used a blade on its end to saw through the lines holding the net in place. As it floated free, Agenta saw a severed arm in its links.

Stretching out her legs, she tried to make herself comfortable. If anyone was watching from the rooftops, let them see she wasn't overawed by her impending meeting with the *Gadfly*'s hijackers. To the contrary, she was looking forward to the encounter. It was said tollen deadened the mind such that users had to take risks in order to extract any color from life. That wasn't what drove Agenta, though— she had long since freed herself of the drug's effects. No, her rationale was simpler. When Shroud could crush you underfoot at any time, what use was there in trying to hide from him? Would her brother have been spared the fever if he'd cowered behind a wall somewhere?

Beside the kalischa, Trita Warner Sturge shifted on the bench. Moonlight reflected off his pate through his thinning black hair. Beside him sat the young water-mage Balen, dressed in the same black shirt and trousers as Warner. Doubtless Balen could have used sorcery to propel the boat more swiftly than Enix's pole, but Agenta had told him to keep his powder dry in the hope he'd be mistaken for just another bodyguard. The remaining members of her entourage, Iqral and Jayle, occupied the bow of the boat. Iqral, a Kalanese, was testing the point of a shortspear against a finger, while Jayle, a follower of the Lord of Hidden Faces, sat stroking the wooden mask that concealed her face.

Just three soldiers and a water-mage, then, to protect Agenta if tonight's meeting went to the Abyss. Her father had sent a dozen other soldiers dressed as civilians to trail her at a distance, but what chance would they have of tracking her through this watery rats' maze? And even if they *did* follow her to her destination, what difference would twelve more swords make when there could be an army of foes hidden on the rooftops? Even now Agenta saw two shadowy figures materialize on the roof of a building ahead, only to retreat at a whistle from Enix. No, she was on her own out here, but how was that different from any other time?

She checked the straps holding in place the throwing stars at her wrists, then looked at the boatman. Thin as the pole he was holding, he steered the boat deftly in spite of the hook where his left hand should have been. His bare forearms were crisscrossed with scars.

When the kalischa spoke, her voice sounded unnaturally loud in the stillness. "Those scars on your arms, what do they signify?"

"Saberfin hunter," he replied. "Blood draws the fish."

Warner said, "You will address her as my Lady."

Agenta shot him a look. If Enix was in the pay of the man—Sticks— that she was going to meet, the revelation that she was noble-born would not sit well with her cover as a trader in stolen duskstones.

Enix continued as if Warner had not spoken. "Of course, not all saberfin hunters use their own blood to attract their prey, if you takes my meaning."

The kalischa remembered the severed arm in the net. "And if the blood draws the sharks, too?"

"How do you think I got me this?" Enix said, grinning as he held up his hook. Then his gaze flickered to something farther along the alley. "Best keep your voice down now, *my Lady*. Folks round here can get a bit jumpy like, if you takes my meaning."

The street opened out, and Agenta saw a building rising from an expanse of rippling water, like a fortress at the center of a lake. *The perfect hideout.* No chance of anyone creeping up on its occupants unnoticed, and there was easy access to the open sea if a quick get- away was required. The windows on this side were boarded up, but light spilled into the night along its south-facing aspect. At first Agenta thought the houses surrounding it had been demolished, but when she looked over the gunwale, she saw the apex of a roof a finger's width beneath the surface. A man carrying a crossbow came strid- ing along that apex, appearing at first glance to be walking on water. Another whistle from Enix stopped him in his tracks, but his cross- bow remained trained on the boat as it glided past.

The sea was choppier here than it had been in the flooded alleys, and between two partly submerged houses to the south Agenta caught a glimpse of foaming waves. Enix poled the boat to the building at the center of the lake and brought it to a stop beside double wooden doors. He rapped on the doors, and they opened outward to emit wisps of smoke and a burst of laughter. Warner stepped up and into the building, followed by Jayle, Iqral, and Balen. As Agenta made to climb from the boat, the water-mage offered her a hand. His palm was moist, and the kalischa saw his unease written plain in the pallor of his face. She flashed him a smile, reminding herself her brother would not have been cowed by what awaited him inside.

"You'll wait for us here?" she said to Enix.

The boatman inclined his head.

As the doors closed, Agenta turned to examine the interior of the building. The inner walls had been knocked down to create a vast open space that was filled with a haze of smoke so thick the far side of the room could not be seen. Many of the marble floor tiles were cracked or missing. Through the gaps in the floorboards below, the kalischa could make out lapping water. To her left, in front of the flue of an immense chimney, was a bar. Tables were scattered about the room, and at them sat a ragged crowd of patrons. On each table was a lantern that gave off a pool of murky light.

From within the smoke at the far end of the room came the sound of breaking glass, then a shout and the thud of a body hitting the floor. The bar's patrons paid no more attention to the fracas than they had to the arrival of Agenta and her companions. And if they weren't interested, neither was the kalischa. Warner strode to the bar and spoke to a woman behind it. She responded to his question by pointing to a man sitting at a table in the corner—Sticks, Agenta presumed. Agenta crossed to join him, waving Warner away as he made to follow.

Sticks studied her as she approached. A few years older than the kalischa, he had short-cropped hair and a scar on his left cheek that ran from his mouth to his ear. On the table in front of him was a glass of what smelled like juripa spirits. He gestured to a chair, and Agenta sat down before looking over her shoulder to check on her companions. They had seated themselves at one of two tables nearby. The other table was occupied by a pair of grim-faced men who returned the kalischa's gaze.

Agenta looked back at the scarred man. "Sticks?"

"And you're Meliani Inessa," he said, using the false name Lydanto had given when he'd arranged the meeting.

She nodded.

Sticks glanced at the bar. "You not drinking?"

"I'm here for the duskstones."

No response.

"Can you deal?"

"Slow down. First we get to know each other a bit better." He sipped his drink. "I've been doing some asking round. Seems no one in the Jewelry Quarter ever heard of a Meliani Inessa."

"And Sticks is your real name, is it?"

"Whether it's the name your ma gave you or not, a face as pretty as yours ain't easily forgotten."

After tonight it certainly wouldn't be, but hopefully Agenta's business in Olaire would soon be concluded and she'd be on her way back to Gilgamar. "I'm not from these parts. I come from Bethin."

"You're a long way from home."

"My employer has extensive interests across the Sabian League."

Sticks's eyes narrowed. "Your employer?"

"Did you think that he would come himself?"

A heavy tread sounded to Agenta's right, and she looked across to see a man in a string vest emerge from the smoke covering the eastern part of the room. Over one shoulder he carried an unconscious woman. Reaching the doors, he threw them open and tossed his burden outside. Agenta heard a splash as the woman hit the water. Then the doors were closed once more. But not before the kalischa had noticed Enix's boat was gone. Most likely he'd parked the craft a short distance away to await Agenta's summons, yet still the kalischa found her heart beating a little faster.

When she turned back to Sticks, he was rolling his glass of spirits between his hands. "You don't look like someone from Bethin," he said. "Your skin ain't dark enough. And your accent—"

"Have you ever been to Bethin?" Agenta cut in. Truth was, she'd only been once herself. She could only hope that was one time more than her host.

"Aye, tipped my hat at the Sender's Temple on King Street." When Sticks grinned, his scar stretched his smile to his left ear. "Even sampled the wares of one of your flesh pits in the Temple District."

Agenta pretended irritation. "There is no Sender's Temple in Bethin. And the flesh pits are in the Speaker's District, not the Temple District." Whether any of that was true she had no idea. She suspected, though, that Sticks didn't either, and that he'd merely fed her some names to see if she'd agree with him and thus blow her cover. "Now, if you're finished, you never answered my question. Can you deal?"

Sticks leaned back against the wall. From the roof overhead came footfalls, but the scarred man ignored them. He tapped the side of his glass. "I can deal."

"Have you got one of the stones?" the kalischa said. Keep pushing, pushing, keep the conversation on her terms.

"First show me the color of your gold."

Agenta took from a pocket a folded sheet of parchment and passed it to him.

Sticks opened it. "What the hell is this?"

"A letter of credit."

"I can bloody see that." He tossed the parchment onto the table. "You expect me to hand over the stones in return for a Shroud-cursed scrap of paper?"

"No. But I expect you to accept it as proof that I am good for the sum of fifty thousand imperial sovereigns." When Sticks stayed silent she added, "Did you think I was going to bring the money here with me? With those duskstones weighing me down I'd have made it, what, a dozen steps from this table before suffering some unfortunate accident?"

The scarred man took another sip of spirits. Smoke from the lantern was stinging Agenta's eyes, but she dared not close them in case Sticks took it as a sign she was hiding something. Finally he grunted, then produced a duskstone from a pocket and put it on the table. The kalischa took out a white cloth and a loupe. Placing the jewel on the cloth, she examined it through the loupe. Even by the flickering light of the lantern, she could see both the cut and clarity were superb, with a single pinpoint inclusion in one of its pavilion facets.

"How many do you have?" she asked.

"Enough for your fifty thousand imperial sovereigns."

"How much per stone?"

"Fifty."

"Thirty."

Sticks's sour expression almost brought a smile to Agenta's face. "You'll get five times that in Bethin."

"And yet it's nearly double what you're selling them for in Olaire. You flooded the market, drove the price into the gutter. And if after three weeks you've still got enough stones for fifty thousand sovereigns, that tells me you're having trouble shifting them."

"For thirty I might as well take the damned things to Bethin myself."

"Then why don't you?"

No reply.

The door behind and to Agenta's left opened again, and this time when she looked across she saw four women stepping down into a boat outside. They had fish-spine swords strapped to their backs, and each wore a tattered ballroom gown and heavy black boots. A strange combination, the gowns and the boots, but then in the Deeps a night on the tiles doubtless meant getting your feet wet.

Still there was no sign of Enix.

When the kalischa looked back at Sticks, something in his expression had changed. It occurred to her suddenly she might have made a mistake. *And if after three weeks you've still got enough stones,* she'd said. Three weeks ago was when the *Gadfly* went missing, so Sticks would now know that *she* knew where the jewels came from. And yet that didn't mean the ship was hers, did it? It just meant she'd done her homework.

The silence dragged out. Stick's gaze bored into Agenta, but the kalischa wouldn't be the one to blink first. She drummed her fingers on the table.

The scarred man looked at her hand. Then he snatched up the duskstone and pushed himself to his feet. "Wait here."

Agenta felt a flutter in the pit of her stomach. "You said that you could deal!"

"You want to speak to my boss, you got to get through me first." With that, he strode over to talk to the two grim-faced men at the nearby table before making his way toward the far end of the room.

Agenta watched him vanish into the smoke. Things were not proceeding as they might. Sticks's hasty withdrawal told her that he had suspicions, but then the kalischa had suspicions of her own. There was something about the man that didn't fit. Few pirates, she suspected, would know what a letter of credit was, never mind be able to read one. And why had he put up so little resistance over the price? She'd expected him to feign outrage at her offer of thirty. To wheedle and to bluster and to threaten until a figure somewhere between their opening bids was agreed on. Instead, he'd scarcely seemed interested. But perhaps he was just leaving the real negotiations to his superior.

Agenta wished she could believe that.

Did she have any choice but to wait until he came back, though? If she walked out now there would be no second meeting, and then how would she find out who had hijacked the *Gadfly*? Moreover, running brought its own risks. Who was to say she wouldn't get a crossbow bolt in her back the instant she left the building? Or while she was returning to dry land through the flooded avenues?

Her thoughts were interrupted by footfalls. Warner strode toward her. "We're leaving!" he said.

Agenta frowned at his tone.

"Didn't you hear me? I said we're leaving."

She glanced at Sticks's friends at the next table to find them watching her in turn. "Calm down," she said to Warner. "You're drawing attention to us."

"So what if I am?" Warner replied. But he'd lowered his voice all the same. "This whole thing stinks! That Sticks is a Shroud-cursed soldier. I knew it the moment I set eyes on him. Hells, the man's boots are shinier than mine! As for his two sidekicks, it was all they could do to stop themselves saluting when he came over. And if I recognized Sticks, odds are he knows what I am too."

Agenta regarded the trita dubiously. Lots of bodyguards would have once been soldiers, so there was no reason to assume Agenta's cover was blown on that score alone. And even if Warner's suspicions about Sticks were correct, that didn't mean this was a setup. Agenta had suspected all along that one of the Storm Lords was behind the *Gadfly*'s disappearance, so it made sense that Sticks was a soldier and not a pirate.

Then again . . .

She scanned the common room. Of the patrons she'd seen when she arrived, half had now melted away, and none of the ones that remained were sitting close to Agenta's table. *As if they were expecting trouble.* Was she reading something into nothing? Perhaps, but she was minded to trust her instincts on this, and her instincts were telling her it was time to leave.

She looked at Warner. "Go back to the others—"

"The Abyss, I will!" he cut in, seizing her arm. "If anything happens to you, I'm the one who gets it in the neck!"

Agenta added a touch of steel to her voice. "Take your hand off me."

For a heartbeat Warner's fingers continued to dig into her arm. Then he released her.

"Go back to the others," she repeated. "Tell Balen to prepare a diversion in case we need it. The next time someone goes through those doors"—her eyes darted to the right—"I want you ready to move."

CHAPTER 6

KARMEL STARED at the Dragon Gate in the distance. With its crisscrossing bars it reminded her of a castle's portcullis, yet unlike a portcullis it was made up of two parts, the lower of which could be raised to allow ships to pass underneath. Atop the upper part were crenellated battlements, and at the center of those fortifications was a sea dragon's skull. Fires had been lit in its eyes and mouth. A gust of wind tugged at the flames, and it appeared to Karmel as if the head were breathing fire.

Through the bars of the gate she could see nothing of the dragons lurking in the waters of the Cappel Strait, but she could hear their trumpeting like the blare of a thousand century horns. As the noise briefly died away, a vast shadow reared out of the gloom beyond the portcullis. Karmel heard a clank as the dragon pushed its head against the gate and set it rattling. That clank was followed by a deep lingering *clunk* as the beast butted the portcullis in earnest, and the priestess imagined the structure toppling into the sea to leave nothing but darkness between her and the creature. Her mind went back to her training at the temple. What advice would her weapons-master, Foss, have given about fighting a dragon? she wondered.

Don't, most likely.

The sound of laughter brought her back to her senses. The torchlit cliff terraces below Dian and Natilly were crammed with revelers. Their celebrations would go on through the night, Veran had told Karmel, yet the real festivities started at dawn when prisoners from around the Sabian League would be thrown into the sea beyond the gate for the dragons to feast on. Tradition had it that any captive who made it back to shore received a pardon, but in Karmel's lifetime not a single soul had swum to safety. Indeed, the only person said to have survived the ordeal was a Corinian Storm Lord who, centuries ago, had been accused of plotting to seize power from the then emir. Accounts of the time reported that the Corinian had confounded the dragons by using water-magic to fill the sea with bubbles before escaping south to a kingdom across the oceans. There he had raised an armada of devilships and returned to bring fire and blood to the Storm Isles.

Perhaps that was why the only Storm Lord to be cast to the dragons since—an Untarian archmage from the turn of the century—had been sent on his way blinded and chained. With weights tied to his ankles. And drugged to the eyeballs on oscura.

The guild ship Karmel had seen this morning was anchored at the mouth of the Cappel Strait. Dian had no harbor, perched on a cliff as it was, and so anyone traveling to the city had to go west to Gilgamar before completing their voyage overland—except the privileged few, for whom access to Dian could be gained by way of a huge basket lowered from a guardroom in the bowels of the citadel. If Veran had come here hoping to see the thing in operation, though, he was going to be disappointed, for judging by the stillness of the guild ship its passengers had long since made the journey up to the city.

Karmel looked at the fortress. Was this basket how Veran planned to get inside? No, she decided, for whoever manned the contraption was unlikely to lower it at the request of strangers. And then even if it *was* lowered, who knew what welcome might await the Chameleons when they reached the guardroom above?

No witnesses, Caval had said.

The boat rocked as Veran came to stand behind Karmel. He'd spoken little since sunset, and the priestess had sensed his mood darkening as the color leached from the sky. Now when she glanced back she saw him gazing at the Dragon Gate with an expression so bleak he might have been staring at his own headstone. Perhaps the enormity of the task he'd taken on was finally coming home to him, or perhaps he'd seen his death written in the flames billowing from the mouth of the dragon's skull. If he wanted someone to hold his hand, though, he'd have to look elsewhere.

"Maybe now would be a good time to make peace with your god," she said.

When Veran met her gaze, the night was heavy in his eyes. "I was thinking the same of you."

"*I've* never been at war with him. Never. In any case, I intend to leave this place alive."

"You don't know what's waiting for us up there."

Something in his tone sent a prickle along the priestess's skin. "And you do?"

"Some."

"Well?"

Veran did not respond. Naturally.

Returning to the oar-bench, he shipped the oars before turning the boat west. Karmel studied his back for a moment, then shrugged. The man was clearly trying to unsettle her, but if he thought she would scare so easily he was even more of a fool than she'd taken him for. True, her heart was hammering, but that was from excitement. This mission was the chance she'd been waiting for to prove herself.

And yet there was no denying she would have liked to know a *little* more of what the next two days held in store.

Her gaze shifted back to the Dragon Gate, now partly obscured by the flank of the cliff. The guild ship lay between her and the port-cullis, and to see the vessel's mast rising to only a third of the gate's height gave Karmel a new perspective on the structure's size.

"How could anything so big have been built by human hands?" she wondered aloud.

Veran surprised her by answering. "Took them thirty years, it's said."

"The Storm Lords?"

"Storm Lords didn't take power until after the gate was built."

Karmel raised an eyebrow. "But the construction of the Dragon Gate marked the start of the Seventh Age, didn't it? I thought the Storm Lords were on the scene long before that."

Veran tutted his disgust. "Read your history, girl. At the end of the Sixth Age the Storm Lords were just so many water-mages employed to protect Sabian shipping from dragons and pirates."

The priestess succumbed to her curiosity. "And?"

"And as the cities of the League grew, those mages came to realize their value to trade. So they started banding together, elected leaders to bargain for higher fees. The League had no choice but to pay. Pirates they could take their chances with, but only a ship with a water-mage on board could hope to outrun a dragon. In the end the mages got greedy and began demanding a cut of the profits from the shipments they were transporting. League decided it would be cheaper to build the Dragon Gate than keep paying."

"Then why weren't the mages sent packing when the gate was finished?"

"Because they weren't idiots, that's why. Thirty years for the League to build the gate meant thirty years for the mages to plan their response. They formalized their ties, took the Storm Isles for their own, started calling themselves the Storm Lords. When the gate went up, piracy went up with it." Veran paused to check his bearings before hauling on the oars once more. "Oh, no one could prove the Storm Lords were the pirates, of course, because no one could hunt down their ships on those waves of water-magic. Back then there were dozens of the bastards too—Storm Lords, I mean. Slowed trade to a trickle until the League caved in and agreed to pay them tribute."

Karmel's mouth twitched. "So the League spent thirty years building the gate and ended up paying the mages anyway."

Veran grunted.

As the boat passed the last cliff terrace, the Dragon Gate disappeared from view. On that terrace a storm dance was being performed by torch-bearing dancers, and Karmel watched the flaming brands swirl through the night. "If there were dozens of Storm Lords in those days, why are there only six now? What happened to the others?"

"Fell fighting among themselves most likely, or died and weren't replaced. Fewer to share the Levy, that way." Veran adjusted his grip on the oars. "Of course, today's rabble won't let the numbers fall any further. Have to be enough Storm Lords to stop whoever's in power from trying to stay on once their time is up."

Karmel covered a smile. Evidently the emira hadn't been deterred from taking her chances, but then the woman was said to be the most powerful sorcerer ever to have sat Olaire's throne. Karmel wondered whether Caval had told Veran about Imerle's scheme to hang on to power. Probably not, for her brother couldn't trust him with such information in the same way he could Karmel.

From the city above, the ghostly melody of an ashpipe floated down—a Hundarian elegy Karmel remembered from her childhood. One of her few memories that didn't sting, in fact. As the boat glided westward the music of the pipe, together with the babble from the terraces, faded beneath the splash of oars and the lapping of waves against the cliff. Quarter of a bell later the boat drew level with the edge of Dian. The city was bounded by a fortified wall so high Karmel could not make out its battlements in the blackness. The torches of the soldiers patrolling the fortifications drifted through the darkness like firewights.

As Dian fell behind, Karmel noticed Veran had turned the boat toward the cliff. Tapping him on the shoulder, she gestured to her left. "West is that way, I believe."

Veran grunted. "There are caves at the base of the cliff."

Karmel could see them now she was looking for them—black arches in the rock face ahead and to her right. She could also make out a cluster of submerged rocks off the bow, their presence betrayed by the foaming waters around them. As the boat edged forward, Karmel used her scabbarded sword to push off from the rocks—the hardest she'd worked the blade, she realized, since she'd won it three months ago. Still the hull scraped against stone, and the priestess glanced nervously at the bottom of the boat, expecting the trickle of water seeping through the boards to become a torrent. "What happens when we reach these caves?"

"We'll secure the boat and swim round." Veran gestured with his head to the west. "There's a beach with a stairwell cut into the cliff. Once up top we'll find somewhere to sleep, then enter the city in the morning. Less chance of attracting attention if we go in at dawn."

Karmel peered in the direction he indicated. "How far is the beach?"

"Quarter of a league, maybe."

"I'm supposed to swim a quarter of a league with my pack on my back?"

"We take what we can carry, nothing else."

The priestess cast an eye over the boat before looking back at her companion. "You seem to have traveled light. You can help me with some of my things."

Another grunt was Veran's only response.

———

"Told you he'd do something stupid," Kempis said.

Half a bell had passed since he'd parted company with Enli Alapha, and the merchant was finally making his move. As the old man left his offices, the mole on his nose was visible in the light coming through the glass door. In his right hand he clutched what might have been a book or a batch of cards.

"How do you know he's doing *anything*?" Sniffer whispered. "He could be going home. Hells, he could be on his way to complain to Hilaire . . ."

Her words died away, for the merchant had turned to look toward the alley where the Watchmen were waiting. Had Enli heard them? No, the old man's gaze was already moving on to scan the main street. A scattering of lights showed in the windows of the offices and countinghouses, but the road itself was deserted. The only sounds were the hum of voices floating up from the lower city, along with the ululating cry of a prayerseeker in the Temple District.

"Five sovereigns says he leads us to our girl," Kempis said to Sniffer.

"Let's say ten."

She could make it a hundred for all he cared. It wasn't as if he had the money to pay if he lost.

Kempis could almost hear Enli's bones creak as he shuffled in the direction of the Round. The septia frowned. The coiffured secretary hadn't yet left the offices. What if the old man was a decoy? What if he'd told his secretary to deliver a message to the assassin? Perhaps Kempis should leave Sniffer behind to watch—

The Untarian touched his arm. Enli had walked barely a dozen paces along the street when a figure—a woman judging by her height— detached itself from the shadows ahead. Her features were hidden by a hood. The merchant had seen her too, and his footsteps slowed. The two figures came together—a chance collision, it seemed to Kempis, though what were the odds of that when they were the only people in the street?

Then Enli was on the ground. The woman crouched beside him.

Comprehension dawned on Kempis. He drew his sword. Not something he ever did lightly, since there was always the risk he'd have to use it.

At the scrape of steel, the hooded stranger raised her head. Within her cowl her blue eyes shone with some inner light. *The assassin from the Shallows.* How had Colm Spicer described her eyes? *So bright they glowed in the dark.* She must have seen Kempis arrive at Enli's office earlier and was taking no chances on the old man's silence. And yet, now that she had killed her agent, how was she going to collect her fee? Hope kindled in Kempis. What was the point in continuing the job if she wasn't going to get paid at the end of it? Could her killing spree be over?

As if I'm that damned lucky.

Kempis left his hiding place, and Bright Eyes straightened. She was holding whatever Enli had been carrying.

"Stay where you are!" Kempis called.

The assassin cocked her head.

Then she turned and bolted along the road. Just like they always did.

Kempis set off in pursuit, Sniffer at his heels.

Bright Eyes tore round a corner into Junction Street, her sandals skidding on the flagstones. Ahead was the Thaxian embassy, and Kempis saw four soldiers in yellow cloaks standing outside. He shouted at them to stop the assassin, but the soldiers just watched as first Bright Eyes, then Kempis and Sniffer, ran past. The guards' laughter followed the septia into the night.

A right turn took his quarry into Templer Avenue. She flowed like a shadow through the gloom, her footsteps sounding on the metal plaque on the pavement outside the Petty Court. Kempis was already struggling to keep up, his heart pounding, his scabbard bouncing against his thigh and threatening to tangle in his legs. Gods, the woman was quick. She ducked beneath the fish-spine sword in the outstretched hand of a statue of the Sender. At any other time Kempis would have lost sight of her already, but at this hour the streets were empty of people—

A man stepped into his path from the door to the Commodities Exchange.

Kempis had time only to register a whiff of expensive scent before he hammered into the stranger. The blueblood, his eyes as large as plates, gave an "oof!" then lurched back into the doorway. Kempis was half spun round by the contact, and he found himself momentarily running sideways, his legs overtaking the rest of his body. He threw out his arms to regain his balance, but the ground seemed to buck and heave. He stumbled.

Then he realized the ground *was* moving. A wave rippled through the street, pitching Bright Eyes from her feet and depositing her on her ass. It might have been funny if it hadn't been Kempis's turn next to go down. As the tremor reached him, he fell and scuffed his palms on the flagstones. To either side the buildings wobbled, their windows rattling. A rumble shook the air, then crashes sounded as roof tiles came raining down. Sniffer crouched beside Kempis, her webbed hands over her head. From all around came the tinkle of breaking glass, the cries of people inside buildings.

Earthquake. Or rather, *another* earthquake. Last week a quake had opened up cracks in the walls of the Watchstation's armory, but the tremors now were far stronger than they had been then. They went on for a dozen heartbeats, though at the rate Kempis's heart was beating, perhaps that wasn't saying much. A crack opened in the road. Bright Eyes was in its path. *In you go,* Kempis thought, but the woman pushed herself upright and rolled aside just as the road yawned wide.

The fissure reached toward the septia.

The tremors subsided.

Kempis groaned. The road had stopped moving, yet a part of him still felt like he might fall off it at any moment. He swung his gaze to Bright Eyes to see her levering herself to her feet using the railings in front of a building. What, up already?

She staggered off.

Kempis rose on legs as shaky as a newborn foal's. Shouting at Sniffer to follow, he set off after his quarry.

In the wake of the quake, an eerie hush had descended on the city. The slap of Bright Eyes's sandals echoed off the buildings to either side. It was clear the woman was a stranger to Olaire from the way she would veer into side streets as if she hadn't known they were there. Her route took her downhill in the direction of the Untarian Quarter. With each corner turned, the distance between her and Kempis grew. It would not be long now before she shook him off entirely, but why was she running at all? When she'd been spotted by Colm Spicer two nights ago she'd just vanished, so why not repeat the trick here? Did she need time to work whatever sorcery she used?

Kempis's lungs were burning as if the blayfire from Enli's office had moved down from his nose to his chest. He wished he had more backup. What was the point of being a septia, after all, if you couldn't get someone else to do your running for you? Behind, he heard

Sniffer's steady breathing. She didn't seem to be busting a gut to get ahead of him, but then when had she ever *not* taken things easy in the Watch?

The assassin passed between two of the trees that lined Orchard Lane before swerving into Park Alley . . .

Kempis smiled. *Dead end.*

He drew up outside the passage. Bright Eyes stood at the far end, a deeper smudge of black within the pooled shadows. To her left was a windowless wall three stories high, while to her right was a wall only four armspans tall but still too high to scale. Beyond, a gate set into another wall led to the Golding Cloister. But that gate would be locked at this hour, and sure enough Kempis heard it rattle as the woman tugged on it.

He hesitated. He didn't want to take on Bright Eyes alone. The alley was only two paces across, meaning there wasn't room for both himself and Sniffer to attack. There was no need for him to play the hero here, though—he only had to keep the assassin from escaping while he waited for a Watch patrol to pass by. And if he stayed *outside* the alley there would be space for both himself and Sniffer to bring their weapons to bear. No matter how formidable Bright Eyes was, there was no way she could take on the two of them together, right?

Kempis licked his lips. The woman had turned and was studying him with those infernal blue eyes. She hadn't drawn a weapon. *Must know the game is up.* He was about to tell her as much when she raised her right foot and placed it against the left-hand wall. Kempis snorted. Did she think she could climb three stories without so much as a handhold . . .

His thoughts trailed away.

For the assassin had pushed up and off with her right foot, twisting in midair across the alley to plant her left foot an armspan or two higher on the opposite wall. She repeated the maneuver once, twice, gaining height each time, until she was level with the top of the single-story wall. She landed nimbly on its roof and flitted away into the darkness.

Kempis's mouth dropped open.

"Sender's mercy," Sniffer said.

The septia moved to the wall and put his hands together to form a cradle. "Here," he said to the Untarian, "I'll give you a leg up."

Sniffer stared at him.

"You can follow her across the roofs and shout to me where she's heading."

"Right. Or I can lose my footing, take a fall, and come down on that thick skull of yours."

"You got a better idea?"

"Yes, as it happens—"

"It's you or me, Untarian," Kempis cut in, gesturing to his interlocked hands. "And last time I looked, the septia's stripes were in my pocket, not yours. Now shut up and climb."

The sea about Senar was black as the Abyss. Braziers lined the walls of the throne room, and the barriers of water beside them rippled in the heat from the coals. The ceiling was smeared with streaks of light. A memory stirred in the Guardian of a night two years ago in Erin Elal's capital, Arkarbour. Senar had been waiting in the shadow of the Black Tower—the stronghold of Erin Elal's mages—and the building's sorcerous defenses had shimmered the sky like a heat haze, making it seem as if the stars were weeping. The tower itself was quiescent, but Senar knew that that stillness was a sham, for the mages could not have failed to notice the Guardians massing outside.

Li Benir had been with Senar as they waited for the signal to attack. His master's good cheer was forced, and in his eyes Senar saw his own doubts reflected. That night had been the last time he'd stood at Li Benir's side, for while his master had initially survived the assault on the Black Tower, the sorceries unleashed against him had condemned him to days of suffering before he finally succumbed to his wounds. Other memories of the attack came flooding back to Senar: Kylin Jey engulfed in black fire, shrieking as he threw himself from a window; a nameless Guardian apprentice cut in half by a demon summoned to the mages' defense; Jessca's face pale with shock as Senar wrenched a knife from her shoulder . . .

Grimacing, Senar shook himself free of the images.

The throne room was cold and dank in spite of the heat from the braziers, and the Guardian could feel the weight of the sea about him. Imerle was seated on the same throne as yesterday, the executioner behind her. To her right sat the chief minister, and to her left one of the Storm Lords—a thin-faced man with ginger hair. There were more new faces present, too. By the wall across from Senar stood a tall black man in the robes of a Chameleon priest—Caval Flood, the chief minister had named him. He was speaking to two other Storm Lords: Thane Tanner—a bear of a man who looked more like a warrior than a sorcerer with his crooked nose and scarred chin; and Mokinda Char—an Untarian male with long black hair who returned the Guardian's gaze with bright curiosity.

Senar had no wish to join the discussions. Instead he let the murmur of voices wash over him. In those voices was a noticeable edge of restlessness, for Gensu had still not arrived. Earlier the emira had dispatched a water-mage in her service, Orsan, to find the Storm Lord, but Orsan had not come back.

The conversation in the room broke off momentarily, and Senar looked round to see Mazana Creed striding toward him from the direction of the underwater passage. Round her neck hung her air-magic pendant, and she wore a black dress no less revealing than her red dress had been yesterday. A lady should always leave something to the imagination, Jessca had once told Senar. But the alternative did have its advantages. The light from the braziers struck copper notes in Mazana's hair and cast a ruddy glow on one side of her face. As she joined Senar, he detected no trace of awkwardness from their encounter yesterday.

The Guardian bowed. "You are alone tonight, my Lady?" he said.

"I am. The belligerent Greave wanted to come, but I said no. He demands a rematch, by the way. Something about your use of the Will giving you an unfair advantage."

"And no mention, I take it, of the armor that spared him from my first strike."

"His memory can be a little selective, it's true."

A male servant approached carrying a tray of drinks. Mazana waved him away.

"I owe you an apology," Senar said. "For last night. I had no right—"

"Nonsense," the Storm Lady cut in. "As it happens I learned much from our conversation. It seems I have allowed myself to become too close to my brother, and in doing so lost sight of the threat he represents. I have you to thank for restoring my objectivity."

Senar winced. She was mocking him, but perhaps he had earned as much. Abruptly he sensed he was being watched, and he looked round to see the emira staring at him. Her expression was unreadable.

Mazana said, "I could not help but notice the insignia on the pommel of your sword. Four crossed blades . . . that is the emblem of the Guardians, isn't it?"

"The sword belonged to my former master, Li Benir."

"Former?"

"He is dead," Senar said flatly, not wanting to talk about it.

Mazana was unperturbed by his tone. "And the ring?" she said, nodding at Senar's right hand. "It bears the same insignia, does it not?"

The Guardian had forgotten about the ring. It felt heavy on his finger, and he covered it with his halfhand. He'd had it made for Jessca shortly after the attack on the Black Tower. But just two months later he'd had to reclaim it from her corpse when she was brought back to Arkarbour . . .

He shook his head. No, he would not think on that. Too often of late his thoughts had slipped toward the maudlin. To allow that to continue would be to focus on one bad memory to the exclusion of the good ones.

The Storm Lady's voice softened. "Strange," she said, "for a man to have a ring so small he wears it on his little finger. Unless of course it was once a woman's ring."

"Mazana!" a new voice said, and Senar looked across to see the Storm Lord who'd been talking to the emira approaching. The man drew up in a fog of moonblossom scent. In one manicured hand he held a roll of parchment. "A delight, as ever," he said to the Storm Lady, taking her hand and kissing it.

Mazana was slow to look away from Senar. "Lord Cauroy," she said eventually. "You have met Senar Sol? A Guardian from Erin Elal."

Cauroy's gaze remained on Mazana, exploring her. "And what are you here to defend?" he asked Senar. "Not Mazana's honor, I trust. I assure you my intentions toward her are as honorable as she wishes them to be."

"I can breathe easy then, my Lord," Senar said. Perhaps he should have felt grateful to Cauroy for arriving to spare him some uncomfortable questions, yet oddly he found himself resenting the man's intrusion.

"Would you like a closer look at my pendant?" Mazana asked the Storm Lord, lifting it from where it hung between her breasts. "You appear to be staring at it a great deal."

Cauroy cleared his throat. "Ah, yes, remarkable craftsmanship." He pretended to admire the jewel.

Mazana gestured to the scroll he was holding. "Is that your summons? May I?"

"Of course."

She unrolled the parchment and read its contents. "The wording is the same as mine. Now I think of it, the handwriting bears a striking resemblance to your own, my Lord, wouldn't you say?"

Cauroy's cheeks reddened. "Certainly not!"

The look Mazana shot Senar had a flash of mischief in it, together with something else he could not place. "No, see here," she said, "the slant of the characters, the ridiculous ostentatiousness of the loops."

"If the summonses had been mine, I would hardly have composed them in my own hand."

Senar said, "You got someone else to write them?"

"Yes! I mean, no!" Cauroy's mouth opened and closed. "What do I stand to gain by calling the Storm Lords together? Answer me that! And if I had, why would I keep up the charade now with everyone but Gensu here?"

"By the same logic," Mazana said, "all of those present would be absolved from suspicion."

"Precisely! Gensu sent the summons—it is as I have always said!" He leaned closer, his voice dropping. "Although my chamberlain tells me that the man who delivered the parchment to my house was an Untarian." His gaze flickered to Mokinda.

Mazana raised an eyebrow. "Why not just sign his name on the summonses and be done with it?"

Cauroy seemed not to have heard. "Then there is our friend Thane. Apparently he received a consignment of dyes and iron ingots three weeks before the summonses arrived." When Mazana and Senar remained silent, he went on, "Don't you see? They are just what he would need to make a copy of the emira's seal!"

Senar nodded. "You may be on to something there. What other possible use could Thane have had for such a cargo?"

Mazana said, "Although since we're dealing with dyes, would not the vessel carrying the shipment have sailed from Peron Ra? We cannot discount the Peronians, surely."

"I knew it!" Cauroy crowed. "The Peronians have always coveted . . ."

His voice trailed off as a male servant appeared at the end of the underwater passage and made his way toward the thrones. When he spoke to the emira, it was in a voice too low for Senar to hear. The message was evidently a lengthy one. Through it all Imerle listened without emotion. Beside her, Pernay frowned. Cauroy drummed a foot, while Thane stood clasping and unclasping his hands. Only Mazana seemed unmoved by the growing tension, for when her gaze met Senar's she rolled her eyes at the theatricality of it all.

Finally the servant finished speaking. At the emira's nod, he retreated to the passage.

Just then a rumble sounded, deepening in pitch as if something were stirring in the deep. Tremors shook the chamber, each more intense than the last. The mosaic floor rippled. Instinctively Senar looked up at the horizontal span of water above him, but the throne room had no ordinary ceiling that it could be brought down by a few shakes. A brazier to his left toppled into the sea, and its glowing coals were smothered by the darkness. Opposite, a second brazier fell. The shadows about the chamber closed in. A crack opened in the mosaic floor, tracing a jagged line along the Sender's forehead and giving the god a look of disquiet that must have mirrored Senar's own.

As quickly as the quake had come, it subsided.

The Guardian stood motionless, expecting an aftershock.

None came.

The tremors had lasted for perhaps ten heartbeats, but the silence that followed went on much longer. The Storm Lords exchanged looks. Cauroy had seized Mazana's arm during the quake, but his touch now lingered, and she threw him off. Pernay sat white-faced in his chair, his hands quivering so violently it seemed the room must still be in the grip of the tremors. In response to a word from the emira he gathered himself and rose.

A brazier beside the executioner chose that moment to topple, spilling coals under the thrones. Pernay flinched, then spun with flashing eyes toward the giant as if he thought the brazier had been overturned deliberately. Senar wished he'd had the idea himself.

The executioner remained staring at nothing.

Clearing his throat, the chief minister turned back to the chamber. "My Lords and Lady," he said. "The harbormaster reports a ship flying Gensu's flag has been sighted in the Causeway. He will be with us shortly."

Agenta heard the scrape of wood on stone as a handful of the bar's patrons pushed their chairs back from their tables and lurched upright. The sea had begun to ooze up through the gaps between the floorboards.

Balen.

At the next table the water-mage wore a look of such concentration it would surely catch the eye of anyone glancing his way. Agenta tutted. She'd ordered Warner to tell him only to prepare a diversion, not to initiate it, meaning either the mage had got twitchy or the trita had ignored her instructions. She looked at Sticks's companions. The two men were watching her, and she rose and strode to their table in an effort to keep their gazes from Balen.

"What's going on?" she said.

Blank looks.

"Where's Sticks? I'm not waiting here—"

"Sit down," the man on the left interrupted, nodding at Agenta's table.

Or what? the kalischa wanted to say. Instead she turned and walked toward her companions. Warner, Iqral, and Jayle stood up. Behind Agenta, the sound of creaking floorboards told her Sticks's men had also risen. When she looked round, she saw them making for the doors through which Agenta had entered. Evidently Sticks had commanded them to stop her leaving, and why would he do that unless he had seen through the kalischa's disguise?

"Let's go," Warner said as she reached him.

Agenta paid him no mind.

A splash of footsteps signaled the approach of three of the bar's Untarian patrons—two women and one man. They were heading for the doors now watched by Sticks's companions. As they drew near, the guards' hands strayed to the hilts of their swords. Agenta thought Sticks's men would turn the Untarians back, but after a pause they stood aside. One of the Untarian women looked at them askance as she threw the doors open. There was no boat waiting outside, so she raised two fingers to her lips and whistled.

"Let's go," Warner said again.

"And do what, swim for it?" Agenta said. "We wait for the Untarians' boat."

A breath of wind blew through the doors, carrying on it the smell of rotting fireweed. Agenta looked outside, searching the night for an ambushing party. She could see nothing except a line of distant buildings and the reflection of the moon in the water—a reflection that disappeared as one of Sticks's men moved across her line of sight. The guard was eyeballing Warner, and the trita looked him up and down before smiling faintly as if to say he'd taken the man's measure and found him wanting.

Agenta lowered her hands to her sides. Keeping her motions slow and steady, she flexed her wrists just so. Her throwing stars slipped from their sheaths into her palms. When the trouble started, the guards would expect the threat to come from Warner and his soldiers rather than from the apparently unarmed kalischa. With luck she might be able to take one of them down before they realized their mistake.

A hundred heartbeats passed and still the Untarians' boat had not arrived. Agenta looked over her shoulder, expecting to see Sticks emerge from the smoke that covered the bar. Was he reporting to someone at the other end of the room? Or had he left the building through a door hidden from Agenta's view? Maybe he'd suspected all along she would try to flee and was now waiting outside to attack her, but then why order his two companions to bar her exit? A thought came to her. Perhaps she should take one of Sticks's men captive to interrogate later.

She was about to suggest as much to Warner when she heard a splash of water outside.

The Untarians' boat.

Then she noticed one of Sticks's guards nudging his companion and pointing at something behind her.

Agenta turned to see Sticks thirty paces away, approaching through the smoke with four men at his back. There was a hardness to the scarred man's gaze, an unmistakable purpose in his stride.

A stride that increased in length when he saw the kalischa's party on its feet.

Agenta hesitated. For all her misgivings, was it possible she'd misread his intentions? Could he have returned to resume the negotiations? But if so, where was his boss? Not among his companions, that much was clear, for Sticks's friends were all walking behind the man, not alongside where a superior would be.

"Balen!" the kalischa called.

The air about her convulsed. With a hissing noise the water on the floor vaporized to form clouds of steam that rose up to engulf Sticks and his entourage.

From behind Agenta came the whisper of swords being drawn from their scabbards. She remembered the two guards at her back. In one smooth motion she spun and hurled the throwing star in her right hand. It took one of the men in the neck, and he went down clutching his throat. Jayle sprang to engage the other guard. Agenta saw nothing of their clash, though, because Warner was already pushing her toward the open doors and the boat waiting beyond.

Ahead, Iqral barged between the Untarians, a shortspear in each hand, before leaping down into the craft. Agenta arrived in time to see him tugging a spear from the chest of a man—the boat's owner, she presumed—who toppled backward into the sea. The Kalanese extended a hand to her, but before she could take it Warner shoved her in the back. Cursing, she pitched forward into Iqral's arms, and they staggered into the starboard gunwale, teetered, almost followed the boatman over the side. Agenta untangled herself just as the trita stepped down behind her. She lurched to the bow to make room, stepping over the oar-bench.

From within the smoky common room came a burst of light as if someone had overturned a lantern. The clang of swords sounded. Agenta saw Jayle aim a cut to her opponent's chest before a wall of mist rolled over them. If Balen had been in the boat, Agenta would have ordered him to take off, Jayle be damned, but the water-mage was only now appearing from the steam.

To the kalischa's right, a crossbowman advanced along the apex of a submerged roof. He pointed his weapon at the boat. Transferring her second throwing star from her left hand to her right, Agenta pulled back her arm—

Just as Balen jumped into the boat. It rocked precariously. The kalischa stumbled a pace to her left, then grabbed for the gunwale, missed, and fell to her knees.

A crossbow string twanged, and she felt a disturbance in the air as a bolt whipped past her face. She smiled. Life or death decided by a hairbreadth. That's just the way it was.

The crossbowman began reloading his weapon. Agenta clambered upright. Her throwing star was cold against her palm. She tried to set her feet for a throw, but the boat twitched beneath her again, and she swayed as the crossbowman pulled back on his weapon's crank. At that moment a wave rippled over the rooftop. The man was set staggering too. The absurdity of their plight struck Agenta, and she felt laughter rising inside her. She drew back her arm once more.

One of Iqral's shortspears buried itself in the crossbowman's chest. He gave a squawk and fell into the sea.

More men were approaching across the submerged roofs. Of Agenta's companions only Jayle remained unaccounted for, but the masked woman suddenly materialized in the bar's doorway and half jumped, half collapsed into the boat. Iqral caught her, and the two went down in a heap.

Agenta's gaze found Balen's. The mage was staring at her like he needed telling what to do next. "Get us out of here!" the kalischa said.

Wide-eyed, he nodded.

The boat rose a handspan into the air on a wave of water-magic. The bow swung north to take them back the way they had come.

"Not that way!" Agenta said. She gestured south. "The sea!" Better to be out on the open waves than run the gauntlet of the Deeps' flooded alleys.

Another nod from Balen, and the boat changed course before skimming away across the waves at a speed that set the kalischa's hair billowing.

A man appeared in the doorway to the bar. Agenta thought it was Sticks come to wave them good-bye. But then a ball of flames sparked to life in his hands, making flickers of light dance across the waves. The fireball swelled to an armspan in diameter.

The man thrust out his arms and sent it streaking toward the craft.

"Fire-mage!" Iqral shouted, as if Agenta might have missed the signs.

"Left!" she ordered Balen, pulling on his sleeve.

The boat veered in that direction, and the kalischa stumbled into the gunwale again. Heat seared her face as the fireball roared past, leaving a trail of steam behind. It struck a house to her right, demolishing a section of wall before detonating inside to send flames spouting from the windows. A man flung himself shrieking into the waves. Tough luck, your house getting hit by fire when it was surrounded by the sea, but at least the man wouldn't lack for water to put the blaze out.

Just then a crossbow bolt thudded into the boards between Agenta's feet. To her right two crossbowmen stood on the roof of a building. As the first man reloaded, his companion placed a quarrel in the slot of his weapon and fired. Agenta never saw where the missile struck because Warner was already bundling into her, bearing her down into the bottom of the boat. She stretched out her hands to break her fall, but still her temple struck the boards, making her vision swim. The grain of the wood was pressed against her cheek. She smelled tar and pine pitch.

Swearing, she tried to lift her head. Warner held her down. She shouted at him to release her, but her words were lost beneath the sound of the keel scraping against stone. The bow began to rise. In veering left to evade the fireball, Balen must have taken the boat across the submerged roofs, and the craft now rode up the pitch of one before lifting into the air.

A moment of weightlessness, then the boat hit the water, rebounded, and came down again.

Warner came down with it, slamming Agenta's head into the boards once more, and crushing the air from her lungs. She tried to take a breath, only to get a mouthful of the trita's sleeve. For all she knew she might have been about to get smothered, but all she could think of was how this fumbling and grunting reminded her of the last time she'd had a man on top of her, and she found herself fighting down laughter again. A loud crack sounded as the bow ricocheted off the wall of a building. The impact made her bite her tongue. Over the ringing in her ears she heard muffled shouts that fell quickly behind, followed by a deep-throated rumble. At first she thought the house struck by the fireball had collapsed.

Then the rumble grew louder. The boat shuddered as if a clap of thunder had broken beneath its bows.

Earthquake, Agenta realized. And yet she was in no danger, she knew, for judging by the rhythmic pounding of waves against the hull, the boat must now have reached the open seas. No buildings out here to fall on her, or for crossbowmen to perch on. Which meant no reason for Warner to still be lying on her. Twisting round, she pushed at his chest, only for one of his arms to come down across her throat.

"Get off me!" she screamed.

The trita raised his body, and she wriggled free.

Sitting up in the bow, Agenta shot him a look. Warner's attention, though, was elsewhere. She followed his gaze north to see the Deeps receding off the stern. A ribbon of foam marked the path the boat had taken. The house struck by the fireball burned fiercely, staining the night sky orange. The earth tremors had subsided, but the damage to the building had evidently already been done, for with a groan its east-facing wall fell into ruin. Then the rest of the structure crumbled into the sea.

A short distance to the west, a huddle of figures stood watching the Gilgamarians' retreat from a rooftop. No one was making any effort to pursue them, so Agenta looked at Balen and said, "I think we've come far enough, don't you?"

Huddled amidships, Balen gave her a sheepish smile.

The boat settled onto the rocking sea as the wave of water-magic beneath it dispersed.

There was blood in Agenta's eyes, and she leaned over the gunwale and cupped water into her hands before washing her face. To her right Warner tore his left sleeve from his shirt. Only now did the kalischa notice a gash to his arm where a crossbow bolt must have grazed it. Served him right for getting in the way of a missile meant for her. Behind him, meanwhile—

Agenta started. Slumped against the oar-bench was Jayle, her shirt torn and bloody round a quarrel protruding from her chest. Beside her sat Iqral, holding her hand and speaking softly in her ear. Her head lolled against his shoulder. He reached down to pull out the quarrel, but the pressure drew a sob from the masked woman and he withdrew his hand.

Agenta looked away, uninterested. The guard meant nothing to her. She'd always made a point of keeping her distance from her father's troops, not because she considered their company unworthy, but because soldiers had a habit of dying. And the kalischa knew better than to fill her life with people who were more likely even than most to be snatched away at any moment.

Each of Jayle's breaths came shallower than the last until a death rattle sounded in her throat. From the corner of Agenta's eye, she saw Iqral release the woman's hand and reach out to lift her mask. He studied her face before shaking his head and turning away.

"Now I know why she wore the damned mask," he said.

Kempis drew in a rasping breath.

Bright Eyes had not stayed long on the rooftops before descending again to street level. Sniffer had directed Kempis to where the woman had come down, but with no time to wait for the Untarian to rejoin him he'd been forced to continue the pursuit alone. He'd briefly gained company in the form of two other Watchmen who'd crossed his path, but both they and Bright Eyes had swiftly outdistanced him and disappeared from sight. For a time Kempis was able to follow them by the sound of their footfalls or the occasional shout. When the noises faded, though, the septia drew up gasping, doubled over a pain in his gut so sharp it felt like he'd been punched.

He looked round to get his bearings. A dozen paces away was the junction of the Catway and Fletcher Street. The Watchstation was a mere stone's throw to the east, and the Forge Barracks a similar distance to the west. Why had the assassin come this way? It was possible she was running blind, going downhill simply because it was easier on the legs, but Kempis doubted it. Indeed the longer the chase had gone on, the more he'd become convinced he knew where his quarry was heading: the alley in the Shallows where the septia had interviewed Colm Spicer two days ago. But why?

Kempis pushed the thought aside. All that mattered now was getting to the passage ahead of Bright Eyes. If he was right about the woman's destination she was following a tortuous route, but then a stranger to Olaire wouldn't know the quickest path. With the aid of a few shortcuts Kempis might cut her off. And if his hunch proved to be wrong . . .

He shrugged. What did he have to lose?

He stumbled south.

His nose was running faster than his legs, but he found an extra burst of speed as he skirted the Untarian ghettos—a Watchman never *walked* through this part of the city. In Abbot Street he was forced to clamber over the rubble of a collapsed building. The destruction wrought by the quake here was worse than it had been in the Commercial District, but the houses in this area were so ramshackle you could bring them down with a shove. Kempis had done it enough times to know.

The strengthening stench of excrement told him the Shallows were getting close. His stomach lurched as he caught the sound of lapping waves. Then above that came a crackling *whoosh* of flames as the skyline ahead and to his right flashed crimson. Elemental magic. A fire-mage, and a powerful one to have unleashed such a blast after the sun had set. The explosion had come from the Deeps. Was it a coincidence a fire-mage should be abroad at the same time as Bright Eyes?

Kempis hoped so.

He swerved into Seaford Lane. In front he saw the right turn that would bring him to his destination.

Approaching at a dead run from the opposite direction was a shadowy figure chased by two Watchmen. *Bright Eyes*. The dash across the city hadn't slowed her at all. She reached the alley before Kempis and vanished along it.

The septia swore and followed her in.

The brothel was ahead and to his left, the sea a shimmer beyond. Bright Eyes had covered half the distance to it already, but her way was blocked. In front of her were three figures, all turned the other way: a Drifter and the two Watchmen who had been assigned to hold his hand tonight.

She was trapped.

Kempis yelled a warning to his colleagues, and the men spun round.

The first to react was a bearded spearman named Joren. Sizing up the danger, he set his feet and lowered his spear as if he expected Bright Eyes to run obligingly onto its point. The second Watchman, Clapp, grabbed the hilt of his sword, only for his helmet to slip over his eyes. Between them, the Drifter dropped to his knees, gibbering.

The assassin ran at Joren. She feinted to go one way, then flowed round his spear tip on the other side. Silver flashed in her hand, and the Watchman gave a gurgling cough, clutching at his throat as blood bubbled between his fingers. He fell to the ground, his spear jarring free of his grasp. Clapp was still trying to draw his sword as Bright Eyes sprinted past. She didn't slow when she reached the sea. Her feet kicked up spray as she ran a handful of paces before leaping into deeper water. Bottles clinked around her.

Reaching Joren's side, Kempis sheathed his sword and scooped up the dying man's spear. But as the septia pulled back his right arm to let fly, the Drifter bolted in front of him, and he was forced to check his throw.

"Out of the way!"

Bright Eyes was in water up to her waist. She turned to look back at Kempis just as he hurled his spear. The weapon flew true, straight for the woman's chest. A surprise, that, but a welcome one.

There was a flash of teeth from within the assassin's cowl. Then for a stomach-churning heartbeat the flooded alleys and dilapidated buildings of the Shallows were overlain by an image of heaving waves that stretched into the darkness.

The assassin vanished, and with her the shadowy vista of the sea.

Kempis's spear passed through the air where she had stood moments earlier, skipped off the water, then splashed down and sank beneath the waves.

"About bloody time," Thane said in response to the news that Gensu was on his way. "Finally we can bring this farce to an end."

The faintest of tremors passed through the floor beneath Senar's feet. It was followed by a distant growl like retreating thunder. None of the Storm Lords seemed to notice it, though. A change had come over the throne room. The mood of strained solidarity that had prevailed while Gensu was missing had fled, and the looks now being cast about the chamber were laced with suspicion and rancor. The Storm Lords were readying themselves for the battle of wills to come.

Predictably it was Mazana who fired the first salvo. To Thane she said, "While we're waiting for our wily colleague Gensu to arrive, perhaps you would care to explain what the two of you discussed when you visited him on Airey five days ago."

Thane stared at her.

"You forget, my island is next to his. I make it my business to know what ships pass through my waters."

Thane shrugged. "We were discussing piracy."

"How very candid of you."

"Not ours!" he snapped. "Two weeks ago Gensu spoke with the Master of Courts, and what he discovered troubled him enough for him to call for me. I think we all knew about the rise in piracy over recent months, but the scale of the problem is much greater than I thought. The number of claims against the Storm Council for lost ships has increased tenfold since midsummer."

"I fail to see—" Pernay began.

"I'm not finished! While most of these claims are mired in legal technicalities, some have been settled with unseemly haste. One in particular caught Gensu's eye—a payment of two hundred thousand imperial sovereigns for a galley, the *Swift,* carrying Androsian silks that went down in a storm off Rastamira." Thane's voice was rising. "The *Swift* flew the Mercerien flag, yet she does not feature on Mercerie's shipping register, nor has the Shroud-cursed merchant who owned her ever signed the Charter of Warrants! None of this, I'm told, will come as news to our chief minister."

The emira was looking at Senar. Doubtless she didn't want him watching the Storm Lords bicker. He thought she would dismiss him, but instead she said to Thane, "We are not clear what you're suggesting."

"I'm suggesting information about these claims has been withheld from us. That money is being siphoned from the treasury."

"Quite an accusation," Pernay shrilled. "You have proof, of course."

Thane rounded on him. "I'm not talking to you! If I have my way, you'll be out on your ear before this night is done!" He cast a look at Mazana. "If Mazana has stopped playing games, that is."

Imerle sounded uninterested. "And that's all there is to these summonses? Surely this could have waited until the next Council session."

Cauroy said, "So it was Thane who sent the summonses?" He flashed a triumphant smile at Senar. "I knew it! Didn't I say—"

"The summonses aren't mine," Thane interrupted. "Nor do I think Gensu is behind them. He didn't mention them when we last spoke."

"Then perhaps," the emira said, "Gensu is playing you as much as he is the rest of us."

The silence that followed was broken by footfalls approaching from the underwater passage. The newcomer was a young woman wearing a servant's livery. As all eyes fell on her, she stumbled to a halt, then moved forward again at Imerle's impatient gesture. She knelt at the emira's feet. Such was her fear that her eyes misted with tears, and her words came out in a tumble. Senar heard only the occasional snatch: ". . . when Orsan arrived . . . with all haste . . . found the ship . . ."

Imerle's already ashen face had become corpse-pale. The flames in her eyes flared brighter until they eclipsed the glow from the braziers. When the servant finished speaking, the emira barked a question. The girl shook her head, eyes downcast. Imerle waved her away, and she fled the room as if the executioner were snapping at her heels.

The emira and Pernay exchanged a look, and Senar caught something in Imerle's gaze that had him holding his breath.

This time the chief minister did not keep the other Storm Lords waiting. He stood to address the room.

"My Lords," he said, his voice grave, "another message has arrived from the harbormaster. It seems that while the ship coming in to dock flies Gensu's flag, Gensu himself is not on board, but rather his son, Polin." He paused, then went on, "Gensu is dead. His ship was ambushed off Airey two days ago."

PART II

A STORM IS COMING

CHAPTER 7

THE SUN was strong against Karmel's face as she looked down on the Cappel Strait. Far below, dragons writhed and snapped in a melee of silver and steel and copper that churned the sea into a spitting cauldron and sent waves crashing against the Dianese and Natillian cliffs. Beneath the froth, huge scaled forms slithered through the water, intertwined like the knotted coils of some immense sea snake. A tail struck the Dianese cliff a blow that Karmel felt through the soles of her sandals. Stones were dislodged from the rock face and went raining down to clang off the dragons' scales like arrows off plate armor.

Into the Natillian cliffs across from her had been carved dozens of terraces which, along with the stairwells connecting them, were as crammed with people as the Dianese gallery on which Karmel stood— so crammed, in fact, that the priestess had to wait for those around her to breathe in before she could do likewise. The air thrummed with anticipation. Someone's elbow was jutting into Karmel's back, but she didn't have space to turn round and complain. To her right an Untarian man with the rasping voice of a blackweed smoker shouted a bawdy greeting to a woman on the Natillian side. If the recipient of that greeting responded in kind, her reply was lost beneath the cacophony of jeers and insults being traded across the strait.

Just then the eighth bell sounded, and a hush settled on the assembled multitudes. Karmel shifted her gaze to the lowest of the Natillian terraces. From beneath a canopy of golden cloth emerged the city's governor, resplendent in a yellow robe. At arm's length he

held a silver goblet as if it were a wither snake. The cup contained
dragon blood, Karmel knew, drained from the corpse of the creature
slaughtered in last year's Hunt. Over the past few weeks drops of
that blood had been sprinkled into the sea to draw the dragons here
from their haunts in the Southern Wastes. Now, as the Natillian
governor stepped to the rail and emptied the contents of the goblet
into the water, the creatures flew into a frenzy of claws and teeth
that momentarily stilled the watching crowds.

A steel-colored beast started ramming its head over and over into
the Dragon Gate, while another creature, copper-scaled, swam to the
cliff beneath the governor's terrace and sank its talons into the rock
before pulling its front quarters from the waves. Panicked cries
sounded as a handful of dignitaries scrambled for the stairs leading
up to the next gallery. The forerunners had made it no farther than
the first step, though, before the stone beneath the dragon's feet crumbled. The beast tumbled back into the sea with a crash that sent
water fountaining into the air.

The Natillian governor had been among those fleeing, but he now
recovered his poise and sidled back to the rail. Karmel saw his lips
move but could not hear his words over the trumpeting of the dragons.
He clapped twice. A century horn blared from one of the Natillian
terraces. Then another horn sounded—from Karmel's right this time—
and another, and another, until the priestess's head rattled with their
call. A roar went up from the crowds. Karmel was standing at the
front of her terrace, and as the people behind her surged forward
she was squashed against the rail at its edge. She struggled to draw
breath. As the pressure grew, she wondered what she should fear most:
that she would be crushed to death against the rail, or that it might
give way to send her plummeting down to join the waiting dragons.

Such was to be the fate of the hapless souls clustered on one of the
Natillian terraces below and across from her. Shackled to steel rings
in the cliff were criminals from around the Sabian League. Their
executions were to form the curtain-raiser to today's festivities, and
as the century horns faded the first of the captives—a shaven-headed
woman with a face dappled by bruises—was released from her chains
by two guards and dragged to a gap in the terrace's rail. A plank had
been extended over the strait. Beside it stood a man in the white robes
of a Beloved of the White Lady. When the woman drew level with
him, she fell to her knees to receive his benediction.

An impatient murmur went up from the people around Karmel—a murmur that changed to heckling as the heartbeats passed. Finally the Natillian soldiers lifted the woman under her arms and deposited her, still kneeling, on the plank. When she refused to move, a guard used the butt of his spear to push her along the board and over the edge.

As she fell screaming, a dragon arched its neck and snatched her from the air.

The crowds cheered.

The next prisoner in line—a bare-chested man with a tattoo of a redback spider on his torso—was freed from his manacles. As he was jostled toward the plank, he stumbled. That stumble proved to be a ruse, however, for he pulled away from his minders before ducking under the spear of a female soldier and driving his shoulder into her midriff. She fell back. He tore her spear from her hands and jabbed its point at another guard, forcing the man to retreat. The people about Karmel must have known the prisoner, for they began chanting a name the priestess couldn't make out.

Three Natillian soldiers rushed to engage the tattooed man, while others moved to block his path to the stairways leading to the upper and lower terraces. Evidently the prisoner had no intention of escaping that way, though, for he dropped his spear and sprinted past the Beloved to the northern end of the terrace. Hurdling the rail there, he launched himself into the air and tumbled down, arms wheeling, until he hit the water below. His leap had taken him close to the cliff on the Natillian side where, he must have hoped, the dragons would find it more difficult to reach him. Karmel gauged the distance between the man and the Dragon Gate. *Less than a hundred armspans.* If he made it to the portcullis, he could pass through its bars to safety. The priestess never saw if he got that far, though, because her view was obstructed by the crush of people leaning forward to her left.

Strangely, she found herself hoping he had.

Karmel returned her gaze to the line of manacled prisoners. It struck her that she might be joining their ranks if she were caught trying to sneak into the citadel. Not that there seemed any imminent prospect of that. Within less than twenty-four bells she and Veran were supposed to have infiltrated the fortress and located the chamber housing the mechanism that raised the Dragon Gate, yet since entering Dian at dawn this was as close as they'd come to the Shroud-cursed place. Looking left, Karmel could see the citadel's slender turrets rising into the sky, their dragon-scaled roofs flashing like mirrors in the morning sunshine. She should have been standing out-side the gatehouse right now, trying to find a way inside. Instead, though, Veran had insisted on dragging her across the length of Dian to the terraces. He hadn't explained why, of course. Maybe he wanted to soak up some of the carnival atmosphere.

Turning to her companion, she tugged his sleeve.

Veran ignored her.

He was staring at the Dragon Gate. Karmel followed his gaze. With the dragon's skull on the battlements now pointing away from her, the portcullis was not half the spectacle it had been last night. Imme-diately above the waterline its bars were rusted and tangled with fireweed, and in the sea about it bobbed a layer of scum and detritus Karmel could smell even from dozens of armspans above. Patrolling the battlements atop the gate were four soldiers, two on the Dianese side, two on the Natillian. As the priestess watched, the Dianese guards removed their full-face helmets and started walking along the forti-fications toward the cliff where, Karmel knew, a door gave access to the citadel. She couldn't see that door from her vantage point, how-ever, much less look through it to the control room beyond, so what in the Chameleon's name Veran thought he could learn here . . .

She grabbed the priest's sleeve again.

At last Veran looked away from the gate. Then he began push-ing through the crowds toward the stairwell leading to the upper terraces.

Shaking her head in disgust, Karmel set off after him.

It took them half a bell to climb to street level. Karmel had never seen so many people in one place. The roof of every building that offered a view of the dragons was groaning with people, as were the branches of the ketar trees along the edge of the cliff. Snowy-haired Maru, rusty-skinned Sartorians, flare-nosed Corinians, even a scat-tering of Melliki with their pierced cheeks and eyebrows: all had come to join in the festivities. A Mellikian with a pointed beard winked at Karmel as she passed, and the priestess scowled. Caval's instruc-tions had been to keep a low profile, so obviously Veran had brought them to the part of the city where the crowds were thickest. Admit-tedly there was little chance of a stranger remembering their faces, but what of the Olairians here? If just one of them recognized the Chameleons, the game would be up before it even started.

A hunchbacked man approached holding skewers of runefish flavored with ganda spices. He thrust one of the skewers at Karmel, but she waved him away. She'd yet to break her fast this morning, yet for some reason the sight of the dragons breaking theirs had made her appetite fly. In any event she'd had her fill of fish. The journey in Veran's boat had left her reeking like a fishmonger's armpit. Before she entered the citadel she would have to find somewhere to scrub the stench from her skin. What use being able to move through the fortress unseen, after all, if the guards could simply follow their noses to her?

Veran led the way as they skirted a marketplace. Today the stalls were gone, and in their place were fire throwers and acrobats, doom-criers and snake charmers, musicians and mirage weavers. On a stage, a group of performers was acting out the Drowning of To-maney. Beyond them a troupe of dragon-masked dancers spun and leapt and stamped time to a breathless jig played by two ashpipers. Karmel's gaze lingered. For years she'd longed to take part in the Dragon Day celebrations, yet now she was here amid the noise and the color, she barely noticed them. But then she needed all her attention just to keep Veran in her sights. He had reached the far side of the square a few steps ahead of her and now ducked into an alley. The priestess broke into a jog to catch up to him.

She tapped him on the shoulder. "The citadel is over there," she said, gesturing behind.

"We ain't going to the citadel."

"I can see that," Karmel snapped. "The question is why?"

Veran did not respond.

The priestess searched his eyes for some clue to his thoughts. His expression betrayed no hint of agitation. It was almost as if . . .

As if he already knows how we're going to get inside the citadel.

A light went off in her head.

And suddenly she understood why her companion hadn't shown any interest in the fortress's gatehouse.

"You mean to climb the Dragon Gate, don't you. *That's* how we're going to get into the citadel."

Veran looked along the alley toward a man retching in the shadows. "Not here," he said, spinning on his heel and moving away.

Karmel stared after him, fighting an urge to turn and walk in the opposite direction.

Then she whispered an oath and set off in pursuit.

The morning sunshine was bright in Senar's eyes as he accompanied Mazana through the palace gates and into the streets of Olaire.

Following the arrival yesterday night of Gensu's son, Polin, Senar had been ordered from the throne room—along with Pernay, Caval, and the executioner—so the Storm Lords could quiz the young man in private. With no other demands on Senar's time he had retired to his quarters. When he returned the next morning he was surprised to find the doors to the throne room still shut and guarded by the executioner. A whole night the Storm Lords had spent in there, much of it waiting for Imerle's pet mage, Orsan, to appear and give his take on things. It was not until the eighth bell that they had finally emerged from their deliberations, grim-faced and bleary-eyed.

Except for Mazana, of course—her step as she now led Senar up Kalin's Hill was as light as if she were walking on her enemies' corpses. She told him what the Storm Lords had learned from Polin the night before. Apparently Gensu had set sail for Olaire two days ago. His family was only alerted to his disappearance when Orsan arrived. Search parties were sent out, and one of them found Gensu's flagship smoldering in a sheltered cove on the southern side of his home island. His burned body was nailed to the mainmast.

"According to Polin," Mazana said, "the summons Gensu received ordered him to Olaire a day earlier than the rest of us, meaning—"

"Meaning his killer was most likely another Storm Lord."

"Very good. That extra day gave whoever sent the summonses time to lay a trap for Gensu, clean up afterward, and still arrive in Olaire on the same day as the other Storm Lords so as not to arouse suspicion."

Even without that extra day, it would have been clear to Senar the killer was a Storm Lord, for who else would have dared to take on a water-mage of Gensu's power on the open seas? "Did Gensu's son say anything that might help identify the killer?"

"Sadly, no. As you can imagine, there is no shortage of suspects. The emira, obviously. Thane, as we only have his word regarding what he discussed with Gensu at their meeting. Then there is Cauroy, since with Gensu's demise, he has now become our emir apparent."

"You are forgetting yourself," Senar pointed out helpfully.

Mazana's eyes slid sideways. "Yes, Imerle did have the gall to mention that my island's proximity to Gensu's gave me the ideal opportunity to lay a trap. As yet, though, we don't know whether the ambush took place in Gensu's waters or mine, or even if he was lured ashore before he was killed and only later nailed to his ship's mast." She slowed to make way for a sedan chair. "In the end we agreed our gilled comrade Mokinda should go to Gensu's island to find out what he can."

"Mokinda? The Untarian?"

"Indeed. As last in line to the throne, he is the most trusted—or should I say the least mistrusted—among us. His abilities as an Untarian will also enable him to sniff out any trails the killer may have left in the water."

A note of amusement in Mazana's voice gave Senar pause. "You don't think he will find anything?"

"Of course not. Whoever carried out the ambush is unlikely to have left a calling card. And even if Mokinda should discover something incriminating, anyone he points the finger at will claim the accusations are politically motivated or have been fabricated to conceal Mokinda's own guilt."

"But if one of the Storm Lords *is* found responsible . . ."

"Then he or she will be trussed up, blinded, and tossed to the dragons on Dragon Day."

High stakes indeed.

The avenue Senar and Mazana were following cut across the flank of Kalin's Hill, and having reached the road's high point, they began the descent to the Commercial District. Last night's quake had opened cracks in the plaster of some of the buildings to either side. When Senar looked down on Olaire he saw other parts of the city had suffered more extensive damage, notably the Shallows, where waves foamed along alleys choked with the debris of fallen buildings.

Between the houses to Senar's left he caught glimpses of the sea. Rectangular metal frames—blue oyster fields, Mazana told him—protruded from the water, and beyond them a flotilla of boats bobbed on the sparkling waves. The Guardian shielded his eyes. For all of the Sabian Sea's tranquil allure, it lacked the soul of the gray, ill-tempered waters that thundered against Erin Elal's shores. But then the Sabian was not *his* sea, Senar reminded himself, any more than Olaire was his city. True, there was a languid elegance to the Storm Isles' capital, with its sun-drenched avenues and its white-plastered buildings, but it had none of the brooding majesty of Erin Elal's first city, Arkarbour.

Senar looked south. "Is that Dian I can see?" he asked Mazana, pointing to a smudge on the horizon.

The Storm Lady shrugged. "You have been there before?"

"Once, many years ago, in the lead-up to Avallon's attack on Cenan. The then governor, Tatin, was selling blayfire oil to Cenan's sacris-tens. Li Benir and I were sent to encourage him to stop."

"And you succeeded?"

Senar smiled. "My master could be very persuasive when he had to be."

The Round loomed ahead of them, with its rooftop of glass and its façade of arches stacked one on top of another. It stood at the center of a square decorated with a mosaic that stretched to the doorways of the courts and embassies round it. The people in the square ob-scured much of the mosaic's design, but Senar could still make out images of hydras and denkrakils and other creatures of the deep amid splashes of gold, silver, and blue. The crowd was as colorful as the mosaic's stones. Senar saw a white-haired Maru woman with arms covered in fish-bone bracelets, a barefooted man in orange robes carrying an armload of scrolls so large he could not see over it, an Untarian woman blowing air through her gills as she harangued a crowd from atop an upturned crate.

Mazana led him across the square before turning into a road that passed between the Mercantile Court and the Mercerien embassy. A stone's throw from Mazana's house they found their way blocked by a line of Storm Guards. Ahead the road had collapsed, bringing down the walls of the houses to either side. A few armspans below, Senar saw a gloomy subterranean chamber buried in rubble. Amid the de-bris were human bones, piled knee-high, and at the opposite end of the chamber was the shrunken body of a man—little more than a skeleton—seated on a throne of skulls.

Beside the throne crouched a black-robed figure, and Senar rec-ognized the Remnerol shaman Jambar. The old man looked up. His thoughtful expression was quickly replaced by the customary inane smile. The shaman was the only person Senar knew who left him wanting to see what his scowl looked like.

"Hunting for treasure?" Senar asked him.

"One does not find treasure in the ground, Guardian, unless one shares the vulgar notion that treasure comprises wealth and luxury. I, on the other hand, consider the virtues of prudence, temperance, and justice to be the real treasures of this decadent world."

Senar glanced at the skeleton seated on the throne of bones. Long, dark hair hung down in a tangle from his skull, and there was a crack along his left temple. "Who was he?"

The Remnerol shrugged. "I have only a passing familiarity with the history of these lands. The empire of the Storm Lords was born in the Sixth Age, so this tomb must date back to some earlier, more primitive civilization . . ."

His voice trailed off as a tremor shook the street and set the bones in the chamber clacking together in a macabre cacophony. The edges of the crater crumbled with a patter of mortar, and the tomb belched up a cloud of dust. Senar reached out a hand to Mazana's arm. Such was the heat of the day that sweat sprang up immediately at the contact.

Jambar had returned to his study of the seated man.

Mazana said, "You had best come out of there unless you want to be the tomb's next occupant."

The way she said it, you'd have thought that would be a bad thing.

"If there were a risk of that, don't you think I would have fore-seen it?" Jambar replied. He turned his body to obscure Mazana's and Senar's views of the skeletal figure, but the Guardian still saw him detach the little finger from each of the man's hands and slip them into a pocket.

"You are taking his fingers?" Senar said. "What makes you so sure his bones are worth adding to your collection?"

"I am not. But knowing, as I do, which are the least efficacious of the bones in my possession, I can substitute those for these and com-pare the prophetic abilities of my collection before and after."

"And how will you do that? By rolling dice?"

"Perhaps."

Senar caught a flash of white hairless legs as Jambar hitched up his robes and began wading through the bones toward him. When the old man reached the wall below the Guardian's position, he clambered onto a block of rubble and stretched out a hand. Senar took it, then hauled him out of the chamber. For a heartbeat Jambar kept a grip on Senar's hand, gazing at it intently as if he were picturing the knuckle bone of the Guardian's little finger in his collection.

Senar snatched his hand away. He'd lost enough fingers already, thank you very much.

Mazana was staring along the street. As another ripple passed through the ground, she turned to Jambar. "These quakes, Shaman . . . How long have they been going on in Olaire?"

"A few months. With each week that passes, the strength of the tremors increases."

"Has anyone discovered the cause?"

Jambar held her gaze before shooting an unreadable look at Senar. "The cause? I fear not. But the origin?" He waved a hand at the fortress visible above the rooftops to the northwest. "Unquestionably the Founder's Citadel yonder."

Senar glanced between them. There was a strange formality to their speech—almost as if they were reading from a script.

"The citadel?" Mazana said to the Remnerol. "You are sure?"

"Of course I am. I was walking past it when last night's quake struck."

"Well then, if the citadel is linked to the tremors, don't you think the emira should be told?"

The old man stroked his chin, his simple smile fading. "Yes," he said after a pause. "I suppose she should."

Agenta stood on the first-floor balcony of the Gilgamarian embassy, squinting against the dust on the breeze. To the west, between the Round and the Mercantile Court, she could see a section of Olaire's harbor where a number of ships rocked at quayside. Yet more vessels waited at anchor beyond the Causeway for a berth to become free. Among their flags Agenta saw the three stoneback scorpions of Nain Deep, the black and gold stripes of Hunte, Sealow's hartfish impaled on the prongs of a trident, together with a host of others she did not recognize. Those unknown ships would belong to fortune hunters, she knew, come to take part in the Dragon Hunt in the hope of winning the riches bestowed on the crew that brought down the dragon.

Though why anyone would *choose* to pick a fight with one of the creatures . . .

This day six years ago Agenta had been in Gilgamar looking out over the harbor and the sea beyond. A southerly wind had blown in a storm, and along with the stinging rain had come a Rubyholt trader ship seeking shelter in Gilgamar's harbor from the silver-scaled dragon pursuing it. With Dragon Day so close, the chains across the port's entrance had been raised to prevent dragons getting in. It was too late to lower those chains even if the harbormaster had been minded to do so. Agenta had watched with a mixture of horror and fascination as the silver dragon overtook its prey and smashed the vessel to splinters with a flick of its tail. She had hardened her heart to the plight of the ship's crew, telling herself only fools would set sail at the height of the dragon season. For days afterward, though, her dreams had been haunted by the cries of the sailors as the dragon dragged them down one by one.

Thank the Sender she would be far from Dian when the next batch of hapless souls was sent shrieking through Shroud's Gate by way of a dragon's maw.

A tinkle of crystal shook her from her reverie, and she looked back to see Lydanto enter his office. She went inside to join her father. The ambassador helped himself to a glass of an orange-colored liquid from a decanter before stumbling to the chair behind his desk. He sat down heavily. Along the wall behind him was a crack from floor to ceiling that must have been caused by last night's quake.

"Apologies for keeping you," Lydanto said, green-faced. "An upset of the stomach, yes?"

Agenta said, "Something you ate, no doubt."

Lydanto's chuckle degenerated into a fit of coughing.

Rethell motioned to her. "Tell him."

She recounted her meeting with Sticks. Her father had heard the story twice already, yet still he listened intently as she spoke. When she finished he said, "And that's it? That's everything you discussed?"

Agenta knew what he was thinking: that she'd committed some slip to put Sticks on guard and was now keeping it from them to save face. The reality was, she'd gone over her conversation with Sticks a hundred times and still she didn't see how she could have played things differently. "What if we go back to the Deeps for another look round?" she said. "That building hit by the fireball shouldn't be hard to locate."

Rethell shook his head. "Sticks and his cronies will have long since moved on. We're better off waiting for *him* to come to us."

"Oh?"

"You came back through the harbor, remember? A boat with one corpse and four bleeding bodies draws attention."

"Would it make things easier if I hadn't come back at all?" Agenta said. So what if someone has seen her at the port? The fact Sticks had moved against her suggested he'd already guessed her identity. It might not even be Agenta who had given the game away, for of the dozen men sent to follow her last night, four had failed to return. If they'd been captured and questioned by Sticks's crowd . . .

Rethell returned her gaze blankly. Then his expression softened. "You did well."

Agenta snorted. Was praise ever delivered so grudgingly? She was becoming accustomed to her father's disappointment, but then how was she supposed to compete with the memory of her dead brother?

And yet, there was no denying last night's operation had been a failure. What had she achieved save to drive the *Gadfly*'s attackers deeper undercover and place a target on her chest for Sticks and his men to fire at?

Lydanto cleared his throat. "Did you manage to swap the stone, Kalischa?"

Agenta nodded. She withdrew from a pocket the jewel Sticks had given her to inspect, and which she had switched for one she'd bought beforehand in the Jewelry Quarter.

The ambassador looked at Rethell. "You have been examining it already?"

"It's one of ours. I'm sure of it."

"The hijacker of the *Gadfly* . . . one of your competitors, perhaps?"

"A competitor desperate enough to resort to piracy?"

Lydanto blinked. "You are right, of course. I was merely—how do you say?—thinking in the loud."

Rethell rose and crossed to the table to pour himself a glass of water. "What have you been able to find out about these loans to the emira?"

"Little as yet," the ambassador conceded. "Imerle has been covering her trail well using nominees and guilds, but I am confident I will be sniffing it out eventually." His eyes glittered. "I have, however, heard something on another matter that might be interesting you. There are rumors Lord Gensu Sensama is dead, ambushed off his home island of Airey."

"I've heard nothing of this."

Lydanto tapped his rosy nose. "The Storm Lords are keeping it quiet, I am thinking, until they have discovered who is responsible."

Agenta raised an eyebrow. As if it weren't obvious already. Things were coming together in her mind. Imerle, intent on raising funds to finance a coup, had ordered her soldiers to hijack the *Gadfly*, along with the other missing ships. Now she was targeting her fellow Storm Lords in advance of launching an attack. The problem for Agenta and Rethell would be proving their suspicions—or at least proving them sufficiently to force the emira to negotiate over the stolen duskstones. *While all the time hoping we don't learn so much that we become a liability.*

A knock sounded at the door.

"Come!" Lydanto called.

A messenger entered wearing the emblem of the Storm Lords on his uniform. He carried a roll of parchment which he handed to Rethell before departing. The kalisch put down his glass, then broke the wax seal and unrolled the scroll. Agenta could see only a few lines of writing on the parchment, yet her father took an age to read them. At last he grunted and tossed the scroll onto the desk. He looked at Agenta.

"It seems your adventures in the Deeps have caught the emira's eye. We are summoned to another audience at the palace this evening."

The crowds thinned as Karmel and Veran reached Dian's Temple District, but even here it felt to the priestess as if a dozen sets of eyes tracked her every step. The doors to the White Lady's Temple were open, and through them came a woman's voice singing a melody pure and bright as sunlight. Karmel paid it no mind. Her thoughts were a whirr. Climb the Dragon Gate? Was Veran serious? He'd neither confirmed nor denied her hunch, but his lack of reaction to her words spoke volumes.

Unless he's just pulling my leg.

No, that would mean having to credit him with a sense of humor.

She studied her companion's back. Had scaling the gate been the plan all along? Or had the withdrawal of whichever Chameleon she'd replaced left insufficient time to infiltrate the citadel the orthodox way? It had to be the latter, Karmel decided, for it smacked of desperation to try to climb the portcullis in full view of the crowds on the terraces and with the dragons waiting below.

Desperation? Madness!

The singing from the White Lady's Temple died away as the Chameleons turned into an alley and passed the entrance to a weed-infested boneyard. At the bottom of the steps leading down to their basement lodgings was a pool of urine, and the smell followed Karmel inside as she entered behind Veran. She flung herself onto her bed. When Veran had brought her to this fleapit earlier, she'd despaired at the prospect of having to lie low here for a few days once their mission was finished. Now that seemed the least of her worries.

Veran removed flint and steel from his pack and lit an oil lamp. Overhead, footfalls sounded as someone walked across the floor of the room above. The priest's gaze held steady on Karmel as he waited for the noise to fade.

"Using the citadel's front door is a nonstarter," he said at last. "The gatehouse will be crawling with sentries this close to Dragon Day, and there's precious little chance of us slipping past them when their guard's up."

"Right," she said. "About the same chance of us climbing the Dragon Gate without anyone seeing."

"They didn't see me last time I tried."

Karmel covered her surprise. "You've done this before?"

He nodded.

"You climbed all the way to the battlements?"

"No, just to the top of the gate."

"When?"

"Eleven days ago."

"Eleven days ago wasn't in the middle of a Shroud-cursed festival." Karmel was sounding increasingly agitated, but she didn't care.

"Shut up and listen," Veran said. "Where the Dragon Gate meets the cliff, the rock has been carved away to form long vertical grooves. These grooves are deep, meaning there's a section of the gate two armspans wide that is hidden by the cliff. That's where we'll climb."

"It's a costly fall if we slip."

"You won't slip because you won't be making the initial ascent. I'll climb up, then lower a rope for you."

Karmel scowled. "I think I can manage—"

"You'll do as you're bloody well told."

A door slammed in the room above, then a man's voice rang out. His words were muffled by the floorboards. A woman shrieked something unintelligible in response. Karmel felt like doing some shouting herself, but before she could open her mouth Veran went on, "Midnight tonight we go back to the beach, then swim round to the gate. Dragons won't give us any trouble because they'll be on the other side."

"Why did we bother coming to the city at all, then? We could have stayed in the boat."

"Because while you were gawping at the dragons earlier, I was watching the soldiers on the battlements. According to our reports the guards are swapped every four bells, but I wanted to see for myself. And I'll be going back today at the noon bell, and every fourth bell after that, to check there ain't been a change in the routine."

The priestess swung her legs round and sat on the edge of the bed. "So we hit them tomorrow after the switch at the fourth bell?"

Veran grunted in confirmation. "Dawn is after the seventh bell. Gives us plenty of time to climb up and silence the Dianese guards before it gets light."

"What about the soldiers on the Natillian side of the battlements? They'll be sure to see—"

Veran shook his head. "Dragon's skull splits the fortifications in two, and the thing's big enough to hide whatever's happening on the other side. If we do things quiet, the Natillian guards won't know what's going on." He reached into his pack. "Hard part will be getting onto the battlements unnoticed. They're wider than the gate itself, so we can't just climb up from the gate below." He pulled out a grappling hook wrapped in black mexin and tossed it onto the bed beside Karmel. "We'll use these. Cloth will deaden the sound of the hooks biting on the merlon."

The priestess eyed him skeptically. He was speaking so confidently he might have been reporting something that had already happened, but there were countless ways this plan could go to the Abyss. The battlements were wider than the gate, he'd said, which meant when the time came for the Chameleons to throw their grappling hooks, they'd be doing so blind. It also meant they wouldn't be able to see which way the soldiers on the battlements were facing.

Her companion must have read her thoughts for he said, "Guards will most likely be looking south at the dragons, so I'll go up on the north side."

"*You'll* go up," Karmel said. "Am I here just to clap in the right places, then?" Even through her dread she could still feel anger at his condescension.

Veran grunted. He had a grunt for every occasion, the priestess was coming to realize. This one conveyed impatience and a hint of scorn. "When the guards are dead," he said, "I'll strip them and use a rope to lower the bodies to you on the gate. We can't toss them to the dragons in case someone sees them fall. You'll have to wedge them as best you can between the gate and the cliff. No one should spot them unless they're looking for them."

Strip them? "You want us to take the soldiers' places?"

" 'S the only way we're going to get into the citadel. Door to the control room is locked from the other side, so we'll have to wait for someone inside to let us in."

In the room above, the argument was becoming more heated. A third voice—another woman's—had joined the first two.

Karmel said, "So we put on the dead soldiers' uniforms and wait on the battlements until we're relieved at the eighth bell? And what happens when the next pair of guards don't recognize us?"

"Dianese soldiers wear full-face helmets. If we keep our mouths shut"—he looked at her pointedly—"no one should notice the switch."

"And if the guards we replace are both men? Or women?" Karmel's said, her voice rising. "Or flame-eyed Manixian firebloods?"

Veran grunted again—a rueful grunt this time. It appeared that was all the answer he would give, though, for he turned his back on Karmel, then took out a roll of parchment and a stick of charcoal from his pack. Moving to the table beside the priestess's bed, he unrolled the parchment. It was blank. He began drawing on it by the smoky light of the lamp. Karmel leaned forward and watched him trace the outline of a room, adding short heavy lines along two walls, together with various other markings and annotations.

"Control room looks like this," he said when he'd finished. "Twelve paces long, ten wide, with doors leading to the battlements and the citadel"—he gestured to the short heavy lines—"here and here. The chain that raises the Dragon Gate enters the room through the floor near the eastern wall then runs along the ground to a mechanism like a ship's capstan"—he pointed to a circle with eight lines coming off it—"here."

Karmel was finding it difficult to hear his words over a string of curses from one of the women upstairs. "How many guards?"

"Usual complement is two. Tomorrow there'll be another eight working the capstan, one overseeing."

"Eleven, then." Karmel left a pause. "Eleven versus two."

"With surprise on our side, we should be able to thin their numbers before they know they're in a fight."

That would still leave two or three opponents each to fight, but those were odds Karmel could live with. After the shock of this morning's revelations, her heartbeat was finally beginning to return to its normal rhythm. She looked back at the drawing. "Eight men on the capstan, right? So assuming there's the same number on the Natillian side that makes sixteen in all. Sixteen men to lift a gate that big? What are these soldiers, titans?"

"The chains that raise the gate are invested with air-magic. Lightens the load."

"You know that for sure, or you're guessing?"

Veran ignored her. "When the shit goes down, our priority is to lock the door to the citadel to stop reinforcements arriving. That's where I'll be. You give me cover."

From overhead came the sound of smashing glass, followed by a man's yelp. The shouting started up again, twice as loud.

Karmel struggled to marshal her thoughts. It seemed Veran had an answer for everything, but instead of reassuring her that just left her feeling wary. Something was niggling her, something to do with what Caval had said in their conversation at the temple. She let her mind drift . . .

It came to her. Killing the guards in the control room was all well and good, but when the Dragon Gate failed to rise, more soldiers were sure to come knocking. Even if Veran barred the door to the citadel it wouldn't keep the guards out for long, and when they broke through, what was to stop them raising the gate in place of their dead colleagues? The best Karmel and Veran could hope for was to delay the Hunt, yet according to Caval the reason for sabotaging Dragon Day was to discredit Dian's governor in the eyes of his supporters. Would a delay be enough to light a fire under Piput's ambitions?

When Karmel put this to Veran his face went still, and she realized she'd touched on something he'd hoped she would overlook. He glanced at his pack. "Dragon Gate won't be rising once we're done. I've got something to take care of the capstan permanently."

"Something powerful enough to destroy the capstan, but not so powerful that it takes us out with it?"

Veran did not respond.

The priestess let the silence drag out, but her companion didn't fill it. Even now he was keeping secrets from her, but why? What else could there be about the mission he hadn't told her? How could the picture be any bleaker than the one he'd already painted? Her gaze flickered to his pack. Perhaps when he went out at noon to watch the changeover of the Dianese guards she would find an excuse to stay behind and sneak a peek inside.

When she looked back at Veran, though, she saw from his eyes that he'd read her intent.

Damn him.

"What happens after this capstan is destroyed?" she said. "Odds are, more soldiers will be coming along the battlements from Natilly. The dragon's skull won't hold them forever. We'll be trapped."

"So what if we are?"

She stared at him.

"Dianese won't know they're dealing with Chameleons," he said. "There's no reason for them to look for something they can't see." Veran stabbed a finger at the plan. "Northwest corner of the chamber is screened by a weapons cabinet. That's where we'll wait for the dust to settle."

They might even get away with it, Karmel conceded. When the soldiers broke into the control room it would be from the citadel first, and the guards would find a room full of corpses and the door to the battlements locked from the inside. They'd probably assume some of their own had turned traitor, and that the two factions had wiped each other out. "So first chance we get we slip out to the battlements—"

"We're not going back to the battlements."

Karmel was incredulous. "You want to leave through the citadel?

So, what, the fortress is too well-guarded for us to break in, but we'll have no trouble getting out?"

"The difference is time. If we can keep from under the soldiers' feet for a few bells, we'll have all the time we need to pick our way out."

"But the battlements—"

"If we go back to the battlements someone from the terraces might see us."

Karmel shrugged. "So we make a break for it at night—dive into the sea on the north side of the gate then swim round to the boat."

"Too risky."

"Whereas trying to sneak through the citadel—"

"It's too risky, I said!" Veran snatched up the plan and put one end in the flame of the oil lamp. As the parchment burned, he tossed it to the floor and watched it blacken to ash.

Karmel opened her mouth to speak, but her companion glowered at her. The words died in her throat. It wasn't that she was cowed by him; she just knew that he wouldn't answer any more questions.

"We've got sixteen bells before things kick off," Veran said. "I suggest you check your gear and get some rest." Another crash of breaking glass sounded from the room overhead, and Veran cast a dark look at the ceiling. "If the bastards upstairs let us, that is."

Agenta watched the sun dip beneath the palace's roofline. For half a bell she and her father had been kept waiting in the corridor outside the throne room. As the light started to fade, so too did the kalischa's expectations for the coming meeting. Imerle's summons had not disclosed the reason for the audience. Agenta had wondered whether that business with Sticks had convinced the emira to strike a more conciliatory tone in their discussions over the stolen duskstones. As the heartbeats passed, though, the kalischa began to suspect Imerle had called them here not to smooth ruffled feathers but to deliver a warning about prying into her affairs. If that were the case Agenta saw no reason to waste any more time in this place. Before she could suggest to her father that they leave, though, the doors to the throne room swung open, and a Storm Guard beckoned them through.

Beyond stretched the underwater passage, its walls rippling like sheets of steel-gray silk. As Agenta descended into the murk behind Rethell, the noise of the waves breaking against the seawall died away.

The doors closed behind her with a noise like rolling thunder.

The throne room was lit by braziers of glowing coals that did nothing to alleviate the chill in the air. Imerle was dressed in a black gown that accentuated the pallor of her skin. To her left sat the chief minister, smiling as if at some private joke. Behind him stood the executioner, his gaze fixed on infinity.

Agenta drew up alongside her father.

Rethell bowed. "You wished to see us, Emira."

Imerle's gaze was on Agenta. "We understand you have been keeping yourself busy since we last met."

"If you are referring to what happened in the Deeps," Agenta said, "you are remarkably well-informed."

"You will find there is little that goes in Olaire that we do not know about."

"Indeed. You'll be able to tell us who's selling our stolen duskstones, then."

"Ah, so you went to meet the hijackers of your ship. Were you able to apprehend one of the pirates for questioning?"

It was plain from Imerle's expression she already knew the answer to that. Agenta was about to call an end to this charade when her father spoke.

"These were no pirates, Emira," he said. "They were soldiers."

"Soldiers?" Imerle repeated. "Did they wear some insignia on their uniforms? Address each other by rank, perhaps?"

"I trust my daughter's judgment in this."

"Of course you do."

What little daylight remained was leaching from the sea, transforming the walls of the throne room into dark mirrors that reflected the smoldering glow of the braziers. Imerle's eyes, too, were smoldering as they focused on Agenta. "If you are right in thinking the hijackers are soldiers, perhaps you should leave the job of tracking them down to our Storm Guards. The Deeps can be a dangerous place. We would hate for your next visit there to be your last."

Rethell's voice was cold. "Oh, there won't be any need for Agenta to return to the Deeps. She left last night with what she went for."

"You found your missing duskstones?"

Agenta held up the jewel she had taken from Sticks.

Imerle smiled. "A single stone? We'd have thought you would set your sights higher."

"I was not referring to the duskstones," Rethell said. "Agenta returned with something much more valuable: information."

"You know which pirates stole your cargo?"

"Better than that. We know the identity of the power behind the pirates' mask."

"And?"

"And when our inquiries are complete, we will present our findings to the Storm Council."

The emira looked bored. "Well, if there is anything we can do to help, you know you have but to ask."

Agenta glanced at her father. She'd told him earlier that Imerle wouldn't fall for such a feeble bluff, but what now? They had yet to raise the matter of Imerle's loans, but then Lydanto's inquiries at the Round had uncovered nothing thus far. Rethell had been reluctant to raise the matter until they had proved the emira was the beneficiary. Even if such proof existed, though, there was no guarantee they would find it. More important, if Imerle *was* planning a coup, how long did they have before she made her move? A month? A week? If they didn't confront her now, they might squander their chance to force her to the negotiating table. Because once she'd made her play for power there would be no need for her to strike a deal. Better to kick the nest now and see what came of it than risk leaving their trump card unplayed. Better to do something than nothing, even if it turned out to be the wrong thing.

Rethell must have come to the same conclusion, for a note of resignation entered his gaze. He nodded to Agenta.

She turned to Imerle. "Perhaps there *is* something you can help us with. It seems a merchant trading in our stolen duskstones has been using the profits to make loans to someone in Olaire—someone who has gone to great lengths to conceal their identity. Naturally we will be doing everything in our power to unmask this person, but if the Storm Council can assist—"

"A moment," Pernay cut in. "This merchant . . . He has a name?"

"Galaman Vesta."

It was the turn of Imerle and her chief minister to exchange a look—a good sign, Agenta decided, for it told her she had their attention at last.

"Vesta is known to us," Pernay said eventually. He appeared to be sitting a good deal less comfortably than he had been before. "But as a trader in Androsian silks, not duskstones."

"Perhaps you do not know him as well as you thought. Or perhaps someone made him an offer regarding the stones that was too good to pass up." That someone had been an agent from the Xiatan Trading House, employed by her father to broker a deal between Vesta and a second merchant already holding a sizable stockpile of the jewels—a deal that had been set up this morning in secret, and at considerable expense to Rethell, with the sole purpose of fashioning a false link between the missing stones and the emira's loans.

Imerle spoke. "What proof do you have that the recipient of these loans is connected to the *Gadfly*'s hijackers?"

"None as yet," Agenta said, "but the possibility of a link needs to be investigated, wouldn't you agree? Perhaps Vesta is in league with the hijackers and is using the loans to launder his profits. Or perhaps we have read the situation wrongly and the loans have been made for an altogether different purpose. Whatever the truth of it, you may rest assured we will pursue this path to its end, no matter where or to whom it may lead."

The emira considered this, her mouth a thin line. Doubtless she believed she had hidden her trail well, but with luck the threat of having the spotlight turned on her dealings would be sufficient to make her parley. Agenta looked at the executioner. Unless, of course, Imerle intended to unleash the giant on the kalischa and her father. A pity Agenta hadn't thought to bring her throwing stars with her.

"Perhaps there *is* something we can do to help you in your investigation," the emira said finally. "We will, of course, need to see the evidence implicating Vesta in this affair."

"Our ambassador has the paperwork," Rethell said.

"Indeed." Imerle paused, then went on, "As for your missing duskstones, we have been thinking further on your plight since our meeting yesterday. Perhaps you and your daughter would do us the honor of joining us on our flagship for the Dragon Day festivities tomorrow. We can continue our discussions on board. You can even bring your ambassador with you."

Agenta's lips quirked. Yes, they were all friends now. It seemed their gambit had paid off, for why else would the emira have extended such an invitation unless she wanted to build bridges? And yet, to look at Imerle you wouldn't know she had just been outmaneuvered. Moreover, when Agenta glanced at her father, it was clear from his frown he didn't share Agenta's satisfaction. His gaze shifted from Imerle to the chief minister, then back again. For a moment Agenta thought he would decline the offer.

Then he bowed to the emira and said, "The honor would be ours."

CHAPTER 8

KEMPIS COULDN'T believe he had agreed to this madness.

It was a sign of his growing desperation, he supposed, what with Hilaire's breath tickling the back of his neck and his last lead having gone Shroud's way with Enli Alapha's death. Earlier he'd drawn a blank wading through contracts and card catalogues at the merchant's office. But then doubtless anything incriminating was now in Bright Eyes's hands after she'd snatched whatever papers the old man had taken with him last night. The septia still had the task of sifting through Enli's remaining contracts at the Round to look forward to, but even if he were to find further irregularities, that wasn't going to stop the killings—there had been two more this evening alone.

Which left Kempis here in the alley where Bright Eyes had disappeared yesterday, about to take a chance on a harebrained scheme Loop had thought up.

The septia looked about him. A few paces away the sea lapped at the cobbles. To his right a pile of vomit lay against the wall of the brothel, and next to it was a patch of dried blood that marked the place where Joren had fallen. Bright Eyes's body count had now reached double figures, yet so far as Kempis could determine she'd used her magic only twice to vanish. On both occasions she'd been here in the alley.

"What's special about this shithole?" he wondered aloud.

"Sir?" Loop said.

"Help me out here, mage. Bright Eyes is a sorcerer, right? Means she has to draw energy for her power from somewhere. Fire-mages draw on fire, water-mages draw on water, I get that. But what energy does someone draw on to make themselves disappear?"

Loop had no answers.

Kempis scanned the moonlit buildings to the south. His gaze came to rest on the yellow house covered in graffiti, and he stared at the scrawled letters as if they held the answer to the riddle of the alley's significance. There had to be something unique to this location—something that created energies the assassin could tap into. If so, though, the source of those energies was well hidden. This morning Kempis had sent Loop and Duffle to search nearby buildings for anything out of the ordinary. He'd even ordered Sniffer to investigate the flooded lower levels of the partly submerged houses in the hope the sea might be concealing something.

Nothing.

The sound of whistling gills marked Sniffer's arrival, and Kempis shot her a look. "You bring the ten sovereigns you owe me?"

"You mean our bet last night?" The Untarian shook her head. "You said Enli would lead us to the killer."

"And?"

"And he didn't. She came to him."

"You're kidding, right?"

Sniffer grinned. "Hilaire's looking for you. Said she left a message for you to come by her office this morning. When you didn't show, she thought you were dead. I let her down gently, of course."

"You told her where I was?"

"No. I just said you were avoiding her."

Loop cleared his throat. "If we're doing this, sir, we'd best get a move on. There's rain in the air, I'm telling you."

Kempis looked up at the starry sky. Barely a cloud in sight. Shame, too, a shower might be the closest thing Loop got to a wash this year. "What's keeping this spirit of yours?"

"Still got to be summoned."

"Summoned? By who?"

"Me."

Kempis's eyes narrowed. "You ain't one of them corpse-huggers, are you?"

"Necromancer, you mean? Not likely."

"What's your power, then?"

Loop examined his grimy nails. "Oh, bit of this, bit of that. You know, whatever my ma passed down."

Kempis studied him, then shrugged. He'd be getting a look at the mage in action soon enough. "This spirit—the Drifter who died here—shouldn't he be cluttering up Shroud's Gate by now?"

"Should be, yeah. Looks like Shroud and his cronies have got more to worry about just now than gathering souls, though." In response to Kempis's questioning look Loop added, "Trouble out west, sir. Seems Shroud is in a bit of a scrap." He cracked a yellow-toothed smile. "Pity the poor bastard in the other corner, eh?"

A thought came to the septia. "Does that mean there are more of these spirits in Olaire?"

"Yeah. Everyone who's snuffed it these past few days."

"Then where in the Nine Hells are they?"

"All about us. You ain't gonna see them, though, unless they wanna be seen."

Kempis felt hidden eyes on him, but he resisted the temptation to look round. "This Drifter—Irlon, weren't it?—you said you had to summon him. Where's he been all this time?"

"Haunting his missus. Seems the grieving widow weren't grieving for long."

Kempis eyed him suspiciously.

"Ain't me she's been getting her comfort from, if that's what you're thinking."

"Who, then?"

"One of the lads—Moric. Went round to break the news of her old man's death two days ago."

Sniffer barked a laugh. "Sounds like she needed lots of consoling."

Kempis said, "Shame this Irlon didn't think to haunt his killer instead of his other half. If he had, he might've been able to tell us where to find her."

"Maybe he can," Loop said. "That's what I'm gonna ask him. Even if he don't know where Bright Eyes is hiding, though, might be he remembers something about the night of the killing. Something that could help us."

From the other side of the wall to Kempis's right, he heard a man's grunting, a woman's exaggerated squeals of delight. The squeals rose steadily in volume, and when the septia next spoke he had to raise his voice to make himself heard. "Get on with it, then," he said to Loop.

The mage spat on his palms and ran his hands through his hair.

A tingling in Kempis's skin told him Loop was summoning his power. It wasn't until the temperature in the alley began to drop that the septia realized the mage was drawing on the ripples of energy created by Joren's death. *Not a corpse-hugger, my ass!* For a while nothing happened, and Kempis wondered whether Joren's energies were too weak to fuel whatever Loop was trying to do. Then a deeper darkness gathered in the passage.

A few years ago Kempis had seen the emira calm stormy seas to save a Rastamiran galley driven toward the rocks off Ferris Point. Blueblood she might be, but he'd had to admire her control as she spun myriad threads of energy together like the weaver of an Elescorian carpet. Loop, by contrast, put Kempis in mind of someone trying his hand at the loom for the first time, for the sorcerous shadows he conjured were a knot of tattered threads and discordant energies. The septia looked at the mage. "You've done this before, right?"

"Quiet," Loop said through clenched teeth. "I'm concentrating."

The unnatural blackness in the alley spread, tendrils of power snaking out to brush Kempis's skin. He took a pace back. Of all the magics he'd encountered, necromancy spooked him the most. The way he saw it, for him to be able to sense sorcery, the power had to be acting on him somehow. And in the case of death-magic it felt as if the sorcery was stealing more from him than just the warmth of his blood. Why should the act of dying release energy? What if corpse-huggers robbed the departed soul of some of its life force?

Then again, wasn't it spirit-mages who consumed souls to fuel their power?

Kempis retreated another step. A smell reached him—a mustiness not unlike that of the Mausoleum this morning when he'd gone to search Enli Alapha's body. Where the septia had been standing moments earlier was now a yawning emptiness. Within the gloom, wisps of gray began to form. They came together to create the outline of a figure before dissipating again. *Irlon is resisting the summons.* Loop must have been winning the battle of wills, though, for the figure rematerialized. First Irlon's body took shape, then his features— hooked nose, widow's peak, dark eyes set too far apart in his face.

Kempis recognized him from when he'd seen him lying next to Enli in the Mausoleum.

Irlon's gaze took in the alley before settling on the septia.

With a shriek the spirit surged forward, hissing and swearing.

Kempis stumbled backward.

The Drifter jerked to a halt a few armspans away as if he were shackled to a chain that had run out to its full length. He thrashed against his spiritual bonds. Kempis waited for his heart to crawl back down his throat.

A woman's querying shout came from above, followed by an intake of breath. A window slammed shut.

Irlon fell still. The hatred in his eyes chilled Kempis as much as Loop's death-magic had done. Puzzled him, too, but then it was entirely possible he owed the man money. A voice sounded in his head.

"Send me back! She was about to . . . Send me back, damn you!"

Kempis's expression darkened. "I'll send you back when I'm good and ready. Till then, I've got questions."

"Is that a fact?" Irlon flexed his arms. "I can sense my bonds weakening, Watchman. When they fail, I will come for you." His gaze shifted to Sniffer. "Or maybe for you, my dear."

Kempis stepped in front of the Untarian. "And maybe I'll tell my mage here to bind your soul to a Shroud-cursed rock and toss it in the harbor. How does an eternity with the fishes and the gallow crabs sound to you?" He had no idea whether Loop could deliver on his threat, but the mage played his part, nodding as if in readiness to carry out Kempis's bidding.

Irlon edged closer to the septia. Was it Kempis's imagination, or had the invisible chains holding him slackened a fraction? Joren's necromantic energies must be dwindling. Loop would need another death to restore his strength, but this was the Shallows, wasn't it? It could only be a matter of time before one of the locals obliged.

Kempis said, "We're trying to find your killer, man! You telling me you don't want the woman who pricked you to get what's coming to her?"

"Maybe I like what she did for me."

"Then when we catch up to her, you can shake her by the hand! Oh no, wait, you can't, because your hand's still attached to the rest of your Shroud-cursed body in the Shroud-cursed Mausoleum!"

Irlon's features briefly lost cohesion as if a breath of spiritual wind had tugged at his form. He leaned forward as if testing his ethereal chains again. Then he shot a glance at Loop's sweat-sheened face before looking back at Kempis. "You'll let me go when I've answered your questions?"

"I'm a reasonable man."

"Make it quick."

The septia let his breath out slowly. "The assassin . . . you remember anything about her?"

"I remember her eyes glowing. And she was quick. I always carried a dagger in case the locals got frisky, but the woman had her pigsticker in me before I could draw it." He sneered. "Is any of this helping?"

"What about when she disappeared? Did you see where she went?"

The Drifter's sneer gave way to a brooding expression. "I saw darkness. The buildings faded. And there were waves—big waves, too. Not like the ones round here."

Kempis nodded. He'd witnessed the same last night. "You sensed her open a portal?"

"No," Irlon said sharply. Then more hesitantly, "No. She didn't open a gateway, I'm certain of it. It was as if the gateway was already there, and she just tugged aside the veil concealing it. Does that make sense?"

Perfect sense, Kempis thought. Bright Eyes steps through a portal that wasn't there moments before, but which she didn't create, and transports herself far out to sea so she can swim all the way back to shore. What wasn't there to understand? "Have you seen her since three days ago?"

"Sure. She came by to check there were no hard feelings."

"You ain't gone looking for her?"

"I've had better things to do."

"Could you find her if you wanted to?"

"Maybe if I knocked on every door in Olaire—"

"You could keep an eye on the other Drifters," Loop cut in. "Follow the assassin to her hideout if she showed again."

"I could do," Irlon said. Then he jabbed a finger at Kempis. "Except *you* said I'd be free to go after I answered your questions."

"And I meant it. What about the other Drifters the assassin did for? You come across any of them since you bought it?"

"One or two."

"They see anything more of Bright Eyes than you?"

"Ask them yourself!"

Kempis looked at Loop. "Doesn't have to be the harbor where we throw that stone. I reckon here would do just as good—"

"Jilane saw nothing," Irlon interrupted. "But then the old man is as good as blind anyhow. Gordan caught a glimpse of the assassin's pigsticker—blackened steel, in case you're wondering. As for Rill"—he shrugged—"I've not had a chance to speak with him yet."

"Rill?" Kempis looked at Sniffer and Loop, and saw his confusion mirrored in their expressions. "Which one is Rill?"

"The Corinian. Does the Wharf District. Speaks with an accent as thick as he is."

The septia's mouth was dry. "When was he killed?"

"Half a bell ago, maybe."

"You said the Wharf District. Where, exactly?"

"Dell Street."

One of the alleys underwater, meaning Bright Eyes would have got her feet wet. And since Kempis hadn't sensed her using her power, she must have exited the sea on foot instead of doing another disappearing act. *Leaving a trail Sniffer can follow.*

The Untarian had already broken into a run along the alley. Kempis gave Irlon a wide berth as he set off after her. "Find Duffle," he called to Loop. "Sort us out some backup."

Loop's voice followed him. "What about this guy? What am I supposed to—"

"Keep him," the septia shouted back. "I may have more questions later."

Irlon wasn't impressed. Or at least Kempis assumed that was what his sudden screeching was about.

"Questions?" Loop said. "Like what?"

Like whether that stone-in-the-harbor idea would work, for starters.

From the shadows of an alley, Senar watched the entrance to the temple of the Lord of Hidden Faces. The shrine was a squat gray structure with a porch flanked by two statues of masked men, one with the legs of an alamandra, the other those of a flintcat. The ramp leading up to the porch was covered with debris from more figures that must have fallen from the roof of the temple—there were gaps in the ranks of statues atop the cornice. Weeds grew between the ramp's ebonystone slabs.

Senar had long harbored doubts concerning the identity of the Lord of Hidden Faces. Decades ago the immortal had risen from obscurity with none of the fireworks that usually accompanied the emergence of a new player in the pantheon. Then, a dozen years later, the god's cult had vanished as quickly as it had appeared, leaving behind only empty temples and unanswered questions. Even the name the Lord of Hidden Faces aroused suspicion, for what immortal needed to hide behind a mask? And just how many faces did the god have? It was as if the deity had been a front for some other power—a power that had abandoned it when it lost its novelty or purpose.

The cult of the Lord of Hidden Faces seemed to be going through a revival in Olaire, however, for at sundown scores of people had converged on the shrine. Untarians, for the most part, though Senar had seen mixed in with them as many different races as there were cities in the Sabian League.

And among the worshippers had been Mazana Creed and her champion, Greave.

After escorting the Storm Lady to her house this morning, Senar had been summarily dismissed. Suspecting something was afoot, he had kept a discreet eye on her home from a small park along the street. At midday he'd spotted her leaving with her dutia, Beauce, and he had followed them to the Commercial District, only to lose them in the crowds. Returning to the Storm Lady's house, he'd seen her reappear at the seventh bell, then head out again shortly afterward, this time with Greave in tow. Senar's curiosity had grown as he trailed them north into a run-down district with narrow streets lined by rows of dust-streaked buildings. Mazana evidently didn't want to be followed, for she and Greave would stop frequently in doorways or double back on themselves in an effort to shake off any pursuers. By reaching out with his Will, though, Senar was able to track them at an unobtrusive distance.

He was beginning to wish he hadn't. For almost two bells he'd waited outside the temple as the darkness deepened and the breeze blowing off the sea cooled to give some blessed relief from the heat. Night had fallen, and the worshippers had long since departed. Except for Mazana and Greave, that is. Had the Storm Lady come for a private audience? If so, what business did she have with the Lord of Hidden Faces? Somehow Senar couldn't see her bending the knee to anyone, mortal or immortal.

For a while longer the Guardian listened to the murmur of the sea and the shouts of dockhands working at the harbor to the southwest. *The harbor.* How simple it would be for him to steal away to the docks, or maybe to the Erin Elalese embassy he'd seen while trailing Mazana round the city. The ambassador might be able to hide him or even smuggle him off the island, but could Senar afford to trust him? Odds were the man would be Avallon's creature, and the Guardians had learned from experience to look for hidden blades in the hands of their kinsmen. Another charge Senar intended to make the emperor answer for when he returned to Erin Elal.

His leg muscles started to cramp. Why in the Nine Hells had he waited this long? Crass stupidity could not be ruled out, he supposed. Most likely Mazana had left by another exit or slipped away in the crowds. It was time to return to the palace, inform Imerle of Mazana's movements, and leave to *her* the task of puzzling over the Storm Lady's new spirituality. Certainly Senar wasn't going to discover any answers out here, and if he risked entering the temple then of course Mazana would choose that moment to appear. That was the way things worked, wasn't it?

Time to go.

Then he noticed movement amid the gloom of the temple's porch. He shrank back into the passage. A man appeared, hands on hips. There was no mistaking Greave's bulk, or the puffed sleeves of his shirt. He looked along the street, his gaze lingering on the alley where Senar sheltered.

A cloud passed in front of the moon, and blackness descended like a curtain.

Senar blinked against the dark. From along the street to his left came footfalls. A lone, gray-robed figure materialized from the shadows—a woman, judging by her height. Her hood was drawn up, and she kept her head down as she walked. An acolyte of the Lord of Hidden Faces? No, for she didn't turn on to the ramp leading to the temple. Instead she continued past the shrine and the entrance to Senar's alley. He lost sight of her behind the corner of the building to his right.

The moon reemerged, and the Guardian looked back at the porch.

Greave was standing where Senar had last seen him. On his cheek was the cut the Guardian had given him in their previous encounter. Even in the darkness Senar could tell he was smiling. Did Greave know he was being watched? There was no way he could see the Guardian in the gloom of the passage—unless he had a second pair of eyes . . .

A second pair of eyes! The hairs on the back of Senar's neck stood up. He looked over his shoulder, expecting trouble.

Nothing stirred.

He swung back to the porch in time to see another figure come out of the temple—Mazana. As she made to step past Greave, he lowered an arm to stop her. Senar heard the Storm Lady voice a question, and the champion growled a response. Mazana tried to step past him again, but again his arm blocked her. Senar frowned. Had Greave seen something the Guardian could not? With Senar's restricted view, the champion would be able to make out more of the street than the Guardian. Senar was tempted to surrender the cover of the shadows for a better look. If he did so, though, he risked giving away his position.

When Mazana next spoke, her voice held a note of irritation. Greave chuckled. *He senses me,* Senar thought. *But then why hasn't he called me out?* Greave's huge frame nearly filled the porch, all but obscuring the smaller figure of Mazana behind. She tried to push past him a third time, and for a moment Senar thought he would relent.

Then he seized the Storm Lady's wrist.

Another cloud passed in front of the moon, and darkness rushed in.

Senar muttered an oath. His senses strained to pick up whatever the champion had detected. The street remained deserted, but an assassin could easily be hiding out of Senar's sight in a doorway or alley. He looked up. The cloud obscuring the moon was dusted with silver. It floated slowly through the sky. *Come on, come on!* Senar thought he heard a sound from inside the porch, but it was lost beneath the cawing of a limewing. The noise came again—a scuff of a boot on stone, followed by a muffled gasp.

This had gone on long enough.

Senar left the cover of the alley, glancing all about. The buildings were silent and watchful. He halted at the foot of the ramp. The animal-legged statues reared up to either side of the porch, and it felt like inhuman eyes were staring at Senar from behind their stony masks. *Someone* was watching him, of that he was certain. Mazana and Greave? How was he going to explain his presence here? Just taking a walk, saw the shrine of a god he doubted even existed and thought he'd stop by to pay his respects?

Within the porch, the door leading into the temple was framed by threads of light, but the glow was not bright enough to illuminate Mazana or Greave. Then the moon came out, softening the darkness. Senar saw twisting shapes in the gloom, charcoal gray on black. A smothered cry reached him, cut short.

Understanding came to him.

Blood pounded behind his eyes, and he sprang up the ramp. Stone chippings crunched underfoot. Reaching the top, he saw the champion had forced Mazana back against the temple wall, his left hand pinning her right, his other hand lost in shadow. His mouth was pressed over hers. As she struggled to turn away, he released her right hand and seized her chin to hold her still. Mazana's free hand now pummeled his shoulder.

Senar increased his pace, heat rising to his cheeks.

He was a dozen steps away when Mazana brought her elbow thumping round into the champion's chest. Then she drove a heel into the back of his leg, and he dropped to his knees.

Just as Senar lashed out at him with his Will. Greave pitched backward. As he fell, he grabbed for Mazana's arm, half pulling her with him before the Storm Lady wrenched free and stumbled into darkness.

Senar moved to stand over the champion. He drew his sword and rested its tip against the man's throat. Greave held still, his gaze locked to Senar's. The Guardian's Will-blow had torn loose the stitches on his cheek, and blood now oozed from the wound. Senar was finding it hard to breathe. The urge to drive his blade through Greave's throat was strong, yet he held back. There was a line you didn't cross—even with men like the champion—and killing Greave now would have been the wrong side of it. In any case, it was not Senar's place to pass judgment here; that responsibility was Mazana's. He looked at her for direction, but she remained motionless, a silent shadow in the porch.

"Mazana?"

No reply.

Greave's lips curled back. He shuffled backward out of range of

Senar's sword. Pushing himself to his feet, he stood with his back to the temple door. Then he hawked and spat at the Guardian's feet. His hand hovered over the hilt of his blade. "Well, well, look what the wind blew in."

Senar did not respond. His Will was still bunched up inside him, but his grip on it was slipping. Anger could spoil your concentration if it was strong enough. This was different, though. Some form of deadening sorcery was seeping from the shrine's walls, making it difficult for Senar to focus his power. He took a half step back to take him away from the magic's influence. Greave must have thought he did so out of fear, for he laughed. For an instant Senar believed—even hoped—the champion would challenge him. Instead Greave moved his hand away from his sword hilt and held his arms wide to show he meant no threat. A mocking bow to Mazana, then he strode past Senar, his shoulder brushing the Guardian's as he did so.

"Later, pretty boy."

Senar watched him walk down the temple's ramp and head toward the alley where the Guardian had hidden. As darkness claimed him, Senar tried to shake off the feeling he would one day come to regret not killing him when he had the chance.

One day? Hells, he was regretting it already.

He sheathed his sword and turned to Mazana. Her back was pressed to the temple wall. Senar could make out the shape of her nose and mouth, but her expression was concealed in shadow. Her breathing was ragged.

He took a pace forward.

"Stay away from me," the Storm Lady said.

Senar drew up.

"I didn't need your help! I don't need any of you! Soon, soon you will see . . ."

That would need considering later, but for now Senar couldn't think past the tremor in her voice. He stepped in and took her in his arms. Her arms remained by her sides, but after a moment she tilted her head the merest fraction so her cheek came to rest on his chest.

Maybe it was the ring on the little finger of Senar's right hand pressing into Mazana's back, or maybe it was the Storm Lady's hair stained black by the gloom, but suddenly it was not Mazana he was holding, but Jessca. They were standing atop one of the Sacrosanct's towers in Arkarbour, staring out across the wide emptiness of the night and listening to the Gamala Clock Tower ring the tenth bell. Even two days after the attack on the Black Tower, ripples of magic still illuminated the sky over the building, and sorcerous fires raged through its upper levels.

He released Mazana at the same time as she pushed him away. The shadows were bruises beneath her eyes. "You followed me here?" she said. Her voice was empty.

"Yes."

"Because the emira told you to watch me?"

He nodded.

A pause. "Then you will have lots to tell her when you make your next report."

"I will escort you home."

"I can find my own way."

"Nevertheless. After Gensu . . ." He offered her his right arm, and she hesitated before taking it.

They started down the ramp.

The thrum of a crossbow string was Senar's only warning. He didn't see the quarrel, only heard it rip through the air. It came from the right—Mazana's side. Senar threw up a Will-barrier even as he pulled the Storm Lady round to shield her with his body, knowing it was too late.

Tensing himself, he waited for Mazana's cry or the punch of a quarrel in his back.

From a few streets ahead of Kempis, a shout shattered the stillness of the night. Bright Eyes's work? It had to be.

Quarter of a bell ago the septia had arrived in Dell Street with Sniffer to find the body of the Drifter, Rill, being picked clean by a gang of urchins. According to Sniffer, Bright Eyes had exited the sea at the junction with Yew Lane, and the assassin's trail was still strong enough for the Untarian to follow. Her steps led north across the city, past the Sanctorium and the Artisan Quarter, until coming finally to the Temple District on the west-facing slopes of Kalin's Hill.

Now, as a second shout sounded, Kempis found himself running through Olaire's streets once more.

———

Senar felt the crossbow bolt strike his Will-shield and deflect away. Drawing his sword, he pushed Mazana behind him and turned toward where the crossbow had been fired from. He expected to see Greave advancing. Instead, a woman clothed in gray—the one he'd mistaken for an acolyte earlier?—detached herself from the shadows of a doorway. Her eyes glowed with a smoky blue light.

She drew two longknives. Then she surged forward, angling her blades to flash moonlight into Senar's eyes.

He sprang to meet her.

Kempis turned into Princes Street to see a man and a woman battling on the ramp outside the temple of the Lord of Hidden Faces. There was no mistaking the assassin with her luminous blue eyes. Her long blond hair hung in a plait down her back, and she wielded two longknives in a blur of glittering steel. Her opponent was a black-haired man with skin so pale it marked him as a stranger to Olaire. Not a Drifter, clearly. So why in the Sender's name had Bright Eyes picked a fight with him?

People had gathered in the street to watch the duel, but they melted away as Kempis and Sniffer approached. All except for one figure standing at the foot of the ramp. The septia's face twisted. Mazana Creed. So Bright Eyes had gone after one of the Storm Lords, had she? *Just as Dutia Elemy Meddes had predicted.* Were the deaths of the Drifters so much smoke, then, to conceal the assassin's true targets? No, that made no sense. Why risk putting the Storm Lords on alert by killing the Drifters first? Why not go straight for the big game? Kempis thought back on his meeting with Elemy two days ago. The old man knew something—something he hadn't seen fit to share with the septia. Perhaps a night in the cells would loosen his tongue, especially if he was sharing that cell with Bright Eyes. It was almost worth doing just to see the look on Hilaire's face when she found out.

Kempis drew up a handful of paces from Mazana. Her attention seemed to be fixed on the duelists, yet her eyes were glazed as if she was staring not *at* the fighters but *through* them. She was in shock—still reeling, no doubt, from the realization there were people in the world who didn't love her as much as she loved herself. The pale-skinned man must be her bodyguard, but the Storm Lady appeared in no hurry to go to his aid. *Not that the bastard needs it,* Kempis thought as he watched the swordsman counter a series of cuts and thrusts with precise, unhurried strokes.

Then the man went on the attack. A lunge at Bright Eyes's chest was only half parried, and the bodyguard's sword scored a hit to her right side. He followed up with a backhand slash. When the assassin lifted her left blade to block, it struck an invisible sorcerous barrier, leaving the man's weapon unimpeded as it flashed for her neck. Somehow Bright Eyes managed to duck beneath it before stepping back and raising her guard in time to meet her assailant's next swing. Parrying frantically, she was driven backward up the ramp.

Kempis considered. If he went to the bodyguard's aid, he would probably be more hindrance than help. And yet, if Bright Eyes landed a lucky strike and Hilaire found out he'd just stood by and let it happen . . .

The septia drew his sword.

Bright Eyes leapt back and hurled one of her longknives at the bodyguard. He batted it aside with his blade, but the assassin used the moment's respite to dive off the edge of the ramp. Rolling on the flagstones below, she came up running and set off along Princes Street. Kempis looked at Mazana's bodyguard, expecting him to follow.

The man held his ground.

Cursing, the septia lurched after the woman.

Every muscle in his body ached from yesterday's dash across Olaire, and his legs felt so heavy he might have been wading through water. If Bright Eyes meant to lead him on another chase, he had no hope of keeping up. Then suddenly he noticed she was limping, her left hand clutching her thigh on that side.

The septia slowed. There was only one thing worse than trailing Bright Eyes across Olaire, and that was catching up to her. For having seen her in action against Mazana's bodyguard, Kempis knew he was outmatched, even with Sniffer behind him. He didn't need to fight the assassin, though; all he had to do was keep her in his sights while he waited for reinforcements to arrive. At the pace she was going, she'd have half the Watch for company by the time she reached the Shallows.

Just then power rippled outward from Bright Eyes. A portal opened before her with a sound like snapping sailcloth. The buildings ahead and to either side of the street were overlain by the shadowy image of a boundless gray plain broken only by a circle of standing stones.

In the sky were two small blue moons that bathed the landscape in a ghostly glow. Bright Eyes hesitated on the portal's threshold before stepping through. Her form lost focus.

Kempis ground his teeth together. And to think he'd believed she could only do her disappearing act in the Shallows. Damn the woman, she wasn't playing fair! A heartbeat ago he'd thought she was done for. Now he'd have another near miss to explain to Hilaire. He didn't even have a spear this time to speed her on her way—

With a start, he realized he was just a few paces from the portal and in danger of following Bright Eyes through. He tried to draw up, only for his left boot to catch on a raised flagstone. He sprawled to the ground and rolled forward before coming to rest on his stomach.

He froze.

Mist clung to his eyes. Bright Eyes stood a handful of paces away. Looming all about her were Olaire's spectral buildings, but Kempis suspected she wasn't seeing them because she was peering across the plain at a range of mountains the septia hadn't noticed before. The overlapping images made his head swim. Sheets of dust blew over him. He lifted a hand to shield his eyes, only to discover he could feel neither the grit nor the wind that stirred it. And yet the crash of waves against the Olairian cliffs was still audible.

Kempis struggled to order his thoughts. Had he passed through the portal or hadn't he? Beneath him he felt the reassuring solidity of flagstones, but he could barely see those stones for swirling dust. Had he fallen on the gateway's threshold? Was he straddling two worlds, his body as much in Olaire as it was in whatever place the portal had opened onto?

He wasn't hanging around to find out. While the portal remained open he still had a chance of returning to the city, and he began rolling back the way he had come.

Before he'd completed his first revolution, though, the mist about him thickened to the consistency of the winter fogs that swept in from the Sabian Sea at the turn of each year. Another snap of air sounded, loud enough to make Kempis's ears pop.

Then the mist and the plains and the mountains vanished, and the septia was back among Olaire's shadow-clad buildings.

Breathing hard, he stared up at the sky—a sky lit by just one moon, not two. What in the Nine Hells had just happened? He hadn't got clear of the mist when the portal shut, so how had he made it back to

Olaire? More important, where had Bright Eyes transported herself to? Yesterday when she'd vanished in the Shallows, Kempis had seen waves beyond the gateway. If the assassin could choose where the portal took her, why had she paused on the threshold just now as if she were unsure whether to pass through? If the place with the two moons didn't suit her, why open a gateway to it? Why not choose another destination she liked better?

Kempis felt a ripple of power to his left—an echo of the portal's closing, perhaps? He clambered upright. Looking round, he saw Mazana's bodyguard had descended the ramp to join the Storm Lady. The bastard wasn't even out of breath. It would be unreasonable, Kempis knew, to berate him for not chasing Bright Eyes, because in doing so he would have left Mazana at the mercy of any other assassins skulking in the shadows.

Kempis, though, was in no mood to be reasonable.

He made his way back to the ramp.

Mazana did not spare him a look. That suited the septia fine, though, if it meant he could give her yes-man the once-over. Standing half a head shorter than Kempis, the bodyguard wore an expression that told the septia his interruption was unwelcome. With his fine-boned, almost feminine, features and immaculately tailored clothes, he looked more like a courtier than a swordsman.

"You let her get away," Kempis said.

The bodyguard shrugged. "The woman will be dead soon, anyhow. I caught a glimpse of the world beyond the portal. Two blue moons, correct? It seems your friend has wandered into the Shades, third of the Nine Hells."

"So?"

"So the Kerralai demons that live there do not look kindly on unwanted visitors. They will hunt the woman down and kill her, no matter where she flees to or how long it takes."

"Well, if they're hunting her, they're doing a worse job of it than even I am. This ain't the first time she's done her disappearing act. And there ain't been so much of a sniff of a demon since."

"Was it here? That she last jumped between worlds, I mean."

"Does it matter?"

The bodyguard looked at Mazana Creed, perhaps hoping she would step in to end Kempis's questioning. The Storm Lady, however, would not meet the man's gaze. There was something here Kempis was missing—something important, since he'd never known a blueblood woman to keep her mouth shut for so long. While Mazana's silence lasted, though, he'd take it as permission to carry on quizzing her yes-man.

"I asked you a question," he said.

The swordsman was a long time in answering. "Are you familiar with how portals are created—the idea that the release of strong magic can burn a path through to wherever the sorcerer gets his power from?"

"Maybe if you spoke real slow."

Senar sighed. "When a mage draws on the power of another world, he draws that world closer to his own. If the power unleashed is great enough, the two worlds will overlap, creating a gateway between them. Some people—your assassin among them—are able to jump between those worlds before the connection is strong enough to form a portal."

Kempis was silent, thinking. If what the bodyguard said was true, it meant the gateway Bright Eyes had fashioned here—insofar as it existed at all—was one that only she could use. Which in turn explained why Kempis hadn't followed her through. It also explained why the assassin couldn't jump between worlds whenever she liked, and why the portals here and outside the brothel opened on to different places.

It didn't explain, though, how Mazana's bodyguard knew so much about this business. "You crossed paths with Bright Eyes before?"

"No."

"One of her kind, then."

The swordsman nodded. "A Kalanese man. Fifth campaign—"

"You're from Erin Elal?"

He held out his right hand. "Senar Sol."

Kempis didn't shake it. *A Guardian.* He'd forgotten how much he hated Dragon Day. Ships had been arriving in Olaire for the past week, bringing with them nothing but trouble from the Sabian League and beyond. Mazana Creed's crowd in particular was said to be a regular freak show, and this Senar Sol was certainly living up to his billing. True, he didn't have the arrogant air of most bluebloods, but Kempis wasn't fooled by the polite words and extended hand. The more courteous a blueblood was, the more likely he had something to hide.

"This Kanalese—" Kempis began.

"Kalanese," Senar corrected him.

"How did you catch him?"

The Guardian withdrew his hand. "We didn't." He gestured to where Bright Eyes had vanished. "Like your friend here, I suspect he traveled blind through a portal he hadn't used before and found himself . . . out of his depth."

Out of his depth? Was that aimed at Kempis? *Showing his true colors at last.* "You're saying Bright Eyes didn't know where she'd end up when she opened the gateway?"

"Either that or she didn't know what greeting Kerralai demons extend to uninvited guests."

"Imagine that."

Sniffer had crossed to the doorway of a house fronting the temple and now returned with a small crossbow. Over the wooden stock were plates of tarnica engraved with writhing wither snakes. "This the assassin's?" she asked Senar.

The Guardian shrugged, then looked at Kempis. "Now, if you'll excuse me, much though I've enjoyed our conversation—"

"I ain't finished with you yet."

Senar seemed unsure whether to be amused or insulted. "I must have missed your name."

"Careless of you. How many of these crossover points are there going to be in Olaire?"

"Your guess is as good as mine."

"Then how's the woman going to get back to the city?"

"The same way she left."

Kempis started. "Hang on, you mean we've just got to wait here till she shows her face again?"

"It's too late for that. You did not sense the second burst of power when you were lying on the ground?"

The septia stared at him.

"The point at which worlds overlap will cover an area greater than this road. When the assassin came back, she must have returned a street or so away from here, out of sight behind a building."

"And you didn't think to warn me sooner?"

Senar looked like he might finally be running out of patience. But gods, Kempis had had to work hard for it. "You must forgive me," the

Guardian said. "I was unaware until now of the depths of your ignorance."

"You mean there's something you don't know?"

The ninth bell roused Mazana Creed from her reverie, and she looked at Kempis as if seeing him for the first time. He braced himself for a tongue-lashing, but instead the Storm Lady said to Senar, "Let's go," before spinning on her heel and making her way along Princes Street in the direction Bright Eyes had taken. The Guardian inclined his head to Kempis, then set off in pursuit.

Sniffer whistled through her gills. "Nicely done, sir," she said. "You ever thought of becoming a diplomat when you hand in your stripes?"

"Damned blueblood," Kempis grumbled. "He's hiding something. They all are."

"Well, if he thinks of anything he's missed, I'm sure he'll now be beating a path to your door."

CHAPTER 9

ENAR WAS beginning to regret escorting Mazana to the palace to inform the emira of the assassination attempt. The Storm Lady had been silent during their walk through the city, but her old spark was now returning as she recounted to Imerle in colorful terms Senar's encounter with the assassin—leaving out any mention of Greave and the Lord of Hidden Faces, of course.

"So you see," the Storm Lady said, "were it not for Senar's intervention you would have been forever deprived of the pleasure of my company."

The emira occupied her usual throne. Her gaze bored into Senar. Beside her sat the chief minister, his expression as sour as sandfruit juice.

Mazana twisted the knife a little deeper. "I am touched you were so concerned about my safety that you thought to send Senar to watch over me."

Imerle let the silence fester. "Anything you'd care to add to that, Guardian?" she said finally in precisely the same tone that she might have said, "Any last words?"

Senar cleared his throat before repeating what he'd told the belligerent Watchman about the assassin's abilities. It wasn't the answer the emira had been looking for, but then he suspected there wasn't any answer that would have satisfied her.

Imerle closed her eyes as she listened. "If the assassin did indeed pass through to the Shades," she said when he finished, "we had best hope she does not stay long in Olaire—or that she leaves again promptly when the demon tracks her here. It is a pity that we did not get an opportunity to speak to her."

Mazana said, "To wish her better luck next time, you mean?"

"We mean, to find out who sent her."

"Oh, I agree. It can be no coincidence, surely, that an assassin should strike at me so soon after Gensu's death. Perhaps the attempt on my life is linked to these mysterious summonses. Perhaps someone wanted all of the Storm Lords in the same place so we could be picked off one at a time." She gave Imerle a pointed look. "I would have been particularly interested to hear why, of those in Olaire, the assassin chose to target me first."

Pernay clasped his trembling hands together. "Hardly first. Almost a dozen water-mages have been killed in the city over the past few days."

"Really? And you didn't think to warn me?"

Senar's gaze flickered to Mazana. Her indignation was feigned, he knew, for even the Guardian had heard about the wave of assassinations sweeping the Shallows.

Pernay licked his lips. "There was no reason to think the Storm Lords would be targeted."

"Not even after Gensu's death? Thane and Cauroy should be informed."

"Mazana is correct, of course," Imerle said. "And we are grateful to her for bringing this matter to our attention so promptly." Her eyes opened to reveal flames in their depths. "Just one thing puzzles us. The assassin attacked you half a bell ago, you say? Whatever were you doing wandering around the city at this time of night?"

Before the Storm Lady could respond, footfalls came from the underwater passage. Senar turned to see two figures enter the throne room. The first was the Storm Guard officer who had escorted him to the roof terrace two days ago. The second was an old woman with rheumy eyes and the suggestion of a mustache on her top lip. She wore a white robe, and there was an ink smudge on the right side of her nose. Her mouth hung open as she looked about the chamber, and Senar realized he'd stopped noticing the walls of black water around him.

"Emira," the Storm Guard said, bowing. "Mistress Darbonna of the Founder's Citadel," he introduced the old woman.

Darbonna cocked her head. "What's that?"

"I said, Mistress Darbonna of the Founder's Citadel."

"Yes," she said, nodding. "I am she."

The Storm Guard muttered something, then inclined his head a second time to Imerle before spinning on his heel and retreating. The old woman watched him go with a puzzled expression.

Mention of the Founder's Citadel had made Senar stand straighter. The building bore an unsettling resemblance to certain other fortresses he'd encountered on his travels. Built by the titans, it was said. Senar didn't know if that was true, but what he *did* know was that people had a habit of going missing in them—and that they were the source of only bad memories for him personally, not least that time in Karalat two years ago.

And this woman, Darbonna, lived there?

The chief minister spoke. "Mistress Darbonna."

Darbonna was still staring after the Storm Guard.

"Mistress Darbonna!"

"What's that?" the old woman said, turning. She seemed to remember suddenly what company she was in, for she attempted a curtsy. As she struggled to straighten afterward, Senar offered her an arm. "Bless you, my dear," she said as she took it.

Pernay rose from his throne. "Mistress Darbonna, I am Chief Minister Pernay Ord. We are grateful to you for coming at so late an hour."

"Oh, think nothing of it. In truth I had expected your summons much sooner. You are curious, no doubt, to know what I and my associates have been getting up to these past few months."

A pause. Even Senar watched her closely.

"What you've been getting up to?" Pernay said.

"Yes, indeed. Work on the library continues apace. There is much still to do, of course, for while every scroll has been logged, and many translated—"

"You misunderstand."

"—just last week all six of Abologog's Treatises on Reverence were found in a chest washed up on—"

The chief minister held up a hand. "You misunderstand," he said again. "We did not call you here to talk about the library. We wish to discuss the quake."

Darbonna's eyes brightened. "Cake?" she said, looking round. "Most kind."

"Quake, I said! You must have felt the tremors yesterday."

"Oh, the tremors," the old woman said, her face falling. "I should not worry about those. True, they are becoming stronger, but as yet the citadel has suffered no ill effects." She frowned. "Though Master Barlaby did have an unfortunate fall—"

"We are more concerned with what the tremors are doing to the rest of the city."

Darbonna waved away the fate of thousands with a casual hand. "Oh, I rarely leave the citadel. So much work to do, yet so little time to do it in. Even I cannot go on forever, aha." This last was an attempt at humor, Senar realized. Darbonna shot him an expectant look, and he forced a smile. Entertaining though it was to see the chief minister struggle with the old woman, Senar was too busy readying himself for his imminent showdown with Imerle to appreciate it.

Pernay said, "From where in the citadel do the tremors originate?"

"What's that?"

"The tremors! Where do they come from?"

"I really couldn't say. There are leagues of passages, you understand, and thousands of chambers. My assistants have explored only a fraction of them." Her look became thoughtful. "Although . . ."

"Yes?"

"In the East Wing there is a ramp that leads down to a lower level. The way is blocked by a sorcerous barrier." She looked at the faces about her. "These are earth tremors, are they not? Perhaps something under the fortress is causing them."

Mazana snorted. "Yes, perhaps there is a titan blundering about in the basement. Maybe we should call down and ask him to stand still."

Senar suspected he was the only one to see Darbonna's eyes narrow in response to the Storm Lady's words.

"Whatever the cause," Pernay said, "it needs to be investigated."

"I'd have thought," Mazana said, "we have more immediate things to worry about. Earlier today I was speaking to our irascible Master of Coin, and he told me of a rumor of the treasury borrowing from merchants in Olaire—perhaps to finance the payouts to mysterious owners of mysterious disappearing ships that Thane told us about."

"We have already discussed Thane's groundless—"

"As I recall, the issue was just put to one side after Gensu's death. Perhaps now is the time for a meeting of the full Storm Council to discuss these matters." A twinkle in Mazana's eye made it clear she believed Imerle had something to hide.

The emira exchanged a look with Pernay, and Senar wondered at the strength of their bond that they seemed able to communicate with a mere glance. The chief minister's slow smile suggested Mazana was about to regret goading Imerle.

"Mazana," the emira said, "maybe you should investigate this ramp."

The Storm Lady stared at her. "Me?"

"It was you who suggested Jambar speak to us about the tremors, wasn't it? Clearly you thought them a cause for concern."

"In case you had forgotten, Imerle, tomorrow is Dragon Day. The Gate rises at the ninth bell—"

"Then you'd best make an early start. We are sure Mistress Darbonna would be delighted to show you around the citadel."

"What's that?"

"Imerle—" Mazana began.

The emira spoke over her. "Chief Minister, perhaps you would arrange a suitable escort for the Storm Lady."

"At once," Pernay said, already striding toward the underwater passage.

"I hardly think—" Mazana tried again.

"Guardian," Imerle said, looking at Senar, "would you stay with us." Then to the Storm Lady, "Don't let us keep you."

Senar couldn't see Mazana's expression, but he sensed her anger in the pause that followed the emira's words, then in the clicking of her heels as she retreated from the chamber. Darbonna glanced from one woman to the other, her look bemused. She made to speak before appearing to think better of it. She shuffled after Mazana.

Their footfalls faded.

Imerle's mouth was a thin line as she regarded Senar. The flames in her eyes had not subsided. "Tell us again what happened this evening," she said at last.

The Guardian took a breath. Now was the time, he knew, to fill in the gaps Mazana had left in her account. Something made him hold back, though. He found himself questioning his hesitation. Why should he protect Mazana's secrets? Earlier he'd saved her life, and she'd repaid him by dropping him in the brown stuff from a great height. And while the emira had done nothing to earn his loyalty, the same was true of the Storm Lady. Admittedly there was a certain vulnerability in Mazana he felt drawn to, but that just made it more important that he maintain his distance. His concern here was not to commit himself to either woman, but rather to keep his head down until he could return to Erin Elal.

He could only hope that by refusing to choose sides he didn't make himself an enemy of both.

In response to Imerle's words he shrugged. "What more do you wish to know?"

"You can start by answering the question Mazana did not. What was she doing out at this time of night?"

There was nothing to be gained by withholding the truth, since the belligerent Watchman would be reporting to the emira soon enough. "She was visiting the temple of the Lord of Hidden Faces."

"You followed her to the shrine but did not enter?"

"Correct."

"And the assassin attacked as she came out?"

The Guardian nodded.

"Then why," Imerle said, articulating each word clearly, "did you intervene?"

Senar did not respond. In his world, you didn't need a reason to help someone against an assassin. Unless you were the assassin, of course—and that had been Senar's job on more occasions than he cared to remember: that Falcon krel in Pagan; the Arapian sacristen; a dozen minor lordlings in the estates around Kal Kartin. But killing in cold blood was something he'd always done with a sense of regret, and never to further his own ends. As a Guardian you didn't get to choose what missions you were given. And Senar trusted the Council to know when a death was necessary, even if he didn't agree with their judgment.

Not the emira, though. He would not kill for her, whatever was at stake.

His skin prickled, and he looked at the executioner. As ever the giant was staring at some point in the distance. It just so happened, though, that that point was now between Senar's eyes. Was saving Mazana's life about to cost the Guardian his own? He looked back at the emira. "You told me to watch her."

"That is right, we told you to *watch* her."

"Was the assassin yours?" he asked to buy time.

"Did you stop to consider she might have been?"

"If that were the case, I'd like to think you would have warned me beforehand."

"And if we *had* warned you?"

Senar drew himself up to his full height. For what that was worth. "My sword is yours, Emira," he said. He spoke the words with as much conviction as he could muster, yet they sounded hollow even to his own ears. The lines about Imerle's eyes tightened, and the Guardian wondered again what Jambar had seen in his future that could make her overlook her obvious mistrust of him. The shaman would not want to tell him, of course, but if Senar made it out of here alive he would track down the old man and shake him until he rattled like that bag of bones of his.

The emira broke the silence. "Perhaps you should go with Mazana to the citadel."

So he could have the same accident she did? "As you command."

Imerle closed her eyes once more, and for a while the only sound was the hiss of waves breaking against the seawall. Senar was beginning to think he was dismissed when she spoke again. "*This* assassin was not ours, Guardian."

But the next one might be—was that what she was saying?

Senar studied her, then nodded. "I understand."

The buzz of the crowds grew louder as Karmel swam round the cliff toward the Dragon Gate. When she entered the Cappel Strait a wave of feverish noise rolled over her. The gate was a stone's throw to the south, and through its links she could make out the Dianese and Natillian terraces bathed in torchlight. Midway between the two cities a wooden platform invested with air-magic hovered high above the sea. On it, Veran had told her, a champion brawler from each of Dian and Natilly would be battling to pitch his opponent over the edge and into the dragon-infested waters below. The fight had been going on since Karmel set out from the boat, yet a resolution still seemed some way off. For while the priestess could see nothing of the combatants from her vantage point, she could hear their seesawing fortunes in the alternating cheers and groans of their supporters.

Karmel's hand brushed something as she swam, but it was only a sandal floating on the greasy waves. The strait smelled as foul as an open grave, yet that wasn't surprising considering how many bodies the priestess had spied in the water during her swim. Victims of too much revelry, no doubt. Beyond the gate there was no sign of the dragons that had whipped the channel to froth this morning, but they would be out there somewhere, she knew, waiting to claim whichever fighter fell from the platform. And while the priestess kept reminding herself the creatures were on the *other* side of the gate, still she found herself expecting the sea in front of her to erupt as one of the beasts rose from the depths.

Suppressing a shudder, she quickened her pace.

Ahead Veran pulled himself through the water with powerful strokes, staying close to the cliff to lessen the chance of being seen from above. When he reached the gate his shadow seemed to dissolve into the rock face. Karmel blinked, then remembered the groove in the cliff he'd told her about. Three more strokes and she saw it—a vertical indentation perhaps two armspans wide and as many deep. Within the recess Veran had hauled himself onto the lowest of the gate's horizontal bars. As Karmel drew near he offered her a hand, but she did not take it, for at that instant a collective gasp had escaped the people on the terraces. Curious, she looked south.

In time to see a figure fall from the platform. No, two figures, she realized: one short and thick-necked and naked but for a loincloth, the other tall and long-haired and wearing silver bands round his wrists and ankles. It seemed the result of the contest would be a draw, though Karmel doubted the two fighters would get a chance at a rematch.

The fools were still grappling as they hit the water.

Veran growled something at the priestess. She ignored him. What would happen if one of the champions swam to the gate and saw her? The dragons would have been alerted to their tumble by the splash, but the men were only fifty armspans from the portcullis. Surely one of them . . .

Her thoughts trailed off as a vast shadow materialized from the darkness at the end of the strait—a shadow that burst into golden light as it entered the waterway and caught the glow of the torches on the terraces. The dragon glided forward, silent as moonlight yet swift as a landslide, and Karmel watched transfixed as jets of water spurted from its nostrils to strike one of the champions where he'd surfaced. The man had time only to voice a strangled cry before he was plucked from the sea.

Crunch, crunch.

Another growl from Veran. This one had a note of warning in it, and Karmel noticed rushing toward her a wave of water displaced by the dragon's coming. It would be on her in moments. She cursed and twisted round, snatched for her companion's hand.

Missed.

Veran, though, did not. His fingers closed round her wrist like bands of iron, and he heaved her into the recess just as the wave came hissing through the gate's links. She collided with the priest before slumping down to sit astride the rusty bar on which he stood. A groan escaped her lips. Her arm felt as if it had been wrenched from its socket, yet she'd escaped lightly, she knew. Another heartbeat and she would have been swept by the wave along the strait and into the Sabian Sea. She could feel Veran's glare on her back, but she did not turn to look at him. Instead she massaged her shoulder and listened to the clink of bottles bobbing on the sea outside the recess.

A second shriek sounded from the strait, quickly cut off.

A grunt from Veran brought Karmel's head round. Evidently he was keen to make a start on climbing the gate because he had un-slung a length of rope from his shoulder and was coiling one end to form a noose. The distance between the horizontal bars of the port-cullis was such that he could not simply reach up and grab the link above. But the end of each crosspiece stood out from the gate, allow-ing him to cast his noose up and over the bar immediately overhead. That done, he tugged on the rope to secure it before shimmying up like a deckhand up a ship's rigging. Karmel watched him repeat the maneuver once, twice, three times.

He vanished from sight into the gloom above.

And not so much as a word of farewell, either.

She leaned back against the cliff to wait.

The recess was as cool as a cave. Karmel's wet clothes were plas-tered to her body, and she moved her hands along her arms to rub some warmth into them. Then she stood up. It would take Veran half a bell of muscle-numbing toil to make the ascent, but after a day spent prowling their basement lodgings, Karmel would happily have ex-changed his role for hers. If there'd been room to pace in the recess she would have done so. Instead she had to settle for rocking backward and forward on her feet. Why could she not stay still?

There was a splashing sound, and she stiffened. It came from the south—the dragons' side of the gate. Looking out of the recess, Karmel saw the golden-scaled beast swim close to the portcullis and dip its snout into the sea. When its head next rose, its luminous eyes seemed to fix on Karmel's position. She drew back. There was no way the creature could see her in the recess, and even if it did it wouldn't be able to get to her. If it came sniffing round, though, might it attract the attention of someone on the terraces?

The priestess waited, senses straining for the ripple of water or the rustle of scales that would signal the dragon's approach.

After a hundred heartbeats she risked another look out.

The dragon had retreated to the cliff below Natilly and was now rubbing the top of its head against the rock face.

Just then a fizzing crackle sounded, and a curtain of fire roared into life in the sky to the south, momentarily blinding Karmel with its flash. When her vision cleared she saw flames coalescing over the Ribbon Sea to form an image of ships on a turbulent swell. She realized she was about to witness a sorcerous reenactment of last year's Dragon Hunt. There was the fiery Dragon Gate, its lower half streaming water as it lifted clear of the waves. Beneath it kindled a spark that grew in size to become a dragon. Wreathed in flames, the creature hurtled like a comet toward the waiting ships. A hail of arrows and spears arced out to meet it, only to deflect off the beast's armor.

Karmel's skin tingled as she watched the drama unfold. What with the cold and the wet, she'd managed to forget that tomorrow was Dragon Day. Earlier Veran had wearied her ears with his endless retellings of the plan to reach the control room—or, at least, those parts of the plan he'd confided in her. As Karmel had expected, he'd kept his pack with him at all times to ensure she couldn't look at what he'd brought to disable the capstan. With little else to occupy her mind, the priestess had spent much of the day thinking on what his secret might be, but the riddle had defeated her. If that secret had been cause for alarm, though, wouldn't Caval have told her about it in Olaire?

Like he told you about the plan to climb the Dragon Gate?

A memory stirred of her brother's remoteness when they'd parted on the beach. A distance had grown between them of late—a distance that had first opened when Caval was made high priest at a secret meeting of the temple's elite last summer. The events of that day remained fresh in Karmel's mind. Her brother had come to her to break the news of his accession, and they'd walked arm in arm to their father's quarters to tell him of his ousting. Afterward Caval had wept, and Karmel had held him until the sobs subsided. It was the only time she'd ever seen him cry. Even after the beatings he'd taken from their father, it had always been Caval consoling her. Looking back, she'd hoped that by gaining some measure of revenge over their father, Caval might have exorcised the ghosts of his past. If anything, though, his gaze had grown more haunted than ever.

Then came the contest to become Honorary Blade. When Vallans had died, Caval had defended Karmel against the people who'd said she had killed him on purpose. Afterward, though, they had argued. Karmel had said things she regretted. As tempers rose, Caval had raised his hand like he meant to slap her. For an instant it had seemed to Karmel as if she were looking not at her brother, but her father. The episode had sent Caval into a despair from which it had taken him days to surface. After that he'd avoided Karmel for a while. He had hidden from her—or so it had felt.

And she had started to hear stories about him. Stories she'd refused to believe.

The sky flashed red, and Karmel glanced up to see the sorcerous dragon attack a Corinian vessel with orange-trimmed sails. A flick of the creature's tail shattered the forecastle—

Something struck the priestess on her right shoulder. She flinched, almost slipped into the sea. It took her a moment to make out Veran's blackened rope swinging in the shadows of the recess.

So much for the climb taking him half a bell.

Holding a hand out to the cliff for balance, she pushed herself to her feet. As Veran had done before her, she tugged on the rope to check it was secure. A look up revealed only dizzying blackness.

She began to climb, trying not to think about what awaited her at the top.

Nothing ever went to plan, Karmel thought as she huddled on the Dragon Gate.

Things had started well enough after Veran's rope fell on her: the

ascent to join the priest just below the battlements had passed un-
eventfully; the changeover of the Dianese guards had taken place at
the fourth bell, as expected; the Chameleons had even had a slice of
luck with the genders of the new soldiers—a man and a woman judging by the voices floating down from the ramparts. The problem was
that those guards, since beginning their watch over a bell ago, hadn't
strayed more than a dozen steps from the door to the control room.
And until they moved along the battlements—and thus away from the
Chameleons' position next to the cliff—Veran had no hope of scaling
the parapet undetected.

Dawn was still far off, but the Chameleons were running out of
time to silence the soldiers, relieve them of their uniforms, and take
their places on the battlements. At this rate Karmel might still be
waiting on the gate when the crowds started gathering for the Dragon
Hunt, and what was she going to say when they asked her why she'd
climbed up here? That she'd done it for the view?

Alongside the priestess Veran stood motionless on one of the gate's
links. His eyes were closed, his bearing relaxed, but Karmel could
read his unease in the ever-deepening furrows across his brow. To
the south the terraces below Dian and Natilly were empty of people,
and the torches affixed to the cliffs had been extinguished to leave
the strait veiled in darkness. In spite of the gloom Karmel felt exposed on the gate with the wind threatening to tug her from her perch.
Above and to her right the edges of the battlements were stained red
from the fires in the dragon's skull, and she could hear the crackle of
fluttering flames. Then over that came the voice of the male Dianese
guard—Clemin, she'd heard him called. He was describing to his
female companion how a prisoner thrown to the dragons had been
seized by two creatures and torn apart in the ensuing tug of war.
Clemin gave a raucous chuckle.

One of those where you had to have been there, obviously.

Veran's voice in Karmel's ear startled her. "Stay here," he murmured. "I'm going to cross to the middle of the gate and climb there."

Cross to the middle? And surrender the cover of the deeper shadows near the cliff? Okay, so the Dianese guards on the battlements
wouldn't be able to see him make the traverse, but what if someone
had lingered on the terraces and saw him inching through the blackness?

It seemed Veran wasn't interested in Karmel's opinion, though, for he'd already begun making his way across the gate, wrapping his arms about each vertical link before placing a foot on the other side and swinging round. It wasn't until he'd passed out of whispering range that Karmel realized they hadn't discussed what to do if he was spotted. Should she climb up and attack the Dianese soldiers? What would be the point? Even if she could silence the two guards before they called for help, there would still be their Natillian counterparts to consider. And since there'd be no getting into the control room if the alarm was raised . . .

We only get one chance at this.

Overhead the voices of the soldiers were becoming animated. Clemin was bemoaning his ill fortune after betting heavily on the Dianese champion in the duel over the strait. Apparently the fighter had knocked his opponent off the platform, only for the Natillian to seize a handful of his foe's hair and drag the Dianese with him. A tie, then, all bets annulled—though Clemin seemed to think he was entitled to a proportion of his winnings on account of what he saw as the Dianese fighter's moral victory.

Of course, he'd first need to explain to his bookmaker what the word "moral" meant.

Veran had reached the center of the portcullis. He unslung his pack and took out a grappling hook. He raised it in one hand.

Just as a shout sounded from the Natillian end of the gate.

Karmel's blood ran cold. Had someone spotted Veran? A watcher on the terraces, perhaps? No, the shout had come from along the battlements. Could the Natillian guards have leaned over the parapet and spied him? Karmel switched her gaze to Veran. She couldn't make out his expression in the gloom, but she could see his left hand held out, palm facing toward her.

Wait.

She snorted softly. What the hell else was she going to do, lie down and catch up on some sleep?

Above, the Dianese guards had broken off their conversation. Karmel heard footfalls heading along the battlements toward the dragon's skull. Steady footfalls, she decided. Not the tread of soldiers who thought they were facing an imminent threat. Clemin called something the priestess couldn't hear. A query as to what the Natillian guards had seen, perhaps? Or what they should do about the idiots climbing the gate?

The footfalls halted near the center of the battlements. Words were exchanged between the Dianese and the Natillians. The speakers were too far away for Karmel to make out what was said, but the tone of the voices was unflustered. Good-humored, even. Then Clemin gave a loud chuckle, and Karmel blew out her cheeks. Evidently the guards knew each other and were chatting across the dragon's skull. The fact the Natillian soldier's shout had come just as Veran was readying his grappling hook must have been pure coincidence.

Karmel felt Veran's gaze on her again, and she looked over. She could guess what he was thinking. With the Dianese soldiers distracted, this was the perfect time to climb to the battlements. The trouble was, the guards were now above Veran's position. He could rejoin Karmel, of course, but by the time he moved back the soldiers might have finished their conversation and returned to their former station. And all the while the sky in the east was paling.

Veran hesitated, then pointed a finger at Karmel and up to the battlements.

It was a heartbeat before she understood his meaning.

The priestess swallowed. *Me?*

He wanted her to climb. How had she not seen that coming?

Karmel wet her lips with her tongue. Earlier she'd complained about him treating her like a fifth wheel, yet now that he was offering her the chance to prove her worth, she found herself wishing they could swap places. She could always signal him to join her, she supposed—wait for him to cross back and pretend she hadn't climbed because she'd thought she heard the guards returning. He would know it for a lie, though. He was probably expecting her to try something like that, and she'd be damned if she would measure down to his low opinion of her.

I can do this.

She unslung her pack so she could take out her grappling hook. Her fingers fumbled at the bag's clasp. Her whole body was trembling. At last she opened the pack and withdrew the grapple. It was attached to a length of black rope. Holding the rope in both hands, Karmel faced north. *I can do this.* She let the hook fall a few armspans, then swung it back and forth, judging the grapple's weight as she pictured the cast she would have to make. It would be a difficult throw, she knew, trying to snare a merlon she couldn't see. Too little rope and the hook would clatter into the parapet. Too much and it would overshoot the battlements and land on the walkway. And there was no way the mexin round the grapple would disguise *that* sound. To make matters worse, she'd need both hands to control the rope, meaning she couldn't hold on to the portcullis at the same time. If her balance was wrong or the wind should gust at an inopportune moment . . .

Setting her feet, Karmel swung the rope and let the line run through her fingers. The hook arced up into darkness.

She knew immediately she hadn't given it enough. The grapple struck the merlon with a muffled clang. The noise was so loud it seemed the Dianese guards *must* hear it. Instead of the expected challenge, though, all Karmel heard was another of Clemin's booming chuckles. She whispered a prayer of thanks to the Chameleon. The soldier's laugh must have covered the sound of the hook.

She wasn't in the clear yet, though, because the rope was swinging back down, and she had to snatch the grapple from the blackness to prevent it hitting one of the gate's bars. As her fingers closed round it, she took a half step forward, wobbled, then lunged for the bar beside her to stop herself tottering into oblivion.

She closed her eyes for a moment, leaned her head against the bar and took a breath. Veran's disapproving gaze felt like two fingers pressed against the back of her head, but he could go swim with the dragons so far as Karmel was concerned. A handful of heartbeats to steady herself, then she played out the rope again and prepared for another cast. *I can do this.* Maybe if she thought it enough times, she'd start believing it.

Her next throw was judged to perfection. She heard a scrape of metal as the hook bit into the merlon.

A tug on the rope to check it was secure, then a pause to ensure there was no change in the guards' voices. Those voices had become louder as their owners argued over which ship would triumph in tomorrow's Hunt. Karmel let the banter wash over her. Now for the hard bit. Veran hadn't told her how he'd intended to dispose of the two Dianese soldiers once he'd climbed to the ramparts, but until Karmel had assessed the lay of the land, there was little to be gained by playing out scenarios in her head. Better to get up there and get on with it.

The moon slid behind a cloud. When Karmel looked down she saw the silver-flecked sea had faded to black. Below, the links of the portcullis receded into the gloom, and it felt to the priestess as if she were standing on the brink of the Abyss.

This wasn't helping.

Gripping the rope with both hands, she leaned forward and swung out into emptiness. Her momentum took her away from the gate, and she clung to the rope while she waited for its pitch to slow. If the Dianese soldiers had looked down just then they would have spotted her, but when Karmel glanced left in their direction she saw only the snout of the dragon's skull protruding from the ramparts. She climbed the rope until her head was just below the parapet. The merlon shielded her from the guards' view—

"What was that?" Clemin said from along the battlements.

Karmel froze. Had he caught the sound of the rope creaking as she climbed? Or the grinding of the hook on the merlon? Sucking in a lungful of air, she forced herself to relax. It didn't have to be her he'd heard, and even if he came to investigate, he wouldn't be able to see her. Yes, the breeze was tugging her this way and that on the rope, but so long as *she* didn't move, her sorcery would hide from sight not just her but also the rope and the hook over which she'd extended her powers.

There was a low buzz of conversation between Clemin and the female Dianese soldier. Then Karmel heard footfalls heading toward her.

She held her breath, her right cheek pressed against the merlon.

The footfalls stopped a few armspans away on the other side of the battlements. Karmel adjusted her grip on the rope. Within moments the guard was on the move again, crossing to the priestess's side of the walkway. She caught a whiff of cheap perfume—the female soldier then.

Karmel waited. She tried imagining this was a training exercise at the temple, but a trumpeting from the distant dragons made it hard to sustain that illusion. Footfalls sounded again. Perfume's tread came closer until it stopped above Karmel's position. The soldier could be no more than an armspan away now—so close that when a puff of wind ruffled the priestess's hair she could almost believe it was Perfume's breath. Her arms started to ache. The grapple was hanging from the merlon by just one of its claws, and Karmel caught the faintest groan of metal as it shifted. Had Perfume heard? Clearly *something* had grabbed her attention for her to spend so much time in this place.

Clemin barked a question.

Perfume's response—"I'm looking, damn you!"—blared so loud in Karmel's ears she almost surrendered her grip on the rope. Her muscles were burning now, and she silently counted heartbeats in an effort to take her mind off her discomfort. A swish of cloth told her Perfume was leaning over the battlements. Karmel fought an urge to seize the woman and help her over the side. Then a thought came to her. *The grappling hook.* If Perfume's hand should brush against it . . .

The soldier drew back. Karmel tensed, expecting to be sent plummeting as the hook was prized loose from the parapet.

Instead Perfume spat over the merlon.

Then retreated along the walkway toward the dragon's skull.

Karmel's shoulders sagged with relief, but this wasn't the time to count her blessings. Now that Perfume's back was turned, the priestess had a chance to climb to the battlements unseen. She seized the merlon with her left hand before boosting herself up. Raising her right leg, she placed her foot in one of the crenels. Then she paused in a half-crouch, her scabbard tangled in her legs, her right hand still clutching the rope. She glanced along the battlements after the retreating Perfume.

The woman's stride had not faltered. Beyond her Clemin was looking south over the Cappel Strait, oblivious.

So far, so good.

Karmel stepped onto the walkway before lifting the grapple from the merlon and dropping it over the side. There was a danger someone might see it fall, but what choice did she have? The instant she released her hold on the hook, it would become visible to the Dianese soldiers, because she could only extend her powers over something she was in contact with. And she couldn't leave it hanging from the parapet any more than she could put it back in her pack.

Looking to her right she saw a sheer cliff face. Set into it was the metal door that led to the control room, bathed in the glow of two torches affixed to the rock on either side. High above, Dian's citadel loomed dark and still, an immense shadow broken only by a window of fuzzy light in one of the towers. To Karmel's left, Perfume had rejoined Clemin and was now shrugging in response to some unheard question. Behind them the dragon's skull spanned the battlements, half again the height of a man and massing so large it hid from Karmel's view the Natillian soldiers beyond. The fires within the skull made the bone appear semitranslucent. In its part-open mouth were dozens of teeth, each as long as the priestess's arm and charred black from the flames licking at them.

Karmel studied the Dianese guards. Clemin was pale-skinned and blond-haired. A head taller than his female companion, he had the slouch of a man used to stooping as he went through doors. Perfume, by contrast, was trying to make herself look taller by standing stiffly at attention. Both soldiers wore swords at their waists, but no armor. Their helmets were on the walkway opposite Karmel. Across their jackets were yellow sashes marking them as citadel guards—the elite among Dian's defenders. But they were still just soldiers. And, more important, soldiers who weren't expecting company.

Karmel drew a throwing knife. Her best chance of disposing of them quietly would be to kill her first victim out of sight of the second, yet that meant waiting for them to separate again. By striking the hilt of her knife against the merlon she might lure Perfume this way a second time, but the sound would surely put the soldiers on guard, and Karmel wanted them breathing easy. What options did that leave? If the Dianese returned to this end of the battlements, Karmel might be able to silence them simultaneously with two well-placed knife thrusts. Yet one or both might cry out and alert their Natillian counterparts.

Karmel's conversation with Veran in the boat came back to her, and she realized this would be the first time she had killed anyone up close. She'd hunted lots of people in her training at the temple, though. Why should this be any different? Fortunately there wasn't time to dwell on the matter, because the conversation between the Dianese and the Natillian guards had ended. The Dianese moved toward the priestess. The hilt of her throwing knife was slick in her palm. Two soldiers represented no threat, she told herself. It was the doing-it-quietly part that was the challenge.

Only then did it occur to Karmel that the battlements were just four paces wide, and that unless the Dianese soldiers halted they would walk straight into her.

Shit.

She fought down panic. If she'd thought to draw two knives, she could have tried bringing both guards down at a distance. But "if" wasn't helping her now. It seemed she'd be forced to take out Clemin with her first blade and hope there was time to draw a second before Perfume reacted. *One victim at a time,* she thought. Make that first knife count.

She tensed the muscles of her right arm.

Clemin drew up.

Karmel remained still, struggling to keep her rasping breath quiet.

Perfume checked her stride and glanced back at her companion before tutting in disgust and continuing on. She halted two paces away from Karmel. Turning to look over the strait, she adjusted her sash. Clemin, meanwhile, had untied the laces of his trousers and was urinating over the parapet.

Karmel could have done with relieving herself too. She took a shuddering breath. Now was her chance to strike at Perfume. No time for hesitation or second thoughts. She'd have preferred to go for Clemin first, but Perfume, with her back turned to the priestess, was the easier target.

Two steps brought Karmel behind Perfume. The woman couldn't have heard her approach, for she made no move to turn. Karmel stabbed her under her right ear, angling the blade up into the brain. The soldier spasmed, then went limp.

And started toppling forward over the battlements.

Karmel inwardly swore. She'd need Perfume's uniform to trick her way into the citadel, so she curled her left arm round the guard's throat and hauled her back even as she withdrew her blade from the woman's skull and twisted to face Clemin. Clemin had half turned toward her, spraying urine onto the walkway. For a moment he stared at her, his mouth hanging open, his manhood hanging out. Then he reached for his sword, his neck muscles bunching as he made to shout.

Karmel threw her knife. It seemed to come out of her hand all wrong, yet still it took him in the throat. His yell emerged as a gurgle. He reached up as if he meant to tug the priestess's blade free. Then his eyes rolled back in his head, and his legs buckled. Karmel knew she should try to catch him, but her limbs felt like they were made of mud. She could only watch as his head thudded into the walkway, the knife tearing loose from his throat.

Silence.

The priestess looked toward the dragon's skull and the Natillian guards beyond. Had they heard anything? If either of them called out a question, Karmel would have to try imitating Perfume's Dianese burr—maybe blame the noise on Clemin tripping over his feet, or mumble something unintelligible and hope that allayed the Natillians' suspicions.

A dozen heartbeats passed, but no challenge came—or at least none that Karmel could hear over the pounding of blood in her temples.

Perfume's corpse was starting to weigh on her arm, and she lowered it to the ground. The woman returned her gaze with glassy eyes. Her skin was waxy-pale, her hair soaked with blood. Clemin lay on his side, his mouth open, his teeth stained pink. Karmel's knife had torn open his throat to leave a gash a handspan long, the flesh inside glistening red . . .

Grimacing, the priestess looked away.

Her hands were trembling again. Perhaps she should have felt triumph at having silenced the guards, but instead she felt only relief that her ordeal was over. Tired, too. Earlier she'd spent the evening pacing her basement lodgings. It had left her feeling drained even before she'd set out for the gate, and there was only so far adrenaline could carry her. Now it set her down with a bump. She sagged against the merlon.

When she looked up again, she saw Veran watching her from a short distance away. He had made no sound in climbing to the battlements, but then the whole of the Dianese citadel could have crept up on Karmel at that moment and she wouldn't have noticed. His gaze was characteristically cold, but it thawed a little when he took in her shaking hands.

Only to darken again when he looked at the corpses of the Dianese soldiers.

"You got blood on the damned uniforms," he muttered.

CHAPTER 10

AGENTA CLOSED the door to the White Lady's Temple behind her. The buzz of the city fell to a whisper. Watery light trickled through the cracked and grimy windows, bathing the chapel in a chill, otherworldly glow. The walls were blackened with age, and the flagstones had been worn smooth as glass. With each step Agenta took, the silence about her deepened until it seemed as if she'd left Olaire far behind.

The chapel was empty but for her father, dressed all in black, seated on a warped wooden bench at the front. Before him was a statue of the White Lady, her features so lifelike that Agenta thought she saw the mouth twitch in an enigmatic smile. The kalischa halted behind Rethell. He sat with head bowed and shoulders hunched. When he'd slipped away from the embassy earlier, Agenta had known instinctively where he was going. The fact he hadn't asked for her company meant he didn't want her here, so why had she followed? On this, the anniversary of her brother's death, she had no wish to intrude on his grief, for it was a grief she felt a stranger to. Even in death Zelin shared a bond with her father she would never know.

"Why are you here?" Rethell said without looking round.

"I could ask the same of you."

He stiffened. "You can't have forgotten—"

"Of course I haven't."

"Then why are you surprised I should remember him today of all days?"

Agenta sat down on a bench. It creaked beneath her. "Because you grieve for him every day."

"*I'm* not the one still in mourning."

"I finished mourning Zelin months ago."

"No you didn't. You just convinced yourself you didn't care."

Agenta recoiled as if she'd been slapped. He was accusing *her* of still brooding over Zelin's death? Was this the same Rethell whose grief had whittled him down to a mere sliver of his former self? Who walked with Zelin's shadow hanging over him even now? So what if Agenta had taken tollen to rid herself of her grief at her brother's passing? What was so noble about grief that one had to suffer through it?

A ruddy-faced old man wearing a white robe appeared from a side door Agenta hadn't noticed. He shuffled to an altar at the front of the shrine. The hem of his gown swished on the flagstones.

Rethell's gaze tracked his progress. To Agenta he said, "I am sorry you had to take on the burden of Zelin's duties after he died."

"Were you sorry he had to carry out those duties while he lived?"

"You were never meant to assume his role. You weren't ready for it."

"Perhaps that's why I always disappoint you in it," Agenta said, hating the note of self-pity in her voice.

And yet Rethell didn't bother to refute her words.

She glanced back at the statue of the White Lady. Was it was her imagination, or had the goddess's expression become more sober since Agenta last looked? "Perhaps I see no purpose in taking on your mantle, Father. Perhaps soon there will be nothing left to succeed to. You spent a lifetime building your empire, but only now do you realize it is made of sand."

"Is that how you see things, Agenta? Nothing has value because everything we have can be lost?"

If she attached no value to something, how could she feel loss when it was taken from her? When she said as much to Rethell, he opened his mouth to speak before closing it again.

Agenta searched his gaze for some hint of what he had been about to say. Something to do with Zelin's passing, she suspected. Was he going to tell her that death was the price we pay for life? That she should live for the happiness in each day? He didn't believe such platitudes any more than she did. He only *told* himself he did to make it easier to manage his grief, else why was he here now and not back at the embassy toasting Zelin's memory? That's what Agenta had done earlier with Lydanto. A part of her wanted to shake her father by the shoulders. To strip away the pretenses and make him confront the absurdity of his self-deception. But she did not. He was a broken man, after all. Who knew what might happen if she kicked away the crutch he leaned on?

A rustle of cloth signaled the priest's approach. Agenta looked up to see the old man lighting a taper from a candle in the hand of the White Lady's statue. Sensing the kalischa's attention, he gave her a smile. For some reason the gesture irritated her, and she looked away.

Rethell waited until the priest had retreated, then said, "It is time we were going. The emira's ship sails in a bell."

"At our meeting, you seemed concerned when she invited us onto the *Icewing*. Why?"

"I don't know. Something in her look."

"If Lydanto's sources are correct we won't be the only people there. The emira would never risk treachery in front of witnesses."

"Yet she intends to negotiate with us over the duskstones before those same witnesses?" Rethell swung his gaze back to the statue. "Perhaps it is nothing."

There was no conviction in his voice, though. Agenta wondered what he was keeping from her. Was he afraid of encountering a dragon on the Hunt, and trying to pass off that fear as unease at Imerle's motives?

Yes, that had to be it.

Agenta pushed herself to her feet. Rethell made no move to follow, and she realized his talk of hastening to the *Icewing* had simply been his way of dismissing her. "I will leave you to your ghosts," she said, striding toward the rear of the shrine.

No response.

A wall of noise hit her as she opened the door to the street and stepped outside. Such was her preoccupation that she didn't at first see the fat man in the pink shirt standing a pace away. His round face showed an expression of comical surprise as she collided with him. The two mitrebird eggs he was holding smashed against his chest, spattering him with amber goo.

Without a word, Agenta walked past.

Quina Hilaire Desa was ranting again, but Kempis had long since stopped listening. He was thinking about what Senar Sol had said concerning overlapping worlds and the gateways between them, and wondering how he could use that knowledge to his advantage. Now that he knew Bright Eyes used the portals to return to Olaire as well as to leave, maybe he could ambush her after her next vanishing act. To that end, Storm Guards had been stationed at the approaches to the gateways in the Shallows and the Temple District. But how could those soldiers set a trap when no one knew how large an area the portals covered? Moreover, what if the presence of the Storm Guards deterred Bright Eyes from traveling through the gateways she'd already used? How was Kempis supposed to find out if there were other portals in the city, and where they were located?

As Hilaire continued her tirade, she took out a looking glass from a desk drawer and began smearing red lipstick over her lips. "And now you tell me," she was saying, "the city is infested with the spirits of everyone who's died in Olaire these past few weeks . . ."

So that was Kempis's fault too, was it? He made a mental note to kick Shroud's soul-gatherers into shape when he got out of here.

". . . and what in the Nine Hells were you thinking, telling Loop to bring the spirit of that Drifter here . . . ?"

Right on cue Irlon's wailing started up from the direction of the exercise yard, followed by the lowing of a temlock.

". . . Lady's blessing, does he ever shut up? And as for those temlocks—"

"It's Loop, sir," Kempis cut in, glad for an opportunity to pass the buck. "Needs a death every few bells to give him the power to keep Irlon bound."

"Then he can take the Drifter to the slaughterhouse! This isn't a Shroud-cursed cattle yard! That spirit's howling has turned the temlocks' bowels to water. All morning I've done nothing but wade through shit!"

Welcome to my world. Not that he'd have swapped it for Hilaire's, of course. Before the quina's time, the bluebloods had tried once to offer her position to Kempis. As if he was going to fall for that one.

Movement through a window caught his eye, and he looked left to see the tip of a spear held by someone outside. When he'd arrived at the Watchstation earlier, he'd spotted two Storm Guards loitering near the armory. He'd assumed they were the escort of some blueblood come to visit Hilaire, but since there was no blueblood in sight . . .

"What are those soldiers doing here?" he asked the quina.

Hilaire gazed into her looking glass, pouting her lips. "Dutia Elemy Meddes sent them."

"Gray-Face reckons Bright Eyes might come here, does he?"

A pause. "The soldiers are now part of your team."

"The Sender they are."

Hilaire scowled. "I'm not asking for your blessing, Septia. Twice now you've had the assassin in your grasp, and twice you've let her slip."

"That's why we've stationed Storm Guards at the gateways. So I can drive Bright Eyes toward them."

"And Elemy's soldiers can help with the driving." Hilaire brought the looking glass so close to her face Kempis thought she was going to kiss it. "With their assistance, maybe next time you won't steer your quarry into a Storm Lady."

"That weren't my fault. Bright Eyes had already found Mazana Creed when I caught up to her. I saved her life."

"As I heard it, Mazana's bodyguard had the assassin right where he wanted her until you blundered in and scared her into running."

Nothing to do with the beating she'd been getting from Senar Sol, then. "You'd have preferred it if I'd sat back and watched?"

"I'd have preferred it if you'd done your job properly and caught the damned woman! Instead it seems we may now have a Kerralai demon to worry about."

Kempis shrugged. "If the demon tracks Bright Eyes down, that's a good thing, ain't it? We just wait for the creature to sniff out her trail, then follow it to her."

"Through the smoldering ruins of the city, you mean? Gods below, Septia, this is a *demon* we're talking about! If it tracks her here from the Shades, do you think it's going to worry about a few buildings that get in its way?"

Kempis kept his silence, knowing no matter what he said it would be the wrong thing.

Hilaire returned her looking glass to its drawer. "Now, in case it has slipped your mind, today is Dragon Day, which means every water-mage worth his salt is about to set sail for the Dragon Gate. I want you at the harbor in case the assassin shows her face. Take Elemy's men with you."

Her tone told Kempis he was dismissed, so he turned and headed for the door.

"And find your bloody stripes!" Hilaire shouted after him.

Kempis left Pompit smiling in the outer office and entered the exercise yard. Elemy's soldiers stood to his right. Both carried spears and had bucklers strapped to their arms. The taller man—a white-haired Maru with bulging eyes—was a septia too, judging by the stripes on his shoulder, and for the first time in a long time Kempis was tempted to take his own stripes from his pocket. Instead he nodded to the men and gestured over his shoulder. "Quina wants a word with you. I'll wait for you here."

The soldiers exchanged a look before disappearing inside, leaving their spears propped against the wall.

As the door to Pompit's office closed, Kempis hurried for the gate leading to Meridian Street, picking his way through piles of temlock dung.

Sniffer's voice startled him from the shadows of the guardhouse. "Morning, sir."

Kempis ignored her, striding through the gate at a pace that had the Untarian half jogging to keep up. Ahead a cart laden with crates of gallow crabs was trundling toward the fish market on Crofters Lane. Its driver was fighting a running battle with urchins intent on lightening the cart's load. The septia took a right turn, then a left, before finally slowing as he drew level with the Amarr Observatory. Behind him in the Watchstation's exercise yard he could still hear the wails of Irlon and the temlocks as they competed in their misery.

Sniffer was whistling through her gills. "Where are we going?"

Kempis did not reply. He'd been hoping to get some time alone to think. As he swung into Vale Street the seventh bell sounded.

"Seventh bell, sir," Sniffer said.

"You don't say." Insight like that, she'd be after his job soon.

"Seventeen more and I'm out of here."

Kempis had forgotten today was the Untarian's last day in the Watch. His mood brightened.

"Any idea," Sniffer went on, "who your new partner's going to be? I was thinking maybe Duffle. The children are our future, right?"

"Whoever I get, he'll be a lot easier on the ears than you."

"You sure of that? There's a blueblood among the new recruits. Apparently he's so unimpressed with our efforts to guard the city he's decided to show us how it's done. I told him to ask for you personally."

"Maybe I won't get another partner at all. Not when they see how bad you turned out."

Sniffer laughed. "I'll miss you too."

The next right turn would take Kempis to the harbor. He went left. "I'm sure we'll be seeing each other again sooner than you think." Criminals like the Untarian never stayed straight.

"But not for long at the speed you run, eh, sir?"

As Kempis opened his mouth to retort, a shadow passed overhead. The septia looked up to see a dark shape glide over the rooftops.

A roar shook the houses to either side.

From the quarterdeck of the emira's flagship, the *Icewing*, Agenta tugged her gaze from the creature sweeping low over the distant buildings and looked down on the docks. At the end of the quay a cordon of Storm Guards held back a sea of faces. As Agenta watched, a young woman carrying a garland of dewflowers pushed through the cordon and approached the ship. She threw the garland up to the main deck where it was caught by a soldier who stared at it before hooking it over a spear in the weapons rack behind him. A comment from the man drew chuckles from his companions, but the laughter was halfhearted. It died away to be replaced by a strained silence.

It was not difficult to determine the reason for the soldiers' edginess. During the past half-bell a procession of vessels had left the harbor bound for the Dragon Gate, yet still the emira's flagship remained at quayside. Agenta had heard the same question voiced by a dozen of her fellow passengers: why had the *Icewing* not set sail? After all, the best starting berths for the Hunt—those immediately facing the Dragon Gate—went to whichever ships claimed them first. Not even Imerle would be able to command the captain of another vessel to make way.

Footfalls to Agenta's left signaled Lydanto's approach.

"Magnificent, is she not?" he said, his sweeping gesture taking in the *Icewing*. "Sixty-two paces long she measures—I have been striding her out myself. The largest ship on the Sabian Sea, I am hearing, though the prince of Hardangill is said to have commissioned a galley with four rows of oars on each side. Four!" He paused to allow Agenta or Rethell, standing a telling distance to one side, to share his wonder. When they kept their silence he went on, "Truly we are in exalted company, no? The man on the aft deck in the ankle-length red gown, that is Karan del Orco, pasha of Shamano, and one of the critics most outspoken of the emira's decision to raise the Levy this year. Beside him, flanked by his bodyguards—imagine wearing chain mail on a ship!—is Gerrick Long—"

"*The* Gerrick Long?" Rethell said. "Of Palana Utara?"

"The very same." Lydanto looked at Agenta. "In case you are not knowing, Gerrick is the successor to Page Calabra, the man who famously bowed to Imerle three years ago before bringing his city into the Sabian fold for the first time in its history. Alas, the move proved unpopular with his people, and he was unseated the following year in a coup led by the man you are looking at."

"What is this Gerrick Long doing here, then? I assume that he withdrew his city from the League as soon as he came to power."

"Indeed he did. But protocol demands he is retaining *some* links with the Storm Isles." Lydanto leaned in close. "Rumor has it also that on a recent visit to Olaire he was—how do you say?—losing his heart to the emira."

"She can use it to fill the hole where hers should be."

The Grantorian did not respond, but then his eye had been caught by a serving-girl emerging from the captain's cabin with a tray of drinks.

"Ambassador?" Agenta said.

"What? Ah, yes, I was speaking of our fellow passengers." He glanced to Agenta's right. "Across from us—no, Kalischa, do not look now—is a man wearing a gold shirt. That is Samel Fletch, one of the merchants believed to have lent money to Imerle." Lydanto tapped his nose. "A chance to quiz him may present itself later, I am thinking. A few discreet questions over a glass of wine will doubtless elicit more information than any amount of sifting through dusty scrolls at the Round."

Agenta's brows knitted. "Curious, isn't it, that the emira should invite us on board when she knew Samel Fletch would be here. I would have thought she'd want to keep us as far away from him as possible."

"Your scheme in the throne room worked, did it not? Clearly Imerle does not see you as a threat now that she has indicated her willingness to deal."

And yet, to risk putting the Gilgamarians with the merchant before the deal was closed, that seemed a little out of character. Now Agenta thought of it, what was Samel doing here at all? From what Lydanto had told her, the emira had done everything that she could to hide her dealings with him. So why was she now flaunting their association in public?

The ambassador's attention had wandered again, his gaze following a second serving-girl as she handed out drinks to the passengers on the aft deck. Rethell, too, was taking no notice of Agenta, his distant look suggesting his thoughts were still with Zelin in the White Lady's Temple. But then he'd long preferred to spend his time among the dead rather than the living.

"Who are they?" Agenta asked Lydanto, gesturing to two men on the forecastle. One was bald and wore the blue robes of a watermage, the other the uniform of a Storm Guard. A cluster of dignitaries had gathered about them, and raised voices reached the kalischa.

"The sorcerer is called Orsan," the ambassador said. "A close confidant of the emira, I am believing. The soldier is Dutia Elemy Meddes."

Karan del Orco had joined the group of dignitaries round the two men and now jabbed a finger into Elemy's chest with such force the dutia was driven back a step.

Something was bothering Agenta, but she couldn't think what. "They don't appear to be the most popular men on board."

"The delay, perhaps—"

"No," she interrupted. "See, we are casting off."

Ropes were being thrown up to the deck, and the hum of the watching crowds rose to a roar. As the *Icewing* pulled away from the dock the throng surged forward, pushing through the cordon of Storm Guards and sending a handful of soldiers toppling into the water. People came running along the quay as if they intended to grab one of the ship's lines and climb aboard. Fast as they were, though, the *Icewing* was faster, as a wave of water-magic swelled beneath the vessel and swept it toward the Causeway. It passed a berthed galleon flying the gauntleted fist of Storm Lord Thane Tanner. Strangely, its decks were all but empty.

Agenta scanned the ranks of the remaining ships at quayside. "I don't see the *Crest*," she said to her father. Those were the first words she'd spoken to him since leaving the temple.

"I sent it on ahead."

The kalischa looked at him. "To the Dragon Gate? Why?"

"Why not?"

Because he cared nothing for the prestige that would come if the *Crest* brought down the dragon, that's why. Because with the loss of the *Gadfly*, he could ill afford to lose another ship. Agenta didn't get a chance to voice her thoughts, though, for Rethell was already walking toward the steps to the aft deck.

Lydanto set off after him, rubbing his hands together. "Time to sample the hospitality of the emira, I am thinking," he said.

Agenta made no move to follow. She could do with a drink herself, but not if it meant rejoining her father.

The *Icewing* entered the Causeway. The kalischa saw people staring at her from the roofs of the flooded buildings, as they had when she arrived in Olaire. Unlike the crowds on the quays these spectators watched silently, sullenly. But then anyone unfortunate enough to live in the Shallows had little reason for good cheer. Starbeaks bobbed on the water in the *Icewing*'s path, and they took flight as the vessel bore down on them. A fishing boat was approaching from the opposite direction. The wave created by the passage of the emira's ship sent it bumping into the wall of a building.

When the *Icewing* reached the open sea, a cry of "hands aloft!" went up. Sailors scrambled up the rigging and began letting out the sails. As the bow swung south, Agenta's breath was tight in her chest. In her enjoyment at outwitting Imerle she had overlooked what her reward for doing so entailed. And while courting risk was one thing, courting a dragon was another entirely. The trader ship she'd seen destroyed six years ago was small in comparison to the *Icewing*. Yet a single flick of a dragon's tail that day had been enough to send the vessel to the bottom of the ocean. It had been decades since a Storm Lord's ship was last lost on the Hunt, but even with both Imerle and Orsan on board there could be no guarantee . . .

Agenta's thoughts trailed off. Both Imerle and Orsan.

She studied the faces on the aft deck, then the quarterdeck, then the forecastle, but the person she was looking for was not among them. Could they be belowdecks? Or in the captain's cabin, perhaps? On the

forecastle, the number of dignitaries clustered about Orsan and
Elemy had swelled, and so too had the sound of their voices now that
the bustle of the harbor was fading behind. The people about Agenta
were looking in their direction. A hush settled on the quarterdeck as
everyone tried to hear what was being said.

The kalischa, though, had already worked out the reason for the
altercation.

Imerle. She's not on board.

Kempis skidded to a halt at the edge of the marketplace.

Sender's mercy!

Black-skinned and horned, the Kerralai demon swooped over the
Round. It banked left and landed on the roof of the Mercerien embassy. Roof tiles torn loose by its claws came raining down onto the
street, and a blueblood exiting the embassy looked up before dropping the armful of scrolls he was carrying and darting back inside.
The people in the marketplace were similarly running for cover, save
for a handful who stared slack-jawed at the apparition. Among them
Kempis noticed a woman dressed all in midnight blue outside the
Round's East Gate. The assassin? It had to be, for while her eyes did
not glow in daylight as they had at night, she stood out from the
finery about her like a crow in a field of peacocks.

The demon unfurled its wings and leapt into the air.

Bright Eyes turned and bolted toward the Round.

The East Gate was guarded by four Storm Guards. They held their
ground as the demon bore down on them, and Kempis found himself
admiring their courage if not their intelligence. A fifth soldier ran
from the South Gate to support his colleagues. As the Kerralai descended, he hurled a spear at it. The creature veered out of the weapon's path before turning its blood-red gaze on the thrower. Twin jets
of flame shot from its eyes, and the Storm Guard became a shrieking
firebrand.

Kempis drew his sword. "We need to get in there," he said to
Sniffer, nodding at the Round.

She looked at him like he'd sprouted a set of horns to match the
Kerralai's.

"I ain't planning on stepping into that thing's path, if that's what
you're thinking."

"Then why go in? Why not wait for the demon to flush Bright Eyes out?"

" 'Cause we can't see the North and West Gates from here, that's why. Only place you can see all the exits from is inside."

"So she leaves without us seeing, so what?" Sniffer said. "The creature found her once, it'll find her again."

"And if she gets to a portal before it catches her?" Kempis watched Bright Eyes enter the Round. "If the demon takes her down, I want to see it. If not, we drive her to one of the gateways we've got guarded. Either way, this ends now." After the stunt he'd pulled at the Watch-station, he would only have this one chance to save his stripes.

The Kerralai alighted in the marketplace near the East Gate. Its taloned feet scraped on the square's mosaic. The Storm Guards facing it crouched behind their shields, their spears stabbing out.

"Are you with me?" Kempis asked Sniffer.

She squinted at the demon, then muttered something and nodded.

"We go on three, right?"

"Bugger that," the Untarian said, sprinting for the Round.

The septia scampered after her.

Sniffer reached the South Gate ahead of Kempis, and he followed her beneath the portcullis set into its ceiling. The walls of the counting-house were so thick it was like running through a tunnel. Kempis had to fight through a crowd of people coming the other way, but at last he emerged into the light streaming down through the Round's domed glass roof.

He drew up beside the trading floor. From his right came a deep-throated growl, followed by a crash as someone lowered the port-cullis over the East Gate. The Storm Guards facing the demon were trapped on the wrong side. Through the bars of the gate Kempis saw one of them jab his spear at the Kerralai, only for the creature to bat the weapon aside and rip open its assailant's throat with its talons. As the demon closed on the remaining guards, its body blocked out the light in the tunnel until all Kempis could see was its blazing red eyes.

Inside the Round, bluebloods ran in every direction. A woman wearing a feathered hat tripped and fell, then took a boot in the face. Some of the desks on the trading floor had been overturned. The ground about them was covered in coins and papers. Amid the chaos knelt a rusty-skinned Sartorian who had slipped out of his purple cloak and was now lifting coins onto it, doubtless intending to use it as a makeshift carrier. Bright Eyes was at the North Gate in the middle of a scrum of bluebloods. Her plait bobbed as she was swept along the tunnel.

Another growl came from Kempis's right, then an explosion of fiery light. The septia saw a wave of demonic magic hit the East Gate. The surviving Storm Guards had been pleading for someone to raise the gate, their arms pushed between the bars. As the sorcery struck them they screamed and collapsed into dust. The rails of the port-cullis fared little better, melting like ice and dripping molten metal to the ground. The magic rolled into the Round. On the trading floor the purple-robed coin-gatherer had time only to hug his gold-laden cloak to him before the sorcery engulfed him. He and his burden erupted into flames.

Kempis frowned. Waste of good gold, that.

Screams started up from his left as the power devoured the people trying to escape through the West Gate. In the wake of the magic the trading floor glowed red. The desks had been set alight, and charred papers flapped and swirled on the scorched breeze. From the East Gate came another growl. Kempis looked that way, expecting to see the Kerralai. Instead all he could make out was a cloud of smoke. The concussion of beating wings reached him. Was the Kerralai retreat-ing? Had more Storm Guards arrived to drive it off? Or had the demon sensed Bright Eyes fleeing and taken to the skies in pursuit?

Bright Eyes . . .

Kempis looked for the assassin again at the North Gate, but she had already vanished outside. He set off after her. As he crossed the trading floor, he felt the heat of the stone through the soles of his boots. A scattering of bluebloods were huddled in the tunnel leading out. They looked relieved to see him—as if they thought he was going to protect them. Kempis couldn't decide what was more stupid, the idea that he might risk his life against the demon, or that he'd fare any better than the Storm Guards if he tried. Pushing through the crowd, he emerged from the Round in time to see Bright Eyes duck into Imperial Road.

Kempis groaned. Another Shroud-cursed chase. But at least for now there was no sign of the Kerralai.

The septia pounded after the assassin. A left turn into Manor Road brought him a glimpse of the Watchtower at Ferris Point, but it disappeared again as he passed the Scriptorium. Ahead was the Artisan Quarter with its warren of alleys, and beyond that lay the Temple District. Could Bright Eyes be making for the portal near the temple of the Lord of Hidden Faces? There seemed little sense in escaping a demon by traveling to the world from which it had tracked her, but if the creature couldn't follow the assassin through the gateway she might at least buy herself time to catch her breath.

The gap between Kempis and Bright Eyes was closing, and he recalled the limp Senar Sol had given her yesterday. Sniffer overtook him as he swung wide round the fountain outside the Carlatian Pleasure Gardens. The Untarian hurdled a broken cart wheel and stumbled as she entered Baker Alley.

The stumble saved her life. Bright Eyes had been waiting round the corner, and her thrown dagger flashed through the air where Sniffer's head had been. The assassin cursed and drew her longknives.

Kempis charged.

The alley rang with steel as Bright Eyes parried his wild attacks. For a heartbeat she was forced to give ground. Then the battle turned, and a thrust to Kempis's face had him swaying back. The cut that came next narrowly missed his chin. He retreated, his sword jerking from side to side as he tried to follow his opponent's intricate feints. A nick to his hip drew a grunt from his lips. It occurred to him it could have been Elemy's soldiers, rather than him, soaking up the assassin's knife strokes, and he found himself almost regretting the deception he'd played on the two Storm Guards at the Watchstation.

Almost.

A dagger thrown by Sniffer flashed past his right cheek, straight for Bright Eyes's chest.

She blocked it with ease, but in doing so gave Kempis an opportunity to disengage. He stepped back out of range—where he should have been all along. What was the point of being a septia, after all, if you couldn't get someone else to do your bleeding for you?

A creak of leathery wings sounded overhead, and the Kerralai glided low over the rooftops. Smoke curled from its nostrils. The touch of its shadow sent a prickle along Kempis's skin, yet he was relieved to see it all the same.

Relieved? Not a feeling he'd ever thought he would associate with a demon's coming.

Bright Eyes's gaze followed the creature as it banked to the right for another pass.

Then she turned and fled along the alley.

Senar looked about the temple courtyard. At the far side was a wall covered with carvings of animal-headed figures, and before the wall stood a white-robed man wearing a gold mask—the high priest of the Lord of Hidden Faces, Senar presumed. The Guardian watched from the shade of a colonnade as the man paced along the length of the wall, bellowing at a congregation seated on the sandy ground. The priest's voice filled the courtyard.

". . . and when a man is unwilling to submit freely to the will of his Lord, it is because his base nature is untempered! Learn to obey His will . . ."

Mazana stood a pace to Senar's left, fanning herself with one hand. She hadn't seemed surprised earlier when he'd told her he would be accompanying her to the Founder's Citadel, and from the glint in her eyes she knew why Imerle wanted him there. But then why had she chosen him, and not one of her bodyguards, to escort her here this morning?

He suspected he was about to find out, for moving toward them along the colonnade was a woman wearing a featureless mask of white wood. Long auburn hair fell about her shoulders, and through her mask's eye slits Senar saw brown eyes that never rested in one place for more than a moment. Her fingers fluttered as she walked. She halted before Senar and Mazana.

"Priestess," the Storm Lady said, inclining her head, "may I introduce Senar Sol, a Guardian of Erin Elal."

He bowed. "An honor."

"Guarrrdian," she said, making a little trilling sound as she rolled the "r."

Senar looked from the masked woman to the worshippers in the courtyard. "I confess, I am surprised to find the cult of the Lord of Hidden Faces flourishing here in Olaire when it has died out everywhere else."

"No more than I am, I assure you," the priestess said, her voice hinting at amusement.

Senar waited for her to explain the remark, but she kept her silence. His gaze strayed to the golden-masked figure on the opposite side of the courtyard. "The high priest is a . . . powerful speaker."

"Artagina is a man devoted to his god. But then the Lord of Hidden Faces makes an ideal master for such as he."

"How so?"

"The Lord is so much less prrrescriptive than other immortals, and thus his cult is one the high priest can truly put his mark on." The priestess tilted her head to listen to Artagina's sermon.

". . . the words of the Lord's priests," he boomed, "cannot be weighed by man's understanding, for they are His words! They are to be heard in silence, and received with humility . . ."

The masked woman's hands caressed the air. "He seems particularly keen on obedience, you may have noticed."

"Most leaders are," Senar said sharply, picturing the emperor. Even when it wasn't owed to them. Especially then, perhaps.

"That is because they believe their judgment to be infallible. As Artagina is so fond of telling us, a man doing his god's will can never be wrong. We are truly blessed to have a high priest so in tune with the desires of his Lord."

Senar wished he could see what expression the priestess's mask was hiding. Something about her bothered him—something beyond her apparent irreverence to the leader of her own order. He reached out toward her with his Will and sensed . . . nothing. *As if she were a mere illusion.* Perhaps he should not be surprised that a dedicate of the Lord of Hidden Faces could conceal herself so artfully in her own temple, but still . . .

If the priestess was aware of Senar's scrutiny, she gave no indication.

Mazana said to her, "Do I have you to thank for Imerle's rush of blood last night?"

Senar shot her a look. Rush of blood?

The masked woman laughed. "I harrrdly think you need my help when it comes to goading the emira."

"And when I *do* need your assistance, how shall I call on you?"

"You won't need to. I'll be keeping a close eye on what happens in the fortress."

"How reassuring."

From across the courtyard Artagina's voice droned on, but Senar had ears only for the conversation of the two women.

Mazana added, "You've yet to tell me the price for your aid. No doubt you will want your Lord represented on the Storm Council."

"No doubt."

The Storm Lady waited a moment for her to continue then said, "And?"

"And I'm sure whatever boon I ask of you will be as nothing compared to the help you are about to receive."

"Then why not tell me—"

"I see you still have much to think on," the priestess cut in, turning away.

Mazana's voice brought her up. "What do you know of the assassin who attacked me yesterday?"

"Assassin?"

"I was accosted just a few steps from your front door, yet you expect me to believe you knew nothing about it?"

The masked woman's gaze flickered to Senar. "What I knew was that you were in capable hands. Is that not so, Guarrrdian?"

Senar looked at the stubs of his missing fingers. Capable hands? What was left of them, perhaps. He tried to wrap his head round what he'd been hearing. So the priestess had agreed to assist Mazana in the Founder's Citadel? How? By thwarting whatever accident Imerle had arranged for her? No, there had to be more to it than that, for if the Storm Lady had tricked the emira last night into sending her to the fortress, that could only mean she *wanted* to go. But why?

He thought about what he knew of the citadels. Following the titans' defeat to the pantheon in the Eternal War, legend had it that most of the titans fled their conquerors through portals to other worlds. A few, though, had retreated to the fortresses where they were besieged and ultimately slain by the gods. Whether or not those tales were true, the citadels had been deserted for centuries and doubtless stripped of anything valuable. What could be inside that might have snared Mazana's interest? Something behind the sorcerous barrier Darbonna had referred to in the throne room? If so, how did Mazana know it was there?

What disturbed Senar most about this whole business, though, was that the Storm Lady was letting him hear it at all. Mazana had chosen him to accompany her because she wanted to drag him into her schemes. With each passing bell, he was getting pulled deeper into matters that he had no interest in. Any deeper and he was likely to drown.

His thoughts were interrupted by a distant sorcerous concussion, then a howl that stole the warmth from the air—a howl from a throat that was anything but human. *A demon.* A Kerralai, perhaps? Had the creature already tracked Mazana's would-be assassin back from the Shades? Another howl sounded, closer this time, followed by a crackle of lightning. Mazana's face lost some of its color, and the high priest's voice trailed off before picking up again with renewed vigor. Only the priestess remained unflustered. Her eyes were smiling, and her fingers fluttered feverishly.

"It might be better," she said to Senar, "if you were somewhere else when the Kerralai arrives."

The Guardian needed no encouragement, but he paused as the implication of her words sank in. She had said "when" the Kerralai arrived, not "if." How could she be sure the demon was coming this way?

"What of you, priestess?" he said. Something told him the woman was capable of looking after herself, but he had to ask. "Will you be safe here?"

"But of course. I have the high priest and his cerrrtitude to protect me. Now, if you will excuse me, I have work to do."

Kempis gaped at the rubble of the building. Destroyed by the Kerralai's sorcery, it had collapsed into the passage to block his way. He staggered to a halt and doubled over with his hands on his knees, gasping. It felt as if he'd spent his whole Shroud-cursed life running, yet his body showed no sign of getting used to the exertion.

Sniffer pulled him into a side alley. "Come on, sir. Temple is only a few streets away."

Kempis pushed himself into motion again.

Bright Eyes had given the two of them the slip in the Artisan Quarter, but the demon circling overhead was not so easily shaken off, and for a while the septia had set his course by the creature's nightmarish form. Then, when he lost sight of the Kerralai too, he'd followed the sound of its wing beats or the crash of collapsing masonry as it unleashed another eye-watering blast of magic. With each sorcerous detonation Kempis would pray that Bright Eyes's running days were over. Each volley, though, would be followed by the demon's growl of frustration, and the chase would continue.

As Kempis swung into Elder Lane he saw the temple of the Lord of Hidden Faces ahead. A figure darted from left to right past the end of the alley. Bright Eyes. She'd lost her longknives and her limp too, but then having a demon on your tail would cure all manner of minor discomforts, Kempis supposed. Another flash of the Kerralai's sorcery darkened the air about the woman, followed by a crack and a rumble of stone. Clearly the demon had not given up on its pursuit of the assassin, but was it too much to ask that the creature had finally hit its target?

As if I'm that damned lucky.

Kempis labored to the end of the alley. Looking right he spied a two-story house that had been hit by the last burst of magic. It was missing the whole of one wall and part of another. A corpse lay amid the devastation, and the septia's heart leapt . . . until he realized the figure was wearing black, not the assassin's blue. A patter of mortar sounded, followed by a creak of masonry. Then the roof of the building collapsed onto the lower levels, and the walls slumped outward, spilling debris into the street. A cloud of dust billowed up to cloak the house and the road beside it.

Bright Eyes was nowhere to be seen.

Damn it, the woman was going to escape again! With the portal just a short distance away she would surely . . .

Kempis's thoughts trailed off.

For Bright Eyes had emerged at a run from the murk, heading straight for the septia. The flesh round her left eye was swollen, and her hair had come loose from its plait. Seeing Kempis, she swerved toward the temple. The ramp leading up to it was littered with chunks of stone, some of them burning with black sorcery. Bright Eyes tried to weave a path through them, only to stumble on a fallen roof tile.

A cold wind hit Kempis from behind. He looked up to see the Kerralai glide overhead. The membrane of its left wing was torn, and a broken spear jutted from its shoulder on that side—courtesy of a Storm Guard at the Round, no doubt. With a shriek it unleashed a blast of magic at Bright Eyes's back, and the street was plunged into shadow again.

The darkness must have alerted the assassin to her danger, for she flung herself to one side and skidded to the edge of the ramp. The wave of power swept past her, leaving in its wake a glowing pathway of rock.

The sorcery rolled toward the shrine.

Kempis's eyes widened. The shrine! From inside the temple he could hear a man's booming voice—the high priest's, probably. Doubtless a congregation had gathered for his sermon, but it was too late for Kempis to shout a warning. Even if the worshippers heard him, they wouldn't be able to escape before the magic hit.

The sorcery incinerated one of the masked statues flanking the temple's porch, then struck the building's façade.

And fizzled out like a burning torch plunged into water. Tendrils of smoke curled into the sky.

Kempis stared. What had just happened? The Kerralai's magic was as strong as anything he'd encountered, yet someone had neutralized it with an ease that was almost dismissive. The temple must be shielded by formidable wards. But then why couldn't Kempis sense them? A power as strong as that should have been simple to discern. The septia felt nothing, though. Not nothing as of something being hidden, just . . . nothing.

Bright Eyes had regained her feet and now entered the temple's porch. As she vanished inside, the Kerralai landed on the shrine's roof. Sparks flew as it touched down. It took to the air once more with a beat of its massive wings. Again it tried to alight, and again there was a flash of sorcery. Coils of magic traveled up its legs. The creature gave a snarl that quickly turned into a squeal. Didn't seem right to Kempis somehow, a noise like that coming from a demon's throat.

Four Storm Guards appeared along Princes Street from the direction of the portal, and Kempis understood suddenly why Bright Eyes had returned this way rather than pass through the gateway. Two of the soldiers carried crossbows that they raised to fire at the Kerralai. Stupidity like that deserved a slab in the Mausoleum, but Kempis didn't want the demon mistaking him for the shooter. He barked at the Storm Guards to lower their weapons. The leader of the quartet, a female octa with the gray eyes of an oscura addict, gave him a disdainful look before gesturing for her companions to stand down.

The Kerralai was hovering above a house next to the temple. Each beat of its wings buffeted Kempis. Lifting a hand to the shaft of the broken spear in its shoulder, it tugged the weapon free, then licked the blood oozing from its wound. The taste seemed to stoke the fires of its anger. Its eyes blazed, and its wings beat faster until it rose to the height of a hundred armspans. Kempis retreated into the passage. The demon seemed to fill the sky above him, two red eyes in an ocean of black.

Another shriek, and it plunged toward him.

Then it leveled off just above the height of the rooftops and sailed away south.

The septia stared after it, his thoughts a mix of relief and confusion. What, that was it? The demon had given up? But hadn't Senar Sol said it would hunt down its quarry, no matter where she went or how long it took? It wasn't as if Bright Eyes could shelter in the temple forever. Why hadn't the Kerralai waited until the high priest threw her out, or until the assassin made a break for the portal?

Kempis put such thoughts from his mind. The path to the temple was clear, and Bright Eyes—without her longknives now—was somewhere inside. He needed to find her before she found a different way out.

Sheathing his sword, he strode toward the ramp.

CHAPTER 11

"MAY I join you?"

Agenta looked across at the speaker and found herself staring into the dark eyes of an overweight man in a lurid pink shirt with a stain over the right breast. A few years younger than the kalischa, he had a round, open face.

"You're the one from outside the White Lady's Temple," Agenta said.

"You recognize the stain?"

"The color of your shirt, actually. You should have taken advantage of the excuse that I gave you to change it."

The man chuckled.

Agenta turned away, hoping he would take the hint that she wanted to be alone. For all the *Icewing*'s size, the decks felt claustrophobic with so many people on board. Quarter of a bell ago she had descended to join the Storm Guards on the main deck in an effort to escape the prattle of her fellow dignitaries. But apparently that detail was lost on her new companion, because he cleared his throat and said, "My name is Farrell." He extended a hand.

The kalischa hesitated before shaking it. "Agenta."

"And what were you doing at the temple earlier? If you don't mind me asking."

"I do mind."

To the south and east, Agenta noticed the *Crest*. It ran ahead of the *Icewing* on a wave of water-magic half the height of that which bore the emira's flagship, and the kalischa suddenly understood something of the grip the Storm Lords held over the Sabian League. For if Orsan, who was not even one of their number, could conjure up a wave ten paces high, what damage could the Storm Lords wreak on the cities round the Sabian Sea if they were to act in concert against them? What was power, after all, but possession of the greatest threat of force?

Even accounting for the difference in size between the waves under the *Icewing* and the *Crest*, though, the emira's flagship was catching up to the Gilgamarian vessel at an improbable rate.

Farrell must have guessed her thoughts for he said, "We have an air-mage on board. See how the *Icewing*'s sails bulge, yet the sails of that ship"—he nodded at the *Crest*—"barely stir?"

"An air-mage?"

He pointed to an enormously fat man talking to Orsan on the forecastle. "Selis, he is called." Farrell grinned. "What else could he be but an air-mage? Without sorcery to lighten the load, how would he ever haul his vast bulk around?"

"Maybe he can teach you a trick or two before the day is out."

Her companion bellowed with laughter, and Agenta frowned as a dozen sets of eyes turned toward her.

When Farrell's laughter was spent he said, "It seems Orsan has finally gained a respite from Karan del Orco's questioning."

"Why would the emira invite us aboard her flagship and then not turn up?" Agenta mused aloud.

"Orsan claims not to know."

"Claims, yes."

Orsan looked at the kalischa and smiled. *He's hiding something.* Up until now Agenta had assumed some urgent business had kept Imerle from taking part in Dragon Day, but what if she'd intended all along not to come? But if that was so, why had she invited Agenta and Rethell on board? To get them out of Olaire, presumably. What was about to happen in the city that the emira did not want them to see? Her coup, perhaps? No, for even if she managed to seize Olaire, her triumph would be short-lived when the other Storm Lords returned from the Hunt.

A serving-girl approached carrying a tray of drinks. Agenta took a glass of red wine from it; Farrell chose white. It seemed he had no intention of leaving the kalischa to her solitude, so she sighed and said, "How did you come by the honor of being stood up by Imerle today?"

"Oh, the invitation wasn't to me. Not really." He pointed toward the aft deck. "That's my father there, Samel, speaking to yours."

Agenta looked across to see Rethell talking to the man in the gold shirt Lydanto had indicated earlier. She gave Farrell a calculating glance. So this was the son of one of the merchants who had lent money to the emira, was it? Had Farrell been sent to Agenta by his father to determine what she knew about the loans? If so, perhaps *she* should be taking this opportunity to find out what she could about *him*. "What do you and your father trade in?"

"Elescorian brandy."

"I didn't have Imerle down as the Elescorian brandy type."

"Nor is she."

"And yet she must be a client of yours to have asked you here today."

Farrell took a sip of wine, then winced and peered at his glass—a pretense, Agenta suspected, to give him time to think. "Of sorts. My father is one of the emira's . . . supporters."

"I didn't realize Imerle's authority relied on the support of the merchant classes." She pretended understanding. "Ah, you mean a *financial* supporter."

Farrell's voice was flat. "It is forbidden by the Storm Lords' charter to offer monetary inducements to members of the Storm Council."

Monetary inducements? *Someone's choosing his words carefully.* "I assume there is a way round these edicts."

"The councils of Olaire's merchant guilds are permitted to make certain donations to a Storm Lord's cause, yes."

"So Samel supports the emira in these councils?"

"Precisely."

"And what does he receive in exchange?"

"Why, the honor of Imerle's patronage. Along with the chance to be let down by her on occasions such as this." Then, "Have you ever taken part in Dragon Day before?"

Agenta was silent, considering. She'd hoped her questions would prompt Farrell to brag about his father's relationship with the emira, but for all the man's youth, there was a glint of intelligence in his eyes. Clearly he was anxious to change the topic of conversation, and if she pressed him further she risked arousing his suspicions. Better to wait for the wine to grease his tongue before steering the discussion back to his father's dealings with Imerle. In answer to his question she said, "No, I haven't. You?"

"Once, three years ago. My father was negotiating a contract with Prince Ellifah of Hardangill. Both my father and I were invited onto Ellifah's flagship."

"And?"

"And I never saw a dragon all day. Ellifah's starting berth was to the east of Natilly. By the time we got to the Dragon Gate the Hunt was over. Afterward I learned that three Storm Lords had converged on the dragon as soon as it passed beneath the gate. The honors had to be shared between them because no one could agree on who delivered the killing blow. The poor beast didn't stand a chance."

"Somehow I find that difficult to believe."

Farrell's eyes twinkled with amusement. "Are you familiar with the armaments on the *Icewing*?"

"No."

"Then allow me to enlighten you. The ship has two ballistae, one on the forecastle, one on the aft deck." He pointed to the giant contraptions. "The weapon on the forecastle can fire weighted nets up to a hundred paces. The one on the aft deck fires bolts attached by ropes to barrels of sorcerously lightened air—see them? Spear a dragon with a few of those, and even the largest creature won't be able to sink beneath the water."

"Spear a dragon? I thought their scales were impenetrable."

"They are."

"Then what use are missiles against them?"

Farrell sipped his wine. "Even a dragon's armor has weak points: its belly, its eyes, its mouth. The neck too—when a dragon turns its head, small spaces can open up between the neck plates."

"Even if you hit one of those spaces, though, the blow will feel like a pinprick to a creature that size."

"If you're using normal missiles, yes." Farrell gestured to a weapons rack behind him. "Some of the arrows we're carrying, though, are invested with sorcery—the black-shafted ones with water-magic, the white-shafted ones with air-magic. Find a gap between two of the dragon's scales with these, and the sorcery released into the creature's flesh will tear the scales clear from its body. Put an arrow in the beast's eye, and you'll blow it out of its socket."

Agenta saw again the trader ship destroyed off Gilgamar. "Assuming the dragon lets you live long enough to get your shot off."

"That's where Orsan comes in. A powerful water-mage can blind a dragon by vaporizing the sea in front of it, or create currents to flip the creature onto its back and thus expose its belly."

The kalischa studied the merchant. "For someone who has taken part in Dragon Day only once before, you seem to know a lot about it."

"That time I was telling you about, when I was invited onto Ellifah's flagship, I got stuck next to some Dragon Day veteran who insisted on boring me rigid with his ramblings."

"I know how you must have felt."

Farrell roared his laughter again, and Agenta smiled in spite of herself. Turning to the weapons rack behind her, she took out a white-shafted arrow from a quiver.

"It's light."

"The air-magic invested in it makes it fly farther than a normal arrow. Archers using the arrows for the first time have difficulty adjusting their aim."

"A bad workman always blames his tools."

The merchant's eyebrows lifted. "You are skilled with a bow?"

Before Agenta could reply, a bow was thrust in front of her. She looked across to see a Storm Guard in a red head scarf. His eyes were bright with challenge. The kalischa hesitated. She had no wish to draw the attention of the other passengers again, but nor was she one to back down from a challenge.

She nodded to the Storm Guard. With a practiced motion, he slipped a string over the ends of the bow. Agenta passed her wineglass to Farrell, then took the offered weapon. It was a composite bow with a hand-grip of honey-colored wood. Two strips of alamandra horn were glued to the front, and a strip of sinew was attached to the back. A memory came to Agenta of the last time she'd held such a weapon, a month before her brother's death. The two of them had been on the Key Tower, shooting at the starbeaks diving for fish in the Ribbon Sea. Late in the day a bird the kalischa was aiming at aborted its dive, but Agenta had kept the bowstring drawn to her ear in readiness for another target. Such was the weight of the draw that by the time the next bird began its descent, her arm was shaking. When she finally fired her arrow it fell so short that Zelin had collapsed in gales of laughter. Agenta had laughed too. It had been hard not to laugh when Zelin was around.

She looked again at the white arrow. The shaft was scored with glyphs, and her flesh tingled as she brushed a finger over them. "The carvings will have warped the shaft."

"Yet the air-magic invested in the arrow will ensure it flies true," Farrell said.

"Assuming the air-mage who did the investing is worth his salt."

"Getting our excuses in early, are we?"

Agenta shot him a look. She'd deserved that, she supposed, what with her line about bad workmen. "I'll need a target," she said, lifting the white arrow to her bowstring.

From the corner of her eye she saw the soldier with the red head scarf go still. He spat over the rail and said, "If it's all the same to you, m'Lady, I'd rather you didn't. Use that arrow, I mean. There's precious few of them on board, and they're best left for the dragon if we meet one."

The kalischa shrugged, then returned the arrow to its quarrel and selected another with a standard shaft. "I still need a target."

Farrell scanned the sea. "There!"

At first Agenta thought he was indicating the *Crest,* a stone's throw off the port quarter and falling farther behind with each heartbeat. Then she noticed a fin break the waves fifty armspans away, just beyond the ripples of foam created by the *Icewing*'s passage. A briar shark, judging by the shape of the fin, and a big one too. A simple enough shot, then, provided the fish remained on its current course parallel to the *Icewing.*

Agenta tested the bow's draw-weight—heavy, but not as heavy as the weapon she'd used on the Key Tower that day. She nocked her arrow to the string and took a moment to assess the conditions. The wind was from the north and west. With the *Icewing* riding a wave of water-magic, the pitch of the deck was less pronounced than it would have been had the ship's bow been cutting through the waves. The slow, rhythmic movement would make the shot only marginally more difficult than if she'd been standing on dry land.

Pulling back the bowstring she sighted on her target, squinting against the glare of the sun on the sea.

Then she let fly.

Her arrow splashed into the water three paces beyond the shark and as many behind.

"Not bad," Farrell said, his voice even. He put the two wineglasses down on the deck and held out a hand for the bow.

"That was only a sighter," Agenta snapped, snatching another arrow from the quiver in the weapons rack. She checked its shaft for imperfections before nocking it to the bowstring. Picturing the flight of her first arrow, she realized she'd underestimated the power of the bow. She'd also overcompensated for the wind, for while the *Icewing*'s sails were bulging, that was due more to Selis's air-magic than to the force of the breeze. She adjusted her aim. A stillness had settled on the main deck, and she could feel the Storm Guards' gazes on her. She blinked sweat from her eyes as she pulled on the bowstring—

The shark dived beneath the waves.

Laughter rang out to Agenta's right, and she lowered the bow. Her cheeks felt hot. Unwilling to meet the looks of those around her, she kept her gaze focused on the spot where the fish had vanished.

Farrell pointed. "Look!"

The shark had resurfaced a dozen paces farther from the ship and forward of its last position. But the shot was still on. Composing herself, Agenta tugged on the bowstring again, aiming for the point where the fish's fin met its body. She blocked out the sensation of the arrow's flight against her cheek, the bite of the bowstring on her fingers.

The shark's fin dipped beneath the water once more, only to reappear an instant later in the same place.

Stay still, damn you!

A muscle in Agenta's left arm twitched. She'd been holding the bowstring at full draw for twenty heartbeats, and her strength was beginning to fail. If she let fly now she risked embarrassing herself as she had with her brother, and yet would it be any less humiliating if she declined the shot?

Taking a breath, she released it at the same time she released the bowstring.

From the moment the arrow left the weapon Agenta knew she had missed her target. Biting back a curse, she watched the missile flash over the sea. She lost sight of it in the dazzle of the sun and was about to turn away when she saw a puff of spray beside the shark.

The fish sank beneath the waves again.

But not before Agenta had glimpsed the arrow protruding from its flank. The water where the shark had been swimming was now tinged red.

Sardonic cheers sounded from the Storm Guards round her, and the soldier with the head scarf gave a whistle of appreciation. "I'll be damned."

Agenta's mouth had dropped open. She shut it again, then looked hopefully at her father on the aft deck. Either Rethell hadn't seen the shot, though, or he wasn't acknowledging it, for his attention appeared fixed on Samel.

"Impressive," Farrell said. The kalischa offered him the bow, but he gestured to the now-empty waves. "It seems the shark has grown tired of the game."

"I'm sure you'll get a chance to test your aim once the Dragon Gate goes up. Whatever dragon passes beneath it will make for an easy target."

Farrell's smile was rueful. "You forget, with the *Icewing* setting off so late, we'll be left with a starting berth far from the gate. Odds are we won't even see a dragon today."

As Kempis entered the temple's porch, the high priest's voice filled his ears. From what the septia had heard at the Watchstation, the man was committed to the liberation of Olaire's lowborn, yet in his pompous tone Kempis heard only another blueblood in the making—someone who wanted not to overthrow the elite but to take their place. His sermon hadn't stopped during the Kerralai's attack on the shrine. Evidently he was confident in the efficacy of his temple's wards, but then why was Kempis still unable to detect any trace of those defenses?

He passed into the anteroom beyond the porch. In the far wall was a rectangular opening of light through which he could see a courtyard filled with a crowd of seated figures. The corner of the anteroom ahead and to Kempis's right was occupied by a statue of a masked, alamandra-legged figure, while to his left . . .

The septia's breath hissed out. Lying on the floor next to an overturned bench was Bright Eyes, her arms folded across her chest as if her body had been arranged for a funeral bier. Her blue-tinged skin and perfectly still chest told Kempis she had passed through Shroud's Gate, yet there was no mark on her corpse to show how she had died.

Beside her knelt a priestess wearing a mask of white wood. The woman's right hand rested on the assassin's chest, her fingers drumming against her breastbone. When she looked at Kempis, the brown eyes visible through her mask's eye slits sparkled with humor. And why not? What could be funnier than having a stranger blunder into your temple and die in your arms?

Unless, of course, Bright Eyes was no stranger. Could the assassin be a follower of the Lord of Hidden Faces?

Kempis gestured for Sniffer to wait at the doorway, then approached the priestess.

"She is dead," the woman said to him.

"Explains the not-breathing thing," Kempis replied. "What happened here?"

"Your friend attempted to travel from this place to another realm. But the distances between the worlds were too great."

"She thought there was a portal here? Why?"

The priestess's fingers fluttered. "Why indeed?"

Kempis slammed his sword into its scabbard. He should have been pleased to find Bright Eyes dead, but there was something in the masked woman's manner that left him feeling like he'd won a hand at flush only to discover the pot was empty. Was it possible she'd played some part in the assassin's death? But how, exactly? It wasn't as if she could have tricked the assassin into believing a gateway existed when there was none.

Kempis's gaze shifted from the priestess to Bright Eyes's corpse, then back again. Something about this business didn't smell right. "She one of yours?"

"I am new to Olaire. You will have to ask High Priest Artagina."

"I mean to. How come you know she was trying to jump between worlds?"

"We are in my temple. Nothing takes place here without my knowledge."

"You sensed her open a portal?"

"I sensed her spirit depart her body—as did the Kerralai. Why else do you think the demon left?"

"Her spirit passed over to this other world, then, but not her body?"

"So it seems." The priestess placed a hand on Bright Eyes's brow as if she were checking her temperature. Was that a whisper of magic Kempis detected? No, he must have been mistaken.

A suspicion came to him. "Were you the one who neutralized the demon's sorcery?"

The masked woman ignored the question. "Your hunt for this woman is at an end, Watchman. You may leave her body with me."

Kempis squinted at her. "What do you want with it?"

"I'm sure I'll think of something."

The Abyss, she would. Knowing Hilaire, the quina would want to see Bright Eyes's corpse for herself—Kempis's word alone that the assassin was dead would not suffice. In any event, he hadn't spent days chasing down his prize just to surrender it to a stranger. Perhaps he would have Bright Eyes stuffed and mounted in the Watchstation's common room—

"What's going on here?" a man's voice boomed.

The high priest's sermon had ended, Kempis realized, and a figure wearing a gold mask was now striding through the doorway to the courtyard. It felt to the septia like he was being run down by a lederel bull, so he drew his sword and pointed it at the priest's stomach.

The man drew up. "You dare threaten me in my Lord's temple?"

His Lord? So this was Artagina himself? "Keep your voice down," Kempis said to him. He jabbed a thumb over his shoulder in the direction of Bright Eyes's corpse. "You want to wake her?"

"Wake who?"

"I was hoping you could tell me, but you'll have to wait your turn. I ain't finished with your priestess yet."

"Priestess, what priestess? What are talking about, man?"

Kempis glanced behind. Then blinked. The masked woman was gone, and with her the body of the assassin. He turned to Sniffer. "Where'd she go?"

For a moment the Untarian couldn't speak. "I was looking at you . . ."

Cursing, Kempis scanned the room. There were only two doors: the one that Sniffer was guarding and the one the high priest had come through. And if the priestess had dragged Bright Eyes that way, Kempis would have seen her circling behind Artagina. That meant she had to have vanished herself using sorcery. But then why hadn't he sensed anything? He looked back at the high priest, wondering if the man held the answers. Judging by the puzzlement in Artagina's eyes, though, he was as much in the dark as Kempis.

The septia heard someone enter the room behind him. He swung round, expecting to see the priestess, but instead he found Duffle standing in front of him.

"Sir, Septia, sir!"

Kempis scowled. "How did you find me?"

"Followed the carnage."

At a safe distance, no doubt. "Well? Spit it out."

"Another assassination, sir, Septia, sir. One of the Storm Lords—Thane Tanner."

Kempis's pulse kicked in his neck. "Impossible."

"Happened outside the Oaken Arena. Crossbow bolt through the right temple." Duffle raised a finger to show where the missile had struck. "Messy—"

"When?" Kempis cut in.

"Half a bell ago, maybe."

Half a bell ago Bright Eyes had been in the Round. And while Kempis had lost sight of her during the pursuit to the temple, there was no way she could have sneaked down to the arena and killed someone in that time—especially not with a Kerralai on her tail. Which could only mean . . .

Another Shroud-cursed assassin.

Feeling nauseated, Kempis exchanged a glance with Sniffer.

The Untarian grinned. "Hilaire's gonna love this."

From atop the Dragon Gate, Karmel looked down at the dragons in the Cappel Strait. At dawn a Natillian official had poured dragon blood into the sea on the Sabian side of the portcullis, and now the creatures were taking it in turns to try to smash their way through. Every strike of their armored heads set the battlements juddering and Karmel's teeth rattling. From beyond the door to the control room she heard voices, but as yet no guards had emerged to relieve her and Veran. The eighth bell had sounded an age ago, and the sun seemed to have become stuck in its flight across the sky. What in the Chameleon's name was keeping the fools? The priestess just wanted to get *on* with this.

She fingered the damp collar of her shirt. Earlier she and Veran had stripped the corpses of the two Dianese guards, only to find the soldiers had pissed themselves, leaving their uniforms stained not just with blood but also with urine and—in Perfume's case—excrement. Karmel had used water from her flask to wash the worst of the stains from the woman's shirt and trousers. Then, with the eastern skyline brightening, she'd been forced to don the still-wet uniform. With the heat of the day building, the marks on the trousers had soon faded, but there remained a blotch on her collar below her right ear. The priestess could only pray anyone seeing it mistook it for nothing more sinister than a sweat stain.

Veran had grumbled all the time he'd cleaned the blood from Clemin's shirt. Karmel had long since given up hope of receiving any praise from him for having silenced the guards, but then it wasn't like she was Veran's pupil that she needed his approval. The truth was, he couldn't have dealt with the soldiers any better than she had. *That* was what really irked him. He'd taken out his frustrations on Karmel by trying to order her to clean the naked corpses in case the stink of them alerted whichever guards came to relieve them. As if she was going to stand for that! Instead she'd climbed down to the gate, and Veran had reluctantly lowered the unwashed bodies for her to lash to the portcullis in the recess. It was only a matter of time before someone spotted—or smelled—them, but with luck the two Chameleons would be safely inside the control room before they did.

Karmel's throat was burning. She had used the last of her water washing blood from the battlements, but more worrying was the size of the uniform she'd inherited from Perfume. The sleeves of the jacket ended a finger's width short of Karmel's hands, and while her boots concealed the shortness of her trousers, they also pinched her toes. She'd hoped to hide her sandals beneath her jacket and change into them in the control room. But Veran had feared someone might notice the shoes, and in the end they, along with the priestess's pack and everything in it, had been cast into the sea. All Veran had allowed her to keep was her sword and her baldric of throwing knives, now concealed beneath the sash across her chest.

The priest, too, had retained a baldric of knives, together with two battered armguards which he'd clipped round his lower arms beneath his shirt sleeves. He wore Clemin's blade at his hip, but no swordsman worth his salt would enter combat with an unfamiliar weapon—meaning Veran intended to fight bare-handed when his knives ran out, using his armguards to parry his enemies' attacks. It seemed Karmel finally had an explanation for the abundance of scars on his arms, if not for how the man had managed to stay alive so long in the Chameleon's service.

Dian and Natilly had stirred to life with the coming of dawn, and the noise of the Dragon Hunt crowds had swelled from a murmur to a hum and finally a drone. South of the Dragon Gate, the terraces overlooking the Cappel Strait—the same terraces that had been crammed with people for the executions—were almost empty, for they offered a poor vantage of the seas where the Hunt would take place. Instead most of the clamor came from the galleries along the cliffs fronting the Sabian Sea. On the towers of Dian's citadel had assembled scores of dignitaries, each arrayed in a costume as colorful as a coral bird's feathers. Karmel scanned their ranks. Governor Piput would be among them, but even if she'd known what he looked like she wouldn't have been able to pick him out. That would change when the Dragon Gate failed to rise: he'd be the one from whom the other dignitaries hastened to distance themselves.

Movement above and to Karmel's left caught her eye, and she glanced up to see two gaudily dressed men in one of the citadel's windows. When they pointed in her direction, she lowered her gaze. In all likelihood it was the dragon's skull and not the priestess herself that had attracted their attention, but in any event there was no way they could make out her features at this distance. All the same, for an uncomfortable heartbeat it seemed to Karmel as if the gazes of *all* the people in Dian and Natilly were focused on her. Her throat closed up like someone had grabbed her round it. And yet hadn't she always wanted the eyes of the world on her? Wasn't that why she had accepted this mission—for the opportunity for notoriety it offered?

Half a league to the north, ships had gathered at the buoys marking the starting positions for the Hunt. Karmel saw Androsian corricks with their high-rounded sterns, Corinian galleys with their green-trimmed sails, Thaxian brigatinas with their black-and-white-banded hulls. Among the flags being flown were the red and yellow stars of Rastamira, the sunburst of Elescori, the white cross on gold of Peron Ra. Of the emira's flagship, there was no sign. Had Imerle chosen to stay away, knowing the gate would not be rising? No, Karmel reasoned, for the woman's absence would have aroused suspicions. Most likely the *Icewing* was anchored to the east or west, concealed from the priestess's view by the cliffs.

Her bladder felt ready to burst. She shifted her weight from one foot to the other. Veran, a pace to her left, was speaking in a low voice, telling her again what to expect when they entered the control room—as if the previous nine hundred and ninety-nine times might not have been enough. Karmel had wanted to attack as soon as they were inside, but Veran said they needed to know exactly what they were dealing with first, and the priestess had conceded the sense in that. The point was rapidly becoming moot, though, for if they were kept waiting much longer there wouldn't be time to waste on planning and reconnaissance . . .

The sound of bolts being drawn back jolted her from her reverie. She had just enough presence of mind to snatch up her helmet and pull it over her head before the door to the citadel opened. Two soldiers appeared, anonymous behind their faceplates, yet unquestionably both men. Veran was already striding toward them. The first newcomer raised a hand as if he meant to challenge him, but Veran pushed past, muttering a rebuke to the guards for their tardiness. He kicked open the door to the control room and plunged through.

The two Dianese soldiers stared after him, then swung to face Karmel as she followed. One of them said something as she drew level. Karmel did not catch his words. She was too busy trying to peer through the yawning doorway into the gloom beyond, but the darkness was too deep for her to see anything. As she passed the second guard she felt the prickle of his gaze on her back. Her hand strayed to the hilt of her sword.

Then the soldier slapped her on the buttocks, and it was all she could do not to spin round and give him a piece of her mind.

The air in the control room was heavy with heat and blackweed smoke. Within moments the padding of Karmel's helmet was soaked through. Such was the limited visibility afforded by her helmet's eye slits that she had to turn her head to scan the chamber. The room was windowless. Light came from a brazier in the corner to her right, and from an oil lamp on a table diagonally opposite. To her left an immense chain rose from a hole in the floor, turning at right angles over a smooth lip of rock before passing through an oversized metal chest with four large circular holes in the top. The chain finished at an upright drum from which eight spokes extended at chest height. To Karmel's right was a cabinet that reached from floor to ceiling. On the wall opposite, a closed but unbolted door led deeper into the citadel.

All exactly as Veran had said it would be. Except . . .

In the room were two male soldiers, one shaven-headed, the other bearded, both flushed and wearing shirts stained beneath the arms. *Just two.* Karmel had expected the guards manning the capstan to be in position already. Her thoughts raced. The Dragon Hunt wasn't due to start for another quarter-bell, but there was nothing to say the Chameleons had to wait that long before attacking. Yesterday Veran had told her he had a device to disable the capstan permanently, so if he used it now the Dianese wouldn't be able to repair the damage before the Hunt commenced. Karmel wanted to laugh. It was suddenly all so easy: kill the guards, disable the capstan, then activate their powers and lie low until the dust settled. If they left the door to the citadel unlocked, when more soldiers arrived they would assume whoever had destroyed the capstan had already slipped away into the fortress. It was perfect!

Karmel tried to catch Veran's gaze, but his back was to her. In her peripheral vision she saw Beardy close and lock the door to the battlements. A red-tinged gloom descended on the chamber. The noise of the crowds fell away to a whisper, but the floor still shivered to the beat of the dragons butting the gate.

Veran spoke to Baldy. "Why were we left out there so long? Thought we'd end up watching the Hunt from the gate."

The guard shrugged. "Should have asked Hook when you passed him. Bastard overslept, is my guess."

"We still on for a start at the ninth bell?"

Another shrug.

Karmel watched nonplussed as Veran began walking toward the door to the citadel. Where the hell was he going? Did he think they had time for a tour of the fortress before they got down to business? Or were two guards not enough of a challenge that he had to go looking for more? Perhaps he wanted to lock the door to the citadel to ensure there were no gate-crashers. Yes, that had to be it.

Even as the thought came to her, though, Veran drew up and spun to face Beardy and Baldy once more.

Frowning, Karmel turned with him. *Now* what? Had he changed his mind and decided to kill the soldiers while their attention was elsewhere? Beardy was picking his nose, while Baldy had crouched to polish his boots with a sleeve. Karmel tensed to strike.

Instead of attacking the Dianese, though, Veran said to them, "You hear that?"

Blank looks. The men seemed as confused as Karmel.

"From the battlements," Veran added. "Sounded like Hook calling."

The soldiers exchanged a glance. Then Beardy turned for the door, his companion watching him.

Both guards were now facing away from the Chameleons, and Karmel sensed Veran release his power. She followed his lead—though why he had to make himself invisible before attacking was beyond her. As Beardy opened the door and called out to Hook, Karmel drew a knife from her baldric. She'd have to wait for the door to close again before letting fly—

Veran seized her wrist. Faintly above the din from outside she heard him say, "Wait."

"Wait for what?" she wanted to ask, but Beardy was already closing the door once more, and she was forced to bite her tongue.

"What did he want?" Baldy asked his companion.

"Nothing." Beardy scanned the room. "Say, did you hear them other two leave?"

"They ain't here now, are they? Work it out, genius."

Veran's grip was still tight on Karmel's wrist. He waited until both Dianese were turned away again before drawing her back, step by painstaking step, into the corner beside the weapons cabinet. Such was the size of the cabinet that it shielded the Chameleons from the guards' sight. Karmel resheathed her knife, then lifted her helmet and perched it at an angle on her head. When Veran also raised his helmet, she leaned in close.

"What are you doing?" she whispered. "There are only two of them! Two!"

"Wait."

"Wait for what, damn you? What is there—"

She fell silent as the door to the citadel opened. A soldier entered, then another, and another, all chatting and laughing, and Karmel hissed her fury until Veran clamped a hand over her mouth. One of the newcomers, a sleepy-eyed man with a limp, must have heard the noise, for his gaze fixed for a moment on the corner where the Chameleons stood before sliding away again.

More and more guards appeared. The priestess's anger gave way to apprehension. *Nine, ten, eleven* . . . But hadn't Veran said there would be eight on the capstan and one overseeing? Still they kept coming. *Twelve, thirteen, fourteen.* Veran's hand remained over Karmel's mouth, but he removed it when she elbowed him in the ribs. When she looked at him, she saw her confusion mirrored in his eyes.

Her count ended at sixteen.

And understanding dawned.

Eight spokes to the capstan, yes, but *two* soldiers to each spoke, not the one they'd anticipated. Karmel ground her teeth together. Now, instead of two opponents she and Veran had almost ten times that number to deal with. Veran's expression had a wry cast to it, and he murmured something that sounded like "one more thing you should know." Whatever the hell that meant.

"Idio—"

His hand covered her mouth again.

Another soldier entered the room, sallow-skinned and wearing a red sash—an officer, Karmel presumed. He slammed shut the door to the citadel. Karmel pulled a face. How many did that make it in all? Just seventeen? There was room for another dozen, surely, if everyone shuffled along.

The officer scented the air like a bloodhound, then started reproaching Beardy and Baldy for the blackweed smoke.

Still Veran made no move to attack.

A suspicion surfaced in Karmel's mind. What if Veran had never intended to attack the guards? What if the Chameleons' real target here was not the Dragon Gate but Governor Piput? If the emira wanted to bring an end to Piput's troublemaking, a dagger through the heart was a more effective solution than this elaborate plot to discredit him. Karmel shook her head. No, that made no sense. There was no reason Veran would have kept such information from her. And in any event, if you wanted to assassinate Piput the very last day you'd choose to do so would be a day such as Dragon Day when the citadel's security was at its tightest.

Meaning this really was the balls-up it appeared.

Karmel elbowed Veran until he removed his hand from her mouth, then elbowed him once more for good measure. Damn the man! Why hadn't he gone for Beardy and Baldy when he had the chance? Even when the first of the new soldiers arrived, he could have driven them back and barred the door against them. But no, he'd just stood there frozen in indecision.

Unless . . .

She cast him a speculative glance. Unless he didn't care how many guards were present because the device he'd brought to destroy the capstan would kill anyone close to it . . .

Her thoughts trailed away. *The device.* It had been in Veran's pack when he climbed the gate, but he'd thrown his bag over the battlements at the same time Karmel tossed hers. So where was the device now? Had he hidden it somewhere about his uniform? Was it so small that it could fit in a pocket?

Her breath caught.

Or had the thing never existed at all?

All at once the pieces fell into place.

"We're not here to stop them raising the gate, are we?" Karmel whispered. "We're here to stop them lowering it again once it's up." *That* was why Veran had passed up the chance to attack Beardy and Baldy. *That* was why he'd refused to tell her about the device in their basement lodgings, and why he'd been opposed to returning to the battlements once the mission was complete—they could hardly escape back that way if there were dragons in the Sabian Sea.

Karmel put her face in her hands. Gods, what a fool she had been! She'd known Imerle was conspiring to stay in power. Well, here was the woman's chance to eliminate the other Storm Lords, all of whom would be out there now on their ships, waiting for the Hunt to start. And the emira herself? With her feet up in Olaire, no doubt, or on her flagship a safe distance from the Dragon Gate, ready to turn and flee once the dragons were released.

Had Caval known the real plan when he briefed her in the temple? The emira had trusted him enough to tell him she was plotting to remain in power, so why wouldn't she trust him with the finer details of the mission? Something he'd said on the beach came back to the priestess—something concerning Veran. *You're to do as he tells you out there, understood?* At the time she had wondered at the intensity of his words, and at what instructions Veran might have for her that Caval could not convey there and then. Now she realized he'd been referring to just this moment.

He knew this would happen. All along, he knew.

But then why hadn't he told her?

Another thought surfaced. Her predecessor on this assignment— the one who'd backed out at the last instant—had he or she withdrawn when the true nature of the mission was revealed? Had Caval feared

Karmel would do the same? She pictured the ships on the Sabian Sea. On most Hunts a vessel or two would be destroyed by whichever dragon was released, but only a handful of passengers lost their lives because other ships would engage the creature before it could feast on them. This time, though, with as many as fifty dragons on the loose . . . *They're all going to die.* Had Caval feared she might balk when she understood how many would perish? Would she have done?

He doesn't trust me. The realization struck her like a punch to the gut. Oh, he trusted her abilities well enough, else he wouldn't have sent her on the mission. It was her conviction he evidently doubted. Her stomach for the job. Her loyalty to the Chameleon cause.

And yet he'd trusted Veran. A man who had walked out on the priesthood.

An outcast.

When Veran spoke, she could barely hear him over the whine of the Dianese officer and the muted crash of the dragons ramming the gate. "Glad you've finally woken up to the real world, girl."

"Why?" Karmel said, her tone bitter. "Why wasn't I told?"

"Ask your precious brother."

"But he said . . ."

She got no further because the officer had finished lecturing Beardy and Baldy and was now crossing to the cabinet. He opened the doors and reached inside. Karmel couldn't see what he tried to take out, but it must have been heavy because he growled at his men, "Help me with these, damn you!"

Eight soldiers hurried to obey.

There was a thud as something hit the floor, then a grinding sound as two guards dragged a huge T-shaped object made of tarnica across the ground. At the officer's direction they left it leaning against the chestlike construction through which the chain passed. Three more such objects followed.

The other soldiers took up their positions at the capstan, their faces ruddy in the light from the lamp and the brazier.

Veran whispered to Karmel, "When the ninth bell rings, they'll start raising the gate. Are you listening, girl? As soon as it's up, those two"—he nodded at Beardy and Baldy—"will lower four metal stays into that chest, where they'll pass through the links of the chain and into holes in the floor. The stays take the weight of the gate so the soldiers at the capstan can relax until a dragon passes through the strait. When that happens—are you getting this?—a horn will sound outside. Then the stays are removed, and the gate is lowered again."

Through the numbness that had seeped into Karmel, she registered that Veran still meant to go through with the plan. In spite of the numbers they faced, he would still go through with it. And in doing so drag her with him through Shroud's Gate, most likely.

"We're not waiting for that horn, though," Veran continued. "We attack as soon as the stays are lowered. First you go for those two." Beardy and Baldy again. "I'll cover the door."

Karmel made no response. The priest began repeating his instructions, only to break off as the officer crossed again to the cabinet and closed its doors.

The priestess had stopped listening anyhow.

He doesn't trust me.

CHAPTER 12

AT MAZANA'S side, Senar entered the gatehouse of the titan fortress. The light was as somber as stone, and when the Guardian looked behind he saw the sunshine streaming through the open gates was held back by a barrier of chill gray air. Powerful sorcery seeped from the walls—the same sorcery that had defeated the attempts of Senar and a handful of other Guardians to punch through the gates of the titan fortress in Karalat two years ago. Memories of that day came back to him: shoving Luker Essendar aside so he could be first up the ladder to the battlements, arrows flitting through an evening sky shot through with bronze, Taluin shamans in the citadel chanting as they whipped their followers into a frenzy of bloodlust. Senar had lost the two missing fingers of his halfhand in that Shroud-cursed fortress.

Ahead the Guardian made out a group of soldiers, sixteen in all, dressed in uniforms with the emblem of a fiery wave on their breasts. The soldiers wore fish-scale armor and were armed with spears as well as the swords scabbarded at their waists. Across from them were four figures, and Senar's expression tightened as he caught sight of Greave among them. With the champion was the Everlord Kiapa, together with a man and a woman Senar recalled seeing at Mazana's house. The man was squat and thick-jawed, and he wore a bearskin cloak and carried a butterfly-bladed ax. The woman was taller and broad-shouldered, and her slanted eyes glittered blood-red.

Mazana's bodyguards were standing as far from the emira's soldiers as the gatehouse would allow. A bristling silence hung in the air, and more than one hand hovered over the hilt of a sword. Not an encouraging start to the expedition, though Senar had a feeling it would represent the high-water mark in relations between the two sides.

"What is he doing here?" he asked Mazana, gesturing to Greave.

The Storm Lady ignored him. "My, my," she said to a bearded officer at the head of the emira's troops. "What a lot of soldiers! And from Imerle's personal guard, no less. Our cause must be dear to her heart indeed."

"With your safety," the man replied, "the emira is not about to take any chances."

And said without even a hint of irony, either. Senar was impressed.

Mazana crossed to speak to Kiapa, and the bearded officer—Septia Cilin Rai, he introduced himself—said for Senar's ears only, "We'll wait for your signal."

Senar hesitated, then nodded. He'd wondered if Imerle would expect him merely to stand aside when the attack on Mazana's forces came, but it appeared she wanted him to lead it. This would be a test of his loyalty, he knew, and if he failed it the septia and his troops would be on hand to cut him down along with the Storm Lady and her followers. Assuming Cilin's talk of awaiting Senar's signal wasn't just a ruse. For all the Guardian knew, the septia's orders might be to plunge a knife into Senar's back at the first opportunity.

Still, at least that would deprive Greave of the pleasure of doing so.

From the direction of the citadel Mistress Darbonna came shuffling toward the company. She drew up a few paces away.

"So many of you!" she said, aghast.

"Is there a problem?" Mazana asked.

"No," the old woman replied, recovering quickly. "No, of course not. We are just not set to receive such a large number of guests." Her eyes brightened. "You will be wanting a tour of the main reading room, I presume? Abologog's Treatises on Reverence are the prize exhibit, but there are countless other treasures . . ."

Her voice trailed off as she scanned the faces of the assembled men and women, her gaze coming to rest finally on Greave's scowling countenance.

"Ah, yes," she said. "Perhaps some other time."

———

As the last of the stays were lowered into the chest, Karmel watched the soldiers manning the capstan slump against their spokes. The echoes of clanking chains died away, and with them the tremors that had rocked the chamber as if the priestess were trapped in the belly of some monstrous creature of metal and stone. Outside, a dragon must have discovered its path to the Sabian Sea lay open, for a triumphant trumpeting sounded. *Not long now,* Karmel thought. As soon as the beast passed through the strait, the gate would be lowered again.

The priestess's insides were clenched so tight she wanted to vomit. She placed her helmet on the floor, knowing the limited visibility afforded by its eye slits would be the death of her if she tried to fight in it. Veran followed her lead, then raised an eyebrow to inquire if she was ready. Karmel screwed up her face. Would it make any difference if she said no? She'd considered repaying Caval's lack of faith in her by refusing to attack, but what would that achieve? Veran would doubtless go through with the assault anyway, and even if she remained still and silent in the corner, she was sure to be discovered once the Dianese knew there were Chameleons on the loose.

Better death than capture, she reckoned. Better she was cut down by a sword than cast into the sea for the dragons to fight over.

Drawing four throwing knives from her baldric, she arranged them in a fan shape in her left hand. Her stinging eyes and the lump in her throat reminded her of the night's sleep she'd missed, but there was nothing to be done for that now. If she was to going to survive, she needed to clear her head. A nod to Veran. He held her gaze, his expression unreadable. Then he drew two of his own throwing knives.

Without ceremony, he stepped out from cover and hurled one at the red-sashed officer. It took the soldier in the back. He pitched forward onto his face.

For a moment the other Dianese guards stared at the body in stunned silence.

Karmel threw her first knife. Beardy was her target, just visible to the left of the soldiers at the capstan. The tightness of Perfume's shirt caused the priestess to drag down her throw, but her blade still thudded into her victim's stomach.

The room exploded into motion.

Karmel transferred another throwing knife from her left hand to her right. The key to this grisly business was not to throw aimlessly into the melee, but rather to pick her victims before releasing. Blades two and three flew to their targets: a long-haired man who'd been first to look in her direction, then a barrel-chested soldier quick to draw his sword. Her next target—an olive-skinned man wearing his hair in a topknot—surprised her with the speed of his charge, and her throw went high and wild. Fortune was on her side, though, for the guard tripped over one of his fallen comrades.

Karmel unsheathed the Chameleon's blade.

Two soldiers rushed at her with swords drawn.

She froze and employed her power.

Her assailants halted, shouting in bewilderment.

Karmel, now invisible, allowed herself a smile. It seemed the guards had never crossed blades with a Chameleon before, for if they had they would have known she'd merely stilled her movements. Instead they looked round as if they expected her to rematerialize in some other part of the chamber.

Their confusion gave Karmel time to draw a fifth throwing knife and let fly. She'd done so with her left hand rather than her preferred right, but still her weapon found its mark in a soldier's chest. He stumbled back into the arms of his friend with the topknot. Lunging forward, Karmel sliced open that man's throat.

The priestess had now accounted for five of the Dianese, but even if Veran had killed a like number that still left nine to deal with. Glancing at the priest she saw he'd locked the door to the citadel but was now being driven back toward the table with the oil lamp. A blond-haired soldier dashed for the door. As he made to throw back the bolts, Veran grabbed the lamp and flung it against the wall above the door. The lamp shattered to leave a black smudge on the stone. Glass and burning oil rained down onto Blondie's head. He went up in flames with a *whoosh* and staggered, shrieking, back among his fellows, setting light to the jacket of another guard. The flailing of the stricken men sent shadows cavorting around the room.

In throwing her fifth knife Karmel had made herself visible to the enemy once more. Three men now edged toward her: a Maru, a stocky man with a maniacal smile, and a bucktoothed man who fought left-handed. Behind them Baldy had found a helper, and the duo were lifting one of the stays from the chestlike construction. Karmel considered her next move. Apparently it needed two to raise the stays, so if she could bring down Baldy, one of the three soldiers facing her might be forced to make up the numbers. How to reach Baldy, though? She had two daggers left in her baldric, but she would need to buy herself time to draw and throw.

Above Blondie's screams the priestess heard a horn blare outside. *The signal to lower the gate.* A dragon must have swum through the strait into the Sabian Sea.

A crack of metal on stone sounded as the first of the stays was dropped onto the floor.

Karmel retreated toward the corner with the brazier. Grabbing its stand, she toppled it toward her opponents. They backpedaled as hot coals rolled across the floor. The priestess used the heartbeat she'd bought to draw a knife in her left hand and hurl it at Baldy. It took him in the small of his back. He stiffened, then sank to his knees.

This was beginning to feel too easy.

The priestess's assailants hesitated. She could guess what they were thinking: one of them should take the place of their fallen comrade, but who?

Not the man with the mad smile, it seemed, for he launched himself at Karmel. She parried a cut before turning her body to evade a slash from the Maru on her right. A lunge at Smiler forced him back. His heel came down on one of the red-hot coals, and he went over on his ankle, swearing. Karmel blocked a strike from Bucktooth, letting his weapon slide off hers to bring him stumbling forward. Knocking aside his parrying sword, she ran him through.

Movement beyond the priestess's adversaries caught her eye. She looked past them to see that a soldier—one of those who'd been battling Veran, presumably—had joined the surviving guard at the chest. Together they lifted the second stay. A groan of metal sounded. The weight of the gate would be exerting enormous pressure on the remaining stays. Would it prevent the soldiers from raising them from the chest? If the third was pulled clear, might the fourth be sheared away?

The room filled with the stench of burned meat. Blondie lay motionless a few paces away, flames flickering over his body. As those flames began to dwindle, the light in the room faded. Beyond, Veran was a whirlwind of motion as he ducked and twisted amid the shadows. He used an armguard to deflect a blow from a soldier's blade before retaliating with a kick that hurled his opponent from his feet. Veran was already leaning out of the path of a sword swing from another guard. As his enemy's weapon clanged against the wall behind, Veran jabbed an elbow into the man's throat. The soldier went down clutching his neck.

A pounding started up on the door to the citadel, while from outside another horn blast sounded, shrill and insistent. The two soldiers at the chest tugged at the third stay. With a squeal of metal, it jerked up a handspan.

Smiler clambered upright to stand alongside the Maru. The reddish light from the cooling coals gave their faces a devilish cast.

Karmel edged forward. Thus far the men had shown nothing to suggest they could beat her. The soldiers must have known they were outmatched too, for they retreated toward the capstan. A mistake. By standing off, they gave Karmel a chance to draw her final throwing knife. She flung it at one of the men at the stays.

Smiler batted the weapon out of the air with his blade.

Cursing, Karmel thrust her sword at the soldier's midriff. The Maru blocked the strike, then hacked at her with his blade, and she was forced to leap back out of range. A feint had the Maru retreating, only for Smiler to reenter the fray. He shouted to distract Karmel, stabbing his sword at her chest.

She sidestepped.

Time was running out, she knew. Sooner or later her opponents would fall to her blade, but the way things were looking that "later" might be *too* late. Maybe Veran would come to her aid before the remaining stays were pulled free, but Karmel was damned if she was going to let him sweep in and play the white knight. She started leaving gaps in her defenses in the hope one of her foes might launch an ill-judged attack. Those gaps were ignored, though, for the soldiers knew they had only to keep her at arm's length until their comrades at the chest lifted the final stay.

"Come on, you cowards!" Karmel screamed. "Fight me!"

Smiler's grin grew wider.

From the other side of the door to the citadel, the pounding of fists became more frantic. Karmel glanced at Veran and saw he'd been backed into a corner. A kick to the ankles of one of his assailants sent the soldier toppling. As Veran tensed to hurdle him, though, another guard reached the door.

He raised a hand to throw back the bolts.

The blare of a distant century horn sounded.

"That's the signal to raise the gate!" Farrell said, his voice tight with excitement.

Agenta shaded her eyes and peered east. There was nothing for her to see yet because the Dragon Gate was hidden by the Dianese cliffs. Earlier the *Icewing* had arrived at the buoys marking the starting berths for the Hunt only to find, as expected, that the best places had already been taken. Karan del Orco had called on Orsan to sail along the line of ships in the hope one of their captains, looking to win Imerle's favor and unaware she was not on board, might give up his space. Instead Orsan had brought the *Icewing* directly to its current position, farthest west of all the vessels in the Hunt and perhaps an eighth of a league from shore.

Atop the cliffs to the south was a scattering of people—latecomers to the festivities in Dian, Agenta supposed, or townsfolk who had fled the city to watch the Hunt away from the noise and bustle. To the west of them rose the fortified wall that bounded Dian, and beyond that was an expanse of pointed roofs, each taller than the last as if the buildings were straining upward to compete for light. Towering over them was the citadel with its sparkling dragon-scaled towers. Below, the galleries overlooking the Sabian Sea were a blur of color, and from across the water came a babble of sound that fell away momentarily as the screech of grinding metal filled the air. *Chains,* Agenta realized, her stomach knotting. *The gate is rising.*

The noise of the crowds swelled to a roar.

A Storm Guard officer bellowed at his troops to take up their positions, and the boards trembled to the pounding of feet. Soldiers lined up along the rails of the main deck and the quarterdeck. Every fourth man carried a pike; the remainder were armed with bows and spears. A septia moved among the archers, handing out white- and black-shafted arrows, and the soldiers began stringing their bows. To Agenta's left two Storm Guards used hatchets to breach barrels. They then emptied the contents of the barrels into the sea, and the kalischa wrinkled her nose at the stench of offal. Farrell had told her the captain would use it to try to entice the dragon here, though why the beast should be drawn by such paltry fare when there were tasty morsels such as Agenta to be sampled, she couldn't imagine.

It *had* attracted *some* attention, though, for cutting through the bobbing entrails and temlock heads was the fin of a briar shark. Agenta wondered if this was the same fish she'd hit on the journey from Olaire, but there was no arrow protruding from its flank.

To the east the ship closest to the *Icewing* was trimming its sails. It was a three-masted vessel of a size with the emira's flagship, and it flew a flag showing a golden octopus. Agenta touched Farrell's arm. "Whose ship is that?"

"Cauroy Blent's, I believe—the *Majestic*. I'm told he has a habit of arriving late to the Hunt, hence his position out here on the fringes with us."

"He's afraid to fight a dragon?"

Farrell nodded. "Most people say he's the weakest of the Storm Lords, and they're not just referring to his skill at sorcery."

The merchant's voice rose at the last, because a second horn note had sounded from Dian.

A dragon had passed beneath the gate.

And the Hunt was under way.

Agenta scanned the water at the exit from the Cappel Strait for a sight of the creature, but the surface of the sea remained undisturbed. Ships surged forward on waves of water-magic in an effort to be first to engage the beast, and Gerrick Long shouted for Orsan to follow their lead. The *Icewing*, though, remained where it was. Agenta frowned. Was Orsan as timid as Cauroy that he was content to watch from a distance as the other hunters contested the prize? Where was the mage, anyway? Last time the kalischa had spotted him, he'd been conferring with the captain beside the binnacle. When she looked that way now, though, she couldn't see his blue robe.

"We should move away from here," Farrell said.

"Oh?"

"If a dragon attacks, Orsan guards the aft deck and Selis the forecastle. The people on the main deck and the quarterdeck get no such protection."

Agenta nodded her assent, then followed him toward the aft deck where the other guests were being shepherded. Lydanto was there, one hand holding a glass of red wine, the other clasped so tightly to the rail it might have been the only thing keeping him upright. A short distance away stood Rethell, talking to Karan del Orco—or at least listening as the pasha denounced Imerle's hospitality in a voice intended to carry.

Agenta had made it as far as the quarterdeck when a shout came from a lookout above.

"Dragon from the east!"

The kalischa's mouth was dry. She drew up beside the mainmast and peered between the heads of the Storm Guards along the starboard rail. For a moment all she could see was blood-sheened waves. Then a shape half as long as the *Icewing* appeared in the water off the bow, glittering like a shoal of silverfins. Its passage created a breaker that slapped against the hull.

"We're lucky," Farrell said as the dragon glided past. "The creature's little more than a baby. Any bigger, and it wouldn't have been able to keep to the shallow waters near the cliff."

Agenta grunted. Oddly, she didn't feel too lucky just now.

The dragon drew level with the *Icewing*'s stern. The ballista on the aft deck was mounted on a revolving stand, and it tracked the beast as it circled to the port side. An arrow flashed out and struck the water above it.

"Hold your fire!" a Storm Guard to Agenta's left roared.

The dragon continued its circuit of the *Icewing* before moving from the kalischa's sight behind the forecastle.

The noise of the crowds on the Dianese galleries had fallen to a whisper, while on the cliff top the spectators were shouting and pointing east. Agenta turned to see Cauroy's ship, the *Majestic*, approaching on a wave of water-magic. "It seems the dragon is so small that even Cauroy is prepared to face it," she said to Farrell.

The merchant bared his teeth. "He's come for a share of our spoils . . ."

His voice trailed off.

Because a second dragon had appeared in the sea off the starboard side of the *Majestic*. Armored in steel-colored scales, it was half again the size of the silver beast circling the *Icewing*. Panicked shouts rang out from Cauroy's ship, and the sorcerous wave on which it was riding began to subside.

Agenta shot a look at Farrell. "What's going on?"

Her companion hesitated. "Sometimes two dragons make it through the Cappel Strait before the gate can be lowered. It happened many years ago when Whin Whorl was emir."

Two dragons that both swam west along the cliffs rather than heading for the deeper waters to the north? Agenta looked east again. The *Majestic* had come to a stop, and soldiers were taking up positions along its rails. Beyond, a single-masted galley was running north away from the Dragon Gate—

"Gods below!" Farrell breathed.

Agenta's skin prickled. A *third* dragon, bronze-scaled this time, rose from the sea off the galley's port beam, shattering the oars on that side. Screams sounded across the waves. From the Storm Guards around Agenta a murmur went up, but it died down at an order from an officer. Gerrick Long, who moments before had been demanding Orsan take the *Icewing* forward, now called for the ship to flee north.

"Eyes to port!" someone cried, and Agenta looked left to see the silver dragon lift its head from the waves. Sunlight glittered off its scales. It studied the ship through slitted eyes, then trumpeted a challenge that sent water spraying from its nostrils.

Agenta was shouldered aside by a pikeman rushing to join his companions at the port rail. As one, the pikemen lowered their weapons to form a line of steel.

"Archers!" an officer shouted, and there was a creak of flax fibers as the bowmen drew back on their bowstrings.

"Fire!"

A hail of arrows whipped out.

The dragon was already sinking beneath the waves, though. Most of the missiles sailed past. A handful clipped the top of its armored head. The invested arrows among them exploded with a booming hiss as if a crate of tindersparks had ignited.

The sea rippled silver as the dragon swam beneath the *Icewing* to the starboard side.

All eyes followed its passage, but the beast did not resurface.

From the east Agenta heard screams, wood splintering, the trumpeting of dragons. A dozen of the creatures now prowled the Sabian waters, and a chorus of voices joined Gerrick Long's in calling for the *Icewing* to retreat. Still the kalischa could see no sign of Orsan. From Dian a horn started up again, shrill and insistent. Then above that . . .

"What's that noise?" Agenta said to Farrell.

The merchant stared at her blankly.

She cocked her head. Had she imagined it? No, there it was again. A rustle of water building to a roar.

And now she was not the only one to have heard it, for cries of warning went up from the Storm Guards at the port rail.

Agenta swung round to see a wave half a dozen armspans high rushing toward the *Icewing* from the north.

Tears stung Karmel's eyes as the soldier unbarred the door to the citadel. So this was it, then. Her first mission, and she had failed. When the Dianese reinforcements burst in, all that would be left to her was to take as many as she could with her through Shroud's Gate. Shuffling back, she wondered at the despair that gripped her. She'd known all along that nineteen guards would be too many—that was why she had resolved to sell her life dearly rather than be captured. And yet she'd come so close! Just one opponent fewer, and she would have fought through to the capstan by now. One Shroud-cursed opponent! She wanted to scream at the injustice of it.

The guard who'd thrown back the bolts made to open the door. Before he could do so, though, the door must have been pushed from the other side because it hammered into him and sent him stumbling back. Light spilled into the chamber. Then a Dianese soldier appeared in the doorway, sword in hand. It took Karmel a moment to register he was facing not toward her but away from her. And that he was bleeding from a cut to his scalp. As he retreated into the room, he brought his blade up to a guard position . . .

Just as a sword thrust from some unseen assailant punched through his chest and emerged from his back. The killing weapon was tugged free.

The soldier crumpled to the floor.

A stillness fell on the control room. Even the whisper of the Dragon Day crowds seemed to recede. Beyond the door to the citadel, shadows swelled. Then darkness descended on the chamber as a man stepped forward to fill the doorway. Silhouetted against the light as he was, Karmel could make out nothing of his features, but where the glow of the torches caught the edges of his face, his skin sparkled as if there were diamonds set into it. Not a Dianese soldier, that much was clear. He carried a broadsword that dripped blood to the ground.

He surveyed the chamber, his gaze lingering on Karmel for longer than she liked.

Then he attacked the soldier who'd been knocked back by the door. The guard parried a slash from the newcomer's weapon, but such was the power of the stroke that he was spun around by the impact. The stone-skin didn't stop to dispatch him. Instead he surged past to engage the soldiers at the stays.

Karmel switched her gaze to the Maru and Smiler before treating Smiler to a grin of her own. *Well, well, this changes things.* The two Dianese seemed more shocked than even the priestess was at the stranger's entrance, and when she lunged with her sword at the Maru her stroke was only half blocked. She scored a cut to the man's right wrist. His hand spasmed, and he dropped his blade. Smiler hesitated before advancing to cover his companion—a brave move, but Karmel could see the defeat in his eyes. Sidestepping a thrust, she kicked out at his lead leg just as his weight came down on it, catching him below the knee. The leg gave way, and he fell on his side, bellowing like a hamstrung lederel.

Karmel's backhand swing opened his throat.

The Maru had more sense than his friend. Abandoning his fallen sword, he bolted for the door to the fortress. *Oh no you don't.* The throwing knife Smiler had batted out of the air earlier lay on the ground a pace away from Karmel. She scooped it up and hurled it at the retreating soldier. It took him in the back of the neck. For an improbable heartbeat his legs continued to pump. Then he collapsed.

Veran had dispatched his final opponent. He moved to guard the door. A glance at the priestess, then he began dragging into the room the corpse of a soldier lying across the threshold. Karmel scanned the room, hardly able to believe she was still alive. Alive! Not a single Dianese soldier remained upright.

A distended arch of light reached from the citadel door toward the capstan. At its edge was the stranger with the broadsword, standing next to the bodies of the guards who'd been lifting the stays. His skin was gray, as if he'd been carved from granite—like a statue come to life. Judging by his lurid green silks he had been Governor Piput Da Marka's guest for the Dragon Day festivities, yet so absurd did the hulking warrior look in his finery it was a wonder how anyone had mistaken him for a dignitary.

Veran closed and bolted the door. The control room was plunged into near blackness.

A pounding started up from the door to the battlements, but Karmel did not take her gaze from the stone-skin. On entering the chamber his first concern had been to stop the Dianese raising the stays. Did that mean he was on the Chameleons' side? Could he have been sent by the emira as insurance in case Karmel and Veran failed? If so, though, why hadn't he made his allegiances known to them by now? And why did his look say he was as puzzled by Karmel as she was puzzled by him?

Not a friendly look, it had to be said, but then she hadn't yet sheathed her sword.

Neither had he.

Veran crossed to join her. The cooling coals gave off enough light for Karmel to see that he left bloody footprints behind. His sleeves were sliced to ribbons over his armguards, and he had gashes to his forehead and chin.

"More scars to add to your collection?" Karmel said.

A grunt was Veran's only response.

The Dragon Gate's chain, stretched taut across the floor, shifted a hairbreadth. Two stays remained in the chest. The stone-skin bent down and lifted another off the ground as easily as if he were picking a dewflower. He slammed it into the chest.

"Who is he?" Karmel murmured to Veran. "*What* is he?"

"A witness."

The priestess didn't like the sound of that. Now that the immediate danger had passed, the sting of Caval's betrayal was coming back. All Karmel wanted to do was put this place behind her and return to Olaire. "Let's get out of here."

A shake of Veran's head.

The fourth stay lay on the floor in front of the stone-skin. He went to pick it up.

"Get ready," Veran said to Karmel.

"For what?"

The swordsman attacked.

His first strike was directed at Veran, and the priest leapt back from a cut that narrowly missed his chest. Such was Karmel's surprise it took her an instant to gather herself. The fool wanted a fight?

Did he really think he could defeat two Chameleons? Even over her disbelief, however, she felt a stab of indignation. The stone-skin had attacked Veran first, meaning he considered Karmel the lesser threat. He would soon come to rue his error, though, because his last stroke had left his flank exposed. It was the simplest thing in the world for the priestess to lunge forward—

Her blade met thin air. Somehow her opponent had twisted to evade the blow. He countered by thrusting his sword's crosspiece toward her face. She tried to sway aside—

Stars exploded in her head.

The next thing she knew, she was lying facedown in a pool of blood—not *her* blood, fortunately, yet for some reason that came as scant consolation. She sat up hurriedly, only for lights to start dancing before her eyes. The right side of her face felt as if she'd been hit with a hammer. When she tested her swollen flesh, though, she found she'd escaped with nothing worse than a loose tooth. Her right ear was ringing with a high-pitched note like the whistle of a kettle. Over that she heard a man's grunt, the grating whisper of metal sliding off metal.

Looking up, she saw Veran and the stone-skin circling each other. The coals scattered across the floor had dimmed to a smoldering gray, and the combatants were mere shadows in the gloom. Karmel saw Veran land a kick to the swordsman's midsection. Any normal opponent would have been winded by the blow, but the stranger merely took a half step back before coming on. His sword was a band of dull crimson light as it cut through the darkness. Veran dodged easily, but Karmel wasn't about to sit back and watch the duel play out. In a contest like this, her money was always on the man holding the sharp pointy thing.

She pushed herself to her feet.

Her vision blurred once more, and she staggered to the capstan. Vomit burned the back of her throat. Checking the ground, she saw her sword a few paces away . . .

The blade had been snapped a handspan from the hilt.

Karmel unleashed a stream of curses. Had the stranger stamped on it after she'd dropped it? Or had it snagged on something as she fell? Either way, she needed a new weapon, and quickly. Baldy lay at her feet, his shirt bloody round a throwing knife buried in his stomach. Karmel crouched to tug the blade free before straightening. She hefted the dagger. Disorientated as she was, she risked hitting Veran if her throw went awry.

Then I'd better make sure it doesn't.

Drawing back her throwing hand, she waited for an opening.

She'd never admit as much to Veran, but she had to concede he showed a certain skill in defending himself against the stone-skin. The strength of the stranger's attacks was such that if they had landed plumb on Veran's armguards the broadsword would have sheared through metal and flesh. Veran, though, was twisting his wrists at the point of impact to deflect his enemy's blade. But his resistance couldn't last much longer. With the gloom about the room deepening, it was just a matter of time before he misjudged a parry or stumbled over one of the bodies on the ground.

Even as the thought came to Karmel, Veran stepped on a corpse's leg and staggered back. The stone-skin surged forward.

Karmel's hand holding the knife shot out. A smudge of black went streaking through the darkness.

The stranger leaned out of the dagger's path, and it clattered into the wall behind.

Karmel blinked. How was that even possible? The stone-skin would have had a mere heartbeat to see the knife coming, yet he'd moved out of the way like its flight had been a thing preordained. At least her throw had given Veran time to recover, though. Closing on the stone-skin, he landed three punches to his opponent's solar plexus.

The man shrugged off the blows like he'd been hit with a pillow. His sword whistled round in an arc and glanced off one of Veran's armguards.

Sparks flew.

Karmel looked round for another knife.

"The battlements!" Veran shouted. "Open the door!"

It was a moment before Karmel understood his thinking. *Of course, the Dianese soldiers who relieved us at the eighth bell!* The men had been hammering at the door since the Dragon Gate failed to go down. If she let them in, they were sure to mistake the uniformed Veran for one of their own and come to his aid.

Karmel strode to the door and threw back the bolts, before realizing it might be better if the Dianese didn't see her—the sight of a woman in a room where there had been only men might give them pause. Stepping to one side, she stilled her movements.

The door swung inward.

Daylight flooded into the chamber, and Karmel squinted against the brightness. A gust of wind washed over her, moist and warm, yet still invigorating after the bruising heat of the control room. On the threshold stood the two Dianese soldiers with swords in their hands. The man in front had his fist in the air, frozen in the act of knocking. He peered into the gloom before tearing off his helmet to reveal a flushed face and a drooping mustache. His eyes widened as he took in the devastation.

Come on! Karmel wanted to shout to him. *What are you waiting for?*

From behind her came the retort of the stone-skin's sword striking one of Veran's armguards. Then Veran yelled to the Dianese, "Get in here, damn you!"

The soldiers lurched into motion.

Shouts sounded from along the battlements. Karmel looked across to see the dragon's skull on the walkway rise a handspan into the air. *The Natillians.* If they succeeded in lifting it and gaining access to this end of the gate—

A hand shoved her from behind, and she stumbled onto the ramparts.

"Keep moving," Veran growled.

Move where? Karmel tried to ask, but with her aching jaw, she managed only a strangled grunt.

She would have been wasting her breath anyhow, for Veran had already disappeared inside again. What, had his conscience pricked him that he wanted to help the Dianese soldiers? And why push her out here? Her gaze took in the dragon's skull blocking the battlements, the sheer cliffs above the door to the chamber. Where was she supposed to go? Without rope and a grappling hook there was little chance of her climbing down to the gate. And even if she managed it, what then? Hail one of the dragons and hitch a ride?

Bells rang out across Dian and Natilly. From the north came the noise of wood splintering, screams, a dragon's trumpeting. When Karmel looked that way she saw a ship flying the Rastamiran flag being lifted into the air by a rust-scaled dragon that had surfaced beneath it. The vessel slid off the creature's flank before hitting the sea. A score of its passengers were pitched shrieking into the water.

All about, the waves were covered with fragments of wood, scraps of sail, broken bodies.

Just then an oath in Dianese came from the control room, followed by a shriek—not Veran's, for the priest had just materialized on the threshold, his back to Karmel. The priestess retreated to give him room.

A second cry sounded. Both Dianese soldiers were down.

The stone-skin emerged from the gloom.

Veran attacked. The narrowness of the doorway hindered the stone-skin's sword strokes, and the priest was able to bat aside a thrust before countering with a kick that sent his opponent reeling back. In Veran's left hand was Karmel's broken sword—the Chameleon's blade. The priestess grimaced. Of course, that was why he'd gone back into the control room—to retrieve the one thing that could have tied the Chameleons to the scene. She should have thought to recover it herself.

"Jump!" Veran shouted to her.

Karmel thought she must have misheard. "What?" she croaked.

The stone-skin reappeared, and Veran parried a slash with an armguard. "Do it! There's no other way!"

No other way? A short while ago Karmel had resolved to die by the sword rather than let herself be thrown to the dragons, yet now Veran wanted her to jump of her own accord?

"Jump!"

The priestess looked over the battlements at the sea below. A silver-colored dragon glided through the surf, displacing waves of water that thundered into the cliffs. In Karmel's mind's eye she saw yesterday's spider-tattooed prisoner. If she jumped close to the rock face, maybe the dragons wouldn't notice her in their eagerness to get to the ships in the Sabian Sea. More likely, though, she would crack her skull on a submerged rock, or be picked up by a wave and smashed into the cliff.

This wasn't about escaping, it was about choosing how she wanted to die. Or how she least wanted to, rather.

More shouts sounded from along the battlements. A helmeted head appeared over the dragon's skull. The Natillians had given up on trying to raise the skull and were now clambering over it instead. Perhaps Karmel should wait for them. When they reached her they would see Karmel's and Veran's uniforms and help them as the two Dianese guards had done before. And yet, there would be no slipping away once the stone-skin was dead. The Natillians, and later the Dianese, would have questions about what had happened in the control room, and they were questions to which the Chameleons would have no good answers.

Karmel made a sour face. Like as not she'd end up taking a dip with the dragons anyway. Might as well get it over with.

A curse from Veran made her turn. She watched the stone-skin drive him onto the walkway. The slump of the priest's shoulders betrayed his weariness. When his opponent's blade next came scything round, Veran lifted his left arm to block, but a heartbeat too late. Instead of deflecting the strike, he took it near full on the armguard.

There was a crack of bone.

Veran gasped but still managed to duck under a decapitating swing. The broken sword he'd been holding had been torn free of his grasp by the stone-skin's last attack and came skittering along the walkway toward Karmel. She scooped it up. Should she go to help Veran? With a broken blade? She couldn't abandon him, of course, but what if he was just waiting for her to jump so he could disengage from his opponent and follow her over the parapet?

Over the parapet. Karmel shook her head. She couldn't believe she was even considering this.

A last look down at the strait. The waters of the channel heaved and pitched like a storm-tossed sea, but at least they were empty of dragons for now.

Putting a foot in one of the crenels, Karmel closed her eyes and jumped.

PART III

THE DRAGON HUNT

CHAPTER 13

S THE wave of water-magic bore down on the *Icewing*, Agenta wrapped her arms round the mainmast. From all sides came shouts to jump, shouts to hold on to something, shouts to turn the ship about to face the wave. Then one by one those shouts were drowned beneath the roar of onrushing water. The wave grew in height, rising above the level of the main yard. Its coming was like the roll of a thousand drums, and it brought with it a darkness as if dusk lay in its wake.

Farrell stepped round to the opposite side of the mast from Agenta and gripped it as she had. His face was chalk white. A Storm Guard behind the kalischa put his arms round her so he too could grasp the mast, and she was crushed against the wood. To either side she saw soldiers seizing the ship's backstays and lower shrouds, or diving for the companionway. *The companionway.* Why hadn't Agenta thought of that herself? There was no chance of reaching it now, though, for the wave was rumbling ever closer—forty armspans, thirty, twenty. On the sea in its path a floating starbeak realized its danger too late and took off squawking, only to be snatched up and devoured. The water off the *Icewing*'s port rail receded, and the vessel slid down into a dip before rising again.

Agenta braced for impact.

The wave caught the ship beam-on. It tipped to starboard. The mainmast shuddered, and the kalischa felt as much as heard the wood snap above her. Then the sea's chill embrace claimed her. The roar of the wave was replaced by ringing silence. In the watery gloom

Farrell's eyes were bulging like he'd forgotten to take a breath, while behind her the Storm Guard was torn away. Agenta tightened her grip as the *Icewing* pitched and rolled. For a heartbeat she didn't know if the ship was still fighting the pull of the wave or already sinking, and it occurred to her that she might be clinging to the vessel even as it was hauled down into the deep. The image made her snort with laughter, and a bubble of air escaped her nose.

Then as quickly as the surge had come, it was gone.

Agenta felt the wind against her face once more. She took in a heaving breath. Farrell stood across from her, his pink shirt plastered to his chest, his eyes dull with shock. Somehow the *Icewing* was still afloat, though all three of its masts were broken and now floated in the sea off the starboard rail amid a tangle of sails and rigging. The wave of water-magic had moved on to the south where it struck the cliffs with a noise like a peal of thunder, sending spray fountaining into the air and dislodging starbeaks from their perches. In its wake the sea gushed and swirled.

Agenta looked east to see that, of the ships taking part in the Hunt, only the *Icewing* had been hit by the wave.

And suddenly it all became clear: why Imerle had stayed away from the Hunt; why Agenta and her father had been invited on board; why the *Icewing* had taken up a position so far to the west of Dian where there would be fewer witnesses to the emira's treachery—for the wave had surely been conjured up by Orsan at Imerle's command to leave the *Icewing* crippled beyond any hope of escaping this place. It also made sense why Farrell and his father were here, for with Lydanto on the merchants' trail the emira must have decided to dispose of them before that trail could be followed to her.

And to think Agenta had believed it was Imerle who'd been outwitted.

Farrell spoke. "The wave. It's coming back."

The kalischa looked south to see the water had rebounded off the cliffs and was surging back toward the *Icewing*. Much of its force had been spent against the rock face, and when it reached the ship it did no more than lift the vessel into the air before setting it back down. Agenta's stomach rose and fell with the wave. Scanning the ship, she saw the main deck and the quarterdeck had been swept clear of all but a handful of Storm Guards. On the aft deck two soldiers manned the ballista, and around them stood half a dozen bedraggled dignitaries. Lydanto was there, still clutching a glass in one hand. The glass was now filled not with wine but with seawater, yet he couldn't have realized because he raised it to his lips.

Agenta tensed. Where was her father?

She scanned the passengers on the aft deck, but Rethell was not among them. She shifted her gaze to the sea. Most of the people who'd been swept overboard were on the starboard side of the ship. Some had been carried halfway to shore and were now swimming back to the *Icewing;* some were treading water beside the shattered masts; others floated facedown in the waves or stared sightlessly up at the sky. But there was no sign of Rethell.

Agenta forced herself to take a steadying breath. Could he be in the sea off the bow or the stern, hidden from view by the aft deck or the forecastle? Or under one of the sails, perhaps—she could see shapes moving beneath the canvas. Even now a gash appeared in the main course as a Storm Guard used a knife to cut himself free.

"Father!" Agenta called.

No response.

She crossed to the port rail. To the north and east, the *Majestic* was under attack from the bronze- and steel-scaled dragons she'd seen earlier, and in the span of Agenta's gaze she saw the bronze beast rear up and snap the bowsprit before a wave of water-magic— fashioned by Cauroy, no doubt—slapped the creature down. Farther west, and a stone's throw from the *Icewing,* the fat air-mage, Selis, hovered above the sea. He must have lifted himself out of harm's way before the wave struck, and only now did Agenta appreciate how far the ship had been carried shoreward. Below Selis bobbed the motionless body of a Storm Guard, while another soldier was trying to clamber onto a barrel of sorcerously lightened air that had been knocked off the aft deck.

Behind the man a silver shadow rose from the depths.

"Sender's mercy!" Agenta said.

She'd forgotten the dragon. The waves swelled and burst as the creature's head broke the surface. The sound of splashing must have alerted the Storm Guard to its presence for he looked over his shoulder. With a cry he abandoned the barrel and began thrashing toward the *Icewing* as if he believed he could outpace the beast. Perhaps Agenta should have been appalled at his plight, but all she felt was relief that it was him in the dragon's way and not her.

Or her father.

Swift as thought, the dragon closed the gap on the soldier, its jaws hinging wide.

But its target was not the Storm Guard. It swept past him and came for the *Icewing*. From the quarterdeck a lone arrow flew out to intercept it, and it disappeared into the creature's yawning maw. The missile could not have been invested with sorcery, for no explosion issued from within. The dragon let out a deep-throated growl. Lowering its head to butt the ship, it came on faster and more terrible than any battering ram. Sprouting from the top of its head were curved horns.

Two pikemen ran to the port rail to meet its charge. Resting their pikes on the wood, they angled the weapon heads down. The first pike deflected off the dragon's armor. The second found a gap between two scales and buried itself in the creature's flesh.

The dragon trumpeted.

The soldier holding the pike was driven back across the boards. As the dragon's head came up, the pike lodged in its flesh came up with it. The weapon's shaft was braced under the Storm Guard's arm, and Agenta watched openmouthed as he was lifted into the air and flung, shrieking, over the dragon's shoulder. The creature's momentum, meanwhile, carried it into the hull. To the sound of crunching wood the deck beneath Agenta tilted, and she grabbed the stump of the mainmast. An archer near the starboard rail stumbled against the gunwale before toppling into the sea.

The dragon backed away from the *Icewing*. The pike was still wedged in its skull, and the beast shook its head in an effort to free the weapon. With every twist, the scales across its neck rasped against each other, opening up gaps between them. If Agenta had been holding a bow with an arrow nocked to it . . .

She hesitated. Her first instinct was to climb to the aft deck and search the seas off the stern for her father. If he had been knocked overboard, though, the best way to help him was to drive the dragon away, or at least keep its attention focused on the *Icewing* long enough for him to make it back on board. She looked round. The weapons rack on the quarterdeck was empty of bows, but on one of the still-stacked spears was impaled the body of a Storm Guard. In the soldier's left hand he clutched a bow. Agenta scampered across and prized the weapon from his fingers. His quiver had some arrows in it, including three with white shafts. The kalischa looped the quiver off his shoulder before returning to the mainmast.

Farrell had vanished, but there was no time to look for him now. To Agenta's right an octa had gathered four archers to him as the remaining pikeman moved to stand in the dragon's shadow. The creature had succeeded in dislodging the pike from its flesh, and its head now swayed above the soldier as if it were a bedra cobra mesmerizing its prey.

A twang sounded from the trebuchet on the aft deck. A bolt ricocheted off the dragon's scaled neck, but the creature paid it no mind. Its teeth snapped at the pikeman's weapon. The Storm Guard pulled the pike back, then jabbed for an eye, the weapon head coming up short.

"Fire!" the octa shouted.

Four arrows flew out.

The dragon's armored eyelids snapped shut, and the missiles pinged off.

Agenta grabbed the first arrow in her quiver that her fingers closed round—a nonmagical one—and nocked it to her bow before pulling back on the string. There were no longer any gaps visible between the plates on the dragon's neck, but its nostrils made for inviting targets. At a distance of forty armspans she could hardly miss. Her arrow flew true to its mark, and the creature flinched and growled, its eyes springing open.

Its head swung round.

And suddenly its attention was fixed not on the pikeman but on the kalischa.

She stood frozen. The beast seemed too big to be real, yet what had Farrell called it? A baby. *Come to Mummy,* Agenta thought, making ready to duck behind the mainmast.

Then jets of water spurted from the dragon's nostrils, hitting her and spinning her from her feet.

The stink of rotting fish met Karmel as she hauled herself into Veran's boat. There were several fingers' widths of water in the bottom, but she was too tired to start bailing, and for a while she lay in the wet looking up at the roof of the cave and listening to the waves lapping at the hull. The boat drifted round, pulling against its anchor.

After jumping from the battlements she'd plunged into the murky waters of the strait before resurfacing amid clinking bottles and strands of fireweed. She'd made for the recess in the cliff intending to wait there for Veran, but before she could reach it a wave created by a dragon's approach had picked her up and carried her clear of the strait. Close behind the wave came the dragon itself, submerged beneath the bulging blue. By stilling her movements Karmel had made herself invisible to the creature, but even so she was forced to endure twenty of the longest heartbeats of her life as it glided beneath her in a dazzle of scales. Only when it vanished to the north did she kick for the Dianese cliffs, watching the strait all the while in case another dragon appeared.

As she drew near to the cliff her knees scraped against submerged rocks. Clinging to the stones, she stared up at the battlements to see the stranger with the broadsword battling a handful of uniformed men. Veran was not among them, though, nor was there any sign of him in the turbulent waters beneath the gate. He could have jumped already and now be sheltering in the recess, Karmel supposed, but she wasn't going to swim back against the tide of dragons to find out. Having resolved to give him a count of a fifty, she'd reached only half that number when a second dragon surged past, the swell of its passage almost tugging her from her perch. Suspecting it was just a matter of time before one of the creatures detected her—she didn't know, after all, whether dragons hunted by sight or smell—she began making her way west toward the cave where she and Veran had left the boat two days ago. If the priest was still alive, he would find his way there eventually. If not . . .

Karmel shivered. The air in the cave was cold as a tomb's. She had a change of clothes under the sailcloth cover, but it was too much of an effort to move. *He's dead,* she realized. What point in denying it? Her throat constricted. Even if Veran had somehow evaded the stoneskin and survived the jump from the battlements, he wouldn't have been able to swim to the cave with a broken arm. She should have gone to his aid on the walkway, maybe waited longer at the entrance to the strait in case he made it that far. Taking a breath, she pushed the thoughts aside. If their roles had been reversed, he'd have done the same as she did. And after the things he'd kept from her these past few days . . .

I owe him nothing.

Sitting up in the prow, Karmel tried to rouse herself. She was alive, wasn't she? Against all odds she'd completed her mission, and when she returned to the temple she would make damned sure she received the recognition she deserved. Whatever satisfaction she might have felt at her success, though, was overshadowed by her brother's duplicity. For all that she and Caval had drifted apart of late, she would never have believed him capable of such a betrayal. And if he could lie to her about the purpose of the mission, what else might he have lied to her about? Had there ever been a predecessor whose shoes Karmel had stepped into? Or had her brother wanted her for this assignment from the start, but held off on telling her to cut down on awkward questions?

And yet, could it be that she was judging him too quickly? Perhaps he'd assumed she would work out the true goal of the assignment for herself, or perhaps he had wanted to shield her from the burden of responsibility for as long as possible. Perhaps he'd even been commanded to silence by the emira.

Perhaps, perhaps.

Whatever the truth of it, her brother would have some explaining to do when they next met.

How long would it be, though, before she could return to Olaire? Caval's instructions had been to go to ground in Dian, and even if she'd been minded to ignore him, no ship would risk the journey to the Storm Isles while there were dragons on the loose. But the emira needed to know about the stone-skin, didn't she? Like Imerle, his goal had been to unleash the dragons on the Sabian Sea. Why? To kill one of the ships' passengers? There were easier ways to dispose of an enemy. But maybe the stone-skin's actions were directed not at one ship but at *all* of them. Maybe the emira was not the only one interested in seeing the power of the Storm Lords broken. The stone-skin could be from the Rubyholt Isles, or some more distant empire such as Erin Elal or Metisca. If so, his exploits in Dian amounted to nothing less than a declaration of war.

Outside the cave, Karmel caught sight of a ship with three broken masts wallowing in choppy seas a stone's throw offshore. The head of a silver dragon reared above its port bow, and a ragged volley of arrows fired from the vessel's quarterdeck bounced off its scales.

Then above the dragon's trumpeting and the clanging of the bells in Dian and Natilly, Karmel heard splashing.

She straightened.

A man appeared at the mouth of the cave, swimming on his back toward her, one arm laid across his chest.

The dragon came for Agenta. She scrambled to her feet and threw herself behind the shattered mainmast. The creature's snout slammed into the wood, sending a jolt through the deck that threw the kalischa onto her back. She found herself staring up into the beast's eyes. Within those swirling cauldrons of liquid gold was a boundless cunning, and she was pinned to the boards by the weight of its gaze. With a grating whisper its lips peeled back to reveal teeth the color of ivory. Its salty breath washed over her, and she heard a rumble in its throat.

The remaining pikeman charged from the left, stabbing his weapon at the dragon's neck. Foolish of him, but Agenta wasn't complaining. A hollow retort sounded as the weapon's head deflected off the dragon's scales and down toward the deck. The creature turned on its assailant. The soldier raised his weapon to fend off an attack.

Too late.

The dragon's head snapped forward, its teeth closing over the Storm Guard's waist. A muted scream came from within the beast's mouth, but it died away as the dragon tossed back its head and gulped down its prey. Its throat bulged in a ripple of scales.

Agenta's stomach heaved.

The soldier's pike fell to the deck with a clatter.

A thrumming noise marked the firing of the ballista on the aft deck. Its bolt must have found a gap in the dragon's armor because the creature recoiled, then roared and swung toward the stern. Lifting its tail from the waves, it brought it whipping down, narrowly missing the catapult and shattering the skylight over the captain's cabin. Lydanto had been standing a few paces away. He ducked behind the broken mizzenmast. Other dignitaries flung themselves wailing over the rail into the sea.

The soldiers manning the ballista held their ground. Agenta saw one of them fumble a bolt in his haste to reload the weapon. Before he could recover the missile, the dragon's tail came whistling down again. This time it found its mark, smashing the catapult to shards and crushing one of the Storm Guards into the deck. The second soldier reeled back with a strangled cry, his face a mask of blood, a sliver of wood protruding from his eye.

Agenta climbed to her feet. The cause was hopeless. True, the meager contingent of Storm Guards on the *Icewing* would soon be supplemented by soldiers climbing from the sea, but what use would a hundred troops be now that the weapons racks were all but empty of sorcerous arrows and spears? And even if the Storm Guards *could* defeat the dragon, what then? With the *Icewing*'s masts shattered, the ship couldn't sail from this place. Nor was a rescue likely with the other vessels on the Hunt beset by dragons.

A high-pitched whine sounded, and a black-shafted arrow buried itself between two scales on the dragon's neck, releasing a gush of water. There was a popping noise, and a plate came away from the creature's flesh. The dragon huffed spray from its nostrils, then scanned the *Icewing* for the archer responsible. The Storm Guards on the quarterdeck scattered. One man dived behind the ship's wheel. Another darted for the steps to the main deck, only to trip on a stray line and sprawl to the boards.

The dragon pounced.

Its snout cannoned off an invisible shield in front of the soldier.

For a moment Agenta thought her eyes were playing tricks on her. Then understanding dawned.

Selis!

She'd forgotten the air-mage. Looking up, she saw the fat man hovering above the quarterdeck, his robes billowing about him as his hands traced patterns in the air. The dragon had seen him too. It lunged upward with neck extended, straining every muscle as it sought to bite one of the mage's legs.

Selis was safely out of reach, though, and the creature's teeth closed on nothing. It fell back into the sea with a crash, throwing up sheets of water that raked the *Icewing*'s decks.

Agenta nocked a white arrow to her bow, trying to think of a plan—any plan—that might work against this beast. She saw again the scale being blown clear of the dragon's neck. If she hit the uncovered spot she could wound the creature, but when the dragon next appeared off the port rail she was on the wrong side of the beast for a shot. Dare she risk catching its eye by making a dash for the forecastle?

Patience.

As the dragon reared over the gunwale, an octa scooped up the dead pikeman's weapon. Behind him five archers loosed a volley that rattled off the creature's scales like rain off a tin roof. The octa inched backward, all the while jabbing his pike at the dragon's snout. The beast could not devour him without also swallowing a length of pike, so instead it snapped its teeth shut on the weapon, crunching through the shaft to leave the octa staring wide-eyed at an armspan of splintered wood.

Agenta hesitated. If she did nothing the soldier would suffer the same fate as the pikeman before him, yet she could not afford to waste one of the precious white arrows on distracting the dragon. Octas were replaceable; the magical missiles were not.

Then she noticed a barrel of sorcerously lightened air floating in the sea tight to the dragon's flank.

A smile touched her lips. Pulling back on the bowstring, she sighted on the cask and let fly.

The arrow thudded into the wood.

Four years ago Agenta had seen a galley carrying tindersparks and smokeshells explode in a fireball in Gilgamar's harbor. According to the only crew member who survived, the disaster had been caused when a deckhand tossed a smoldering blackweed stick into the hold. The blast that followed had shattered the windows of every building on the waterfront and was heard as far away as Airey. To Agenta, standing on the Key Tower, it had felt as if her eardrums would burst.

The explosion of the barrel beside the dragon was louder. The cask disintegrated in a hail of splinters, and the air concussed, slapping Agenta to the boards. Chunks of wood came raining down. She shielded her face with her hands. Through a gap in her fingers, she saw a Storm Guard stumble against the steps to the aft deck, his hands clasped over his ears. Another soldier tottered to the port rail, blood trickling from one of his nostrils. His lips opened and closed, but Agenta couldn't hear his words over the ringing in her ears.

A moment to collect herself, then she clambered upright and looked down into the sea. The dragon's shimmering form could be seen wallowing in the deep to the north. The creature wasn't dead—Agenta could see its barbed tail flickering—but with luck the explosion had ruptured something inside the beast, for at close quarters the blast must have felt like a punch from a titan. At the very least the kalischa now had a chance to search for her father. She looked round. Farrell had tied a rope to the mainmast and cast it over the starboard rail. A Storm Guard's head appeared at the gunwale before the merchant hauled the man onto the deck. There was no sign of Rethell, though—

Someone tapped Agenta on the shoulder. She swung round to see Selis beside her. A handspan shorter than the kalischa, he stank of sweat and wine. His dark, beady eyes explored her body, and she crossed her arms over her chest. When he spoke, his voice was strangely high-pitched and so muffled he might have been standing on the other side of a wall.

"Where's Orsan?" he demanded.

Agenta bridled at his tone. "Halfway back to Olaire by now, probably."

"Meaning?"

"Where do you think that wave came from?"

Selis's eyes narrowed. "Another water-mage—"

"Then why didn't Orsan counter him? And where is Orsan now? How many water-mages have you known to *drown*?"

Before the fat man could respond, one of the Storm Guards shouted a warning. The dragon was on the move again, circling the stern toward the starboard side of the ship. So much for the beast being injured.

Agenta looked back at Selis. "What can you do against this creature?"

"Little, while it stays underwater."

She pointed to one of the remaining casks of sorcerously lightened air in the sea. "Can you levitate the barrels and bring them close to the dragon for us to fire at?"

"I could, but what do we gain by stunning the beast? Better to raise the mainmast"—he gestured, and the mast began to lift from the waves—"and then summon up a wind—"

"What about the other masts?" Agenta cut in. "Can you raise those too and still call the wind?"

"No, but—"

"Will the sails of one mast give us enough speed to outdistance a dragon?"

The mage's frown was all the answer she needed.

More shouts from the Storm Guards. Agenta saw the dragon, still submerged, reappear in the sea off the port rail. For an instant it held its position, its tail moving back and forth. Then it rushed the ship, gathering speed with every heartbeat. It flashed beneath the water like a shaft of lightning.

It means to ram us again.

This time the dragon remained beneath the waves where weapons could not reach it. A barrel of sorcerously lightened air floated on the sea in its path. Agenta thought to detonate the cask, but the dragon was already surging past, setting the barrel bobbing in its wake.

"Brace yourselves!" the octa called.

Agenta seized the stump of the mainmast.

The dragon's head slammed into the *Icewing*. The vessel lurched to starboard, and from the hull came a scraping noise, then a crack. The dragon must have tried to surface beneath the ship because the *Icewing* tipped and lifted an armspan before sliding down and hitting the waves. The jolt put Agenta on her back. Again. It must have broken Selis's concentration too, for the mainmast fell back to strike the sea. Cries sounded from those in the water.

The *Icewing* swayed. When it finally came to rest, it was listing to one side.

Another groan from the hull, and Agenta exchanged a glance with Selis, now hovering a handspan above the deck. She heard footfalls from the companionway. A man's sweat-sheened face appeared to deliver the good news.

"We're taking on water!"

Veran.

Karmel smiled. The chill about the cave seemed to lift. Veran hadn't turned to look at the boat, and the priestess waited until his head thudded into the hull before seizing him under the arms. He stiffened at her touch, then twisted round to stare at her. Karmel blinked. Was that unease in his expression? Resignation? The look was gone before she could focus on it.

Just the pain of his wounds, she decided.

Hauling on his good arm, she helped him scramble into the boat. He closed his eyes and lay panting for a while before dragging himself through sloshing water to the oar-bench. Head bowed, he sat cradling his injured arm. His face was gray and drawn and streaked with blood from the gashes to his forehead and chin. More blood leaked from a cut to his left shoulder beside the strap of his now-empty baldric. Karmel wondered if he was as proud of his scars now as he'd been on the crossing from Olaire. His armguard was dented where his arm had been broken. When Karmel reached out to inspect the arm, Veran flinched.

"Let me look," she said through the pain of her swollen jaw. Her mangled words echoed round the cave.

The priest shook his head. "I'll make a sling for it later. Till we can find someone who can set it properly."

Properly? Didn't he trust her with something as simple as making a splint? "What about your cuts?"

"I've been cut before, girl," he growled. "As you seem so keen on reminding me."

Karmel was silent, stung by his hostility. No doubt he was feeling sorry for himself, or maybe he was sulking at having been beaten by the stone-skin. Either way the priestess was in no mood to let him take out his frustrations on her. "I'm fine, by the way. Thanks for asking."

Veran made no response.

Karmel turned away in disgust. And to think she'd been pleased to see him when he entered the cave! She remembered the time they'd spent together on the journey from Olaire. Just a few bells with the priest then had left her wanting to get out of the boat and swim to Dian. Now she faced spending weeks in the man's sour company. Weeks of uncomfortable silences and indecipherable grunts. Weeks in a basement that smelled of piss and had neighbors who bickered more often even than she and Veran did. Her face twisted. The hardest part of this Shroud-cursed mission was doubtless still to come.

She started as an explosion sounded from the ship outside. The noise was like someone had clapped their hands next to her ear. But when she glanced outside to find the cause, she could see nothing to account for the blast. Had the dragon rammed the far side of the vessel? No, if the impact had been violent enough to cause such a noise, the ship would be halfway to the bottom of the sea by now. What then? Sorcery?

The priestess looked back at Veran. From the belligerence in his gaze it was clear he didn't want to talk, but Karmel had questions that couldn't wait.

"What happened on the battlements after I jumped?"

Veran was a long time in answering. "Natillians came to help. I bailed out before they got a look at my face."

"And the stone-skin?"

"Jumped a while after I did. I was in the recess when I saw him hit the water. He landed ahead of a dragon. Thought the creature would do for him, but the stone-skin must be a water-mage because he went shooting off north. Dragon trailed him for a time, then let him go."

Karmel paused, wondering whether the stone-skin's escape was the reason for Veran's ill temper. True, the stranger was a loose end, but not one that could hurt them—it wasn't as if he'd be dropping in on Piput to give him a description of the Chameleons. "Have you seen anyone with skin like his before?"

"No. Hope I never do again, neither."

"But you said he swam *north*," Karmel said. Toward Olaire. Was it a coincidence the stone-skin's flight had taken him in the direction of the Storm Isles? The priestess doubted it, and judging by the bleakness of Veran's look, so did he.

Outside, the mainmast of the stricken ship rose a few armspans into the air. Evidently there was an air-mage on board, and an idea took form in Karmel's mind. An idea as harebrained as jumping off the Dragon Gate. She'd survived that well enough, though, hadn't she? What was the point of having luck if you didn't push it a little? "The emira has to be warned about the stone-skin."

"She will be. In time."

"And if she doesn't have that time?"

Veran looked from Karmel to the damaged vessel and back again, his expression darkening all the while. "I know what you're thinking, and you can forget it."

"If we could reach that ship—"

"We wait here till nightfall, then head back to the city. We ain't come this far for you to risk it all because you're getting homesick."

"Risk what? The emira's in the clear now, and you know it. *In the clear.* Piput will look no further than the stone-skin for someone to blame. Even the Natillians who saw us on the battlements won't have seen past our uniforms."

"And if someone on the terraces noticed us swimming round just now?"

Karmel regarded him skeptically. "I hardly think—"

"Damned right! You don't *think*, you do as you're told! Our orders are to lie low, and that's what we're going to do."

The priestess scowled. "The stone-skin changes all that. Imerle will want to know—"

"Since when have you given a shit what Imerle wants?" Veran's lip curled. "If you want to spit your dummy out at your brother, you'll have to do it on your own time."

Karmel groped for a response, but none came. Did Veran think she would risk a swim with the dragons just because she was sulking? She wanted to kick spray over him. Instead she turned her back on him and looked out at the ship. The mainmast streamed water as it crept higher into the air, dragging the sodden mainsails with it. Then it toppled once more.

But not before Karmel had glimpsed the flag the vessel was flying. The *Icewing*. "That's the emira's ship," she breathed.

The oar-bench creaked as Veran shifted his weight. "So what if it is? Imerle won't be on board."

"You don't know that."

He barked a laugh. "She knew the damned gate wouldn't be coming down, didn't she? You think she's stupid enough to put her head in a dragon's maw? Most likely she's tucked up in her palace, hammering the last few nails into the other Storm Lords' coffins."

"She wouldn't just give up her flagship like that. No way."

"Ships can be replaced."

The silver-scaled dragon had risen beneath the *Icewing,* and the vessel was half lifted into the air before sinking down again.

"Even if Imerle's not on board, another water-mage will be," Karmel said, determined not to back down.

"Then why's the ship still here? You don't think whoever's commanding it would have fled by now if they could?"

"There are people in the water. Maybe the captain wants to rescue them before he sets sail."

Veran snorted.

"If we swam across now, we might be mistaken for passengers who'd been swept overboard."

The priest gestured to his broken arm. "You reckon I can make it all that way with this?"

If Karmel had thought there had been a chance of that, she'd have broken his other arm too. "Then I'll have to go alone. I'm sure you can survive without my company for a few days." The gods knew, she could survive without his.

Veran pushed himself upright, setting the boat rocking. "You'd leave me here like this?"

There was something in his voice that gave Karmel pause. Was he worried she might steal the glory if she returned to Olaire? Or that Imerle might not believe her story without Veran there to back her up? "You swam all the way from the gate, didn't you? The beach is, what, a few hundred strokes from here? Once you get there, you won't need my help making it up to the city." Unless he'd begun walking on his hands.

Veran opened his mouth to speak, but Karmel was already turning away. She was done talking with him. Truth be told, she hadn't yet decided whether to try for the *Icewing,* but when she reached a decision it would be hers, not his. She'd played the good girl until now, and look where that had got her. It was time they started doing things her way.

The priest's tread sounded behind Karmel, but she did not glance round.

Then his right arm curled round her throat, and she was lifted off her feet.

Chapter 14

A BREEZE BLEW into Senar's face as he followed the passage into the belly of the Founder's Citadel. There was space for only two people to walk abreast, and the Guardian found himself next to Mistress Darbonna. Her every breath was a wheeze as she shuffled into the gloom. Ahead, two of her assistants led the company: grim-faced men carrying torches and wearing swords strapped to their waists. Strange, Senar mused, that librarians should bear arms. But then in a citadel built by the titans, one learned to prepare for all eventualities, he supposed.

A murmur sounded in the Guardian's ear, but when he looked round to see who had spoken he found the people behind him—Mazana and the Everlord—were walking silently several paces away. A number of times Senar had heard noises carried on the breeze: a snatch of conversation, or a whispered rasp like wind playing across sand, or a clank of metal as of a sword striking stone. There were footfalls too from along the side corridors. When he peered down them, though, he could make out nothing through the cloying darkness. In the end he decided he was hearing echoes of the company's own footsteps, or perhaps the footfalls of those who had walked this way long ago, for doubtless the breeze roaming the corridors carried sounds that were as old as the fortress itself.

Senar had passed the entrances to scores of chambers, yet not one of them had contained a book or a scroll. Most of the rooms were dark and empty. On occasion, though, he would see signs of past use such as potsherds or coins or—as now—the ashes of a fire. He placed a hand on Darbonna's arm and pointed to the ashes.

"Is the fortress inhabited?"

The old woman stared at him. "Good gracious, no, my dear. Unless of course you are referring to our humble community of librarians."

"What about before you came?"

"There were some people here, yes. The sick and the destitute."

"And you drove them out?" Senar said, glancing at Darbonna's sword-bearing assistants.

"What's that?"

"The people here before you, you drove them out?"

"Certainly not. They were merely . . . encouraged to leave. It is the scrolls, you understand? We cannot risk the texts being damaged or stolen."

Yes, how could the needs of the fortress's former occupants possibly compete with those of a book?

As Senar passed a side corridor he heard a fragment of his conversation with Darbonna repeated, then above that a snatch of disembodied laughter, faint as memory. When he looked at Darbonna she gave no indication that she'd heard it. But then the maker of that laughter could have been standing right next to the woman, and she still wouldn't have noticed.

"How many librarians are in the fortress?" Senar said.

"Not enough," Darbonna replied with a sigh. "The demands on our time are endless. Mexin leaves are so susceptible to mold, did you know? Of course you did. And as for our more ancient texts . . ."

Senar was only half listening as she proceeded to explain at length the properties of various writing materials and the efforts of the librarians to preserve them.

"How long have you been here?" he said when she paused for breath.

"Oh, less than two years. The emira herself gave her blessing to our community. A great and a wise woman . . ." She broke off as if she'd just remembered Mazana was walking behind her.

The torchbearers turned right into an unmarked windowless passage, and Senar found himself wondering at their ability to navigate the corridors without hesitation. Following the attack on Karalat's fortress by Erin Elalese forces, a single enemy sacristen had escaped to flee into the citadel's warren of passages. Neither he nor the three squads of Breakers sent to find him were ever seen again.

"What do you know of the fortress's history?" Senar said.

A look flitted across Darbonna's features. "A little," she said. "The citadel was constructed by the titans and abandoned at the end of the Second Age. It must have been occupied by primitives some time after because occasionally we encounter rooms with wall paintings or"—she suppressed a shudder—"the remains of their dead. We have found nothing, though, to suggest the fortress has been occupied by large numbers in recent times."

"The Storm Lords never claimed it?"

"The Storm Lords have no interest in a building where their powers would be blunted by the weight of stone separating them from the sea."

The librarians leading the company turned into a wider passage lit by torches in holders on the walls. Those torches bothered Senar for some reason, but it was a moment before he could put his finger on why. "You are mapping the fortress?"

Darbonna checked her stride. "What's that?"

Perhaps it was Senar's imagination, but the old woman's poor hearing only seemed to trouble her when he asked certain questions. "We've been walking now for nearly quarter of a bell, yet we still haven't reached the ramp. How is it you librarians came across it?"

"Oh, we explored widely in the early days when we were clearing the fortress of unwanted guests."

"And the torches along our route?" As if this were a well-trodden path . . .

Suddenly an earth tremor set the floor quivering. Senar was pitched into the wall to his left. A rasping groan came from along the passage, and the quake grew in intensity until the corridor thrummed like a bowstring. The Guardian looked at the ceiling, expecting to see fissures develop in the rock. There were no cracks, though. No cracks at all, even to mark the joints between blocks of stone. It was as if the passage had been carved from a single piece of rock, yet there were no tool marks on the walls.

The tremors subsided, and Darbonna moved ahead.

"Ah!" she said. "We are here!"

The torchbearers had reached the end of the corridor, and the light from their torches expanded into the black emptiness beyond. Senar's eyes widened as he entered a circular chamber so large the torchlight breathed only a hint of form and color into the far wall. Around the base of the wall were arches leading into passages, and carved into the rock above each arch was a face as tall as Senar himself. *Titans.* To the Guardian's left was a male with a heavy brow and a beard. Alongside was a female with a bulging forehead and thin lips parted to reveal filed teeth. Time had in no way softened the chiseled lines of either face, but then, as Senar was coming to understand, the titans had been workers of stone without compare.

The Everlord moved up to flank him. "Magnificent," he said, and so it was—in a creep-the-shit-out-of-you kind of way.

The word was repeated by one of the stone faces, then another and another, to create an otherworldly harmony that filled the room. With each repetition the sound grew more distorted, merging with the words of the other titans until finally it became unrecognizable.

Slowly the whispers faded.

Senar hadn't noticed the floor sloping down as he walked through the fortress, yet the dank smell in the chamber made it feel as if he were deep underground. From the far side of the room came a drip, drip of water. When the Guardian took a breath, intense cold tickled the back of his throat. He coughed, and the noise was spat back at him by the stone faces.

The last of Imerle's soldiers entered the chamber and spread out to half encircle Mazana and her bodyguards. The move did not go unnoticed by Greave and the Everlord, for while the two men pretended an interest in the titan faces, they took care to keep the soldiers in view at all times. This was the chance Imerle's forces had been waiting for to spring their ambush, for the size of the chamber would allow them to exploit their superior numbers. And while there were many exits from the room through which Mazana's bodyguards could flee, the torchlit corridor that the party had taken here was now guarded by Imerle's men. Senar could feel the septia's gaze on him. Doubtless Cilin was waiting for the Guardian to signal the attack.

Let him wait. Maybe Imerle thought she'd been clever, sending Senar here. Maybe she thought he had no choice now but to kill Mazana. But the more someone pushed the Guardian, the more he wanted to push back. If he had to pick a side, it wouldn't be Imerle's; the two of them could never be friends. Perhaps Jambar had been right, and he would one day save her life. But if he did so, he wasn't fool enough to think Imerle would stay thankful for long. Soon her thoughts would turn to the Merigan portal. Senar's knowledge about the gateway made him a threat to the Storm Isles, and the emira wasn't the sort to let gratitude get in the way of expediency.

The torchbearers moved farther into the chamber, driving the gloom before them. At the center of the room was a ramp leading down, and at the bottom of the ramp was a wall of sorcerous shadows that the torchlight could not penetrate. As the librarians descended to stand before it, ice crystals crunched beneath their feet. Such was the chill given off by the barrier that the flames of the men's torches darkened through purple to blue, and Senar wondered whether he would feel heat or cold if he reached his hand out to those flames.

The sorcerous wall was made up of scores of different threads of magic, suggesting many hands had contributed to its construction. A number of those threads were frayed, and the barrier was pitted and scarred as if someone had attempted to tear it down. Senar shot a look at Darbonna. Could someone have mounted an attack on the wall without her or the other librarians knowing?

An aftershock of the earlier quake shook the fortress. The ground lifted and settled as if the citadel had drawn in a breath. A rumble sounded beneath Senar's feet, and the stone faces sent echoes booming around the chamber. As the noise died away, Mazana forced a smile. "I'd say we've found the source of the quakes, wouldn't you?" she said to the Guardian.

Quakes, quakes, quakes, the titans whispered back at her.

Senar leaned in close, trying to pitch his voice so the faces wouldn't share his words with the rest of the room. "Someone tried to bring that thing down"—he nodded at the sorcerous wall—"and failed. Recently too, I'm guessing. No doubt that person is hoping you will finish—"

"Then I'd best not disappoint them," Mazana cut in, moving away.

Senar tutted his disgust as he watched her descend the ramp. What in the Matron's name was she up to? She couldn't be blind to the hidden hand at play here, any more than she could be ignorant of the tension between her forces and Imerle's. Yet she acted as if neither were her concern. Senar felt the septia's gaze on him again. Cilin wouldn't wait on his signal for much longer. Would the soldier attack, though, when there was so much going on they didn't understand?

Any of them except Mazana, that is.

She reached the bottom of the ramp to stand between the two librarians, then extended her hands to the wall of blackness. The barrier started to weaken, layers of wards peeling away with a sound like the tolling of a spirit bell. The chill in the room began to lift, and the flames of the librarians' torches turned through green to yellow to orange. Another tremor shook the chamber, faint at first, then growing stronger as the barrier dissolved. It was as if the wall had been holding back whatever force was responsible for the quakes. Was something trapped on the level below? Something the Storm Lady was about to release. Something the titans had seen fit to cage behind magic strong enough to last millennia.

Senar reached out with his senses to explore the power flowing from Mazana's hands. Whenever he sought to focus his Will on it, though, it escaped him. Not water-magic, that much was clear. So what was its source? *The priestess of the Lord of Hidden Faces—it has to be.* The priestess had agreed to help Mazana in the fortress, and now she was delivering on that promise.

The last few strands of the sorcerous barrier unraveled. The darkness before Mazana dissipated to leave her standing before a vast arched portal decorated with more snarling titan faces. There was movement in the gloom beyond, and a swirl of ice-blue light swelled outward.

The Storm Lady stepped back.

A wave of mist rolled through the portal to engulf her.

Senar heard her gasp. He reached for his sword. Around the chamber, Mazana's bodyguards and Imerle's troops were doing the same. The Guardian wondered if the tension was about to erupt into battle. The soldiers had lowered their spears, and Greave half turned toward them, baring his teeth. Below him the wave of mist had broken against the ramp and now came surging up to curl round the legs of those in the chamber. The shuddering cold returned, and the flames of the librarians' torches guttered, before burning once more with a blue so deep it verged on black.

The light in the room faded.

But not before Senar had seen Mazana's form reappear in the mist at the foot of the newly exposed archway. Hugging her arms about herself, she strode through the portal and into the murk beyond.

The coming of the mist had put an end to any prospect of a fight, because with the darkness so deep it would be hard to tell friend from foe. *As if I'd known the difference before.* For a heartbeat no one stirred. Then Senar flinched as Darbonna brushed past him. She started down the ramp, her movements showing no hint of the frailty she'd displayed on the walk through the fortress. As she drew level with the torchbearers, they fell into step. Together they passed through the archway. The Everlord went next, followed by Mazana's other bodyguards.

Four of the emira's soldiers moved to take up positions at the top of the ramp. They looked at Cilin for a signal. The septia was frowning, but in the gloom Senar couldn't have said if that frown was directed at him. The Guardian stared again at the stone titans. The face across from him was the woman with the filed teeth. A sound escaped her lips—the same ghostly laughter he'd heard on the walk to the chamber. The Guardian thought he saw movement through the archway beneath her, but it was only the swirling fog.

Then another noise reached Senar—a sound on the edge of silence. It came from his left. The stone faces picked it up and sent it bouncing about the room. A word. *Follow? Sorrow?* With each repetition it became more mangled until it was transformed into something no human throat could have uttered. Senar looked at the passage from which he thought the noise had come.

Nothing stirred.

Moving alongside Cilin he said, "Give the word to your men, Septia. Tell them to watch their backs."

Kempis was sweating in spite of the chill. The emira's throne room was as large as the Watchstation's exercise yard, yet still he felt hemmed in by the walls of water. To make matters worse, prowling the sea to the septia's left was the meanest looking kris shark he'd ever set eyes upon. Try as he might, Kempis couldn't keep his gaze from straying to the fish, and the Shroud-cursed thing seemed to be watching him in turn. For all the septia knew this could be the same shark that had chewed on his leg twenty years ago. He could even convince himself he saw a glint of recognition in the creature's eyes.

Right now, though, Kempis was more worried about the big fish *inside* the chamber. On a throne sat the emira, her hands steepled as she listened to his account of Bright Eyes's passing. Her chief minister frowned at the septia from the chair to Imerle's right. Behind, the twins Mili and Tali looked bored, the executioner vacant, while the Chameleon high priest, Caval, wore a smile that suggested he was reveling in Kempis's discomfort.

Hilaire was two paces to the septia's left, standing so rigidly at attention she might have had a spear shoved up her ass. She'd insisted on coming with him to answer the emira's summons, though doubtless only to ensure that, of the two of them, *he* was the one thrown to the sharks for Thane Tanner's untimely demise.

When Kempis finished speaking, Imerle turned to Caval. "We had understood, High Priest, that your counterpart at the temple of the Lord of Hidden Faces was a fraud."

"And so he is. Artagina has usurped a dead religion in order to acquire some small measure of power. There must be another explanation for why the shrine survived the demon's attack."

In other words, the bastard thinks I'm making this up.

Imerle switched her gaze to Kempis. "Septia, you say you couldn't sense the temple's wards?"

"I'm sure—" Hilaire began.

"Are you a septia?" the emira cut in. "Because that can easily be arranged."

Hilaire's mouth snapped shut

Kempis found himself warming to Imerle. "I've seen sorcery used to cover a trail before, and it leaves a shadow. There weren't nothing like that here."

"Meaning we are dealing with someone skilled at covering their tracks."

Kempis stayed silent. His back was starting to ache. Before entering the chamber Hilaire had insisted he put on his stripes, but without needle and thread to secure them to his shoulder the only way to stop the damned things slipping off was to match Hilaire's wooden stance.

Pernay spoke. "Is it your view, Septia, that the assassin intended all along to take shelter in the temple?"

"No."

"But the priestess you mentioned protected her, did she not?"

"If you call making off with her corpse 'protecting,' yes."

The more Kempis thought about the masked woman, the more questions arose to plague him. Most likely the priestess had taken

Bright Eyes's body to prevent her being recognized as a follower of the Lord of Hidden Faces. But then why had Artagina seemed oblivious to the whole affair? Was it possible the priestess wanted the corpse for herself? Kempis had heard rumors of aging bluebloods employing necromancers to shift their souls into younger bodies, but the priestess had appeared no older than Kempis himself.

"What about Artagina?" Pernay said. "Did you get a chance to speak to him?"

"The high priest claimed he knew nothing about the assassin or the priestess or the Shroud-cursed Kerralai demon for that matter. Otherwise, he was real helpful. Maybe we should bring him and the priestess in."

"Leave the Lord of Hidden Faces to us," Imerle said.

Kempis scowled, and Hilaire hurriedly said, "Of course, Emira."

Imerle's gaze remained on the septia. "What have you been able to find out about Thane Tanner's killer?"

"Nothing yet. What with having come straight here from the temple, and all."

Hilaire cleared her throat. "There are no reports of anyone seeing the assassin, but I remain hopeful a witness will come forward. The perpetrator *will* be found."

"We have your word on that, Quina?"

"I have the utmost confidence in Septia Kempis Parr."

There she went again, talking Kempis up when he least wanted her to. There'd been no suggestion Thane's assassin was a sorcerer, so there was no reason why Kempis of all people should be given the case. Except that he was here now, and Hilaire needed someone to take the fall for her if the killer wasn't found.

Just then shouts came from the underwater passage behind, and the septia looked round to see a one-eyed old man enter the throne room. In his right hand was a bag; in his left, a monocle, which he pointed at Imerle.

"Emira! Look to the seas behind you!"

Kempis scanned the wall of water at the back of the chamber and saw a dark shape speeding through the deep toward them. At first he thought it another shark. Then he detected a flicker of water-magic.

The rear wall rippled and parted, and a woman stepped into view. Green-eyed and hugely muscled, she clutched a longsword in her left hand, a throwing knife in her right. She wore a sleeveless leather jerkin and a necklace of fireweed. Her most striking feature, though, was her skin—charcoal gray with glittering flecks. She stiffened at finding her arrival expected, then sent her throwing knife flashing toward the emira.

Imerle sat frozen.

The executioner stepped into the dagger's path. He made no move to bat the blade aside, merely let it strike him at the level of his navel. The knife bounced off the metal links sewn into his skin and fell to the ground.

The stone-skin transferred the longsword in her left hand to her right.

Mili and Tali sprang at her. The newcomer was fast with her blade—faster even than Bright Eyes, perhaps—but the twins were faster still. Cuts blossomed across the stone-skin's arms and chest. Kempis saw one twin thrust her needlelike sword into the assassin's thigh before twisting and withdrawing it. The stone-skin's leg almost gave way, but she managed a counterswing that was blocked by the second sister. The first twin lunged again, for the newcomer's chest this time, and the stone-skin pushed the blade aside with her free hand.

Then she flung herself into the wall of water at her back.

Mili and Tali stabbed their swords into the sea after her. From where Kempis stood, it was difficult to make out whether their weapons found their mark. He doubted it, though, for the stone-skin was already retreating swiftly into the sunlit waters. The shark Kempis had seen earlier didn't even try to follow her. Evidently it was having too much fun tormenting the septia with its stare.

Kempis realized he hadn't so much as drawn his sword in the emira's defense. But then the clash between the twins and the stone-skin had lasted only a handful of heartbeats. The assassin had taken a risk trying to beard Imerle in her own den, yet it might have paid off had it not been for One-Eye's warning. Kempis looked back at the old man to find him smiling inanely. So this was the Remnerol shaman, was it? The one who could read the future in his knuckle bones. Clearly he'd foreseen the threat to the emira and arrived in time to alert her, but why hadn't he also foreseen the attacks on Mazana Creed and Thane Tanner?

Maybe he did, Kempis thought. *Maybe he just decided not to share his knowledge with the targets.* He looked at Imerle. At her order, perhaps?

The emira was studying Kempis, and he stilled his expression lest she read his suspicions in his look. She appeared unruffled by the attempt on her life, but Kempis was beginning to wonder if she was capable of any emotion at all.

"We suspect we may have just found Thane Tanner's killer for you," she said to Kempis.

The septia's gaze flickered to the sea. "Found and then lost again."

"And yet she used water-magic to get here, did she not? We assume you would recognize the signature of her sorcery if you encountered it again."

He nodded warily.

"Then why are you still here?"

Kempis licked his lips, remembering the stone-skin's speed with her blade. He looked at Mili and Tali. The twins hadn't sheathed their swords and were now prowling the rear of the chamber. "Don't suppose I could borrow your bodyguards, could I?" he said. "Just until the stone-skin is caught. I promise I'll bring them back afterward."

Imerle raised an eyebrow.

Sighing, Kempis turned away.

Forget I asked.

Senar descended the ramp into mist so dense the thickest curls felt like fingers brushing against his skin. Reaching the base, he paused on the threshold of a chamber. Its walls and ceiling were hidden by the fog, but Senar could sense the size of the room in the weight of emptiness before him. Ahead the torches of the two librarians were smears of blue light. That light had stained the mist through which the men passed, and the fog held the glow to leave a spectral trail that was now fading to black. Mazana walked in front of the torchbearers, her breath steaming in the chill.

Senar set off in pursuit.

He didn't notice the corpse until he stumbled over it. Skidding on ice crystals, he threw out his arms to regain his balance, then turned to inspect the body. A male titan lay curled up in a fetal position, his right hand reaching for a sword just out of reach. His skin was encased in frost. Doubtless he'd been dead for millennia, yet somehow the mist had preserved—

The Guardian started as someone touched his shoulder. Cilin. The septia's expression was bleak as he pointed back the way they had come. The ramp was barely visible through the murk, but Senar could see two soldiers stationed to either side of the base. One of them, a woman, was crouching beside the wall just inside the chamber. Through a curtain of fog, she appeared pale as a spirit to Senar's eyes, but it was the wall that held his attention. The lowest handspan was a deeper gray than the rock above it, and the soldier scratched a fingernail along that darker section. She rubbed the nail against a thumb.

"Blood."

Echoes of the word came at Senar from all directions—evidently there were titan faces carved into the walls of this room as there were above. When the Guardian looked for them, though, he could make out nothing through the mist. Other sounds reached him: a rustle of metal, fragments of words, a faint rumble like the growl of an approaching storm. It was only then that Senar realized the floor was trembling. Not the erratic jolts of an earth tremor, but a regular pulse like a heartbeat. The Guardian's own pulse kept time.

Cilin stood watching him, irresolute. Senar could guess what he was thinking. The septia's orders had been to attack Mazana, so why was he guarding her back? Why had he trailed her down here at all? Senar shared his misgivings. To follow is to let your fate be decided by another. He wanted to act, but act how? He knew nothing of what was happening here, and if he picked his course blindly, he was as likely to hit rocks as he was to find a safe harbor.

Mazana had halted a short distance in front, and Senar crossed to join her. Icy stone shavings cracked and popped beneath his boots. The Storm Lady cupped her hands through the mist as if she were scooping up water. When she opened her hands again, the fog sank down.

"Titan magic," she murmured to Senar. "The air is thick with it, even after all these millennia. It deadens sorcery, did you know? My power is useless here."

"And the priestess's?"

Mazana gave a rueful smile, then moved deeper into the chamber.

Ahead and to the right were more titan corpses scattered about like discarded dolls. None of the bodies showed any wounds. All were perfectly preserved. Almost as if the titans had just been killed, in fact. But no, that wasn't possible. Nothing could have survived down here on the wrong side of that sorcerous barrier. The Guardian reached the edge of a ring of fluted pillars curling away into the mist to either side. The columns to his left stretched upward into darkness, but the pillar immediately in front and to his right had collapsed to leave only a waist-high stump. The floor around it was strewn with chunks of rock, while on top . . .

Senar blinked.

A torch, its blue flame flickering weakly. A second torch lay atop another shattered pillar a few paces away. Of the librarians who had been carrying them, there was no sign. Darbonna, too, had disappeared.

A whisper sounded to Senar's left—not the whisper of a hushed voice, but of a blade being drawn from its scabbard. Shadows gathered at the edge of the torchlight, and the Guardian pushed Mazana behind him.

"Weapons out!" he shouted to his companions, unsheathing his own sword.

Then the first screams started.

Sniffer and Duffle were waiting for Kempis at the palace gates. The Untarian shot him a black-toothed smile. "Never thought we'd see you again, sir."

"Had them eating out of my hand by the end," Kempis said, taking his stripes from his shoulder and putting them in a pocket.

"And Hilaire?"

"Stayed behind to brown-nose one of her Storm Guard contacts."

As they climbed Kalin's Hill he told them of the conversation in the throne room and of the assassination attempt on the emira.

When he finished, Sniffer said, "You want me to swim round to the chamber and see if I can pick up the stone-skin's trail?"

Kempis eyed her suspiciously. On her last day in the Watch? What was she after, overtime? "Did you miss the part about that Shroud-cursed shark eyeballing me?"

"Untarians can swim as fast as most sharp-teeths over short distances."

"But not as fast as water-mages, I'll bet."

"Why, Kempis, I never knew you cared."

"That's 'Septia' to you."

At that moment a tremor shook the ground. Not as strong as the quake the other day, but still intense enough for Kempis to cast a wary eye over the buildings to either side. To the west the towers of the Founder's Citadel, along with the tenement blocks around it, were shuddering like an old man's palsied hands. Screams floated up the hill. From a house to Kempis's right came the sound of breaking glass and a baby's crying.

"It's the denkrakil," Duffle said as the tremors subsided.

"What is?" Sniffer asked.

"These quakes. Denkrakil's got its tentacles wrapped round the island. One of these days it'll give Olaire a shake and the whole city will slip into the sea."

The Untarian snorted.

"On my life! Fisherman saw the thing a few weeks back off Ferris Point."

"Then how in the Sender's name did he survive to tell the tale?"

Kempis said, "Maybe it was hunting bigger game."

Sniffer looked across. "Tell me you don't believe this shit."

The septia shrugged. "Why not? Suits the Storm Lords to have a denkrakil on the loose in the Sabian Sea. If the creature takes the odd ship, so what? Gives the emira an excuse to raise the Levy each year."

"And if she's on that floater when the thing attacks?"

He shrugged a second time. "Friend of mine knows a soldier in Dian who saw the Dragon Gate rise in the dead of night a couple of years back. Weren't nothing to do with Dragon Day neither." He looked between Sniffer and Duffle. "Don't you get it? Not long after that is when the tremors started, right?"

The Untarian studied him, then grinned. "Now I know you're kidding. A friend of yours knows a soldier in Dian?"

Kempis returned her gaze blankly.

"Since when have you had any friends?"

And with that, Sniffer spun on her heel and headed back the way they had come.

"Where the hell are you going?" Kempis shouted after her.

"To the palace, of course. To follow the stone-skin."

The septia thought to call her back, then decided against it. Where was the harm? It wasn't as if he could detect the assassin's magical signature just now, so until the stone-skin used her sorcery again, the Untarian was the best chance they had of tracking her down. Assuming Sniffer meant to follow the assassin at all. Most likely she'd just wait until Kempis was gone before finding somewhere quiet to sit out her last day.

Duffle said, "What about us, sir, Septia, sir?"

Kempis resumed climbing the hill. "Back to the station. We'll find Loop, see if anything's come in on Thane Tanner's killing."

"And if Sniffer can't find the stone-skin?"

"Then we hit the streets. If the stone-skin's been in Olaire these past few days, odds are someone will have seen her. A woman with skin like hers can't just blend into the scenery."

Duffle's long legs were eating up the slope, and Kempis found himself struggling to keep up. As he drew level with the Chameleon Temple, he saw two priests standing outside its gates. One of them—a middle-aged man with receding blond hair—was returning Kempis's scrutiny, and the septia was oddly glad when a turn in the road took him out of sight.

Duffle placed a hand on his right arm. "Sir, look!"

Kempis swung his gaze to where the youth was pointing. He'd reached a position on Kalin's Hill from where he could see the whole of Olaire, and to the west he spotted a dozen small ships approaching the Causeway, their gray sails filled by the strengthening east wind. At first he thought they were blueblood vessels returning from the Hunt. Then he noticed that none of the ships was flying a flag.

And that their decks were heaving with armored figures.

The lead vessel entered the Causeway. On the main deck, gray-cloaked troops were lining up along the rails. Ahead of the ship the docks were awash with color and noise from the crowds awaiting the arrival of whichever captain brought back the dragon's corpse. It sounded like they had a party going on down there, but Kempis suspected someone was about to call time. As the galley entered the harbor, a cheer went up, only to die away as the revelers did the math.

People on the rooftops of the houses overlooking the Causeway ducked and scrambled away across the roof tiles.

Here it comes.

A volley of arrows flew out from the deck of the lead ship to strike the people on the docks.

As one, the crowd flinched.

A second hail of missiles rained down. The townsfolk nearest the water turned to flee, only to find themselves boxed in by the multitudes behind. Some threw themselves into the harbor and started swimming toward the shipyard to the north. Others tried to claw a way through the press behind. Kempis could taste the fear from up here. Fights broke out as the throng turned on itself.

Another volley of arrows.

Those at the rear of the crowd—the lucky ones—began streaming into the streets of the Maiden District. The Storm Guards who might have returned fire on the enemy were swept along with them. A lone arrow arced toward the gray ships. Kempis did not see where it landed.

Duffle stared wide-eyed at the mayhem. "What are they doing?"

"Sowing panic, lad," the septia said. "Ain't no way the Storm Guards can organize a defense with that stampede going on."

"But, the ships . . . They're attacking Olaire? The Storm Lords . . ."

Kempis did not respond. Out of the corner of his eye he'd seen movement in the flooded streets of the Deeps. When he looked across he caught sight of a flotilla of small boats gliding toward the Shallows. Sunlight glinted off the armor worn by their passengers. The septia tried to count numbers—ten boats, twenty, thirty, and still more were materializing from behind the buildings.

"Let's get out of here," he said to Duffle, striding in the direction of the Commercial District.

Above the tumult from the docks, the bells from the Maudlin Watchtower started to ring their note of warning across the city.

The two former torchbearers rushed at Senar from the mist beyond the ring of pillars, chanting in a language the Guardian did not recognize. He parried a strike from the first, then ducked under a head-high cut from the second and slammed his blade into the man's groin. With a cry the injured swordsman staggered back into his companion, and they went down in a tangle.

Senar stabbed out twice and they fell still.

He swung back to Mazana. The Storm Lady stood behind a half circle of her bodyguards, none of whom had made any move to help Senar. Greave watched him with a hint of a smile. The others peered into the fog beyond the torchlight, their weapons held ready. From the direction of the ramp came the clash of metal on metal, chanting, bellowed war cries. It had to be more of these so-called librarians; they must have followed the company down from the upper level, meaning the emira's soldiers, at the rear of the party, would bear the brunt of the assault.

White-robed figures came swarming out of the gloom. Mazana's ax-wielding bodyguard leapt to meet them, his weapon a glittering arc that cut the mist to ribbons. The Everlord was calmness personified as he stepped between the flailing swords of two female assailants. He ran one through, then delivered a punch to the throat of the second. She dropped to her knees gasping for air. A black man carrying a shortsword and a shield came for Senar. The Guardian dispatched him with a feint and a slash to the neck, and the man toppled into the back of Greave's legs. Senar thought the champion would go down, but he kept his balance and blocked the attack of a male assailant, pinning his foe's blade on the barbs of his fish-spine sword.

Senar crouched to collect the black man's shield, fumbling the strap with his halfhand.

A shout from Mazana.

Two swordsmen materialized from the fog to Senar's right and advanced on the Storm Lady. She tugged a dagger from a scabbard at her waist and flung it at the nearest enemy. The throw went high, but it bought Mazana time to skip behind a pillar and out of her attackers' reach.

Senar hurled himself at the newcomers. The first man had his back to the Guardian and died before he could raise his sword. The second retreated, parrying feverishly, until a push from Senar's shield drove him back toward one of the broken pillars. Mazana rose up behind and brought down a chunk of stone on the back of his head. His skull caved in with a wet crack. He slumped to the floor, his blade slipping from his fingers.

The Storm Lady gazed at her blood-spattered hands, then dropped the rock on the corpse. Her breath came quickly, and her face was flushed.

She shot Senar a grin.

The Guardian scowled. Something funny in all this, was there? Maybe someone had cracked a joke that he'd missed.

Thus far the sound of fighting had been loudest from the direction of the ramp, but the titan faces had taken up the clamor so that now it seemed to Senar as if he were standing in the middle of a pitched battle. Of Mazana's bodyguards only Greave and the Everlord remained visible in the mist, fighting back-to-back against half a dozen assailants. As Kiapa cut down a woman to his left, a man appeared from the fog to his right, swinging a saber in a decapitating stroke.

The Everlord spun to catch the attack.

Only for his foe to trip on the body of one of his white-robed companions. The librarian's sword dipped beneath Kiapa's block, slamming into the top of his right leg and cutting cleanly through the limb.

The Everlord toppled wordlessly.

Greave, sensing his back was now exposed, carved his fish-spine blade through the chest of an opponent, then grabbed the man and threw him into the librarians approaching from behind. Before the champion could dispatch the fallen swordsmen, another enemy emerged shrieking from the mist.

Senar cast a look at Mazana to find her watching him in turn. He raised an inquiring eyebrow, only for her to repeat the gesture at him.

Sighing, he went to help Greave.

Three librarians rushed the champion, and he swung his sword in a wide arc to meet their attack. Two of the foe checked their advance, but the third was struck on the chin and fell in a spray of blood. A thrust from one of Greave's remaining assailants pierced the champion's defenses only to deflect off the armor beneath his puffed shirt. Greave's countercut lifted the swordsman's head from his shoulders.

A white-robed young man appeared from the shadows behind him, chanting in a voice that quavered with fear. Senar moved to intercept. It was clear to him the librarians weren't librarians in truth, but nor were they warriors of any distinction, for when the youth attacked he raised his sword high overhead as if he were chopping wood. Senar parried the blow, then ran the youth through.

Two more assailants closed in, a man and a woman. Senar smelled juripa spirits on the woman's breath as she spat the words of her chant at him. Holding her sword two-handed, she swung the weapon so violently that, when Senar swayed back, she stumbled off balance. The Guardian flashed his blade across her throat. This was beginning to feel more like slaughter than fighting, but the work still needed doing. A sword in a novice's hands cuts just as sharp as one in a weaponsmaster's—as the Everlord's example had proved.

The second attacker wielded his longsword like a dueling rapier. Senar blocked his first thrust with his shield, then countered. His opponent was plainly not accustomed to the weight of his weapon, for the Guardian's lunge took him through the heart before he could lift the blade to the guard position. As he collapsed, the fingers of his left hand curled round the rim of Senar's shield and tore it from his grasp.

Senar looked about him for the next enemy. The chanting and the sounds of fighting had started to fade as if the battle were moving away from him—or the librarians had been put to flight. More than a dozen white-robed figures lay sprawled in death within the range of the torchlight. None remained upright.

And there was no sign of Mazana.

The Guardian's stomach knotted. He cast a fearful eye over the corpses about him, but the Storm Lady's was not among them. Could she have slipped away during the clash? Senar hadn't seen her after he went to Greave's aid because his attention had been fixed on his opponents. It would have been simple enough for one of the enemy to circle round and attack her from the rear, but then wouldn't she have shouted a warning?

A bank of mist swept over him, concealing everything beyond an arm's length in each direction. Abruptly the clash of combat started up loud again to his right. A man's roar sounded, followed by a startled cry, a clank of metal, a woman's scream. But no chanting. If the librarians had indeed retreated, whose scream had Senar just heard? The image of Mazana's female slant-eyed bodyguard appeared in his mind's eye. Had the emira's soldiers turned on the Storm Lady's followers when the danger posed by the librarians had passed? Would they be coming now for Greave? *For me?*

The mists parted, and Senar caught sight of Greave crouching among the white-robed bodies. Of all the people to survive, it would have to be the champion. One of the librarians—a woman—was also alive. The champion smiled as he seized a handful of her hair and wrenched her to her knees before drawing the barbs of his fish-spine sword across her throat. Wide-eyed, the woman tried to take up her chant again, but her words bubbled in the blood gushing from her neck. Greave gave her a push, and she toppled forward. Her forehead cracked against the floor.

Another tremor shook the chamber. Senar leaned against one of the pillars. For a moment he thought he heard laughter from deeper in the room, but it was swallowed by the fog. Then a new sound reached him.

Footfalls.

Greave had heard them too, for he straightened and turned toward the noise.

A shadowy outline in the murk resolved itself into Septia Cilin Rai. He staggered toward Senar. His hair was matted with blood, his uniform dark and torn round a cut to his side. Halting a few paces away, he took in the corpses on the ground before squinting into the mist beyond the circle of pillars.

He's looking for Mazana.

The soldier took a breath as if summoning up his strength. His gaze flickered from Senar to Greave, then back again.

"Kill him," Cilin said to the Guardian.

CHAPTER 15

THIS CAN'T *be happening,* was all Karmel could think.

When Veran's forearm curled round her neck, her first instinct was that he'd lost his balance and thrown an arm about her to stop himself falling. Even when she was lifted into the air she expected his grip to ease after he'd warned her what would happen the next time she questioned his orders. Instead the cold metal of his armguard continued to press against her throat. She gasped for a breath that would not come.

He really means to kill me.

The realization froze her heart, then she began to thrash about, her indignation as much as her fear giving her strength. This was all because she was considering returning to Olaire? Did secrecy matter so much to Veran that he would kill her for it? She wanted to scream at him to release her, but when she opened her mouth all that came out was a wheeze. She hooked her fingers round his armguard and attempted to pry it from her neck.

His grasp did not falter.

Karmel thrust her head back, trying to butt him in the face, but she succeeded only in wrenching the muscles of her neck. She kicked back with her right leg, hoping to catch him where it hurt, but instead she dealt him only a glancing blow to the inside of his knee. Frantic, she reached over her shoulder, intending to gouge his eyes or grab a handful of hair. He ducked his head out of range.

One of her flailing hands brushed the empty sheaths of her baldric.

She inwardly cursed. If she'd brought back just one of her throwing knives from the control room—

Then it came to her.

My sword!

The blade was broken, yes, but even a broken weapon could deliver a mighty sting. She grabbed the hilt.

Veran's hand closed round her wrist. But since his right arm was about her neck, he had to be using his left hand to hold her. And if that arm was broken . . .

Karmel pulled on the hilt with all her strength. The blade shifted a finger's width, but no farther. In an effort to break the priest's grasp, she twisted her wrist until her skin burned in his grip. Nothing. She yanked her hand from side to side, knowing each wrench would send a spike of agony up Veran's arm. Still he held her tight. His breathing was ragged, and Karmel pictured the broken bones of his arm grinding together. She couldn't imagine what it cost him to keep her still, but he managed it.

Karmel tried to tense her neck muscles against the force of his grip, but to no effect. Her eyes were watering from the pain of her swollen jaw. She'd bitten her tongue, and she tasted the metallic warmth of her blood. The boat started to rock. For an instant Karmel's boots touched the bottom of the craft. It dawned on her that Veran must be leaning back to keep her feet off the ground.

And an idea surfaced.

Her gaze fixed on the prow, a couple of paces away. She let her struggles diminish, hoping the priest would think her strength was failing. His grasp didn't ease, but then she hadn't expected it to. All she wanted was the slightest relaxation in his stance . . .

Now!

She threw her weight forward, dragging Veran with her a step.

A step was all she needed, for with the bottom of the boat curving up to the prow she could now place her feet on the boards. Tensing, she pushed off to propel herself backward.

Veran teetered before stumbling back a pace. Karmel thought he would steady himself, but his feet must have tangled because suddenly he was toppling backward, taking her with him.

The cave tilted.

Karmel heard Veran's head crack against wood—the oar-bench?— then she landed on him. He grunted. His grip on her throat loosened, and she clawed at his arm, twisting her neck left and right, ignoring the stabs of white-hot pain each movement caused in her jaw.

She was free.

Scrambling on all fours, she splashed through shallow water to the prow. If she threw herself over the side there was no way he'd be able to swim after her with a broken arm. As she tried to clamber upright, though, Veran seized her right foot, and she sprawled to the boards. She kicked out at the hand holding her, then flipped onto her back and snatched for her sword. Desperation made her fingers clumsy.

The blade slid clear.

She'd only intended to use it to keep Veran away, but the priest had already closed the distance between them. The fingers of his right hand reached for her throat, his weight bearing down on her.

Her sword buried itself to the hilt in his gut.

Air hissed between his teeth. For a few heartbeats he remained on top of her, his face a handspan from hers, his eyes fever-bright, a muscle in his cheek twitching. Blood trickled from the corner of his mouth. She tried to get her hands under him so she could push him away, but her strength was gone, and in the end it was Veran who levered himself up—Karmel's blade pulling free—before rocking back on his haunches and collapsing against the oar-bench.

The priestess lurched to the prow, her sword held out in front of her in case he came for her again. Her right hand was trembling on the hilt, so she moved her left to join it. Strangely, that only seemed to make the trembling worse. Veran was shaking too. Blood oozed from his stomach wound, and Karmel saw her own exhaustion and despair mirrored in his features. He watched her in silence, his chest heaving in and out as if *he'd* been the one nearly strangled. Each breath brought a grimace to his face. His eyelids began to droop.

When he spoke, his voice was a whisper. "Forgive me . . . girl," he said through red-flecked lips. "Just . . . following orders."

Karmel's hackles rose. "Whose orders?"

Veran did not reply. His right arm moved, and the priestess raised her sword higher. But he was only reaching for the wedding band on his left hand. He tugged it off his finger and held it out.

"Don't let her—" His voice cracked. "Don't let her be alone at the end."

Karmel's voice rose an octave. "Whose orders?"

But Veran's chest had already fallen still. His eyes rolled back in his head. The ring slipped from his grasp and clattered onto the boards.

Fearing some final deception, the priestess watched him for a time, her head thick with incomprehension. What had she done? What had he *made* her do? He'd left her no choice, she told herself, but when had she ever had a choice in this Shroud-cursed business?

This can't be happening.

Her anger and fear came boiling up, and she staggered across the boat. Seizing Veran by the shoulders, she shrieked, "Whose orders?"

His head lolled backward, banging off the oar-bench.

Karmel released him.

She wasn't sure when she'd started weeping, but she could feel the tears running down her cheeks. She retreated a step, only to trip and fall, taking the impact on her elbows just as she had three days ago when Veran launched their boat from that Olairian bay.

The priest had slumped onto one side, his face half submerged, his right eye staring back at her. The water round him was streaked red. When Karmel looked at her hands she saw they were bloody too, and there was more blood—Veran's blood—on her shattered blade.

With a sob, she flung the sword into the gloom.

It clanged against the wall of the cave and splashed into the sea.

Agenta watched the dragon bear down on a Storm Guard halfway to shore. The soldier had tried to swim for the caves at the base of the cliff, doubtless hoping the creature's attention would remain fixed on the *Icewing*. The dragon, though, having punched a hole in the ship's hull, seemed content to pick off stragglers in the water while it waited for the vessel to sink. And sink the *Icewing* surely would, for while four Storm Guards had been sent below to help at the pumps, on each occasion Agenta looked over the rail she found the sea was closer than the last time she'd checked.

The distant swimmer shrieked as the dragon reached him. He was tugged beneath the waves. Bubbles broke the surface. Then all was still.

Agenta scanned the waters near the *Icewing* for her father. Beneath the rope that Farrell had tossed over the rail, a mob of dignitaries, apparently unaware the ship was going down, kicked and splashed as they battled to be next to climb. Other passengers, Dutia Elemy Meddes among them, sat on the shattered masts, waving their arms for attention as if they thought those on board might not have noticed them. Yet still there was no sign of Rethell.

He's dead, a voice inside Agenta said.

She refused to hear it.

If he were alive, you would have seen him by—

Shut up!

Footfalls sounded to the kalischa's left. She turned to see the Storm Guard octa approaching, thumbs tucked into his belt. He halted in front of her.

"Got any more of them white arrows?"

"Two."

He held out a hand.

Agenta did not move. "What's your plan?" she said.

The octa gestured to where the dragon had claimed the Storm Guard. "Can't go on pricking that thing one needle at a time. When it next comes within range, we hit it with all we've got, all at once."

Agenta considered. A volley concentrated on the dragon's eyes or nostrils might do for the creature, but the beast had been quick to protect its vulnerable areas thus far. And if the attack proved unsuccessful, those on the *Icewing* would be left with no way of repelling the dragon's next assault. With the ship sinking, though, what choice did they have?

"How much is all you've got?" Agenta asked.

"Including yours, eight arrows. Two shortspears."

"Eight arrows. And how many archers?"

"Seven."

She regarded him coolly. "Sounds to me like you're one short."

"Sounds to *me* like you're wasting my time."

A shout came from a lookout near the starboard cathead. "Ship to port! Coming this way!"

Agenta looked north and east, expecting to see Cauroy's vessel bearing down on the *Icewing*. The *Majestic,* though, was in no position to mount a rescue, for its mainmast had been toppled and a bronze-scaled dragon was even now lifting its front claws to the starboard rail, only to trumpet as the sea about it vaporized. The vessel that the lookout had spotted was farther west, riding a wave of water-magic . . .

Agenta's breath caught. The *Crest!* There was no mistaking its flag or the shape of its bow. But how could that be? At the speed the *Ice-wing* had overtaken it, Agenta had expected the Gilgamarian ship to still be far to the north. But then perhaps Balen had merely let the other vessel pass so he could follow it at a discreet distance. Had Rethell anticipated Imerle's treachery and made sure help would be at hand?

The octa said, "I don't recognize the flag she's flying."

"It's my father's ship."

The soldier squinted at her. If he realized the balance of power between them had just shifted, it did not show in his manner. "The water-mage on board, is he strong enough to hold off the dragon while we move people across?"

"I don't know."

"How about sorcerous arrows? Got any on board?"

"No."

"Then we finish this now." He held out his hand again for Agenta's arrows.

She did not move.

The octa muttered something, then spat on the deck. "Have it your way, lady. If you want in on this, though, you do what I tell you. I pick the target, right? The dragon's eyes, nose, mouth, whatever. Got it?"

"I'm just about keeping up so far."

He turned away.

Agenta looked at Selis. "Mage, use your sorcery to get people back on deck. Start with whoever the dragon targets." *And find my father,* she almost added.

Selis gave a mocking bow.

The octa had rejoined his troops near the steps to the aft deck. Aside from the officer there were a dozen soldiers, seven holding bows, two spears, and three pikes. Among the archers was the man in the red head scarf who had lent Agenta his bow for the shot at the briar shark. His clothes were soaked, and he had a cut along his jawline that leaked blood into the collar of his shirt. He was the only archer without a sorcerous arrow nocked to his bow, so Agenta passed him her spare. He accepted it with a flash of teeth.

"No sighters this time, right?"

Right.

The octa began lecturing his troops on what he expected of them, but the kalischa was only half listening. Yet again she scanned the sea for her father. If Rethell had been caught under one of the sails, he should have swum clear by now—

Agenta's heart leapt. There, at the end of the mizzenmast!

Rethell's face was turned away from her, but it had to be him because he was the only one wearing black on this day of festivity. His arms were draped over the mast, his head lowered onto his arms. Agenta let her breath out slowly. She hadn't realized how much tension was in her shoulders until that moment, and she rolled them to relieve the tightness. Her father was alive! And safe while the creature's interest remained focused on the people farthest from the *Icewing*.

A scream went up from a blond-haired serving-girl off the starboard bow. The dragon was gliding through the water toward her, and she started swimming for the ship. If Agenta had still been with Selis she would have told him to lift Rethell on board first, the serving-girl be damned, but it was too late to return to the mage now. The girl was plucked from the sea as if by an invisible hand. Sobbing, she held down her sodden skirt as if she thought the dragon might try to look up it. The beast's head broke the waves below her, and she screamed a second time.

She was too high for the creature to reach, though. The dragon, after considering its escaped prey, sank down into the water again.

The next swimmer to draw its eye was a balding Storm Guard off the *Icewing*'s starboard quarter. From beside Agenta the octa swore— not, the kalischa suspected, because the dragon had targeted one of the octa's troops, but because it had selected another victim too far from the ship. *As if it knows we're waiting to shoot at it.* The dragon drew close to the balding Storm Guard, and he was snatched into the air like the serving-girl before. The girl, meanwhile, fell back into the sea with a wail.

The dragon swam past the soldier.

Agenta shifted her gaze to Rethell. Then frowned. Her father hadn't moved since she'd last looked at him. An odd time to take a breather.

A growl from the octa. The dragon had chosen its next victim: a dignitary swimming on his back abeam to starboard. Improbably, the man still had on his head the hat he must have been wearing when the wave struck.

"Get ready," the octa told his troops.

Because the dignitary was in arrow range.

Agenta nocked her white arrow to her bow.

The dragon sped toward its prey. The man stopped swimming and began treading water, apparently unconcerned at the creature's approach—but then he'd already seen two others lifted to safety, and no doubt expected the same would happen to him. Sure enough, as the dragon came near, the balding Storm Guard fell into the sea and the dignitary started to rise, though not as quickly as the serving-girl and the soldier had before him. He stopped when he was only a few armspans above the waves.

Agenta's eyes narrowed. Was Selis tiring? No, she realized, he was using the dignitary as bait to entice the dragon to lift its head from the water. Good thinking that, though the man in the hat clearly thought otherwise, for he shouted at Selis to raise him higher.

The dragon's head broke the sea below.

"Draw!" the octa bellowed, and Agenta pulled back on her bowstring until her arrow's flight brushed her ear.

Up, up, the dragon's head came. The dignitary rose higher too, staying always just out of reach. The man drew his sword and swung it wildly. The blade clinked off a tooth, and the dragon flinched back before snapping at its prey. Its head was half turned away from the *Icewing,* meaning the archers had no shot. Agenta feared the octa would give the order to fire anyway, but instead he shouted, "Rabid, Walker, get that thing's attention!"

Rabid and Walker turned out to be the two spearmen. They sent their sorcerous weapons flashing across the water toward the dragon.

The creature had given up on catching the dignitary and was sinking into the sea. Selis tried to keep it interested by lowering the man, and the dragon paused in its descent.

The two spears, both black-shafted, struck it on the side of its head, showering it with spray.

The muscles of Agenta's right arm were trembling from holding the bowstring at full draw, but she dared not ease up in case she missed the chance to shoot when it came.

"The eyes, you hear me!" the octa barked to the archers. "Go for the eyes!"

"Fire as soon as the creature turns," another man said. "Don't give it a chance to close its lids."

The dragon's head came round.

"Fire!"

Agenta's arrow was already on its way. Remembering Farrell's warning that the white arrows stayed in the air longer than normal missiles, she'd aimed lower than she otherwise would have done—just above the center point of the dragon's right eye. Seven other bowstrings twanged about her, and she lost sight of her arrow as the volley whistled to the target. The dragon must have recognized its danger for it started to close its eyes. Agenta heard explosions of air and water as one, two, three arrows cannoned off its armored lids.

Only three.

Meaning the other five had found their mark?

For a heartbeat nothing happened.

Then, to the sound of cracking bone, the dragon's head bulged as if the creature had blown out its cheeks. Agenta smiled. Blood and milky spray jetted from its nostrils and eye sockets, and its jaws sprang open. An immense tooth flew out, sailing fully fifty armspans before plopping into the sea beside a startled swimmer. *Got you!* Agenta wanted to shout it from the top of the mainmast—before remembering that the mast was now floating on the swell.

The dragon's head wavered then fell forward and struck the water with a noise like a hand clap.

Cheers erupted from those still in the sea and from the passengers on the aft deck. When one of the Storm Guard archers slapped the man beside him on the back, though, the octa said, "All right, you whoresons, which of you missed? I counted five hits, meaning three of you wasted your stingers. And don't you go gawping at the lady here"—he nodded at Agenta—"because I watched her arrow split the right lids clean as a virgin's conscience . . ."

The kalischa left him to his ranting and returned to the mainmast.

By the time she reached it, Selis had raised two dignitaries to the quarterdeck. Neither of them was Rethell. Agenta looked to where she'd seen her father earlier. He remained slumped over the mizzenmast. Alone of the people alive in the water, he was not celebrating the dragon's demise. Agenta called to him, but he made no response. Something was wrong. Her stomach was aflutter as she turned to Selis and tugged his sleeve.

"The man in the black shirt, he's next."

The mage shrugged.

A Storm Guard was already in the air over the starboard rail. So slowly did Selis lower him to the deck, he might have been made of glass. Even after the soldier touched down it took a while before Rethell started to rise, his body twitching like a puppet on limp strings. Was he asleep? When he was lifted clear of the water his arms hung slack by his sides, and his chin rested on his chest . . .

Agenta gasped, then covered her mouth with her hands.

The lower halves of his legs were missing, the remaining stubs dripping watery blood.

The deck seemed to tip beneath Agenta. She leaned against the mainmast. No, it wasn't possible. She'd had the silver dragon in eyeshot for the whole time since the wave struck. There was no way it could have reached her father. When it first attacked the *Icewing* it had targeted the port side of the ship, not the starboard side where Rethell must have been. And after the hull was breached it had kept its distance from the vessel until it was lured in close . . .

Agenta's thoughts trailed off.

The shark.

In her mind's eye she saw again the fin gliding through the blood-sheened water after the barrels of offal were tipped into the waves. Evidently the fish had refused the offal for the richer pickings offered by the *Icewing*'s passengers. Agenta's eyes burned. She should have realized the threat the shark posed. She should have been quicker to locate her father and get him on board instead of playing hero against the dragon. If she hadn't insisted on joining the Storm Guards for that volley . . .

People made space for Rethell as he was lowered to the deck. His head bumped against the wood. Agenta stared, numbed, at the shattered bone protruding from the ruined flesh of his legs. Then she fell to her knees beside him. His face was so pale she thought he was dead, but his eyes cracked open, and his bleary gaze fixed on hers. Blood oozed from the corners of his mouth. He coughed. Was he trying to talk? The kalischa leaned in close.

He did not speak, though. Instead he wrapped his arms about her and pulled her to him.

Agenta held herself still in his embrace. Silence had fallen on the *Icewing,* and she could hear a distant dragon's trumpeting; the rustle of water as the *Crest* drew near on its sorcerous wave; screams from the survivors on the *Majestic*. Shroud could take them all. Closing her eyes, she tried not to think about the other passengers staring at her, or her father's ruined legs, or how long it had been since he'd last held her like this.

She remained that way until the strength in his arms faded.

Whose orders?

The answer to that question haunted Karmel.

The emira's. It had to be. The great and the good of the Sabian League would have turned out for the Dragon Hunt, and if it became known Imerle was to blame for today's carnage, the response of the Sabian cities would be swift and uncompromising. Even a sorceress as powerful as the emira couldn't hope to stand alone against the whole of the League—for alone she surely would be now she had turned against the other Storm Lords. With Karmel's mission complete, the priestess had outlived her usefulness. Why should Imerle take a chance on her silence when a dagger in the back would eliminate the risk? It seemed so obvious now, Karmel wondered why she hadn't seen it before.

And yet she would never have suspected the hand wielding the dagger would be Veran's. If the emira was concerned about loose tongues, after all, why had she trusted Veran to keep his mouth shut but not Karmel? More to the point, how had she known he would be willing to betray a fellow Chameleon? *Because he walked out on the priesthood, that's why. Because his loyalty is to Imerle, not his god.* But then why had he been so outspoken in his criticism of the emira during the journey from Olaire? *Because he wanted to hide from me where his true allegiance lay.* What was one more deception when all he'd told Karmel since they met were lies?

The priestess hugged her arms about herself. Her teeth chattered. Veran lay facedown in the water at the bottom of the boat, his hair fanned out about his head. It should have been Karmel in his place, she knew. It *would* have been if Veran's arm hadn't been broken by the stone-skin, or if he hadn't retrieved from the control room her shattered sword—the sword of the Chameleon's Honorary Blade—for fear of it being recognized.

Had he attacked her because she'd suggested returning to Olaire early? Or had his orders from the start been to silence her once the assignment was finished? Karmel remembered his look when she'd helped him into the boat—a pained expression that she had attributed to the discomfort of his broken arm. The truth, she now suspected, was that he'd been hoping a dragon would take her while she swam to the cave, thus sparing him the need to dirty his hands. And if that was the case he must have been planning to kill her all along, for he had only found out *after* he reached the boat that she was thinking about trying for the *Icewing*. Doubtless he'd never intended to waylay her when he was unarmed and wounded. He would have been expecting the two of them to lie low in Dian for weeks, giving him time to heal and pick his moment. By threatening to leave early, Karmel had forced his hand.

Something troubled her, though. Hadn't it been Caval who insisted she stay in Olaire after the mission was over? Why, if he hadn't been in league with Veran? *Because he knew the seas would be impassable once the dragons were released.* He had no reason to want her dead, after all. If he'd been told whoever went on the assignment would have to be silenced, he'd have picked someone other than Karmel to go. Someone disposable. *Unless there was no one else. Unless I was the only one he trusted not to ask questions.* Could he have sacrificed her for the sake of his ambition?

No, not Caval. He'd never *had* any ambition—unless it was to escape their father's ambition for him.

Something he'd said on the beach in Olaire came back to her: *Stay close to Veran. He'll take care of you.* Karmel shivered. *He'll take care of you.* She replayed the conversation in her mind, straining to remember any detail that might give a clue as to how the words were meant. Had his expression been earnest? Sardonic? It was so difficult to recall. She closed her eyes and tried to place herself on the beach with the waves breaking against the shore, the gray stones crunching beneath her sandals.

He'll take care of you.

Each time Caval spoke the words his intonation was different, but never was there any hint of irony in his voice. Could she trust herself, though, not to imagine things as she wanted them to be?

Opening her eyes, she rubbed a hand across her bruised jaw. In all likelihood she was making something of nothing. But her doubts would not go away. So many questions unanswered. Her gaze settled on the *Icewing*. And only one way to get them resolved.

The ship had drifted to the east, leaving only a small section of its stern visible through the mouth of the cave. A man bobbed in the sea a short distance from the vessel, waving his arms and yelling. Then he was lifted into the air and drawn toward the ship.

Karmel's eyes widened. *The air-mage.*

The silver dragon would have to be dead if the sorcerer had started fishing people from the water. What would happen when the last of the passengers were on board? Might the air-mage try to raise the masts again? If so, and if there *was* a water-mage on the *Icewing*, when the ship finally got under way the combined powers of the two sorcerers would propel them faster than any dragon could swim. Propel Karmel, too, if she could find a way to join them.

Where would the *Icewing* go, though? The most likely destination was Gilgamar to the west. But there was always a chance the captain might make for his home port of Olaire. Truth be told, Karmel didn't care where the ship went as long as it took her away from here. If she stayed in Dian, as the emira would expect, she would forever be looking over her shoulder, wondering if the next stranger she encountered was an assassin come to finish the job Veran had started.

And all the while her suspicions about Caval would eat away at her.

A dragon's trumpeting sounded from the northeast. Karmel drew in a shuddering breath. She was shivering so much now her teeth were clacking. If she was going to reach the *Icewing* it would mean chancing the sea again, but then she'd have to brave the water even if she chose to swim for the beach to the west. Moreover, the risk she faced was surely less than it had been when she'd jumped from the battlements, because the Dragon Gate would now have been lowered to stop more dragons passing through the strait. As for the creatures already in the Sabian Sea, wouldn't they be dead or busy attacking other ships?

Her mind made up, Karmel lifted the sailcloth cover in the bottom of the boat to search for her change of clothes. Her gaze fell on Veran's corpse. What should she do with him? She couldn't just tip him into the water, could she? No, better to let him lie here in the boat. Once the craft sank, the fish could fight over the body. Then she remembered the priest's Chameleon ring. She should remove it from his hand to avoid anyone identifying him, she knew, but that would mean touching him, and in the end she decided to leave it behind.

A glimmer at the bottom of the boat caught her eye. She hesitated, then crouched to pick up Veran's wedding ring. It was a plain band of gold, scratched and tarnished. *Don't let her be alone at the end,* he'd said. He had no right to ask that of her. No right at all. Karmel considered tossing the ring overboard to join her broken blade at the bottom of the sea.

Then she slipped it into a pocket.

The air in Agenta's cabin on the *Crest* was thick with shadows. She had retreated here to escape the sight of Rethell's corpse, yet no matter where her gaze settled she saw something that tugged free a memory of her father: the traveling chest on which he'd sat when he came to speak to her on the crossing from Gilgamar; the sword that he'd given her when she became kalischa; the statuette of the White Lady that had been a present on the anniversary of her naming day. Images from her past pressed in on her, suffocating as the heat, and she seized the statuette and hurled it across the cabin. It shattered into pieces against the opposite wall.

Breathless, Agenta sat down on her cot. She could hear her father's spectral voice berating her irreverence. Rethell had always been a devout follower of the White Lady, but where had the goddess been when the shark took his legs? Agenta curled her lip. The gods cared nothing for the fate of mortals, and those who prayed to them for benediction were no less fools than those who railed against them when the winds of fortune turned contrary. The truth was, people believed in divine stewardship because they *wanted* to believe the gods would protect them. Because it was safer to have faith in some higher order than it was to acknowledge the precariousness of their lives. Agenta, though, would not deceive herself. Shroud's fist fell where it would, and she could no more predict its coming than she could save those in its path. Hadn't she learned that lesson from her brother's death? Hadn't she long ago steeled herself against the inevitability of her father's demise?

Her eyes misted, and she cuffed at them in irritation. Why was she crying? If she'd died instead of Rethell, would he have wasted tears on her? Doubtless he was happier now he'd been reunited with her mother and brother on the other side of Shroud's Gate.

And doubtless with what Agenta was planning to do next, she would soon be joining them all.

There was a knock at her door. She did not respond, but the door opened anyway, and she looked up to see Lydanto leaning against the door frame.

"Kalisch," he said, "the last of those in the water are being lifted to the deck. Dutia Elemy Meddes is asking if we are going to the aid of the *Majestic*."

Agenta stared at him. *He called me Kalisch.* She looked out of the window. To the north and east Cauroy's ship was sinking beneath the waves. Beside it bobbed the motionless form of a bronze-scaled dragon. The second creature that had attacked the *Majestic*—the steely-scaled beast—had survived the clash and was now gliding among the survivors in the water. Their screams sounded across the sea. Agenta turned back to Lydanto. "Cauroy is finished. I won't risk the *Crest* to fish a few corpses from the waves."

"But the dutia—"

"Has no authority over me or this ship. If he doesn't care for my orders, he can stay on the *Icewing*. Tell him that."

"You are wishing to sail for Gilgamar?"

Agenta hesitated. The temptation to return home was strong—a chance to bid a proper farewell to her father, perhaps get hold of some more tollen. Just a little to help see her through the next few days . . .

Then she saw again the wave of water-magic bearing down on the *Icewing*. Anger sparked inside her. Odds were, Orsan was back in Olaire reporting to the emira on the success of his mission. Imerle would think Agenta was dead, or else paralyzed by grief, whereas in truth the sting of Rethell's death was already fading. Now was the time to strike back. Now was the time to make Imerle and Orsan pay for their treachery.

In response to the ambassador's question she said, "Tell the captain to set course for Olaire."

"You are going after Orsan."

"What else would you have me do?"

Lydanto's mouth was a thin line. "Orsan will be denying having responsibility for the wave that struck the *Icewing*. He will be pinning the blame on another water-mage, saying he gave chase to the culprit—"

"He can say what he likes."

"You are not thinking, Kalisch. The failure of the Dragon Gate to be lowered was no accident, I am believing. The emira knew the dragons would be unleashed, meaning she has moved today not just against us but against *all* of those on the Hunt. We must be gathering the survivors together, making them aware of what we know."

"To what end? You said yourself, we have no proof Imerle is behind this."

"We have the merchants. Perhaps now they will be willing to tell us about their dealings with the emira. Given time—"

"Time?" Agenta cut in. "What time do you think we have? With every heartbeat, Imerle's stock will rise. If the other Storm Lords are dead, the Sabian League will have no choice but to tow her line. Who else but the emira can hunt down the dragons now they are loose? Who else can keep open the shipping lanes the League relies on for its precious trade? We have to act now!"

"You are forgetting your teachings—the words of Gorbel and Tsufon, yes? 'To proceed without proper intelligence is to seek to cross blindfolded the stepping-stones of a river in flood.' There is still much we are not knowing. For what purpose was Imerle borrowing money from the merchants? What other schemes has she set in play?"

"We will find out when we reach Olaire."

"And if you are walking into a trap? The emira has been trying to kill you once already. Why should the lion not snap shut its jaws if the alamandra is placing its head inside?"

"She is welcome to try."

Lydanto took a breath. "It is not so simple, Kalisch. You are having your father's responsibilities now. Be reckless with your own life if you must, but you should be thinking also about the lives of your men."

Agenta's voice was cold. "I had not forgotten."

Footfalls sounded outside the cabin. Lydanto looked across at the unseen newcomer before shaking his head. Then he entered the cabin and closed the door behind him. The pieces of the broken statuette crunched beneath his sandals as he crossed to the traveling chest and sat down. He held Agenta's gaze for a while then said, "I was hearing the rumors about you joining the Seekers. Are they true?"

The change of subject took her aback. "No."

"But you were taking the tollen?"

Agenta did not respond. What, was he going to give her a lecture? Did he think he could take on her father's role now Rethell was dead?

Lydanto said, "The tollen took your grief at Zelin's passing, yes, but that was not all it was taking, am I right? You lost also some of the memories from before his illness—memories of better times." Again Agenta kept her silence, and Lydanto nodded. "I am sorry for your loss."

"Don't be."

"Was your father ever telling you how I came to enter his service? The reasons for my—how do you say?—fall from grace from the Ruling Council?"

Agenta looked at him, wondering where this was heading. "No."

"Fifteen years ago Rethell and I were both minor players on the Council when a business opportunity was presenting itself. Pasha Ygren of Kal Kartin sought a buyer for a shipment of ganda spices. Naturally both your father and I were having an interest. Of more importance than the profit we stood to make was the prestige that would come from gaining the pasha as a patron. I was determined to beat whatever price Rethell bid, but your father had something to offer Ygren that I could not match. You."

Through the window Agenta could hear voices raised in argument on the quarterdeck. She ignored them.

"You were a beauty even as a child, Kalisch," Lydanto went on, "and the pasha was wanting you from the moment he set eyes on you. He asked your father to give you up as part of the price for the spices. Rethell said no."

"You think I should respect my father for not selling me out?"

"I think a daughter should not be needing to look for reasons to respect her father." The ambassador's tone softened. "When Rethell refused to hand you over, I offered Ygren my own daughter to seal an understanding between us. He accepted. As for the remainder of the price for the spices, the pasha was insisting on settlement in advance. I agreed to pay half. You can no doubt be guessing what happened next. The caravan carrying the shipment from Kal Kartin was attacked by tribesmen on the Sun Road west of Arandas. Or so I was being told. The pasha sent me the heads of one hundred of the soldiers who died protecting it—though they could have been the heads of anyone, it is true. Ygren declined to return my money, for he argued he had lost both the merchandise and the unpaid half of the fee. I was still having his patronage, however, and he promised me another shipment soon. Then three weeks later, he and his entire household—my daughter included—were put to the sword by an Erin Elalese Guardian."

Lydanto's voice faltered, and an uncomfortable silence descended. Perhaps he was waiting for Agenta to console him, but if so he would be disappointed. He'd given away his own daughter? When Agenta looked at him now she felt nothing but contempt. Though judging by the ambassador's expression, she wasn't the only one.

Lydanto continued, "I had borrowed heavily to fund the cost of the spices, and now found myself unable to settle my debts. I had lost my money, my reputation, my seat on the Ruling Council . . . and my only child." He bowed his head. "Your father took pity on me—gave me a position on his staff, even helped to repay my creditors. Perhaps the kindness came from knowing how close he had been to making the same mistake I did."

"Or perhaps he put you with me as a lesson—to remind you of what you had lost."

"Perhaps. But if so it was a lesson worth the learning."

"And what is the moral of this story for me, Ambassador?"

"Moral?"

"Why are you telling me this?"

Lydanto's eyes glittered. "In my culture we are honoring the dead by sharing tales of their memory. Is it not the same among your people, Kalisch?"

Agenta looked away.

Karmel hauled her weary arms through the water. The wind had stirred up waves an armspan high, and each breaker picked her up and tossed her back so that whenever she glanced up to check the *Icewing*'s position, it appeared no closer than when she'd last looked. On another day she would have reached the ship by now, but the events of the past few bells had left her battered and bruised and tired beyond measure. It was as much a weariness of the spirit as of the flesh, she knew, and all the more sapping for that.

It was only after Karmel had swum clear of the cave that she'd seen the approaching Gilgamarian galleon, now drawn up on the opposite side of the *Icewing*. She'd also spotted the motionless body of the silver dragon a short distance to the west, rising from the sea like the upturned hull of a metal-plated ship. A cloud of starbeaks had descended to blunt their beaks on the corpse, and now all Karmel could see of the dragon was the occasional twinkle of scales beneath a blanket of white feathers. More birds hovered in the sky overhead, squabbling as they tried to alight.

Currents bore the carcass across the priestess's path, and as she swam up to it a handful of the starbeaks took flight. She'd come as far as her strength would allow, yet she remained over a stone's throw from the *Icewing*. More troubling still, she'd seen a shark's fin skidding through the waves to the west, and while the fish had been moving away from her, she had no wish to stay in the water when others of its kind might be prowling nearby. If she wanted to evade the creatures—and make sure she was spotted by the ship at the same time—she would have to climb onto the dragon's back.

Scanning the huge silver carcass, she saw she was at the creature's rear end. To her right the covering of starbeaks was broken by a ridge of triangular plates—hooked and tapering to wicked points—that traced the line of the dragon's spine. She swam to where those plates entered the sea. Boosting herself out of the water, she raised a leg and swung round so she was seated between two of the scales. Then, by shuffling forward and lifting her buttocks over each plate in turn, she began inching her way up the dragon's back, her sopping robes dragging at her all the while.

The vast corpse rocked and tipped in the water like some wallowing scow. With each plate traversed, more scolding starbeaks took flight, only to land again behind the priestess. The dragon's scales were slick as ice, yet warm to the touch as if blood still flowed in the creature's veins. The triangular plates were getting bigger as they rose up the dragon's back, increasing the chance of Karmel goring herself if she slipped. She paused to look round. This was as high as she was going to get. From her new vantage she could see another ship to the northeast. The vessel was sinking, its prow pointing almost vertically into the air. A few passengers clung to what remained of the bowsprit as if they thought being last into the sea would save them from whatever horrors lurked beneath the waves. Dozens of figures were swimming toward the cliffs, but as Karmel watched, a steel-scaled head broke the water and scooped a shrieking woman into its maw.

The priestess looked away.

Then swore. Farther east a second dragon had surfaced, golden-scaled and twice the size of the beast on which she perched. It was heading for the *Icewing* and the Gilgamarian galleon. By now the

Icewing's passengers had all moved across to the other vessel, and the crew of the Gilgamarian ship were casting off. Cries of warning rang out at the dragon's approach, followed by the shouted orders of whoever was in command—a woman. The emira? No, what Veran had said in the cave made sense: there was no way Imerle would have risked coming here if she knew the dragons were going to be released.

The last line between the vessels was thrown clear, and the ships began to drift apart.

Karmel was about to get left behind.

By gripping the dragon's carcass with her thighs she was able to steady herself enough to raise her arms, but the instant she let go of the triangular scale in front of her, she almost slid down its flank. Grabbing the scale again, she lifted a single arm this time and started waving to the ship, expecting to be plucked into the air like the man she'd seen from the cave. Nothing happened. The focus of those on board must have been fixed on the gold dragon, and Karmel had little enough time in which to bring their heads round. Rising on one knee, she tried calling to the vessel—"Here, over here!"—but her throat was so raw after Veran's attack that her voice came out as a mere rasp.

"Here, here!"

A wave of water-magic burgeoned beneath the Gilgamarian ship. If the vessel fled, not only would Karmel be left marooned on an island of dragon flesh, she might also find her efforts at drawing the attention of the galleon's crew brought the onrushing gold dragon down on her. And yet if she used her powers now to hide herself from the beast, how would those on the ship know she was here?

Not that being visible was helping at present, for the Gilgamarian galleon had begun to move away to the west. The sails bulged as the air-mage on board released his power, and the ship jolted forward. The dragon, seeing its prey escape, trumpeted its fury. Startled by the sound, the birds round Karmel took flight.

And in doing so saved her life, most likely, for the raucous explosion must have drawn the gaze of someone on the ship. Moments later the priestess was snatched into the air.

She let her arms fall. Her stomach was doing somersaults from the swiftness of her ascent, but she had more important things to worry about just now. The Gilgamarian ship had swung toward her. She looked from the vessel to the dragon, gauging their respective speeds. The creature was quick, seeming to double in size in as many heartbeats, but the galleon was faster still as it came rushing toward her on its wave of water-magic. Karmel could now make out individual faces among the crowd of people on board. Her spirits lifted.

She was going to make it.

Now she just had to hope the emira wasn't waiting on board to welcome her.

CHAPTER 16

SENAR LISTENED to Cilin's retreating footfalls. The septia must have been using his sword as a crutch, for along with the tread of his boots the Guardian heard the occasional scrape of metal on stone. Then a scuff and a grunt sounded as if Cilin had fallen, but Senar did not take his gaze from Greave. It hardly seemed fair now he should have saved the man from Darbonna's followers only to have to fight him, but he doubted the champion would see it that way. Greave had crouched to clean his blade on the robe of one of the dead librarians. Rising again, he reached into a trouser pocket and took out a black gourd with a wax cap.

The champion said, "Mazana ever tell yer why I'm with her, pretty boy? What she said she'd give me to follow her?"

Yes, what better time for a story? They should pull up some chairs, make themselves comfortable. "No," Senar replied. "Nor do I wish to know."

Greave barked a laugh. "Yer think yer any different from the rest of us? She'll give herself to yer like she has to every other sword in her pay, then keep yer sniffin' round for more till something better comes along."

Senar's tone hardened. "This is not the time."

"Oh, but it is. This is the Shroud-cursed perfect time. Yer weren't listenin' to the bitch, were yer? No sorcery down here, she said. Means yer Will has gone to the Abyss!"

Senar's eyes widened. Was he right? The Guardian hadn't tried to use his power against the librarians because there had been no need. Now when he groped for his Will he felt it melt away like a half-remembered dream. *Shit.* Again he reached for it, and again it eluded him, seemingly just beyond his grasp. For an instant he considered using one of the Guardians' mind exercises to hone his concentration, but such an exercise would require him to block out the world around him. And Greave would surely attack when he lowered his guard.

The champion used a thumb to flick off his gourd's cap. He poured liquid from the gourd onto the blade of his fish-spine sword, turning the weapon round so the liquid ran down to coat its barbs. Senar caught a smell of rose petals. *Red solent,* he realized, his chest tightening.

Greave flung the gourd aside. "First blood again, pretty boy? One scratch is all it'll take."

"That sword cuts both ways."

"What do yer mean?"

"I mean, unless you're expecting to take me down with your first strike, some of the poison will transfer from your blade to mine when our weapons touch."

Greave scowled. "Then I'd best make this quick."

He attacked.

Without juripa spirits to dull his senses, Greave wielded his sword as fast as an arrow's flight, yet his strokes were no less weighty than Senar remembered from Mazana's house. No doubt Greave would argue the loss of Senar's Will had put the two of them on an equal footing, but things weren't as simple as that. The Guardian had disciplined himself over the years to use the Will only when it was necessary—too much power can become a crutch, if you let it—but still it had become an integral part of his fighting style. So when Greave now aimed a thrust at Senar's midriff, the Guardian's first instinct was to block with his Will, and he lost a precious heartbeat overriding that instinct before bringing his sword up to parry.

On this occasion he succeeded in deflecting Greave's weapon, but next time the heartbeat might cost him his life. When one dueled an opponent of the champion's skill, one relied as much on instinct as on training. Each move and countermove was effected without conscious thought because in the time it took to frame that thought,

Greave's blade could have pierced Senar's defenses. The Guardian found himself battling his natural instincts as much as his opponent, and with red solent on Greave's sword it needed only one slip . . .

When Senar blocked his adversary's next stroke, the champion pinned Senar's blade on the barbs of his fish-spine sword, then stepped in close and shoved the Guardian back. Senar's head slammed against a pillar behind, but he recovered in time to spin away from an attack that would have cut him in half. Greave's blade clanged against the column in a shower of sparks.

Senar retreated.

Out of the corner of his eye he saw one of the torches abandoned by the librarians atop a broken pillar. He picked it up in his halfhand before turning to face Greave again. The champion came on, his sword held high. The corpse of a female librarian lay on the floor to Senar's left, and the Guardian edged away from it, then thrust the burning torch at Greave's face.

The champion sidestepped.

Senar lunged with the torch again, only for Greave to bring his blade whistling down to intercept. The brand was severed in two, and as the flaming part hit the floor it flickered and died.

Shadows closed in.

The remaining torch lay on top of a column to Senar's right, the circle of light surrounding it a mere dozen paces across. The Guardian retreated toward it, flinging the stub of the first torch at Greave. If he could reach that second torch he could extinguish it, but how was darkness going to help him, exactly?

The champion rushed him.

Senar parried two cuts and countered with a thrust to his opponent's chest. Greave twisted his body as the blow landed, and Senar's sword glanced off the armor hidden beneath his shirt.

Chuckling, Greave came on again.

Kempis and Duffle passed through the Watchstation's gates and entered the exercise yard. It was deserted but for a lone temlock cropping the weeds that grew between the flagstones. The door to Pompit's office was half open, and a gust of wind sent it crashing into a wall. Inside, papers swirled across the floor. There was no sign of Pompit.

Someone had smeared temlock dung on the door to Hilaire's office, and there was more dung on Pompit's desk.

"Where in the Nine Hells is everyone?" Kempis mused aloud.

As if he didn't know. Without Hilaire to crack the whip, the Watchmen had fled rather than be enlisted into the defense of the city. Kempis couldn't blame them. On the contrary, he just hoped whatever place they'd found to crawl into, they'd left enough space for him. The invasion of Olaire was no business of his. The raiders' targets would be the Storm Lords, and so far as the septia was concerned a few less bluebloods round the place could only be a good thing. Whichever side emerged victorious, Kempis's world wouldn't change. The boot pressed to his neck would remain even if the foot inside it was different.

The door to Hilaire's office opened, and Kempis feared the quina had beaten him back from the palace. Then Loop emerged. The mage had swapped his uniform for a black shirt and trousers, and he was carrying the medal Hilaire had worn when Dutia Elemy Meddes came calling three days ago.

When Loop caught sight of Kempis, he dropped the medal on the floor.

"Report!" the septia said.

"City's going down the sewer, sir."

"The docks?"

"Holding, last I heard. The ship of that Thane Tanner guy was still moored when the attack came. Seems there was an air-mage on board, and he downed one of the gray-sailed ships before he got studded like a pincushion. Bought some time, though, for the Storm Guards to sort themselves out."

Whatever success the soldiers had enjoyed thus far would be short-lived. On the walk down from Kalin's Hill, Kempis had seen the raiders from the Deeps take the Forge Barracks without a fight. Now the Harbor Barracks was under attack, and if it fell the Storm Guards at the port would find themselves fighting on two fronts. "And you were just off to help them, right?" he asked Loop.

The mage looked down at his clothes, then shrugged. "Wouldn't want anyone confusing me for someone who gives a shit."

"This ain't over for us yet." Kempis told Loop what had happened in the throne room.

The mage's tone was incredulous. "You wanna go after the stone-skin? Bugger that. The emira's finished."

"Either that or she's just getting started."

Duffle spoke. "You reckon she's behind this, sir? Then why's she attacking her own Storm Guards?"

"Storm Guards are loyal to the Storm Lords, not the emira. As for whether she's the one pulling the strings, ain't no one else stupid enough to try to take Olaire. An invader might conquer the island, but they'd never leave it again while the Storm Lords controlled the seas." He hawked and spat. "One way or another, the emira will come out on top, you'll see."

Loop ran his hands through his hair. "And you're worried she'll be pissed if you don't hunt down this stone-skin?"

"I don't give a damn about the stone-skin. I'm going after Sniffer."

"Sniffer?" Loop looked about as if noticing for the first time she was missing.

"She went to pick up the assassin's trail. Odds are she'll have tracked the woman to the Shallows." A while ago Kempis had detected a familiar whisper of water-magic from the south of the city. Strange that the stone-skin had swum round the island instead of finding a quiet cove on the northern shoreline, but maybe she'd wanted to put some distance between herself and the throne room.

Loop frowned in response to his words. "It's Sniffer's last day."

"Yours too, if you like."

"That ain't what I meant. Sniffer won't stick her head where someone's gonna shoot at it."

"Then you've got nothing to worry about going after her!" Kempis said, his temper rising.

Okay, so Loop was probably right about Sniffer not getting caught up in the invasion. But she'd know that Kempis would have detected the stone-skin's sorcery, and if she was waiting in the Shallows for him to come and investigate . . .

Footfalls sounded from the street beyond the Watchstation. It occurred to Kempis that, after the docks and the two barracks complexes, the Watchstation would be high on the raiders' list of targets, so he was relieved when the footfalls receded. He looked from Loop to Duffle, not liking what he saw in their expressions, but knowing better than to try ordering them to come with him. He'd have preferred not to slow himself down with their company, but if the city had gone to the Abyss, then the Shallows was no place for a Watchman to be wandering alone.

Like Sniffer is now.

Kempis blew out a breath. Truth was, he was tired of putting all his partners in the ground. Before Corrick it had been Pleat, who had lost his head fighting smugglers down at the Jetty. Then there was Jingle, who'd been nibbled on by a shark when he trailed a thief into the Deeps. Afterward, Kempis had had to break the news to the fool's missus, then say some words over his shroud at the funeral. That was typical of Jingle, though: the man was the other side of Shroud's Gate, but he still found a way to make work for the septia.

"Look," Kempis said to Loop and Duffle, "I'm a reasonable man. I don't want to get drawn into this shit any more than you. We find Sniffer, then we go somewhere quiet to weather the storm, that's it. Now, are you with me or not?"

Loop exchanged a glance with Duffle before looking at Hilaire's medal on the floor. Kempis could guess what he was thinking: if the mage hadn't stopped to plunder Hilaire's office he might have escaped the Watchstation before the septia arrived. There was a lesson there somewhere, though Kempis was damned if he knew what it was.

Eventually Loop sighed and nodded. "If we're doing this, we'd best get a move on. There'll be rain before the bell's out, mark my words."

Kempis turned away, pretending not to notice when the mage stooped to retrieve the medal.

Senar's duel with Greave had been going on for a tenth of a bell. During that time the Guardian had been content to defend while he analyzed his opponent's technique. On two occasions Greave had overbalanced when Senar angled his sword to make the champion's weapon slide off it. If it happened again Greave might find his blade out of position when the Guardian countered, but Senar had learned to expect tricks from the champion, so the next time Greave seemed to lose his balance the Guardian merely feinted to his foe's midsection rather than going through with the attack.

Greave was already stepping to one side to evade the thrust, and he retaliated with a cut to Senar's neck.

Senar parried with ease, knowing now that the apparent flaw in his opponent's technique had been a ruse.

Greave began cursing the Guardian's luck, his caution, his cowardice. Then, when that brought no response, he started telling Senar what he would do to Mazana if he found her alive after the duel. The Guardian's thoughts shifted to the Storm Lady. With Cilin injured, she should be able to outrun the soldier if she saw him coming—

Greave roared and delivered a slash of such power it knocked Senar's parrying blade into the pillar behind. The champion made to follow up the blow, only to check his sword arm midstroke. Senar hesitated, expecting Greave to repeat the tactic he'd used in Mazana's house when he had thrown his weapon from one hand to the other so as to change the angle of his attack.

Instead the champion's left hand snapped forward, and a dagger flashed for Senar's chest.

His first instinct was to block the throw with his Will, and he was therefore late in raising his sword to parry. Rather than batting the knife aside, he could only deflect its course. Fortune was with him, though, for he did enough to spoil the dagger's flight.

Its hilt thudded harmlessly into his shoulder.

Swearing, Greave renewed his onslaught. Senar blocked three crunching blows, retreating all the while. Suddenly his right heel slipped on the stone fragments on the floor, and he went down. He turned the fall into a dive that took him behind one of the pillars, then slipped again as he tried to rise. The champion was on to him, but Senar swung his sword round at ankle height, forcing his opponent back. He regained his feet in time to meet Greave's next thrust.

The Guardian blinked sweat from his eyes. That had been too close for comfort, but the slip had given him an idea.

It was time to try a trick of his own.

A high cut from the champion gave him his chance. He dived under the swing, then came up on one knee, his blade darting out toward his opponent's groin. Greave's parry was unhurried, but Senar's attack hadn't been the purpose behind his maneuver. This time when he'd rolled he had scooped up some rock shavings in his halfhand, and as he lurched to his feet he flung those shavings into Greave's face.

The champion flinched as the grit struck, turned his head away.

Too late.

Blinded, Greave pawed at his eyes with his left hand. Now it was the champion's turn to backpedal, and Senar pressed after him to stop him fleeing into the mist. Greave began swinging his sword in broad arcs to keep Senar at bay, but the Guardian didn't need to get in close in order to finish this. When Greave's blade next lashed out, Senar stepped to his left and lunged with his weapon to score a cut to the back of his foe's right hand. The champion's sword flew from his fingers and skittered away into the murk.

Greave retreated, then tripped over a white-robed corpse. He hit the floor and let out a stream of curses. His hands searched the ground for his lost blade but closed instead on the shield of one of the dead librarians. He seized it, holding it out before him as he clambered upright.

Senar did not advance. The red solent would already be doing its job, and there were no extra points on offer for killing the champion twice.

Some of the chippings he'd scooped up had stuck to his palm, numbing the skin. He wiped his hand along his trousers, then spun on his heel and strode deeper into the chamber. Somewhere in the mist Cilin was hunting Mazana, and the Guardian wouldn't stand aside and let her die, even if it meant stepping into the soldier's path. As for what happened after . . .

Senar grimaced. "After" would have to wait until he was clear of this place.

Kempis peered out from a doorway on Flask Street. To his right the road, slimy with mud and fireweed, led down to the sea. Moments ago another quake had shaken Olaire, and the north-facing wall of one of the houses on the waterline had collapsed. Beams jutted from the ruined building like broken ribs. From within the darkness of the exposed first floor, a boy sat watching Kempis.

The septia's gaze strayed to a familiar partly submerged house. It was covered in the same flaking red plaster he recalled from six months ago. He hadn't returned to this place since Corrick's death. He remembered his partner's blood oozing from his mouth; a crossbow bolt thudding into Kempis's shoulder; the slap of waves against his face as he swam toward the red house and struggled through a window just above the waterline. Inside, he'd treaded water, sensing his hunters were waiting for him beyond. He'd been lucky to survive, he knew, for the tide had crept in through the window after him, the sea rising first to his ears, then his nose and eyes . . .

Perhaps, Kempis mused, whatever secret he and Corrick had stumbled onto that day was tied up with this invasion. Perhaps the blueblood they'd followed to the Shallows had been on his way to a meeting with the raiders. The incident was a reminder of what happened when you involved yourself in blueblood affairs, but that wasn't what Kempis was doing now. All he wanted was to find Sniffer and get out of here. The problem was, the Untarian didn't use magic, so he couldn't track her the same way he could the stone-skin. The only chance he had of locating Sniffer was to hunt down the assassin and hope his partner was close by. But while the lingering ripples of water-magic on the air told Kempis the stone-skin had exited the sea in this place, that was quarter of a bell ago. She could be anywhere now. The septia could do nothing except wait and hope she used her power again soon.

Loop and Duffle were getting increasingly twitchy. The mage was muttering something over and over, while Duffle was sharpening his longknife so fervently it was a wonder there was anything left of the blade. If Kempis stayed here much longer he would lose them both, but what was he supposed to do? Wander blindly through the streets and hope he bumped into the stone-skin?

As if I'm that damned lucky.

This was beginning to feel like a waste of time. Kempis didn't know for sure whether Sniffer had managed to pick up the assassin's trail outside the throne room. She could be sitting somewhere with her feet up, laughing at him. It wouldn't be the first time either. On one occasion she'd arranged for them to meet with a snitch in the Shallows, only to stand Kempis up. Half a bell he had waited with the sea lapping at his boots, thinking all the time that someone must have done for her. Just a misunderstanding, Sniffer had claimed afterward when he found her in the mess hall. But the smile in her eyes had said otherwise.

A flicker of water-magic to the west, and Kempis stiffened. The stone-skin.

With a nod to Loop and Duffle, he set off.

Loop hadn't been exaggerating earlier when he said the city was going down the sewer. The sky was stained with tendrils of smoke, and above the murmur of the sea Kempis heard glass smashing, flames crackling, shrieks, laughter. And not a raider within a stone's throw, he'd warrant. He took a left into Berry Street. The locals were out in force, looting all manner of stuff they hadn't wanted yesterday and wouldn't want tomorrow. Two strangers were struggling under the weight of a sedan loaded with slabs of flamestone. Farther along, three women were using a statue of the Sender as a battering ram as they pounded on the door of a house. Screams came from inside. Kempis checked his stride for an instant, then breathed a curse and continued on. What was he going to do, arrest the whole district? As yet no one had noticed his Watchman's uniform, and he'd prefer that it stayed that way.

If there was one advantage to this chaos, it was that the air would be flush with necromantic energies. Glancing at Loop he said, "You ready with a blast if we need it?"

The mage inclined his head. His expression betrayed his lack of enthusiasm, but then doubtless he would rather have been joining the looters instead of picking a fight with them.

Ahead a shaven-headed man with scratch marks on one cheek turned into the road from a side alley. He was dragging a young girl by the hair. Her hands were round his wrist, her sandals scrabbling at the cobbles as she sought to gain her feet. Kempis nodded a greeting to her captor.

Then he swung his fist hard, catching the stranger full in the face. The man collapsed, boneless.

" 'Scuse me," the septia said, shaking out his hand.

The girl scampered off.

Kempis turned left into Mount Avenue, then took the next right and halted at the corner of the last building. In front was a square littered with bricks, potsherds, and broken furniture. The sea sloshed at its southern edge. The raiders must have landed in force here earlier, for a handful of boats were drawn up at the waterline, unguarded. To the west a house was on fire, and the wind blew smoke across the square. Muffling a cough with his sleeve, Kempis scanned the windows of the buildings about him. Those at ground level were boarded, while those of the upper floors were empty. If there were people inside, they knew well enough not to show themselves to the undesirables prowling the streets.

"Where's Sniffer?" Duffle said, his voice tight.

Kempis had been wondering the same himself. Then he caught another whisper of water-magic approaching from the sea.

Showtime, he thought.

Before frowning.

Because the signature of the sorcery was not the same as the stone-skin's.

The glow from the torch faded behind Senar as he plunged into the mist. For a moment he considered returning for it even though that might mean another confrontation with Greave. Then far ahead he noticed a glow like moonlight through tattered cloud. With nothing else to guide him he set off toward it, pausing to clean the poison from his sword on the shirt of a dead titan.

For a while the echoes of Greave's curses accompanied him. Then the noises dwindled to leave him walking in silence except for the crunch of stone shavings underfoot. On the floor was a trail of blood—Cilin's, Senar assumed, for the septia had been wounded when the Guardian last saw him. A handprint beside two oval impressions in the chippings showed where Cilin had fallen to his knees before clambering upright again. Maybe the soldier's strength had failed before he tracked down Mazana. Maybe Senar would find his body somewhere ahead in the fog.

Maybe.

A dozen more paces brought the Guardian to another ring of broken pillars. Beyond, the frost-covered ground glittered like a field of silverspark flowers. Senar's step faltered. There was a . . . sensitivity to the air here, a prickle he had come to associate with sanctified ground. Could this be a holy site? If so, who was it sacred to? Considering the titans' ancient enmity with the pantheon, Senar couldn't see them building a shrine to any god or goddess. Except to knock it down, perhaps.

His heart skipped a beat as he caught sight of a woman's body on the ground in front. But it was not Mazana's. The stranger was wearing a blue robe, and her skull was bulb-shaped, twice as broad at the cranium as at the jaw. A Fangalar. What in the Matron's name was she doing here? The Fangalar were an elder race that had disappeared from this part of the world centuries ago. Was she the one responsible for the dead titans Senar had seen earlier? The Guardian doubted it, for while the Fangalar's ability to draw energy from more than one element made them formidable sorcerers, a single mage, however strong, could not hope to match the power of a titan.

A mystery for later.

More corpses came into view—titans this time, maybe fifteen in all—their skins blackened by sorcery, their clothes scorched and torn. One man's legs were bent at impossible angles; another's face had been torn away; a third had a hole in his chest the size of a sandfruit. Senar shifted his grip on his sword, scanned the fog all about. What with the attack by the librarians, he had somehow managed to forget the disquiet he'd experienced in the chamber above. Now it came stealing up on him once more, and the sweat from his earlier exertions beaded cold on his skin.

Then he saw Mazana.

Wreathed in mist a dozen paces ahead, she stood facing away from him, her bare arms wrapped about herself. The knot in his chest—a knot he hadn't even realized was there until now—eased a fraction.

On the ground to Mazana's right, Cilin lay facedown and motionless, a bloody puncture in the back of his neck. Mazana still held the dagger that had made that hole. She must have recognized the tread of Senar's boots, for she did not look across as he drew level. He studied her face. The fog had drained both the color from her cheeks and the warmth from her eyes. There was a fierceness in her expression he had not seen before, a determination in the set of her mouth. She was staring at something in front of Senar, and he turned to follow her gaze.

A short distance away was a pillar as wide as the Guardian was tall. It glowed with a faint luminescence. Chained to the column was a gaunt man with a distended stomach, naked but for a loincloth. His blue-gray skin was so translucent Senar could see his heart beating inside his rib cage. His hair and beard hung down to the ground, where they pooled in lank, knotted coils. From his fingers and toes grew blackened and twisted nails more than an armspan long. His skin was dark with sweat and grime, and the flesh of his wrists and ankles was ragged and weeping from the touch of the manacles.

All at once things started to make sense to Senar: the dead titans; the strength of the sorcery used to seal this chamber; the whiff of sanctification in the air.

He was looking at one of the pantheon. Who else but a god would be imprisoned beneath a titan fortress? Who else could have survived the millennia? Senar just hoped this wasn't the Lord of Hidden Faces he was staring at—an immortal whose existence the Guardian had denied all these years. That *would* be awkward.

The god must have sensed Senar's regard, for he glanced up. From the depths of his bloodshot eyes shone the misery and loneliness of centuries of imprisonment. Senar staggered beneath the weight of his gaze. He tried to look away but could not. He tried to raise a hand to cover his eyes, but his limbs would not obey him. The god's eyes filled his vision as if the immortal were standing toe-to-toe with him. The chill of the mist about Senar began to fade, and he could no longer feel the hilt of his sword in his hand. Instead he became aware of stone against his back, of limbs trembling in a fire of agony, of the touch of cold metal round the burning flesh of his wrists. Pressure started to build in his chest until it seemed his heart would explode.

Then the god's eyes abruptly lost focus and Senar was able to look aside. He drew in a breath.

Mazana's expression was wry. "You may want to avoid meeting his gaze. It packs quite a punch."

"Thanks for the warning," Senar croaked.

His words were whispered back at him by the titan faces hidden in the fog, and the god cocked his head to listen. A snatch of laughter escaped his lips—laughter that became high and hysterical, almost a sob. He began thrashing against his bindings. The chains groaned as their links drew tight, and the pillar at his back quivered. A tremor shook the room. Mazana seized Senar's arm to steady herself.

The god let his chains fall slack. Then he threw his weight against them once more, muscles standing out from his arms as he strained and twisted, pulling first with one arm, then the other, then seizing in his right hand the manacle holding his left and pulling with both, bracing his legs against the pillar for leverage. The floor bucked. Veins pulsed at the god's temples. He let out a choked scream that transformed into a delirious chuckle as his struggles subsided. Moments later the clanking of his chains fell to a rustle, and he became still. His head dropped to his chest.

The tremors receded.

Senar gathered the frayed ends of his nerves. "Who is he?" he asked Mazana after a pause.

"This is Fume—one of the gods who disappeared in the war between the pantheon and the titans."

"Forty thousand years ago." Senar shivered. Forty thousand years chained in darkness and mist with only the whispers of the titan faces for company. It was unthinkable.

"Don't waste your pity on him," Mazana said. "At the height of his powers, our long-haired friend here had a reputation for ruthlessness even Imerle would envy. What he didn't discover about blood sacrifice almost certainly isn't worth knowing. It is said he found a way to prolong his victims' lives until every last drop of blood was extracted from their veins."

"He was captured by the titans?"

"Toward the end of the war, yes. The titans tried to use him to wring concessions from the pantheon, but they were fools to think the other gods cared for his fate. The conflict was as good as over by then, and the cooperation between the immortals lasted only so long as was necessary to secure the titans' defeat."

It sounded like one of the stories Senar's old loremaster had told him back at the Sacrosanct. Yet here was Mazana speaking as if she'd witnessed the events herself. "And you know all this how?"

The Storm Lady smiled.

She rubbed her hands along her arms, then let her arms fall to her sides. She was still holding her dagger. "He's quite mad," she said, nodding at Fume, "but I suppose that's no surprise considering how long he's been imprisoned. The titans abandoned this fortress when they fled the world at the end of the Second Age. As for Fume—they just left him behind."

Senar looked at the god, taking care not to meet his gaze again. Fume was crooning to himself. The notes of his song echoed back to him, jumbled and discordant. The immortal listened before repeating the disjointed melody.

"And the librarians were his disciples?" Senar asked Mazana.

"Very good. The duplicitous Darbonna and her brood are—were—all that remained of the god's cult."

"They've been trying to free him all this time?"

"They've been trying to *find* him all this time, yes. Darbonna told you the truth when she said they came to Olaire less than two years ago."

"How did they know he was here?"

"Most likely they didn't. Most likely they've spent centuries wandering the globe in search of a master they sensed was still alive, yet could not make contact with. When they arrived in Olaire they must have felt his presence, for they begged leave of the emira to occupy the fortress under the pretext of setting up a library. Imerle agreed. The tremors started when Darbonna began chipping away at the barrier of titan sorcery at the base of the ramp. Oh, she didn't have the power to demolish it entirely, but she did enough to weaken it and so expose Olaire to the effects of the god's struggles to free himself. The rest I think you know."

Except what Mazana was doing here, of course. If her intent all along had been to liberate Fume, why had she not approached Darbonna and offered to help? And how did she plan to break the immortal's chains if Fume himself could not? More important, what use was a mad god as an ally in the Storm Lady's struggle with the emira?

"So what happens now?" Senar said.

"Now we release him."

And before the Guardian could stop her, Mazana stepped forward and buried her dagger in Fume's chest.

Senar stood aghast, his mind struggling to make sense of what he was seeing. Then the god's roar of pain battered at him. He raised his hands to his ears only to find that made the sound resonate more strongly through his body. The hidden titan faces added their voices to Fume's, emitting a blast of noise so intense the air about Senar seemed to thicken. A groan was torn from him. He felt blood trickle from his ears. Perhaps if he retreated into the mist it would deaden the sound, and he took Mazana's arm and stumbled back.

She shook him off.

Then, dropping her dagger, she seized Fume's head in her hands and covered his mouth with hers.

CHAPTER 17

SENAR'S EARS were still ringing from Fume's death cry as he left Mazana in order to scout their path back to the ramp. When he arrived at the first ring of pillars he found Greave lying dead in a pool of urine, his tongue swollen to many times its normal size. Mazana's other bodyguards were also dead, except for the Everlord who sat propped against a pillar beyond the light of the remaining torch. His right leg was missing, and he had been stabbed in dozens of places, yet he did not seem to be in pain. The mist of titan sorcery was stopping him from regenerating, so Senar hauled him upright and helped him up the ramp and along one of the passages to a room that was free of the fog.

Scattered across the ground at the foot of the ramp were the bodies of Fume's disciples, along with six of Imerle's personal guard. Some of the emira's forces must have survived the librarians' assault and turned on Mazana's bodyguards, for the corpse of the axman was surrounded by the bodies of four of Imerle's troops, and the slant-eyed woman had died with a soldier's spear in her back. On counting the dead, Senar discovered that of the emira's warriors only Cilin had survived to pursue Mazana into the mist. As for Fume's disciples, there was no telling how many might have fled up the ramp to the corridors above.

When he returned to the Storm Lady he found her cutting off the little fingers of Fume's hands with her dagger.

Another piece of the puzzle fell into place.

Jambar.

A memory came to Senar of the conversation between the shaman and Mazana yesterday at the edge of the subterranean tomb exposed by the quake. Jambar had revealed that the tremors originated from the citadel, and the Storm Lady had said, *Don't you think the emira should be told?* At the time, something had puzzled Senar about the conversation, and he wondered now whether it had been staged for him in the expectation he would convey the words to Imerle. The reason for Jambar's involvement with Mazana was clear enough—with Fume's bones in his collection, his powers of foresight would increase markedly. But what had Jambar done for Mazana in return? Yes, he'd convinced Imerle the cause of the quakes needed to be investigated, but there had to be more to it than that.

"Kiapa's alive," Senar said to the Storm Lady. "Your other bodyguards are dead."

"And the emira's soldiers?"

"All dead, along with more than fifty disciples. I couldn't find Darbonna, though."

The news seemed to amuse Mazana. "Strange, is it not, that a god as savage as Fume should have such pitiful followers."

Senar frowned. "Their god has been missing for forty thousand years, yet these few remained loyal. And you would call them pitiful?"

"Who has been answering their prayers all this time? What do they have to show for their devotion?"

"Is that how you judge the worth of everything?" he said, more sharply than he'd intended.

Mazana raised an eyebrow at him.

Senar took a breath, surprised at his irritation. Why should he be angry at Mazana? Because she hadn't told him what she'd planned to do here? She hadn't asked Senar to accompany her. He'd come to the fortress on Imerle's orders, so the Storm Lady owed him nothing. She hadn't asked for his allegiance. She hadn't asked him for anything.

Mazana tore a strip of cloth from Cilin's shirt and wrapped Fume's severed fingers in it. Senar felt a twinge from his own missing digits, and he scratched at their stubs. As the Storm Lady pushed herself to her feet, she swayed and lowered her head into her hands. Senar resisted an urge to go to her.

"How do you feel?" he said.

"If you are referring to my . . . contact with Fume, I feel no different. But then we are still within the deadening influence of the titans' sorcery. Perhaps when we leave this place . . ."

"You are sure you can steal the god's power from his dying breath?"

"So the priestess assured me."

"And if she is wrong?"

Mazana's eyes twinkled. "You want to know whether I'm now strong enough to defeat Imerle? If you're so worried about finishing on the winning side, perhaps you should kill me while I'm vulnerable. I'm sure the emira would reward you handsomely."

Senar scowled. He didn't know what annoyed him more, that the idea could still tempt him, or that Mazana was so confident of his support that she was prepared to voice the thought herself. He didn't like being presumed upon by the Storm Lady any more than he did Imerle. "You think there will be no repercussions from what you did? Matron's blessing, you killed a god!"

"What I did was put him out of his misery. In any event, it isn't as if he has any disciples left to avenge him."

"I'm not talking about his disciples. The priestess told you Fume's power would ride his final breath, yes? But did she say *why*? Because the only way I can see that happening is if you took in part of his spirit." And absorbing the spirit of a mad god obsessed with blood sacrifice, how could that end badly?

Evidently the prospect didn't concern Mazana, because her expression did not change. Did becoming emira mean so much to her? Was power all she cared about?

"What about the priestess?" Senar said. "What is her interest in all this?"

Mazana did not reply.

"How did you find her?"

"She found me."

"And you think she offered her services out of the goodness of her heart? You're nothing more than a puppet, Mazana, and you don't even know who's twitching your strings."

The Storm Lady's voice was cold. "And if I'd rejected the priestess's aid, where would I be now, do you suppose? In a shallow grave, most likely, dead by the emira's hand." *Or by yours,* her look seemed to say. "If Imerle had acted against me sooner, would you have lifted a finger to help me?"

Would he? Senar didn't know. But that wasn't the point. For Mazana, this wasn't about survival. If it had been, when she'd learned about Imerle's plans to kill her she would have fled or taken the information to the Storm Council. Instead she had come here.

Before he could put that to her, though, she strode past him in the direction of the ramp.

Senar hesitated, then followed.

A glow marked the place where the torch lay on the shattered pillar. Mazana followed the light, Senar a step behind, to where the Guardian had dueled Greave. All about, the ground was slick with blood, and the stench of excrement hung in the air. The Storm Lady paused to kick Greave's corpse before disappearing into the murk. She returned with the dagger she'd thrown at one of the disciples.

Senar caught her gaze and nodded toward the ramp. "What's going on up there? In Olaire, I mean."

"The illustrious Imerle will be making her play for power. Weren't you listening to what I said in the throne room? The emira has been borrowing from merchants to help pay for a company of mercenaries. They, along with troops from Imerle's home island, will have launched an attack on the city by now." She returned her dagger to the sheath at her waist. "With luck, by the time we leave here the emira will have disposed of the other Storm Lords, meaning all I have to do is defeat her and take her place."

Senar's anger was back. "Will anyone notice the difference, I wonder?"

"You think we are alike, she and I?" Mazana said. "Should I take that as a compliment?"

The Guardian's expression tightened. "It was you, wasn't it? The summonses to the other Storm Lords. The assassination of Gensu."

In Mazana's hand the cloth wrapped about Fume's fingers was becoming soaked through with blood. "Of course."

"Why?"

"Besides ridding myself of a contender to the throne?" She shrugged. "To throw the emira off guard. To fluster her into making a mistake. Were you not surprised at how easily I goaded her into sending me here? She wanted me out of the way."

"Why bother goading her at all? Why not just sneak into the fortress when her attention was elsewhere?"

"Because then I wouldn't have had the pleasure of *your* company. I also wouldn't have had Imerle's crack troops to watch my back."

"You knew the disciples would attack? Did you also know Greave would turn on me?"

"I knew that much and more. Our one-eyed friend, Jambar, told me how many disciples we would be facing, that their assault would come when we reached the first circle of pillars, that likely Cilin alone of the emira's soldiers would follow me to the column where Fume was chained. The only thing he *wasn't* sure about was you."

"The shaman didn't know whose side I would take . . . but you did."

The Storm Lady stepped closer. The front of her dress was smeared with Fume's blood, and there was more blood round her lips. "Naturally," she said. "Did you think I wouldn't find out about how you came through the Merigan portal? Imerle has let you live this long, but you know she will turn on you eventually. Only by helping me today do you stand a chance of walking out of this alive. In a way, you've been using me as much as I have you." She held Senar's gaze, challenging him to contradict her. Then she looked down at his right hand. "You never told me about that ring."

He read the unspoken question in her eyes. "Her name was Jessca."

"Your wife?"

"No."

"What happened to her?"

Senar looked away, unsure why he was speaking of this. "It was the aftermath of the Guardians' assault on the Black Tower. Li Benir was dying. Many of my other friends had already passed through Shroud's Gate."

"But not Jessca?"

"No, she died later. When we attacked the tower, the mages summoned demons to defend them. A few of those demons fled Arkarbour when their summoners were killed. Jessca was among those sent to hunt them down." She'd asked Senar to go with her, too, but he had said no. Because of Li Benir's injuries—because Senar had wanted to be with his master at the end.

Mazana's smile was rueful. "Did you know your eyes only ever come to life when you speak of the past? Poor Senar. All you brought with you from Erin Elal are memories. You are like the sadly departed Greave here." She kicked the champion again. "Your life is all behind you."

"It appears you have me all worked out," Senar said stiffly. "A pity you seem unwilling to hold yourself up to the same light you judge me by."

"Meaning?"

"Meaning Greave told me you stop at nothing to buy the loyalty of your followers, yet you've made no effort to win my trust or even my friendship. Instead you appear intent on mocking me at every turn."

"Perhaps I have no further use for you."

"And perhaps you've got so accustomed to using people that you know of nothing else."

Mazana's expression grew sober, and when she spoke again her voice appeared to come from a great distance. "You seem so keen to show me the error of my ways. To make me into something I am not. Are you sure it's even me you see standing here before you and not someone else?"

With that she walked past him, following the trail of corpses toward the ramp.

Agenta stood on the *Crest*'s forecastle, looking at Olaire in the distance. For nearly two bells the ship had sped north on a wave of water-magic. During that time it had overtaken two smaller vessels apparently heading for the Storm Isles, one flying the Cinsarian flag, the other flying colors the kalisch did not recognize. Within a short while of the *Crest* passing the Cinsarian ship, the latter vessel had been caught by the gold dragon trailing the *Crest* from Dian. Agenta had watched impassively as the creature closed its massive jaws about the waist of the small craft and snapped it in two. Meanwhile, another dragon—an enormous copper-colored beast—had approached the *Crest* on an intercept course from the east. The combined powers of Balen and Selis had taken the *Crest* away from its would-be attacker, and the dragon had fallen behind until it vanished in the glare of the sun on the waves.

Since Agenta had come on deck her fellow passengers had shown enough sense to keep their distance, but now she spied movement to her right and glanced across to see Farrell advancing. He halted beside her.

"I'm sorry," the merchant said.

"Don't be."

"If you need to talk, I understand—"

"You understand nothing!" Agenta said, rounding on him. "Are you going to tell me that I should treasure my father's memory? That I should be grateful for the time we had together? Save your platitudes for when you—"

"My father is dead," he cut in.

Agenta stared at him blankly. She'd seen a man in a gold shirt on the quarterdeck earlier and assumed he was Samel. But then there *had* been another man on the *Icewing* dressed in gold, she remembered. She studied Farrell with new eyes. Now that she knew to look for it, she could see the cloak of self-pity about him. It seemed he had come here not to ease her sorrow but to burden her with his own as well.

"He couldn't swim," Farrell went on. "Can you imagine? A man who'd lived his entire life on an island. I looked for him in the water, but I couldn't see him. I hoped he would find his way to one of the masts, or that someone would help him stay afloat." He let out a shuddering breath. "His body was found under the mizzen course, less than ten armspans from where I stood on the *Icewing* helping others climb aboard."

The merchant paused as if he expected Agenta to say something, but she kept her silence. Did he think she didn't know what he was doing? Like Lydanto, he thought that by speaking of his own loss he could encourage the kalisch to talk of hers. He was wasting his time, though. Her grief was already spent.

"I wish I'd had a moment with him," Farrell said. "A chance to tell him . . ." He looked across. "What did your father say to you at the end? When he held you."

"Nothing."

The merchant nodded as if some deep truth had been revealed to him.

Olaire was rushing closer. Agenta could make out the Founder's Citadel in the northwest of the city, the white-plastered buildings on the slopes of Kalin's Hill, the flooded streets of the Deeps, bright with reflected sunlight. A pall of smoke rose from the western districts and drifted east on the breeze.

Farrell said, "You're going after the emira, aren't you."

"Maybe."

"I'm coming with you."

Agenta did not respond, hoping the man would leave her alone now that he'd said his piece.

Instead he gestured to the sword scabbarded at her waist. "Are you as skilled with that as you are with a bow?"

"After my brother's death, my father insisted that I be trained to fight. He said a ruler must know how to defend herself, but how many duels have you seen in a council chamber? The truth is, he wanted me to replace the son he'd lost."

Farrell made to say one thing, then appeared to change his mind. "When you questioned me on the way to Dian . . . You know about my father's dealings with the emira, don't you?"

"Yes."

"Imerle never told him what she wanted the money for, and my father didn't ask. He was curious, though, so he made some inquiries. You have heard of the Revenants?"

Agenta shook her head.

"Neither had I. They are mercenaries from Elipsos—a place to the east of here. The company has just a thousand warriors in it, yet last year they held the walls of Kybor against a Corinian force twenty times that number. The only way to join the group is to defeat one of its members in single combat, and there is no shortage of people willing to try. Such are the fees the Revenants charge, it is said a man need only serve in their ranks for a few years before he can buy himself a kingdom. Before today I had wondered what the emira wanted with a company of mercenaries." He nodded at Olaire. "I guess I have my answer."

Olaire's harbor was partly visible over the Shallows at the western end of the city, and there Agenta could see the masts of a handful of ships with gray sails. Two more vessels were stationed at the entrance to the Causeway. The docks themselves, along with the streets around them, were filled with a heaving melee of combatants, while to the south and east smoke rose over one of the Storm Guard barracks complexes. The kalisch smiled without humor. "I'd been trying to work out how I could convince the Storm Guards to grant me an audience with Imerle. Now it seems I won't have to."

"Where will we dock?"

"The palace fronts onto the sea, does it not? Perhaps we will land there." The closer they could get to the palace, the fewer guards they would have to fight to reach the emira.

"If we circle the island to the west, we risk drawing the attention of the ships guarding the Causeway . . ."

His words trailed off. The *Crest* had begun to lose speed. Its sails still bulged with air-magic, but the wave on which it rode was receding. As the rustle of water died away, the noise of the city became audible—an angry buzz like a beehive shaken to life. Agenta turned to see Balen standing beside the galley chimney.

"Mage," she said, "why have we slowed?"

Balen blushed. "Water-magic, Kalisch. Someone is challenging my control of the seas."

"Who?"

The mage gave an apologetic shrug.

Agenta spun back toward Olaire, her gaze raking the shoreline. Waves foamed over the flooded buildings of the Deeps. On the rooftops of the Shallows she saw a dozen strangers, all facing away from her, and all apparently watching the battle for the city.

Then she spotted him: a bald man standing at the end of a submerged street, dressed in blue robes and with his hands raised in the air. Agenta was too far away to make out his features, but she knew who he was all the same.

Orsan.

Ripples of power drew closer to Kempis along one of the flooded roads. A bald man in blue robes swam between two boats at the far corner of the square. When he reached shallower water, he waded out of the sea before pausing to brush a strand of fireweed from his sleeve. Kempis stifled a groan. Orsan. What was the emira's pet mage doing here? Had Imerle sent him on the trail of the stone-skin? Didn't she trust Kempis to track down the assassin alone?

Out to sea, a wall of water half a dozen armspans tall was rushing toward the Deeps. On its crest rode a three-masted galleon. Was this another enemy vessel come to take part in the attack on Olaire? No, its sails were white, not gray. Orsan set his power in opposition to the sorcerer on board . . .

Duffle leaned in close. "We got trouble."

A figure had materialized in an alley behind Orsan. There was no mistaking the emira's would-be assassin, for her skin glittered in the shadows of the passage. Not here to guard the mage's back, Kempis reckoned. Sure enough, she produced a crossbow and started wrestling with the crank mechanism. The weapon was half as tall as she was. How had she known Orsan would be here? Had she expected one of Imerle's minions to follow her from the palace?

Kempis considered. The woman wasn't paying attention to her surroundings. If he could circle behind her, he might catch her unawares.

He looked at Loop. "Are you thinking what I'm thinking?"

Plainly not, for the mage's eyes flashed. "You said we was here for Sniffer!"

"And I meant it. But we ain't going to get a better shot at taking the stone-skin down. She's distracted, ain't she?"

Loop said nothing.

"What's your problem, man? We've already done the hard part getting here. Raiders are gone, right? And if they show up again, hells, you ain't even wearing a uniform. We walk away now, we could spend a month later trying to sniff out the stone-skin's trail again." To Kempis's mind, it didn't bear thinking about. Another month with Hilaire on his back. Another month reporting to the emira in that watery hellhole she called a throne room.

Still Loop kept his silence.

"Best make your mind up quick, mage, else the stone-skin's going to make it up for you."

Scowling, Loop looked out to sea. Orsan must have gained the upper hand over the sorcerer on the ship, for the wave of water-magic under the galleon had dwindled to a ripple. Closer now, Kempis could see the flag the vessel was flying—the crakehawk of Gilgamar.

For a heartbeat longer Loop stared at it. Then he shook his head in resignation and said, "What's the plan?"

Karmel looked toward the commotion on the forecastle. She was too far away to hear the voices of the people there. But having kept her head down for the past bell and a half, she wasn't about to risk drawing attention to herself by moving closer to eavesdrop. When she'd first set foot on the galleon she'd resolved to find somewhere out of the way to engage her powers and disappear, but with the decks full to bursting she'd been forced to hunker down on the main deck near the surviving Storm Guards from the *Icewing*. For once she was relieved her face was unknown beyond the walls of the Chameleon Temple, for she'd yet to see any hint of recognition in the eyes of her fellow passengers. And while the bruising round her jaw and neck was drawing curious glances from the Storm Guards, such was the air of stunned solemnity about the ship that none of the soldiers had mustered the heart to start a conversation.

There were a handful of people on board that the priestess knew: Dutia Elemy Meddes; Grand Magister Dewar; Lady Maida Saxby. Karmel did not, however, recognize the woman who commanded the vessel—Kalisch Agenta Webb, she'd heard her called. Earlier when the kalisch emerged from the captain's cabin and stalked onto the forecastle, those already there had moved to leave a space round her. It was not difficult to see why, for there was a sharpness to the woman's gaze that could cut. Karmel looked along the main deck to where the bodies of some of those who'd died on the *Icewing* were laid out beneath scraps of sail. From the conversation of the Storm Guards, the priestess had learned Agenta's father was among them. And while the kalisch effected a stern indifference to his fate, Karmel could see her grief in the lines that scarred her forehead.

She tried not to think about what would happen if the woman discovered Karmel's role in his death.

The priestess was struggling to shake off the lingering effects of the shock of Veran's attack. Her hands trembled where they gripped the rail. She looked at Olaire and the gray-sailed ships in the harbor. It had come as no surprise to find the city under assault—the chaos wrought by the dragons gave Imerle the perfect opportunity to sweep aside the remaining elements of the Storm Lord dynasty. Fortunately for Karmel the fighting appeared to be concentrated around the port and the two Storm Guard barracks complexes, so when the time came to disembark it would be a simple matter for her to pick her way through the turmoil to the Chameleon Temple . . .

A shout from one of the Storm Guards brought her head round, and she looked in the direction the soldier was pointing. A ripple of movement blurred the southern horizon, indistinct through the glare off the sea. At first Karmel thought it was another ship fleeing north from Dian.

Then it sparkled with copper light.

A dragon.

Kempis peered round the corner at the stone-skinned assassin. Standing thirty paces away, she was still struggling to load her crossbow, her efforts apparently hampered not just by the weapon's size but also by the wounds she'd taken in the throne room. In the square beyond, the septia could see nothing of Loop or Duffle, but they should by now have used the cover of the rubbish to crawl within striking distance of the stone-skin. All Kempis had to do was distract her long enough for Loop to hit her with a broadside of death-magic—and pray he didn't also get blasted in the attack. There was little risk of that, though. From where Loop was stationed he would be firing at an angle to the alley rather than along it, so Kempis should be safe provided he didn't get close to the woman.

Something he had no intention of doing.

Tendrils of smoke from a nearby burning building curled about him, making his eyes water. As he dabbed at them he heard a sound behind, and he spun round to see a figure approaching.

Sniffer.

Kempis cracked a grin. For once, she'd shown excellent timing. The Untarian's clothes were wet, and she stank as if someone had emptied a piss pot over her head. The image made the septia's smile stretch wider. In one hand she held a half-eaten honeyfish; in the other, her boots—her webbed feet were bare. There wasn't time to explain the plan, so Kempis gestured for her to join him, then whispered, "Follow my lead."

Sniffer took a last bite of her fish before tossing the carcass aside.

When the septia looked round the corner again, he saw the stone-skin had finally locked the crossbow's crank and was placing a quarrel in its slot. Kempis scanned the ground about him. A shout would do fine as a distraction, but much better if he could find . . .

His gaze settled on a rock to his right, and he crouched to pick it up. It fitted snugly into his palm. Who knew, with a good throw he might even take down the assassin without Loop's fireworks.

To the south a rustle of water was building, but there was no time now to worry about what it signaled. The stone-skin was sighting along her crossbow. The weight of the weapon on her supporting arm must have caused her discomfort, for she shifted position before settling again. Kempis hesitated. It was tempting to delay his attack until she'd finished her business with Orsan, but he knew the woman would be at her most vulnerable while her attention was on the kill. If Orsan survived the encounter, that was just a price Kempis would have to pay.

Stepping into the alley, he hurled the rock.

Just as the assassin's head came round.

But not to look at Kempis. Something in the square had caught her eye, and she swung her crossbow over. Her new target couldn't have been Loop or Duffle, because the Watchmen wouldn't have broken cover until Kempis sprung his diversion. Who, then? A looter? One of the raiders, perhaps?

It hardly mattered now, because the die had already been cast. Kempis's thrown rock arced through the smoky air, straight for the stone-skin. It thudded into her shoulder at the same time as the string of her crossbow twanged. The woman did not look round at the septia. Her gaze remained fixed on something in the square. She cocked her head as if she were listening for a sound.

Then she dropped her weapon and flung herself across the alley, rolling against the wall to her left.

Kempis's spirits sank. He knew what was coming next.

A wave of scintillating blackness cut through the space where the stone-skin had been standing. To the noise of cracking rock, Loop's burst of death-magic slammed into the house on the corner, and the walls of the building crumbled. There was a muffled thud from within, followed by an explosion that blew out a shutter. A section of wall groaned and shifted as if the entire structure was about to come down on the stone-skin.

But it remained intact. The woman rose, unhurt.

The best laid plans . . .

Kempis hadn't discussed with the others what to do if plan A failed. With the element of surprise gone, though, there was no point in trying anything fancy. The septia drew his sword and charged.

Dust hung heavy in the alley, but the glittering points in the assassin's skin marked her out in the gloom. As she spun to face Kempis, her right leg—the leg stabbed by one of the twins—almost gave way. He parried her first thrust, then retreated, forcing the woman to come to him. Sniffer took up a position to the septia's left, her right arm drawn back in readiness to hurl one of her knives. There was no need for them to press the attack; all they had to do was keep their foe busy until Loop and Duffle arrived to cut her down from behind. Four on one, even the stone-skin couldn't beat those odds.

Amid the clouds of dust beyond the assassin, a shadow appeared. The newcomer's features were invisible in the murk, but Kempis knew Loop's stink when he smelled it.

"Heads down!" the mage yelled.

Kempis threw himself to the ground.

The stone-skin couldn't have understood Loop's warning, for she turned toward him.

Right into a blast of the mage's death-magic. It struck her at the level of her chest. Fiery darkness enveloped her, clinging to her like burning oil. She shrieked. Her raised sword shattered into shards of glowing metal. Her skin swelled and split like overripe fruit, and her flesh sloughed away to expose organs that spat and hissed like meat on a fire. Then they too disintegrated to leave behind nothing but charred bones.

The sorcery winked out.

The stone-skin's shoulders and upper arms were gone, and her lower arms now fell to the ground. An instant later her legs buckled, and what remained of her body toppled over. Scorched entrails flopped onto the road. Kempis felt the bile rise in his throat. The smell of rotting meat filled the passage.

A few paces away, Sniffer sat with her back to a wall. She seemed puffed, but in response to Kempis's raised eyebrow she nodded to indicate she was unharmed. The septia heaved himself to his feet. A stiffness had settled on him as if he had aged ten years. It was the feeling he always got around necromancy. There was a hole in the left knee of his trousers, and he was bleeding from a cut to his chin. All in all, though, things could have gone a lot worse . . .

Then he remembered the crossbow bolt the stone-skin had fired into the square.

He looked along the alley. Loop's death-magic had left a black stain in the air that was only now beginning to dissolve. Amid the murk stood Loop, white with dust. He was staring toward the square.

Kempis's mouth was dry. Where was Duffle? Had the boy stayed behind so as not to get in Loop's way?

The mage's grim expression didn't auger well for his fate.

Kempis opened his mouth to speak.

A flash of light from the mage's right—the direction of Orsan—and a throwing knife buried itself to the hilt in Loop's neck, snapping his head round. Wide-eyed, Loop raised a hand to the weapon.

His gaze turned to Kempis. "Bastard!" he breathed.

Then he collapsed.

Agenta looked south. The approaching dragon remained a copper smudge on the horizon, but a smudge that was growing larger with each moment. If the creature caught up to the *Crest* there would only be one outcome, for there were no sorcerous weapons on board. And if Balen broke off his struggle with Orsan to attack the dragon, he would leave the other mage free to unleash a wave of water-magic against the ship. Their only chance was to make it to shore; at least they still had Selis's air-magic to fill the *Crest*'s sails.

Suddenly the ship's pace began to slacken, and she glanced up to see the sails hanging limp. The vessel floundered.

The kalisch located Selis near the starboard rail on the quarterdeck. He was staring at Olaire. "You're looking the wrong way, mage," she shouted, pointing south. "The dragon is over there."

Selis's gaze remained fixed on the city. "That's Orsan."

"I know who it is! Now, get us out of here, or I'll make sure you're the first one down that dragon's throat when it attacks. If we're lucky you may stick in its gullet."

The mage sneered. "Your quarrel with the emira is no business of mine. I won't be goaded into taking sides."

"Your side has already been chosen for you. You think Imerle will let you live, knowing what you do?"

"I'll live longer if I remain neutral than if I throw in my lot with you," he said. Then he gestured with one hand and was snatched into the air. He rose as high as the top of the mainmast.

Agenta looked for Warner and saw him standing near the ship's wheel. "Trita! Prick that fat fool's gut with an arrow. Maybe we can let some of the air out of him."

Warner stared at her before nodding. He spoke to an archer beside him. The soldier didn't nock an arrow to his bow, though. Instead he coiled a length of rope to form a lasso and cast it into the air.

It struck an invisible barrier beneath Selis and fell back to the deck.

Agenta scowled. Had her order been so unclear that the trita had struggled to understand it?

Behind her someone cleared his throat. She turned to see Dutia Elemy Meddes. "Kalisch," he said, "I am needed in Olaire to coordinate the city's defense. We must dock immediately."

Brilliant idea. Why hadn't Agenta thought of it? She spoke through gritted teeth. "I'm open to suggestions."

"If we cannot go forward we must choose another course. Take us along the coast—"

"It's not that easy," Balen cut in. The strain of his fight with Orsan showed in his voice. "Whichever direction I try to take the *Crest* in, Orsan will counter my efforts. Our sorceries cancel each other out . . ."

His next words were lost beneath a roar of water as the ship lurched forward. A wave of water-magic had formed beneath the ship and was lifting it into the air. Glancing over the rail, Agenta saw a seething, hissing wall of white. "What's happening?" she called to Balen.

"It's Orsan. Instead of holding us here, he's added his will to mine."

Elemy said, "He's driving us onto the Deeps. The submerged roofs will crack the hull open like a nut."

Agenta pursed her lips. There was sense in what the dutia said, but why hadn't Orsan left the *Crest* to the dragon's mercy? Had he grown tired of his contest with Balen? Could he not see the beast from his vantage point?

The wave beneath the *Crest* began to recede, and Agenta realized Balen had thrown his will against Orsan's to halt the vessel's passage.

She smiled.

"Mage," she said, "stop fighting him. I've got an idea where we can set the ship down."

By the time Kempis reached Loop's side, the mage's chest had fallen still. His eyes stared back at the septia accusingly, and Kempis felt the usual queasy mix of sadness and relief—that it wasn't *him* there on the ground. A look into the square confirmed his fears regarding

Duffle. The youth lay to his left, dead. There was a joke doing the rounds in Olaire's taverns about a Watchman who wore his breastplate on his back, but Duffle couldn't have been fleeing because the assassin's crossbow bolt had struck him between the eyes. Kempis took a shuddering breath. Why had the lad gone for the stone-skin early? Had he heard something he'd mistaken for the septia's signal? Or had he seen the woman train her crossbow on Orsan and given up waiting for Kempis to make his move?

Sniffer came to stand beside him. There was nothing to say, and they stood for a while in silence. Kempis looked toward the sea. Dust from the building hit by Loop's death-magic hung thick in the air—thick enough to conceal whoever had thrown the knife at the Watchman. Orsan? It had to be. Perhaps the water-mage had mistaken Loop for the assassin, or perhaps he'd thought Loop's sorcery was aimed at him. Most likely, though, the bastard had just decided not to take chances. That was the blueblood way, wasn't it? Shoot first and ask questions later. Kempis clenched his hands into fists. If so, Orsan was going down, and to Shroud with the consequences.

The breeze was beginning to tug apart the cloud of dust, and the buildings on the waterline were now blurred outlines in the haze. The invaders' boats became visible, and among them . . .

Kempis's skin prickled. Facedown in the waves lay Orsan, his head banging over and over against the hull of a boat. In the flooded street beyond him, a man wearing green robes was wading out to sea. Big bastard, he was. He must have heard something to alert him to the septia's presence for he turned. Kempis muttered an oath. Another stone-skin. Where had he sprung from? Had he come here to meet the assassin Loop had killed? Or had he followed Orsan to this place just as Orsan had followed the female stone-skin?

Going by the man's expression, he was wondering whether to return to shore and dispose of Kempis. Instead he smiled a humorless smile and looked over his shoulder.

The septia followed his gaze.

By the Sender.

He'd forgotten about the sorcerous wave carrying the Gilgamarian ship. When he'd seen it earlier it had been half a dozen armspans tall. Now it was nearly double that size, and it came surging toward the Deeps with a sound that built from a rustle to the hiss of a thousand wither snakes. On the forecastle of the vessel atop it was a blue-robed man with big ears and goofy teeth—the water-mage who had conjured the wave, presumably. Near him stood a dark-skinned woman with eyes as sharp as flint.

Kempis swore. What in the Nine Hells were the Gilgamarians doing? That wave was going to wash half the Shallows away. Ordinarily the septia would have paid to watch it happen, but his viewpoint was a lot closer to the action than was comfortable.

The sea at the edge of the square began to retreat, taking with it the invaders' boats. Darkness gathered. The wave rose to brush the sky, and a flock of limewings on a rooftop in its path took flight. The wind was now in the septia's face, strengthening all the while, as if it too were fleeing the sea's approach. Around the square, doors were thrown open. People emerged from their homes to gawp at the swell before bolting inland. Kempis should have been doing the same, he knew, but what was the point?

There would be no outrunning that wave.

Part IV

Sea of Blood

CHAPTER 18

SENAR EMERGED from the citadel's gatehouse into bright sunshine. The tenement blocks across the street had been reduced to rubble by the tremors that must have shaken the city while he was in the fortress. From the south—the direction of the harbor—came sounds of battle: the clash of weapons, the screams of combatants, the crackle of sorcery. When Senar looked in that direction he found his view obstructed by the roofs of the warehouses fronting onto the dry docks. No way of knowing, then, which side was winning, but the one thing he could be sure of was that he wouldn't be slipping away on a ship in the confusion. He was trapped in Olaire. Trapped until Imerle's play for power ran its course.

Mazana had stayed in the citadel to wait for the Everlord's severed leg to regenerate. She'd asked Senar to accompany her when she went to confront Imerle, but he'd declined. Instead he had agreed to deliver Fume's bones to Jambar because that would give him space to think—something he should have been doing a lot more of lately. How long had he been in Olaire? *Three days*. Just three days, and he'd managed to make an enemy of the most powerful woman on the island. Three days, and he'd almost lost sight of what his real objective here was. Survival. Anonymity. Getting back to Erin Elal by whatever means necessary.

Of all the possible ways to return, it seemed he'd chosen a casket. *Idiot.*

Mazana's words from earlier came back to him. *All you brought with you from Erin Elal are memories.* There was truth in that, Senar knew. Even before he'd traveled through the Merigan portal he'd dwelled too much on better times, but when the past was so bright, was it not natural his eye should be drawn to it? Conversely, what did the future of the Guardians have to offer? Nothing but a slow descent into oblivion—a descent that had already started with the defection of Borkoth from the Guardian Council, the decimation of the Guardians' numbers in the attack on the Black Tower, the divisions within the Council over how to counter the emperor's schemes. Things would never return to the way they had been, however much Senar might wish it otherwise.

Avallon's image appeared in his mind's eye. He felt the heat rise within him. His anger was a pale thing compared to what it had been after Jessca's death, for the months of imprisonment had seen the fire of it burn down to embers. But they were embers that could be blown back to life. For centuries the Guardian order had served Erin Elal, and the emperor had wiped it out in the span of a decade. And why? Because he resented the check on his power the Guardians represented. Because they had refused to bow at his command. Such a betrayal surely demanded an answer. Didn't Senar owe it to the Guardians who had died to seek vengeance? Didn't he owe it to the friends who still lived to stand alongside them?

He thought of Fume's bones in his pocket—of the risk he would take in delivering them to Jambar. For a moment he was tempted to toss them into the nearest pile of rubble. He'd given his word to Mazana, though, hadn't he?

As you gave your word to the emira?

Shaking his head, he set off for the palace.

The intersections of Olaire's main streets were blockaded and manned by soldiers. Some of them wore the emblem of Imerle's personal guard, others the insignia of the Storm Lords. There were also bands of pale-skinned men in gray cloaks that Senar took for the mercenaries Mazana had told him about. None of the warriors had any reason to pick a fight with a lone, nonuniformed stranger such as the Guardian, though, and by steering clear of the roadblocks he was able to pass through the city unchallenged.

He paused on the flank of Kalin's Hill to look down on Olaire. To the west he saw a dozen galleys with gray sails. Two were guarding the entrance to the Causeway; the rest were in the harbor. One of the ships at quayside had been set alight, and the flames had spread to the quays themselves. The streets round the harbor were swarming with warriors battling amid smoke and flames. More fighting was taking place at one of the barracks complexes, where armored figures had overwhelmed the defenders at the gates and were now pouring into the barracks yard. A single-story building within the compound was struck by a blast of sorcery. Fire jetted from its windows, and its roof lifted into the air. Then the structure collapsed in a cloud of dust that billowed up to hide the battle.

Senar had already seen enough, though, to know the fight was as good as lost for the defenders. Judging by the uniforms on show at the roadblocks, Imerle's uprising had split the Storm Guard, and if she was half the commander he took her for she would have already taken care of the enemy top brass to deprive the opposition of leadership. What force could now oppose her? The Storm Lords? If Mazana was correct, they would be dead already. Mazana herself? There was no guarantee Fume's power would allow her to match Imerle. She might not even make it as far as the palace with the whole city turned against her. Her words from their meeting at her house came back to him: *You backed the wrong horse, Guardian.*

Not once but twice now, it seemed.

A flicker of movement to his left caught his eye. A stone's throw from the Deeps, and borne on a wave of water-magic four times a man's height, was a galleon flying the Gilgamarian flag. And farther south . . .

Senar's eyes widened.

A quarter of a league behind the ship, a copper-scaled head broke the surface of the sea before rising into the air on a long sinuous neck. The dragon sprayed water from its nostrils, then trumpeted, the sound fierce with joy. On Dragon Day the creature that passed beneath the Dragon Gate was supposed to be the one hunted, but evidently no one had told the beast of that fact, for it was driving the Gilgamarian ship toward the Deeps. Senar watched the wave carrying the galleon grow higher and higher. The rush of water built to a roar.

Then he felt a dampness in his trouser pocket, and he remembered Fume's severed fingers.

The need to be done with this business was suddenly strong in him. He spun on his heel and started down Kalin's Hill toward the palace.

"Come on!" Sniffer said, seizing Kempis by the arm.

The septia allowed himself to be dragged to the house hit by Loop's death-magic. A jagged hole had been punched through the corner walls, making it look as if some creature had taken a bite from the building. Sniffer wrestled Kempis through the opening. He found himself in a room that was empty but for furniture covered by sheets. Ahead was a breach in one of the internal walls. The Untarian didn't lead him there, though; instead she took him to a fireplace on the south-facing wall. What, were they going to build a fire? Sit round it and sing a few songs, perhaps?

Sniffer said, "We need somewhere to brace ourselves!"

What they needed was a staircase to the upper floor, but there probably wasn't time to reach it before the wave struck. The ground trembled at the water's approach. Motes of dust vibrated in the air, and furniture danced across the floor with a scrape of wood on stone. A section of wall to Kempis's left collapsed. He looked up at the ceiling, fearing it would be next. Then the absurdity of the thought struck him. If he had to die, he'd always hoped it would be of old age, but given the choice between drowning and being crushed . . .

Sniffer bullied him to the fireplace. Placing a webbed hand on his head, she pushed him beneath the mantelpiece. The grate had been removed, but a pile of ash remained, speckled with bird shit. Kempis sat down with a bump, throwing up puffs of dust. There was barely room for one person inside the opening, but before the septia could object Sniffer crawled into his lap. She grinned as their gazes met. Nothing to fear for her, though, was there? Damned Untarians could stay underwater for several bells, but the last time Kempis had looked his cheeks hadn't sported a set of gills to match hers.

The roar of the sea made his ears hum. His breaths were coming so quickly he was in danger of hyperventilating, but hells, these breaths were likely to be his last so he may as well get in as many as he could. Through a hole in the eastern wall he saw the wave roll over the rubble-strewn square. An instant later a frothing gray flood came crashing into the house. Kempis cursed. Why had he let Sniffer trap him here? At least outside he'd have had a chance of swimming to safety. He started struggling to escape the fireplace, but with the Un-tarian's weight on top of him he succeeded only in cracking his skull against the lintel. Lights flashed before his eyes.

Sniffer seized his head between her hands. "Don't you dare read anything into this, sir, you hear me!" she shouted.

Then she kissed him.

The shock of that alone was enough to quell Kempis's struggles.

A mass of water exploded over him, pushing him against the wall at the back of the fireplace. The sea was in his eyes, his nose, his ears. Through water fizzing with bubbles he saw the gills on Sniffer's cheeks twitch, then felt her warm breath as she blew down his throat. Now he understood. The air had a fishy flavor to it, but it tasted sweet as nectar to Kempis as he drew in a lungful. A moment later he ex-haled before realizing he had blown the stale air back into Sniffer's mouth. She glared at him. He breathed out through his nose instead, sending bubbles floating up past his face.

Water was trickling into his mouth at the corners, so Sniffer pressed her lips more tightly over his. Her eyes were right in front of him, and he looked at the hole in the wall—anywhere to avoid meet-ing her gaze. When he inhaled again, she wasn't ready for him—she was breathing for two people, after all—and he had to wait before her gills moved and the next breath came. For as long as his blood was up he would need air faster than Sniffer could give it to him, so he had to find a way to steady himself—to take his mind off Loop and Duffle and the water all about. Perhaps if he closed his eyes . . .

Behind his eyelids awaited a memory of the night he'd spent in the flooded ground-floor room of the red-plastered house. As the tide had risen he'd scratched his fingers bloody prying loose two rotten floor-boards from the room above. There had been just enough space for him to get his head and right shoulder through. Cold and shivering, he'd twitched at every splash of water outside in case it signaled the approach of the crossbowmen who had killed Corrick. Those had been six of the worst bells of his life—and there'd been some stiff compe-tition on that score recently. The next morning, when he made it back to shore, he'd sworn never to get in the water again.

Trust his luck that the sea should have come to *him*.

After what seemed like an age Sniffer broke off her fishy kiss. Kempis opened his eyes as the Untarian untangled her limbs from his. She pointed a finger at herself before gesturing to the hole in the eastern wall. Then she was off, her kicking legs almost catching him in the face. Beyond the house Kempis could make out nothing but murky water. Yet the sorcerous wave must have broken by now on the rooftops of the Shallows. The septia considered following Sniffer out, but if he left too soon he might find himself caught by the back swell and swept out to sea.

After the wave had retreated, though . . .

For the first time since the surge struck, Kempis began to think he might live out the next bell. He pondered his next move. The temptation was strong to find a tavern and drown the memory of this morning's ordeal, but the sight of Loop's accusing eyes kept coming back to him. Kempis hadn't known the man well. Truth be told, he hadn't liked him much either. Something gnawed at him, though—a feeling he owed the mage for dragging him here when he would rather have been lining his pockets with the other looters. But how was he going to settle that debt? He wasn't seriously thinking about going after Loop's killer, was he?

That wave must have knocked something loose in his head.

There was always a chance, of course, that the stone-skin had been flattened by the wall of water, but the fact Kempis had seen him wading *toward* the swell rather than away from it told him the man was a water-mage. And if that was so, the stone-skin wouldn't have suffered so much as a bruise when the wave fell on him. Normally Kempis would have been able to hunt the sorcerer down in the same way he had the female stone-skin. Except that the septia hadn't been paying attention to the bastard's power's signature when he fled. No way he'd recognize it if he came across it again. And while Sniffer could follow the stone-skin's trail out to sea, that meant the two of them would have to split up once more.

In any case, Kempis already had an idea where the stone-skin was going. The man had probably come here to help his kinswoman after the beating she'd taken from Mili and Tali. Odds were, he wanted to finish the job she'd started, and that would make his destination the throne room.

It wasn't much to go on, but it was all Kempis had just now.

By the time Sniffer reappeared between two pieces of floating furniture, the septia's lungs were burning. She blew another gust of fishy air down his throat, then gestured to the hole in the outer wall and gave him a thumbs up. Time to be going. It proved harder getting out of the fireplace than it was getting in. In the end Sniffer had to grab one of Kempis's arms and haul him free. He twisted round to get his bearings, then braced his legs against the chimneystack and kicked off.

Outside he broke the surface coughing and gasping. The sounds of the city were loud in his ears: the bells of the Maudlin Watchtower, the fighting from the docks, the cries of those who'd survived the wave. The waterline had advanced to Kempis's left, and the square was now completely submersed. Bodies bobbed on the breakers amid froth and scum, knots of fireweed, and pieces of wood.

A current was drawing the septia out to the sea, and he thrashed against it until Sniffer took one of his arms and guided him toward the shore. Eventually the water became shallow enough for Kempis to stand up. He waded the final distance before collapsing onto the slick flagstones of Queens Street.

"Sender's mercy," Sniffer breathed. "I've known fish foods that could swim better than you."

The septia was too busy savoring each lungful of air to retort.

When the Untarian next spoke there was an edge to her voice. "Sir, look."

Kempis gazed in the direction she was pointing. Thirty armspans away and high above the street was the Gilgamarian galleon, wedged between the roofs of two houses. Water streamed from its blackened hull to spatter onto the road, and more water poured from a fissure between two planks. The top of its mainmast was bent at an angle. As Kempis watched, the mast toppled, bringing down a tangle of rigging and sails.

"Not something you see every day," he muttered.

The ship was listing to the left, and people were scrambling from the deck onto the roof on that side. From there, ropes had been lowered to the street. Kempis looked for the water-mage and the flint-eyed woman he'd spied earlier, but there was no sign of them. Perhaps they had been thrown overboard when the ship came down. He could always hope.

At street level one of the survivors was peering along the road toward him, and the septia looked away. He'd recognize that gray skin anywhere, together with those strands of gray hair draped absurdly across the man's bald pate. Pushing himself to his feet, Kempis strode toward a side street, his boots squelching with every step.

"Come on," he said to Sniffer. "We're out of here."

"Septia!" Dutia Elemy Meddes called. "Septia Kempis Parr!"

Kempis ducked his head and kept walking.

Agenta scrambled over the port gunwale and onto the roof alongside. She looked round. Orsan had vanished, but then doubtless the traitor was already scurrying back to the emira to report on what had happened here. The city throbbed like a migraine. In a street to the north, four men were beating a prostrate figure senseless, while to the west a shrieking crowd had gathered about a burning building, taunting the occupants who were shouting for help from the upper windows. One might have thought the threat of conquest would have seen the Olairians unite to repel the invaders, but having witnessed the black-weed riots in Karalat last year, Agenta knew only too well how thin was the skin of civilization over the rotting flesh beneath.

When her turn came to descend, she shimmied down the rope to the street. Dutia Elemy Meddes approached. When he bowed, his carefully arranged strands of hair fell across his eyes. "Kalisch, I am taking my soldiers to the Harbor Barracks. You and your men are welcome to join us."

"My destination is the palace."

His brows knitted. "Our priority should be the defense of the city. Leave the emira to the other Storm Lords."

"What other Storm Lords?"

"We don't yet know what has become of Mazana Creed or Mokinda Char. Even Cauroy may still be alive. We saw his ship go down, yes, but he is a water-mage, is he not? Perhaps he was able to swim clear."

Agenta's voice betrayed her scorn. "And if he was? You think he will come to challenge Imerle?"

Elemy regarded her thoughtfully before unbuckling a scabbarded dagger at his waist and passing it to her. "I cannot spare you any of my Storm Guards, but if you make it to the palace some of the soldiers there may still be loyal to the Storm Council. Show them this and tell them you command them in my name."

Agenta nodded her thanks.

The dutia moved away, and the kalisch turned to see Lydanto, Farrell, and Warner watching her. "So," she said to the ambassador.

"You told me earlier that we should gather our allies together. How many of our passengers will be coming with us to visit the emira?"

Lydanto had the good grace to look aside. "None, Kalisch."

"I am touched by their gratitude."

"They will not be forgetting their debt to you. But they are thinking it wise to strike back at Imerle from a position of strength."

"Or they think it wise to let someone else fight their battles for them."

The ambassador made no response.

"I want you to take my father's body to the embassy. Farrell's father, too."

Lydanto hesitated then sighed. "My personal residence would be a safer choice."

"As you will. Warner, arrange an escort for him."

The trita frowned. "If we're to reach the palace we'll need every—"

"An escort, I said!" Agenta snapped. "And, Trita, the next time you see fit to question my orders, I will find someone else who likes them better. Do I make myself clear?"

Warner kept his expression even. After a pause he nodded.

The *Crest* shifted, sending water raining down onto the road. A handful of roof tiles followed, and Lydanto ushered them out of the vessel's shadow.

"What of the ship, Kalisch?" he said. "You will be leaving some guards to protect her?"

She shook her head. "We cannot spare the men."

"She will be picked clean when we are going."

Agenta did not doubt it. Olairians had already gathered on the nearby rooftops like a flock of redbeaks eyeing a corpse. And yet what did it matter if the ship was looted? With the wind from the west, the fires Agenta had seen earlier would likely soon claim the vessel in any event.

Lydanto made one last effort to dissuade her. "Kalisch, I am begging you to reconsider. The streets of Olaire will be swarming with the enemy."

Farrell spoke. "I know a few shortcuts to the palace. If we stay clear of the main roads, we should avoid any soldiers."

"And the rioters?"

Agenta ignored him. Passing Elemy's dagger to Warner, she checked that her throwing stars remained strapped to her wrists. "Let's go," she said.

"Where is my brother?" Karmel asked.

Two men guarded the entrance to the Chameleon Temple, neither of whom the priestess recognized. The first was of an age with Karmel and had a pimpled face and a sneering smile. His companion, an older man with receding blond hair, stared back at her with a look so blank it bordered on insolent.

"Am I talking too fast for you? The high priest. Where is he?"

The older man's expression did not change. "Which high priest?"

Tutting her disgust, Karmel shouldered past. Either the fool was simple, or he was mocking her. Whichever was the case she had no intention of spending any more time in his company.

The temple's corridors were alive with the sounds of rustling armor and whispered prayers, while in the courtyards priests and priestesses honed weapons or buckled on armor or simply watched from the shade of colonnades as Karmel hurried past. For each observer she knew there were three she did not, and the presence of those strangers robbed the shrine of its familiarity. Not the triumphant homecoming she'd envisioned when she set out for Olaire. Doubtless Caval had summoned the newcomers here from other temples to supplement the emira's forces. But then why were they sitting on their hands as battle raged across the city?

On board the Gilgamarian galleon, Karmel had played out in her mind a dozen times how her meeting with Caval would go. She'd considered keeping quiet about Veran's attack to see whether her brother asked any revealing questions. She'd even wondered whether she should claim Veran *told* her it was Caval who had ordered her death. Her brother would deny it, of course, but if he was deceiving her it would be harder to maintain his innocence in the face of her feigned certainty. Whatever ploy she used, she would be watching him like a crakehawk. She knew him too well for him to mislead her.

And yet, hadn't he misled her all too easily over the purpose of the mission?

When she reached the door to his quarters, she heard voices beyond. She entered without knocking. In the chair she'd occupied three days ago was a man with skin so dark he looked like a shadow bedecked in clothing. Behind the desk stood Caval. He was staring down on Olaire through the transparent western wall. At the sound of her footsteps, he spun round. She searched his eyes, knowing his first reaction to her return would be the most telling. For an instant he gaped at her, his expression one of such bewilderment that, on another occasion, she might have laughed.

Then a look of relief broke out across his features, and she found herself blinking back tears.

How could I have doubted him?

Caval recovered his poise. He glanced at the man across the desk and said, "Ah, would you excuse us for a moment?"

It was a while since Karmel had heard such deference in his voice. She remembered the words of the guard at the gates: *Which high priest?* Evidently Caval's companion was the head of another Chameleon Temple.

The man shifted his gaze from Caval to Karmel, and the priestess was abruptly conscious of how she must appear to him with her bruised neck, tangled hair, and salt-stained clothes. She met his look, and after a pause he nodded and withdrew.

As the door clicked shut Karmel turned to Caval, her verbal plan of attack forgotten. "He tried to kill me."

The high priest stared at her.

"He tried to kill me!"

"Veran?"

"Of course Veran!"

Caval's voice was flat. "Where is he?"

"Dead."

"Ah, you killed him?"

"Yes."

Karmel had expected to see shock or confusion or guilt in her brother's expression, but his face showed nothing. "Why?" he said at last.

The priestess's blood was rising. "Why did he attack me? I was hoping you could tell me."

Still no reaction. "You think I had something to do with it?"

"He said he was following orders. Orders, Caval!"

"What else did he say?"

"What else were you expecting?" Karmel snapped, conscious her brother was asking the questions instead of answering them.

Caval turned away and looked out over Olaire once more. Above the docks a sorcerous concussion sent clouds of fire-flecked smoke mushrooming into the air. "What happened in Dian?" he said.

Karmel's face darkened. He was trying to buy himself time, she thought. To find out what she knew before he showed his hand. She should have insisted he answer her questions before she answered his, but the words were suddenly spilling out of her before she could stop them. She told him about how she and Veran had scaled the Dragon Gate and gained access to the control room. When she reached the part where Veran revealed to her the change of plan, Caval swung round and held up a hand.

"Wait," he said. "You're saying he wanted to stop the gate from being lowered? And you went along with it?"

Karmel opened her mouth and closed it. Then opened it again. "You told me to do what he said! *What he said!*"

"I also told you the gate was not to be raised. Which part of 'not' didn't you understand?"

"I thought—"

"You thought what? That I lied to you?"

Yes, Karmel wanted to say, but the word tripped on her tongue. She struggled to marshal her thoughts. Of all the ways she'd imagined this meeting going, not once had it played out like this. She searched for some way to wrest back the initiative. "Whose place did I take on the mission? Who pulled out at the last moment?"

"What do you mean?"

"Why didn't you tell me about the mission until the day I left?"

Caval threw up his hands. "Because I wasn't told myself! You forget, this is the emira's game, not mine."

The implications of what he was saying were beginning to sink into Karmel's mind. *Chameleon's mercy, what have I done?* The plan had never been to release the dragons into the Sabian Sea—or at least not so far as the Chameleons were concerned. Meaning it had been Veran and not Caval who had deceived her as to the reason she'd gone to Dian.

The priestess looked away from her brother's penetrating gaze. How could she have let herself be fooled? Why had she doubted Caval? Because he'd ordered her to do as Veran said? If Veran alone knew the plan of attack, then of course Karmel would have to follow his lead. Because Caval had told her so little about the mission? From what he'd said, he had been kept in the dark as much as she had. Karmel felt color rise to her cheeks. The one thing he *had* told her was the aim of the assignment, yet when Veran had contradicted that in the control room she'd swallowed his lies without a second thought.

Veran had been clever, she realized: he'd planted doubts in her mind as to Caval's integrity on the journey to Dian and let those doubts fester during their stay in the city. Then, once he and Karmel were in the control room, he'd timed his revelations such that the priestess had no chance to think things through. And yet that was only half the truth, she knew. If she'd trusted her brother, Veran would never have been able to dupe her. She hung her head. In the citadel she'd convinced herself Caval didn't trust her, when all along it was *her* trust in *him* that had been lacking.

The high priest broke the silence. "The emira has played us for fools."

Karmel looked up. "Why would she tell you she was plotting to remain in power but not how she was going to do it?"

"Ah, because she knew I'd never go along with her scheme, that's why. Gods below, do you know how many will die today? Not just on the ships, but in Olaire itself?" He brought himself under control with an effort. "Imerle needed my help—needed our help—to sabotage the Dragon Hunt, but she didn't trust me enough to reveal *all* the cards in her hand."

"And yet she trusted Veran?"

"Have you asked yourself why? Do you even know why he left the priesthood?"

"He was disillusioned—"

"He left because he was our father's man. When Pennick's star fell, so did Veran's. And he was too ambitious to settle for a place in the priesthood's rank and file. Clearly he thought he could do better for himself by throwing in his lot with the emira."

Strange. If Veran had been their father's man, why had Karmel never seen him around? Then she remembered Veran's wedding band in her pocket. "He said his wife was sick. The gray fever. He said the Chameleon agreed to heal her if he performed one last service."

"And you believe him?"

She heard the unasked question in her brother's tone: Do you believe him over me? *Of course not*, she almost said, but then Veran's last words on the boat came back to her. *Don't let her be alone at the end*. Why would he have lied to Karmel with his final breath? Why had he given her the ring? Caval was watching her closely, and she struggled to meet his gaze.

"There's something else you don't know," she said to change the subject. "About what happened in the control room." She told him of the stone-skinned stranger that she'd encountered in the fortress.

When she was done, Caval shrugged. "Another of Imerle's lackeys, most likely."

"But—"

"He came from the citadel, yes? How did he get into the control room?"

Karmel thought back. "The door was barred."

"Ah, and who was watching the door?"

She saw what he was suggesting and shook her head. "Veran was driven off by the guards."

"Or he let himself be."

"But the stone-skin fought him while I was unconscious."

"And yet neither of them died."

"He broke Veran's arm! Broke it! That was the only reason I survived when Veran attacked me on the boat."

Caval shrugged a second time. "I don't have all the answers. But I know a woman who does."

"The emira."

Her brother gave a gap-toothed smile, but there was no humor in it. "Imerle has commanded me to attend her at the palace and to bring the full strength of the Chameleon priesthood."

Karmel's tone was disbelieving. "You're still going to help her?"

"Ah, who said anything about helping?"

The priestess almost found herself returning his smile. Then a thought came to her. Caval hadn't known about the emira's treachery until Karmel told him just now, so how could he be prepared to launch a strike against her? "You've been planning to betray her all along, haven't you?"

"Imerle would have turned on me eventually. Better to strike first while she is exposed. As a swordswoman, you'll know the moment one attacks is also the moment when one is most vulnerable."

"Why didn't you tell me before?"

"What would have been the point? If you'd stayed in Dian as planned, you wouldn't have been here to take part in the attack."

And yet Caval had said the emira had only informed him about the Dianese mission at the last moment. He'd had weeks before that to share his plans with Karmel. "What else haven't you told me?"

If her brother was aware of the edge in her voice, he gave no indication. "Troops from the emira's home island have been arriving in Olaire for weeks. This morning they attacked from the Deeps, while a band of mercenaries known as the Revenants attacked the harbor. Some of the Storm Guards have turned to Imerle's cause, but most remain loyal to the Storm Lords, so if the emira is going to take the city, she'll need every man she's got." His voice was a monotone. "She's left herself short-staffed at the palace. The Chameleons are to act as her bodyguards for the day—or at least that's what she thinks."

"And if you succeed in killing her? How do you intend to hold on to power afterward?"

"Ah, who will take it from me? The Storm Lords? With the dragons released, they're probably dead by now—or wishing they were. The Sabian League? With so many heads of state killed on the Hunt, the League will be too busy licking its wounds to interfere." There was a note of resignation in his voice—as if for all his talk of victory, he believed his cause hopeless. "As for the Revenants, with the emira's gold in my possession I'm sure they'll accept my orders as readily as they took hers."

A knock sounded at the door, but both Karmel and Caval ignored it. Karmel studied her brother, wishing she had time to consider all he'd told her. After the shock of discovering Veran had tricked her, her mind was only just starting to function again. And while she felt sure Caval was holding back as much as he was telling her, she couldn't think what, or why.

There was another knock at the door.

"A moment," the high priest called.

Karmel said, "You're going to the palace now?"

He nodded.

"I'm coming with you." The emira had all the answers, Caval had said. Karmel meant to be there when she gave them.

"Out of the question. When Imerle sees you, she'll know that *I* know she betrayed us."

"By which time it'll be too late for her. We'll already be in the throne room."

"And if one of her cronies should recognize you before we get there?"

Karmel scowled. The more Caval protested, the more she was de-termined to go. "Ever heard of hoods? Remarkable things."

"It's too risky."

"But it wasn't too risky for you to send me to Dian?"

"Ah, Dian had a purpose. One more sword won't gain us anything at the palace, but it could lose us everything."

Karmel's voice betrayed her irritation. "It was *me* in the control room with the stone-skin. It was *me* Veran tried to kill. I want to hear what Imerle has to say for herself."

"You don't trust me to pass on her words?"

"You don't trust *me* to hear them for myself?"

Caval held her gaze, then turned away to look out over the city once more. A third knock sounded at the door, but the high priest seemed not to hear it. At the entrance to the Causeway a copper-scaled dragon had attacked the gray-sailed ships stationed there, and a hail of flaming arrows flew out from the vessels' decks. As Caval watched the dragon sink beneath the waves, he rubbed the shoulder that had been broken by their father. Strangely the sight didn't touch Karmel as it had three days ago.

Turning, he took a breath and let it out.

Then he nodded his assent.

Ahead of Senar the palace gates came into view. Twice on the descent of Kalin's Hill he'd been forced to circumvent roadblocks, and twice he'd lost his way in the maze of tree-lined avenues. The battle for Olaire had obviously not reached this part of the city, for the streets all around were still. The gates to the palace were guarded by Storm Guards—Imerle's minions, most likely. They watched him draw near with grim expressions but made no move to oppose him.

"Where's the emira?" he asked as he passed. If the soldiers thought he was going to report to her, they'd be less likely to inform her of his presence.

"In the throne room."

Inside the palace the corridors were empty but for a scattering of servants. Senar asked one how to find Jambar's quarters, then set off in the direction indicated, whispering a silent prayer to the Matron that he wouldn't bump into one of Imerle's inner circle on the way.

He reached his destination without incident.

As he approached Jambar's door he took Fume's bones from his pocket. The shaman's door was already opening. Jambar stood in the doorway, his gaze fixed on the bloody bundle in Senar's hands.

Understanding came to the Guardian. "You've seen this moment before, haven't you?"

Jambar looked at him. "I see many things—"

"That's why you stepped in to save me from the emira when I first came through the Merigan portal. Not because—as you told Imerle—you'd seen me save her life, but because you saw me delivering the god's bones to you now." It was only a hunch, but the Remnerol was not bothering to deny it. Jambar reached for the fingers, and Senar withdrew his hand. "I wonder if the emira realizes yet that you played her false."

"As I've said before, all I see is possibilities. Imerle understands that not all of them can come to pass."

And yet, the information he'd provided to Mazana about events in the fortress had been unerringly accurate. "If she's in any doubt as to your motives, I'm sure Mazana will be happy to clear up the confusion."

"You think Mazana and I are allies? We are not. I simply performed a service for her, and in return she performed one for me." This last was said with a pointed look at the bundle. "Now, the bones if you please."

Instead of handing them over, the Guardian pushed past the shaman and entered his quarters. Jambar watched him openmouthed, and Senar gave a half smile. For all the Remnerol's powers of foresight, it was nice to know he could still be surprised once in a while.

Jambar's room was as the Guardian remembered it: the barred door, the strange smell, the table with its circular wooden board covered with symbols. There were bones on the board, Senar noticed. He turned to the shaman.

"I have disturbed you in the middle of a reading, I see. Last time I was here, you told me Dragon Day was a blur to you. The dice have been cast. The players are all assembled. Surely the fog must be clearing from your eyes now."

Jambar closed the door. His gaze flickered to something behind Senar—the board, maybe. "I will be able to tell you more once the god's bones are in my possession." He reached for the bundle again, and this time Senar let him take it.

"Perhaps I will stay for your next casting."

"You wish to know which side will emerge victorious? Would you have me believe your allegiance to Mazana Creed is so fickle?"

"My part in this conflict is done."

"Then why are you so keen to know its outcome?" His gaze flickered past the Guardian again.

Senar's eyes narrowed. Something had the shaman unsettled, but when the Guardian looked round he saw nothing except the board with its bones. Was Jambar worried Senar might read something in the bones' pattern? Or was he anxious to return to a reading interrupted? There was something Senar was missing. Something Jambar didn't want him to see.

Then it struck him.

The bones on the board were speckled with blood.

Senar's lips quirked. "It seems I have my answer as to where you draw your power from. Blood-magic, correct? The bones themselves are dead, but blood invests them with an energy you can shape to divine the future."

Jambar's expression indicated annoyance, but his slowly released breath suggested Senar had seen only part of what the shaman wanted to hide. Was it relevant, the Guardian wondered, that the bones he'd delivered to the Remnerol belonged to a god renowned for blood sacrifice? Senar hoped not.

"My secret is flown," Jambar said. "Now, if you will excuse—"

"Where does the blood come from?"

"The blood?"

"The blood on the bones."

The shaman licked his lips. "From my own poor veins, alas. Such is my devotion to my art. Such is my unswerving loyalty to the ideals of reason and civic duty."

"Show me."

"Show you?"

"Show me your cuts, your scars."

Jambar made no move to comply.

Just then Senar heard scratching to his right. It came from the barred door. And suddenly he realized the significance of the bar being on *this* side of the door. His hackles rose. Pernay had told him about the servants who had gone missing when they delivered messages to Jambar's quarters. Now Senar knew what had happened to them.

"Open the door," he said to Jambar.

"Do not rush to hasty judgment, Guardian. Whoever considers his own failings fairly will find no reason to judge others."

"Open the door!"

"If you cannot shape yourself as you would wish, how can you expect—"

Senar lashed out with his Will at the bar across the door, and it snapped in two. One half fell to the floor while the other hit the ceiling before cannoning down to strike the ground a handspan from Senar's right foot.

He crossed to the door and tugged on its handle. Stupid to linger here perhaps, but there were some things you didn't turn your back on.

The room beyond was swathed in shadow and so hot it felt to Senar as if he were standing at the door to a forge. He gagged at the stench of rot and excrement. Through watering eyes he saw a boarded window on the wall to his left. Beneath the window was a cot to which a boy had been chained. Another figure, a woman, was scuttling away from Senar. She halted in the corner farthest from him, then crouched and pushed herself into the wall as if she were trying to squeeze through the cracks between the stone blocks. The Guardian lifted his hands to calm her, only to find he'd clenched them into fists. The air was alive with the buzz of needleflies.

A footfall sounded behind him, and he spun to see Jambar opening the door to the corridor. The shaman was carrying the board of blood-spattered bones. *Not so fast.* Senar tensed his Will to close the door in the old man's face, but Jambar was already halfway through, and the Guardian's efforts succeeded only in propelling the Remnerol into the passage beyond. The door slammed shut behind him. Senar heard the clack of bones falling to the floor.

Scowling, he strode to the door and wrenched it open. He had no idea what he'd do when he caught up to the shaman. But he'd start by dragging him back by the scruff of his neck, and go from there.

A handful of bones were on the ground before him. Jambar had abandoned them and was now standing ten paces along the passage to the Guardian's left.

He was not alone, though. With him were the emira's bodyguards,

Tali and Mili. The shaman was gabbling at them in a high-pitched voice, nodding at Senar as he clutched his board and its remaining bones to his chest. He flashed a triumphant look at the Guardian.

Senar raised the heel of his boot and brought it down with a crack on the nearest finger bone. A pity it had not been one of Jambar's own.

The shaman shrieked and scurried away.

And the twins advanced.

CHAPTER 19

AGENTA HEARD the clang of a crossbow bolt hitting a shield, then a strangled oath as one of her soldiers went down clutching his leg. From a side street came wolf whistles and taunting shouts. Four of her troops, their shields held in front of them, went charging along the passage until a bellowed order from Warner drew them up.

Just as another enemy appeared at the mouth of an alley opposite. Agenta saw him point his crossbow at the four Gilgamarians.

Then the soldiers Warner had assigned to protect her closed in, and her world contracted to the handful of armspans immediately about her.

And to think the expedition had started so well. After leaving the Shallows, Agenta had seen a few scattered groups of warriors, but always at a distance and never of a size to challenge the Gilgamarians. Then, a quarter of a bell ago, the company had turned into a road at the foot of Kalin's Hill to find their way blocked by pale-skinned warriors in gray cloaks. The strangers had retreated from the more numerous Gilgamarians before splitting into small parties to harry the kalisch's men with their crossbows. Not once had they engaged the Gilgamarians blade to blade, and not once had Agenta seen an enemy warrior take so much as a scratch. In contrast, eight Gilgamarians had been killed or injured.

"Much more of this," Agenta said to Warner, "and we'll have no one left to face the emira's troops when we reach the palace."

"The bastards know what they're doing. I can't let my men give chase because we don't know what's round the next corner. But if I send a large force, we may get separated."

"Then we must increase our pace."

"And risk running into an ambush?"

Agenta shook her head. "If these Gray Cloaks are mercenaries, they won't know the city."

"They'll know it well enough to realize we're heading for the palace."

"But not well enough to know which route we'll take. They won't waste time laying a trap that we could just walk around."

There was another crash of a quarrel deflecting off a shield. Agenta looked up to see a gray-cloaked crossbowman crouching on the roof of a building across the street. A Gilgamarian crossbow twanged in response, but the enemy had already ducked down.

Agenta located Farrell and waved him over. The merchant's face was beaded with sweat, and his pink shirt was sodden across his chest and beneath his arms.

"How far are we from the palace?" she said.

"Maybe a quarter . . . of a league," Farrell replied between breaths. "It's downhill from here, though . . . thank the Lady."

"How many gates?"

"Three . . . I'm taking us to . . . the main one."

Agenta considered. The main gate was the one most likely to be open, yet it would also be the one most heavily guarded. If the defending force proved too strong, the Gilgamarians could still try the smaller gates, but what if those too were impassable? Would Agenta then retreat to Lydanto's residence? She grimaced. What would be the point? With the *Crest* stranded in the Shallows, there would be no leaving the island. And if the emira's coup was successful, her troops would soon hunt the Gilgamarians down wherever they went to ground.

A gap opened in the shield wall round the kalisch. She caught a glimpse of the soldier who'd been hit in the leg earlier. One of his companions tugged the crossbow bolt free, and the wounded man's scream momentarily drowned out the sounds of combat to the west.

Agenta sought Warner's gaze and held it. "If we're going to make a run for it, we need to do something with the wounded. We can only move as fast as the slowest man."

Warner spoke grudgingly. "If we break into one of these houses"—
he gestured to the buildings to either side—"maybe we can find
somewhere for them to lie low until this is over."

The kalisch did not hesitate. Like as not she would be condemn-
ing the men left behind to their deaths, but would their chances be
any better if they stayed with the main company?

"Do it."

Tali and Mili slunk forward, quick as flintcats, and as alike to Senar
now as they had been when he first met them. They halted a dozen
paces away. If anything they seemed even taller than he remembered.

He said, "I didn't realize you took orders from the shaman."

"We do not," replied the twin on the right—Tali, the Guardian presumed, since she always spoke first.

"We were sent by the emira," Mili added.

"To find me?" Senar asked.

"No—Jambar."

The Guardian raised an eyebrow, then nodded along the corridor
behind the sisters. "He went that way."

"Finding you here . . ."

". . . was merely good fortune."

Senar crushed another of Jambar's bones underfoot. "Actually I
was just leaving."

"Without paying your respects . . ."

". . . to the emira?"

"Perhaps we should . . ."

". . . take you to her."

Senar hesitated before shaking his head. What would he say when
Imerle asked what had happened in the fortress? How would he
explain his visit to the shaman? "I think not."

Tali and Mili grinned as they drew their needle-thin swords. "The
emira warned us . . ."

". . . your allegiance might have changed."

"We have dreamed . . ."

". . . of this moment, Guardian."

"Dreamed of you."

Senar said, "You share even your dreams?"

The twins did not respond. Instead Tali leaned close to Mili and whispered something in her sister's ear. Mili giggled, then murmured a reply, gesturing toward the Guardian with her blade.

Senar unsheathed his own sword, his mind racing. A clash with the women was sure to draw every Storm Guard in the palace, so he'd have to beat them quickly. Easier said than done, though. For while the sisters looked little more than girls, Imerle was unlikely to have chosen her bodyguards for their fresh-faced charm. Doubtless they were lightning-fast and fought seamlessly together. He needed to find a way to isolate one from the other.

His gaze shifted to the doorway to Jambar's quarters. If he retreated just within the room he could stop Tali and Mili doubling up on him, but then the twins could merely trap him inside and wait for reinforcements. He looked round. Ten paces behind him the corridor opened out, but where he now stood it was too narrow for one of the sisters to circle round and attack from behind . . .

Movement from the twins interrupted his thoughts. They had retreated a few steps and were sheathing their swords. Senar wondered if they meant to withdraw.

Then they sprang forward in unison, tumbling like acrobats.

The Guardian took a pace back, uncertain. At the last moment the woman on the right, Tali, landed nimbly and drew her blade before attacking with a thrust to Senar's midriff.

He parried.

Mili, meanwhile, had continued her tumbling. Her ponytail bobbed as she launched herself into a somersault that took her up and over the Guardian's left shoulder. Drawing her sword in midair, she aimed a cut at his head.

Surprised as Senar was, he was still able to block the strike with his Will.

An instant later he heard Mili touch down in the corridor behind him.

He sighed.

So much for not being attacked from behind.

The sounds of fighting echoed along the palace corridors. Always it seemed to Karmel as if a battle must be taking place around the next corner, but always when she reached that corner she found the passage beyond empty. Evidently a few soldiers loyal to the Storm Lords remained alive within the maze of corridors, yet all the guards Karmel had seen since entering the palace wore the emira's fiery wave pinned to their breasts. Each time she encountered them she watched their faces for anything that might indicate the Chameleons were walking into a trap. All she saw in their expressions, though, was grim weariness mixed with relief at what the soldiers must have thought was the arrival of allies.

A misconception the Chameleons would soon be disabusing them of.

Over two hundred priests and priestesses had made the journey to the palace, but at each intersection a handful separated from the main party until now only eight remained in Karmel's group. To her left walked Caval, his heels clicking on the mosaic floor, while to her right was Wick, Keeper of the Keys, his long blond hair shimmering like spun gold in the light streaming through the high-set windows. A step behind him strode the weaponsmaster, Foss, his expression as sour as if he were walking to his execution. Of the remaining five Chameleons, only the man Caval had been talking to when Karmel entered his quarters earlier—Aminex—was known to her. But the others all had the look of warriors who knew one end of a sword from the other. Caval had brought his best.

He would need them too, considering what awaited them in the throne room. Imerle's twin bodyguards, Mili and Tali, never strayed far from her side, and their prowess with the blade was legendary. As for the executioner, even the Karmel of three days ago would have thought twice before crossing swords with him, slow and clumsy though he would doubtless be. Surely these three freaks would be no match for eight Chameleons, though—not least because the Chameleons would have the advantage of surprise. The thought should have eased Karmel's nerves, yet with each step closer to the throne room she found her breath growing tighter in her chest. It wasn't a clash with Imerle's bodyguards that she most feared, after all, but what she might learn from the emira that Caval had wanted to keep secret.

Along the wall of the corridor ahead were arched double doors thrown wide. In front of them stood four soldiers—three women and one man. Caval nodded to them as he drew near, and they parted to let the Chameleons pass—all of the Chameleons, that is, save Wick and one of the priestesses Karmel didn't recognize, who stayed behind to keep the guards company.

Karmel's steps faltered as she entered the underwater passage beyond the doors. She'd heard tale of the emira's subaquatic domain, of course, but nothing could have prepared her for the wonder of that corridor with its wavering walls of glassy blue light. Beyond, the throne room was fifty paces long and half that across, yet the weight of water all about made Karmel feel oddly claustrophobic. The air was dank and gloomy. As the priestess looked round, a school of hartfish passed overhead, only to scatter as a kris shark floated into view.

Karmel swung her gaze to the six thrones at the far end of the chamber. In the chair right of center sat Imerle. Beside her was the chief minister, and behind her stood the executioner, his eyes fixed on something over Karmel's shoulder. The twins were absent, though, as was the emira's water-mage, Orsan.

Karmel's pulse quickened. Caval's gambit might yet work.

Caval halted before the thrones, and Karmel drew up alongside him.

Imerle's gaze swept the group before coming to rest on Karmel. The priestess had never met the emira before, but Imerle must have known her all the same, for a ghost of a smile touched her lips. She looked at Caval. "What is she doing here?"

Caval stepped forward. "She has news from Dian."

"News of such gravity it required her to return to Olaire against our express instructions?"

"Indeed. It seems you were not the only one with an interest in disrupting today's Dragon Hunt. Karmel had company in the citadel. A stranger. A man with skin like granite."

Imerle's smile faded.

"Ah, I see the stranger is no stranger to *you,* Emira," Caval went on, glancing at Karmel as he spoke.

The priestess looked from her brother to Imerle. At the mention of the stone-skin there had been a glint of . . . something in the emira's eyes. So Caval was right: the stranger must be Imerle's man, for how else could she know of him? And yet something about this business with the stone-skin didn't ring true.

Karmel had too many other things on her mind, though, to chase down the thought. Starting with why Caval had chosen to open with this line of attack. What interest did he have in the stone-skin? Why hadn't he confronted the emira straight out with her treachery?

Pernay turned his oscura-clouded gaze on Karmel. "This stone-skinned stranger, you're sure he was in the citadel to stop the Dragon Gate being lowered?"

The priestess nodded.

"Where is he now?"

"He escaped," she said, her voice still rough from Veran's attack.

The chief minister exchanged a look with Imerle.

"What's going on here?" Aminex said, but whether the question was aimed at Caval or the emira or Pernay, Karmel couldn't say. She'd been thinking the same, as it happened. Imerle and her chief minister must have realized Karmel's presence spelled trouble, yet they appeared more interested in the stone-skin than in the more immediate threat posed by the Chameleons.

It was Pernay who answered Aminex's question. "An assassination attempt was made on the emira this morning by a woman with the same skin as this stranger from the citadel. She too . . . escaped."

Karmel's eyes narrowed. A coincidence that two people with such distinctive skin should be prowling the Storm Isles at this time? Hardly. And if the female stone-skin had tried to kill Imerle, it was fair to assume the actions of her kinsman in Dian had also been aimed at the emira. So it *was* war, then. But over what? Who were these stone-skins? And would the imminent conflict between the Chameleons and Imerle play into their hands?

The emira was staring at Karmel, and the woman's unnerving smile returned. "Grave tidings indeed," Imerle said, scanning the line of Chameleons before looking at Caval. "We do not see, though, why it needed six of you to deliver them."

Caval inclined his head. "Emira, may I introduce Aminex of the Chameleon Temple in—"

"Oh, come now, High Priest, we think this charade has gone on long enough, don't you?"

Caval paused, then shrugged. "As you wish."

He clapped his hands.

From the far end of the underwater passage came a man's scream, then the clash of metal on metal as Wick and his female companion set about silencing Imerle's soldiers guarding the corridor. A dozen heartbeats later all was quiet.

Karmel's companions drew their swords, but Karmel did not follow suit. Her gaze was still on the emira. A whisper of cold passed through the priestess, for throughout the struggle Imerle had not so much as blinked.

And her smile remained in place.

Kempis's head was spinning. For the last quarter-bell he'd been watching the palace gates from the corner of Monks Lane, and in that interval he'd seen them change hands no fewer than three times. When he and Sniffer had arrived, the gates were being opened by Storm Guards to let in a troop of Chameleons. After the priests and priestesses disappeared into the palace, more Storm Guards emerged from the building—come to reinforce their colleagues at the gates, Kempis assumed.

Wrong.

He'd stared slack-jawed as the newcomers fell on their comrades, slaughtering a handful before the defenders rallied. By this time, though, the attackers had unbolted the gates to admit a force of men wearing gray cloaks who'd come running up from the west. Once inside the palace grounds, those warriors had drawn curved swords from scabbards strapped to their backs . . . and begun butchering the Storm Guards, friend and foe alike. A sensible enough strategy, Kempis supposed. If you couldn't be *sure* of the allegiance of the man in front of you, you didn't gamble your life on a guess.

Evidently not wanting to miss out on the fun, some Chameleons had then reappeared from the palace and started firing crossbows indiscriminately into the melee. Finally a company of Gilgamarians from the stranded galleon—Kempis had seen the flint-eyed woman among them—had materialized along Crown Avenue and attacked through the still-open gates.

It almost made the septia want to hang around to see who turned up next.

He slipped out of the gray cloak he'd been wearing over his uniform. A few streets back he'd stumbled across a dead raider and relieved him of his cloak, thinking a disguise might come in handy if the city fell to the invaders. With such obvious confusion among the warring factions, though, Kempis decided the cloak was as likely to get him killed as it was to save his skin. And if he *was* going to follow Loop through Shroud's Gate, he'd rather it be because of who he was than who he wasn't.

The Gilgamarians had driven their opponents into the palace grounds, leaving the gates momentarily unguarded. Kempis wasn't going to get a better chance than this to slip through unchallenged, but still he hesitated.

"Get out of here," he said to Sniffer.

The Untarian ignored him. Odd, she'd never before had trouble hearing his orders to flee. "The way's clear, sir. If we're quick—"

"Didn't you hear me? We don't know for sure Loop's stone-skin will go after the emira. No point in us both risking our lives on a no-show."

Sniffer unsheathed her knives. She wouldn't meet his gaze. "Gilgamarian attack is running out of steam."

Kempis looked back at the gates. The Untarian was right—the tide of the battle was turning, thanks to the arrival of yet more Gray Cloaks from Crown Avenue.

"Reckon we should be going now if we're going at all," Sniffer added.

The septia opened his mouth to speak, then shut it again. What was the point in arguing? In the time it took him to drum some sense into the Untarian's skull, the Gilgamarians would all be dead. And with them would go his chance of getting inside.

To hell with this.

Drawing his sword, he set off at a run toward the palace.

The ground beyond the gates was littered with the dead and dying. The septia slowed as he picked a path through the carnage.

"Coming through! Coming through!"

Ahead a Gray Cloak writhed on the blood-smeared flagstones, his right leg hacked off at the knee. Kempis hurdled him, only for his left foot to come down on a carelessly discarded set of intestines. He slipped and fell, but was up again in a heartbeat, Sniffer urging him on. The crash of swords was loud in his ears. The surviving Gilgamarians had lost more than half their number now and were covering the flight to the palace of the flint-eyed woman and a few others. A Storm Guard noticed Kempis and ordered him to halt.

The septia paid him no mind, increasing his pace as he cleared the tangle of corpses. His shoulders prickled for an arrow or a crossbow bolt that would bring this Shroud-cursed madness to an end.

It never came.

Instead he found himself charging at five soldiers who had appeared from one of the palace's arches. For once Kempis's luck was in, for between him and the guards was a fountain with a statue of a sea dragon at its center. The Storm Guards went left, so the septia went right, sprinting for the arch through which the soldiers had emerged.

Kempis plunged into the palace's corridors. The clamor of fighting faded behind, to be replaced by his wheezing and the slap of Sniffer's bare feet. He had no idea where he was going, but for now his only concern was to put some distance between himself and the combatants. As he approached a T-junction he heard shouts from the right-hand turning. He went left. In front a woman in a servant's livery squealed and vanished into a courtyard.

The corridors flashed by in a blur of white.

The next intersection was strewn with corpses, and beyond them the septia caught sight of two Chameleons, a man and a woman, dressed in shimmering robes. He darted into the right turning, his shoulder brushing the left-hand wall, his sandals skidding on the mosaic floor . . .

He slid to a stop.

A short distance away waited two more priests, facing in the opposite direction. They spun round to confront him. There was blood on their swords, and on the ground behind them lay the bodies of three Storm Guards.

"Back off, lads," Kempis said with as much authority as he could muster. "We're on the same side." Which was true, in a way. The septia *was* on the Chameleons' side, because he was on the side of whichever faction happened to be winning at any given time. And from where he was standing, that was the priests just now, no question.

The men smiled to suggest they weren't taken in by the ruse.

Kempis retreated a pace.

As the Storm Guards drew near, Warner stepped in front of Agenta. She'd tried showing them Elemy's dagger and commanding them to step aside, but their expressions made it clear they were Imerle's creatures. *Of course they are,* the kalisch thought bitterly—the emira would long since have swept the palace clear of enemies.

Though how the Chameleons fitted into the picture remained a mystery.

"Put your weapons down!" a voice said.

It was only then that Agenta saw standing at the back of the Storm Guards a septia in the uniform of one of Imerle's personal troops. Not just any soldier, either. *Sticks.* His scowl told her he remembered her too. From the shadow that crossed his features, he hadn't forgiven her for surviving their encounter in the Deeps.

Agenta bit back a curse. She had barely set foot in the palace, and already the game was up. The Storm Guards outnumbered her party eleven to seven, and of those seven, one—Farrell—was not even armed. If Warner and his soldiers held off Sticks's men for a while, then Gilgamarian reinforcements might arrive from the gates. But the next person to enter the palace was as likely to be an enemy as a friend. And even if Agenta's forces defeated these Storm Guards, what about the next group they ran into, and the next, and the next?

The kalisch looked at Sticks. Giving her voice a note of self-assurance she did not feel, she said, "We have business with the emira. If you escort us to her, then this need not come to bloodshed."

Sticks snorted and gestured to his troops. "Take them."

At the front of Agenta's party, Iqral, the Kalanese spearman who had accompanied her to the Deeps, was the first to react. He leapt at the soldier opposite him, and their shields crashed together. The Storm Guard was thrown back a step. Iqral crouched, then thrust his shortspear under the lower rim of his enemy's shield and into his groin. The man screamed and went down.

Beside Iqral a short-haired Gilgamarian swordswoman aimed a cut at the Storm Guard across from her—a huge man with arms as thick as a blacksmith's. He blocked the effort with his mace, then countered with a blow that smashed through the woman's parrying stroke and caved in her skull. Blood splashed to the wall behind.

Suddenly crossbows twanged from along the corridor, and screams sounded from the rear ranks of the Storm Guards. Agenta glimpsed shimmering robes in the passage beyond the emira's soldiers. *Chameleons.* Had they come to rescue the Gilgamarians, then?

Somehow the kalisch doubted it.

The Storm Guards spun round to face this new threat. Iqral took advantage by slamming his spear into the neck of the soldier who'd killed his female companion. As the Kalanese tried to withdraw the weapon, though, it snagged in his foe's flesh. A sword stroke from another Storm Guard shattered the shaft. Iqral retreated, reaching for the remaining spear strapped to his back.

A crossbow bolt hit the wall to Agenta's right before ricocheting past.

"Run!" Warner shouted, pushing her along the corridor and away from the fighting.

She fled.

Farrell and a Gilgamarian soldier called Spark were ahead of her. Spark turned right into a side passage, and Agenta followed, quickly drawing level with Farrell, who was jogging with one hand over his gut. Spark took the next right, bringing them into a corridor that ran parallel with the one in which they had met Sticks. As they approached a junction Agenta drew her sword, expecting Imerle's soldiers to arrive to block their path.

None appeared.

The kalisch reached the intersection and looked right to glimpse a scrum of Storm Guards and Chameleons. Sticks was in the thick of the fighting, wielding his sword two-handed against a red-haired priestess wearing fish-scale armor. Then Agenta was past the junction, sandals flapping and slapping.

The combatants disappeared from view.

Agenta glanced back to see Balen and Warner behind. There was no sign of Iqral, though, and the kalisch struggled against an urge to laugh. They were down to five. Five, to take on not just the remaining defenders in the palace, but also the emira and her elite guardians. She should not have sent so many soldiers to escort Lydanto. More to the point, she'd been a fool to think she could fight through to Imerle with a mere forty men. And yet, if she could just make it as far as the throne room . . .

An idea was taking form in her mind. One which offered a chance to wrest *some* gain from the ashes of this day. One she dared not share with her companions.

Spark, ten paces ahead, took the next left. Doubtless the man was as lost as Agenta herself, but the sound of the sea was getting louder so he must have been leading them toward the throne room. The kalisch heard fighting from along the side corridors they passed. In one of the courtyards to her right she saw two Chameleon priests battling a Storm Guard, but the passage in front remained mercifully empty.

Then the air ahead of Spark blurred, and he seemed to stumble.

His head lifted from his shoulders.

Spark's body ran on an improbable step before collapsing to the ground. Blood pumped from his neck.

Agenta slithered to a halt. What in the Nine Hells . . . ?

A flicker of movement, and two Chameleons—a man and a woman— materialized in the corridor.

Then someone hammered into Agenta from behind, knocking her to the floor.

Senar lashed out with his Will at Tali and connected with a blow that spun her from her feet. Then he turned just in time to confront Mili, parrying a thrust to his groin before countering with a backhand cut that she blocked. Knowing he had only heartbeats before Tali recovered from his Will-strike, he pressed his assault on her sister. Mili seemed happy to defend, never risking her needle-thin blade in a full-blooded parry but instead just touching Senar's strokes aside. The corridor rang with steel. Over the clamor the Guardian listened for footfalls that would signal Tali's approach from the rear.

Nothing.

He pictured Tali creeping up behind, her blade stabbing for his unprotected back . . .

Cursing, he feinted a cut to Mili's hip, then struck out with his Will. The blow knocked her back a few steps, and she stumbled into a wall.

Senar spun round.

In time to see Tali's sword lunging for his chest. He brought his blade up to parry, turning his body as he did so. Tali's weapon flicked off his own and grazed his shirt. He retaliated with a cut that had her leaping backward. A pace behind her was the open doorway to Jambar's quarters, and Senar, seeing a way out of his predicament, glanced toward it.

As he'd hoped, Tali edged across to block his path to the doorway.

Opening up a way past her along the corridor.

Senar caught her next thrust on his sword and twisted his wrist to pin her blade for the time he needed to move level with her. A nudge of his Will forced her back into Jambar's room.

He stepped past her along the passage before turning to confront Mili.

Mili had recovered her footing and now approached cautiously, her sword held low. Tali reentered the corridor to flank her.

All that effort just to bring the three of them back to the positions where they'd started.

The sisters were grinning.

Senar heard running feet suddenly, and from a side passage behind the women appeared two Storm Guards. One was carrying a crossbow which he pointed at the Guardian.

Tali barked a command, and the soldier lowered his weapon.

Sporting of her.

Another of Jambar's bones cracked underfoot as the Guardian took a pace back. He was already regretting cleaning the red solent from his blade after killing Greave, but it wasn't as if he'd come anywhere close to piercing the sisters' defenses yet. The women were as good as he'd been expecting, but not as good as he'd feared. He had noticed, for instance, that Mili tended to narrow her eyes before attacking. If he could anticipate her next strike and grasp her sword . . .

The twins came on again, and Senar retreated, waiting for an opening. When it came—a high thrust from Mili on his right—he swayed aside and reached out to seize her blade.

Mili must have been expecting the move, though, for she snatched her weapon back, and Senar's fingers closed on air.

The twins' smiles broadened.

When Tali next attacked, Senar used his Will to deflect her sword into the wall on his left, hoping its point would snag on a joint between the stones and shatter. Luck was against him, though, for her blade merely scored the rock. Before he could take advantage of her moment of vulnerability, Mili lunged forward. A blow from Senar's Will rocked her back on her heels—just as Tali rejoined the fray. She feinted a low slash before spinning on her heel and aiming a punch at the Guardian's midriff which he blocked with a forearm.

Mili renewed her onslaught, and the twins' combined assault forced Senar to backpedal. One of Mili's thrusts, turned aside by Senar's sword, brought her chest to chest with the Guardian. Her head snapped forward, and Senar, anticipating a head-butt, leaned back.

It seemed Mili had been intent on delivering no more than a kiss, though, for her puckered lips passed a finger's width from his chin.

The sisters giggled.

"What, not even . . ."

". . . a single kiss, Guardian?"

"We promise . . ."

". . . not to bite."

Senar grimaced. "I fear, ladies, that your kisses may have something of a sting to them."

Laughing, they advanced.

Senar had used the time they'd been talking to gather his Will, but before he could unleash it he heard a scream from behind the sisters. Looking past them, he saw the Storm Guard crossbowman on his knees, blood gushing from his throat. His companion—a woman—was so busy staring in disbelief at the wound that she didn't notice a man in the shimmering robes of a Chameleon priest materialize to her right. He rammed his sword into her side.

Senar allowed himself a smile. An unexpected source of help, that, but he would take whatever allies were going.

A ripple of air, and a second priest appeared a few paces behind the twins. Tali had already turned toward the danger. The Chameleon swung his blade in a decapitating cut, but she caught the strike on her sword and countered with a kick to the man's chest that sent him sprawling.

Mili's gaze had remained fixed on Senar, but now she looked at something over his shoulder.

Her eyes widened.

The Guardian spun round, then realized he might have just fallen for the old look-out-he's-behind-you trick. If he got Mili's sword in his back after that, it would serve him right.

Instead he saw a different blade stabbing for his face—this one held by a third Chameleon priest.

Allies. Right.

"It's over, Emira," Caval said. "As we speak my followers are taking control of the palace. The few Storm Guards stationed here are no match for them, and your troops in the city are too far away to help."

"You wish us to surrender?" Imerle said, examining her nails. Behind her the executioner remained staring into space.

"Ah, I don't see that you have any choice."

"And you expect us to believe you will let us live if we do?"

"I give you my word. You will be my guest until the dust settles on this day's events, but once the transition of power is complete, you will be free to go wherever you wish. So long as it is outside the Sabian League, of course."

Imerle looked at Karmel. "What say you, priestess? Should we take the deal he offers? Can we trust his word?"

Karmel stared back at her, uncertain what the woman wanted her to say. Caval was never going to let her walk out of here alive, but from the emira's expression she knew that as well as Karmel.

"What did your brother tell you?" Imerle said suddenly. "That he knew nothing of what would happen at the Dragon Gate?"

"Enough," Caval said.

"Or perhaps," the emira went on, "that he didn't have time to give you all the details before you left?"

Karmel swallowed. A part of her wanted to ignore Imerle's questions and leave Caval to administer the woman's last rites. But Karmel had come to the palace for answers, and she wasn't about to shy away from them now. "He said you told him about the mission only the day before Dragon Day."

The corners of the emira's mouth turned up. "Yes, that makes sense. Do you have any idea how much planning went into today's proceedings? Into learning about the Dianese control room and sounding out the Storm Guard commanders for support? Into raising funds to hire the Revenants and bring their ships to our island undetected? Months it has taken, yet all would have been for naught if we couldn't have found a way to dispose of the other Storm Lords and those closest to them. For that we required the Chameleons' aid to release the dragons. The success of our venture hung on what happened in Dian, so obviously we would wait until the last moment to speak to Caval."

"Save your breath," Caval said. "You won't make her doubt—"

"Doubt?" Imerle cut in. "Oh, we think you will find she has doubts already." Then, to Karmel, "We assume from the bruises round your neck that Veran turned on you after the mission was over. Did Caval claim the man's attack was our idea? That Veran served us, and not your brother?"

Karmel nodded, not trusting herself to speak.

"And you believed him?" The emira shook her head. "Must we spell it out for you? There were to be no loose ends after Dian—we made this clear to Caval when we first approached him. Once Veran killed you, he was to turn the knife on himself, and why do you think he was prepared to do that?"

"His wife," the priestess whispered.

"Very good. Your god agreed to heal her if Veran accepted this mission, and how could that arrangement have been brokered without your brother's involvement? You think *we* hold any sway with the Chameleon?"

It felt to Karmel as if the throne room were spinning. She couldn't think. She wanted to close her eyes, but the emira's gaze held her.

Caval spoke. "If I'd wanted my sister dead, I could have arranged it at any time. Hells, I could have done it myself when she returned to the temple."

"In front of *witnesses*?" Imerle said. "Do you take the girl for a fool?"

"No, it is *you* who take her for a fool if you expect her to see this for anything other than what it is: a feeble attempt to sow dissension among our ranks so you can save your sorry hide."

The emira laughed. "You think your betrayal comes as a surprise to us? Jambar warned us of your plans, but we disregarded him because we *wanted* you to attack. Why else would we have emptied the palace of soldiers before inviting you here?"

"Perhaps because you overextended yourself."

"Or perhaps because we wanted to leave you with a target too tempting to pass up. You don't believe us? Think, High Priest. The Sabian League will take years to recover from the wounds we have inflicted on it, but recover it will, and when it does so it will come seeking retribution. Who do you think its prime suspect will be for what happened in Dian? Why, ourselves, of course." Her eyes smoldered. "It was always our intention to blame the Dragon Gate on a Chameleon play for power. How much easier do you imagine it will be to convince the doubters now that you are here?"

Karmel stared at her, uncomprehending. So the Chameleons *had* walked into a trap? Were her fellow priests and priestesses even now being rounded up and slaughtered? But then why had Imerle let Caval reach the throne room unmolested? And why had she let her guards in the passage outside be killed?

Caval must have been wondering the same for he said, "Ah, a stroke of genius, Emira, though you seem to have overlooked one point. What good will it do you if your troops hold the palace when you yourself are a captive?"

"But our troops do not hold the palace. If we had warned them what you were planning, you might have seen it in their eyes."

"You're saying you *allowed* my attack to succeed? You expect me to believe—"

"You still don't understand, do you? Look around you, High Priest. What do you see?"

Caval glanced about the chamber, his expression showing a mixture of wariness and puzzlement. Karmel's mind was numb, her thoughts slow to rise as if they were mired in blood honey. There was something here she wasn't seeing, something important, but what? Other than Imerle, Pernay, and the executioner, the chamber was empty of any threat to the Chameleons. Could Storm Guards be massing at the end of the underwater passage, ready to pour into the chamber at the emira's signal? No, Wick would have warned Caval if that were so. But then what was the source of Imerle's confidence? Did she think Caval would stay his hand now that he knew his attack had been foreseen? Why should he, for there would be no witnesses to what took place here, unless the emira counted the fish in the sea . . .

Karmel blinked.

The sea!

She opened her mouth to voice a warning, but Imerle was already gesturing.

And the walls of water came crashing in.

CHAPTER 20

SENAR'S NEW assailant was a Chameleon priest with a hooked nose and green eyes—eyes that widened when his stabbing sword struck an invisible Will-barrier thrown up by the Guardian. The priest had a friend—a shaven-headed woman with a ring through her nose—and she lunged with a long-knife for Senar's chest. He brought his blade up to parry but could only half deflect the stroke, and the priestess's weapon stung his left shoulder. Senar hissed through gritted teeth before countering with a thrust that was blocked by the woman's friend.

The priestess feinted low with her longknife even as her male companion thrust high with his sword. Senar parried the priest's blow but did not retaliate, content to defend while he assessed his opponents' strengths and weaknesses. Neither was a match to Mili or Tali. The man in particular, fighting with a longsword, was struggling to adapt his style to battling in the confines of the corridor, and he was constantly having to check his strokes to avoid hitting his companion. If Senar kept him swinging, the priest would eventually do the Guardian's work for him—assuming the twins didn't stab Senar in the back first, that is. From the sounds of fighting behind, though, it seemed the sisters were being kept well enough occupied by their own Chameleon assailants—

A concussion suddenly shook the passage, and for a heartbeat Senar was back in the titan fortress, the floor pitching beneath him as Fume thrashed against his manacles. But the god was dead, wasn't he? A knife in the heart would have that effect. This couldn't be another quake.

The Chameleon priestess was the first to recover, shifting her grip on her longknife and leaping to the attack. Senar blocked a cut to his head, but before he could counter, another tremor rattled the corridor, followed by a boom of water. It must have been the Guardian's imagination, but it sounded like it came from the next passage. The air quivered, and the floor lurched again as the thunder of water grew to a roar.

The priestess broke off her attack, gaping at something over Senar's shoulder.

What, behind him again, was it?

Glancing back, Senar saw a chest-high frothing tide engulf the twins and the two Chameleons fighting them.

There was no time to fashion a Will-barrier, and he was swept away by the wave.

As Agenta lay on the floor she found herself staring at Spark's severed head. She should move, she knew—the Chameleons would be coming for her—but her limbs felt impossibly heavy. She lay with her cheek pressed to the mosaic. Through the tiles she heard a rumble. Then she felt a vibration that grew in intensity until it shook the corridor and made Spark's head bounce and twist.

An earthquake? she wondered, remembering the tremors during her flight from the Deeps. No, she decided, for the rumble had resolved itself into the unmistakable crash of water.

The two Chameleons spun round to look back along the passage.

"Sender's mercy!" Warner said from behind Agenta.

A roaring, white-flecked wall of water came surging toward her.

"Any ideas?" Kempis asked Sniffer as the Chameleon priests advanced.

"Run?"

"Genius!" he said. "Thank the Sender I brought you along."

Before he'd even finished speaking, though, there were footfalls in the corridor behind. He looked round to see two more Chameleons— the man and woman he'd glimpsed earlier—enter the passage. Both were carrying injuries, the woman a slice to her scalp, the man a cut to his thigh.

They moved to block off the Watchmen's retreat.

Just then Kempis heard a thunderclap from along the corridor to his right. A deep-throated rumble set the walls shivering, followed by a concussion the septia felt through his boots. A wall of water three-quarters the height of the corridor came rushing up behind the two Chameleons. The woman turned toward it first. She gave a despairing cry as she and her male companion were engulfed and swept toward Kempis.

The septia groaned.

Not again.

Karmel gulped in a lungful of air, then gritted her teeth to keep it in as the sea pummeled her from every side. She was plucked from her feet, turned inside out, wrenched this way and that as if by vast watery hands. The waves were shot through with bubbles, but to her right she could make out the hazy forms of Imerle, Pernay, and the executioner, safe within a pocket of air. It stood to reason the emira would have collapsed only that part of the chamber where the Chameleons had been standing. Karmel considered swimming to join them, but doubtless if she did so she would be met by the point of the giant's sword.

There were figures about her in the misty waters—other Chameleons wriggling and straining and kicking. A foot caught her shoulder as its owner swam for the surface. No access to the roof terraces from the sea, though—even Karmel knew that. Her best hope of reaching dry ground was to make for the doorway to the palace, for surely Imerle wouldn't have flooded the building with so many of her own forces inside. Karmel squinted. She couldn't see the doorway through the bubbles, but she *could* see the floor of the now-collapsed underwater passage stretching off to her left. She kicked in that direction, battling against the currents that threatened first to tug her up to the surface, then down into the grainy depths below.

Pressure was building in her lungs. There was no cause for panic, though, with the surface of the sea only a handful of armspans above. If she ran out of air, she could simply swim up for a breath before diving down again.

Then a memory came to her of the shark she'd seen circling the throne room. Where was it now?

She quickened her stroke.

Fish scattered from her path. The bubbles in the water were dispersing, and she glimpsed the doorway ahead—an arch of brightness in the long dark of the seawall with its swaying covering of fireweed. She pulled herself through the water, arms already aching with the effort, breath pushing against her bared teeth. She seemed to be moving away from her target instead of toward it, and she wondered if Imerle had spun chains of water-magic round her legs to keep her from escaping.

Then suddenly she was rushing toward the doorway as if she were being drawn into a whirlpool.

Too late she realized she'd been wrong about the emira flooding the palace. Imerle would have expected the Chameleons to have overrun her forces by now, so there was nothing for her to lose, and everything for her to gain, by flushing out the nest. The palace would have been transformed into a watery charnel house, but it was too late now for Karmel to turn back. When she twisted and tried to swim against the current, she found its pull was too powerful. Stronger and stronger it became as she drew near to the palace, the doorway yawning wide like the mouth of some creature set to devour her, water rushing all about. She was sucked through the opening and hurled into the wall across from it with bone-jarring force.

Air exploded from her lungs. Her mouth filled with water. The weight of the sea crushed her into the stone, and she coughed and thrashed and tried to surface. The corridor, though, was flooded even up to the ceiling, and she succeeded only in striking her head on stone. Through the stars that clouded her vision she saw a square of light ahead—a window!—and she thrust her head through it into the hot glare of the sun. A lungful of air was all she managed before the pull of the current dragged her away. She hooked her fingers round the edge of the window, clung on for an instant. But the draw was too strong, and she was tugged clear and carried along the corridor to her right in a contortion of limbs.

Walls flashed past to either side, windows to her left. The little breath Karmel had snatched at the window was already running out, but the level of water in the passage would surely drop as she moved

farther from the doorway. Sure enough, when she kicked for the surface she found sufficient air for her to steal a breath. She tilted her
head back so her face was pressed to the ceiling. For a while she let
the current take her. Water sloshed and fizzed in her ears. The corridor was trembling. Then it opened out in front, and she glimpsed a
patch of light in the roof to her right, a partly submerged staircase
leading up to the terraces. So strong was the tug of water that she
nearly overshot it, but she grabbed one of the foam-covered steps as
she drew level, hauled herself round and onto it, her knees catching
on the stone.

She turned onto her back and lay looking up at the sky, her legs
still in the water, the air against her face cool with spray. Her scalp
stung from when she'd smashed her head on the ceiling. Overhead the
sky was dazzlingly bright after the gloom of the sea. The angles of
the steps were cutting into her neck and back, but she hardly felt them
for all her other aches and grazes. Distant screams reached her. From
farther along the corridor came the sound of thundering waves as if
there were rapids round the next corner. While from the direction she
had come . . .

Splashing. It was drawing closer.

She sat up, shivering. A man moved into view, floating on his back
with his face pressed to the ceiling as Karmel's had been. It took the
priestess a heartbeat to recognize the weaponsmaster, Foss, his black
hair plastered across his face, his cloak shimmering in the water. She
seized his arm as he came level. He fought her for an instant, his eyes
rolling wildly. Then his gaze locked to hers, and his struggles
subsided.

She dragged him onto the steps. He sat panting with his back to
the wall, his shoulders slumped, his look one of grim disbelief. He
wouldn't meet her gaze. Karmel knew what he must be thinking. How
could they have failed to see what was coming? How could they have
been foolish enough to challenge a water-mage in a room carved out
of the sea? With a mere gesture Imerle had smashed the Chameleons'
ambitions, for even if Caval's forces survived the flooding of the palace
there was no way they could reach the emira in her pocket of air.
Once her troops in the city defeated the remaining Storm Guards . . .

And yet, that wasn't what troubled Karmel most about the events
of the last quarter-bell.

More splashing sounded. Another figure appeared along the passage, wheezing and spluttering. A man. He saw the stairwell and kicked for it. Foss leaned forward to extend a hand.

Karmel's expression hardened. It was Caval.

Pushing herself upright, she walked up the steps to the roof terrace.

Agenta tensed for the wave's impact.

That impact never came. Instead she heard a crash as of a breaker striking a cliff, then a spattering noise as water was driven out through the windows to fall into the courtyard to her right. The light in the corridor dimmed, and the kalisch looked up to see a shimmering blue-green barrier an armspan away. Balen stood beside her with palms extended, his brow furrowed in concentration. The two Chameleons who had killed Spark had been swallowed by the wave. The male one swam along the now-flooded passage toward Agenta's party, and she shuffled backward as first his head, then his shoulders and arms, burst from the water. Gasping for air, he dropped his sword and clawed at the floor, his fingers seeking cracks in the mosaic so he could pull himself into the dry part of the corridor.

Warner stepped forward and plunged his sword into the man's neck.

The priest died with a gurgle.

Behind him his female companion had been making to follow, but she now reversed her course and swam back along the passage. Reaching a window, she thrust her head outside. All around, the sounds of battle had died away. Running footfalls came from the roof overhead. Distant shouts rang out. Then one by one the noises faded until all that could be heard was the swirl and splash of water.

The sea had stolen the heat from the passage. Agenta sat against the wall with her arms wrapped round her knees. That wave had saved her life, she knew, yet somehow she doubted that had been its purpose. Farrell approached the dead Chameleon and stooped to collect the man's sword. Exhaustion warred with sadness in his features.

"You should not have come," Agenta said.

"I should not have talked my father into doing business with Imerle either. But I cannot change that now."

Agenta stared at him. So it was Farrell, and not his father, who had embraced the chance to ally with the emira? If so, the responsibility for Rethell's death lay in part at the merchant's feet, because without him Imerle might never have been able to hire the Revenants. Some of the anger Agenta felt toward the emira should be directed at Farrell too, she realized. When she reached for that anger, though, it eluded her.

"There's no way that you could have known what would happen on the *Icewing*," she said.

"What would happen on the *Icewing*, no. But that Imerle might prove to be an uncertain friend . . ."

Warner crouched to search the priest's corpse. In the wall of water behind, Spark's body and severed head hung motionless.

Farrell's gaze was distant. "My father used to say all roads led to Shroud's Gate, but he wouldn't complain because by the time he'd walked them all he'd be due a rest. He knew the risk he was taking in supporting Imerle. He'd have had no regrets."

Agenta's face twisted. Regrets, she'd always considered, were for those stupid enough to think tomorrow might hold less disappointment than today. And yet, had her indifference to the world made her any more impervious to its hurts? She regarded Farrell impassively. The words he'd spoken just now had been said to convince himself rather than the kalisch. Did he believe them any more than she did? Earlier on the *Crest* she'd wondered at his acceptance of Samel's fate. Where was his anger? His need for vengeance? The truth was, he blamed himself as much as the emira for his father's passing. And guilt would be a harder foe to vanquish even than Imerle.

"Do you think the emira is dead?" Farrell asked. "The only way the palace could have been flooded is if the magic holding back the sea failed."

"We will see for ourselves soon enough," Agenta said.

Warner looked at her sharply. "You still mean to go on?"

The kalisch was tempted to confide in him her plans for Imerle. Instead she turned to Balen and said, "Mage, this wall of water, can you drive it before us as far as the throne room?"

He nodded.

Farrell's voice was urgent. "What about the one behind?" he said, pointing back down the corridor.

For a second wave was rushing toward them.

Arms and legs flailing, Senar was swept along the passage by the wave. A smaller wave surged toward him from the opposite direction, and the two masses of water met with a crash of spray that came splattering down upon him. A current gripped his legs and tugged him under where he tangled with the shaven-headed Chameleon priestess. He shoved her away, broke the surface, and heaved in a breath.

Another wave hit him from behind.

Then he was hurtling along the corridor again, eyes stinging with salt, feet scrabbling at the floor. In an effort to slow himself he kicked against the flow, but the weight of the surge was irresistible. It snatched him under once more, enfolded him, and the roar of the water fell to a muffled gurgle as if someone had pressed their hands over his ears. Blinded by bubbles, he didn't know which way was up. Then he saw the blue-white of the floor mosaic. He pushed off against it and surfaced again, coughing spray from his mouth and nose.

He sucked in another breath. The waves in the passage were rolling high enough to break against the ceiling, and Senar rose and fell with them, water washing into his eyes. An intersection came rushing toward him. He reached it just as a wave lapped into the corridor from a side passage, dealing him a clout to the side of the head. That wave carried him into the point of a corner and pinned him there. It seemed a good idea to escape the drag in the main corridor, so he kicked and twisted and squirmed until he'd reached the less turbulent swell of the side passage.

Sudden calm.

Treading water, Senar drifted for a time. With each junction he passed, the water became less choppy. He had no idea where he was heading. Maybe he should be trying to find a way into a courtyard or onto one of the terraces, but just now he was happy to settle for no one swinging a sword at him. To his left was an open doorway. When he looked through he saw a flooded room filled with bobbing casks. Floating facedown among them was a woman in the uniform of Imerle's personal guard. Along a side passage were more corpses—all Storm Guards. In front of the bodies Senar glimpsed the Chameleon priestess he'd fought, struggling under the weight of her sopping robes. There was no sign of her male companion, or of the twins.

To his right water poured through a window into the courtyard beyond. The sea must have been flowing into the passage faster than it could drain away, because the water continued to rise until the windows narrowed to mere bars of sunshine. He raised his head to keep from swallowing a mouthful of water. The light began to fade. At the next T-junction he was tugged right. From the wall to his left seeped water-magic, and he realized he must be in the corridor that bordered onto the sea. Close by was a partly submerged staircase. The steps fell away from this side, meaning Senar would have to swim past, then double back if he wanted to climb. Was this the same staircase he'd taken to the roof terrace when he first met the emira? He hoped not, because if so the underwater passage would be near. And the last place he wanted to be floating toward now was the throne room.

Something brushed his ankle. He looked down to see a sea snake slither past. There were fish in the water too—silver ones and black ones and blue ones with red-tipped fins that scattered when he kicked his legs. In his mind's eye he saw again the kris shark circling the throne room, and it occurred to him there might be worse things prowling the passages than the twins and the Chameleons. His gaze fell on his wounded shoulder. Blood was leaking from the cut the priestess had given him, staining his shirt red. Doubtless that blood would be attracting predators from the sea.

If they hadn't already been drawn here by the corpses of the Storm Guards.

His weariness forgotten, Senar pushed his sword into its scabbard and started swimming for the stairs. He ignored the complaints from his injured shoulder. The water in the corridor was covered with a layer of fireweed that weighed on him like wet wool. By the time he made it to the steps, the muscles of his arms were burning-tight and the sea had risen to almost an armspan from the ceiling.

His knees bumped into the submerged stairs. He crawled a short way up before rolling onto his back. Waves lapped at his boots, but he didn't have the strength to move. Instead he lay listening to his ragged breath and staring up at the sky through an opening in the ceiling. He hadn't been in the water for long, yet his body felt as if he'd swum all the way to Olaire from Erin Elal. A body drifted by: a Chameleon priest, his eyes staring wide, his open mouth collecting water. It seemed to Senar there should have been more corpses down here, but then maybe anyone else caught in the passages had been quick to climb to the terraces. Were the twins up there waiting for him now? There was no clash of swords from above to suggest the fighting had moved to the rooftops. All Senar could hear was the gush of water, a distant grumble of collapsing masonry, someone's cut-off cry for help . . .

Then the sound of splashing reached him. He looked back along the corridor. Two figures were heading toward him. Mili and Tali. Neither of the twins were looking his way. One was clearly no swimmer for she lay on her back, kicking out with her legs while her sister half dragged, half supported her along the passage. Easy prey while they remained in the water. A lot easier, certainly, than if they gained the stairs and drew their swords.

Senar's hand strayed to the hilt of his blade.

Then a black fin rose from the waves behind the twins. It sped toward the women, cutting a V through the chop and leaving ripples in its wake. The twins had seen it too, and they began thrashing toward Senar's staircase, churning the sea to froth. They closed the distance in heartbeats, only to flinch when they caught sight of the Guardian. A moment's pause, then the nonswimmer lifted a hand to him, her eyes pleading. He hesitated. Yes, the Chameleons had attacked both him *and* the twins, but that hardly made the sisters his allies. If he helped them now, what was to stop them turning on him when the danger had passed? It wasn't as if he had time to quiz them on their intentions. Why take the risk? Why save them now just to kill them later? Or perhaps be killed by them, more to the point.

A huge shadow was now visible in the water behind them. The already meager light in the corridor seemed to dim further with the creature's coming. Its snout glistened as it broke the surface. Senar half drew his sword. If he wasn't going to help the twins he at least owed them a clean death. It would be a mercy, he told himself. They would do the same for him if the roles were reversed.

He had to kill them. It was right thing to do.

The twin thrust her hand at him again.

For a heartbeat longer he stood frozen in indecision.

Then he released his grip on his sword hilt and grabbed the sister's hand. There was no balustrade on the stairwell, and he pulled the woman out of the water and onto the steps behind him.

Senar turned for the second twin. The current had carried her a few paces past. If she'd had the presence of mind she could have swum farther along the passage and clambered onto the submerged stairs to the Guardian's left. With the shark bearing down on her, though, she wasn't thinking clearly, for instead she swam a stroke toward Senar before stretching and reaching out her right hand. He snatched for it.

Missed.

The twin gave a despairing cry and fell back in the water.

Senar glanced at the approaching shark. The creature was almost as wide as the passage. When it opened its mouth he saw teeth a handspan long, a scrap of red cloth trapped between them. The sister standing on the staircase behind him screamed, startling him so much he almost toppled into the water. Her horror was reflected in the eyes of her twin in the waves. Senar lashed out with his Will at the shark's snout. There hadn't been enough time to fully gather his power, though, and the blow barely slowed the creature's rush.

Cursing himself for not acting sooner, Senar grabbed for the sister's hand again. He caught it at the second attempt. Her skin was so slick it began to slide from his grasp, and he seized her wrist with his halfhand also, half lifted her from the water. Her legs hit the submerged steps. As the shark's head emerged from the sea she raised her knees to her chest. Her twin, behind Senar, screamed again. Matron's blessing, did she think that was helping him? Or that he wasn't aware of the danger, perhaps?

With a final effort he yanked her sister toward him.

Just as the shark lunged forward. With a clack Senar felt through his bones, its teeth snapped shut—

A handspan from the woman's feet.

She bundled into Senar. He fell back onto the staircase. His head struck stone, and his vision clouded. Still he was aware of the gray blur as the shark swam past, thought he might have seen its eye swivel to track him.

The sister had landed on top of the Guardian. When his sight cleared he found himself staring at her chest. Her gossamer-thin dress was soaked through, and it clung to her body in a disturbingly revealing manner. Clearing his throat, Senar looked up into the woman's green eyes, a handspan away.

She grinned.

"Perhaps," the Guardian said, "we might postpone the continuation of our duel until we find out whether we're now on the same side."

Her smile broadened.

———

Kempis kicked for one of the corridor's windows and draped his right arm through it. His ears crackled with water when he moved his head. He silently cursed the Sender, cursed the Matron, cursed every damned immortal he could think of. He'd been on dry land— dry land, for Shroud's sake!—yet for the second time in as many bells he'd found himself heartbeats away from a salty grave. If it hadn't been for Sniffer's help in keeping his head above water he would surely have drowned. Even with her aid it felt as if he'd taken in enough of the sea to refloat that stranded Gilgamarian galleon.

The water in the corridor had reached the bottom of the window and was still rising. Kempis wasn't going to wait for it to rise the rest of the way. He looked through the opening at the courtyard outside. To his left steps ascended to a roof terrace, while from an archway in the opposite wall the sea poured into the yard. It dawned on him that, with Sniffer's help, he could escape the flooded passages by swimming round to that archway, but why waste time doing so when he could just as easily leave through this window? He looked at the floor of the courtyard. It seemed a long way down, particularly since he'd be going headfirst. And while the flagstones were underwater, it was only a few fingers' widths deep and thus not enough to break his fall.

The risk of cracking his skull, though, was as nothing compared to the prospect of another of Sniffer's fishy kisses.

Kempis considered the dimensions of the window. It would be a tight fit. With a little wriggling, however, he should be able to make it through. By drawing in his shoulders he managed to squeeze them through the opening. He placed his hands against the exterior wall and pushed to lever his upper body out.

He tipped forward and began sliding into the courtyard.

And stuck.

Bugger. It was his sword, he realized—its hilt had jammed against the wall by his left hip. Kempis tried to haul himself back through the window, only to find he couldn't move because all his weight was tugging him down into the yard.

"Sniffer!" he called. "Pull me back!"

The Untarian heaved on his legs. As he reentered the corridor his head dipped below the surface, and he took in a mouthful of water. Spluttering, he draped his right arm out of the window again.

Sniffer was grinning. "You want me to find you a bigger window, sir?"

"Sword got caught," Kempis said, unbuckling his sword belt and flinging it outside.

"Right."

The water now reached halfway up the window, and the light in the corridor was fading. Kempis struggled once more through the opening.

And stuck.

Curse it all! This time it was the buckle of his trouser belt that had caught. He tried to stretch back to undo it but couldn't fit a hand through the opening, so snugly did his body fill it. Blood rushed to his head.

Sniffer's muffled voice sounded behind. "Maybe if you breathed in . . ."

"Can you reach my belt?" Kempis said. "Undo the buckle?"

A pause. "You're joking."

"Does it sound like I'm bloody having a laugh out here?"

"Relax, sir. In a few days you'll have lost enough weight . . ." Sniffer's words trailed off, and Kempis heard splashing. Then, "Sender's mercy!" The Untarian started pushing at his legs. "Move it, you lump! Get out!"

When the septia looked back all he could see was his body plugging the window. "What's going on?"

"Get out!" Sniffer screamed. "Out!"

The panic in her voice was infectious, and Kempis began thrashing and squirming in an effort to free himself. His struggles, though, served only to grind his belt buckle harder into the stonework, thus pinning him more securely. Water poured through the gaps in the window left by his body. Kempis braced his arms against the wall and pushed with all his strength. His belt strained against his hips, cutting into his skin. He shifted forward a hairbreadth.

Then his trousers rode down his legs, and he fell. He stretched out his hands to cushion the impact, but still his right shoulder jarred as he landed. In an instant he was up again, his trousers flapping round his ankles as he turned to the window. He'd hoped to find Sniffer climbing through after him, but all he saw escaping from the opening was yet more water.

Abruptly the sea spewed from the window in an explosion of

spray as if forced out by the movement of something huge along the corridor.

"Sniffer!"

No reply.

Grabbing the window ledge, Kempis pulled himself up until his chin was level with the bottom of the opening. By leaning forward he was able to look a few paces in either direction along the passage, but he couldn't make out anything in the gloom except pitching water. A wave slapped him in the face, and he dropped back into the court-yard.

He pounded a fist against the wall.

"Sniffer!"

CHAPTER 21

KARMEL STOOD on the roof terrace looking out to sea. Below and to her right Aminex's corpse bobbed in the waves, while farther out the water had been churned to foaming breakers by the wind. The priestess's mind took her back to a time when, as children, she and Caval had stumbled upon an abandoned boat and set out to discover what lay beyond the place where the glittering plain of the sea met the sky. After launching the craft they had taken an oar each and rowed for all they were worth. But her brother was so much stronger that their efforts had succeeded only in turning the boat round in circles. Karmel had laughed until her chest hurt, and with their hopes of adventure dashed, she and Caval had banked the oars and lain in the bottom of the craft with shoulders pressed together until the waves rocked them to sleep.

A smile touched the priestess's lips. For a few short bells the only things in their lives had been the touch of the sun, the pitch of the boat, the lullaby of the sea's whispering voice.

Then the boat's owner had swum out to reclaim his craft, and Karmel and Caval had returned home to their father's cane.

Footsteps sounded behind her. She turned to see her brother climbing the stairs alongside the weaponsmaster. Her smile faded. Caval's gaze when it locked to hers was empty. Strange, she mused. When he'd suffered Pennick's beatings there had always been a spark in him. That spark had faded when he'd surrendered to their father's will and embraced the Chameleon faith, but Karmel had hoped it might return when he ousted Pennick. Instead it had disappeared entirely. Now when she looked at him she saw no trace of the brother who had lain beside her in the boat all those years ago.

She missed him.

Caval opened his mouth to speak, but the weaponsmaster got in first. "We have company."

From along the roof terrace came the emira's twin bodyguards, Mili and Tali, hissing like cats. Struggling to keep up with them was a black-haired swordsman with a face too comely to be that of a warrior. Karmel stared at them. Stupidly, she'd thought she would be safe once she was clear of the passages. Had the twins known of Imerle's plan to flood the palace? Had they been lying in wait for any surviving Chameleons?

Clearly not, since their clothes were as wet as Karmel's.

Caval drew his blade and stepped between the priestess and the twins.

Mili and Tali were evidently in no mood to talk, for as one they leapt at the high priest. He blocked their needle-thin swords with a single sweep of his blade, then countered with a backhand cut that had the sister on the left swaying back. With Caval's power activated he was a blur even to Karmel, and the twins were forced to retreat. Foss, meanwhile, had intercepted their black-haired companion. The weaponsmaster's sword flickered fast as a viper's tongue, but his opponent parried each stroke with an enviable economy of movement, seemingly always unhurried despite his assailant's speed.

Shielded by her two male companions, Karmel released her power. Her right hand hovered over the hilt of her sword. The twins had survived Caval's initial onslaught and were now making their numerical advantage tell with a succession of skillfully staggered attacks. Karmel should go to her brother's aid, she knew, but her mind kept replaying the emira's words in the throne room. There was an inescapable logic to what Imerle had said about the timing of her approach to Caval, and about Caval's role in recruiting Veran. And while the priestess knew Imerle wouldn't hesitate to lie if it served her purpose, what reason had she had to deceive Karmel? As had become apparent, the Chameleons had never been a threat that the emira had needed to set them against each other.

Karmel kept coming back to one thing: if Caval had known the truth about the mission, he would have chosen her to accompany

Veran only if he *wanted* her dead. And what reason could he have for that? She recalled his look of relief when she'd entered his quarters earlier—not the look of a brother who had sent his sister to die.

And yet, why had he felt *relief* at seeing her again? Because he'd been pleased to see her, of course, but then why not just happiness in his expression? *Unless he had expected me to die at the gate.*

Her musings were interrupted by a grunt from Caval. When Karmel looked across she saw a whirlwind exchange end in a thrust from one of the twins to her brother's chest. Caval was bleeding from a cut to his sword arm, and the wound must have slowed his reflexes for while he was able to block the strike, his blade would be out of position to meet the next attack.

A throwing knife was in Karmel's hand. She couldn't remember drawing it.

She hurled the weapon at the nearest twin.

Kempis treaded water in near darkness.

At the time, it had seemed like a good idea to go looking for Sniffer. Having climbed to the roof terraces and found a staircase leading down into the flooded passages, the septia had spent an age summoning up the courage to reenter the water, then even longer struggling back to where he had exited the window. It was only as he reached the opening that it struck him Sniffer would have long since moved on, else why hadn't she answered his calls when he was outside? The sensible thing for him to do now would be to return to the terraces and wait to see if the Untarian reappeared.

If only he could remember the way back to the staircase.

He swam to the next intersection. Along the corridor to his right was the body of a Storm Guard. One side of the man's face had been sheared away by a weapon blow—

The body disappeared.

Kempis rubbed a hand across his eyes. One moment the soldier had been there, the next he was gone. *Must have been tugged underwater.* By a shark, perhaps? The septia fingered the hilt of his sword. Like he'd be able to swing the thing if a fish attacked. He peered into the murk.

And saw approaching not a shark but . . . something else. A dozen armspans away the water in the corridor ended abruptly. Beyond was a gap of perhaps ten paces, and behind that another mass of water into which the corpse of the Storm Guard suddenly bobbed into view again. *A pocket of air,* Kempis realized.

Water-magic.

Inside the pocket he made out the tops of the heads of whichever strangers were coming toward him. Whoever they were, they wouldn't be friends. He considered retreating, but what good would that do? He barely had enough strength left to keep his head above water, so what chance did he have of getting away before the newcomers arrived?

As the pocket of air reached Kempis, the sea about him melted away. He fell. His legs were shaky from swimming, and they buckled as his feet touched down. He slumped to the floor. The water had leached the heat from his body, and he lay shivering on the corridor's mosaic. From his money pouch a handful of coins spilled onto the floor. He watched one roll away until it was trapped by a sandaled foot.

"This one's alive," a woman's voice said.

Kempis winced. The voice was one he knew.

He looked up to find Mazana Creed regarding him with her arms crossed over her chest. There was no hint of recognition in her eyes. Probably just as well, too. Her frown suggested irritation he'd had the gall to drop into her section of corridor. Beside her was a man wearing a bronze cuirass and a white skirt covered with bronze plates—a man who was even now drawing his sword and advancing on Kempis.

The septia tried to coax his weary limbs to move.

A door to his right opened, and a finger's width of water sloshed into the passage.

"Leave him!" a new voice snapped.

The man in the skirt froze.

Looking round, Kempis saw the Remnerol shaman, Jambar, step into the corridor. The old man's hands were red, and there was a bloody thumbprint on the monocle hanging round his neck. In his left hand he clutched a bag; its contents clacked as they moved. Jambar did not appear surprised to discover Mazana outside his door, but then the man was a shaman, wasn't he? No doubt he'd foreseen this meeting as he'd foreseen the assassination attempt on the emira in the throne room.

Mazana looked from the Remnerol to the bag in his hand. "You have Fume's bones?"

A nod.

"Senar found you, then."

"We must talk—"

"Where is he?" the Storm Lady cut in.

"Forget him! We have more important things to discuss."

Mazana held the old man's gaze for what seemed like an eternity before shrugging. "Speak, then."

"In private," the shaman said, stepping aside to allow Mazana to enter the room beyond. Within, Kempis saw an old woman lying on a pallet. Her throat had been cut, and her susha robe was drenched crimson round the neck. Mazana regarded the corpse with arched eyebrows, then shrugged a second time and stepped inside. Jambar followed her in and closed the door.

Leaving Kempis alone with Mazana's skirted bodyguard.

The septia shuffled over to sit with his back to the wall. Through the door he heard the voices of the Remnerol and the Storm Lady. Skirt was watching him, and Kempis started gathering up his spilled coins to hide the fact that he was eavesdropping. The occasional word reached him: "assassin," "emira," "betray"—or was that "betrayal" or "betrayed"? Jambar seemed to be doing most of the talking, and Kempis heard the old man say "stone-skins" before lowering his voice. All that followed was a formless murmur.

The septia's gaze fell on a window behind Skirt. For a moment he imagined himself wedged in the opening with Sniffer pushing at his legs. How much time had passed between him landing in the court-yard and the water being expelled from the window? Enough for the Untarian to escape whatever was prowling the corridors? Kempis snorted. Who was he trying to kid? He should have been quicker through the opening, maybe let Sniffer go first. More important, he shouldn't have brought her to the palace in the first place. The debt to Loop was Kempis's not hers. Now he had another debt to burden him—one he suspected he wouldn't get an opportunity to repay.

The door beside him opened again, and he hauled himself to his feet. Mazana reappeared, Jambar a pace behind. Kempis's hand hovered over his sword hilt. If the Storm Lady meant to unleash Skirt on him, he'd make sure he took one of the bluebloods with him through Shroud's Gate.

Mazana was facing away from Kempis. He heard a tightness in her voice as she said, "Let's go!" to her bodyguard before starting along the corridor.

Skirt set off in pursuit, Jambar in tow.

As the bluebloods moved away, the wall of water at the rear of the pocket of air advanced with them. Kempis hurriedly fell into step with the shaman. Mazana hadn't said he couldn't come with her, and since staying put would mean allowing the sea to reclaim him, Kempis reckoned he would tag along for now. Wherever the Storm Lady was heading in this hellhole, Sniffer was as likely to be there as anywhere else. And if in the meantime he happened upon a flight of steps leading up to the roof terraces . . .

Kempis scowled.

As if I'm that damned lucky.

Agenta stepped through the double doors that led to the throne room. The underwater passage was gone, but Balen was able to maintain a pocket of air about the Gilgamarian party as it followed the mosaic path down into the sea. The light began to fade. When the kalisch looked up she could make out the corpse of a Chameleon priest floating on the waves above. Then Farrell placed a warning hand on her arm, and she peered ahead to see blurred figures.

Abruptly the sea ended and the throne room opened out. Agenta had expected to find the chamber full of Storm Guards. Instead it was empty but for the emira, her chief minister, and the executioner. The kalisch halted several paces from the Olairians. The irony of her reaching the throne room did not escape her, for it was only through Imerle flooding the palace—if indeed it *had* been the emira—that she had made it this far. She realized the last time she'd been here was with her father, but she put the thought from her mind. If her plan was going to work she needed to keep a rein on her anger, to convince the emira she was no less cold-blooded than Imerle herself.

Was that so far from the truth, though?

The emira said, "Well, well, what have we here?" She scanned the Gilgamarian party, her gaze lingering on Balen before shifting back to Agenta. "Of all the people we expected to encounter this day, you were among the last."

The kalisch's voice was flat. "You failed, Emira."

"To dispose of you, you mean? And yet by coming here you have been gracious enough to give us a second chance."

"You don't deny it, then? That the *Icewing* was attacked by Orsan at your command?"

"Would you believe us if we said otherwise?" Pernay leaned across to whisper something to Imerle, but she motioned him to silence. "We confess, we are curious how you survived the wave and made it back here so swiftly."

"Your betrayal was foreseen. My ship, the *Crest*, was on hand to rescue us."

"But from the absence of your father we assume it did not come quickly enough."

For a heartbeat Agenta could not speak. Cracks began to open in her resolve.

Farrell came to her aid. "The game is up, Emira. Dutia Elemy Meddes, Karan del Orco, Gerrick Long: all survived. They know the role you played in the attack on the *Icewing*."

"Then why are they not here now?"

Farrell ignored the question. "When the survivors return home, word of what happened to the *Icewing* will spread. Soon the whole of the Sabian League will know of your treachery."

"Assuming, of course, those survivors make it off the island. The dragons may have something to say about that, don't you think?" Then to Agenta she said, "We owe you a debt. By bringing the *Icewing*'s passengers to Olaire, you have made the task of rounding them up so much simpler."

"And how do you propose to show your thanks?"

Imerle gave a thin smile. Then she gestured with one hand.

The ceiling collapsed.

Agenta flinched as the sea plunged down. Beside her, Balen threw up his arms.

And the water stopped.

The ceiling of the throne room had transformed from a smooth, glassy plane into a misshapen convex dome with threads of water hanging down like stalactites. Droplets fell from those stalactites as if they were made of ice. Agenta saw in Balen's gritted teeth what it cost him to hold the sea in place. Imerle's expression, by contrast, was cool, even sleepy. She cocked her head to inspect the young water-mage.

Then fires kindled in her eyes.

Water began to pour from Balen's face. He sank to his knees. Within moments his robes were drenched. He seemed to age before Agenta's eyes, the flesh of his face melting away even as his skin grew ashen and wrinkled. His lips vanished, his nose withered, black bags formed beneath his eyes. He doubled over, clutching his head in his hands.

Agenta's hackles rose. The emira was drawing the water from his body. Soon he would be nothing but a dried-up husk. She spun to face Imerle. "Wait! We can still deal!"

"And what is it you have to offer us, Kalisch?"

"You talk of hunting down the *Icewing*'s survivors, but there are sure to be some who escape your clutches. And once word gets out that you attacked your own flagship, it won't take long for people to realize that you were behind the sabotage of the Dragon Gate. If I were to support a different account of what happened on the *Icewing*—"

"Agenta," Farrell cut in.

"Quiet!" Then to the emira, "If I were to support a different account—I, who lost my father on the ship—would that not take the sting out of any accusations leveled against you?"

Imerle's gaze bored into her. The kalisch met it without looking away. To her right Balen's breath was a rasp, while to her left she heard Farrell shifting his weight from one foot to the other. Imerle glanced at the merchant. There would be hurt in his expression, Agenta knew, perhaps even anger at the kalisch's betrayal, but she couldn't afford to let the sensitivities of her companions distract her. All of her attention was focused on the emira. There was suspicion in Imerle's eyes, but there was calculation too. Would the emira believe Agenta's proposal was genuine? Would she trust in the kalisch's silence enough to take the deal that was offered?

Imerle drummed her fingers on the arms of her throne, then looked at her chief minister.

It was the opening Agenta had been waiting for. Her right hand snapped forward, and the throwing star she'd been holding went whistling through the air. The throw went straight for the emira's sternum over the heart. Pernay shouted a warning, but it was too late—

There was a clang of metal on metal, and the star fell to the ground.

Agenta stared at the executioner's sword now shielding the emira's chest. Somehow the giant had drawn his blade and brought it down to intercept the missile. Now he returned the weapon to its scabbard and settled back into his relaxed stance, his gaze fixing on nothing.

Agenta cursed.

Points of color appeared on Imerle's cheeks, and the smile she directed at the kalisch was glacial. Then her smile faded as her eyes flickered to something over Agenta's shoulder.

Behind, footfalls sounded.

Kempis was beginning to think he should have stayed behind in the flooded corridors. How in the Sender's name had it come to this? He'd joined Mazana's party in the hope of finding Sniffer, but instead he had walked in on something that smelled as bad as the Untarian's fishy breath. To his left the Gilgamarian water-mage knelt in a puddle as if he'd pissed himself. Sparks were coming off his flint-eyed female companion, and Kempis was guessing the throwing star on the floor near Imerle hadn't been dropped there by the emira. Evidently the different factions here were intent on spilling each other's blood to see whose ran the bluest. To cap it all, Imerle was staring at Kempis like he'd just suggested a tumble behind the thrones. He realized how it must look to her, him standing among the ranks of Mazana Creed's followers.

He shuffled back a pace.

The emira turned her attention to Mazana Creed. "Mazana, what a pleasant surprise."

"We need to talk."

"You wish to discuss the terms of your surrender?"

Jambar said, "Emira—"

"Silence."

"Emira, listen to me!" the shaman continued. "I know who the stone-skins are and why they are here. I know what is coming."

Fires smoldered in the depths of Imerle's eyes. "What you *say* is coming."

"You question my art? I warned you about the assassin, did I not?"

"Because it served your purpose to do so. Just as it served you to lie to us about Senar Sol saving our life, is that not so?"

Mazana spoke to Jambar. "I told you she wouldn't listen. She doesn't know what happened in the Founder's Citadel. She still thinks she is the stronger."

Kempis's eyes narrowed. The Founder's Citadel? How did the fortress fit into all this?

Who cares? he rebuked himself. He should be concentrating on getting out of here alive, not indulging his curiosity in blueblood business. A look round revealed no one was paying him any notice. He retreated another half step.

Jambar's gaze hadn't strayed from the emira. "If I thought this was a battle you could win, do you think I would be standing on *this* side of the room?"

Imerle's tone was mocking. "What do you propose?" She looked at Mazana. "An alliance between us?"

"You need her," Jambar said, then glanced at Mazana. "You need each other. Against what is coming—"

"And do you believe for a moment," the emira cut in, "that she would ever be satisfied with one of these other five thrones?" She gestured to the chairs to either side.

It was Mazana who answered. "Of course not, my dear. But *you* might."

"You expect us to step down graciously, is that it?"

"While you still can, yes. All that has taken place today—the attack on Olaire, the disturbance in Dian—can be laid at the door of the stone-skins."

"And what of us?"

"You would remain a Storm Lady—take your place in the succession and wait for your time to come again."

The flint-eyed Gilgamarian woman snorted. "The hell she would."

Imerle and Mazana ignored her.

Kempis shifted his weight. He didn't understand half of what was being said, but the smell he'd caught when he entered the chamber was getting worse. If the bluebloods meant to cover up the emira's part in the invasion, they would want to dispose of any witnesses whose silence they couldn't rely upon. And since none of those present had any reason to trust Kempis . . .

The throne room had fallen still. Even the susurration of the sea seemed to fade. Then the emira broke the silence. "Strange," she said to Mazana. "Just a short time ago we received a similar offer from Caval Flood."

"You seem to be running thin on allies."

"What makes you think the answer we give you will be any different from the one we gave him?"

The Storm Lady shrugged. "I don't."

Imerle's cold smile was in marked contrast to the heat in her blazing eyes.

Kempis retreated again. The fuse had been lit, he sensed. The others in the chamber knew it too. The chief minister was sitting forward in his chair, ready to bolt. One of the Gilgamarians—a red-faced man with a shield strapped to his back—was edging to position himself between his flint-eyed mistress and the emira. Skirt's right hand hovered over his sword hilt.

Then Imerle's left arm snapped forward. A spear of fire flashed toward Mazana, briefly lighting up the throne room.

In front of the Storm Lady, a curtain of water descended from the ceiling to intercept the emira's attack. The flames fizzled out with a hiss of steam, and what remained of the curtain collapsed into droplets.

Nobody moved. Had it not been for the curls of vapor rising from the floor, Kempis might have wondered if he'd imagined the sorcerous exchange.

Then Mazana wagged a finger at Imerle.

The room exploded into motion.

The executioner bellowed a challenge and hurled himself at Skirt. Mazana's bodyguard unsheathed his blade and leapt to meet him. Pernay sprang from his chair and took cover behind it. To Kempis's left the red-faced Gilgamarian unlimbered his shield and brought it round to screen his flint-eyed kinswoman.

Time to say my good-byes.

Senar dispatched his male Chameleon foe just as the young priestess's dagger buried itself in Tali's left shoulder. Gathering his Will, Senar lashed out at the thrower. The priestess was standing close to the edge of the terrace overlooking the sea, and the blow sent her staggering backward. A futile twist and jerk for balance, then she toppled into the waves.

The impact of her dagger had spoiled Tali's attack on Caval, dragging the twin's sword arm down so that her blade missed his neck and scored a crimson gash across his chest. He countered with a backhand cut, but Mili intercepted the stroke, her sword skewering his arm below the elbow. The arm spasmed, and Mili's weapon was wrenched from her grasp to go skittering across the terrace. She responded by unleashing a kick that caught Caval under the chin and lifted him from his feet. He hit the ground hard and rolled a few paces before coming to a halt. He lay still, most likely unconscious. Or perhaps he just had the sense not to come back for more.

Sheathing his sword, Senar crossed to join Tali. The priestess's dagger was embedded below the twin's collar bone, and its hilt when he seized it was sticky with blood. He looked at Tali. She nodded. From the resignation in her look she knew what pain was coming, but it wasn't as if they could leave the knife in her. Gripping her shoulder with his halfhand, he tugged the blade clear. Tali screamed and sagged into his arms. Senar looked down on her blond scalp. Another woman in his embrace, yet they never seemed to stay there for long. Blood was oozing from her wound onto his shirt. He pushed her upright, then raised her right hand and pressed it to her injured shoulder.

"Keep pressure on this."

Tali nodded a second time, trembling as if with cold, yet the touch of the sun was so fierce it had already started to dry Senar's clothes. He crouched to tear a strip from the robe of his Chameleon victim for a bandage.

The sound of Mili's breath hissing out drew him up. He looked round, expecting to see more Chameleons rushing toward them. Mili, though, was staring not along the roof terrace but out to sea.

Senar followed her gaze.

A short distance away the young Chameleon priestess was struggling to keep her head above water. The fins of two briar sharks were approaching from the north, though whether they'd been drawn by the priestess or by the bodies in the palace, Senar could not say. He should extend the same courtesy to the woman that he'd shown to the twins in the flooded passages, he knew. Then he realized it wasn't the swimmer that had caught Mili's eye. In the sea beyond her, a flash of red light sparked. A reflection on the water? No, this came from beneath the surface. *The throne room.* Evidently someone had fought through to the emira, and a sorcerous duel was now taking place under the waves. Mazana? It had to be, for who else in Olaire could stand toe-to-toe with Imerle?

Senar watched the smears of light sway and sparkle, wondering what his next move should be. He turned to scan the terraces. The closest ones looked deserted, but that meant little when there were Chameleons abroad. On the crest of a tiled roof a gray-cloaked soldier was engaged in a wobbling duel with a Storm Guard. The other warriors scattered about seemed in no hurry to resume the hostilities that had been interrupted when the sea came crashing in. To the west three soldiers were making for a rocky shoreline beyond the palace boundaries. If Senar tried to follow them, would the twins let him go? After the business with the shark they'd forged a fragile alliance in order to meet the Chameleon threat, but he still wasn't entirely comfortable having Tali at his back now, injured though she was.

Then again, he'd never exactly been comfortable having the sisters at his front either. More to the point, if the emira triumphed here she was unlikely to forget his betrayal. She would send her followers to hunt him down, and how long could he hope to hide from them in an unfamiliar city? Where could he go that might offer him shelter? The Erin Elalese embassy? That would be the first place Imerle thought to look. And even if the ambassador didn't hand him straight over to the emira, Senar doubted the rules of diplomatic immunity would hold the embassy's doors against the executioner. Like it or not, his fate was tied to Mazana's.

He scratched at the stubs of his missing fingers. It should never have come to this. He should have gone with her to fight the emira. Her words from outside the temple of the Lord of Hidden Faces came back to him. *I don't need any of you!* she'd said. Maybe that was true now that she'd absorbed Fume's spirit, but Senar wasn't one to leave his fate in the hands of another. He needed to get in on the fight, and that meant reaching the throne room. If he dived down he might be able to enter the chamber through its ceiling, yet the sorcerous light show was more than thirty paces from the roof terrace. The briar sharks would doubtless close on him before he made it that far.

Movement to the north. When Senar looked across he saw a shadow in the sea beyond the Watchtower at Ferris Point. At first he thought it was a shoal of fish. A big one. Then the water began to boil and bulge as something stirred in the depths.

Senar's stomach clenched as the head of a copper-scaled dragon burst from the waves—the same dragon, in all likelihood, that he'd seen pursuing the Gilgamarian ship earlier. Sunlight flashed off its head and neck, and beneath the sea its immense body glittered like a jewel. The creature must have spotted the Guardian and the twins for it trumpeted a challenge and surged forward, its neck cutting through the water like the prow of a ship. In front of it rolled a wave an armspan high.

Senar stood his ground.

Karmel floundered in the sea near the terrace. When she tried to move her left arm, agony ripped through it. Judging by the pains shooting through her side she must have been charged by a lederel bull, yet when she looked back at the terrace all she saw were the twins and their black-haired companion.

A lump came to her throat. Meaning both Caval and Foss were down. Doubtless the priestess would soon be sharing their fate if either twin deemed her worth the cost of a throwing knife, but what did it matter? What did anything matter?

My brother is dead.

Just then she heard an all-too-familiar trumpeting behind. She twisted round to see a horned copper head burst from the waves. *No, it can't be.* Higher and higher it rose, until it seemed to Karmel as if the dragon's head must brush the wispy clouds. It was still several hundred armspans away, but the gap was closing. If it hadn't seen Karmel already, it surely would when it neared the terrace.

Her pain forgotten, she turned and kicked for the seawall.

What would she do when she reached it, though? The terrace was too far above her for her to pull herself up, and it wasn't as if one of her enemies was going to offer her a hand. She could activate her powers to make herself invisible to the dragon. That would mean stilling her movements, however, which in turn meant finding something to hold on to that would keep her afloat. Aminex's corpse bobbed in the water to her left. If Karmel used him as a buoy, though, she might find herself devoured by the dragon if it came looking for easy meat.

That left swimming down to the arched doors and reentering the palace. Drawing in a breath, she prepared to dive.

But she hadn't reckoned on the wave created by the dragon's coming. The sea swelled beneath her, and she was lifted up and over the lip of the terrace to bump and roll across its flagstones. Her hands grasped for something to slow her rush. In vain. She fell headfirst into the courtyard beyond, cracking her skull on stone.

Blackness rose to claim her.

As Kempis turned to flee, his eye was caught by movement in the wall of water behind the Gilgamarians.

He blinked.

Far off in the sea, a shape moved toward the chamber. A shark, perhaps? No, it was too big. Bigger, he realized with a start, than the wreck of a galley he could make out on a reef to the east. As it drew nearer, Kempis saw sunlight glinting off scales. A shoal of fish? But then what were the twin globes of golden flame that suddenly kindled in the deep?

Understanding dawned.

His jaw dropped.

The dragon's head streamed water as it burst through the wall to Agenta's left. For a heartbeat the kalisch's wonder overshadowed her fear as she gazed at the crest of copper spikes atop its head, the scratches and weapon marks across its snout, the tinge of verdigris round its nostrils. Then its lips peeled back and she saw gobbets of flesh and shreds of clothing trapped between its teeth. Its breath smelled of corruption. Flashes of sorcery from the battle between Imerle and Mazana reflected in its eyes, and Agenta felt herself sinking into the oblivion of those glistening golden orbs.

Warner shouted a warning, but the kalisch couldn't move—

Someone bundled into her and she staggered forward a pace before sprawling to her hands and knees. One of her fingernails snagged in the gap between two mosaic stones and was torn loose. She ignored the pain. Knowing the dragon could pounce on her at any instant, she dived forward, then lurched upright and turned so quickly she almost spun herself from her feet.

In time to see the dragon's jaws close about Farrell as gently as if the creature were picking up one of its young. Farrell, who must have given her that push.

The merchant gave a coughing wheeze as his breath was squeezed from his chest. His eyes clouded with horror. The dragon began to withdraw, and Farrell's hands reached out for something to grab on to. If Agenta had been holding her last throwing star she would have hurled it at one of the dragon's eyes, but the missile remained strapped to her wrist. So instead she tottered forward and seized one of Farrell's hands. The futility of the move struck her. What was she going to do, play tug-of-war with a dragon? Would she hold Farrell still while Warner prized the beast's teeth apart, maybe talked it into taking Imerle instead?

Farrell gripped her hand with a strength born of desperation. As the dragon retreated Agenta was yanked from her feet and dragged across the floor. She hit the wall of water and felt a slap of cold. Then the sea closed about her. There were bubbles in her eyes. Ahead an expanse of copper scales marked the dragon's flank, while below a glint of talons showed as one of the creature's feet churned the sea-bed to smoky brown. Agenta hadn't thought to snatch a breath before the water claimed her. Her lungs were already burning. There was nothing she could do to help Farrell, and his gesture in saving her would be rendered meaningless if she died here. She should return to the throne room.

Like hell she would.

Beyond the merchant the dragon's eyes shone like beacons. Perhaps the beast might open its jaws to try to scoop her up too and in doing so give Farrell a chance to swim clear.

Then Farrell's hand slipped from hers, and she realized he had pulled it back to break the contact. She reached after him, but he was already retreating into the blue as the dragon's head twisted up and away. A moment later all she could see of him was a smudge of pink from his shirt. Then that too was gone. She kicked her legs to follow. The currents left in the dragon's wake were already drawing her away from the throne room—

Hands grabbed her ankles, and she was wrenched back into the chamber.

She hit the floor and lay shivering, coughing up water between her choked sobs. Her ears were filled with the clash of swords, the hiss of quenched sorcery, Warner's voice growling something unintelligible. Blood ran from her finger where her nail had been torn away. *You fool!* she silently raged at Farrell. Doubtless he'd intended only to knock her out of the dragon's way, rather than sacrifice himself, but that wasn't the point. It should have been her the creature took, not him!

He had no right.

A shout from Warner brought her attention back to her immediate surroundings. She looked across to see a stranger with skin like granite step into the throne room through the wall of water a few paces away. His sodden green robes were torn and tattered, and in his hand he held a broadsword.

A glance round to get his bearings.

Then he took a stride toward Balen and plunged his weapon into the mage's back.

CHAPTER 22

THE DREGS of the wave created by the dragon's coming swirled about Senar's legs, immersing the roof terrace in ankle-deep froth. A stone's throw away the creature's head rose from the sea. In its mouth was a figure, and the Guardian's blood ran cold. Mazana? No, the unfortunate soul's screams were unmistakably male. The dragon shook its victim like a dog would a rat, then threw back its head and tossed the man into the air before catching him and wolfing him down. One of the emira's followers? Senar shook his head. Not tall enough to be the chief minister, not . . . crunchy . . . enough to be the executioner.

Another burst of red light flashed beneath the waves, and the dragon began to sink into the sea once more.

Senar's expression hardened. *Oh no you don't.* The creature's prey hadn't been Mazana on this occasion, but next time . . .

Gathering his Will, the Guardian delivered a slap to the beast's snout. To the dragon it would feel no more weighty than a puff of air, yet still its head swung round.

Senar's pulse kicked in his neck.

The creature stared at him. Its golden eyes were orbs of smoky glass, and along its neck was a crest of copper spines tangled with fireweed. When it trumpeted, the Guardian caught a whiff of rotting flesh. Protruding from the scales behind its left ear was a spear, a gift no doubt from one of the sailors on the Dragon Hunt. Something told Senar the beast had returned the gift with interest.

Then a light went off in his head. Thus far his only thought had been to draw the dragon away from the throne room, but now an idea had come to him. An idea appalling in its audacity. If he could reach that spear . . .

With a roar that eclipsed the thunder of the sea, the dragon surged toward the roof terrace. It felt to Senar like he was standing in the path of an avalanche. He sensed the twins at his shoulder.

"Stay behind me," he shouted. "I will fashion a shield."

"To the Sender . . ."

". . . with that, Guardian."

"The dragon will not . . ."

". . . leave the sea."

"We should flee this place . . ."

". . . while we still can."

Senar paused. If he told the sisters what he planned to do they would probably turn on him, yet if he offered no explanation for staying he could hardly expect them to stand with him. "You go. I will keep the creature entertained."

"Why?"

"Because if the dragon's attention is on us, it can't also be on those in the throne room."

It sounded weak even to his own ears. How long could he and the twins hope to distract a creature that size? How were they supposed to fight it when their weapons wouldn't even scratch its armor? Yet when he glanced back moments later the sisters were still behind him. Tali's eyes were dull with pain, Mili's wide with fright. They weren't grinning anymore, but neither were they making to flee.

Senar still held the dagger he'd pulled from Tali's shoulder, and he transferred it from his left hand to his right. "Our blades will be useless against dragon scales. If you get the chance, go for the eyes."

Neither of the twins replied.

He spun back to the sea to find the dragon just twenty armspans away. It trumpeted another challenge that doused Senar in spray. Taking a breath, he gathered his Will and began weaving layer upon layer of his power into a barrier in front of him. He angled the shield into the terrace, hoping that when the dragon struck, the force of the blow would be directed down into the roof. Behind him the twins were murmuring a prayer to the Sender.

Ten armspans. The dragon's mouth opened wide in greeting.

Five.

Senar braced himself.

The dragon's head slammed into his Will-shield with a force the Guardian felt as a stab of agony through his skull. Lights flashed before his eyes, and he groaned. It seemed as if the whole palace shuddered at the impact. Senar's bones vibrated in time. He stumbled back into the twins. A fissure appeared in the terrace beside his left foot.

But the Will-barrier held.

The dragon recoiled from the collision, dazed. Then it darted forward again. With a noise like a gauntleted fist hitting an open palm, it smashed into the Will-shield a second time. This time Senar's pain was so intense he thought one of the twins must have stabbed him in the head. The fissure by his foot widened, and water came bubbling up from the flooded corridor below. Any moment now the ground was going to open up and swallow him. But better the ground than the dragon, he supposed.

The creature growled as it readied itself for another attack. Senar let his Will-shield fall. Maybe the barrier could withstand a third blow, but the Guardian's head couldn't. As the shield faded he pulled back his right arm and sent his dagger spinning end over end toward the dragon's right eye. The weapon buried itself in the orb, and the creature gave a salty bellow. It blinked its metal eyelids, then lifted a clawed foot and cuffed at the eye.

Senar drew his sword, his gaze flickering to the spear jutting from behind the dragon's left ear. The weapon was sunk so deep into the creature's flesh that none of its metal head was visible. It was farther back than he'd thought, and higher too, but he might still be able to reach it if he jumped. First he had to stay clear of the beast's jaws, though.

With a shriek that parted his hair, the creature came on again.

"Scatter!" he called to the twins.

As if they needed telling.

Senar hurled himself to his right across a roof terrace slick with water.

Kempis watched openmouthed as the stone-skin tugged his sword from the Gilgamarian sorcerer.

After emerging through the wall to the septia's left, the green-robed man had sized up the chamber before making for Jug-Ears. Kempis's shouted warning had come too late to save the Gilgamarian, and now yet another water-mage would be joining the stampede through Shroud's Gate. What did these stone-skins have against sorcerers? And why had the newcomer killed Jug-Ears when the likes of Imerle and Mazana battled only a short distance away? Perhaps for no other reason than the Gilgamarian had been in his path. The way was open now, though, wasn't it? If the stone-skin wanted to advance on the women, Kempis wasn't going to stop him.

The trouble was, the newcomer had already recognized Kempis and appeared unwilling to turn his back on him. *Smart man.* So rather than attacking Imerle and Mazana, the stone-skin came for the septia instead. Alone, Kempis knew he wouldn't last long against the stranger. Fortunately, though, Jug-Ears's red-faced kinsman—a trita judging by the stripes on his soldier—had taken exception to the stone-skin butchering his friend. He hurled himself at the man, his sword whistling through the leaden air. Kempis held back a smile. The Gilgamarians wanted Imerle dead, the stone-skin wanted Imerle dead, yet here they were fighting each other. Maybe he should step in to clear things up.

He'd have to think about that one.

Kempis hadn't got a good look at Loop's killer when he encountered him in the Shallows. Closer now, he saw the man's face was covered with bruises, and his sodden green robe was slashed in dozens of places. Whoever had inflicted those wounds was a better warrior than Red-Face, though, for the stone-skin easily repelled the trita's initial onslaught before driving him back toward Jug-Ears and the flint-eyed woman. One of the stone-skin's thrusts, only half blocked, sliced open Red-Face's right cheek, and the trita huddled behind his shield as blows crashed down upon it like a blacksmith's hammer on an anvil.

A flash of light from Imerle's sorcerous clash with Mazana roused Kempis from his reverie. It seemed he wouldn't get away with leaving Red-Face to do all the work, so he drew his sword and advanced. His preferred bellow-and-charge style of fighting was as likely to distract Red-Face as the stone-skin, so he moved left in an effort to flank his foe. The stone-skin responded by putting his back to the wall of water through which the dragon had appeared earlier.

Now if the creature would just return for its main course . . .

Red-Face attacked the stone-skin, his sword dancing in his hand. The stone-skin was forced onto the defensive, yet still he managed to keep one eye on Kempis as the septia edged further round. All Kempis had to do was wait for his foe to be distracted by one of Red-Face's strikes—

Got you.

Extending his sword arm, Kempis lunged forward.

And almost impaled himself on the stone-skin's blade. An eye-blink ago the man's weapon had been parrying a blow from Red-Face. Now its tip was in front of Kempis, and he had to twist his body to avoid running himself through. It should have been impossible for anyone to maneuver a broadsword that quickly, yet the stone-skin had already recovered the blade and now swung it in a cut that the septia only just blocked in time.

Kempis grimaced. He'd never been much good at swordplay, but then what was the point of being a septia if you couldn't get someone else to do your fighting for you? He tried to time his attacks now so they landed with Red-Face's—not even the stone-skin's blade could be in two places at once—yet somehow his enemy's sword was always there to parry. It wasn't as if the bastard was only defending, either. A decapitating slash had Kempis jumping back off balance, and he stumbled and went down on one knee.

The stone-skin turned on Red-Face. After blocking a lunge from the Gilgamarian, he stabbed out with his free hand and delivered a punch to the trita's forehead that knocked the man onto his back.

Before the stone-skin could move in for the kill, Kempis bellowed to distract him. He had to admit, he liked how things were going so far—he did the shouting and Red-Face did the bleeding.

Playing to my strengths.

His foe's head swung round.

Senar rolled to evade the dragon's jaws and came to his feet again. Mili stood beside him, but Tali was nowhere to be seen—doubtless she'd dived left instead of right when the dragon came for them and was now hidden from Senar's view by the creature's head. She must have attacked at that moment because from the dragon's opposite flank came a peal of metal as her sword deflected off its scales. As the beast turned to confront her, gaps opened up between the plates on the side of its neck facing Senar. He darted forward, his sword stabbing for one of those openings.

Only for it to close at the last moment as the dragon shifted position. Senar's blade ricocheted off its armor with a tortured scream of steel.

The creature swung toward him, and he scuttled back.

This was hopeless. They could chip away at the dragon's scales all day, yet it would still be their weapons that gave way first. Senar's only chance of ending this was to reach the spear in the creature's neck, but for now the weapon remained tantalizingly out of range, five armspans back along the beast's neck. He needed to lure the dragon farther out of the sea, but how?

Mili skipped past the creature's snout. She could not reach its eyes with her sword so instead she thrust her weapon into its gaping mouth. Her needle-thin blade clattered off its teeth before tracing a red line across its lower lip. The dragon flinched, then snapped at her. Fast as the beast was, Mili was faster, her long stride taking her past the dragon and out of range.

Or so Senar thought.

Jets of water shot from the creature's nostrils, striking the woman and sending her tumbling. She rolled to the edge of the terrace overlooking the courtyard. The dragon raised a clawed foot onto the roof and dragged its front quarters from the sea. The terrace groaned and shifted. Tiles crumbled round its talons, fissures running outward like cracks in shattered glass.

Senar heard Tali attack again from the beast's opposite flank in an attempt to draw its eye, her blade clanging off its armor. The dragon seemed not to notice.

My turn.

The Guardian lashed out with his Will at the side of its head. His stroke landed with a sound like a bell tolling. The dragon paused, and that pause gave Mili time to scramble upright. Pulling back her right arm, she flung her sword like a spear at the dragon's face. No doubt she'd aimed for one of its eyes, but Senar did not see if her blade found its mark. His gaze was fixed on Mili, for in making the throw she'd sacrificed the heartbeat she needed to dive clear.

Ignoring the thrown sword, the dragon lunged forward.

Senar shouted a warning.

Mili stepped back off the roof, her hands reaching out to grab the edge as she fell.

The creature's teeth closed on nothing.

Senar saw his chance. The dragon's lunge had brought its head forward, and the spear embedded in its neck was now within reach. Sheathing his sword, the Guardian sprang forward. A part of him couldn't believe he was doing this. A part of him expected the dragon's head to turn at the last moment, and for Senar to find himself charging down its throat. A fitting end that would have made to this sorry affair. Instead the dragon continued to sniff after Mili, and the Guardian closed to within a few paces of the beast, then gathered himself and leapt.

At the point of takeoff, though, the terrace lurched beneath him, and his leap became more trip than jump.

He crashed into a wall of dragon scales.

When Karmel came to, she was lying on her back. Water lapped at the corners of her eyes, and there was water in her ears too, muting the sounds from the palace about her. As she sat up those sounds burst into life. On all sides water splashed into the courtyard from windows along the walls, and above that came the clank of a sword striking what she assumed was a shield. Karmel frowned. It had come from the terrace. Evidently some newcomer had climbed from the flooded corridors to pick a fight with the twins, and yet how could anyone think of settling scores when there was a dragon on the loose? Had Karmel been unconscious so long that the creature had moved on?

She looked round. Bobbing in the shin-deep water all about were fallen fruits from the malirange trees that ringed the courtyard. A few armspans to her left was the corpse of the weaponsmaster, while to her right . . .

Caval.

Gods, no. She rose and limped to where her brother floated facedown in the water, then fell to her knees beside him. She turned him onto his back and lifted his head. Liquid trickled from his mouth. His eyes stared back at her sightlessly. Death had smoothed the creases from his brow, stripping years from his face, and for an instant

Karmel saw again the brother she'd shared the boat with as a child. Blinking rapidly, she reached out—

A shadow fell across her. She looked up.

Then froze.

One of the twins was hanging into the courtyard from the terrace, and looming above her was the copper-scaled dragon. Rage shone in its eyes, one of which, Karmel noticed, had a sword embedded in it. The creature's gaze swept the courtyard before coming to rest on Karmel and Caval. Absurdly the priestess found herself reaching for her blade. Was she going to fight the beast over her brother's corpse? Had she escaped the dragons in the seas off Dian just so she could serve herself up to this creature?

Still she held her ground, too numbed even to release her power and hide herself.

The dragon's head moved toward her. Its lips parted to reveal red-rimmed teeth, and Karmel smelled the fetid saltiness of its breath. She felt as if she were falling into its shimmering eyes. Then it gave a roar and recoiled, its head twisting round to snap at something behind.

Karmel took a shuddering breath. She should flee before the dragon returned, she knew. But that would mean leaving Caval, and she wasn't yet ready to bid him farewell. The finality of his death hit her. Her shoulders sagged, her breath caught in her throat. If she'd gone to his aid sooner against the twins he might be alive now. It was her hesitation as much as the final sword thrust that had killed him . . .

She stiffened.

The final sword thrust.

So where was the wound? She scanned Caval's body. There was a cut along his chest, a bruise across his chin and jaw, and his shirt was bloody round a puncture in his right arm midway between wrist and elbow. But none of those injuries would have killed him. Karmel pictured the final moments of his fight with Mili and Tali. The priestess's thrown knife had spoiled one of the sisters' attacks, but Karmel had been hurled into the water before she saw what came next. And by the time she'd resurfaced, her brother was down. What if he'd merely been knocked unconscious? What if the twins had been distracted by the dragon before they could deliver a mortal wound?

Hope kindled inside her. The sister she'd seen hanging into the courtyard had now climbed back to the terrace, so Karmel moved alongside Caval and pushed down on his chest to expel any liquid from his lungs. So deep was the water in the yard, however, that all she succeeded in doing was forcing his head and body beneath the surface. *Shit.* She looked round. At the edge of the courtyard was a bench, and she struggled to her feet before seizing Caval by his collar. With her right hand only, she dragged him toward it through bobbing malirange fruits. Lifting him onto the seat required the use of her injured left arm as well, and the effort tore a groan from her.

Caval was lying on his front. She rolled him onto his back and freed his right arm where it had become trapped beneath him. When she applied force to his chest, just below the rib cage, she saw liquid gush from his mouth. She turned his head to one side then repeated the action until the flow of water ceased.

So much water . . .

Karmel took a breath, then bent down and covered Caval's mouth with hers. She blew out the air she'd inhaled—only to feel that breath brush her cheek as it came out of his nose. She cursed. She wasn't thinking straight. Pinching his nostrils shut, she tried again.

This time his chest rose.

Frantic now, Karmel lowered an ear to his mouth to listen for breathing, but she couldn't make out anything over the splashing of water all about. Interlacing the fingers of both hands, she placed the heel of her right palm in the middle of Caval's chest and began pressing. The movement sent pain lancing through her left side, but she paid it no mind. Again and again she pushed, fighting a growing trembling in her arms.

Caval remained still.

Anger welled up inside her, and she increased the rate of her compressions, putting all her strength into it. *Come on, damn you! Breathe!* She felt one of his ribs crack beneath her hands.

Still nothing.

Karmel's eyes misted. She was wasting her time. For all she knew, Caval had broken his neck when he fell from the terrace. Or one of the twins had crushed his windpipe, or landed some other fatal blow on him that the priestess hadn't seen. Even if Karmel was right and he *had* drowned, he could have passed through Shroud's Gate quarter of a bell ago, for she had no way of knowing how long she had blacked out for.

And yet wouldn't his flesh have been colder if he'd been dead all that time?

Karmel stared down at his face. His eyes remained closed, and his expression was peaceful. She wondered if she was right to try to bring him back. What did he have to return to? The Chameleons were finished, and the surviving priests in Olaire would be hunted down by Imerle's forces. If Karmel revived him the two of them might not even make it as far as the palace gates. And if he *did* come back, like as not the lines on his forehead would return too.

Pushing her doubts aside, Karmel blew another lungful of air into his mouth.

Agenta knelt beside Balen and took his hand in hers. His skin felt rough as leather. The mage was younger than the kalisch, but the ravages of Imerle's sorcery had left him shrunken like one of the mummified corpses Agenta had seen in a Karalatian tomb last year. His breath rattled in his throat. She knew she should say something to ease his passing, yet even as she groped for the words the light faded in his eyes. He slumped into her arms. She eased his body to the floor. When she raised her hands she saw his blood was on them. *His and all the others'.* Of the Gilgamarians who had set out for the palace, were she and Warner the only ones now alive? How many had died to deliver her here, and for what?

Thinking of the dead just brought back the image of Rethell on the *Icewing*'s deck. A tightness gripped her chest so she couldn't breathe. She wished her father were here.

Or she were with him.

She looked to where Warner fought alongside the Watchman against the stone-skinned stranger—another of the emira's lackeys, she supposed, for why else had he attacked Balen? Even outnumbered, the green-robed man seemed to be doing most of the attacking, but whenever he carved out an opening against one opponent, the other would move to close it. Agenta's gaze flickered to the Watchman. She'd seen him somewhere before, but where?

A burst of light drew her eye to the northern end of the chamber. Imerle stood enveloped in sorcerous flames, while a handful of paces away was Mazana Creed, almost invisible at the center of a storm of glittering energies. A blast of Mazana's magic ricocheted off an invisible shield in front of the emira before exploding against one of the walls of water in a thousand multicolored sparks. To the women's right, Mazana's bodyguard was battling the executioner. In the span of Agenta's gaze she saw the Storm Lady's man connect with a slash that clanged off the metal threads across the giant's abdomen.

The kalisch's first throwing star lay on the floor where it had fallen, now melted by sorcery. She was conscious of the remaining star at her left wrist. Her route to Imerle was blocked by Mazana, but if she circled to her right she might find a place for a clear throw. If the emira's defenses could shield her from Mazana's magic, though, would they not also shield her from the star?

Perhaps an opportunity would present itself later for Agenta to dispatch Imerle. For now the kalisch's priority had to be helping Warner against the stone-skin.

Even as the thought came to her, she saw the trita floored by a punch. The Watchman bellowed to catch the stone-skin's attention.

Agenta drew her sword.

Kempis swore as the stone-skin advanced on him. Doubtless Red-Face would return to the fray in heartbeats, but the septia wouldn't last even that long against this foe. He took two steps back.

Then realized his mistake. The stone-skin was a damned water-mage, wasn't he? The lull in the fighting gave him time to use his sorcery, and immediately above Kempis the ceiling collapsed. A torrent of water slammed down onto him as if he were standing beneath a waterfall. Through a curtain of spray he saw a blur of green as the stone-skin approached.

He flung himself to his left.

Agenta edged forward, her gaze fixed on the stone-skin's blade. It struck her that, for all her weapons training, this would be the first time she'd fought someone for keeps. She shouted a challenge, and the swordsman swung to face her. His gaze when it met Agenta's was as stony as his complexion.

The flood of water battering the Watchman ceased.

There was movement in the sea behind the stone-skin. Agenta

thought that the dragon had returned, but the shadow of the creature's body remained visible to the south. Closer, she saw what appeared to be a vast serpent, barbed like a flense whip, yet as broad
around as her torso.

And it was coming closer still.

The dragon's tail broke the wall of water, whipping spray across
the room. To the kalisch's right Warner, just climbing to his feet,
raised his shield, and the tail struck it. The trita was hurled from his
feet.

Then the tail slammed into Agenta and she went down.

The collision with the dragon knocked Senar's breath from him,
jarring the ribs he'd bruised in the flooded passages. He threw out
his arms, desperate for something to hold on to. His right hand
missed the spear, but his left—his halfhand—curled round the top of
one of the dragon's scales, and for a precarious moment he hung from
it by two fingers. Through the beast's scales he could sense the heat
of its body, feel the pulse of the arteries in its neck. Just above him
was the spear, and as his fingers began to slip he grabbed for it with
his free hand.

Got it.

The downward force on the weapon must have ground its point
into the dragon's flesh, for the creature trumpeted with rage then
craned its neck round, snarling and snapping. Senar was too close to
the beast's head for it to reach him, but its twisting made the scales
about the Guardian's halfhand pinch tight, threatening to shear
through his remaining fingers. He snatched the hand back and
grabbed the spear with it, praying the weapon was anchored securely
enough to take his full weight.

The dragon trumpeted again then tossed its head in an effort to
dislodge him, shaking Senar until his teeth clattered. Somehow he
clung on. The creature's thrashing was taking it away from the roof,
and when the Guardian looked down he saw waves ten armspans
below, foaming at the dragon's flanks. The terrace was a similar distance to his left and moving farther away. Mili had climbed back up
to the roof to rejoin her sister, and together they stared up at Senar
with expressions of exhaustion and incredulity.

Still, at least it was *him* looking down on *them* for a change.

The spear shaft was beginning to bend under his weight. He removed his halfhand from it and curled its fingers back round one of the dragon's scales. He had to act quickly now in case the creature thought to dunk him into the sea. Moving his right hand along the spear's shaft—away from the dragon's body—he leaned into the weapon with all his strength, driving it into the beast's neck.

The dragon spasmed. Hot black blood spurted from its flesh onto Senar's shirt over his right shoulder and upper arm.

He froze.

Dragon blood.

Matron's mercy!

He recalled the execution of the Untarian three days ago, saw again the poisoned claws of the giant's metal glove stabbing into the condemned man's chest. Senar looked down at his shirt. The cut he'd sustained in the palace had been to his left shoulder, not his right, meaning the dragon's blood would not yet have mixed with his. What effect, though, would the blood have on his skin when it seeped through his shirt? Could it leach through his flesh and into his veins?

Now wasn't the time to worry about that, because the dragon had lifted a taloned foot from the water and was reaching for him. He lashed out with his Will to keep the foot at bay, then adjusted his grip on the spear and leaned into it once more. Grunting and straining, he ground the weapon up and down, round and round. The dragon shrieked and quivered and bucked. And yet for all the pain Senar seemed to be causing it, he still hadn't succeeded in pushing the spear any farther into—

Suddenly the spear slid more than an armspan into the dragon's flesh. The Guardian, with only a short part of the shaft now to hold on to, eased his pressure on the weapon. More blood pumped from the creature's wound. Senar turned his head so it would not splash his face. A groan rattled along the dragon's neck. Music to the Guardian's ears. It gave a hacking cough as if blood was bubbling in its throat.

Time for Senar to take his leave.

Bracing his feet against the dragon's scales he pushed off, twisting in the air to take him clear of a swishing claw.

Now he needed a touch of the Matron's luck.

The terrace was a stone's throne away, but Senar had never intended

to swim back to it. Turning his fall into a dive he plunged toward
the sea, scanning the water below for a telltale flash of light.

Kempis's sternum ached where the dragon's tail had caught him and
sent him flying. When the world righted itself he found himself on
top of the flint-eyed Gilgamarian woman, her face in his left armpit.
She squirmed beneath him, hissing something indecipherable. He
rolled onto his back.

His sword lay in a puddle, and he picked it up and pushed himself
to his feet. Bile rose in his throat. He couldn't remember hitting his
head in the fall, yet the throne room tipped and swayed. The stone-
skin and Red-Face had resumed their disagreement, and he stumbled
toward them, the flint-eyed woman with him. The stone-skin must
have known he couldn't stand for long against three opponents for
he sprang to attack the woman, aiming a slice at her knees. Red-Face
brought his shield round to intercept.

The green-robed man retreated.

Conscious the stone-skin might use a pause to unleash his sorcery
again, Kempis pressed forward. The stone-skin leaned back to evade
a cut, but for once he made no effort to counter. Should have been a
good sign, that, yet for some reason it made Kempis nervous. Red-
Face shuffled left to place himself between his kinswoman and the
stone-skin. He spoke a few words Kempis did not understand, and
the septia risked a look across.

"You talking to me?" he asked in the common tongue.

"You don't speak Gilgamarian?" the trita said, matching his
dialect.

"Next language on my list."

The stone-skin attacked, and Red-Face blocked an overhead strike.
To Kempis he said, "On three, you charge him—"

Kempis's snort cut him short. "*You* charge him! You're the one with
the bloody shield!"

"I'm also the one with the trita's stripes on my shoulder!"

"And maybe that would mean something—if we were in Gilgamar."

Red-Face opened his mouth to speak, but the flint-eyed woman got
in first. "Save your breath, Warner."

"Agenta—"

"The stone-skin can understand what you're saying. I've seen the glint in his eyes."

Kempis regarded the green-robed man thoughtfully. So the bastard knew the common tongue, did he? Perhaps the septia could use that to his advantage.

Warner and the stone-skin traded blows. The addition of Agenta to their ranks had not tipped the balance as Kempis had hoped, for Warner was forever putting his shield between his companion and the stone-skin, thus preventing her from engaging the enemy. Misplaced chivalry, so far as Kempis was concerned, but then was there another kind? The trita parried a cut from the stone-skin and retaliated with a thrust that was turned aside by a deft twirl of his opponent's broadsword. For a heartbeat Warner's blade was trapped—a heartbeat that might have proved fatal had Kempis not attacked at that moment and driven the stone-skin back.

The exchange had given the septia an idea. A few days ago he'd seen Pompit sparring in the Watchstation's exercise yard. The clerk had been showing off a maneuver to a woman among the new recruits. By twisting his wrist at the instant his sword met his opponent's, Pompit had pinned her weapon long enough to steal a kiss. Kempis squinted at the stone-skin. Okay, the kiss might be pushing it, but the pinning-the-sword part had looked simple enough. If the septia could catch his foe's blade, it might give his Gilgamarian allies time to deliver a fatal blow.

One way to find out.

A cut from the green-robed man gave Kempis his opportunity. He blocked the strike, twisting his wrist in the manner he remembered Pompit doing.

Only to find his sword wrenched from his hand. It arced into the air and sailed over his head.

Kempis's eyes widened.

Realizing he would now be defenseless against the stone-skin's next attack, he shouted "Now!" at the top of his voice, hoping to convince his enemy that his blunder had been a deliberate ploy.

The stone-skin hesitated, and Kempis jumped back out of range.

His blade caught briefly in the sea overhead before falling to the floor with a clatter.

The momentum of Senar's fall carried him deep into the sea. Below and to his left were blurred shapes in the water. He swam toward them with frenetic strokes, fearing at any moment he would be plucked from the waves by the dragon seeking revenge. The bursts of red light had come to a sudden end, and it occurred to him the sorcerous contest between Mazana and Imerle might have ended. If that was so—and if Mazana had lost—he would doubtless soon be joining her in a watery grave.

His hands pushed into air. His head and upper body followed, and he took in a breath. Blood rushed to his head as he hung suspended from the throne room's ceiling. Then a kick of his legs, and he was plummeting toward the floor. He twisted to take the brunt of the fall on his left side, but his head still cracked against the ground.

The chamber spun.

Ripples of fire-magic rode the air, hot as a desert's breath. All about he heard the clash of swords, bellowed curses, footfalls pounding the floor. None of those footfalls appeared to be getting closer, though. It was as if his arrival had gone unnoticed by the combatants present.

Maybe I should try that entrance again.

Through the wall of water opposite he saw the dragon retreating to the north, while to his right, within the chamber, two of the six thrones were aflame. The stones of the mosaic beneath them had melted to form a multicolored slurry. In front of the thrones stood Mazana, Jambar, and Imerle.

Senar blinked.

They were talking. Just . . . talking. Or rather, Jambar was talking, and the two women were listening. Imerle's eyes were smoldering, but the look she directed at Mazana would have turned water to ice. Mazana was facing away from Senar, so he could not make out her expression. Her tension was evident, though, in the stiffness of her posture. The Guardian shook his head, bemused. Had he fought a dragon just to watch these three have a heart-to-heart? What did Mazana and Imerle have to talk about, anyway? The differences between them were hardly the sort that could be resolved by a few placatory words and a handshake.

To Senar's left he glimpsed the belligerent Watchman from last night. The Watchman was fighting alongside two strangers against a single opponent—an opponent with gray skin that glittered in the half-light . . .

Senar's breath hissed out.

No, it cannot be.

A crash of swords sounded behind, and he looked round. If Mazana and Imerle had agreed a truce, then clearly no one had told their bodyguards because the Everlord and the executioner were exchanging blows in the corner of the chamber behind and to the right of the thrones. As Senar watched, the giant batted aside Kiapa's parrying sword and drove his own blade through the cuirass over the Everlord's chest before lifting the weapon into the air with Kiapa impaled on it. Kiapa did not cry out. Instead he dropped his sword and wrapped his hands round the executioner's blade as if he meant to pull himself off.

The giant was wearing his clawed metal glove on his left hand, and he reached out with it to seize the Everlord by the neck. The glove's talons scored deep cuts in Kiapa's flesh. Kiapa shifted his grip to the glove and tried to pry the giant's fingers loose. Before he could free himself, though, the executioner hauled him forward into a headbutt. There was a crack of bone, and Kiapa rocked back, his face covered in blood.

Still he struggled.

The giant regarded him blankly. Then he drew back his lips in a snarl. Still holding Kiapa round the neck he tugged his sword from the man's body and hurled him toward the wall of water on his left. The Everlord hit the ground short of the wall and rolled into the sea, where he was snatched down by the weight of his armor.

The giant turned.

Senar stood still. Like he was he going to escape the man's notice that way. It didn't work, unsurprisingly, and the executioner's storm-cloud gaze fixed on him.

The Guardian clambered upright and drew his sword.

Agenta was relieved to see the Watchman disarmed and driven from the fray. It had become increasingly apparent his flailing blade was as likely to hit the kalisch as the stone-skin. Moreover, his absence allowed her to escape Warner's shadow, for the trita, fighting to her right, was forever edging left in an effort to screen Agenta. Now that the Watchman was momentarily indisposed, she had space to bring her sword to bear.

She'd never faced an opponent of the stone-skin's strength or speed before. As his broadsword came whistling down, she raised her blade two-handed to parry. The impact almost took her arms off. Warner countered with a blistering assault, and the stranger was driven back toward the wall of water.

A shout marked the Watchman's return to the conflict. The stone-skin was forced onto the defensive once more. Agenta's sword delivered a gash to his torso, and his shirt turned crimson-black. Well, well. It seemed you could get blood from a stone after all.

Another flash of sorcery lit up the throne room, searing the kalisch's eyes. It was followed by a crackling hiss of warring fire- and water-magic that sent clouds of steam billowing about the throne room. Agenta smiled without humor—the ceasefire between Mazana and Imerle must have ended. And about time, too.

Then a wave of heat broke over her. A shriek came from her right. She looked across to see Warner's sword arm and shoulder were engulfed in flames. The trita dropped his blade and hurled himself toward the wall of water. He plunged his arm into the sea. Had that volley of sorcerous fire been a stray blast from the confrontation between Imerle and Mazana? Or had the emira finally overwhelmed her opponent and shifted her attention to Agenta and her companions?

The stone-skin launched another attack. His sword moved so fast it seemed as if he were fighting with two blades instead of one.

Agenta retreated a step.

Only for her right foot to slip from under her. She fell to her knees. Her left hand came down to steady herself, and she found the ground was sticky cold. *Ice?* Perhaps she shouldn't have been surprised. In the Deeps two nights ago she'd seen Balen vaporize the sea, so why shouldn't the stone-skin freeze the water on the floor?

Off balance, she raised her sword to block his next thrust, but there was no strength in the parry.

The stone-skin's blade punched through her chest.

The executioner's footsteps set the floor quivering as he bore down on Senar. He massed as large as a plains bear yet moved with disturbing grace, always in balance, poised on the balls of his feet. Light shimmered off the metal threads sewn into his skin. Over his stomach were a score of lighter strands where new threads had been woven to replace old. Had the armor there been breached by a weapon? Senar could only hope such a thing was possible. But then perhaps there was some other cause that had seen the executioner renew the strands. Hells, maybe he'd just put on weight.

The Guardian lashed out with his Will, thinking that if he could hurl his opponent through one of the walls of water, then the weight of the giant's armor would seal his doom. There had been too little time for him to gather his power, though, and when his Will-blow struck it succeeded only in driving the executioner back a step.

He came on again.

Senar looked at the clawed glove on the giant's left hand. Was there dragon blood on it, or was it only at executions that the talons were dipped in poison? He saw again the dragon's blood spurting onto his right arm and shoulder. Beneath his wet shirt his skin felt tight, and he wanted to tear the sleeve away to see what damage the blood had caused. The giant wasn't going to wait on him, though, and he covered the last few strides in a rush, his sword a whistling blur. Senar parried, adding a touch of his Will to bolster the block. His eyes watered as the blow landed. The power he'd used in maintaining his Will-shield against the dragon had left his head throbbing. As he fended off the next backhand cut, the impact resounded as loudly in his skull as it did on his sword.

Feinting low, he lunged with his blade for his opponent's chest. The giant made no attempt to block, merely twisting his body so the Guardian's sword glanced off the metal threads without parting them. The executioner countered with a decapitating cut, and Senar ducked beneath it before stepping back and raising his blade to parry a clubbing overhand strike. Rather than meet the blow full on, Senar angled his sword so his opponent's weapon slid off his own. The giant's blade followed through to hit the floor with a clang, throwing up sparks and sending mosaic tiles spinning into the air.

With his foe momentarily vulnerable, Senar dealt a Will-strengthened cut to the man's thigh. The executioner grunted as the sword struck, but his armor held, and he retaliated by swiping at the Guardian with his clawed glove. Drops of the Everlord's blood flicked off its talons.

Senar swayed out of its path.

His thoughts raced. He'd put nearly everything he had into that last attack, but to no effect. If he scored a similar hit to a less fleshy part of the giant's body—an ankle or a knee perhaps—he might break a bone, but he doubted it. What options did that leave? Conventional armor had weak spots. Even plate mail had gaps at the joints. The executioner's armor, though, seemed to have no such holes in its coverage, for the only parts of the man's body not shielded by the metal threads were his head, his hands and his groin. And since his head was out of reach without a ladder . . .

Senar used a nudge of his Will to foul the giant's footsteps before thrusting with his sword for his foe's groin.

The executioner was ready for him, of course. When you had so few vulnerable areas to defend, it was easy to anticipate your enemy's strikes. He slapped Senar's blade aside with his own before countering with a succession of hammer blows that, when parried, left the Guardian's arms feeling numb. Senar backpedaled. He realized he must be drawing near to one of the walls of water. If he could reverse positions with the giant and hit him with every last scrap of his Will . . .

He'd gotten too far ahead of himself, though, for the executioner's next attack proved to be a feint. Senar, with his mind elsewhere, was late in reading his intent. As the Guardian's sword came up to block, the giant's gloved hand snapped out and seized the weapon.

Senar's blade was yanked from his grasp and went skating across the floor before coming to rest near the thrones.

The executioner brought his sword sweeping down.

Kempis watched Agenta's sword slip from her hands. Her eyes lost their sharpness. Then her legs buckled, and she slumped to the floor. As quickly as that, Kempis had gone from having two allies to none. On the plus side, though, the stone-skin's blade had got trapped in Agenta's body as she fell, and it was pulled from the swordsman's hands to leave the septia facing an unarmed enemy.

The kind he liked best.

He aimed a cut to his opponent's neck. The stone-skin ducked under the blow and threw himself forward in a roll that took him past Agenta's motionless body and through the puddle of black blood spreading out from the woman. When he rose once more, his face was smeared red.

And he was holding his broadsword in his hand. Kempis swore.

How the hell had he managed that? Did he have the bloody thing on a string?

The stone-skin brought his blade scything round, and it landed plumb on Kempis's sword. The weapons locked. Kempis came chest to chest with his enemy—or rather his chest came level with the other's man's stomach. Throwing his weight behind his blade, the septia strained to force his opponent back, growling and spitting.

The stone-skin might have been leaning into a gentle breeze for all the effort that showed in his face.

Then he dipped his shoulder and *pushed*. Kempis was thrown back, his feet skidding on the mosaic.

He could think of nothing to say that might slow his enemy down. Nor was there anything he could duck behind or throw in the stone-skin's path—like one of his colleagues from the Watch, for instance. The man's broadsword came sweeping round at waist-level, and Kempis raised his blade to block, but his sword arm might have been lifting the weight of the world, so slowly did it move . . .

Warner's battered shield, flung like a disc from the edge of the throne room, thudded into the stone-skin's side before deflecting away. A blow to the man's head would have served Kempis better, but the distraction had at least spoiled his foe's attack, and it was the flat of the stone-skin's blade—not the edge—that thumped into Kempis's left arm.

Just as the septia's parrying stroke connected with his enemy's sword a hairbreadth below the crosspiece. A dull crash sounded.

The stone-skin stepped back.

Only for his foot to come down on the same patch of ice Agenta had slipped on. Kempis might have said it was justice, if he thought such a thing existed. The stone-skin's ankle went from under him. He fell to all fours, his head lolling forward.

In time to meet Kempis's rising knee. There was a crack of bone, and the man's head rocked back, his shattered nose pumping blood. He tried to raise his sword against the septia's next attack, but Kempis batted the weapon aside and slashed at his opponent's neck.

Blood threaded the air as the septia's blade opened the stone-skin's throat.

Kempis leaned in close. "Give my regards to Loop when you see him."

The stone-skin gave a gurgled choke. Sounded like he might have been trying to say something, but it was drowned in a froth of blood. In any event, his scope for witty comebacks was limited. His eyes rolled back in their sockets, and he pitched forward onto his face with a satisfyingly meaty crunch. A leg twitched, then an arm.

His movements ceased.

Kempis wiped sweat from his eyes. He stared down at the stone-skin's corpse, scarcely able to believe he'd beaten the man. Just to be sure, though, he kicked his foe's sword from his hand and planted a boot in his side. It felt like kicking a wall.

No reaction.

His arm was bruised where the stone-skin's sword had hit it. Gods, he felt tired. Flushed, too, though that might have had something to do with the heat coming off the sorcerous clash between Imerle and Mazana at his back. On instinct he started to check the stone-skin's body for valuables, then stopped himself. Not like the warrior would be carrying his life savings with him, and besides, was any amount of gold worth the time looking when Kempis could have been running instead?

Warner approached, his clothes smoldering, his blackened right sleeve fused to the raw and weeping skin of his arm. Made Kempis's own skin prickle just to look at it. The trita's palm on that side was a ruin of red flesh, the imprint of his sword's hilt branded into it. He was grinding his teeth against the agony. Kneeling beside Agenta he lowered an ear to her mouth.

"Is she all right?" Kempis said, regretting the question even as he spoke it. The woman had just taken a sword through the chest. Of course she wasn't all right.

Warner ignored him. He placed his left hand on Agenta's torso and pressed down in an effort to stem the flow of blood. Her chest labored in and out. Kempis suspected she had one foot through Shroud's Gate already, because her eyes were glazed and her skin was as bloodless as Imerle's.

Speaking of whom . . .

The septia looked round in time to see a thunderous blast of Mazana's sorcery break against the interwoven layers of fire- and water-magic that made up the emira's wards. Those glittering shields were cracked and frayed, and now they began to peel away under Mazana's onslaught. And to think people said that Imerle was the power-ful one.

To the right of the sorcerous confrontation, the executioner was fighting . . .

Kempis blinked. Senar Sol? Where had he come from?

The septia shook his head in disgust. Once again he was letting his curiosity get the better of him. He hadn't forgotten Mazana's talk of keeping secret Imerle's part in the invasion, or what such a cover-up would mean for him. For the time being the bluebloods seemed oblivious to his presence. If he slipped away now they might forget he'd ever been here. True, he would have to swim back to the palace's flooded corridors, but with the dragon having moved away . . .

He looked down at Agenta and Warner. The flint-eyed woman lay so still her spirit must have flown her body, but Red-Face continued to push on her chest, all the while urging her to hold on until help could be found. If Kempis did a runner it would mean abandoning his new allies, but so what? He still owed them for dropping that wave on him in the Shallows.

His mind made up, he took a step toward the rear of the throne room.

Senar dived to his left and felt the giant's sword cut through the air where he'd been standing. An expectant hush had settled on the chamber as if the other combatants had halted their clashes to see the conclusion of his duel. He rose on one knee, then lashed out with his Will. The executioner's head rocked back, and he was half swung round.

Senar flung out his right hand toward his sword and used the Will to summon the blade to him. As the weapon sped through the air, the giant surged forward. From the corner of Senar's eye he saw his opponent's sword flashing down, but he couldn't take his gaze from his own blade because if he failed to grasp it at the first attempt . . .

Its hilt nestled in his palm. He pushed himself to his feet, raising the weapon to block the executioner's attack.

But there hadn't been time for Senar to use his Will to reinforce the parry. Without sorcery he couldn't hope to match the giant's strength. His foe's sword punched through his defenses and chopped down onto the Guardian's right collar bone.

A dull clang sounded, and the blade rebounded. The power behind the blow drove Senar to one knee again.

The executioner's eyes widened.

His surprise was nothing compared to the Guardian's. That strike should have taken his arm off. Instead all he felt was an ache. The giant's sword had cut through his shirt, and through the tear Senar saw a ripple of overlapping scales like plates of fish-scale armor. He did a double take. The scales were the same copper color as those of the dragon from the roof terrace.

No time to think on it now, for the giant had lifted his sword above his head, evidently keen to try his luck with Senar's other shoulder. The Guardian lurched upright.

A woman's voice barked an order at the executioner, and he froze.

The voice had been Mazana's. She limped to stand beside Senar. Her dress was scorched, her left leg flash-burned. She was barely half the size of the giant, yet when she met his gaze there was a note of steel in her eyes.

Her blood-red eyes, Senar noticed with unease.

"Put up your sword," she said to the executioner.

The giant held her gaze a moment longer before looking at the emira. Imerle's hair and eyebrows had been burned away, and chains of crackling blue energy bound her wrists. She did not return the giant's look. Instead she stared directly ahead, her chin held high, apparently oblivious to the people around her.

Mazana spoke again. "You serve me now," she said to the giant.

The executioner's gaze swung back to her, his bestial countenance giving no hint as to his thoughts. His blade was still raised in the position it had been when Mazana commanded him to hold. The muscles of his arm did not even twitch under its weight. With the giant's speed it would take only a heartbeat for him to cut Mazana in half, and Senar gathered his Will in readiness to block an attack.

Then in one smooth motion the executioner returned his sword to the scabbard on his back. He settled into his familiar relaxed stance, his gaze fixing on nothing.

Senar released his breath, but did not sheathe his own blade. An allegiance that had changed so swiftly could easily shift again. If anyone should know, it was the Guardian. And yet, with Imerle shackled it would surely be suicide for the giant to challenge Senar and Mazana together. This was victory, then. A strange victory, perhaps, that left an enemy as implacable as the emira alive, but something told Senar it wasn't mercy that had stayed Mazana's hand. Most likely the Storm Lady had plans for Imerle—plans that involved a public execution and a spike on a wall.

He looked across at Mazana to find her studying him in turn. He knew better than to expect her to thank him for coming to help, but still he'd hoped to see something in her eyes. Some recognition of his presence, at least. There was nothing.

To his left were the two strangers he'd seen fighting with the Watchman against the stone-skin. The woman lay on the floor, apparently unconscious or dead, her shirt torn and bloody round a wound to her chest. Her male companion was kneeling beside her, pressing on her injury. His right hand was burned and blistered, his sleeve on that side stuck to his arm. Behind them the belligerent Watchman was pretending an interest in the mosaic floor as he sidled toward the rear of the chamber. The stone-skin was dead, and another body, burned beyond recognition, lay beyond what remained of one of the thrones.

"Pernay," Mazana said, following Senar's gaze. "It seems Imerle's fondness for the gallant chief minister did not extend to shielding him from my magic."

"Considering the sorceries you unleashed, I'm surprised more weren't caught in the cross fire."

Mazana did not reply.

"I saw you talking to Imerle and Jambar earlier," he said. "What was that about?" He paused, then nodded at the body of the stone-skin. "It has something to do with him, doesn't it?"

"You know him?"

"I know his people."

"I've never seen his like before."

Nor had Senar, but he'd read enough about the stone-skins in ancient texts to know who the man was. An Augeran. Erin Elal's ancient nemesis. It was a name that had all but passed into legend. Centuries ago the stone-skins had driven Senar's ancestors from their homeland across the Southern Wastes following a war that had lasted five years. There had been hundreds of Guardians then, but the stone-skins had rolled over them like a wave. Strong, ruthless, devastating. Out of a population of millions only tens of thousands of Erin Elalese had survived to take ship and sail into exile.

Senar was about to tell Mazana as much when she called out, "Septia Kempis Parr, stay with us awhile, if you please."

The Watchman scowled at her from the rear of the room. Senar thought he would throw himself into the waves. He must have recognized the pointlessness of trying to escape a water-mage through the sea, though, for he came slinking forward, kicking the ground like a petulant child summoned to heel.

Senar looked again at his shoulder—as if he might have imagined the scales the first time. Where the executioner's blade had landed, the plates were marked by an indentation that was even now fading. His shoulder ached when he rolled it. Maybe he owed his life to the scales, but he was still struggling to see them as a good thing. A crackle of sorcery drew his attention back to the emira. A movement of her hands set her magical shackles hissing. The sorcery must have caused her pain for the lines about her eyes tightened.

"Why is she still alive?" Senar asked Mazana.

The red glow had receded from the Storm Lady's eyes, and with it had gone some of the remoteness in her look. "Because from what Jambar tells me, this stone-skin is not the last we're going to see of his kind. Perhaps Imerle will have her uses."

The emira's lip curled.

Then a throwing star sprouted in her forehead, just above her right eye. She crumpled to the floor.

Senar seized his sword hilt, but the thrower of the star—the woman he'd assumed was unconscious or dead—was already collapsing into the arms of her companion with the burned arm. Senar saw a look of satisfaction flicker through her pain. Then her breath died in her throat, and she fell still. Properly dead this time. As dead as Imerle herself, for the emira's eyes were staring sightlessly up at the ceiling. A trickle of blood ran down her left temple.

With her passing, the magic holding back the walls and ceiling of the throne room faded. The barriers wavered until a gesture from Mazana stilled them. The Storm Lady's last words came back to Senar. *Perhaps Imerle will have her uses.* He gave a wry smile.

Mazana must have guessed his thoughts for she sighed and said, "And then again, perhaps not."

Karmel pushed on her brother's chest once more, and Caval spasmed and hacked up water. The priestess helped him to sit up, then slumped onto the bench beside him, her legs suddenly shaky, her mind rocked in every direction. A fresh bout of coughing seized Caval. He wrapped his arms about himself. When the convulsions subsided he looked round, evidently confused as to how he came to be in the courtyard when his final memory was of fighting Mili and Tali on the terrace. His gaze met Karmel's, and she saw consternation in his eyes.

Then his mask came down.

They sat in silence. It was clear Caval wasn't going to break it, yet what was Karmel supposed to say? A hundred thoughts flitted through her mind, but she dismissed them all. Then she noticed movement above and to her right. She held a finger to her lips. Caval nodded his understanding before stilling his movements and releasing his power to make himself invisible. Karmel followed suit.

And not a moment too soon. On the terrace appeared one of the twins, her robe smeared with blood. She was joined by her sister—Mili, the priestess heard the other woman call her. Their gazes swept the courtyard before fixing on the body of the weaponsmaster. Karmel could see their confusion: three Chameleons had been washed into the courtyard by that wave, so why was only Foss's corpse floating in the water? Doubtless the twins had heard Caval coughing, but would they assume he and Karmel had moved on? The priestess could only hope so, for while Tali was injured—and while there was no sign yet of their black-haired male companion—there was little doubt in Karmel's mind as to which side would emerge victorious in a fight.

With an unheard comment to her twin, Tali began hobbling away along the terrace. Mili paused before setting off in pursuit. Catching up to Tali, Mili threw her sister's left arm about her shoulders to support her.

A dozen stuttering steps took them out of Karmel's sight.

Karmel sensed Caval looking at her, yet she remained staring up at the terrace. The twins' apparent retreat might just be a ruse, but more important, she wasn't ready to meet her brother's gaze. Now that the initial relief of his survival had passed, her doubts were resurfacing. *No, not doubts,* she realized. She had stopped deluding herself about Caval's betrayal when she was on the terrace. What she didn't know was *why.* She hesitated. Part of her wanted to quiz Caval now, but another part wanted to put the questions from her mind and pretend the past few days had never happened. The hurt went too deep for that, though. She could no more let it go than she could have left her brother to die.

Caval's breaths came in wheezes. His face was drawn. At last he said, "When I climbed to the terrace earlier, you were thinking about that time when we took the boat, weren't you?"

Karmel nodded.

The barest hint of a smile touched his lips. "I tried so hard to forget that day, yet always when the memory faded you found some excuse to bring it up again."

The priestess stared at him. "I thought it would lift your spirits."

"Ah, because you remembered only the freedom and the adventure. For me, it was the day I realized there would be no escaping Father."

Her expression tightened. "Why were you so stubborn, Caval? Why did you have to fight him for so long?"

"I never *stopped* fighting him, even when I took my vows as he wanted. I just fought him in a different way."

Karmel looked at him blankly.

"You think my sudden devotion to the Chameleon was because I'd seen the light? You think I wanted to be high priest?" He shook his head. "I only wanted it because that meant *he* couldn't have it."

"You were fifteen. Another few months, and you would have reached majority. You could have walked away."

"And left you behind?"

"Then you could have let him *think* he'd won! You could have made things easier for yourself!"

"As you did?"

Karmel's eyes narrowed. "You think I should have stood up for you? I was a girl—"

"There was nothing you could have done," Caval cut in. "In any case, whatever you did, he'd have found a way to blame me for it."

There was truth in that, Karmel knew. Caval alone had borne the weight of their father's expectation, while Karmel herself had felt anonymous. Even rejected. Was that why she'd always felt driven to compete with her brother? Why she'd resented his elevation to high priest even as she celebrated it?

Caval's gaze swung to the opposite side of the courtyard. The flow of water from one of the windows had stopped where the body of a Storm Guard blocked it. Caval stared at the corpse, then said, "Do you know how many times I prayed to the Chameleon for the beatings to end? The god never responded, of course . . . Until one day I stopped begging for his help and asked what *I* could do for *him*. Have you never wondered why he supported me in my bid to become high priest? Because for all Father's devotion, he wasn't ambitious enough. The Chameleon isn't interested in prayers. He wants power. Power I promised to give him."

Karmel's voice was flat. "So you allied with Imerle."

"The Chameleon told me about Imerle's plans for Dragon Day long before *she* did. He thought she would be vulnerable with her forces committed. He thought if the Chameleons ruled Olaire, the faith would spread like wildfire across the Sabian League."

A starbeak alighted on the weaponsmaster's corpse and began pecking at his eyes. Karmel looked away. The moment was upon her. "Why did you pick me?" she made herself say. "To go to Dian."

"Because you're good," Caval said. Then, "And because you alone would trust me enough not to ask questions about the true purpose of the mission."

"You sent me to die. To die!"

Her brother opened his mouth to speak, then shut it again. He bowed his head.

And with that simple gesture, finally admitted his betrayal. Karmel's vision blurred. At least this time he hadn't denied it. She'd expected him to try to turn her uncertainties upon themselves. To deflect and refute and confound. The fact that he hadn't came as a relief. The truth she could deal with—perhaps. It was the lies she hated, and she'd started to fear Caval was incapable of telling the truth.

But he still hadn't given her the *whole* truth, she sensed.

Their hands were close on the bench, and when Caval lifted his, Karmel snatched hers back, thinking he meant to take it. Instead he began massaging his injured shoulder. If he noticed her snub, he gave no sign. "Do you remember the time we confronted Father after I became high priest? What he did when I taunted him?"

"He smiled."

"He smiled," Caval agreed. "I wanted to see his anger. To see he knew he was beaten. But he wasn't. Perhaps I was doing what he wanted. Perhaps he'd been hoping all along that I would depose him." His hand paused on his shoulder. "Or perhaps he knew the scars he'd left me would never fade. And that for so long as they remained, I would never be free of his influence."

"If you hated him so much, why didn't you send *him* on the damned mission?"

"Because he's dead."

For a while Karmel could not speak. *Dead?* No, that wasn't possible. He'd left Olaire for Benaldi two weeks ago. Since becoming high priest, Caval had found excuses to send their father as far away as possible, as often as possible. "His commission to Benaldi—"

"A ruse to keep people from wondering at his disappearance. In time I would have broken the news that his ship had been taken by pirates or gone down in a storm."

"You killed him?" Karmel whispered.

"Yes."

It felt like a pit had opened up in her stomach. Not because of her father's passing—he'd been dead to her from the moment she was old enough to escape his clutches. No, what sorrow she *did* feel was at Caval's part in his death. For all that her brother had been through, she would never have believed he could so such a thing. And yet he had tried to have her killed too, hadn't he?

Caval's look was distant. "He knew why I'd come. He didn't even put up a fight. Every time I saw him I remembered the beatings, the sneers, the years of humiliation. I was the new high priest, yet with him I would always be the boy who had cowered as the cane fell. Since I replaced him I haven't slept more than a few bells at a time. I relive the beatings each night, and each morning when I wake up my shoulder feels like the bone has been broken again. And now the oscura has lost its bite—"

Karmel started. Oscura? Now that she looked for it, the whites of his eyes *were* a little dull.

"You didn't know?" Caval said, his mouth twitching. His smile did not reach his eyes, though. "I thought when Father died there would be some respite from the memories." The look he turned on Karmel was pointed. "But there wasn't."

And suddenly everything became clear to the priestess. "Because those same memories you had when you looked at Father, you had when you looked at me. After Father, I was your link to the past. You thought if I died you could sever it."

Caval lowered his gaze. "I'm glad Veran failed. Your death wouldn't have helped. Father's didn't—though I only came to realize that after you had gone."

Karmel felt color rise to her cheeks. "So you would do it all again if you thought it *would* work?"

"Nothing will work. But that hardly matters now."

"Why?"

He studied her. "You're not going to finish this?"

It was a heartbeat before Karmel understood what he meant. *He thinks I'm going to kill him.* More than that, he wanted her to. The realization came as yet another blow. He really thought her capable of that? How broken must he be that any of this made sense to him? Vengeance had never been on her mind. All she'd wanted was to be wrong in her suspicions. For things between her and Caval to return to the way they'd once been. And that, she knew, could never happen.

Her brother's gaze shifted to the weaponsmaster's corpse. A second starbeak had joined the first, and they began squabbling over the choice pickings. When Caval next spoke, his tone was rueful. "The Chameleon chose me over Father because I promised him power. I promised him the League, and look at what I have brought him instead. He will be finished with me." He glanced at Karmel. "And I cannot tell you what a relief that is."

Karmel did not respond. For the first time in a long time her brother's look wasn't closed to her. Along with the self-loathing, she saw resignation in his eyes. Resignation at the fact she wouldn't grant him the release he sought? At the fact he would have to live with the knowledge of what he'd done? She searched his face, wondering what he now felt when he looked at her. And what she would feel in the coming days when she looked at him.

The metallic chatter of swordplay started up in the distance, followed by a whistle and a shout, much closer. Karmel scanned the roofline before looking back at Caval. They couldn't stay here. They'd been lucky to evade Mili and Tali earlier, but who was to say the twins might not come back? Or a squad of Imerle's soldiers?

"Can you walk?" she asked Caval.

He raised an eyebrow. "Walk where?"

"To the gates. With the corridors flooded, we'll have to cross the terraces."

Her brother's gaze was intense. "And then?"

Karmel shook her head. She had not thought that far ahead. "One step at a time, Caval," she said.

One step at a time.

With a heavy tread Kempis climbed the stairs to the roof terrace. Mazana Creed had started draining the palace's flooded corridors, but the septia wasn't going to stay down there with the sharks while she finished the job. He emerged blinking into bright sunlight and seated himself on the top step. A strand of fireweed was tangled round his legs. He tugged it free before pulling off his boots and emptying them of water.

To his right a section of seawall had collapsed. All around, the flagstones were cracked and scratched. The dragon must have tried to climb to the terrace here, but there was no sign of the creature now. How had the beast managed to slip through the net of ships at the Dragon Gate? And why had none of those vessels followed the dragon here? Something Mazana had said in the throne room came back to him—something about a disturbance in Dian that she would blame on the stone-skins. Were there more of the strangers running amok in Dian and Natilly? Had they disrupted the Dragon Hunt in some way?

Kempis scanned the palace rooftops. To the south he saw two Chameleons—a man and a woman—shuffling along a terrace in the direction of the main gates. The man looked familiar, but Kempis was too far away to make out his features. On a rooftop a stone's throw to the left, four Storm Guards stood staring out to sea, while on a terrace midway between Kempis and the soldiers . . .

His eyes widened.

Sniffer.

The Untarian was stretched out on the sun-drenched flagstones, her shirt pulled up to expose her midriff, her trousers rolled up to her knees. She lay so still that Kempis thought she was dead.

Then he noticed the half-eaten runefish beside her.

The corners of his mouth turned up, but he caught the smile before it could spread. He'd spent an age in the flooded corridors searching for the woman, and all that time she'd been up here, topping up her tan? She'd *known* the stone-skin's target was the emira. She'd *known* Kempis had been heading for the throne room. It should have been a simple matter for her to swim down and check if he was there. But then perhaps she had. Perhaps she'd seen him battling the stone-skin and decided she didn't like the odds he was facing.

Slipping on his boots, Kempis crossed to her terrace. He stood over her.

Sniffer's eyes remained closed. She had to know it was him, else she would have looked up at his approach.

He drummed a foot on the ground.

At last Sniffer opened an eye. "Do you mind, sir? You're in my sun."

Kempis scowled. Then, when no suitably caustic retort came to mind, he stepped past and continued south along the terrace after the two Chameleons.

Damned Untarian, he thought. Everything that had gone wrong today was her fault. If she hadn't gone after the female stone-skin, he would never have been in the Shallows when Orsan came ashore. Loop and Duffle would still be alive, and then Kempis would not have come to the palace seeking revenge against Loop's killer. He couldn't even say the worst of this business was over, what with Mazana Creed having waylaid him in the throne room. On the contrary, his troubles were just beginning. How typical of Sniffer that, on her last day in the Watch, she should stir up the manure for him.

The slap of the Untarian's webbed feet sounded behind.

"I came looking for you," she said as she drew level. "When you weren't on the terraces or in the courtyards, I assumed you were fish food."

"I can see that cut you up real bad," Kempis muttered. "What happened when we got separated? I thought a shark—"

"I've told you before, Untarians can swim as fast as most sharp-teeths over short distances."

"Then why all the squawking?"

"To warn you, idiot! What do you think the sharp-teeth would have done if it'd caught you with your legs in the water? Tickled your feet?"

There was nothing Kempis could say to that, so he kept his head down and continued walking.

The heat was building to a head-throbbing intensity, and the septia wiped a hand across his brow. Not all of the palace buildings had terraces, so as he worked his way southward he had to scramble over gently sloping roofs that creaked beneath him. He passed a courtyard still submerged in water, the archway leading into it plugged by bodies. In the next yard five servants had gathered to escape the floods and the fighting. With hollow eyes they watched Kempis stride by. An old woman shouted up to him for news, but the septia was in no mood to respond.

Sniffer whistled through her gills as she walked beside him. "We're leaving, then? It's over?"

"For now."

"You found the stone-skin?"

"Yeah."

"And?"

"Dead."

The Untarian waited for him to continue. "That's it?"

Kempis shrugged. Mazana Creed had told him to keep his mouth shut about what had happened in the throne room. Normally that wouldn't have stopped him, but in this instance he suspected Sniffer was better off not knowing.

"So what now?" the Untarian asked as they clambered over a terrace railing and onto a roof of ebonystone tiles bleached gray by the sun. "We just forget this business with the stone-skins?"

"I wish."

"Oh?"

Kempis hesitated, then said, "Turns out those two stone-skins might not be the only ones in Olaire. I've been told to sniff out the others."

"By the emira?"

"Emira's dead."

"Then who?"

"Mazana Creed," the septia said, his tone betraying his disgust. "I'm to report to her personally from now on."

There was a smile in Sniffer's voice. "For someone who claims not to like bluebloods, you sure seem to be spending a lot of time round them lately."

Like he had a choice! If Kempis had refused the Storm Lady's request, he would have been feeding the fish by now. He had no option but to dance to her tune—until he worked out how to leave this wretched island without setting foot on a boat, that is. Nothing good ever came of mixing with the bluebloods.

The distance between Kempis and the two Chameleons was closing, so he slowed lest the strangers think he was following them. As he crossed the next roof one of its tiles shifted underfoot, and he windmilled his arms to keep his balance. Sniffer, waiting for him on the terrace beyond, chuckled.

"There's one thing I don't understand," she said as he joined her. "Bright Eyes wasn't a stone-skin, right? So how does she fit into this?"

"Woman was a hired sword—remember Enli Alapha?"

"Hired by the stone-skins?"

" 'S my guess. Stone-skins only went for the emira once Bright Eyes was dead. Maybe they were forced to get their hands dirty when their lackey screwed up. Or maybe they meant for her to be a decoy."

"What makes you so sure the stone-skins were the ones pulling her strings? How do you know they weren't hired swords themselves?"

Because of what Jambar said in the throne room, that's how. Kempis did not voice the thought, however. *I know who the stone-skins are and why they are here,* the Remnerol had told Imerle. *I know what is coming.*

Kempis had a fair idea himself. After the stink the stone-skins had kicked up today, the septia didn't need a shaman to tell him they meant trouble. Odds were, war was coming, but why? Before this morning he'd never heard of a stone-skin, never mind seen one in the flesh. What reason did they have for setting their sights on the Storm Isles? And why had they gone not just for Storm Lords but for any water-mage that crossed their path? What threat did the sorcerers pose?

Ahead the roof came to an end, and beyond it Kempis saw the main gates. He snatched a look into the grounds below. The sea must have risen and receded here previously, for the flagstones glistened with moisture. Corpses lay in the street beyond the gates. More were crushed against the flanking walls, as if some broom-wielding titan had passed this way recently and swept the bodies aside like so many fallen leaves. Among the corpses a figure moved: a young Gray Cloak with a wispy red beard. Curled up round a chest wound, he shivered as if with fever.

Kempis cocked his head to listen for any noise that might signal a hidden force in one of the palace arches. The only sounds he could hear, though, were the hiss of the sea behind, the cawing of starbeaks overhead, and screams from the west of the city. He lowered himself backward from the roof before dropping the final way.

Ignoring the pleading cries of the wounded Gray Cloak, he led Sniffer through the gates.

He took a winding course round the flank of Kalin's Hill, avoiding the main roads and pausing at each intersection to check for trouble. A short while later he came to the place where he and Duffle had watched the emira's forces launch their assault on Olaire. He looked down on the city. Fires raged through the Shallows, and a pall of smoke hung over the district. The Gilgamarian ship remained suspended where he'd last seen it. Its decks were crawling with figures— scavengers, most likely, come to plunder what they could before the vessel was claimed by the flames.

The sea had retreated from the areas flooded by the wave of water-magic. The streets of the Deeps were choked with floating corpses, and Kempis realized that Loop's and Duffle's would be among them. He made a sour face. When he'd left the throne room earlier he had vowed—not for the first time—never to come within spitting distance of the sea again. If he was to retrieve his companions' bodies, though, he would have to make an exception.

To the west the battle for the docks had ended. Half a dozen gray-sailed ships were now berthed at quayside. Gray Cloaks patrolled the waterfront. Farther east the Harbor Barracks must have fallen to the invaders, for the flag flying from its tower was the emira's fiery wave. The only fighting still taking place was going on in the streets round the Founder's Citadel. The fortress's gates had been shut. Its battlements were manned by Storm Guards, but there were too few defenders to withstand a concerted attack from the raiders if it came. The Storm Guards wouldn't need to hold out for long, though—just until news reached the invaders that their commander and paymaster, Imerle, was dead.

"Where to now?" Sniffer said.

Where indeed? Looking south Kempis saw the black-tiled roof of Lappin's gambling den at the edge of the Gambler's Quarter. Lappin would be doing a roaring trade, what with looters coming by to gamble away their ill-gotten gains. The septia's palms began to itch. "You can go where you like," he said. "I'm off to spend a little time at Lappin's, play some flush, and see if I can win back what I owe."

Sniffer raised an eyebrow. "I've always wondered why someone with your luck spends so much time gambling."

"With the day I've had my luck's due a change. When that happens I want to be somewhere I can make some money from it."

Not that he'd need luck if the plan he'd been working on for the last quarter-bell came good. Loop had given him the idea yesterday when he'd spoken about the spirits haunting Olaire. The ghosts were only visible, the mage had said, if they wanted to be seen, so what was to stop Kempis from using one to keep a discreet eye on his opponents' cards? How he was going to find one of the ghosts and persuade it to help him was a matter he hadn't figured out yet, but he'd think of something. *If Sniffer ever stops buzzing in my ear, that is.*

A burst of light came from one of the partly submerged buildings beside the Causeway. Kempis looked over to see a house topple into the water. *Fire-magic.* At first he thought a fight was going on there.

Then he saw a dragon's head break the waves at the mouth of the Causeway.

Sunlight reflected off the creature's blood-red scales, making it appear to Kempis as if the beast were aflame. The dragon had eyes like cauldrons of fire and a neck as long as the masts of the ships in harbor. Was this the same creature that had plucked the fat Gilgamarian from the throne room? *Must be,* the septia decided—only one dragon was ever let through the Dragon Gate on Dragon Day. And yet he could have sworn the beast he'd seen earlier had had copper scales, not red ones.

The dragon entered the Causeway and devoured some fool who had climbed onto a roof for a better look. Ahead of the creature another explosion flared, and a second house crumbled into ruin. The Gray Cloaks were trying to block off the Causeway, Kempis realized, and thus prevent the beast from reaching the ships in the harbor. So far their efforts had succeeded only in stopping up those parts of the channel closest to the buildings. The center of the Causeway remained clear.

Sniffer's voice interrupted his musings. "I've been thinking about staying on for a while. In the Watch, I mean."

The septia thought he must have misheard. "What?"

"Just until the stone-skins are caught. Be a shame not to see this through, don't you think?"

A pause. "You're serious?"

"Of course. Wouldn't want you getting lonely now Loop and Duffle have gone."

Kempis studied her expression. A twinkle in her eyes made him hope she was having him on, yet there was something about the set of her mouth . . .

Scowling, he turned away. "And I thought my day couldn't get any worse."

EPILOGUE

SENAR STOOD on the roof terrace, looking out on a storm-tossed sea bathed in the light of the Watchtower at Ferris Point. Waves heaved and crashed, and rain swept down from the blackness overhead. Not one drop fell on the terrace round Senar, though. Instead it ran down invisible barriers of water-magic above and to either side, making it appear to the Guardian as if he were standing in a glass shell. Alas, those barriers did not blunt the bite of the westerly wind, and Senar clutched the terrace's handrail as his cloak billowed about him.

Beside him stood Mazana. She was wearing the same red dress and air-magic pendant he'd seen her in when they first met. Her arms were drawn about herself, and Senar took off his cloak and placed it round her shoulders. She gave a small smile but did not thank him. A full day and more had passed since she'd defeated Imerle, yet still the reserve she'd shown in the throne room was evident. The only time Senar had seen that reserve thaw was this morning when she'd been reunited with her half brother, Uriel.

Imerle, the Guardian learned, had sent soldiers to Mazana's house yesterday with orders to snatch the boy. Mazana, though, had anticipated the move and commanded her dutia, Beauce, to hide Uriel, as well as himself and his troops, in the temple of the Lord of Hidden Faces—leaving just Greave's followers to greet Imerle's soldiers when they arrived. Earlier Senar had gone to the temple to collect Uriel and Beauce and bring them to the palace. The journey through Olaire had proved uneventful, but then the fighting between the Storm

Guards and Imerle's forces had quickly died out yesterday when Mazana sent the executioner to parade Imerle's severed head through the streets.

Senar felt a twinge from his right shoulder and rubbed his hand across it. Through his shirt he could feel the coldness of the dragon scales. When Mazana spoke, he had to lean forward to catch her words above the wind.

"The scales are causing you discomfort?"

"There is no pain. Just a little stiffness."

"Each year the dragon killed on Dragon Day is butchered for its meat, and each year some of the workers are splashed with its blood. It is said to burn like acid."

"Then I am fortunate the blood splashed my shirt and not my skin. Clearly the sea weakened its effects when I swam to the throne room."

"Clearly," Mazana said, a note of . . . something in her voice. Senar wondered what she wasn't telling him. Was there some effect of the dragon's blood beyond what he already knew?

He rolled his right shoulder and felt the scales rubbing together. The plates ran from the bottom of his neck down his shoulder and arm to just above his elbow. Perhaps it was only his imagination, but it seemed that overnight the scales had extended a hairbreadth farther up his neck. If they were to reach his face . . .

"What about you?" he asked Mazana, remembering her blood-red eyes in the throne room. "Have you felt Fume's presence since you left the Founder's Citadel?"

"I have felt his *power*," she said in a tone that indicated the matter was closed. "As did Imerle."

Senar pursed his lips, suspecting now was not the time to mention the price she'd paid for that power. For while the priestess of the Lord of Hidden Faces hadn't made an appearance when Senar called at the temple this morning, something told the Guardian she wouldn't forget Mazana's debt.

And that Mazana would not like the cost when she remembered.

In response to Mazana's words he said, "You are lucky that that woman—that kalisch from Gilgamar—killed Imerle when she did. Whatever deal you struck with the emira, she would have betrayed you in the end."

"Of course she would."

"Then why did you bargain with her? Because of something Jambar foresaw? The shaman himself will tell you, all he sees are possibilities."

"What our learned friend Jambar saw, he saw not just in *some* futures but in *all*."

"Then why didn't he get a whiff of the Augerans' coming before now? This would not be the first time he has manipulated his patron to serve his own ends. Perhaps he wanted Imerle alive."

"And pass up the chance to add her knuckle bones to his collection? That is not something he would do lightly, I think."

Senar's scowled. Before Imerle's blood had even cooled, Jambar had severed the little fingers of both her hands. He had taken the stone-skin's fingers too. "Even if you are right, with a shaman's art there can be no guarantees. He failed to foresee Imerle's death, after all."

"Yes, he blames you for that. The addition of Fume's bones to his collection increased his power, but much of what he gained was lost with the bones you destroyed outside his room—he told me of your little disagreement yesterday."

"Did he also tell you how his power is fueled? By the blood of innocents."

Mazana's face darkened. "Stay away from him, Guardian. Soon I may need his gift of foresight."

Senar did not respond. He had no intention of standing aside while the shaman practiced his grisly work, but Mazana's expression showed she was in no mood for an argument. In any case he had other things on his mind. After Imerle's death he'd overheard Jambar telling the Storm Lady about the Augerans' role in the raising of the Dragon Gate, but when they'd moved on to what the future held, Jambar had steered Mazana out of earshot. When Senar asked Mazana earlier she'd refused to be drawn on the subject, so perhaps it was time to try a different tack. "I understand there was an Augeran in the control room at Dian," he said. "Evidently Imerle was not the only one intent on smashing the power of the Sabian League."

"Fortunately for me."

"Oh?"

"The cities of the League have long bridled beneath the Storm Lords' yoke. Imerle's antics might have galvanized them into taking action, but with so many heads of state now lining a dragon's stomach, those cities will be too embroiled in their own power struggles to challenge me."

"Giving you time to shore up your position."

Mazana inclined her head. "Gensu and Thane are dead. With luck, Cauroy too. Which means that even if Mokinda survived, I am now Imerle's rightful successor."

"The Storm Lords' heirs will want to take up their places on the Storm Council."

"If those heirs are still alive, yes. Thoughtfully, Imerle left no successor. Cauroy's brood doubtless went down with him on the *Majestic*"—she ticked them off on her fingers—"and Gensu's son, I hear, got himself killed in the fight at the harbor. In any event the children of a Storm Lord have no divine right to succeed their parents. First they must prove they are worthy of the honor, for it is only by recruiting the most powerful water-mages that the Storm Lords have maintained their stranglehold on the League." A smile touched her lips. "As the only surviving Storm Lord, the task of judging the merits of each aspirant will fall on me. Such an important decision cannot be rushed, you understand."

Senar did not return her smile. "What of the Revenants?"

"The mercenaries will care only about receiving whatever gold Imerle promised them. I'm sure my money is as good as hers—it should be, since they are now one and the same. And if the Revenants' commander has ambitions above his station . . ." Mazana shrugged. "We shall find out for ourselves soon enough."

"He is coming here?"

She nodded.

That explained Mazana's choice of attire, Senar thought, glancing at the air-magic pendant round her neck. He should not be surprised, he knew, that she was making overtures to the Revenants. For while Olaire's streets were quiet at present, many of Imerle's troops still occupied the city. Beauce's men patrolled the palace but they numbered only a few dozen, and there would be no reinforcements arriving from Mazana's home island while the dragons prowled the seas. As for the Storm Guards, securing their loyalty would mean dealing with Dutia Elemy Meddes. Earlier Elemy had come to the palace requesting an audience with Mazana, but she had sent him away. True, the dutia had been a critic of Imerle, but only because she had abused her power in the final months of her reign. Most likely Elemy would want to keep the same influence he had enjoyed under the old regime, and to see the Storm Council retained as a check on Mazana's authority. And Mazana had not just won power from Imerle to give it away to the dutia. In order to deal with Elemy from a position of strength, though, she would first need to strike a bargain with the Revenants.

Thunder ripped up the sky, and Senar thought he saw a figure up there in the maelstrom, riding the gusting winds. No, he must have imagined it. A wave exploded into spray against the seawall, setting the roof terrace shuddering. Senar cast an uneasy eye at the ground. The place where he and the twins had fought the dragon was thirty paces to his right, yet even this far away the flagstones were cracked from when the creature had tried to clamber onto the roof. The trumpeting of a dragon momentarily drowned the roar of the storm. When Senar peered out to sea, though, he saw nothing except churning waves.

"What of the dragons?" he asked Mazana. "Will you hunt them down?"

"Why would I? For as long as they remain this side of the Dragon Gate, the League will need my help protecting their ships. Besides, the harder it is for my opponents to travel, the harder it will be for them to plot against me."

"Or to unite with you against the Augerans when they come."

Shadows swirled in Mazana's eyes. "The Augerans do not have to be my enemies."

"Their actions at the Dragon Gate hardly qualify them as friends."

Mazana said nothing.

"And the assassination attempt on you outside the temple?"

"*If* that was their doing, I suspect it was nothing personal. In case you've forgotten, I wasn't the only water-mage targeted."

"And why do you think the Augerans set their sights on Olaire's water-mages? Because when they come next time it will be in force, and they do not want you endangering their fleet."

"When they come next time it may not be to these lands. Perhaps they merely wanted to ensure the League did not interfere in whatever plans they have for *your* people."

"And perhaps you would be correct if the League and Erin Elal were allies. We are not. Why would the Augerans risk the enmity of the Storm Isles unless they knew their plans for you would make such enmity inevitable?"

Mazana looked away. "Maybe you are right." Then, "And maybe you would just like to think such enmity is inevitable because it means your kinsmen will not have to stand alone against the stone-skins when they come."

There was something in her tone that gave Senar pause. He wondered suddenly if the invasion of Erin Elal had already begun. It was ten months since he'd passed though the Merigan portal. Ten months in which that invasion could have been launched. Since coming to Olaire he hadn't asked about his homeland, but surely he would have heard something if his kinsmen were under attack. *Would Mazana tell me if she knew?* Of course she would. What reason did she have to keep the information from him?

He scratched at the stubs of his missing fingers. Was the emperor aware of the Augeran threat? If so he would no doubt be regretting his part in the Betrayal two years ago, and the consequent weakening of both the Guardians and the Black Tower. Oddly enough, the coming of the stone-skins could see the Guardians' star rise once more, for Avallon would have no choice but to restore them to their position of preeminence. The emperor had been grooming his elite soldiers, the Breakers, to replace the Guardians, but the Breakers hadn't had time yet to master the Will. Alone they could not hope to resist the might of the Augerans.

And yet how could even the Guardians and the Breakers together hope to turn back the Augeran tide? Eight hundred years ago the Guardians had been at the height of their power, and still they had been defeated. What chance would they have now with their numbers down to barely twenty? Senar pushed the thought aside. This was not the time for doubts. After the initial shock of seeing the stone-skin in the throne room, the return of Erin Elal's age-old nemesis had left him feeling strangely energized. The old rivalries within the empire would have to be set aside. Senar's vengeance against the emperor would have to wait. Avallon would need every man he had to stand against the enemy.

The Guardians will need me.

Mazana's voice was distant. "You must be keen to return to your people."

Senar looked at her. There she went again, reading his thoughts.

It dawned on him she might no more want him reporting the presence of the Merigan portal in Olaire to his kinsmen than Imerle had done before. Would she stop him leaving if he tried? "I had not decided."

"And you want me to help you make that decision?"

The Guardian hesitated, unsure how she meant that. "For now there is no decision to make. No ship will leave Olaire while the dragons remain at large." In truth, a part of him was grateful for that fact because it meant he had time to get his thoughts in order—to let the dust settle on the events of the last few days.

"Then perhaps I should make clearing the seas a priority after all."

Before Senar could reply he saw Beauce climbing the stairwell to his left. The dutia halted on the top step. "Emira, the commander of the Revenants is here."

For a while Mazana did not answer. Senar wondered whether she still hadn't got used to people calling her Emira. She stared toward the Watchtower at Ferris Point. Senar searched her eyes for some hint as to where her thoughts had flown, but in them he saw only a reflection of the beacon's flames. For all that she was right next to him, he felt a distance between them as great as if they were standing at opposite ends of the roof terrace.

Then she met his gaze and flashed him a smile that made his breath catch.

"Shall we?" she said, slipping an arm through his.

Acknowledgments

Many thanks as usual to my editors, Marco Palmieri and Natalie Laverick, for helping me knock the book into shape. Thanks also to my publicists, Ardi Alspach, Ksenia Winnicki, Lydia Gittins, and Cara Fielder, for their tireless efforts in promoting this book and the series as a whole.

I should also say thank you to the various bloggers, reviewers, and readers who have enjoyed my books and helped to spread the word. You know who you are! Your enthusiasm and support are invaluable and much appreciated.

Finally, thank you to my son, James, for keeping me smiling and to my wife, Suzanne, for being a constant source of advice and encouragement along the way. I couldn't do this without you.